AS THE AGE OF ICE ... S
BEGIN A LONG T ... E
GREAT RIVER—ON ... E
PATH TOWARD PEACE AND FRIENDSHIP LEADS
THROUGH A MAZE OF TABOOS AND TREACHERY.

Tôrnârssuk—Once feared as the Great Ghost Cannibal of the North, the powerful Palaeo-Inuit headman has never doubted his own strength or wisdom as a leader . . . until now. Suddenly, he sees in the heavens and earth the signs of his own demise—and the need to make the ultimate sacrifice.

Hasu'u—As Tôrnârssuk's woman, she is closest to the great leader and dearest to his heart. But not even she knows the struggle he is undergoing or the difficult path on which she herself will be forced to follow if she hopes to save his tortured soul.

Ne'gauni—An intense young man, he had his life saved but only at the cost of one of his legs. Now he struggles to find his place among the People even as he harbors a secret love for a woman it is sacrilege for him even to dream of possessing.

Mowea'qua—A child of the wolf, the hotheaded child-woman flagrantly disobeys the ways of the People, yet her talents as a healer belie her outcast heritage. Her rebellious nature will lead her on a mission of her own—and a surprising passion that could destroy the tribe.

Avataut—Once Tôrnârssuk's best friend, he has fallen out of favor with the People and nurses a grudge against his old boyhood hunting partner over the beautiful Hasu'u. Now he has set in motion a plan to utterly destroy Tôrnârssuk and reclaim his woman—and the best part is that Tôrnârssuk will voluntarily give up his woman and destroy himself.

BANTAM BOOKS BY WILLIAM SARABANDE

SPIRIT MOON

William Sarabande

BCI Producers of **The Holt Family Sagas** and **When The Horses Came.**

Book Creations Inc., Canaan, NY • *George S. Engel, Executive Producer*

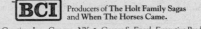

BANTAM BOOKS

New York Toronto London
Sydney Auckland

SPIRIT MOON
A Bantam Book / August 2000
Produced by Book Creations, Inc.
Lyle Kenyon Engel, Founder

ISBN 0-553-57909-6

Published simultaneously in the United States and Canada

Bantam Books are published by Bantam Books, a division of Random
House, Inc. Its trademark, consisting of the words "Bantam Books" and the
portrayal of a rooster, is Registered in U.S. Patent and Trademark Office and
in other countries. Marca Registrada. Bantam Books, 1540 Broadway, New
York, New York 10036.

PRINTED IN THE UNITED STATES OF AMERICA

OPM   10 9 8 7 6 5 4 3 2 1

To Hannah, the newest runner in my sacred Circle
To Dorothy and Ferdi for the most precious gift of Hannah
To John, who listens and inspires along the way
And once again, always and forever, to Charles
All of you make the run worthwhile

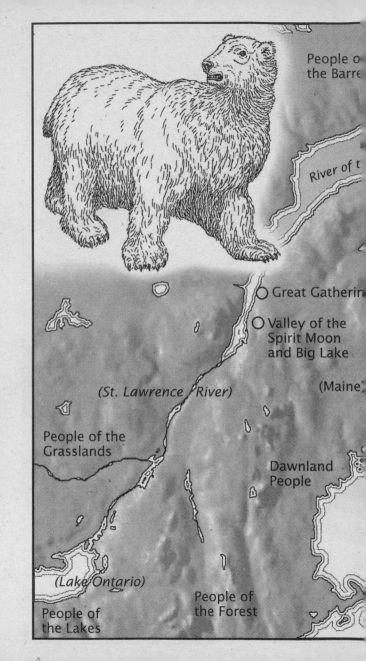

People o
the Barre

River of t

O Great Gatherin

O Valley of the
Spirit Moon
and Big Lake

(St. Lawrence River)

(Maine)

People of the
Grasslands

Dawnland
People

(Lake Ontario)

People of
the Forest

People of
the Lakes

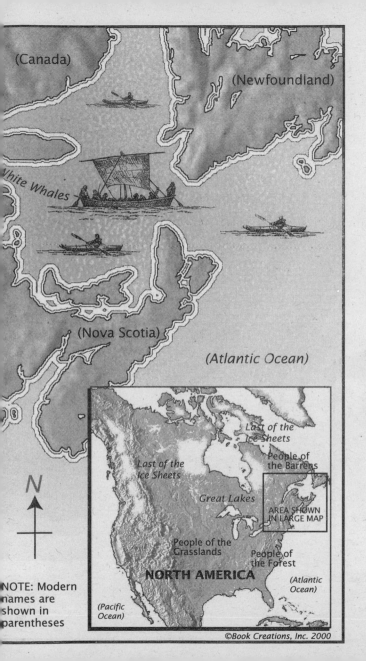

(Canada)

(Newfoundland)

White Whales

(Nova Scotia)

(Atlantic Ocean)

Last of the Ice Sheets

Last of the Ice Sheets

People of the Barrens

Great Lakes

AREA SHOWN IN LARGE MAP

People of the Grasslands

People of the Forest

NORTH AMERICA

(Pacific Ocean)

(Atlantic Ocean)

N

NOTE: Modern names are shown in parentheses

©Book Creations, Inc. 2000

Come!
Let it be told in the old way
Beneath the Spirit Moon
The Old Ones beckon
The great herds sing the song of life
The ghosts of man and whale and wolf are dancing
Come!

Part One

TO SEE THE SKY

▼▼▼▼▼▼▼

*"Raven made the world
Man knows this, for Man and Raven are One."*

—CREATION LEGEND, NORTHEAST COAST

Chapter One

▼▼▼▼▼▼▼

The forest was alive with spirits. Cannibal spirits. All men knew this. And all men were afraid. Or so a woman of the People had once told him.

Now, standing motionless at the shadowed edge of the primordial woodland, the solitary hunter reminded himself that he was not a man of the People. He was a man of the far north, of the vast Barrenlands and open skies of the distant tundra, a man of many potent spirit names and magic amulets, a man who had dared to hunt white whales on the Great River of the North, a man of the True People! He was not afraid of the ghosts and demons of lesser tribes. The spirits of his Ancestors were with him in this eternally dark and hostile realm of sky-eating trees and legendary monsters. The Ancient Ones would protect him. He would not waste his thoughts worrying over the warnings of women. His enemy was out *there*! Somewhere to the south, White Bear was moving his followers north.

White Bear! Warrior of the True People! For over a moon I have seen you dead within my dreams. Now the shaman Inau has come from the Cave of the Winds to foretell your coming. It seems that it has not been enough for me to ask the spirits of our Ancestors for your death!

The hunter ground his teeth until the muscles in his jaw bunched and crawled like serpents writhing beneath his well-greased skin. Bad spirits walked with White Bear's band. Dangerous, malevolent, man-and-woman-and-dog-eating spirits. He could not let White Bear bring them north. Not when he had at last seen a way of stopping him!

The hunter's head went high. He had told no one of his plan. And wisely so. There was not a single member of his band who would approve of it; it was far too dangerous. But sometimes, for the good of all, a brave man must be willing to risk all. And so he had come alone into the forest on the pretext of seeking solitude in which to better commune with the spirits of the game. It had not been a lie. He had simply neglected to inform anyone that the game he sought was man, not meat.

No one had questioned. No one had followed. With the wind at his back and the spirits of the Ancient Ones at his side to guide and protect him, he had made his way southward from the wide arm of the great river and the sprawling encampment of his band. A day and a night had passed upon the long and often circuitous route. Now, in the thinly diffused light of morning, he had come at last to this long-remembered break in the trees.

His wide, meaty lips tightened into a down-curving smile. It was good to see the open sky again, and to look once more upon the meadow. The broad, undulating span of grassland was as he remembered it. Only its color had changed. Although summer was young, after two consecutive moons of little rain the grasses were already bleaching from springtime green to autumn sere. As he had hoped they would!

A shiver of excitement tingled up his spine. Everything

was going almost exactly as planned. Except that there were deer on the meadow. This was a surprise. And a pleasant one! He had not eaten since yesterday, nor had he partaken of fresh meat since leaving the river camp. Salivating, he willed himself to remain motionless as, finding himself fortuitously downwind of the herd, he summed a full hand-count of bucks and twice as many does, many with fawns at their teats or gamboling close by.

His heartbeat quickened. The wind was stinging his face. There was grit in it, a fine, sharp, granular sand that he recognized as the airborne residue of the far north, of his birthplace, of an immense and distant land laid bare to decomposing bedrock by the grinding retreat of ancient ice sheets. He fortressed up his eyes but did not turn away. Not from North Wind! Not from Winter Wind Blowing in Summer! Not from this cold, perverse, potentially deadly river of air that had come blustering down across the world in the tender light of yesterday's dawn to awaken and inspire him. This wind was a gift from the spirits of his Ancestors! This wind was the weapon with which he would dare to drive back his enemy . . . or kill him.

He trembled. North Wind was rising. All signs portended a storm in its wake. A great storm. There would be rain in it, and thunder and lightning, perhaps even hail and snow. But all signs also portended that the storm would not come for another day, perhaps two, and surely not before he had made his way safely back through the tinder-dry depths of the forest to the more or less open country along the river and the encampment of his band. By then North Wind would have accomplished all that he intended to ask of it.

In the meantime, there were deer on the meadow. And he was hungry. Certain that the spirits of his Ancestors had summoned the herd to the clearing as demonstration of their power to look after their own in this dark and demon-haunted world of trees and monsters and lesser tribes, he could not resist reaching over his shoulder to draw an arrow from the sealskin quiver that he carried on his back. As tense as his sinew bowstring, he nocked the arrow and positioned his bow. Scanning the herd for his most promising target, he could feel the spirits of his Ancestors moving all around. The Ancient Ones would grant strength to his shooting arm! They would guide his arrows! They would see to it that he would feast on the hot blood of a kill that would strengthen him for all that he must do this day!

But suddenly, in a screaming fury of black wings, a raven flew out of the forest.

The hunter was so startled that he nearly dropped his bow and arrow. Taloned feet grazed his scalp. He felt the rake of claws and the warm ooze of blood as the bird flew overhead to cut a shrieking, purposeful swath back and forth over the meadow and the now-flagging herd. Watching in dismay, he saw his prey scatter and disappear into the trees. As the raven swooped after them, it occurred to him that the bird might not be a bird at all, but a spirit, a manitou, a winged demon of the forest come to challenge the powers of his Ancestors by informing the deer that Death, in the guise of True Man, was trespassing at the edge of their meadow this day.

He hissed an unarticulated curse and, once again, found himself recalling a warning of the woman of the People.

"Beware of Raven. Inside his feathers he is not Bird, but Man, a creature of two tribes, a warrior spirit born of both Earth and Sky, loyal to none but himself."

Annoyed, as he sent questing fingertips to determine the extent of his wound, he was less troubled by what he found than by the realization that words spoken so long ago by one small doe-eyed female kept returning again and again to lance his mind. Surely neither the woman nor her words were worth remembering! Yet, when he drew his hand from his scalp to stare indignantly at his bloodied fingertips, lust for White Bear's captive heated his loins as surely as loathing chilled his soul.

She had disgraced him. She had leaped into the ice-choked waters of a flash flood and dragged him out by his hair. As though he had ever needed the assistance of a woman! No man should have been asked to share the same camp with such a shameless female. Yet White Bear had asked this of him. And so he had gone his own way. And was better because of his decision. But he would never forget. He would never forgive.

He shivered. Not at unbidden and unwelcome memories of the captive—she was nothing to him now! And not at the extent of his wound. It was minor and would not need stitching. He shivered because he remembered that White Bear's war mask was a representation of Raven. Glowering across the yellow blaze of the sunstruck meadow to the green wall of wind-riled trees into which the bird had flown, he tongued his fingers clean of blood and wondered just who was hunting whom in the forest this day.

Worry settled in his gut. He recalled his enemy. So powerful! So dangerous! As compelling and uncompromising as the tide! And, if the shaman was right, coming toward him even now, leading his slavering war dogs and cursed captive and surviving warriors ever northward. And bringing his man-eating bad spirits with him!

"No! I will stop you! I will . . ."

He blinked, distracted—not by the virulent intensity of the proclamation that he had not intended to speak aloud, but by the sight of a doe returning to the meadow. He caught his breath. Raven, be it bird or phantom, had not won its

way. The spirits of his Ancestors were still working on his behalf, seducing the doe from cover. He *would* taste of the flesh
of deer this day! When the doe paused belly-deep in high
grass, stamped a foreleg, then uttered a series of high, nick-
ering blasts of air, he marveled at the brilliance of the Ancient Ones.

There was still a fawn on the meadow. The *doe's* fawn!
She was calling to it in the way of her kind. He squinted into
the distance and could just make out the form of the little
animal lying on folded knees at the far side of the meadow. It
struck him that the fawn's youth and inexperience must
have coupled with an unusually brave—or stupid—nature
and prevented it from following the herd; but he preferred to
believe that the spirits of his Ancestors were detaining it in
consideration of his needs. His broad face split with a grin as
he saw the doe match the fawn's bravery—or stupidity—by
venturing farther onto the meadow, only to stop again,
stamp again, and nicker again in a vain effort to summon her
offspring into the shadowed safety of the forest.

A tremor of elation shook the hunter. In just such a way
had the doe-eyed woman of the People made herself vulnerable to captivity. To save her infant she had risked all and
lost all. His brow furrowed. There was meaning in this.
Something to think about . . . later. Now his eyes fixed on
the ruddy, sun-dappled silhouette of the fawn as it lay almost
perfectly hidden in wind-bent russet grasses, browning ferns,
and desiccated white meadow flowers. Almost. It was not
good enough.

He did not hesitate. His blood was up for the kill. So were
his bow and arrow. He took aim, pulled back, released the
arrow, and, even as the fawn was struck, could not forgo the
pleasure of reaching back to pull another arrow from his
quiver.

The doe turned and ran.

But not in time. In the instant before she whirled and quartered away, the hunter's second arrow struck her head on, penetrating the soft hollow between her shoulder blades and driving deep to bury its stone head in her heart.

And still she ran.

Astonished, the hunter stood his ground. The doe was dead and did not know it! As the upraised white banner of her tail faded into the shadows between the trees, a scowl tightened his face. He recalled elders speaking of seeing heart-struck deer break and run, but, having never witnessed such an incredible sight, had not believed it possible until now. Still scowling, assuring himself that the Ancient Ones must have a special reason for not killing the doe outright, he strode onto the meadow and followed his prey. He doubted the doe could go far. Her race for cover would increase the flow of blood to her heart; soon the organ would burst and collapse around the arrowhead. She would drop dead then, as surely and suddenly as though brained by a battle club. Guided by the spirits of his Ancestors, he would find her with ease, but first, smiling now at the prospect of the feast to come, he paused to retrieve the fawn.

It was very young and small, all limbs, it seemed, but its smooth, spotted skin would make a handsome cape for his fat little son, and its soft flesh would make a welcome meal for his equally plump and perpetually sore-gummed woman. Nevertheless, his smile vanished when he knelt beside it, surprised to see that, although his arrow had pierced its side, it lay stunned, bleeding profusely, but still alive. He had failed to kill it.

Far off within that part of the forest into which the wounded doe had disappeared, the raven cawed. Or laughed?

Once again the hunter hissed an unarticulated curse.

The bird *was* a spirit! A bad spirit! An emissary of White Bear! The gash at the top of his head was throbbing. Blood was trickling down into his eyes. He backhanded it irritably away. He was certain that there were omens in the moment. Bad omens. Two arrows sent from his bow, each guided by the spirits of the Ancient Ones, neither making a clean kill! And Raven, harassing him, hurting both his flesh and his pride. As White Bear had done. And would do again if he succeeded in bringing his followers north.

"No. I say it will not be!"

The declaration made, he straddled the fawn and gripped it hard between clenched knees. The spirits of his Ancestors might suddenly have lost the power to work their will in this forest, but he had not! Imagining that he was handling the body of his enemy, he twisted the arrow from the flesh of the fawn as painfully as he knew how, then, ignoring the little animal's bleats of pain, thrust the projectile point into one of its eyes and downward straight into its brain. He turned the arrowhead. Worked it. Felt the fawn go lax in his grip. It was lifeless now. Let Raven chortle over that!

The bird was silent.

The hunter, glaring southward, remained kneeling with the dead fawn between his knees. Under any other circumstances he would have cut out its heart and gouged out its other eye to consume both on the spot, but the circumstances that had brought him to this moment perplexed him and deprived him of his appetite. Where were the spirits of the Ancient Ones now? He could no longer feel their comforting presence. But North Wind was still rising, still combing aggressively back through the fringes of his buckskin hunting shirt and the oiled strands of his unbraided black hair, still streaming past him to flatten the parched ferns and grasses of the meadow as though pointing the way to the part of the forest into which the doe had run and Raven had flown . . . and out of which White Bear would come to reclaim everything the hunter had dared to take as his own since breaking company with the man and hurrying north to warn all of White Bear's former trading allies along the great river that White Bear walked with bad spirits now.

Anxiety pricked him. And something else. Guilt? No! He would not consider it. It was time to do what he had come here to do.

Impatiently, using the dead fawn's ears, he wiped his arrow clean of hair, blood, tissue, and the black ooze of vitreous fluid. As he reinserted the projectile into his quiver, an utterly disconcerting wave of restlessness surged through him. The hunting traditions of his Ancestors obligated him to go in search of the wounded doe. To squander her life would be an offense to Great Spirit of All Deer. And if Great Spirit of All Deer was offended, in the future, deer—be they white-tailed or caribou or moose—would not yield their lives to the spears and arrows of True Men.

Frustration heated his mood. There was anger in it. And righteous indignation. He had not entered the forest intending to hunt deer. It was White Bear he wanted dead! White Bear and his doe-eyed captive and his remaining warriors and all the dangerous, malevolent, man-and-woman-and-dog-eating spirits that followed him! He knew now that the deer had not been sent to the meadow by the spirits of the Ancient Ones. The herd had been a diversion, a trick devised by Raven to dissuade him from his purpose. But for the good of all whom he had inspired to name him Headman in White Bear's place, he would not be dissuaded! With North Wind still rising at his back and the sun-seared meadow stretching to the southern flanks of the tinder-dry forest that lay beyond, he would not allow himself to squander time or energy in pursuit of the doe.

"Great Spirit of All Deer, you will understand, or you will not!"

The arrogance of the exclamation surprised him. It also set fire to his intent. He slung his lynx-skin fire-starting bag from his shoulder and rummaged eagerly in its depths. He needed only a pair of flints to accomplish his purpose now.

Soon sparks were flashing. Soon North Wind was breathing hot new life into the ready tinder.

"Burn!" he commanded the fire he had made. "Blow hard and strong!" he ordered the wind. As he watched the first bright tongues of flame leap high and begin to dance southward across the meadow, he shouted to the black winged demon that had come close to making a fool of him this day. "Fly now or die, Raven!"

Hefting the fawn and slinging its limbs forward around his neck, he took up his fire-making bag, rose, turned his face into the wind, and set his moccasined feet back into the forest toward his distant camp.

North Wind would not turn to betray him. He was confident of that. It would be his weapon now! With any luck at all, it would consume everything—and everyone—in its path.

Chapter Two

▼▼▼▼▼▼▼

"Something is wrong. We must not continue north!"

"Why say you this, Ne'gauni?"

Startled out of a daze by the sound of his name, the young man paused upon the forest trail. Disoriented, he leaned on his crutches and stared blankly at the girl who had just spoken to him. Who was she? Why were her strange, pale eyes so full of questions? He frowned. Somewhere far away, a raven was calling. A shiver went up his spine. He did not like ravens. And this one seemed to be part of a dream. A bad dream. A fading dream. And then, suddenly, through a haze it seemed, he heard the girl speak his name again, more sharply than before. He flinched. Wide awake and scowling, he looked around, vexed, not by the imagined soundings of the dream bird or the now-familiar gray-eyed inquisitor's intrusion into his befuddled thoughts, but with himself.

It had happened again. He had allowed himself to become lost in the Darkness. The inner Darkness. That insidious black lethargy of mind that had, of late, been stealing into his head to feed upon his spirit until there was nothing left of him. Nothing! Others might count him among the living as he made his way among them, a mindless, mumbling, broken shell of a man, but, in truth, he was not there. He had slipped away into some other place. No one ever saw him go. Softly, silently, insidiously the Darkness came upon him, emerging like a warm little spider from the innermost core of his brain to cast deceptively innocent arms around his consciousness until, suddenly stinging, it gathered his thoughts into a poisonous black web of memories and mind-numbing despair from which there was no escape, no reprieve until—

"Ne'gauni!"

The young man winced. It had almost happened again, in the blink of an eye: memories, despair, and then Oblivion. Only this time the girl had anticipated the coming of the Darkness and called him back from it. Unlike the raven, Mowea'qua was no dream—although there were those, himself included, who behind her back named her Nightmare. Still, looking at her now as she stood before him in her crudely cured cape of black wolfskin, with her unkempt hair falling in unnatural waves around the strangely elongated oval of her face, he had to admit that the daughter of Kinap the Giant, itinerant storyteller from the distant Land of Grass, knew how to break the spell of the Darkness. She simply shouted at it. And at him. Loudly. Impatiently. And imperiously. As she shouted at the dogs and children and other young women of the band and anyone else who happened to annoy her. Ne'gauni's scarred mouth tightened. He knew that he should be grateful to the girl for rescuing him from the black web of despair, but gratitude was something that Mowea'qua would never win from him. Never!

"Go away," he commanded.

She did not obey. "Sick you are, think I," she told him. "Maybe lying down and riding on a drag frame you should be?"

"Sick I am not! And the day I consent to be pulled along

by the dogs on a drag frame like a pile of meat or baggage, on that day I will make my death song. So do not again suggest this to me!" His words had ripped from his mouth on an angry snarl that stressed the still-tender scar that striped his once-handsome features from the top of one ear to the lobe of the other. A tremor of revulsion and frustration shook him. Would the wound never heal? Would there never come a day or night when he would be free from the cruel ache and the grossly disfiguring shame of it?

"Mmph!" Mowea'qua was not about to be put off. "Know I sickness when see it I. If you will on a drag frame not lie, then for you from a medicine bag will take I a healing powder dark and strong with dogbane and—"

"No!" He cut her off with another snarl. The girl's over-bearing manner and hopelessly tangled Old Tribe dialect irritated him nearly as much as the sight of her equally tangled hair, perpetually dirty face, and unnaturally pale eyes. "I have had more than my share of your attempts at so-called healing, Mowea'qua. Take your place with the other women and girls of the band, or with your father, and stop shadowing me! If I am sick of anything, it is of you."

Not one to wilt at either insult or repudiation, the girl stood her ground and informed him coolly, "My spirit is at ease not with women and girls. And Kinap with the widow walks. No eyes has my father for his Mowea'qua when he is with Suda'li. But my eyes tell me that if the band is to be on the far side of the Gap of Many Stones by sundown, as our headman wishes, my steadying hands are needed to keep you from falling as along through the forest you go asleep on your crutches muttering, 'Something wrong, something wrong, not go north, not go north!' What kind of talk is this? Sick! Very sick talk! The will of the headman and council you challenge, Ne'gauni. Good this is not, think I!"

He scowled. *Something wrong!* Had he said that? *Not go north!* Why would he give such advice? Defensive, he mumbled, "My words and dreams are my own concern."

"Think you so? Wrong you are! Watching you has old Ko'ram been. Many call him Wise Man. And says he that maybe bad spirits are feeding inside your head. If he hears your sick words he—"

"Ko'ram is so old that he can barely hear himself break wind! Call him what you will, but I will not name a man Wise One simply because he has outlived all but his grandchildren and seen more winters than anyone else within the band. I do not care what he thinks, Mowea'qua. I care only that I keep myself upwind of him!"

"Others care. Others heed him. And Kinap about you worries. He has said to me that I must keep you well and strong, because if bad spirits are truly inside your head you will from the band be driven. This is the way of the People. And then what to you will happen, a one-legged half-healed man hopping through the forest like a grounded bird with no one to protect you? Mmph! To the north you should *want* to go. You are Ne'gauni—He Walks Ahead—boldest and bravest son of the hunt chief Asticou!"

"I am now the only son of Asticou. And the name my mother gave me mocks the truth of what I have become— He Walks Behind, now Half a Man, now Scar Face, now—"

"Truth a man puts to his own name, Always Sorry For Yourself! In this band you are not the only man to carry on your face a scar. One leg you have lost, not two, Grateful for Nothing, and under past moons great skill with a bow have you gained! All say that when the wide river we reach, we will in the finest of all hunting grounds be. All there will see and admire the skill of Hunts on One Leg. And all will envy us our headman. Leads us well does Tôrnârssuk! Many are the battles he has won! Many are the captives he has taken! Many are the tongues he speaks! Many are the bands and tribes that cower and shiver like frightened dogs in fear of his name! It is good that we have come to travel with him. And with Chief Ogeh'ma and his family, too! Once three bands were we, each from a different tribe. Now we are one people! Together we are strong! So why should we to the north go not? With Tôrnârssuk as headman we are safe. Walking together with three bands, we have no enemies!"

"I have heard Tôrnârssuk say that no one is ever safe. And there are always enemies, Mowea'qua. Always."

"Mmph!" snorted the girl. Then, with more than a hint of reproof, "And so walk you along to yourself mumbling . . . because you are afraid!"

Once Ne'gauni would have challenged her. Once he would have said that he was afraid of nothing. Once it would have been true. Now, grimacing against emotions too corrosive to entertain, he said tightly, "Our last camp was a good camp. We took much meat. All we needed was there. Why move on?"

"Why not?" The girl's exclamation was an unrestrained burst of pure enthusiasm. "Everyone who has to the Great Gathering been says that a wonder it is to see. So many bands! So many people! So many dogs! So many lodges! So many strange and good things to hunt and eat! So many cooking fires that by night it is as though the stars to the earth come down to light the land! And Chief Ogeh'ma says that mammoths swim in the great river. Bald as eggs are they, with tails and fins instead of legs. 'Whales' he calls these mammoths. White and blue and gray whales as many and as shining sleek as the stones that at the bottom of the great river lie. And to the sun and moon and stars they sing! Can this you imagine? Ah, Ne'gauni, would you these things not see and hear?"

The young man stared at her blankly. Mammoths were so rare that only a few men he knew of had ever set eyes on a living tusker. He, for one, had never seen one, but he had heard the trumpeting of its kind and found it so terrifying that he hoped never again to hear its like—or come close enough to view any animal capable of equaling it. But a bald blue mammoth swimming along singing beneath the stars? Now that would indeed be a sight to see! He shook his head, amazed by the extent of Mowea'qua's gullibility, but no more so than by his own inability to raise an eyebrow or snicker at her willingness to believe yet another of Chief Ogeh'ma's fanciful exaggerations. Perhaps the girl was right after all? He must be sick! Or perhaps he was simply being worn down by the time it was taking for his wounds to heal. With a sigh of acquiescence to fatigue and befuddlement, he stared off, willing his trance-dulled eyes to readjust to the light of morning.

They had been traveling since dawn. It worried him to realize that much of that time was a blank, a part of the Darkness, but he knew that they had come far. Pain told him. The stump of his left thigh throbbed. No matter how many moss-stuffed rabbit pelts he twisted around the braces of his crutches, extended travel never failed to chafe the skin and bruise the muscles of his armpits. And there was something different about the light. It was no longer the cool, substanceless gray of dawn. It was warmer, richer, ripening toward noon. And the wind, still rising steadily out of the north, was wafting transparent eddies of dust, pollen, stray leaf fragments, and winged insects into yellow sunbeams that were angling through the surrounding conifers.

His head went high as he squinted ahead. It was a

beautiful morning. The pungent scent of the ancient boreal forest was strong around him, unseasonably dry yet intensely fragrant with the heavy smell of balsam and a fragile, sweeter scent that told him that shinleaf and pipsissewa flowers were still in bloom. The combined fragrances were heady, soothing; he breathed them in and felt his troubled spirit ease a little as he watched his band moving far ahead within the sun-streaked shadows between the trees.

Then, with a start, Ne'gauni's gut tightened. The sweet scent of blossoms and balsam flew from his nostrils along with an exhalation of disgust. The girl was definitely right about him. He *was* sick. With shame. With confusion. And, suddenly, he *was* afraid. He had fallen behind again. As he always did when the Darkness took him. But this time the distance that he had placed between himself and the band was larger than it had ever been before.

He frowned, deeply shaken and at a complete loss to understand his behavior. Ever since the headman had agreed to the decision of the council to break down the band's last hunting camp and resume the journey to the Gathering of Many Tribes, he had been slipping in and out of the Darkness by day and suffering headaches and cold sweats by night. Unable to secure a decent night's sleep, he found himself glowering at each new dawn and rising irritably to grumble his way through each new day, half the time not knowing where he was or that he was mumbling aloud at all. Everything anyone said or did put him on edge. Only this morning he had angrily pitched stones at the dogs for no other reason than to protest the loudness of their usual *yarf*ing greeting to Ningao and the other handlers. And soon after, over a minor childish infraction that he could barely recall, he had lost all patience with old Ko'ram's ever disruptive grandsons, the twin boys of the widow Suda'li. For this outburst he had won the widow's ire and, with the entire band looking on, endured the humiliation of standing to her scalding accusation that he was behaving not like a mature hunter of nearly sixteen winters but like a sore-nippled, puff-bellied, foul-tempered female on the brink of shedding moon blood.

Ne'gauni flushed with righteous indignation. How the entire band had laughed at him! All except the headman, the headman's woman, and old Ko'ram. Tôrnârssuk never laughed. The headman's woman was always conciliatory. And the Wise Man never found Ne'gauni in the least amusing. But Suda'li had been right about him. He was not behaving like himself. Indeed, of late his conduct had been so strange and unpredictable that, as surely as Halboredja, the ever wandering sun, rose out of the east and journeyed to find sleep beyond the western edge of the world, Kinap's worries were bound to prove well founded. He was either going to say or do something unpardonable or simply fall behind once too often. On that day he would come blinking out of a daze to find himself alone, surrounded by medicine bags and protective fetishes and, if he was at all lucky, offerings of food left by his fellow travelers as a farewell gesture of hope that he would somehow free himself of demons and manage to survive.

He trembled. Perhaps it was meant to be. Once before he had been abandoned, left for dead by his own brothers, but that had been long ago and for other reasons that he refused to think of now—just as he would refuse to fault the council when and if his behavior forced the decision to leave him behind. A band, like a team of dogs, was only as strong as its weakest member. All men knew this. And Ne'gauni's band, an alliance of three distinct peoples, was newly formed and only beginning to define its strengths and weaknesses.

The young man's eyes narrowed against the wind as he watched the others moving northward through the trees. Forest dwellers like himself. Men, women, and children from the coastal marshes, estuaries, and beaches of the Dawnland. Traders and onetime raiders from the northern barrens. And Kinap, the giant storyteller, from the interior grasslands. All had come for their own reasons from their own far portion of the world, and not one of them could have said why the Four Winds had swept them into the same part of the forest. But wise men did not question the will of the Four Winds, and now, having stood successfully against a common enemy, they had put aside old enmities, forgiven past grievances, and, with language no longer a complete barrier, taken pleasure and comfort in each other's company as they journeyed together to the annual Gathering of Many Tribes. There, along the shores of the great and still-distant river, they would trade. They would hunt. They would make new alliances. They would greet old friends and relatives among extended families that they had not seen in many a long moon. Unmarried women would find husbands. And men would take or exchange wives.

"Some men."

Again Ne'gauni winced. Had he spoken? He was not sure. But the bitterness of the words lingered in his mouth as he heard the wife of Tôrnârssuk, headman of the band, lift her light and lovely voice in song.

He held his breath, transfixed, listening. Hasu'u's song was beautiful. As Hasu'u was beautiful! And too long had it been since this kindest and fairest of all women found cause to sing.

Something deep within Ne'gauni's chest gave a hurtful little lurch that felt all too much like love. Hasu'u's song, like the fragrance of flowers and evergreens and the woman herself, captivated his spirit. Her presence within the band centered his world, for she had been a part of his life long before either of them had come to walk with Tôrnârssuk: first in his father's inland village, to which she had been brought from the Dawnland as his eldest brother's bride; then on that now-distant and ill-fated trading trail along which he had journeyed toward the coast with her and his brothers. What a small, careless, and contented band they had been! Until the day the raiders came.

Tôrnârssuk's raiders!

It made Ne'gauni light-headed to think of it. On that day, struck down by weapons he had never before seen, he had been swept away by the savage waters of a wild and icy creek. On that day Hasu'u's newborn infant had been torn from her arms and drowned. On that day he had seen her carried off into captivity. And on that day he had lain stunned and bleeding in the creek, his left leg hopelessly shattered, his face slit open, his body battered, unable to move, unable to save her.

But the Circle of Life turned forward, never back. And the whims of the forces of Creation took men and women where and how they would. The manitou spirits of the forest had been watching over Ne'gauni and Hasu'u in their own perverse way on that long-gone day. And eventually the Four Winds swept the Dawnland woman and the youngest son of Asticou together again onto the path of Chief Ogeh'ma and his band—Hasu'u's own family—even as Tôrnârssuk's raiders, long on the trail and yearning for home, wearied of their marauding ways. Now, reunited with one whom they had maimed and nearly killed, they named Ne'gauni Brother. Now Hasu'u, once their slave, was the honored wife of their widowed headman and milk woman for his motherless infant. Proudly, along with the discreet, traditional tattooing of her

Dawnland band, she wore the intricate spiral facial tattooing that now marked her as a woman dedicated to her new tribe. The baby, Tiguak, brought her joy, and Tôrnârssuk was proving to be a more considerate husband than Ne'gauni's brother M'alsum had ever been.

The young man clenched his teeth. He did not want to think of the past. And most assuredly he did not want to think of his brothers. To save their own skins, M'alsum, Sac, and M'ingwé had taken their dogs and trade goods and fled from danger, leaving him alone to defend Hasu'u from certain death. And he had defended her. Boldly! Bravely! With no thought for his own safety, he had stood his ground, placing himself between his brother's woman and the raiders' arrows as he challenged Death for her. But Death had other appetites that day. Later, in other parts of the forest, it consumed his brothers. Ne'gauni did not grieve for them; they had been the worst of men, and he would forever regret the day he so trustingly put his life into their hands and left his father's peaceful little village in their company. But regret counted for nothing in the violent, unforgiving, and all too often confounding world that he had found beyond the hunting grounds of his Ancestors. And the old adage was true—just as an infant could not return into the birth lodge of its mother's belly once it had been born, no man of pride could return to beg meat and shelter of his father once he had chosen to go his own way and make his own encampments in the world.

"Ne'gauni! Blank-eyed you are staring off again! Do you hear Hasu'u not? Her song calls us on! Come! We must follow! Or ahead I will go, Wounded One, to ask the headman for a drag frame upon which you shall lie whether you wish it or not."

The girl's words cut him. *Wounded One*. She did not

often call him that these days. He glared at her. Hated her. Wondered if she had any idea just what her threat meant to him and how much he despised that name and all that it recalled.

"Have you not shamed me enough?" he asked. By the expression of utter incomprehension on her face he knew he had his answer. She would never understand. Too long had she lived wild, all but deserted by her wandering father to the shadowed depths of the inland forest and to the care of a solitary Old Tribe grandmother who spurned and despised the civilized ways of the People.

Ne'gauni shook his head. Memories were crowding him again. Intense. Unwelcome. Blacker than the Darkness. More ominous than that far and haunted portion of the forest within which the manitous had led the wild girl to find him after his brothers had forsaken him and the raiders had taken Hasu'u and gone their way. Colder than the bleak and bitter shank of winter that he had passed with her and her feral old grandmother against his will, mad with the agony of his wounds and desolate with grief within their hidden lodge of bark and bones and the tusks of long-dead mammoths.

He caught his breath.

Somewhere near, a raven was calling, raising the hackles on his back. He reminded himself that winter was over. The old woman was dead. The wild girl had been claimed by her nomadic father and brought from the forest along with "her" Wounded One to live among the People. And so Ne'gauni had come to this moment and would never again set eyes on that dark and bloodied lodge of bones within which his youth had died and he had been reborn as half a man when—to save his life—Mowea'qua and her grandmother had cut off his leg.

He exhaled violently, attempting to cast out memories

along with the air in his lungs. It was no use. As his eyes fixed on the girl, he knew that he did not want to forget, or to forgive her—ever. He cursed the day she had found him. He cursed the moment in which she had chosen to drag him from the creek and take him into her care. Tôrnârssuk and his raiders had at least been compassionate enough to leave him to the forces of Creation once they had struck him down. They had known that, wounded as he was, he would welcome Death. And so he had—until, against his will, Mowea'qua had chosen life for him, without asking, as she took all things.

He turned his gaze from the girl and stared ahead. Standing very still, he closed his eyes as he listened to Hasu'u's song, inviting it to filter through his troubled thoughts and salve his restive spirit.

"*Hay ya, ya! Hay ya, ya!*
The trail is long. Together we go. Together we go!
Hay ya, ya! Hay ya, ya!
Our hearts are strong. Together we go! Together we go!"

Ne'gauni's throat constricted. Shame burned him. If the Dawnland woman, a mere female, and a very small one at that, could find strength enough within herself to make accommodation with all that had befallen her, how could he allow himself to do less? Hasu'u, Woman Who Sings Always, did not bemoan her losses. She did not look back. Instead she had come resiliently through tragedy to give new meaning to her name as she rejoiced in her resounding faith in the ultimate goodness of the forces of Creation and, through her forgiving and understanding heart, inspired others to share and act upon this faith. To walk once more within the same band with such a woman was the one blessing Ne'gauni could count among the endless curses that the forces of Creation had rained down upon his head. As for Mowea'qua, what was she to him now? Only what he allowed her to be. A shadow that recalled the past, no more, no less.

Now, opening his eyes and watching Hasu'u's lithe form walking gracefully with the other women while the men of the band tended to the dogs and heavily loaded drag frames and the children kept up with the adults by playing a frantically happy game of Kicking the Fir Tree Cone Ahead, the young man actually felt a smile begin to take shape upon his mouth.

What a joyful and thoroughly amazing scene it was: one-time marauders and their victims walking happily together, the past forgotten, the future looming ahead, promising good things to all. Even the dogs appeared relaxed and at ease, fully confident in Tôrnârssuk's leadership as he guided them ever northward, while old Ko'ram hop-danced along behind him on spindly legs and big feet, no doubt—judging from the distance the others were keeping—cutting copious wind as he shook his deer-hoof ankle janglers and turtle carapace rattle in vigorous accompaniment to Hasu'u's song.

One by one the women began to take up the chant and weave new words into the melody. The men followed suit. The girls and boys joined in. Onen'ia, one of Ogeh'ma's two sons, took up his willow flute. Kinap the Giant began to beat the rhythm of the song upon the broad round face of his story drum as Musquash, his adopted little son, helped keep the rhythm with a beater of his own. Gray jays, offended by the resounding clamor of this human invasion of their domain, scolded from the deep green heights of the forest canopy to remind that they—and not the noisy stream of human passersby—were the chiefs of all they surveyed in this land of trees. One of the babies of the band, riding securely in its cradleboard on its mother's back, squealed in delight at the noise of the rising chorus of man and bird, or perhaps only at the sound of its own newly discovered voice.

Ne'gauni allowed his smile to take control of his mouth. He was feeling better. Much better. Almost himself again. His eyes shone ahead to see that Hasu'u was stepping out from the other women, turning to walk backward as she smiled and raised a slim arm in salutation, then sang out, just to him:

"Hay ya, ya! Hay ya, ya!
The great river waits. Together we go. Together we go.
Hay ya, ya! Hay ya, ya!
Old friends together. Together we go. Together we go!
Hay ya, ya!"

Ne'gauni's spirit soared. The morning—like the headman's woman—was transcendently beautiful. To be young and alive and sharing the world with Hasu'u on such a morning was a gift from the forces of Creation! To be near her was the best of all things that he could hope for in what was left to him of his life, but it was enough. More than enough! How could he be less than grateful? And how, on such a day, even with sullen Mowea'qua glowering by his side, could he have thought for even the merest shading of a moment that anything in all the world could possibly be wrong?

▼▼▼▼

Heat.
  Smoke.
  Flame.

Far to the north—in a deeply wooded hollow midway between the still-smoldering meadow and that part of the forest within which Ne'gauni followed in the footsteps of Tôrnârssuk and his band—an exhausted woman crumpled to her knees in a choking rain of ash and fire.

"I can go no farther. Nor will I be carried another step by any of you. Go, I say. This baby in my belly will not be born! You must leave me. Now!"

No one spoke. In the gray-brown light of a morning turned to dusk by smoke, the woman had raised her voice in an effort to be heard above the roar of the wind and approaching fire, but no one wanted to hear her words. They stood around her in a protective circle, a small band: her husband, another adult couple, one old man, five children, an adolescent girl, and a few dogs. The moment seemed unreal to them.

They had traveled a great distance since North Wind first brought smoke and ashes to warn them of what might soon come to them if they did not break camp and move on. At first, observing the discolored sky, they had seen no real danger to themselves. Long had they lived within this part of the forest. Longer still had it been since this part of the forest had burned. All knew the old stories of Wildfire, daughter of Lightning, and of how she danced across the world at will, burning up everything in her path, but no one could recall a single tale that spoke of her ever dancing anywhere near. So no one was afraid. Indeed, they might not have moved on at all had the hunting not been poor for the past few weeks and their current encampment not begun to reek from prolonged habitation. It was time to move on. Since they had already been discussing the benefits of relocating to higher and more open country where they could air out their lodge skins and where biting blackflies might find their flesh less sweet, they all agreed that it would be a good day to set off for their distant hunting grounds at Hidden Springs.

The hasty gathering of belongings, breaking down of lodges, securing of cache pits, and even the bedding down of Grandfather upon a twin-poled carrying frame for the dogs to drag had seemed a timely and welcome diversion from the routine of their days. Everyone looked forward to fresh meat and a clean camp and fine fishing.

The woman had, perhaps, been the most eager of all to journey on. At close to seven full hand-counts of summers, she was not young, but she was over nine moons full of baby. Convinced that a long, strenuous walk was just what she needed to bring on the birth of her child, she had made a praise song to North Wind and Smoke and Fire, thanking these spirits for forcing the movement of her band as she walked on, strong in the certainty that she would soon prove to all that she was still young enough to bear. How could she have known that, although the baby would refuse to be born, her birth pains would come on with such intensity that they would soon wear her down, or that, along with her water, she would pass so much blood that she could now no longer stand? And who could have imagined that North Wind would carry Wildfire so fast and far that they could not outdistance it?

Now they were trapped in the hollow, with Wildfire burning all around. Above their heads the wind-whipped treetops were beginning to catch fire. Somewhere high in the canopy of the forest a branch as thick as a man's thigh exploded, and superheated sap swelled to burst its containing bark with an explosive crack.

"Go!" screamed the woman as burning brands flew through the smoke and fell upon the band.

"We will not leave you. Get up, my woman! We cannot

stay! Look! Even Grandfather is on his feet and ready to walk on his own. I *will* carry you. We will find cover! We—"

"No!" Splaying her fingers wide upon the ash-grayed, blue-quilled buckskins of her husband's shoulder, she gripped him hard as he knelt beside her. "There is no time . . . not with me to slow you down. You must loose the dogs! Leave everything! Pick up the little ones and run!"

He had lost track of how long he had been carrying her. Forever, it seemed now. It had not been so bad at first. Indeed, he had been glad for the chance to prove his strength to her and to the others. A small man, he had always rejoiced in his big, strong woman. What a wife she was to him! A good cook, a competent mother, a maker of enviable garments, a renderer of fat that did not smoke too much in the winter lamps. Under normal circumstances she could drag the lodgepoles all day long and carry a baby and a fully loaded pack on her back at the same time without complaint. And by night she was always ready to lie under him like a big, soft, smoothly padded skin, all warm and receptive, spread wide to receive his need. But these were not ordinary circumstances. She was now so weakened by pain and loss of blood that she could no longer stand. And having willingly borne her weight—doubled, it seemed, by her pregnancy—his arms and back and thighs ached so cruelly that he knew that he would stumble and fall and be unable to rise again if he attempted to lift, much less carry, her once more. But he *could* carry a child, his three-winter-old son. The other boys were old enough to scamper along on their own feet ahead of their parents, who could scoop them up if they faltered. The girl could carry the toddler. And Grandfather could make his own way . . . or form his death song alone.

"Go!" the woman begged him again. Then, gripping his

shoulder even harder, her voice softened, broke, became a resigned and mewing plea. "Only first . . . please . . . do not . . ."

He interrupted her with a kiss. Long. Deep. All his love for her was in it. He wanted her to have that now. There was no need for her to speak. He knew where her words would lead him. And he was already there.

Drawing back, he nodded consent to her unfinished request, but anguish choked him as he turned up his face to the rain of ashes. He could now barely find air enough to sustain his breathing, and what little he managed to rake into his lungs seared them with heat and smoke. Cinders stung his skin. His eyes smarted. His nostrils burned. He could smell the hair on his head and the backs of his hands beginning to scorch. And everywhere around and within him was the stink and sound of the burning forest—as though the entire world was going up in flames, screaming as it died.

"May the forces of Creation take pity on any man, woman, child, or beast who walks in the way of the wind within the forest this day!"

The invocation came on a sob. To stay in this place was to be burned up alive in this place, and although he was not a young man, he was not yet so old that he was ready to die. Or to turn his back on his big, strong woman and allow her to die in agony.

He reached to his belt. "We will not forget you," he vowed. Bending to kiss her one last time, he slipped his stone dagger from its birchbark sheath.

▼▼▼▼▼

They were still singing.

Ne'gauni lowered his head, squinted into the wind, and swung out and down with his crutches, resolutely making his way after the band.

Pain was his constant companion—pain and Mowea'qua. He was doing his best to ignore both when, his eyes fixed stolidly ahead, he was startled to see a veritable tidal bore of small, pale, black-masked birds come flying out of the forest to swoop madly over the band. Startled, he ducked and nearly fell as the entire flock flew overhead to disappear into the trees through which he, Mowea'qua, and the others had just come.

"Chickadees!" exclaimed the girl with delight.

Ne'gauni did not share her enthusiasm. "Among my people it is said that when chickadees fly like that, they are not chickadees at all, but messengers of the forces of Creation, emissaries of the Four Winds come to warn of approaching danger or a change in the weather or—"

"Mmph! Rain I would see! And out of your own mouth have you said that there is always danger."

"Always enemies," he corrected.

"It is the same. And it is for Tôrnârssuk and old Ko'ram and the council to determine signs, not for you, say I."

His brow furrowed. The entire band had been brought short by the feathered disruption. One of the dogs was sneezing and spitting feathers, apparently all that remained of a hastily snatched snack of bird on the wing. Old Ko'ram was gesturing wildly at the dog with his turtle-shell rattle. Tôrnârssuk, Chief Ogeh'ma, and Kinap the Giant were coming together to converse while the women shushed the children and the other men spoke together in low tones until Hasu'u, laughing, called out to the headman for help.

Ne'gauni went as rigid as his crutches.

"Look!" directed Mowea'qua with a merry chortle at the other woman's expense.

Ne'gauni felt tension drain from him as he saw the headman go to Hasu'u and, surrounded by children, proceed to gently assist her in freeing a bird that had ensnared itself in her hair.

The young man's breath snagged in his throat. Once, long ago, on the day Hasu'u came to his father's village for the first time, all had delighted to see a butterfly alight upon her head to fan her brow as though it recognized her loveliness and chose to do it homage.

"All living things acknowledge her kindness and beauty," he sighed, lovesick, intoxicated by his memories and the woman who engendered them.

"Not all living things are of kindness deserving," said Mowea'qua dourly. "But Old Tribe people say that all things are alive. And that all things are beautiful."

"Not you," he slurred. His eyes caressing Hasu'u, he observed as she reached to take the bird from Tôrnârssuk and cup it gently between her palms.

"Go now, little one!" Hasu'u cried as she opened her hands and set the chickadee flying high, to the approving *aahs* of the women and children of the band and the furiously supportive shaking of old Ko'ram's rattle. "Fly high! Fly far! Tell your brothers and sisters and all who would hear within the great forest that the followers of Tôrnârssuk walk strong and with peaceful intent toward all . . . especially chickadees. Go! Join your band! You are now free of mine!"

Mowea'qua snorted again. "A foolish woman is Hasu'u. Her words she wastes. There is need not to tell a chickadee how and where to fly! It will its band seek. It will with its own kind hide from what it fears."

Fear.

The word tore the moment for Ne'gauni. He was on edge again. And he was vexed and offended by Mowea'qua's willingness to find fault with Hasu'u. "Just what does a chickadee fear? The nets of Old Tribe scavengers like you and your grandmother, who, like dogs, would catch and eat such unfit meat?"

The girl's long, full mouth went white against her teeth. "The Old Tribe is no more. And you will speak no bad words of Kelet. Your spirit lives on in your body only because of Grandmother's magic!" She thrust her thumbs under the shoulder straps of her backpack and glared at him. "Mmph! Maybe our Old Tribe magic was on you wasted. And why ask me what the chickadee fears? That bird into Hasu'u's hair flew to tell its secrets, not into mine!"

"Any bird careless enough to fly into your hair would be ensnared and soon no more than bones and beak and feathers—like the leftovers of a mouse in the puked-up hair ball of a lynx or owl . . . or in the turd of a wolf."

Even Mowea'qua had her limits. "Comb I my hair when I see fit! And mice do not have feathers!" she snapped and walked on without him.

Ne'gauni was surprised not to be more relieved to see her go, but he had riled the girl and was glad about that, even though he remained troubled about the chickadees. If the birds were truly messengers of the forces of Creation, what had their message been? They had flown south, ahead of North Wind, as though fleeing into that very part of the forest out of which Tôrnârssuk insisted upon leading the band. Logic mocked his concern. The rising wind, coupled with the booming of Kinap's drum and the hiss of Ko'ram's rattle, was enough to rile any bird and inspire it to seek a roosting place in a quieter and more sheltered part of the forest.

He sighed. The band was moving on. He set himself to ignore pain again and soon succumbed to an almost lyric sense of longing as he walked on, imagining what it must be to fly . . . to soar . . . to rise above the earth . . . to wing as light and free as air among the trees. He was actually smiling as, gradually, he felt himself relaxing into the pleasant, albeit more earthly distraction offered by the continued music-making of his fellow travelers.

Hasu'u was singing again, still leading the refrain as she walked once more with the other women. Old Ko'ram was now embellishing the end of each stanza with ululating screeches that sounded like the rasping yowls of an aged mountain lion in the throes of its last and most stupendous passion. Even Mowea'qua was singing as he fell into step beside her. Although he found her nasal "hay ya yas" only slightly more harmonic than the would-be Wise Man's cater-wauling, he had to admit that, as she leaned forward into the press of her browband to more evenly distribute the weight of her antler-framed backpack, she was doing her best to keep the rhythm and echo the words of the song.

> "Hay ya, ya! Hay ya, ya!
> The trail leads on. Together we go. Together we go.
> Hay ya, ya! Hay ya, ya!
> Boldly we walk. Together we go. Together we go!"

"Sing, Negauni! Sing, say I!"

He expelled a taut breath. Annoyance, exasperation: Both were in it. She was commanding him again! He would not sing. Not to please her. But, scanning ahead, his eyes fastened on the headman's woman, and softly, to please himself, he said, "Together we go, together we go. Always and forever together we go!"

"That is how the song goes not!" the girl protested. "There are two 'together we goes.' Then come two 'hay ya, yas.' Then come words telling about the journey, three or four words, as many as the song caller says. Then come two more 'together we goes.' And then over again it all starts, with new song caller words each time. But there is no 'always and forever' after the second 'together we go'!"

"There is if I say there is."

"Not in this song, say I!"

Ne'gauni clamped his jaw tight. The girl was only just learning to sing in the manner of the People, and already she was convinced that she knew everything about the subject. He was, however, in no mood to argue with her. The distance he had put between himself and the others remained considerable even though he had been doing his best to close the breach. Wanting to be closer to Hasu'u and determined not to fall behind again, he lengthened his one-legged stride.

"Down you will fall if a crutch you snag on a root or stone or sapling," warned Mowea'qua. "Slow your step!"

"Mind your own!" he warned her back and walked on even faster.

The headman was leading the band uphill now. The grade was slight at first, in all likelihood barely noticeable to Tôrnârssuk and the other travelers and certainly not enough to trouble Mowea'qua, but it was gradually increasing and was enough to stress a one-legged man. Ne'gauni broke a sweat as he made his way doggedly onward, keeping his grueling pace, alternately stabbing down and swinging out with his crutches, maneuvering over and around broad outcroppings of lichen-scabbed rock and patchy areas of leafy ground cover that, under a later moon, would be thick and sweet with berries.

It was difficult and thirsty going. He salivated, imagined soft pulp and tiny seeds sluicing between his teeth, red and purple-blue juices running down his throat, coloring his lips, satisfying his thirst. Frowning, he swallowed the small amount of spit his imagination had summoned from his salivary glands and fought back the urge to reach to his side for the bladder flask of water that he carried attached to his belt. To stop for a drink now, so soon after pausing, would no doubt win some sort of unwelcome comment from the girl—and add to the distance he had already placed between himself and the headman's woman. He would not do this. He would drink when the others stopped to rest and drink. Not before. In the meantime, he would try not to think of water.

It was impossible. Not because cool freshets burbled enticingly alongside the trail. And not because fat drops of morning dew dripped from the trees or glistened beckoningly on every leaf, frond, and sapling within the undergrowth. It was impossible because as he stomped along, scattering dry leaves, fallen needles, and bits of crumbled bark every time he lifted the tips of his crutches, he was also breathing in the dust raised by the band. Miserable, he lowered his head and attempted to breathe through his mouth, but dust backed up into his nostrils anyway and brought with it the scent of desiccated fungi and dried leaf mold. Slowly it began to dawn on him that he had never seen a forest so dry. There had been dew this morning, but not enough to drip from the trees or do much glistening upon the undergrowth, and for many a morning before this there had been no dew at all. And even before the wind had shifted and begun to blow strong and steady from the north, after two moons without rain the brackens and trilliums that grew in the usually moist shade of the deep woods had shriveled and gone as dry as the mossy embankments of many of the shallower stream courses that the band had traversed since leaving its last hunting camp.

Now, scanning to his left and right as he walked on, he noticed that on either side of him the forest floor stretched away between endless distances of trees, its surface covered by a deep, loosely woven mantle of fallen forest debris that was the color and texture not of spring, but of late autumn. Here and there the sundered branches and shattered trunks of last winter's blowdowns lay tangled and scattered about like the cast-off bones of slaughtered giants. And everywhere were broken stands of browning ferns and parched thickets of low-lying shrubs. All dry. So dry. No sign of moisture anywhere. None!

Ne'gauni swallowed again. His mouth felt as parched as the woods. Again he thought of berries, but, despite his earlier fancy, he knew that there would be none this year. Not here. Not in this part of the forest.

"By all the powers of the forces of Creation," he sighed, "why does it not rain?"

"Old Ko'ram says that if our band a true shaman had, he or she would know the way to call down Rain," said Mowea'qua.

Ne'gauni made a rude noise. He had never known a true shaman. Nor was he comfortable with what he had heard about them from those who did. And, since he had little faith in magic, he said mockingly, "We could ask young Musquash to be our shaman. Old Ko'ram seems to think that the power will be his one day. And Kinap claims that the boy's father was a great Squam, a keeper of ancient wisdom and a magic maker upon a far and enchanted island that—"

"Mmph! The spirits choose who will a shaman be. A father cannot this power give to his children. A shaman must of the spirits be worthy. And a bad man was Musquash's father. Good it is that he is dead. Better still that Kinap stole his son and took Musquash as his own. And again better still that my father has no one told of all that he saw take place upon the far island. A baby only six summers old is

Musquash, with dreams of that island so terrible that in the night he still pisses his bed furs. Mmph! No power has he. Nor wants he any. But to a true shaman in the ways of magic schooled the forces of Creation would listen and give Rain permission to come."

Ne'gauni made another rude noise. "Then why do you not ask for rain, Mowea'qua? Work some of your Old Tribe magic for the band! You and your old grandmother had such faith in that! Not that it ever did me any good."

"Alive you are, Grateful for Nothing, because of Old Tribe magic. But the Old Tribe is no more. And our ways are healing ways. We are not shamans. We can speak to the kami and offer gifts and prayers but we cannot expect the spirits to—"

"You can do nothing correctly, Mowea'qua, nothing!" He kept on his way, doing his best to work up what little saliva he could to moisten his mouth as he walked beneath the shadowing canopy of trees so ancient that he suspected they might have been old when First Man and First Woman came, following the great white mammoth, Life Giver, out of the time beyond beginning to people the world.

The legends of Creation drifted through his mind. Thinking of them helped to pass the time. They were such wondrous tales, of a vast sea of ice, of mountains that walked across the land and offered shade to perpetually misted rainforests and evergreen grasslands within and upon which the children of First Man and First Woman lived and loved and hunted and prospered unto this very generation. But where was the sea of ice? How gladly he would journey along its shores this day! Where were the mountains that walked and offered shade to evergreen grasslands? And why had the lush forest suddenly gone as dry as old bones? He worried about the dryness. He did not understand the long absence of rain. It was unnatural, threatening in ways that he could not even begin to comprehend.

He tried not to think about it, or, for that matter, to think about anything else that would draw his thoughts from the immediate task at hand. Having nearly just tripped over a hidden root, he won an immediate "Warned you I it would be so!" from Mowea'qua. Not sure with whom he was more annoyed, himself or the girl, he decided that it would be best to concentrate wholly upon the physical manipulations necessary to keep his body advancing upright along the trail.

"Slow your step, say I!" commanded the girl.

"Keep up or fall behind!" he challenged. "Or would you have Tôrnârssuk accuse you of being the one to keep the band from reaching the Gap of Many Stones before sundown?"

"Fall behind I do not . . . except to you look after!"

"We will see," he taunted and, deliberately quickening his pace for no other reason than to irritate her, set himself to the task of maintaining it.

It was not easy. He clenched his jaw and willed the proper sequence of movements. First, swing out with the crutches. Second, ram the fire-hardened tips down hard. Third, assure an even and solid purchase. Then, gripping the hardwood staffs securely with both hands, press down and lift up and hold, reach out with the good leg, swing the torso forward and then . . . careful . . . balance . . . balance . . . then plant the foot down firmly and begin the entire process all over again . . . only this time faster than before, just to see how long it would take for Mowea'qua to break a sweat.

Swing. Ram. Lift. Reach. Step.

Again.

Swing. Ram. Lift. Reach. Step.

And again.

Swing. Ram. Lift. Reach. Step.

And again and again and . . .

He was sucking in a smile now, eyeing the girl with a side-ward glance, delighted to see that she was glowering at him. Her thick black eyebrows were so deeply veed over the high bridge of her narrow nose that they looked like the wings of a swooping blackbird. And perspiration was very definitely dewing her upper lip and showing along the lower edge of her headband as it ran downward over her cheeks to streak her dirty face.

Immensely satisfied, Ne'gauni slowed his step and settled into a more comfortable and less hazardous pace now that he had proved to himself that he could physically stress the girl if he chose to do so.

"Mmph!" snorted Mowea'qua, unwilling to acknowledge either relief or gratitude, or to concede to him, or to herself, that she had just lost a battle of wills.

Ne'gauni made no comment. He was again concentrating on each step, finding the process to be more than a little like Mowea'qua's instructions for song making. Rhythm and balance could both be achieved through carefully metered repetition of essential patterns, and there was something inestimably soothing about allowing his thoughts to flow on and on into a tranquilizing monotony that assured his safe progress along the trail even as it dulled the pain that came with every step and enabled him to ignore all but Hasu'u's voice as she continued to lead the band in song.

▼▼▼▼

He was not sure just when he became aware of a chill creeping up his back.

He stared ahead as he walked on, frowning, realizing that it had happened again. The Darkness had taken him! His mind had indeed been tranquilized by monotony. So much so that he had allowed his thoughts to once again go wading blithely out into Oblivion. He had no idea where he had been in the past few moments.

Following the band?

"Yes," he assured himself. He could see that much. But he could also see that he had slowed his pace considerably since drifting off into wherever it was the Darkness took him and had thus failed to close the gap between himself and his fellow travelers. He cursed himself for that. And for the fact that Mowea'qua no longer looked miserable as she stepped out beside him.

His frown became a scowl. As he scanned ahead, he realized that time had passed. There were subtle changes in the air and the angle of the light as it came through the trees as well as in the heightened level of pain that prolonged movement was causing him.

Hasu'u was still singing.

The band was still echoing her song.

Kinap's drum boomed on.

Old Ko'ram was still shaking his rattle and uttering his feline screeches.

And the headman continued to resolutely lead his followers uphill through increasingly dark and wind-riled groves.

But something had definitely changed.

The trees were much closer together now, their branches low to the ground, deflecting the wind, dispersing the light of morning and giving it a gray and somehow muddy glow. The song of the women possessed an element of tension that had not been there before. The sounding of the drum was slower. The click of the deer-hoof ankle janglers and the hiss of the rattle were barely audible above old Ko'ram's caterwauling as other men counterpointed his noise-making with howlings of their own so that, as Ne'gauni listened, it seemed as though a great force of men and not a small band of casually allied families was passing through the forest. Had words been put to the sound, their meaning would have been no clearer: "Beware! Stand back! The people of Tôrnârssuk come! Boldly we come! Unafraid!"

The hackles went walking up and down Ne'gauni's back again.

Something is wrong! Yes! They feel it, too! We must not go north! We must not! Danger awaits us there!

He shook his head. There it was again! The inner sense of dread! The unwelcome warning! The words that, this time, he would not allow himself to speak aloud. What was there to fear? Shadows? The all too readily conjured and wholly unsubstantiated terrors that dogged a man's step whenever he found himself journeying into the unknown? He would have no part of them! Not now! Not ever again if he could make it so! And yet everything about the moment raked his senses.

The trail the headman was making through the groves was ascending sharply, growing steeper with every step. And yet Tôrnârssuk kept the pace steady. Relentless. Not once had he looked back to see if anyone was finding his chosen path too difficult to follow. Ne'gauni's scowl became a disapproving grimace. With his mouth still so dry that it parched his very spirit, he leaned into his stride, straining to maintain his pace, frustrated by his infirmity, and resenting the headman for making absolutely no accommodation for the difficulty that his chosen route through the forest was presenting, not only to a one-legged cripple, but to the women and children of his band.

Squinting, the young man settled his gaze on Hasu'u. She

was plodding stalwartly along at the headman's side, but, although bent under the weight of her baby carrier and fur-wrapped traveling roll, she showed no signs of stress as Tôrnârssuk led her and the others steadfastly in and out among the trees.

A purely reflexive animosity toward the headman hardened Ne'gauni's heart. The man might well call him Brother these days, but he would never forget the specter of Tôrnârssuk as Raider, nor would he ever hold the Northerner less than fully responsible for initiating the ruin of his life. Yet now, as he saw Hasu'u cast a loving gaze upward at her husband, his feelings of enmity toward the other man had little to do with past grievances. He was jealous. He knew it. And named himself Fool. Sometimes, when the band paused to rest upon the trail, he would see Hasu'u look at Tôrnârssuk in that special way she reserved only for him. The headman almost invariably looked back. Hasu'u would then smile as at some wondrous secret and give the baby, Tiguak, into her mother's arms while she and Tôrnârssuk discreetly drew apart. Ne'gauni would avert his gaze and pretend that he had not seen them go off together, as though by ignoring their union he could somehow cancel the reality of it. Truly, he *was* a fool! The Dawnland woman was a hunt chief's daughter and, as such, rightly a headman's wife. She was the best among women and deserved the best among men. And Tôrnârssuk was that.

Grinding his teeth as he appraised the headman, Ne'gauni tasted truth and found it bitter. Tôrnârssuk was in his prime. A broad, powerful man, he wore no unusual garments or adornment to set himself apart. Indeed, only rarely had Ne'gauni seen him don these things—the raven mask, the bear shirt, the leggings said to be painted in blood and fringed with the hair of those he had slain along the raiding trail. Such raiment was designed to impress the spirits, terrify his adversaries, and confirm his rank and superiority when among strangers. Among his own people Tôrnârssuk needed nothing to define him as special among men. Ne'gauni had only to look at the man to know why his mustached kinsmen from the far north remained loyal and added to the name Tôrnârssuk—One Who Gives Power—the name Tunraq, Guide and Guardian and Man Who Walks in the Favor of the Spirits. Everything about Tôrnârssuk bespoke his natural strength and intelligence and conveyed an aura of absolute authority to which others yielded as easily and unquestioningly as they drew breath. When Tôrnârssuk spoke, others listened. When Tôrnârssuk gave advice, others took it. Where Tôrnârssuk raised his lodgepoles, there, in the protective shadow of his residence, other men chose to bring their families. And where Tôrnârssuk walked, others followed.

All except Ne'gauni.

He stopped. He had to rest. Just for a moment. He had to stand still. He had to even out his breathing and, as he felt sweat cooling on his brow, will the poison of envy from his heart. But it was no good. He ached with love for the headman's woman. As Mowea'qua paused beside him, she gave him a conciliatory look that made his headache worse.

"The way is long . . . difficult for all," she said.

He fought back the urge to strike out at her with one of his crutches. He wanted no pity from her. Or from anyone. Yet every muscle in his body was afire. And every fiber of his being was again telling him that something was wrong.

"Look!" exclaimed Mowea'qua.

He was scowling again as he saw her scurry forward a few paces and, instead of urging him on, promptly drop to her knees. "What are you doing?"

"Ah!" The girl reached to finger something up from the ground, then turned to display an object long and dark and as slender as the lanceolate leaf of a willow tree, something that even in the light of the shadowed sun shone sleek and black as . . . "A feather from the wing of Raven!" she proclaimed. "A sign it is from the kami! A gift from the Old Tribe spirits of the forest! An omen, think I. A shaman could us tell if it is for good or bad."

Deep within the cortex of Ne'gauni's brain, something shifted, darkened, then went very bright. He gasped. The brightness burned him. Hurt him. He closed his eyes, shook his head, tried to clear it, and, only half succeeding, batted open his lids to stare ahead in utter disbelief.

Mowea'qua was no longer there. An older woman was kneeling in her place.

The young man stared. Uncomprehending. Unable to believe his own eyes. "What kind of trick is this?" He was angry as he turned, looked all around for the giant's daughter, and saw no sign of her. Leveling his gaze upon the kneeling woman, he demanded, "How can this be? Who are you? Where is Mowea'qua?"

She did not speak. Her head was down. She did not move, nor did she seem to be in the least aware of his presence.

He was again aware of a chill creeping up his back. Only now it rose straight up his neck to tingle in his scalp and shoulders and down his arms to his fingertips. He recognized it for what it was: dread. There was something very strange at work here. He did not know the kneeling woman. Even though he could not see her face, he was certain that she was not a member of his band, or of any other band he knew of. Her garments gave no hint of tribal origin. Their style was that of most any forest woman traveling through the woodlands at this time of year: leggings; high-cut moccasins; a well-worn buckskin dress made of two unpainted, work-soiled deer hides laced together at the sides, shoulders, and sleeves, with generous fringing to foil the blood-sucking insect war bands of Mici'cak, Master of Biting Blackflies. If there was anything unusual about her at all, it lay in the fine quality of the intricate blue cross-hatched quillwork banding that was stitched down the sides of her sleeves and leggings—that and the fact that she was so enormously pregnant that she appeared a moon past ready to give birth.

"From where have you come, woman?" he asked.

She remained as she was. Motionless. Silent.

"Where are your people?"

The question seemed to hang in the air between them before at last she said quietly, "My people have gone to the north." And then she turned up her head. "You should not journey there."

Again Ne'gauni gasped.

The woman had no face! She had no eyes. She had no nose. Where her facial features should have been, there was only a smooth span of skin, and below that, in line with what should have been her lower jaw, a long slit of a mouth gaped wide. But it was not a mouth. It was a livid slash, a hideous wound, and as her head lolled back, it gushed blood . . . and fire.

Ne'gauni cried out.

The woman burned.

He moved to save her. Too late. She was encased in flame, ablaze like pitch burning high in the special burning baskets of twisted bark that the men of his father's village used to lure fish to the surface of creeks and pools by night.

And then, in an instant, she was gone.

Mowea'qua was kneeling in her place, looking up at him with the strangest expression on her face. "Ne'gauni? What is wrong, Ne'gauni . . . ? Why do you at me look and speak as though to another?"

He stared down at her in stunned incredulity. He wanted to answer. He wanted to shake himself free of whatever it was that had taken control of his thoughts, but the little black spider that usually crept so benignly from his brain to seduce him into the Darkness was spinning its mind-numbing web again and, as it did, metastasized into something else entirely.

The Beast of Remembered Terrors had him.

It held him, brutalized his senses, took him down into the Darkness, drowning him, burning him with recollections of the hot smell of his own blood and the shock of unendurable pain as he saw himself sprawled helplessly on his back, arms and legs splayed wide, wrists and ankles bound fast to the bottom of a crushing vault of bones as a pair of black wolves circled him.

"Go away," he told them.

They did not go away.

They stopped on either side of him. Stared. Showed their teeth. Their manitou teeth. And then, growling, they were transformed. It was Mowea'qua and her grandmother who leaped upon him, savaged his body, tore at his face, ripped off his leg, and then, with his dismembered limb in their jaws, ran off into the Darkness.

He cried out again.

The ghosts of his brothers were dancing within his mind. Mocking. Jeering. They were no longer men. They were manitous. Spirits. Dangerous, hateful spirits, jealous of his life.

"Follow the burning woman!" urged M'alsum.

"Join us, Little Brother," invited Sac.

"Come north!" implored M'ingwé.

"Bring Hasu'u! Together you will die!" they vowed as one.

"I will not go north!" he railed at them, hating them, wanting them gone, dead forever. "I will not allow you to harm Hasu'u. And I will not follow you! I—"

"Ne'gauni!"

He could hear Mowea'qua call his name. He could not respond. Her voice was far away, part of another world, a world that he had somehow left behind. Once again a light flared inside his head. Hot. Bright. It was a single flame until, suddenly, it burst wide, then imploded, setting fire to every quadrant of his body.

Did he cry out yet again? It seemed so. He stared. Inward. Unable to move. Unable to speak. Somehow his spirit was loose within himself, a two-legged being, trapped, desperately seeking a way out, running, screaming down the branching corridors of his own veins and arteries until, beating for freedom within the great pulsing inner chamber of the drum that was his own heart, he at last broke free and ran on, only to find that—although in his vision he could move on two strong limbs—he was not free at all.

Across a flaming world of endless trees he ran. And ran. The wind drove him on, a furious wind, mating with Fire, feeding the flames. Somewhere ahead a man ran before him, looking back over his shoulder as he ran, faceless, a laughing stranger disappearing into the Darkness beyond the flames as a mammoth trumpeted, its voice the sound of thunder, its footsteps shaking the earth. He fell. Rose. Staggered against the wind. Then ran on again as all around him the forest burned and the wind laughed and a woman screamed and animals and people fled ahead of the flames, only to be consumed. Burning . . . in agony . . . he fell again and plummeted alone into the Darkness, sobbing and calling out for the wind to turn and the rain to come.

Chapter Three

▼▼▼▼▼▼

N e'gauni!"

He heard Mowea'qua call his name. Softly she called it. Whispering close to his ear. Strange, he thought, wondering why the girl refrained from her usual shouting when he could feel her strong hands curled tightly upon his shoulders, shaking him hard.

"Ne'gauni . . . you must wake up . . . please, Ne'gauni, please!"

Please? Now, that was a new word for Mowea'qua. He gave it careful consideration and decided that he must have heard her incorrectly. Yet, even if he had not, he would have been unable to bring himself to respond. The Darkness had taken him and cast him out again. But this time it had burned him up alive. There was nothing left of him. Nothing at all.

"Ne'gauni!"

"What!"

For the third time this day, the young man came blinking out of a daze. There was a rank, inexplicable stink of smoke at the back of his nostrils, but he barely noticed it. The girl had slapped him! His left ear rang. His cheek stung from the impact of her blow. It occurred to him that he should strike her back, but, as he stared at her in stunned bewilderment, her expression stayed his intent.

Her eyes were enormous. Her dirty, sweat-streaked face was as tense as a drumskin. As the raven's feather that she had braided into her hair blew across her cheek, she drew her mouth so tightly against her teeth that her lips were flat. "Listen to me you must, Ne'gauni. Please."

Again that word.

Ne'gauni raised his left hand and pressed his fingers against his ear and the side of his face. The ringing and the sting eased a little, and the stink of smoke vanished from his nostrils, but the expression on the girl's face continued to hold his complete attention. If he had been looking at anyone else in the world he would have been convinced that he was beholding someone who had just suffered the fright of a lifetime. But he doubted that Mowea'qua knew the meaning of the word *fear*.

"Wake up now you must, Ne'gauni. You must, say I!"

His eyes held on her face. She certainly looked worried. And now she was peering nervously back over her shoulder in the way of one who dreaded the approach of another, or feared being overheard. Odd, he thought. Although he wanted to ask her why she was behaving so strangely, he was slipping back into a daze, in no mood to speak to her concerns, whatever they were.

She turned to face him. "Ne'gauni, I . . ."

He was staring at the raven's feather in her hair. A gift from the spirits? An omen for good or bad? He had no idea, nor at this moment did he care. The feather had come to Mowea'qua, not to him. He closed his eyes as a signal to her that he did not wish to hear her words. Or look at her face. His head was aching and thick with the dissolving residue of daydreams he would just as soon forget. His return from the Darkness had left him weaker than ever before, empty somehow, as though it had cost him some inner portion of himself. And his forehead hurt. As did his nose. Half asleep again, he sent both hands questing gingerly upward in search of the cause of these two new and thoroughly unexpected sources of pain. Then his eyes batted open as he discovered a cracked layering of mud packed across the bridge of his nose and a wrap of defurred rabbit skin bound around his aching brow.

"Tripped you over a snarl of roots and on your face fell flat," the girl revealed in a whisper. "Warned you I this would happen! Yah! Magic it is that your nose still stands tall between your cheeks. But after you fell, wake you could I not. Others came to help. Musquash from his own flask gave you water. Old Ko'ram his rattle shook over you and said maybe this time you would not return from wherever it is your spirit wanders." She paused and, chewing her lower lip, seemed to need a moment to steady herself before continuing. "Now more closely than before must you listen, Ne'gauni, because after that Suda'li to Kinap said that we should leave you before the bad spirits that feed inside your head decide to feed upon the band."

He made a rude and dismissive noise. "I would expect nothing less from her."

"Against you she was not the only one to speak. Kamak said that if you are truly a bad spirit man, we should kill you and scatter your bones to make sure that your bad spirits would follow us not when we go on from this place. And Niñgao said that, if Tôrnârssuk asked it of him, he would hack off the head of the man who at his dogs throws stones, then smash that head with his braining club and burn it up in fire with all the bad spirits inside. And Moraq said that he would bury the ashes of your head and pile stones so high over them that the bad spirits of Ne'gauni could not fly away on the wind to haunt the people. But Hasu'u spoke for you, Ne'gauni, and so Tôrnârssuk did not—"

"Hasu'u!" Appalled as he was by the girl's revelations, his heart still gave a lurch of joy. "Hasu'u spoke for me?"

"Yah! What difference who? Only with the headman's consent could Kinap and I have brought you here, all the way to the Gap of Many Stones. And so now heed me you must, Ne'gauni! When Tôrnârssuk from the overlook returns, he will with questions come to you. If your answers do not his spirit ease, the council has decided that you a man apart will be. No food or shelter will be yours. And when the band moves on it will be . . . without you."

Stunned, he sat bolt upright, his head spinning. For the first time since waking, he realized that he was no longer standing on the forest trail but seated on the ground with his back propped upright against the cool base of a massive boulder. His crutches were at his side, along with Kinap's drag frame and his own pack, assorted carrying bags, fox-skin quiver, lances, and ashwood bow. "How . . . ?"

"Told you I! Dragged you here we did! And now, say I, when Tôrnârssuk comes, you must tell him that your bad words were a mistake, that there are no bad spirits in your head, only fever spirits that Mowea'qua's medicines will—"

"Bad words?"

"Challenged the headman did you, Ne'gauni, shouting out for all to hear that to the north we should not go, that you will follow Tôrnârssuk no more . . . and that you will no harm allow him to bring to his own woman."

His head swam. Her disclosures shook him now. Deeply. He did not remember speaking against the headman. And he had no memory of tripping, or of falling, or of landing on his face. And he certainly had no recollection of being picked up, bundled onto a drag frame, and hauled off through the forest like a sickly elder.

Now, however, to his utter dismay, he knew that it must be true. His surroundings were unfamiliar. He could see that time had once again passed him by. A great fat fistful of time! The sun—although barely visible through the trees and further obscured by a high, thin gauzing of clouds that seemed to be discolored by wind-borne dust—was in a different portion of the sky than when he had last seen it. How was this possible? Unless it was no longer morning at all! His gut tightened. It was afternoon!

He looked around, deeply troubled, aware now of the sound of running water and of the voices of women and children. Mowea'qua handed him a freshly filled flask of cold water. He took it absently. The wet bladder skin oozed moisture into his palms from tiny leaks in the stitching along its well-worn sides. The coolness felt good as he drank deeply, squeezing and twisting the flask until it was drained, feeling better as he handed it back without a word.

The band had come to pause in a stony glade on the banks of a fast-running stream. Massive boulders and monoliths identified the place as the Gap of Many Stones. Scanning around, Ne'gauni assumed that the overlook of which Mowea'qua had spoken must lie somewhere beyond the trees and that Tôrnârssuk had not gone there alone. Of the adult male members of the band, Ne'gauni could see only Kinap the Giant, old Ko'ram, Ningao, Moraq, and Onen'ia.

The women had found a deep-water pool and spread a fishing net across it. Stringy little Segub'un, Hasu'u's mother, had her fringed leggings off and, with her traveling dress knotted up across her belly, was thigh-deep in the pool working the net with Hasu'u, her three unmarried daughters, and the wives of her two sons, Onen'ia and Kanio'te. Tsi'le'ni, Ningao's woman, sat on the nearest bank seeing to the swaddlings of the babies with help from Onen'ia's busy little girls. Not far away, young Musquash was immersed in the creek up to his chin, paddling and diving happily about in a good imitation of a muskrat. Old Ko'ram had found a spot of sunlight atop a boulder in the middle of the creek and, apparently drying himself after a swim, sat stark naked, cross-legged, hands on knees, fast asleep and snoring in explosive spurts and lip-bubbling sputters. Farther downstream, close to where Ningao and his favorite dog were leading the rest of the pack to do their own fishing, the widow Suda'li's twins were sloshing through the shallows, viciously piking the underside of the embankments for frogs and turtles, while the widow and Kinap, the giant storyteller, sat hand in hand looking on.

After the long uphill walk through the dry forest, it was a scene that should have soothed his senses. But, under the circumstances, a ripple of hopelessly tangled emotions slurred through Ne'gauni. Sadness. Envy. Indignation. Resentment. And anger. Everyone appeared so cheerful and content! How easily they laughed and fished and played together now that they had decided amongst themselves what they must do with the raving cripple among them.

Suda'li laughed.

Ne'gauni cringed. The widow was young and comely, but her laughter sounded like the flat, throaty blast of a crow. One of her twins, either Ka'wo'ni or N'av—he could not tell the siblings apart from where he sat—had just tossed a small turtle to his mother. Suda'li caught it and, deciding to instigate a game of catch, tossed it back. When the boy eagerly returned the throw, the game continued in furious earnest until Kinap joined in to intercept the turtle and send it flying in a high arc that had the twins splashing backward and savagely flailing at one another as they competed to make the catch.

Ne'gauni shivered with anger as he watched Suda'li excitedly goading her boys and flirting with the giant. She had been the first to ask for his abandonment! She had not hesitated for so much as a single breath of time when she had seen her chance to humiliate him before the entire band. And today, seeing him unconscious and in need of assistance upon the trail, had she shown kindness? No! She had again asked that he be left behind. He glared at the widow, longing to see her slip from the embankment into the stream, crack her pretty head on a rock, and drown or bleed to death before anyone could save her. The longing passed. The stream below where she sat was relatively shallow. Even if it were not, Kinap would save her.

The young man pulled in a sigh of resignation. The widow and the giant had become close. And, unlike Suda'li, Kinap had long since proved to be friend; he wished no ill to the man. In his painted summer buckskins and wolfskin cowl, and with row upon row of elaborate fetish necklaces and feathers adorning his massive neck, Kinap was an imposing figure. Even seated he was enormous. Huge hands. Bigger feet. Limbs the size of tree trunks. Shoulders and chest the breadth and hardness of the boulder upon which old Ko'ram lay sleeping. In his day, the man must have been magnificent. Now, with his face hidden within the dark recesses of his cowl, as it almost always was, the truth could not be seen. But Ne'gauni knew that truth. It was simple enough. Kinap was the ugliest man alive.

Only in nightmares were such faces as the giant's seen. Alone among his bison-hunting tribesmen from the distant Land of Grass, Kinap had danced with the demon Wildfire and lived to tell the tale. Yet, although the giant would be the first to claim that he was the finest teller of tales in all of Creation, he needed no words to describe the horror of what he had endured. And survived.

Ne'gauni frowned. He found himself recalling his most recent encounter with the Darkness. He saw himself running, fleeing across a burning land while people and animals ran ahead of him screaming. It was Kinap's story! His daydream had been no daydream at all; it had been a recollection of the giant's tale! The realization was startling, and reassuring, for surely anyone who had ever set eyes upon what the demon Wildfire had done to Kinap's face must also suffer tortured dreams.

Like rendered tallow that had overboiled a stone lamp and oozed over the sides to eventually congeal and set, the skin of Kinap's face appeared to have melted and then thickened into a hideous coalescence of lumps and streams of liquefied flesh that now lay pale and shining and almost translucent over his skull. There was little left of his nose or lips or ears. His dark eyes, perpetually tearing, looked out at the world from beneath a smear of lashless lids. And only from the very top of his great round head did hair continue to sprout, as though by some perverted magic from a single circlet of unseared skin and follicles—a long and lustrous growth of hair, a shining cascade blacker than a moonless midnight and as thick as the strong man's wrist, a braid of singular beauty that was all that was left to the giant of the Kinap of old—of a man whom other men had once envied and whom all women had desired.

Ne'gauni pitied the giant. And was revolted by him. Raising his hands, he set his fingertips gently exploring the ruin of his own face. Battered brow. Now swollen and mud-packed nose. These things would heal quickly enough. But the arrow that had laid open his features had cut deep, even if it had cut clean. In the hands of an experienced and competent healer new tissue would have grown to mesh smoothly with the old; indeed, among the many Forest and Grassland tribes that marked the maturation of a male with ritual scarification, such a scar would have been seen as a thing of beauty, proof of his ability to face and endure pain. But the hands that had stitched Ne'gauni's face had not been competent to the task at hand. Mowea'qua's nervous fingers had sutured the gash too tightly; as it healed it had puckered the skin, distorting one nostril and lifting the left corner of his mouth into a perpetual sneer. Yet he knew that, compared to Kinap's scars, it was no scar at all.

Another deep slur of emotion rippled through Ne'gauni. His hands drifted to rest upon his thighs as he continued to observe the giant and the widow holding hands and talking softly together. This time, although he had not felt it in so long that it seemed a stranger to him, the young man recognized the emotion for what it was: hope!

His heart quickened.

Later he would remember the moment and find cause to once again name himself Fool. Now, swept up in a rush of pure euphoria, he told himself that if he could only manage to stave off the Darkness and dispel the belief of others that bad spirits were feeding inside his head, all might not be lost for him. Because if Kinap could win himself a woman, there might yet be a chance for Ne'gauni to do the same. He was young—as Hasu'u was young; he knew that she would not see eighteen before the rising of the Moon of Leaves Falling. Tôrnârssuk, on the other hand, had a band of white streaking his hair, the result, some said, of an unseen scar given to him in his youth by the raking claw of a white bear that had nearly scalped him before he had slain it. But the headman was no longer young. Nor would he live forever.

A chill fluttered in Ne'gauni's breast. Had he just wished death on Tôrnârssuk? No. He would not accuse himself of that, but, given all that stood between them, when the man died he would not grieve for him. His eyes narrowed. Kinap was getting to his feet, extending his hands to Suda'li as he looked down at her out of the wolfskin cowl that shadowed his ugliness.

Ne'gauni held his breath.

The widow did not rise. Instead, she tilted her head and, settling back on straight arms, stared up at Kinap with her spine arched and her breasts stressing the soft dun doeskins of her traveling shirt. Then she shook herself.

"Mmph!" said Mowea'qua, returning from the creek with a newly filled flask just in time to follow Ne'gauni's gaze and express disapproval. "Worthy of my father that one is not!"

Ne'gauni had no cause to disagree, but he did not speak to affirm the girl's judgment. The widow's movements were pure provocation. His loins warmed and stirred in response as he watched Suda'li reaching up to the giant, wordlessly inviting him to take her hands and draw her to her feet—and to so much more than that.

Kinap did not hesitate.

Ne'gauni gasped as he saw the widow swept onto her feet and then into the giant's arms.

Suda'li laughed. A raucous whoop of delight. And then she cried out loud enough for everyone to hear, "Yes! Now, Kinap! Now! There is time before the headman returns with the others and we must move on again!"

The giant's rumbling roar of anticipation of sexual pleasure filled the glade, as did the gleeful catcalls and shouts of encouragement from the watching women and men of the band.

Suda'li laughed again. Another whoop of delight.

On his rock in the middle of the creek, old Ko'ram blinked and stared like a sun-baking lizard reluctantly roused to wakefulness by the calling of distant birds.

And Suda'li's twin boys, eight summers old and of an age to fully understand, paused in their spearing of turtles and frogs to gape as their mother and Kinap disappeared into the trees.

Ne'gauni was suddenly bitterly cold. It took two strong legs to carry a woman off like that. Two! Shivering again, his loins ached for want of a pleasure that had never, and would never, be his. Hope faded within him. Pity and repugnance overwhelmed him. Not for the giant. For himself. What did it matter that his facial scar did not come close to equaling Kinap's revolting disfigurement? The giant was a *whole* man! A man as wise and wary as the black wolves whose skins he and his wild daughter wore! A man whose hunting skills were as valuable to any band as were his talents as a teller of tales and maker of music and dispenser of fetishes and amulets for the wounded and worried and unwise! A woman would surely avert her eyes from Kinap's face when he came down on her, but his body could fully pleasure her, and at his lodge fire there would always be much meat and pride.

Ne'gauni bent up his leg and laced his fingers around his folded knee. What had he been thinking of? Hasu'u would never be his. She would never return his love. No woman worth anything at all would ever look his way. Without the charity of the band, a one-legged man would find it difficult to provide adequate food and shelter for himself, much less for a woman and any children he might make on her. Perhaps, if they chose not to abandon or kill him and burn and scatter his bones today, in the future one of his bandsmen might take pity on him and send a second-rank wife to sate his need, or some juiceless, toothless old widow would creep into his tent and slither under his sleeping furs to sate her own need. He would not accommodate a hag! He would have Hasu'u or no woman at all. And he would accept pity from no man!

He blinked.

Tôrnârssuk was walking toward him.

▼▼▼▼▼

The headman was not alone.

His closest confidants among the council were with him. Stern, strong, hard-eyed men all. From among Tôrnârssuk's own initial band of Northerners, Kamak and Itiitoq and Inaksak. From Chief Ogeh'ma's Dawnland family, Ogeh'ma himself and his son Kanio'te.

Ne'gauni looked around for the other Northerners and realized that they must have remained at the overlook or were taking their time returning from it, but he could see Moraq and Onen'ia hurrying to take their place close to the headman. Ningao, after pausing only long enough to assist old Ko'ram off the rock, was slogging out of the creek with his big, skinny, favorite dog at his side.

Mowea'qua was on her feet. "Get up, Wounded One!"

Ne'gauni found her voice a bludgeon to his ears. She had used the hated name again, demeaning him with it. And she had not asked him to rise. She had commanded! And shamed him before the others with her careless disregard of whatever the forces of Creation had left to him of his masculine pride. His face flushed with indignation as he looked up at her standing tall and unkempt beside him, lanky as a young moose, he thought, and brazenly close to eye level with every man there. It was unnatural for a girl to be so tall! Glowering, it struck him in this moment just how much she had grown since she had first shed a woman's blood during those long dark moons that he had spent with her against his will within the haunted forest. Truly no one could doubt that she was the giant's daughter, or that she was the most obnoxious female ever to walk with any band . . . unless, of course, he considered Suda'li. But at least the widow was soothing to a man's eyes.

Tôrnârssuk's long, dark, heavily lidded eyes were, however, not focused upon Mowea'qua. The headman's gaze was fixed on Ne'gauni. As Moraq, Onen'ia, Ningao, and old Ko'ram took their places among the rank of men who stood beside him, Tôrnârssuk did not speak. Nor did the others. They observed. Fixedly. Measuringly. Critically.

Ne'gauni lowered his eyelids. How dare they look at him like this! There was not a man or woman born to any tribe who did not know that the eyes were the entranceway to the spirit. To stare directly into the eyes of another was to trespass into his inner being, to say without words that he was weak, that his spirit could not prevent their invasion of his private self, much less dare to glare them down with an invasion of his own.

A tremor of frustration went through him. They were right. He *was* weak. His encounter with the Darkness always left him so. If they looked into his eyes, they would see the truth. And so he glared off, avoiding their eyes, squinting past them into the wind as he tried to distract himself by watching the women hurriedly hauling in the net and asking for the assistance of the children in bringing in the dogs while they tended to the quick killing and gutting of the few fish they had caught. The happy scene had, with the return of the headman, become one of undefined tension. Already

Segub'un's three unmarried daughters were chattering busily and worriedly amongst themselves as, preparatory to moving on, they repacked whatever they had taken from their family drag frames. And Hasu'u was standing stock-still, apart from the others now, facing him yet not looking at him as she held her head down, slumping on one limb, her hands hanging loosely at her sides.

Ne'gauni's mind reeled. She was standing like a heart-struck doe! Had Tôrnârssuk communicated something to her as he had come through the trees from the overlook? Did she already know her old friend's fate? And was she now grieving for him?

Ne'gauni's heart sank. The moment he feared had come. The headman had made his decision! There would be no questions, no chance to plead his cause. The band was going to cast him out. Or kill him. And Hasu'u was going to stand quietly by and allow it to happen.

The realization hurt him more than he thought possible. He had risked his life for her. When his brothers had left her and fled from danger like frightened dogs, he, too, could have turned and run and left her to fend for herself. But he had stayed. For her! He had risked all. For her! He had lost all. For her! And now his heart ached so with the intensity of his love that he nearly wept. If Tôrnârssuk chose not to consent to his death, given his skill with a bow, he might just possibly survive abandonment if the winters were not too harsh and the forces of Creation saw fit to show compassion to a lonely cripple. But how could he live beyond the fall of Hasu'u's shadow? And why would he wish to?

Ne'gauni turned up his gaze. As expected, Tôrnârssuk's eyes were as piercing as stone awls; they cut deep into the meat of his spirit. And yet, unexpectedly, the cut drew, not despair, but a sudden outrage at the unfairness of his situation.

He knew that the headman and those who stood with him must find him far short of whatever measurement they used to sum the worth of a man. But, with the exception of Ogeh'ma and his sons, these men were the same raiders who had struck him down in the first place. How dare they judge him when they knew that it was their actions that had caused him to be as he was! Would they fare any better were they in his place? Would they not suffer from the endless pain of their wounds or from the torment that their memories brought them?

Tôrnârssuk saw the anger in the young man's eyes. His head lowered. His own gaze sharpened.

Ne'gauni refused to look away. Why should he? Before he was killed or abandoned, he could at least regain some semblance of his pride. He had nothing to hide. And he surely had nothing to lose. Let the headman and the others see into the very heart of his spirit! Let them know the Darkness! Let them share the dreams! And then let them see if their own spirits could measure up to the bruised and bloodied valor of his own!

Clenching his jaws in anticipation of pain, Ne'gauni reached for his crutches, positioned them, and, sucking in a deep breath of resolve, pulled himself upright into a stance of pure belligerence. If they were to kill him, let it be now, and if they were to cast him out, let it be like this—with the memory of him standing boldly and defiantly and unafraid before them.

"What do you want of me?" he demanded combatively. He would make them say what they had come to say. Now. On his terms, not theirs.

Tôrnârssuk's head went high.

Mowea'qua, only moments ago so bold and blatantly commanding, looked more worried than before.

Ningao's dog began to growl and threaten with its teeth.

Ningao held the animal by a handful of neck fur; his expression was not unlike that of his animal.

The other men exchanged glances. Only old Ko'ram remained motionless, arms crossed tightly over his chest, eyes fixed and wary.

Ne'gauni looked the old man up and down. In the excitement of the moment, Ko'ram had not bothered to snatch up his clothes from the embankment when he had come wading from the creek. He was stark naked. Gooseflesh dappled his skin. As he attempted not to shiver in the wind, his jaw clacked and his shriveled stub of a penis protruded from the gray tuft of his genital hair like the skinny little nose of a defurred mole. With the frayed feathers of his browband blowing back and the skin of his face shrunken into the hollows of his skull and stretched so tautly across the arching beak of his nose that it was thinned to near transparency, he resembled nothing so much as a tough old hawk plucked and ready for the boiling bag. Ne'gauni felt nothing but distaste for the man. "My spirit has returned from its wanderings," he informed the elder coldly. "If you have something to say, say it now and to my face, not when my mind is lost to dreams!"

Ko'ram rattled phlegm around in his throat, but his face remained expressionless as he replied, "The words I would hear spoken must come from your mouth."

"What words?"

"Ko'ram wonders what you have seen for us in the dreams that bring you to sob and wail and challenge my leadership." Tôrnârssuk's voice was low, deep, and unhurried as he spoke the language of the People, not in the halting manner of his fellow Northerners but as flawlessly as he spoke his own.

Ne'gauni was not soothed by the lambent flow of words. He recognized a threat when he heard one. "My dreams are my own," he replied defensively.

"No," countered Tôrnârssuk. "A man's dreams are gifts from the spirits. When they involve others, they are meant to be shared."

"My dreams are memories. Nothing more." Ne'gauni frowned. He had opened his spirit to them, and they had looked into his eyes and seen nothing. Nothing! And now the smell of smoke was back in his nostrils. Visions of a burning woman and burning world were flaring again at the back of his eyes. What kind of memories were these? Recollections of Kinap's misfortunes? Yes. And no. Somehow he suspected that they were much more than that.

"Only bad spirits would make a man speak aloud to challenge the will of Tôrnârssuk and the council." Moraq's tone was as flat and threatening as his weatherworn face.

"And only bad spirits would make a man throw stones at dogs or shout at children and fall down upon the trail to thrash and cry out like a woman bearing new life," added Ningao.

"Sick he is!" Mowea'qua spoke out in Ne'gauni's defense. "Suda'li's boys are all the time fighting, and dogs are noisy beasts! See you not Fever in this Wounded One's eyes? It is there taking life from his wounds. It burns him. It gives him bad dreams. It makes him shout and throw stones. But I have from the stream gathered healing willow and—"

The low agitated hiss of old Ko'ram's turtle-shell rattle interrupted the girl. "It is not for a female to speak now. Go away, daughter of Kinap."

"Where is your father?" Tôrnârssuk asked Mowea'qua sternly.

"Kinap on Suda'li lies!" she snapped with a sneer and an upward jab of her chin that fully revealed her displeasure with the match.

"No. I am here."

Ne'gauni was relieved to see the giant coming forward with a loincloth-clad young Musquash trotting at his side.

"The boy came to tell me that you had returned." Kinap was readjusting his garments as he joined the others, his voice emerging from the shadows of his cowl as a harsh, grainy rasp forced out of a larynx thickened by scar tissue. "We . . . we did not think you would return so soon!"

"You were left behind to guard the band, not to pleasure yourself."

The giant's head drooped at the open censure.

"There was no danger to guard against," piped a dripping-wet Musquash as he beamed up at the headman and flashed a wide, confident smile that was filled with small, pointed, perfectly even white teeth.

The headman's face darkened. "You may be the son of a shaman, boy, and favored by some of my band because of this, but I warn you, Musquash, if you are to survive to manhood in this world you must learn that there is always danger and that you must always be on guard . . . especially with me."

The boy wilted, and his handsome little face went as white as a bunchberry blossom.

Mowea'qua, grasping yet another opportunity to speak on Ne'gauni's behalf, said eagerly, "So also says the son of Asticou—that there is always danger, always enemies. Always!"

Tôrnârssuk was not pleased. "Take the boy. Go. Your place is with the women and children, daughter of Kinap. Ko'ram has told you that you are not wanted here."

Mowea'qua stiffened. Resentment pulled her face into a knot of hostility. Then, slowly, her features expanded as suspicion filled her eyes. She made no attempt to disguise it as she looked steadily for a single piercing moment at every man there. To the headman she said, "Know I what you would do, but say I that the kami have to Ne'gauni given back his life through me. Soon will he be healed. Soon will he be strong. Angry will the Old Tribe spirits be if one who has to the People been returned is cast out and again left to die. It is Ne'gauni's time not to walk the wind forever."

A collective gasp seemed to suck the oxygen from the air as every man present caught his breath. The tension in the air was palpable. Old Ko'ram shook his rattle at the girl until it hissed like a viper poised to strike.

Kinap, hearing it, went as rigid as a tree. "My daughter speaks with the tongue of one inexperienced in the ways of the People. Her ways are Old Tribe ways. The fault for this is mine. I beg forgiveness for her words."

"For truth I need no forgiveness," declared Mowea'qua.

A flustered Kinap bristled like a threatening bear. "You will do as our headman commands, Mowea'qua. Now!"

She did not move.

A restlessness was visible in Tôrnârssuk as the faces of the men around him congested with anger.

Ne'gauni was amazed. The girl was standing up to the headman for him! Truly she did not know the meaning of the word *fear*. With the wind at her back and sunlight glancing through her hair and across her face, she stood as resolute as stone, the raven's feather lost to view within the chaos of her hair, her features granite hard, her eyes glaring verification of her ancient race and implacability of spirit. He cringed. As the others must be cringing. No one had eyes like Mowea'qua's. A composite of every imaginable color of the earth and sky, combined in intricate striations of gray and black, with flecks of green, brown, yellow, and amber glinting bright as pebbles on the graveled bottom of the cold, clear running stream, they were unnatural. Old Tribe eyes. Manitou eyes?

Old Ko'ram began to shake his rattle again.

"Come, Mowea'qua." Musquash reached out and tugged imperatively at the girl's hand as he attempted to pull her away. "You must learn to obey."

Indignant, she snatched her fingers free of his grip and, only after a loud and defiant "Mmph!" turned to stalk away, warning over her shoulder, "Remember my words, say I. Remember!"

Ne'gauni watched her break into a run with the little boy dogging her heels. His brow came down. Musquash was loyal to a fault, and it was no secret that he was enamored of Mowea'qua, but what the child saw in the girl was a mystery to all. Now, as she hunkered down close to where the other women were shaking the fishing net dry—and stubbornly made no move to assist them—Ne'gauni was certain that she was the most recalcitrant girl alive. Yet never before had he imagined that he would ever be sorry to see her leave his side. And now, with a sinking feeling, he noticed that some of the other men had returned from the overlook and were hurriedly slinging side packs onto some of the dogs and harnessing others to the drag frames, obviously intent on having the band up and on its way again as quickly as possible. Only Hasu'u remained unmoving, still with her head bowed . . . still looking like a heart-struck doe.

"We have wasted enough time with talk," said Tôrnârssuk. "We cannot camp here for the night as I had hoped. I want the women and children on the far side of the gap and safe at the lake by sundown."

"Lake . . . what lake? Where—"

Kinap cut into Ne'gauni's question as though the young man had not even spoken it. "Then . . . what was seen from the overlook was . . ." There was an odd edge to the giant's voice, as though he hesitated to fully form his words into a query because he dared not consider where its answer might lead him.

"We saw what we feared to see," replied Tôrnârssuk. "It is far, but, yes, it is all that we feared and more."

"Ah!" The giant actually swayed on his feet. "And this lake . . . we can reach it before the wind brings—"

"We must." Tôrnârssuk was emphatic. "And we will."

"And the spirit dreamer?" pressed old Ko'ram, his rattle at his side and silent at last.

Ne'gauni smelled his own death in the moment.

Even the eyes of the dog were burning into his skin.

The other men held their positions. Waiting for what they knew must come now.

And yet Ne'gauni saw only the face of Tôrnârssuk. The face of the man who was about to take his life. He knew this as surely as he had once known when his father was about to crinkle up his eyes and smile over some small foolish thing that he did as a child, or when his mother was about to pout, whine, and cajole him into bringing her one more small morsel from the roasting spits. He stood to his full height, balancing proudly and defiantly on his crutches, reminding himself that he had faced Death before; boldly and unflinchingly he had faced it. Now, it seemed, the Circle of Life had indeed come full circle for him, and once again he stood upon a forest trail beside a swiftly flowing creek facing the same deliverer—the same Death—at Tôrnârssuk's hands.

It was meant to be.

Ne'gauni accepted his fate.

He kept his eyes fixed upon the headman. He was glad that Tôrnârssuk wore no mask today—no carved and painted raider's face shield of wood and bone designed to make others cower as it disguised the true face of the man who, even now, among the peaceful forest and coastal tribes of Ne'gauni's people, was feared as Wíndigo, inheritor of the black and bloodied cloak of Raven, Great Ghost Cannibal, Winter Chief of the many and malevolent manitou spirits of the forest deeps, a manitou himself, master of demons, lord over the Djeneta and Djigáha, hideously deformed giants and dwarfs who danced under the stars in the skins of flayed human captives, or over the wild and immortal wolf woman, Mowea'qua, who howled to the moon and prowled the hidden vastnesses of the northern forests in eternal search of human prey.

Irony twisted Ne'gauni's mood. Mowea'qua's grandmother had named the girl to honor—or placate—the wild wolf woman of legend. Kinap, when he shook loose his cowl, was no less hideous than any giant spoken of in the ancient tales. When Tôrnârssuk, Chief Ogeh'ma, and Kinap had become allies, they had vanquished an enemy whose shaman was said to have danced in the skins of flayed human captives—among them the boy Musquash's own Old Tribe mother. And although Ne'gauni was no dwarf, the forces of Creation had certainly seen fit to deform him.

As his eyes continued to hold on Tôrnârssuk's face, it struck Ne'gauni that his people were right. The man who had first threatened his life from behind a raiding mask was all that they feared. And much worse than that. He was not a manitou. He was a man. And he was about to take the life of one whom he had come to name Brother.

"Your eyes offend me," said Tôrnârssuk.

"My eyes see you as you are." Ne'gauni saw no reason to hold his tongue. "Perhaps you see your own reflection in them and do not like what you see?"

The headman stiffened at the provocation as, on either side of him, Moraq and Ningao went livid and the others murmured amongst themselves.

"I have asked you before," Ne'gauni reminded him. "Just what do you want of me?"

"Moraq and Ningao would like you to die," replied Tôrnârssuk evenly.

Ne'gauni was suddenly cold again. And yet he would not allow himself to tremble. "I am not afraid!" Only after he had spoken the words did he know that he lied.

"No?"

"I—"

"You are brave. We have all seen this," conceded Tôrnârssuk. "But you are a man with one leg who throws stones at my dogs, shouts at my children, questions my judgment, falls down shouting into thin air, slows the progress of my band, and puts my people at risk. Were it not for my consideration of the needs of a wounded man and my willingness to oblige my woman's pity for an old friend, my Northerners would have left you behind long before now. Had we done this, we would now be taking our ease at the Great Gathering of Many Tribes. So why should I allow you to continue to walk with my band?"

"I—"

"And why do you say that we should not go north?" It was Chief Ogeh'ma. Stolid. Pragmatic. Steady as the beat of a well-paced drum. He was a small man by any standard, but now, standing in his quilled and painted caribou-skin garments with his back straight as an arrow and the wind whipping the many shell-beaded braids of his black hair forward around his intelligent face, his dignity gave him a stature that equaled the height of any man. "You must speak, Ne'gauni. You must tell us this." His features were so tense that they appeared ready to crack. His heavily lidded eyes held on the young man with a fixedness that betrayed his hope that the worst was not about to befall one toward whom he felt the deepest and most sincere compassion.

"I do not remember saying that we should not go north," Ne'gauni told him defensively, riled by what he could only interpret as pity in the older man's sympathetic tone and manner.

Old Ko'ram had had enough. Suddenly overcome by the passion of his emotions, he loosed a single explosive break of wind as he stepped out from among the others to advance on Ne'gauni with the aggression of a charging elk, shaking his rattle so vehemently in the young man's face that he forced him to stagger back.

Taken completely off balance, Ne'gauni fell. Flat on his buttocks, good leg extended, still holding his crutches, he bent forward and crossed the twin staves over his head just in time to prevent Ningao's dog from going for his throat. The dog *yarfed* as Ningao reclaimed his hold on the animal and pulled it back.

Ne'gauni was shaking. Angry. Humiliated. Unable to rise. He remained as he was. His nostrils pulled in against the heavy stink of the old man's flatulence and the sour smell of warm dog slobber running down his wrists. The backs of his hands began to ache; he could feel where the dog's teeth had bruised him, perhaps even broken the skin. And all the while Ko'ram leaned over him and shook his rattle more aggressively than before.

"What have you seen in the dreams that bring you to challenge Tôrnârssuk?" demanded the old man.

Ne'gauni did not move.

"Tell us!" insisted Ko'ram.

Ne'gauni did not speak.

"We will know if the spirits that speak through your mouth are good spirits or bad!" the old man insisted again.

"No spirits that challenge our headman can be good spirits," said Moraq sourly.

It was over. Ne'gauni knew it. He was suddenly tired beyond bearing. Beyond caring. Why not give them what they wanted and have done with it? And so he began at the place where the Darkness and his dreams began. "There is a spider in my head—"

"A what?" Moraq was as openly contemptuous as he was disbelieving.

"A spider," repeated Ne'gauni, looking up now. "It spins a web of Darkness. And in this Darkness my spirit wanders unknowing."

Moraq's face went blank.

Ko'ram leaned closer. "And yet you speak . . . you cry out of this darkness." His voice was softer, his rattle resting quiet at his side again.

"I cannot say if I do or not. But today in the Darkness I have seen blood and I have felt pain . . . my own blood, my own pain. I have seen the spirits of those who abandoned me . . . my own dead brothers. And I have run with wolves and strangers and seen a faceless woman burning as Wind mated with Fire to consume the forest and—"

"Enough!" Ko'ram raised his hands, one palm out, the other curled tightly around the bone handle of his rattle as he shook it with even greater vehemence. Within the turtle carapace that formed the sounding box, dried seeds and the teeth of small mammals struck madly together as they were shaken and swirled back and forth against the convex, bone-plugged walls of the rattle. Then, suddenly, Ko'ram brought the noisemaker to silence by abruptly slapping it against his other palm. "Do not speak the words lest you make them so!"

"It *is* so," said Tôrnârssuk grimly.

No one spoke. They stared. At one another. At the headman. And then at Ne'gauni.

He stared back. Had he thrown rocks at them they could not have looked more astounded than they did now. All hostility had vanished from their eyes. Something else had taken its place. Apprehension? Yes. And something else. Even Ogeh'ma no longer appeared solemn or troubled by regret; he was, like the others, gape-jawed with amazement.

"To the north, between us and the great river, fire burns," Tôrnârssuk revealed solemnly to those who had not been to the overlook with him. Turning up his face to the canopy of the trees and all that he could see through it of the sky, he set his gaze on the wind-borne clouds that were now reddening the sun. "Smoke," he said, pointing upward. "It colors the clouds. If the wind does not turn, the fire that is spawning that smoke will come here. Kinap can tell you what this will mean to our band."

Now it was Ne'gauni who was staring gape-jawed with amazement as the headman turned down his head and fixed him with a censorious stare that was hotter than any flame.

"In this Darkness that you speak of you have looked to the north and seen a danger that you could not have known was there."

"And yet he has known!" Ko'ram's proclamation was a sigh of wonder. "The spirits have spoken through his dreams in warning to the People! Good spirits, not bad!"

"It may well be so," acknowledged the headman with a marked absence of enthusiasm as his eyes held unwaveringly on the young man's face. "Why did you not come to me or to any other member of the council with your concerns?"

"I did not know that I had concerns . . . only headaches, only bad dreams and worries that I could not place."

"Then let me tell you of a headman's concerns. And of a

headman's worries. And of a headman's *responsibilities*. Listen well, Dreamer, because I will tell you only once. At our last encampment the dryness of the forest brought much concern to my heart. By day I watched the sky for gathering clouds that would speak of coming rain. By night I lay awake thinking of the tales that the old men of the forest and Barrenlands all tell: of Wildfire whispering to Wind, promising to mate with him and bear him many dancing children if only he will carry her away from enslavement in the well-banked fire pits of the People so that together they can recreate the world in flame and fury. And tales of Cloud, who sometimes shadows Land and forgets to bring Rain to quench the children of Lightning when he mates with Earth to create Fire. And so, with the rising of North Wind, the big lake that lies beyond the Gap of Many Stones was much on my mind. For this reason I called a council. For this reason it was decided that the band must journey north out of the depths of the dry forest to the shores of the lake, for only there will my people dare to rest until Rain at last comes to cancel the dangers presented to this band by the threat of Wind and Fire."

Ne'gauni was aware of the intense whispers and impassioned nods of the others, but could not bring himself to speak.

"And so, Dreamer," Tôrnârssuk continued, "know now that I have chosen to lead my followers to the north, not to bring them to harm as you have accused, but to keep them from it! If you do not choose to follow me, so be it. But I warn you now for the first and last time: You may have foreseen the danger of Wind and Fire in the Darkness of your dreams as surely as I have anticipated it in the core of my *experience*— but I will not suffer you to challenge me again."

Without another word, the headman turned away, and,

as one, the others followed him. Not even the dog looked back.

Ne'gauni's heart sank. They were not going to kill him. They were going to abandon him after all.

And so he sat. Too weary to move. Too relieved to utter a sigh. And so bereft at the realization of what must happen to him now that he let his crutches fall as he buried his face in his hands and wept like a baby.

It was the sound of deer-hoof ankle janglers, the hiss of a rattle, and the unmistakable whiff of flatulence that brought him pause.

He held his breath, peered through his fingers, and saw that old Ko'ram had returned to shake his noisemaker in his face again. Disgusted, Ne'gauni slapped the rattle away.

"You must take it, Dreamer!" insisted the old man, quickly picking it up, holding it out, and shaking it again. "A Wise Man must make a proper noise when he calls upon the spirits!"

"It is your noise, not mine, and I want no parting gift from you. Go away! I am no more a Wise Man than you are, old man."

"No, you are not," agreed Ko'ram, drawing back the rattle and holding it close, protectively, as though it were a living thing that needed consolation and reassurance after suffering an insult. "You are young and ignorant. And I am old and nearly deaf, but I am not blind. It does not take a Wise Man to know what you are, Ne'gauni, son of Asticou of the inland forest, He Walks Ahead in Dreams to Foresee Danger for the People. And to think that all this time I was so sure that spirit power must eventually come through Musquash. But it is not his. Ogeh'ma was right about that. As was Kinap. A shaman must be worthy of the spirits or they will seek another through whom to speak. The boy's father was not worthy. So why should the spirits speak through the son?"

Ne'gauni drew his hands from his face. "What are you saying, old man? I am a one-legged cripple with only one foot upon which to—"

"Ha! The spirits do not speak to a man through his feet! Why do you sit here bawling like a suckling deprived of a teat? Get up, Dreamer! Gather your belongings! You have much to learn! And I have much to teach you! The forces of Creation have taken your leg and given you a great gift in return. Do you truly think that Tôrnârssuk would allow the band to leave you behind now, when we have at last found ourselves the makings of a true shaman–in you?"

Chapter Four

▼▼▼▼▼▼▼

Nothing was the same.

They called him Dreamer now.

Everyone stared, appraising him—covertly, they thought—as though he was no longer the same Ne'gauni who had been traveling with them these many days, but a stranger suddenly come among them to be observed, evaluated, and held in more than a little awe . . . and, for some, perhaps no small measure of suspicion.

He turned down his gaze.

Let them think what they would of him! They could call him Dreamer. They could call him Someday Shaman. They could call him anything they liked. As long as they did not brain or abandon him! But, no matter what they called him, Ne'gauni knew that he was the same man today that he was yesterday. Exactly the same man. He was certain of this. Even if they were not.

Yet you dreamed of a fire that truly burns.

"Ha!" he said, reminding himself that the headman had visualized the same fire, not in daydreams that caused him to blunder and shout and fall down along the trail like a man possessed by spirits, but in a purely rational, anticipatory fear born of logic and life experience. Anytime there was wind in a dry forest, there was always the threat of fire. It did not take a shaman to know that! He should have guessed the source of his own hallucinations. He shook his head and busied himself rearranging his pack frame, ill at ease and so disconcerted by the recent turn of events that he did not see Hasu'u come to stand before him.

"It is as I knew it must one day be for you."

He stared up. She was as radiant as the dawn. Not even the delicate lines of tattooing that swirled across her cheeks and eyelids could diminish her loveliness. She was as beautiful and welcome as the face of the rising sun after a long winter's night. And he could not think of a single word to say to her.

She knelt, reached out, and laid her hands lightly upon his forearms. "The forces of Creation would not permit Tôrnârssuk to abandon one who has suffered so much and whose heart has been so brave and caring toward others. I knew they would not. Ah, Ne'gauni, do you remember the day the Four Winds brought us together again so many long moons after the raid that took us apart? Do you remember what you said to me that day?"

He hung his head, as he always did when she came close. He could not bear to think of her soft and gentle eyes looking at the ugliness of what her beloved forces of Creation had allowed to become of his face. "I remember seeing you again, Hasu'u," he told her. "I remember how good it was to know that you were alive. I remember that."

"And I remember this: On that day you told me that when others believed me dead, you knew that I was alive because you heard me singing and calling out to you in your dreams. Ah, Ne'gauni! Even then, though we knew it not, the spirits had chosen you to walk upon the shaman's path."

He shook his head, uncomfortable, embarrassed, and deeply troubled. "My father believed that dreams were the shadows of fear and longing. After the raid, I wanted you to be alive, Hasu'u. I wanted this even more than I feared that you might be dead. And so I dreamed of you and—"

"And so I live because of the power of your dreams. You kept me alive in your mind, Ne'gauni! Ah, dear friend, someday you will be a great shaman."

Ne'gauni's lips compressed. He did not believe her. Not for a moment. How could he? He had long since learned that the Northerners had taken Hasu'u captive to provide milk for Tôrnârssuk's newborn son after the headman's first wife died giving birth along the trail. They had never intended to kill her. And they had wounded and left him for dead simply because he had chosen to place himself in the way of their intent to enslave her. He raised his eyes, looked at her face, and willed himself to hold his tongue. If Hasu'u wanted to believe that she owed her life to him, he would be the last man in all Creation to attempt to change her mind.

"I will always be grateful to you, Little Brother," she assured him, using the name she had given him on the day she became his brother's bride. "Always!"

He blinked, too startled to react, for in that moment Hasu'u leaned forward, took his face between her palms, and turned it up to her own.

"You must not turn your face from me, Little Brother. The scar you carry marks your valor . . . your willingness to stand against Death for me. Because of it, in my eyes, you will always be among the most beautiful of men." This said, she kissed him, not one kiss, but many small, lingering kisses along the line of his scar.

He gasped. Closed his eyes. Breathed in the warm sweetness of her breath and the scent of her skin and hair as, trembling at the soft pressure of her mouth moving tenderly across his face, he basked in the most singularly wondrous and transcendent moment of his entire life.

"Mmph!"

There was no missing Mowea'qua's exclamation. He batted open his eyelids and glared at her with murderous intensity as she stood to one side of Hasu'u in soaking wet leggings, her dripping hands holding a brimming burl cup.

"His face is to my eyes also beautiful," the girl informed Hasu'u loftily. "Made it so have I! Seen it you should have on that long-ago day in the creek before my healing skills used the gut of Lynx to sew it back together! My Old Tribe magic has returned Ne'gauni's life to the People, not to you, Headman's Woman. No more will his dreams he waste on unimportant things. The spirits speak through his mouth. Someday a great shaman will he be! And now Tôrnârssuk has told me to tell you that the band moves on. Go! Join your man and the other women. I for the Dreamer will care!"

Ne'gauni was shaking with anger as Hasu'u, refusing to take even the least umbrage at Mowea'qua's impertinence, got to her feet and actually thanked the girl for delivering Tôrnârssuk's message before going her way.

Others were coming to him now. Old Ko'ram. Kinap and Musquash. And Pwaumó, wide-hipped, big-breasted woman of Kanio'te, hurried to his side with her baby in her arms as she begged him to lay his hands upon the head of the teething infant and ask the medicine spirits to lessen its discomfort before the band moved on.

"I . . . I am not yet a shaman."

"But you are Dreamer. The power of a shaman will be yours someday. Even now, the spirits speak through you. They will listen, Someday Shaman. I know they will!"

"But I do not know how . . . or . . . *what* to say," he

stammered, setting aside his pack frame and using his crutches to lever himself upright.

"Like this!" Old Ko'ram was shaking his rattle over the baby's face, causing it to startle and squall as he whispered a quick litany of words into Ne'gauni's ear.

At a loss as to what else to do, the young man laid tentative fingers upon the screaming baby's brow and, in a weak facsimile of what the old man had insisted he offer as a loud incantation, muttered, "Spirits of pain, feed not on the infant of Pwaumó. Uh . . . hear me. Uh, medicine spirits, I am Ne'gauni. Son of Asticou. Bandsman of Tôrnârssuk. Uh . . ."

Ko'ram stopped shaking his rattle and cleared his throat noisily as he gave a weak smile to Pwaumó. "Our Dreamer has just discovered his powers. Take the little one. Hold it close. Sing soft songs to it. Use more of Segub'un's special salve for teething to cool its gums. This, together with the medicine words of our Dreamer, will make the child suffer less upon our journey."

Pwaumó sighed. The old Wise Man's words had proved as soothing to her as any balm suggested for her child, but when she smiled and sighed again, her gratitude was directed toward Ne'gauni. "I thank you for your words to the medicine spirits on behalf of my baby, Dreamer. Look! She has stopped crying. Already her pain has gone. Tonight, Someday Shaman, when we encamp, there will be fish for you. Cooked by my own hand." This said, she bowed her head and rushed off to take her place with the others.

Ne'gauni could not believe what had just happened and said as much to Ko'ram. "I did nothing to deserve a gift of fish or anything else from her. Why did she thank me? The baby stopped crying because you stopped shaking your rattle."

Ko'ram chortled. "Can you be so sure?"

Kinap shook his head. "You have much to learn, Ne'gauni,"

he rumbled, kneeling to lay out some of the young man's belongings upon the drag frame.

"And medicine to take. Real medicine." Mowea'qua held out the burl cup. "This *will* eat your pain."

Ne'gauni hesitated, but only for a moment. He took the cup. As much as he was loath to admit it, although the girl had failed to save his leg or make a decent job of suturing his face, her salves and potions were more often than not as effective as she claimed. And she had spoken up for him today. He owed her for that. And so he drank, fighting to hold down the vile-tasting, mucilaginous liquid.

Musquash, now fully dressed in his buckskin traveling tunic with its ragged headdress of muskrat pelts topped by the whiskered head of a single rodent facing forward and making him look very much like one of the clever little bog rats for which he was named, asked Ne'gauni solemnly, "Is it true, Ne'gauni? Are you really to be Shaman?"

"Dreamer he is!" affirmed Mowea'qua. "Good spirits have through his mouth spoken to warn the People of Danger! And to me now all must give thanks! Old Tribe magic has saved this Dreamer's life so he can be shaman for this band. Mmph! Maybe now others will not so stubborn be? Medicine better than Segub'un's healing salve could I make for Pwaumó to give her baby."

"I think Pwaumó wanted magic, not medicine," said the little boy sagely. Again he asked Ne'gauni, "Are you *really* to be Shaman, Ne'gauni, really so?"

"It is what the others are saying."

The boy stared. Solemn. So intent upon his thoughts that he shivered. "I am glad," he whispered. "I am *very* glad that it is not to be me!"

▼▼▼▼

They traveled in silence.

Ne'gauni insisted on walking. He felt stronger. The girl's medicine had eaten most of his pain and cleared his head. A mouthful of jerked venison had given him strength, but not half as much as did his recollection of Hasu'u's kisses.

Fear and hope walked hand in hand with the travelers as they moved on toward the overlook through the ancient groves, passing through broken stands of birch and aspen that now and then gave space to the odd maple, each hardwood offering silent testimony to the unnatural dryness of the season in its display of leaves already splotched with autumnal color. Other than this, the world was green, dark, illuminated only now and again by a glimpse of ruddy sky, the scarlet flash of a tanager's breast, the bright yellow plumage of a grosbeak or warbler, or the milky blue wash of a blue jay's wings.

"It is like moving under water," observed Musquash, looking up and turning around and around on his moccasined heels, "with the birds swimming through the trees like fish and frogs!"

"Keep moving, Muskrat," Kinap growled. "We dare not linger!"

And they did not.

They went on.

And on.

After a while, old Ko'ram drew Ne'gauni aside and, shooing Mowea'qua and Musquash ahead, insisted that the young man raise invocations to the sky spirits on behalf of the band.

"I have told you before. I do not know how to—"

"Now you will learn! Speak! Ask! Invoke!"

"Rain come! Wind turn!" Ne'gauni obliged the old man, but he was uncomfortable as they walked on together.

Ko'ram's words struck him as presumptuous in the extreme. It was one thing to ask favors of the spirits in hope of receiving an occasional omen in return. It was another thing entirely for a mere man, shaman or otherwise, to actually believe that he could command the powers of the forces of Creation and expect them to obey him.

The old man clucked his tongue and responded as though he had seen into the young man's mind. "Do not command. Ask politely."

Ne'gauni felt more at ease, but not much. "Forces of Creation . . . please hear me?"

"Better. But not firm enough. And who is 'me'? Have you no name? How will the forces of Creation know who speaks to them?"

"Uh . . . forces of Creation, I am Ne'gauni, son of Asticou. Please hear me?"

"You are no longer Ne'gauni, son of Asticou. You are Ne'gauni, Dreamer, Someday Shaman, He Walks Ahead in Dreams to Foresee Danger for the People."

"That is far too much name for a one-legged man to carry."

"The spirits have chosen it for you! Your father, Asticou, is far away in another part of the forest. You walk with Tôrnârssuk now. It is for this band that you must speak. So! Speak!"

"Forces of Creation, hear this man, He Walks Ahead in Dreams to Foresee Danger for the People. Uh . . . make easy the way of those who walk with Tôrnârssuk? For Hasu'u . . . I mean, for all the women and little ones of this band, please smooth the trail to the overlook? Keep her . . . uh, I mean, keep this band safe from Wildfire? Uh . . . uh . . . ask the sky spirits to . . . uh . . . I mean, please ask the sky spirits to convince Rain and North Wind to—"

"Too many uhs. The sky spirits will not listen to uhs. The word has no meaning. And you must not be so specific. You must allow the forces of Creation to work in and around your words. This way, if they do not respond in exactly the way you would have them respond, no one will be able to hold you accountable. And why do you make questions out of your requests? The band will think that you are unsure of yourself."

"I *am* unsure of myself!"

"Ah, Dreamer, those who look to you for courage must never know this."

"But—"

"No buts! No uhs! No direct commands. You must implore. But not weakly. You must concede that whatever happens is the will of the forces of Creation. And then you must speak to the spirits as Kinap speaks to the band when he recounts the stories and history of the Ancient Ones. Your words must be strong, for only with the utterance of such words will the forces of Creation be able to give strength to the People through you."

"The responsibility for the future of the band lies with Tôrnârssuk and the council, not with me."

The old man's features wrinkled as he shook his head. "Do you not understand that from this day you will be a member of the council? Do you not understand that from this day no decisions will be made until first your dreams are considered? Ah, Dreamer, have you truly never desired the great gift that the spirits have given you?"

"Never." It occurred to Ne'gauni that had he known that the Darkness would bring Hasu'u to his side with kisses and soft words of affection he would have welcomed it, and the black abyss of Oblivion would not have been filled with despair.

"Have you never known a true shaman or marveled at the skill and power of all that is worked through him or her for the good of all?"

Ne'gauni shrugged. "In my father's village there was no shaman. Ours was far too small a band to be accorded such a gift from the spirits. My mother told of wizards she had known among her own people when she was a girl dwelling in the country of the Lake People, good men all. And traders passed through our part of the forest with stories of healers and holy men who caused the spirits to smile upon everyone who came within the fall of their shadows. But I have also been told that in the Dawnland of your people the powers of such magic makers as Musquash's father and stepmother were used to subvert the powers of the chiefs, until half a season's take in meat and furs and fat was yielded to the shaman while the people sometimes went hungry and cold and without light in the winter dark. I would not wish to be such a man as that."

"No! Of course you would not! And so I tell you now, since I was a small boy, I have asked the spirits to come to me in dreams so that I might set my own feet upon the shaman's path—to be a force for good, not bad. But, although I have grown old and wise and have observed and learned from the true and good shamans I have seen upon the many trails of my days, the spirits have not spoken to me. Until now."

"And what do they say?"

"They say that I have not wasted my life observing the shaman's way. Now, as Teacher to Dreamer, I will be able to share my wisdom and, in this small way, walk at last upon the shaman's path . . . with you, He Walks Ahead in Dreams to Foresee Danger for the People."

Ne'gauni frowned. The old man had just loosed a silent but highly potent and noxious miasma. "I will chant, as you bid me," he said. Lengthening his stride, he decided that he might as well begin to live up to his new name by walking as far ahead of the Wise Man as a one-legged cripple could. To his band he might well be He Walks Ahead in Dreams to Foresee Danger for the People, but in his own mind, as long as old Ko'ram was determined to dog his steps, he was going to be He Walks Ahead of Old Man's Wind.

▼▼▼▼▼

He made his chant to the well-remembered rhythm of Hasu'u's song, using Ko'ram's specifications upon which to build his cadences. He asked the sky spirits to summon Rain. He asked North Wind to turn. He asked Wildfire to go to her rest and leave the People at peace this day. Strongly, surely, politely he asked, ending each stanza with "may it please the forces of Creation." And soon the old man was proved right. The steps of the band were noticeably lightened by his invocations. Appreciative glances came back to him from Hasu'u and those walking just ahead. Ogeh'ma's three unmarried daughters whispered amongst themselves and giggled as they appraised him in a way that made his face flush hot with embarrassment.

"They consider you with new eyes, Dreamer," observed Ko'ram with a knowing chuckle. "Females by their very nature must be practical beings. The woman of a shaman ranks high in any camp. Even if her man cannot hunt for her, there is always meat and comfort to be found at the fire of a shaman's wife. Always there are gifts. Food. Furs. Fat for the cooking lamps. Anything a man or his woman could need!"

"I am not a shaman."

"But you will be, Dreamer, you will be! You must begin to think ahead. And even a one-legged man has yet another 'leg' with which to 'kick' a woman, hmm? Perhaps, by the time we reach the Great Gathering of Many Tribes, He Walks Ahead in Dreams to Foresee Danger for the People may well be making himself and all three of Ogeh'ma's daughters smile beneath his bed furs . . . with Ogeh'ma's and Segub'un's permission, of course."

Ne'gauni was amazed. So he no longer need look forward to the sexual pity of second-rank women and juiceless old widows! Ogeh'ma's three unmarried daughters were ripe and plump and ready for first piercing. Any man could see that. And yet he desired only one woman: Ogeh'ma's fourth daughter. The headman's woman. And whenever he turned up his gaze and looked ahead to see Tôrnârssuk looking back at him along the trail, face set, eyes stern and tacitly approving, he remembered Hasu'u's kiss and looked quickly away.

The way ahead continued to be difficult. Despite Ne'gauni's best efforts to clear the way ahead with words, here and there fallen giants, pines and hardwoods in the main, forced the travelers to slow their pace and clamber up, over, and around shattered branches and downed trunks. It was difficult going for all, especially for the dogs, and more than once Ningao and the men of the band worked together to heft both animals and drag frames over deadfall. As Ne'gauni did his best to make his own way, he caught his breath, startled, when he found himself suddenly hefted into the air and slung up onto Kinap's shoulders.

"I can walk!" the young man protested.

"In your dreams." The giant's sarcasm was unmistakable, but affable enough. "For now it is best for the band if you ride on my back. The headman has said that he will not have our Dreamer slow us down. Nor will he have you fall behind again. Besides, it is not seemly for one who will someday be Shaman to be hopping along like a one-legged dog. And, big and strong as my daughter is, Mowea'qua cannot carry her own pack and lift you over this fallen mess of winter without—"

"Try I can!" the girl insisted.

"There is no need, daughter of Kinap," said Chief Ogeh'ma kindly as the giant and his family came abreast of him on the far side of a maze of deadfall. "Long has it been since I have traveled so far north. But I will tell you now, Giant, that the winter blowdowns are worse than I have ever seen them."

Ne'gauni heard the undercurrent of dread in the chief's statement. It did not take a shaman or a dreamer to understand the man's concern. If Wildfire came to this part of the forest, she would find much upon which to feed and grow strong.

"Everywhere it is the same," Kinap rumbled. "Never have I seen a winter as cold or long or storm ridden as the last."

Ogeh'ma was nodding. "It seems that there are more cold moons now than when I was a youth. And always the trees that fall away at winter's end seem to be of the same kind. The big spruces and firs stand strong. The pines and oaks, the hemlocks and ashes, and even the maples sicken and die, as though they have not the heart to survive the long cold or to set seedlings strong enough to endure it. But I have heard it said by traders from the south that there are places where the winters are so much milder that forest dwellers there have chosen to raise permanent villages. Indeed, it has been told that there the maples grow strong and the sugaring is better."

"It is true," confirmed Ne'gauni. "The sugaring huts of my father's village yielded many makuks filled with sweet sap. There was enough for our village, and much more left over to trade north and—"

"Endure what?" It was Ko'ram, falling into step with the

others and worrying over one of the few words that had managed to filter through his ears as he strained to keep up.

"The lengthening winters," answered Ne'gauni from his perch atop Kinap's shoulders.

"The *what?*" pressed the elder, cupping his palms at the back of his ears. "The wind blows your words away!"

"The lengthening winters!" Mowea'qua shouted. "Kinap and Ogeh'ma say that trees are of the cold dying!"

"Ah! It is so!" Ko'ram nodded vigorously. "Winter comes early these days. And it stays long. Too long. Then comes the rain. Too much rain at once! The ice goes out on the rivers . . . more ice than these aging eyes have ever seen . . . and then there are floods everywhere! Tôrnârssuk can tell you about that. Kamak says that before they joined with us the Northerners lost half their number in a washout at winter's end. And now the world has gone dry. No rain at all! But I will wager you all the beaver-teeth gaming pieces I own that it will soon be winter again. As it was last year and the year before. An early winter, long and cold . . . so cold that even on the coast where my people have long made their winter camp the great water freezes solid, and across its icy surface hunts the—" The old man abruptly cut off his words. He had not intended to send his thoughts where his tongue had taken him—to the death of his last surviving son. All knew how Ami'ck had died, dragged off the beach by a marauding polar bear, his spirit lost forever, consumed. Ko'ram turned up his gaze to Ne'gauni. There was something in his eyes that had not been there before, an expression of inestimable loss and sadness, and then of anger and resolve. "You must implore the spirits of winter to have mercy upon the People. You must ask them not to linger so long in hunting grounds where men are unfamiliar with their ways."

"Rain and Wind and Winter will come as they will," said

Ogeh'ma. "The forces of Creation have already given men the intelligence to learn from the trees and attempt not to stand against that which will in time surely break them. And so we will go to Big Lake to seek safety there in case the wind does not turn and the rain does not come. And so the People must follow the seasons as they follow the game—to the coast in late winter and spring for sealing and fishing and the taking of shell meat, inland to the caribou crossings in autumn when it is time to take prime hides and horn and meat and beaver. Then back to the coast again to avoid the deep winter snows of the interior. It is the only way to survive."

Kinap was grumbling, to himself or to the others—it was difficult to tell. "Everywhere I have traveled during the past many seasons it has been the same—shamans asking the winter spirits not to linger. The spirits do not seem to be listening."

"Maybe they are," suggested Musquash thoughtfully. "But not to the northern Forest People or to the Dawnland tribes."

"What said you, boy?" pressed Ko'ram.

"I said that maybe the spirits are listening to different shamans. The Northerners like the cold. I have heard Tôrnârssuk talking to the other men of the True People. He says that after we have reached the great river and hunted there awhile he will continue north into the far country of his Ancestors where it is always winter."

Ogeh'ma shivered up his shoulders. "Then we are destined to part company at the great river, Tôrnârssuk and I."

"Why?" asked Mowea'qua. "It no difference makes where you go. Journey north. Stay at the great river. Return to the Dawnland or into the deep forests where the sugar trees grow. The winter spirits will find you. True it is! Old Tribe people say that a day will come when the time of the long dark and lasting cold will return and go away never. It will again be as it was in the time beyond beginning, forever winter, a world of endless snow and ice, with Rainbow a river running across the night and stars as many and bright as fireflies helping Moon to light the way for the sons and daughters of First Man and First Woman as once again they with wolves run wild to hunt mammoths and caribou and—"

"Stop, daughter of Kinap!" Ogeh'ma raised his hands. "Your words chill my bones! Ah, look. Another maze of blowdowns lies ahead."

Ne'gauni was frowning again. And not because of the girl's talk of endless winter; indeed, in a forest as dry as the one through which they were traveling, the thought of snow was not unappealing. He was frowning because, seeing that Tôrnârssuk and a handful of Northerners were already working together with Kanio'te and Onen'ia to clear the way, he felt a captive on the giant's shoulders. "Let me down, Kinap!" he demanded. "I will help the others. I will do my share."

"Then keep asking the spirits to turn the wind or bring the rain, Dreamer! But you will stay where you are, and out of my way!" Ignoring the young man's further protestations, Kinap ordered Mowea'qua to haul the family drag frame as best she could while—with Ne'gauni clinging to his perch atop his shoulders—he moved ahead with Ogeh'ma and old Ko'ram to help the women, girls, and dogs negotiate their way through the blowdowns.

Ne'gauni glowered after Musquash as the boy hurried forward to give what little assistance he could to Tôrnârssuk and the others in opening the trail. He was not sure when he first noticed Suda'li's twins slinking away from the main body of the band like a pair of mischievous young weasels. His brow furrowed as, wondering what they were up to, he saw them darting through the shadows, then climbing high until they hunkered together on a branch directly over Musquash, who, unaware of their presence, hacked away at branches with his hand ax.

With a start, Ne'gauni realized their intent, too late. Before he could open his mouth, the twins were leaping into thin air in a harmony of shrieks to drop onto the younger boy and pummel him to the ground.

"Yah!" N'av guffawed at Musquash's expense as he snapped to his feet and stood triumphant above his prostrate victim.

Ka'wo'ni shook his head in disparagement of the younger boy. "And to think our old grandfather thought a little bug like you could one day grow into the powers of a great shaman. Ha! Ne'gauni is to be shaman. Not you. So—"

"So strong and eager and bold are the sons of Suda'li," observed the headman with quiet disdain as he set down the branch he had been dragging off the trail and came to pause before them.

Kinap was standing to his full height. Ne'gauni could feel the tension in the giant's shoulders as he stared ahead at the twins, standing shoulder to shoulder, breathless, gloating up at the headman, so full of themselves that they had apparently mistaken Tôrnârssuk's calmly stated reproach for commendation.

Suda'li, hurrying forward to stand beside the headman, beamed at her boys. "My sons bring joy to this widow's heart!" she boasted. "I weep that their father cannot see them now! But each night, before I sleep, I send good words about them to the spirit country and hope that the great bear who ate him may be there to hear my words so that the spirit of my lost man may smile and know that he has left such strong, bold sons in the country of the living."

"You do not have to send words about those two to my dead son, woman." Old Ko'ram came to stand beside his daughter-in-law, eyed his grandsons with disapproval, then hacked up a wad of phlegm and spat it in their direction. When the twins jumped back, he chortled at the look of dismay on their faces, but there was no amusement in his voice when he said, "No one has to tell your father about the pair of you. If he is in the spirit world, be he bear or man, he can hear the noise and disruption you two are always making. And I doubt very much that he finds cause to smile."

Suda'li's face congested with anger. "My sons are—"

"In need of a father's guidance in this band within which we walk together . . . one people now, but still with different ways," Tôrnârssuk interrupted. Then, leveling his gaze at the twins, he said evenly, "From your actions, sons of Suda'li and grandsons of Ko'ram, I must assume that you are capable of carrying far more than that which your mother has deemed to be your fair share of your family's burden. So. We must remedy this. Now. Suda'li, come forward. And Ko'ram, too. Let this be done. N'av and Ka'wo'ni, since you have chosen to speak disrespectfully of an elder, you will now honor your grandfather by taking his pack frame and dividing its burden between you. You will also take half of the widow's burden and share it. This will lighten the steps of both Suda'li and Ko'ram and make the journey to the overlook go more quickly for the band. And it will give you each a chance to make your mother proud as you show us all just how strong and brave you truly are."

Musquash emerged from beneath a pile of branches, spitting leaf fragments and shaking a good portion of the forest floor off himself, and vented a righteous snicker at the expense of the twins.

"There will be no laughter." Tôrnârssuk was emphatic.

"We have become one band. One People. Wildfire dances between us and the great river. North Wind carries her southward as we speak. We must be at the lake by sundown. Only there will we find refuge. So come. We must go on. There is neither time nor space for divisiveness among us now."

▼▼▼▼▼

It was the sound of a waterfall that told them the overlook was near.

"There are cliffs ahead—a great and dangerous drop. Keep the children close," Tôrnârssuk commanded the women. He eyed the sons of Suda'li as they came panting through the trees, last in line, trudging beneath the weight of pack frames that nearly bent their noses to the ground as they strained to keep up with the band.

But keep up they did. And without complaint.

Ne'gauni looked back at them. How miserable they looked! He was delighted, especially since he knew that young Musquash was not the only one to be pleased by the manner in which the headman had dealt with the twins. Old Ko'ram's initial grunt of approval had won a self-righteous scowl from Suda'li. Chief Ogeh'ma and Segub'un had exchanged knowing glances with each other and with their sons and their wives, obviously agreeing among themselves that it was long past due for someone to take the twins in line, since Suda'li was either unable or unwilling to do so. Ne'gauni, feeling nothing less than resentment toward the mean-spirited widow, could not resist a smile of satisfaction as he watched her equally mean-spirited boys trudging on in misery.

His smile did not last.

The roar of wind and water was coming through the trees

and, with it, something else, something deeper, wilder, like the call of some mythical beast spoken of in the most ancient tales of the time beyond beginning.

A great roaring filled the forest. Not wind. Not the sound of the falls. Deep at first, growling, it came through the trees as from some vast resonating chamber to become a high-pitched animal scream that ululated across the world like the cry of a defiant giant.

"Great One . . . Earth Shaker . . . Thunder Speaker."

"Silence, Mowea'qua," Kinap rumbled. "Do not speak!"

She did not have to speak. Ne'gauni knew the identity of the demon of which she spoke.

Katcheetohúskw.

His people's name for the five-legged monster who spoke with the voice of thunder and stormed through the forest to crush and devour careless travelers while they slept was as well known to him as his own. It was the beast of a child's nightmares, a demon conjured by parents when they wanted to be certain that, when unwatched, their little ones would not stray far from home.

Ne'gauni's blood ran cold as, once again, the great roaring rent his ears. Beneath the downward press of his thighs, he felt the giant's shoulder muscles tense into the rigidity of solid rock.

He held his breath. Listening. He had heard this sound before.

Once.

Long ago.

In another part of the forest.

On the day when Death had come through the trees and life as he had known it had ended forever. And now, as then, it seemed unreal to him, disembodied, a phantom risen from a world beyond this world, a . . .

"Mammoth!" exclaimed Musquash.

"Be still!" commanded Kinap harshly.

Up ahead the band had paused.

Old Ko'ram was shaking his rattle as though the high, hissing sound might obliterate the terror of the other, much greater sound.

Tôrnârssuk raised his arms to indicate silence.

No one spoke.

No one breathed.

Ko'ram drew his rattle into his chest and held it close, comforting it, and himself.

But there was no need.

The sound of the wind and falls continued to come back to them, but whatever they had heard before was absent—or silent now.

"A trick of the wind and water and dying day," said old Ko'ram, attempting to convince himself.

Mowea'qua looked up, as did Musquash. Disagreement was intense within their eyes, but neither had a chance to speak. There was warning in the giant's face, an unspoken command for quiet and absolute obedience.

Tôrnârssuk was waving them on.

And soon, falling into step behind him, they were there, one moment plodding along within the perpetual shade of the deep woods, the next standing squint-eyed in the blowing mist of a waterfall beneath a soaring vault of open sky.

The wind struck at them, threw grit and water in their faces as it tried to beat them back. They would not be beaten. They stood their ground, poised at the very edge of the world, it seemed, with range after range of forested hills rolling away to the horizon and the sun a ruddy ember glowing low in the west, its heat and brilliance dulled by clouds that were expanding from the north, taking the blue from the sky and transforming it into the color of blood staining wet buckskin.

No, thought Ne'gauni as the giant lowered him to the ground and he positioned himself on his crutches, not only clouds. "Smoke!"

"As you have seen in the Darkness that comes to warn the People of Danger through you, Dreamer?"

"I . . ." He could form no reply to old Ko'ram's question. His heart was pounding. His mouth had gone dry again. And the stench of smoke was back in his nostrils, that rank and heretofore inexplicable stink. Foul. Sour. So revolting an amalgamation of scents that he nearly retched because now, for the first time, he could visualize its source: vaporizing green wood and leaves and needles, charred fur and flesh and bones, bubbling sap and fat and burning hair, as though something—or someone—had been wrapped in freshly picked greenery and thrown into a flaming fire pit to be cooked alive.

He gasped.

And knew in this moment that what he had seen within the Darkness was real.

The burning world.

The burning woman.

Long before the others had gone ahead to confirm their fears, he *had* foreseen them both! And now the burning world lay, not in the Darkness of his fevered daydreams, but ahead. And the burning woman–the faceless woman–was out there even now in the conflagration that raged between the band and the great river.

"No!"

His own exclamation shook him as the true horror of the moment dawned upon him. What if she was not out there at all? What if she was here, standing beside him even now, her fate unrealized . . . and still to be determined?

His gaze flew to Mowea'qua, then past her to the other women of the band, past Segub'un standing with her three round-faced daughters, past bucktoothed Goh'beet, her own little girls drawn near, past Pwaumó and Suda'li and Tsi'le'ni, Ningao's winsome but almost excessively plain young wife. At last his eyes rested upon the face of Hasu'u, the headman's woman, the one he loved more than life itself. "You are in danger," he told her.

"We are all in danger," said Tôrnârssuk bleakly.

"Wildfire *is* dancing," Kinap emphasized. "If North Wind does not soon turn, it *will* bring her here."

"Be it so," replied the headman with a surly impatience that betrayed both anger and defiance. "We will not be here to greet her." He gestured out and down. "The lake we seek lies there!"

No one said a word.

Far below, within a broad valley cupped between the up-folded knees of the range through which Tôrnârssuk had just brought the band, the deeply indented shoreline of a vast body of water mirrored the bloody color of the sky.

"So far down . . ." Ko'ram observed wanly. "And that which we fear is yet so far away. Perhaps we could just stay here beside the falls, close to the stream, and hope that . . ."

"No," Kinap said grimly. "The trees are too dry and close, the stream too narrow and shallow. If Wildfire comes here, everything will burn, even the air, and the falls and the stream will boil."

"We will descend by way of the rockfall to the right of the falls," Tôrnârssuk told them. "My men and I have been this way before. Arnaktark has already supervised the fixing of ropes. We will lower the drag frames, and the dogs and children where necessary. And you, too, Wise Man, if you would have it so. The descent will go easily enough. It will be tedious, but not difficult. Before the moon is fully risen we will be encamped beside the lake, out from under the cursed cover of the forest for a while . . . able to breathe again and to see the sky. If Wildfire comes, we will take shelter in the cool arms of Water. There is no longer need to fear the threat of flames." He paused. Seeing the dubious expressions on the faces of his people, he gestured once more, this time to Ne'gauni. "Our shaman is with us."

Chapter Five

▼▼▼▼▼▼▼

They lowered him to the valley by rope and sling while the giant steadied the line and Mowea'qua and Musquash clambered down the wet, rocky, moss-slick trail beside him.

Ne'gauni made no protest.

He knew that he could not make the descent on crutches. And even if the forces of Creation had chosen this moment to give him back his leg, he would have been too weak to walk on it. Too shaken by his confrontation with Death. Too overwhelmed by the implications of all that had befallen him this day. The strong rope of twisted fiber that supported his weight was biting into his thigh. He barely felt it. Whatever the girl had mixed into the concoction in her highly polished medicine bowl of burled oak was powerful. It ate his pain, but not his lingering dread.

Yet there was no Darkness within his mind.

No little spider emerged from the core of his consciousness to spin black webs of despair in his brain.

Nor were his thoughts wandering off into the abyss of Oblivion.

Ne'gauni knew exactly where he was.

The mist from the falls blew across him like a fine rain, but he was not cooled or soothed by the welcome moisture. The image of the burning world and the burning woman were stamped in fire at the back of his eyes. The smell of smoke tainted his nostrils. And although he was determined not to challenge Tôrnârssuk again, he was certain that the headman was wrong about one thing: Until they reached the lake, they all had every reason to be afraid.

"We must go on." He summoned the strength to make a litany of the words, repeating them again and again, doing his best to be heard above the roar of the falls as he echoed the headman's intention to reach the lake before sundown to everyone who picked his or her way past him upon the trail. "Be cautious, but move as quickly as you can. Our headman is right. We must not linger. You, Ningao, carry that dog if you must, but help your woman to hurry her step. Chi'co'pee, stop staring at me and help your sisters! And you, Onen'ia, why do you move so slowly?"

"They are afraid, Ne'gauni," whispered Musquash, leaning close to be heard above the sound of the falls.

"We will be safe," Ne'gauni assured the boy. "But only when we reach the lake."

"It will be there . . . in the valley . . . waiting."

"No. It is yet too far to the north. As long as we keep moving, there will be time for us to—"

"I do not speak of that which burns," interrupted the boy, his earnest little face pinched with intensity beneath the dripping snout and whiskers of his muskrat hood. "I speak of the one whose roar came to us on the wind. The great mammoth is real, Ne'gauni. No matter what old Ko'ram said, it is there, in the valley, waiting. You will see."

▼▼▼▼▼

The sun had nearly gone to its rest by the time they had all descended from the overlook, gathered up their belongings, and, with the men now carrying their lances and bows at the ready, set off for the lake.

"You see," said Musquash to Ne'gauni as Kinap was about to heft the young man onto his shoulders. "Men do not need lances and arrows to protect the band from that which burns. And look at the Northerners! They are all wearing their bolas, each man ready to send the stones flying. I tell you, Dreamer, the one that speaks with the voice of thunder is out there. As tall as a mountain! As white as a thundercloud standing before the sun! With tusks as long as the tallest lodgepoles and as thick as a grown man's thighs! And they *do* fear it, Ne'gauni, but they—"

"Be quiet, boy," interrupted the giant. "And speak not of this again. Tôrnârssuk will not have you frightening the women and children more than they already are."

"Frightened I am not," Mowea'qua loftily informed him. With a self-assured air she prepared to walk on with her fine ashwood bow in hand, an exquisitely fletched and painted dogwood arrow nocked and ready.

"You should be afraid," warned Kinap. "You to whom the spirits have given the feather of Raven, do you think others have not noticed this? It is a questionable and worrisome gift, daughter, one that you are not wise to wear."

"Mmph! On his raiding mask Tôrnârssuk wears the feathers of Raven. And care I not what others think!"

"You must learn to care! Raven and Bear are totem to Tôrnârssuk. They speak to the power of his wisdom and courage and strength. These things have nothing to do with you!"

"To the Old Tribe all animals are totem. And a hunter am I! Strong and brave and—"

"You are female! And I have told you before that it is forbidden among the Northerners for a woman to handle a man's weapon. The Dawnland people take equal offense. So take the feather of Raven from your hair. Put that arrow back in your quiver, girl, and have consideration enough of the taboos of others to wrap your bow and carry it concealed upon your back so that the sight of it proves no affront to others."

"Of the Old Tribe am I, not from the far country of the Northerners, not from the Dawnland! The kami have given me a gift from Raven. Wear it I will. And this weapon is my own! It belongs to no man! If a bow you did not wish me to possess, you should not have made one for me, my father, or taught me the use of it."

"When I made that bow for you, Mowea'qua, I had no way of knowing that you would ever leave the solitude of the deep forest."

"Mmph! Is this why you never put upon me the tattoo mark of the daughters of your band? Did you think that my grandmother forever would live to take care of me? Or that I would alone stay in the deep forest after her bones were scraped and cleaned and laid out in a sacred circle for the kami?"

The giant shivered. "That was not done! Your grandmother was given a scaffold burial, an honoring in the way of my people, her body left intact, not decapitated and dismembered and set out to be devoured by wolves and foxes in the revolting and ignorant way of the Old Tribe."

The girl went rigid. "Kelet was of the Old Tribe. Good were her ways. My ways."

"You will learn other ways!" Kinap was huffing and hulking up his shoulders like a riled bear. "The Old Tribe is no more, Mowea'qua. And for good reason. You walk with the People now! You must learn their ways. My ways. The blood of the People is yours through me. I will not allow you to dishonor it! And how many times do I have to tell you that you must not name the dead lest you summon a spirit back from the country of the Ancestors?"

"I *will* Kelet's name speak," she told him defiantly. "Welcome in my heart is the kami of my grandmother! It is the only way her spirit can live again. No singing did you allow me to make for her, not in the old way, not within the sacred circle of bones. Nor would you allow me to take her heart and flesh and eat of—"

Kinap struck her across the face with the side of his hand, so hard that the bow and arrow flew from her grip as she spun to one side and went sprawling. "Never speak of that again! Never!"

Ne'gauni was stunned.

The girl lay motionless, facedown on the duff of the trail as Musquash leaped between her and the giant.

"T-Tôrnârs-suk has s-said that there will be n-no dee . . . deev . . . eye . . . eyesiveness among us now!" the boy reminded, fighting his way through the complex word and stammering as he often did when he was upset. "You m-must not hurt her more, my f-father! You m-must not!" he proclaimed, standing as tall as he could, looking for all the world like a brazen little muskrat doing its best to ward off the menacing advance of a towering brown bear.

Kinap looked ahead. The band was still moving on. No one had noticed his loss of temper with his daughter. And he was not about to be deterred from his purpose by a blustering boy. He growled, picked up the child by the scruff of his skinny neck, and roughly set him back on his feet beside Ne'gauni, then stood over his daughter, glowering down at her. "Get up," he commanded.

Mowea'qua did not get up.

Ne'gauni's heartbeat quickened. Was the girl breathing? It seemed not. Until, slowly, she levered up with both hands and turned to glare over her shoulder at her father through the wild tangles of her hair.

"Get up!" Kinap insisted.

Mowea'qua did not move.

Ne'gauni frowned. The girl's upper lip showed red. She was bleeding profusely from both nostrils. And she was snarling, showing her teeth. Like a wolf, he thought. Like a cornered and beaten wolf . . . or like her namesake, the half-human wolf creature who howled to the moon and prowled the hidden vastnesses of the northern forests in eternal search of human prey.

The giant must have seen the resemblance, too. He was shaking, uttering low, barely suppressed rumblings of rage and disgust as, bending to snatch up the girl's bow, he broke it over his knee and cast it aside. "Sometimes, Mowea'qua, I regret the day I did not strangle you at birth." The declaration made, he curled the fingers of his right hand in her hair, jerked her forcefully to her feet, pulled the quiver of arrows from her back, and handed it to Ne'gauni. "Take this. The arrows may be slightly light and short for your bow, but if need arises they will serve you well. I should never have made them for her. Never."

▼▼▼▼

Ne'gauni clamped his jaws together. He knew that there was no point in objecting to being lifted and carried by the giant. Dusk was beginning to gather in the shadows of the deep woods. The band was marching doggedly ahead. Afoot he would surely slow them down. And they must reach the lake by sundown!

"Keep up!" Kinap looked back at his daughter and Musquash.

Ne'gauni swiveled his head around. The girl was moving slowly and sullenly along, head tilted up, one hand to her nose to stanch the flow of blood.

The boy reached for her free hand. "You *must* learn to obey, Mowea'qua! You *must*! Here . . . let me be your eyes until your nose stops bleeding."

She slapped his hand away. "My own eyes have I!" she declared nastily and lengthened her stride until she was walking belligerently along at Kinap's side.

"Take the feather from your hair," he commanded.

"Take it from me if you will, but cast away I will not what the spirits have to me given!"

The giant grumbled but made no move to force his will upon her. "So be it, then, but do not fall behind again, or, by the forces of Creation, I swear that I will cast you away and consider myself better off for the loss of you."

"Mmph!" was all the girl would allow herself to say as, rummaging in one of the many little fur and leather bags that hung from her belt, she pulled up a fingering of moss, tore it in two, and packed it into her nostrils.

"You would n-not really leave her, would you, my father?" Musquash sounded worried to the point of tears.

"Do not tempt me, boy, do not tempt me."

"I will go with her," threatened the child.

The giant looked down. "In this forest, boy, you would all too soon be meat. And as for Mowea'qua, who knows what she would become?"

Ne'gauni shivered. Talk of abandonment unnerved him. And although he had his bow in hand and Mowea'qua's quiver now hung beside his own over his shoulder, there was something about the surrounding woodlands that raised the hackles on his back.

No birds called.

No squirrels scolded.

He frowned, tasted the bitter aftertaste of the girl's medicine lingering at the back of his mouth, and, as he looked around, imagined himself being watched by unseen eyes.

Hostile eyes.

Animal eyes.

Manitou eyes.

He started.

A face was peering at him from the undergrowth . . . furred . . . fanged . . . and yet short of snout and, with its ears sprouting from the sides of its head, somehow human.

He shut his eyes. Tight. Opened them. Cautiously. And, with his bow up and an arrow set to fly, stared again at . . .

"Nothing."

"What said you, Dreamer?" asked Kinap.

"Nothing," he said again as he relaxed his bowstring and shook his head, realizing that whatever he had seen must have been a product of Mowea'qua's potions and his overwrought imagination. There was nothing there. Nothing! Surely if there were faces staring from the undergrowth, he would not be the only one to see them. Yet his skin crawled as he watched from his perch high atop Kinap's massive shoulders the band moving silently ahead through shifting walls of dusty evergreens that swayed languidly back and forth, sighing and groaning and making the low creaking sounds of stress as they yielded to the gentle caress of the wind.

Gentle?

He caught his breath. When had the wind last been gentle? Two days ago?

"The wind . . . it has dropped!" he exclaimed.

"Perhaps," conceded Kinap. "It was stronger on the heights, that much is certain. Here on the floor of the valley, with the hills shouldering up to the north, it is difficult to say if it has lessened or merely been deflected."

"Dreamer has asked the spirit of North Wind to turn," Musquash said. "If he is truly shaman, it will obey him."

Ne'gauni did not appreciate the boy's words of confidence. The thought of being shaman weighted him in ways that he could not fully explain. Not now. Not with his head thick with medicine. Not in this strange and stultifying part of the forest when Wildfire was burning somewhere up ahead and the band had yet to reach the safety of the lake. He frowned, glad to be distracted by the sight of Tôrnârssuk falling back to walk beside the widow Suda'li and talk quietly to her sons.

"He rewards them now with words of encouragement," observed Kinap.

"Rewards them for what?" Ne'gauni was perplexed; in his eyes the boys deserved no commendation for mean-spiritedness.

"Dropping on me from the trees and mauling me like a pair of bears?" Musquash's question was as acidic as a leaf of mountain sorrel.

"He will reward their willingness to abide his harsh discipline without question or complaint," replied Kinap firmly, turning a censoring gaze to an oblivious Mowea'qua.

"I obey him," said the little boy dourly. "He does not reward me."

"That he allows any of us to walk with his band is reward enough."

"I walk with *you*, Kinap." Musquash looked up at the

giant out of anxious and speculative eyes. "You have become my band . . . you and Mowea'qua and Ne'gauni. Is it not so?"

"No." Kinap was adamant. Yet, when next he spoke, he lowered his voice, obviously not wishing to be heard by anyone outside of his immediate family. "One aging, over-sized storyteller, a disobedient half-wild daughter, a son no bigger than a muskrat, and a one-legged dreamer—what kind of band is that? We do not even possess a dog to call our own. Alone we are vulnerable. And so we walk with Tôrnârssuk. We are part of a much larger family now. He is headman over this family, and although he is stern and demanding, I have never known him to be less than fair to any man or boy . . . or even to a dreamer who shouts against him on the trail."

"Tôrnârssuk now Ne'gauni names Shaman." The glumly spoken reminder came from Mowea'qua. Her bloodstained face wore an expression that clearly said she believed herself and her skills as a healer solely responsible for this unprecedented turn of events.

"Mmm. So he has." Kinap did not deign to look at the girl as he made low grumbling sounds, as though chewing over an indigestible piece of meat that he could not quite bring himself to swallow. "Are you listening up there, Dreamer?"

"I am listening."

"Then heed me, Ne'gauni. From this day you must measure every word and action as carefully as Mowea'qua measures and mixes her salves and oils and powders. Make no mistake—Tôrnârssuk would have seen you killed for what you said of him today. In the past, when I have traveled among bands of other Northerners, I have seen good men killed as punishment for far less serious infractions."

"Then the Northerners are not fair," declared Musquash, scowling.

Kinap was rumbling like a storm cloud. "To keep a band strong and invulnerable against its enemies . . . anything is fair, boy. *Anything*."

▼▼▼▼

Loons were calling.

No one spoke, and even the dogs appeared cowed as the avian cries came shivering eerily through the trees like the high, keening ululations of women mourning the dead.

Tôrnârssuk raised an arm and gestured the band forward, resolutely leading his followers onward through the gathering gloom of early evening. At last they came through the trees and found themselves upon a broad, stony beach to the lee of a long, fingering peninsula that jutted well out into the lake, effectively blocking the view to the north and gentling the flow of the wind.

"Thanks be given to the forces of Creation and to the invocations of our new dreamer, the wind *is* down!" proclaimed old Ko'ram, lifting his rattle and shaking it jubilantly at the sky. Followed by Kinap's family and those of his own band, he broke into a bobbing, high-stepping dance that took him zigzagging across the slanting beach to the edge of the water like a frenzied shorebird.

Standing with several other Northerners beside Tôrnârssuk, Moraq scowled as he watched the old man pause, raise his other arm, and begin a chant of thanksgiving to the forces of Creation. "He neglects to praise his headman for remembering the way to the lake and to this sheltering beach."

Kamak was nodding sullenly. "That jut of land out there breaks the back of North Wind. You knew it would be so, Tôrnârssuk, as did all of us who have been to this place before. The new dreamer has had nothing to do with it."

Tôrnârssuk stood motionless, expressionless, staring north.

"Let the old one thank whom he will . . . his people seem to have need of one of their own to speak to the spirits for them."

Ningao did not look happy. "But the cloud spirits have spoken all afternoon of a change in the weather, my tunraq. We needed no one-legged dreamer or wind-making Wise Man to tell us this. We all been looking up and hoping that—"

"Hope?" Tôrnârssuk turned the word as though it were a foul thing, both to his ears and tongue. "Are you willing to wager your life on when the wind will turn, Ningao? Or the lives of your woman and dog on when the rain will come? Have you been so long within this land of endless trees and careless tribes that you no longer wear two knives and would presume to speak for Sila? True men do not hope! True men do not put all of their trust in signs or in dreams! True men fear Sila—the pure and unrelenting power of all the un-expected man-and-woman-and-dog-eating terrors that can and will come against them! Then, strong in this fear, men of the True People make their lives accordingly."

"Yes, Tôrnârssuk." Ningao's head sank a little between his shoulders, rather like one of his dogs anticipating a puni-tive clout. "We all still wear two knives, one hidden on each side within our traveling shirts . . . anticipating danger, ac-knowledging the power of Sila."

"It is so," Kamak affirmed. He was not the only man to press his hands against his ribs to indicate possession of hidden fighting daggers.

Tôrnârssuk had not moved, nor had his expression changed. Now he turned his face to the darkening sky, his wide features showing the strain of fatigue and of long-sustained apprehen-sion. Breathing in deeply, he raised one hand, palm up, and said quietly, "I smell no smoke, and I was certain that there would be more ash falling upon us by now. What little there is feels cool to my skin. This is good. Very good. Perhaps the wind *is* down. Perhaps the clouds *will* bring Rain. But until these changes actually occur, we can be sure of only this: If North Wind holds steady and Rain does not come, that which we fear will continue to advance toward us. She will send her flaming children ahead of her as embers upon the wind. They will settle upon the peninsula before they come to us. Then we will smell smoke, strongly. We will see flames, burning like torches on trees across the water. But even then there will be time for us to take shelter in the lake. There, on that long spit of gravel over which water lies shallow, there we and our belongings will be safe if the sky begins to rain fire upon us. But now, come, let us not stand apart from the others. There is work to be done before we can rest and wait for whatever will come—or not come—to us this night. The dogs must be fed. There are trenches to be dug. We must bury our drag poles and trading goods and all that will not hold up to a good soaking."

"And the other—the source of the thunder that we heard roaring in the wind when we stood on the overlook—how do we protect ourselves against that?" Inaksak stood as boldly as he had posed his question. He was short and muscular, as were most of his fellow Northerners, and with his legs planted wide and his expression one of exaggerated contempt for whatever might befall him, he was doing an admirable job of masking his fear—fear not only of the potential for disaster inherent in the approaching Wildfire, but of the legendary mammoth that he dared not name lest the spirit of the beast overhear and think itself summoned.

Tôrnârssuk rested his palm against his chest as he set his long, dark eyes upon the man who had spoken. "I have seen no sign of its kind in this part of the forest," he replied evenly. "No gouged and broken trees. No trampled earth. No leavings. But if what we heard from the overlook was not a trick of wind and water as old Ko'ram prefers to believe, we will respect and defend against its potential to kill us. And we will draw strength from the knowledge that our Ancestors once hunted and grew strong upon the meat of its kind."

"But what if it is not flesh?" proposed Ningao, doing his best to appear unconcerned but not coming even close to succeeding as he lowered his voice and added in a whisper, "What if it is a spirit, a great white phantom tusker as big as a mountain crashing through the trees to eat our dogs and grind us all into the earth? A living revenge called upon us by the ghosts of the Old Tribe band that we drove before us when last we came through this valley?"

"Then we will look once more into the face of Sila," interjected the headman. His voice was as low and smooth and languid as the valley wind, but there was a tension and underlying anger to his tone that had not been there before, and in his eyes were dark and dangerous undercurrents of bitter resolution. "Have we not each looked many times into the many faces of the many kinds of Death that have confronted and challenged us during our lives? Why should it be different now?"

"We may have left survivors here, my tunraq . . . enemies who will remember that we slew for sport their brothers and wives and little ones."

"Do not speak of it. Chief Ogeh'ma and his Dawnland followers would not understand the way it was for us then. But even the dreamer knows that there are always enemies, old friend. And what happened here between us and that Old Tribe band happened long ago. In all of this land of trees within which men can only rarely see the sky and the face of our father, the sun, this valley and lake offer us the only refuge I know from Wildfire. We will be wary, as we are always wary. And if any surviving 'ghosts' of that band come against our camp, as men of the True People we need be only half as bold as the one-legged dreamer, who, when he stood up to us today, saw the face of Sila in our eyes and did not turn away or whimper or wonder aloud what he should do about it."

Chastised, Ningao hung his head.

Inaksak's head went defensively high.

Kamak and the others stared at their feet to mask their embarrassment.

Moraq continued to scowl. "We will be as bold. As we have always been bold. Since the day we chose to turn our backs upon our people and walk with you out of the great cold Barrenlands of the Ancient Ones to trade and raid and make our way in the lands of lesser tribes, we have never been less than men of the True People. And so I say to your face that you should have let us kill the dreamer, Tôrnârssuk. I still fear that bad spirits feed inside his head."

Chapter Six

▼▼▼▼▼▼▼

Darkness filled the valley.

Stars showed overhead, dull pinpricks of light glinting through a veil of high clouds and smoke. Far to the east, the moon was rising behind forested hills, its face still unseen as the first incursions of moon glow penetrated the trees and sheened the surface of the lake.

Ne'gauni stood alone at the water's edge. With his pack frame and belongings still at his feet, he stared across the lake, too tired to move. Not that there was need. As soon as old Ko'ram had finished his prayer of thanksgiving, Tôrnârssuk commanded the band to tend to the needs of the dogs and assemble a camp. Kinap had put him firmly on his crutches and told him to stay out of the way. And so he had, watching from a distance as the men worked together in teams to dig a pair of trenches and drag several large trunks of storm-washed driftwood up the beach to form a circular windbreak, close to the water, away from the edge of the forest. Now, with their belongings either buried against the potential onslaught of Wildfire or assembled close at hand— ready to be carried into the lake at the first command of the headman—the band was gathered within the bastioning circle of driftwood. Old Ko'ram had just called out and invited him to share in a meal. A cold meal. There would be no fire tonight, not on a night when the wind-borne ember children of Wildfire might be blown overhead to glimpse the flames of a cooking fire and mistakenly believe themselves invited to a feast. No. Tonight the band would eat jerked meat, traveling cakes of pounded fat, roots, nuts, and berries, and the fish that the women had netted earlier in the day. For such food Ne'gauni could summon neither appetite nor energy enough to inspire him to join the others.

He stood unmoving, his back to the encampment. The strangest of moods was upon him. Somnolent. Heavy. An embodiment of fatigue and the residue of Mowea'qua's medicine—of this he was certain. The lake stretched out before him, a vast, shimmering receptacle of starlight. It was beautiful. So beautiful! And to think that only this afternoon he had not imagined that he would live to see the sunset.

"Ne'gauni!"

He frowned. Someone had called out to him again. Not old Ko'ram this time. A woman's voice, distorted by distance and obscured by the slur of waves along the shore.

Mowea'qua? His frown became a scowl. *Chi'co'pee? Nee'nah? Ane'pemin'an?* His scowl became a grimace. *Hasu'u?* His grimace became a smile of longing. He wanted to think that he had heard the headman's woman. Succeeding, he stood his ground, hoping that if he remained where he was, a lonely figure brooding across dark waters, Hasu'u would be moved by her innately caring nature to come down the beach to join him, bringing food and kind words and maybe even another kiss.

"Dreamer?"

Again a woman's voice, and footsteps moving toward him over the stony beach.

Ne'gauni tensed, held his breath, certain that in a moment Hasu'u would be beside him.

"Forgive me, He Walks Ahead in Dreams to Foresee Danger for the People. I bring this fish to you. It is not cooked in fire, but its flesh is sweet, an offering in return for your kind words to the spirits on behalf of my child."

He exhaled, recognizing the voice, and the woman who had spoken. It was Pwaumó, not Hasu'u, who came to stand at his side. True to her promise, the woman of Kanio'te now bent to lay a fish cradled on a spruce bough at his foot.

"You must not stay long alone, Dreamer," she half whispered. "It is good that you send your thoughts to the spirits on behalf of your people, but our headman has told me to advise you that we must all remain within the circle of the band this night." This said, she rose, bowed her head, and hurried back up the beach without another word.

Ne'gauni slumped on his crutches, disappointed by Hasu'u's failure to see to his needs and too fatigued to think of eating or making even the slightest effort to bend down and pick up his dinner, much less of working up the energy to join the rest of the band.

Loons were calling again, far out beyond the headlands, their crescendoing cries rising and falling on unseen swells, more laughter now than wail. A fish jumped and splashed in the shallows over the sandbar. Ne'gauni fixed his gaze northward across the wide channel that separated the beach from the benighted peninsula. No dust or ash or fragments of airborne grit attempted trespass between the dark curtaining of his lashes. The wind was definitely down! And where he expected to see the night sky showing red above the serrated spine of the heavily treed peninsula, there was only a space of star-struck sable. If Wildfire was still advancing southward through the northern forest, he could see no sign of her.

Is it possible the forces of Creation have heard and answered my prayers? Is it—

"Intend you to stand at the edge of the water until you take root like a sapling on this beach?"

Ne'gauni, startled by Mowea'qua's belligerent query, turned to see the girl picking her way aggressively over the rocks as she came toward him with Musquash at her heels.

The boy paused beside the young man and apologized, "We do not mean to disturb you as you stand alone talking to the spirits, Dreamer, but others grow restless as they see you standing outside the circle of the band, and Mowea'qua wanted to—"

"Do not speak for me, Bog Rat! Healer am I! And care I not for the restlessness of others. I have for my Dreamer brought special salves. Too long have you kept your half leg dangling, Wounded One. So sit you now on the smooth back of that big driftwood log over there and I will onto your wound pack healing Old Tribe magic."

Ne'gauni's brow furrowed with annoyance. She had not even deigned to look directly at him before turning away and heading for the log. And she had commanded him again. And used the name he hated. But the day *had* been long and she was right—the stump of his left thigh *was* throbbing. So he followed her obligingly to the driftwood log, sat, and put his crutches down, leaving Musquash to gather up and transfer his belongings, including Pwaumó's fish, to his new position on the beach.

"Mmph." Without looking at him, Mowea'qua knelt and took one of her medicine pouches from her belt. "Heal will you never if to your wounds you do not attend."

He unlaced the buckskin flap of the shortened legging that folded up over the stump of his knee. Her voice sounded unusual. Her breathing was shallow, and through her mouth.

Recalling her confrontation with Kinap, he asked, "Have you attended your own wound? How is your nose, daughter of Kinap? It does not sound as though it is working very well."

"Stopped has the bleeding," she replied obliquely. "How is *your* nose, son of Asticou?"

He had forgotten all about his earlier fall. A quick exploration of his face with questing fingertips brought it all back and required an honest, albeit begrudging, reply. "There is little pain and less swelling. Whatever you added to the mud you packed onto it has done its work well."

"Old Tribe magic," she said tightly.

"Her nose is a big nose now!" Musquash informed him, not without sympathy but with all a little boy's enthusiasm for talk of blood and gore—when they are not his own. "So swollen! So fat! This big is her nose!" He made a fist and brandished it as a comparison. "And the skin around her eyes is turning black!"

"My face will heal," said Mowea'qua, keeping her face downturned and her eyes to her work as she fingered a strong-smelling salve from her pouch and began to daub it gently on the overheated skin and scar tissue of all that remained to Ne'gauni of his left limb.

It occurred to the young man that normally at such a time, he would have chosen to add insult to injury by saying something hurtful to the girl about her unusual appearance, but her ministrations were tender and his feelings toward her had softened since she had spoken out to the Northerners in his defense. And so he said with genuine sympathy, "I am sorry that Kinap hit you. I thought for a moment that he had killed you."

"Mmph! My medicines you would miss?"

"Yes," he admitted, and almost added, *And I would miss*

you, too, for the words were in his heart, startling him, but not enough to concede them to her . . . or to himself.

"His own strength he does not know," said Mowea'qua of the giant. "Hurt me he did not mean to do."

Musquash exhaled a forbearing little sigh as he picked up Pwaumó's fish-laden spruce bough platter, climbed onto the driftwood tree trunk next to Ne'gauni, and handed him his dinner. "Here, Dreamer. Eat. And tell Mowea'qua that she must learn to obey."

Ne'gauni found the boy's request more than reasonable. As he stared down at the trout gleaming silver on its bed of spruce needles, his stomach growled with a sudden reminder that he had eaten nothing save a mouthful of jerked venison since afternoon. "Among all tribes it is a woman's place to be obedient, Mowea'qua," he told the girl. Breaking the spine of the trout and bending it back, he raised the fish to his lips and took a bite of its pale flesh.

"And what of all tribes do you know, son of Asticou, man of the Inland Forest People? Mmph. You may now be He Walks Ahead in Dreams to Foresee Danger for the People, but never out of the deep woods were you until last winter!"

"Nor were you," Musquash reminded her peevishly, then warned, "You must not speak to a shaman like that! And you *must* learn to obey, Mowea'qua. You *must*. You make Kinap so angry. You make everybody so angry! This is not good. Our father is not happy with you. I fear for you, Mowea'qua! You must give the feather of Raven back to the spirits."

"Yah! Nothing do you know, Bog Rat!" The girl closed her medicine pouch, looped it back onto her belt, and snapped to her feet. "If the spirits wanted the feather of Raven, they would not to me have given it. And Kinap's blood is not your blood. Of his flesh you are not. Never could

Kinap hurt his Mowea'qua. Not *really* hurt me. My father he is! And it is his right to hit me. Do you hear me complain?"

Ne'gauni, having voraciously devoured the tender but scant meat of the trout, now bit off the fish's head. He crunched its bland sweetness, sucking and tonguing eyes and juices and bitter guts and gills as he tossed away the skin, spine, and tail. Wiping his hands absently on the fragrant, stubby little needles of the spruce bough, he stared after Mowea'qua. The girl was walking stalwartly back up the beach toward the band. But before she had turned away, even in the cloud-misted glow of starlight, he had at last seen what the giant's blow had done to her face. Anger touched him. He spat out what was left of the bony head of the trout. "No man has a right to strike a woman and leave her looking like that. No man! Not even Kinap. And not even if the woman is Mowea'qua."

"Our father is short-tempered since Suda'li stopped smiling at him." Musquash shared his opinion freely. "I think the widow is angry because Kinap did not speak out against Tôrnârssuk for punishing her bad sons. I think maybe because of this she will not spread her legs for Kinap again." Swinging his own legs back and forth, he thumped his heels against the tree trunk as he stared up at the stars. "I hope that the forces of Creation will see to it that she does not. I would not like to have Suda'li as a woman at my father's fire circle. And I hope that the backs of N'av and Ka'wo'ni will ache forever from the load Tôrnârssuk made them carry today."

"They carried it bravely enough."

"Mmph! They were afraid not to carry it."

"Be careful, boy. You sound like your sister."

"Mowea'qua is not my sister." Musquash turned his gaze from the sky to Ne'gauni and, with his heart in his eyes, confided, "She will be my *woman* someday."

"On the day muskrats fly!"

"Do not make fun of me, Ne'gauni. It will be so. She *will* be mine. I will care for her and protect her against all enemies! This I have sworn! You are to be Shaman. Surely you have seen this for us in your dreams?"

"No, Muskrat. I have not seen this."

"You will. I have wished for it on my sacred stone." He puffed out his meager chest and, laying a hand over the amulet that lay concealed beneath the skins of his traveling shirt, confided, "The spirits of the Ancient Ones live inside the sacred stones. This one belonged to my father and to his father's father before it came to me. Someday it will speak to me. My father promised this. In the meantime the sacred stone listens when I speak. It knows all things . . . about you . . . about me . . . about everything that has ever been and ever will be! Great Squam told me this, and so I know and trust in the truth of it."

Ne'gauni would never understand how the boy could speak of his father without cringing. It was no secret that Great Squam had been hated by all and that he had been slain by one of his many wives, but not before he had allowed Musquash's mother to be killed and then skinned by the hand of the same murderous female who eventually suborned his rank and took his life. Now she, too, lay dead, her bones scattered, her skull no doubt bleaching on the bloody sands of the sacred island alongside the skeletons of those who had so unwisely chosen to follow her. Ne'gauni's lips tightened as he remembered that Musquash, whose hearing was now acute as an owl's and whose voice piped out high and clear as Onen'ia's flute, had been beaten into muteness and near-deafness by his father's slaves and favorite wife. It was Mowea'qua's grandmother, not the shamans of the sacred island, who had healed the child. With Old Tribe magic? No. Ne'gauni knew better. He had been in the lodge of the old woman when Kinap brought the savaged child to her. He had seen old Kelet bathe the boy in medicinal herbs and oils. He had watched her care for him with a maternal gentleness and compassion that he would not have thought the old hag capable of had he not witnessed it with his own eyes. The old woman had healed the boy. But she had not healed Ne'gauni! Not with kindness. Not with curative herbs or oils, and most certainly not with gentleness or compassion. No. For his injuries there was no magic. No cure. There was only compromise. And ultimately concession.

"Our headman wears such a stone around his neck, too! It was a gift to him from a shaman of his tribe. I have seen it!" Musquash babbled happily. "And so I say that it is good that Tôrnârssuk leads us north, good that we will take the spirits of our Ancestors to see new places and gather with new people to trade and hunt new kinds of meat! And I think that this is a good place to which Tôrnârssuk has brought us. A safe camp. No matter what comes."

The hackles went up again on Ne'gauni's back. "No matter what comes?"

"We will be safe from all that we have feared this day. With you as our Dreamer and Tôrnârssuk as our headman and so many armed men on this beach, how can this not be so?"

Safe.

Ne'gauni was just tired enough to find the word as welcome and soothing as any of Mowea'qua's healing salves. All that had happened this past day—the dreams, the threats, the roaring he had heard from the overlook, the conjured face of the burning woman, and the half-human thing peering from the undergrowth—all was forgotten as, looking at the lake, he imagined how it would be to wade out and find equilibrium in water, to float on his back beside Hasu'u and the other members of the band, to fin out with his hands and laugh up at the specter of Wildfire if she dared to come dancing and threatening impotently overhead.

Let the forest burn! he thought. *Let North Wind blow! There will be no burning woman! And there is no sign of mammoths in this part of the forest! Here, in this camp, on the shores of this lake, Hasu'u is safe!*

Safe.

The word was taking on a form of its own within his mind. He could actually see it. A living thing. Small. Gray. It ran around and around within his head like a little deer mouse he had once seen trapped in his mother's carelessly banked fire pit, frantically stirring up ashes, inadvertently rousing heat along with the scent of grease smoke as it scuttled in and out amidst charred embers and fragments of splintered wood and bone and old heating stones, desperately seeking escape . . . freedom . . . safety.

He had freed that mouse with a single kick to a loose curbstone. His brother M'alsum, standing close by and contemptuous of his consideration of a mouse, had ground the tiny creature under his heel before inviting his favorite dog to lick his moccasin clean of blood.

The recollection was unpleasant. He had not thought of it in years. Why recall it now when M'alsum was as dead as the mouse in the fire pit and the band was safe at last on the shores of the lake to which Tôrnârssuk had so wisely led them?

"This will not do, Dreamer!"

Ne'gauni turned his head as Musquash slid to his feet, both of them alerted to old Ko'ram's presence, not only by the Wise Man's statement but by the click-click-click of his deer-hoof ankle janglers and the subtle but unpleasantly pervasive essence of his latest flatulence.

Ko'ram paused before them. He stood unperturbed amidst the miasma of his own wind, his nostrils apparently as unresponsive to stimuli as his ears. When Musquash and Ne'gauni both took a backward step and found themselves blocked from further retreat by the driftwood on which they had been seated, he shook his rattle at them. "Why do you stand here? The son of Squam knows that Dreamer cannot sit on a log apart from his people eating fish and talking about ordinary things with such as you, Musquash. Someday Shaman must know that wherever he is and whatever he is doing, he must always appear to be up to something special . . . thinking important thoughts . . . saying important things . . . speaking or singing to the spirits . . . always sharing with the forces of Creation his concerns on behalf of his band. Your people have need of their Dreamer tonight, Ne'gauni. Tôrnârssuk has commanded me to bring you into the safety of the band circle. The omens are no longer good for us. Behold . . . the moon rises red over the eastern hills."

▼▼▼▼

It was true.

The moon was red.

Ne'gauni stared at it as he made his way up the beach with the old man and the boy. Spirit Moon, the elder called it, whispering worriedly of phantoms warring to the death across the sky and spattering the face of the moon with their blood. Whatever its name, Ne'gauni did not like the look of it. Never in his life had he seen such a moon. Never! To his inland Forest People and to the Dawnland tribes, the moon was Sky Woman, passive and gentle wife of Halboredja, the ever-wandering and all-powerful sun. But there was nothing passive or remotely feminine about this moon. It looked like a great round war shield being raised slowly above the trees by invisible hands. Its face was flushed as though with a warrior's battle fury and streaked by shifting war paint patterns created by fleeting tides of clouds and high-flying birds. And now, in its ascending glow, the entire world seemed awash in watered blood.

"Come, Dreamer, join us." Tôrnârssuk was standing, beckoning, and although his tone was amiable enough, it was obvious that his invitation was a command. "On this night we must all remain close and watchful within the sacred circle of the band."

Ne'gauni looked past the headman and into the sacred circle. It was a solemn gathering. It seemed that he was not the only one of his fellow travelers to be disconcerted and intimidated by the moon this night. Kinap, Kanio'te, and several of the Northerners had placed themselves at various points outside the perimeter of the circle, lances, bows, and bolas at the ready. The rest of the band was seated inside the circle with their backs against the driftwood windbreak, men with weapons close, women with their children near. Segub'un and her three unmarried daughters were sitting together, tented under a single large sleeping fur; indeed, Ne'gauni noticed that all of the women—except Mowea'-qua, who was perched sullenly atop the driftwood bastion with her belongings piled at her side—had blankets over their heads. He knew that they were doing this not only to ward off the increasing chill of the night but to accommodate the Northerners' belief that females could become spontaneously impregnated by the potent light of a full moon.

The young man eyed the moon. He would never

understand how the Northerners could believe that Tatqeq, as they called the moon, could be both sister and wife to the sun, a spirit like his own Sky Woman, capable of giving birth to the stars, yet, as Tatqeq, also capable of impregnating females in the world below. It seemed an impossible amalgamation of sexual opposites. And yet, as Ne'gauni looked at the moon, he could not deny that tonight it wore a masculine face, an angry and wholly unnatural face. Just what would a woman give birth to if impregnated by such a moon as this? he wondered. No purely human infant, of that much he was sure.

He shivered at the thought and, entering the circle through a break in the assembled trunks of driftwood, passed close enough to where Mowea'qua was crouching to notice that the raven's feather she had braided into a forelock of her wild and unkempt hair was snaring the red light of the moon. "Cover your head, daughter of Kinap," he advised, then whispered in passing, "And take that cursed feather from your hair before it brings worse luck to you than it already has!"

"She is safe enough," slurred Chi'co'pee, youngest of Ogeh'ma's daughters. "Mowea'qua is Old Tribe. At the Great Gathering no man will want such a tall, disrespectful, mist-eyed thing. Not a single tattoo does she wear. Not on her eyes or cheeks or chin or breasts, not that she ever walks free of her smelly clothes so that we can see if she is even woman enough to have breasts! Only such a homely girl could live so long and still be unmarked by either band or man. And have you seen her face tonight? Someone has finally struck her a well-deserved blow. Now she is truly ugly. Not even such a moon as that which looks down upon this camp tonight would wish to make her pregnant!"

Ne'gauni's eyebrows lifted as Chi'co'pee tittered an inane and thoroughly unexpected response to the humor she obviously found in her insult. He was perplexed. The youngest of Ogeh'ma's girls, like all her sisters, was usually a pleasant and mild-tempered young woman, but, now that he thought about it, earlier in the day he had noticed her walking along the trail keeping company with the widow Suda'li. Apparently the widow was giving lessons in mean-spiritedness . . . or was it contagious?

"Be silent, my sister!" adjured Hasu'u. "It must be the angry light of Spirit Moon that makes you speak so. It is not like you to be so outspoken or inconsiderate of the feelings of others."

"But does Mowea'qua have feelings?" The widow Suda'li's query came sliding through the moonlight like an eel gliding through thin air in search of prey. "Look at her crouching like an Old Tribe animal with her head uncovered to the moon . . . disrespecting the concerns of our headman . . . and shaming her father again. N'av, Ka'wo'ni, bring to our storyteller a pair of cakes from our traveling parfleche. Kinap has done more than the share of three men in assembling this good camp. It is, of course, for a daughter to show such consideration, but it seems that Mowea'qua has forgotten her obligation to see to her father's needs this night. So this widow can at least—"

"Mowea'qua has seen to the needs of our Dreamer this night." The reminder came from Tôrnârssuk. Cold. Tight. So strained in its control of an underlying irritation that somehow it seemed more ominous and potentially threatening than the red moon. It silenced Suda'li immediately. It caused Chi'co'pee to shrink back between her sisters until she was visible as only a suggestion of a shadow hiding beneath Segub'un's blanket. Then, quietly, the headman spoke to Mowea'qua. "Daughter of Kinap, you are as vulnerable as any other woman. You will cover your head under the light of the red moon."

The girl did not move. Her eyes were fixed upon her father.

Ne'gauni's gut tightened. He knew that she was waiting for Kinap to speak. The giant stood silent. He had yet to utter a single word in defense of his daughter. Why? The young man could not understand. Granted, the girl was as irritating as a hard-shelled beetle crawling around inside a man's sleeping skins, but if Mowea'qua had not given a meal to her father tonight, it was only because she knew that he would have refused to accept one from her. Kinap had lived as an itinerant bachelor storyteller for so long that he expected assistance from no one. When, after the death of her grandmother, the girl had come to permanently share his fire circle only one scant winter ago, the giant was so used to curing the skins of the beasts he hunted, stitching his own clothes, and making his own meat that he had seen no reason to stop. He wore the protective fish-skin gauntlets she made for him and used her salves to keep his face and the backs of his scarred forearms and hands supple and less sensitive to sunburn and insect bites, but he so seldom ate of the food she prepared in her Old Tribe ways that, after a while, she had come to leave the meal making to him. Yet now, without even looking at her, Kinap was gratefully accepting not one cake but two, from the upward-reaching hands of the twins of the widow Suda'li. And although the giant's face was hidden, not only by the night but within the depths of his cowl, it was obvious that he was looking across the band circle at Suda'li. It was just as obvious that she was looking back . . . and smiling at him again from within the blanket that covered her head but did not conceal her face.

"Mmph!" The exclamation came from Musquash as, now

standing beside Mowea'qua atop the driftwood log, he slung off his cape and placed it soundly atop the girl's head. "You *will* obey! You will *not* be disrespectful of the wishes of others. You *will* cover your head!"

"Not with anything of yours!" she snapped. Flinging off the boy's garment of muskrat skins, she reached back to pull up the hood of her own wolf-skin cape.

Ne'gauni rolled his eyes. The girl was impossible! But at least, in her own obstinate way, by covering her head she was making concessions to the command of the headman and consenting, for once, to follow the will of someone other than herself. It seemed an improvement. At least for a while.

▼▼▼▼▼

Wolves were howling.

The loons had long since fallen silent.

The red moon claimed the heights of the increasingly clouded sky.

Within the circle of driftwood, the weary travelers slept to the soft, rhythmic slur of waves washing along the lakeshore while Tôrnârssuk and the appointed guardsmen stood watch, talking low.

"The wolves are close," observed Ningao edgily.

"If they are wolves," mumbled Moraq.

"What else would they be?" Kanio'te asked, perplexed.

"Old Tribe hunters calling to one another in the way of their kind," revealed Inaksak in a whisper. "Howling in the manner of beasts . . . summoning their pack . . . warning their kind that we have returned."

"Old Tribe hunters? Here? In this valley?" The son of Ogeh'ma was obviously shaken.

Even in the light of the red moon, the sudden pallor that leached the blood from Inaksak's face was visible as he looked wide-eyed to his headman. "Forgive me. I did not mean to speak of it." His gaze moved quickly to Kanio'te, and his rush of words was less an explanation to the Dawnland man than an apology to Tôrnârssuk. "Sometimes, Son of Ogeh'ma, I forget that you are of a Dawnland tribe and not one of us, not a man of the True People!"

Kanio'te did not take the statement as a compliment. "My people *are* true people. And in the Dawnland men warn their hunt brothers when they lead them into danger . . . they do not assure them that they are leading them away from it."

"And in the Barrenlands men of the True People do not find it necessary to warn each other of that against which they know they must always be on guard," said Tôrnârssuk sharply. "Danger comes in many guises, Kanio'te. True Men are wary at all times."

Kanio'te, appreciating the logic but uncomfortable with the circumstances, shuffled his feet. "Even so, it is good to know exactly against what a man may be called to fight."

"And best not to name it lest in the speaking of it, it overhear and be summoned," said Ningao.

Tôrnârssuk nodded and conceded quietly to Kanio'te, "When first we passed through this valley, there were others here. A small band. Thieves. Not of the People. Filthy in their ways. They fled before us. It was long ago. There was no need to alarm the women and children among us."

"And so the protective circle you have raised is as much against men as mammoths?"

"They were not men," said Moraq to Kanio'te. "Not like us."

Kinap was rumbling to himself. "I would have sworn that all of their kind were hunted and slain long ago . . . except for the old woman of the wood and—"

"And your daughter." There was an edge to Moraq's voice.

Cut by it, Kinap reminded sternly, "Little of the old blood is in her."

"Truly?" Moraq uttered a low, rude snort of disbelief.

"It matters not to us now," said Tôrnârssuk soothingly. "What is important is that we stand watch together as one band, one people, alert to whatever dangers may or may not exist in this place."

Inaksak shuddered at a sudden, piercing crescendo of wolf song. "Listen to them . . . it is as though they sing to the red moon!"

"Maybe their howling will drive it away?" Kanio'te surmised hopefully.

"Or summon the bad spirits that redden its face." Moraq could always be counted on not to add cheer to any given moment.

"Or to entice our dogs from camp?"

"The dogs are tethered close by, Ningao," Tôrnârssuk reminded him. "No man here is about to let them become meat for wolves. And the wolves *are* wolves. They sing now as they always sing, to call the pack to the hunt, to rejoice in a kill. As we should rejoice now among ourselves because the wind is down and Wildfire will not come here tonight."

"Praise be to the forces of Creation!" Ningao said obligingly. "And to you, Tôrnârssuk, for anticipating the threat."

"It would have been bad for us if we had been caught on the far side of the Gap of Many Stones with nowhere to take refuge from the flames," said Kinap.

"There are other threats," emphasized the headman obliquely, avoiding eye contact with the giant and Kanio'te as, to his fellow Northerners, he again alluded guardedly to their earlier conversation about Old Tribe enemies. "We cannot rest content until we reach the great river."

"Do you think they are safe even in that great camp, Tôrnârssuk?" asked Inaksak. "I mean, the wind has dropped, but if it should turn north, Wildfire could—"

"I cannot say what could or should be," Tôrnârssuk told him. "But you are a man of the far north, old friend. You know as well as I that no one is ever safe. Sila hunts us all."

▼▼▼▼

"Safe . . . ?" Ne'gauni turned the word and did not know that he spoke at all. Sitting next to old Ko'ram, he raised his cheek from his bent knee and, rubbing sleep from his eyes with the backs of his thumbs, followed the little gray mouse out of the ashy fire pit of what had until this moment been dreamless slumber.

"Our Dreamer wakes," Moraq observed with his usual sourness.

"What have you seen for us in your dreams this time, Shaman?" asked Tôrnârssuk.

Ne'gauni frowned as he looked across the band circle to settle his gaze on the headman. "Shaman?" Ah, yes, he remembered now. "Nothing," he said. "I have seen nothing."

"Nothing?"

Ne'gauni winced, not only at Ko'ram's whispered question but at the sharp elbow jab to his ribs that informed him in no uncertain terms that the old Wise Man was fully awake and highly disapproving of what he had just said.

"You are now Dreamer!" Ko'ram whispered. "You must tell them that you have seen *something*! Or else of what use are you to the band?"

Ne'gauni's heart went cold. So he was still in danger of

abandonment or death at the hands of those who now looked to him as a source of spiritual inspiration. *Prove yourself or die. Is that the game? Apparently so.* In the menacing glow of the bloodred moon, he saw expressions of concern on the faces of Ogeh'ma, his family, Kinap, and Hasu'u. Yet, with Tôrnârssuk, Moraq, and the other Northerners staring at him as fixedly as the howling wolves would have done if given a chance to close around him, it seemed that the spirits of the night—both benign and malignant—were haunting the inner circle of the band and threatening his very existence within it.

"Tell us of your dreams!" Old Ko'ram was adamant; he sounded worried.

Ne'gauni responded nervously, "I . . . uh . . . a mouse . . . I have dreamed of a mouse."

"A mouse . . . and before that a spider?" Moraq was scowling. "What kind of dreams are these?"

Ne'gauni was as perplexed as any man there. "I do not know. Nor do I ask for my dreams, Moraq. I have told you before, they come as they will."

"Mmph!" Mowea'qua was awake and sitting upright, bundled in her cape and sleeping fur on the place she had claimed for herself atop the driftwood log, neither inside nor outside the circle of the band. "A great shaman my Wounded One will someday be. Until then Wise Man says that much to learn has he. But when Ne'gauni has all things learned, remember he will your questions, Moraq, and no cause will he find to speak well of you to the spirits."

"Threats!" Moraq did not need the light of the red moon to add color to his suddenly livid face. "I do not stand for threats from the likes of you, Wolf Girl!"

"Moraq, she is my daughter," Kinap reminded him, his voice as dark and heavy as the bearskins he wore.

"Are you so sure, Giant?" Once again a query from the widow Suda'li came sliding through the moonlight like an eel in search of prey. "Or has your kind heart perhaps—"

"Enough!" Tôrnârssuk put an end to discord with a single word, but the girl had gone rigid, and the rising voices of dissension awakened the sleeping members of the band. In the benighted depths of the forest, a pair of owls chose this moment in which to call.

Goh'beet, Onen'ia's bucktoothed woman, uttered a fearful little moan. "Do not listen! And no one must look at them if they fly overhead!" The warning given, she gathered her little ones close.

"Them? What is it she has heard?" Ko'ram asked Ne'gauni.

The young man whispered his reply and felt as well as heard the tremulous sigh that shook the old man. They both understood Goh'beet's fear. All People of the Forest and of the Dawnland knew that owls were more than birds; they were restless ghosts crying in the night to remind of the brevity of life. To hear them was unavoidable, but to witness the passage of their wings across the darkness was to see the image of one's own death—and to know that one's life was over.

Ko'ram began to shake his rattle.

The owls fell silent.

As did the wolves.

The old man rose, slowly and somewhat shakily. He stood a moment, looking around the circle, then, after bending to whisper imperatively into Ne'gauni's ear that he must watch and learn, he cast off his sleeping robe with a flourish.

Ne'gauni wrapped his arms around his bent knee and observed the old man's methodical walk around the inner circle of the band. Chin jabbing skyward, Ko'ram high-stepped over the extended limbs of his people, shaking his rattle at them until, when everyone had scooted up his or her legs and pulled their belongings out of his way, he announced,

"Now! Behold! Ko'ram will banish Fear!"

The old man began to dance. The movements were a variation on his usual Wise Man's hop. Dignified. Intensely focused. The steps were the same as when he had earlier bobbed his way down the beach, looking like an old marsh bird thrusting after frogs, but the pace was slower, graceful and mesmerizing as he swayed his body and extended his arms and waved them up and down like wings. And then he began to chant, deep in his throat, a low, threnodic cry that rose and quickened with the intensifying rhythm of his dance. Soon he was hopping again and screaming like a woman attempting to sing through the pains of childbirth. Coupled with the shaking of his rattle, his dance became so enthralling that even if the owls had flown overhead it was doubtful that anyone would have noticed, unless the birds defecated or regurgitated upon them or chose to land in the middle of the band circle.

But the owls did not fly overhead.

The wolves remained silent.

The people of the band stared at their dancing Wise Man, so captivated by his showmanship that, even though they must have noticed the occasional fluting and unpleasant scent emanating from his hindquarters, they overlooked and forgave him for it.

At last, sweated and heaving, the old man gave a final screech, a final flourish with his rattle. Then, with much grunting and heaving, he folded himself back into a seated position beside Ne'gauni, leaned close, and sighed into the young man's ear, "That is how it is done . . . for the good of the band . . . for the confidence of your people! A one-legged man you may well be, Dreamer, but you must learn the way of it, nonetheless, for I am growing far too old for this!"

Ne'gauni flushed with embarrassment for the elder. In the way of the nearly deaf, the old man's whisper had been loud enough for any of those sitting nearby to hear.

But no one was listening.

It was there again.

A great roaring filled the valley. Not the roar of the wind. Not the cry of owls or wolves or the echo of a screeching old Wise Man coming back to them through the trees. It was the roar of distant thunder . . . or, perhaps, the same sound they had heard from the overlook, a high-pitched animal scream that resonated across the world like the cry of a defiant giant.

"Great One . . . Earth Shaker . . . Thunder Speaker . . . mammoth!"

"Silence, Mowea'qua." Kinap rumbled the command to his daughter just as he had rumbled on the overlook.

Ne'gauni attempted to gulp down his rising apprehension. It was no use. His mouth had gone dry again. All around him the band was murmuring, looking worriedly at the sky and at one another.

"Thunder . . . it must have been thunder," said Ningao on a rush of optimism. "Look—the dogs do not bark! They have barely raised more than a pair of ears among the entire pack. As Tôrnârssuk has said, we have seen no sign of mammoths in this forest. But the cloud spirits *have* been speaking all afternoon of a change in the weather, and those *were* storm clouds we saw gathering on the northern horizon along with plumes of smoke."

"Yah!" Old Ko'ram was on his feet again and jabbing a scrawny arm skyward. "We have all heard our Dreamer, our Someday Shaman, call out to the forces of Creation! He

Walks Ahead in Dreams to Foresee Danger for the People has spoken to Wind and Rain. He has told of the needs of this band. The forces of Creation have heard his words. Wind has dropped. And now Rain will come!"

"You cannot be certain of that," cautioned Tôrnârssuk. "And as long as you walk with me, Ko'ram, do not again say aloud what the forces of Creation will or will not do. No one knows the power of Sila. No man . . . no dreamer . . . no shaman."

Affronted, Ko'ram sat down, visibly stung by the unexpected scolding, and defensively gathered up his robe and pulled it around his shoulders with much unnecessary fussing.

Ne'gauni was startled. Never before had he heard the headman speak sharply to the old man. And now, as his gaze moved across the circle, he saw Hasu'u worriedly drawing her nursling into a protective embrace within her sleeping robe of white bearskin.

"May the words of Ko'ram be as cautious as he is wise," she said softly to the Wise Man, in an obvious attempt to soothe the bruising of her husband's reprimand. "And may the wish of Ko'ram be granted this night—may it be the voice of Thunder that we have heard, for it is within my heart to never again hear that other sound . . . that terrible mammoth cry of—"

"Mmph!" Mowea'qua interrupted disdainfully. "Foolish are you, Headman's Woman, say I, if fear mammoths you do!"

Ne'gauni saw Tôrnârssuk stiffen even as Hasu'u shook her head at Mowea'qua and revealed in a hushed and patient voice, "I fear the Great One, daughter of Kinap. We must all fear it, the dreaded mammoth spirit whose name we dare not speak, the spirit who is said to come to us before the end of our days."

"That one may well walk in this world no more," Kinap said, stepping with ease over the back of the driftwood log behind which he had been standing, then seating himself upon it. "As for the others of its kind, my Grassland People have said that the presence of even one mammoth in a man's hunting grounds is a sign from the forces of Creation that all remains well with the world. Still, I will say that I believe that Tôrnârssuk has wisely led us with caution into this valley. If there are mammoths here, they are great and mysterious and dangerous beasts. And who can say just how many of them share the world with us these days?"

"I, for one, have never seen more of a mammoth than a few bones and tusks lying half buried in river washouts," Moraq said bluntly. "True People say that their kind no longer live beneath the sky." He spoke slowly, not in his own native tongue but in the language of the giant and the Forest People, who were not familiar with the beliefs of the far north. "In long-past days, on the Barrenlands of my Ancestors, the tuskers fell before our lances and arrows until the last of their kind fled from us to make their hunting grounds in caverns beneath the earth. Even here, in this far country, before the ice goes out on the big rivers each spring, you can hear them roaring as their Great Chief, Rises from Below, pushes up the bones of those among his herd who have died, shoving them through the ice into the rivers so that True People can look upon them and fear that which would surely hunt us if mammoths and man still breathed the same air."

"Mammoths do not eat men!" said Mowea'qua.

"They do not have to," countered Ningao's woman, the usually shy and reticent Tsi'le'ni. Pulling in a deep breath, she worked up the courage to say politely, "Here, in the country of my Forest People, my father's father once saw a mammoth. Often he would tell us children of it. He said that there was enough meat on its bones to feed all of the many tribes that gather each year by the great river. He said that it had hair like a bear in winter, and ears like a bat, and two long bones sticking out of its face like lances, and it had five legs! Five! Can you imagine such a thing? One of these legs grew out of its head! And when my father's father threw his spear at that mammoth, it became very angry and used this fifth leg to pull down trees and send flying the lean-tos of my grandfather's hunting camp. All who could not run away were crushed as flat as hearth cakes under its feet!" Tsi'le'ni exhaled a shivering little sigh and, after pulling her sleeping fur far over her head so that no lurking spirits could see her face or place the source of her words, whispered, "My grandmother died under the feet of that mammoth. And so my grandfather always told us that he had seen Ktci'awa that day, the Great Beast, the one who is Death. Ah! A terrible thing is a mammoth."

"I may also have seen the Great One." The revelation came from Onen'ia. "I do not like to think of it. In truth, it may have been nothing more than moonlight breaking through mist to shine on white rock, a confusion of distance and fog. It was back in the Dawnland, on the night the bear came from the sea to take as meat the son of Ko'ram and husband of Suda'li. I was on the beach. I felt myself being watched, and when I turned around, I thought I saw the Great One standing on the cliffs above me . . . big as a mountain, and white, with ears turned forward like the ears of bats in flight, and tusks like those of the barking sea dogs my people call walrus, only bigger, and as thick as—"

"As long as lodgepoles and as thick as a grown man's

thighs?" asked Musquash, peeking excitedly from a pile of sleeping skins beneath which he had curled up unseen on the log next to Mowea'qua.

"Yes," affirmed Onen'ia. "With tusks as long and thick as that."

"Mmph!" It was Mowea'qua again, thoughtful now, her voice lacking all hostility. Ignoring the boy at her side, she revealed wistfully, "Of the tusks and bones of fallen Great Ones did my grandmother and I wall up our lodge. A fine lodge it was. As big as a mammoth. And as strong. Sheltered did we against many storms within that lodge of bones, and often did my grandmother to me speak of seeing mammoths. A great white mammoth, and his mate. And bulls who sometimes wintered with him, and in summer, by the sacred spring, many cows and calves. Never did I with my own eyes see them, but say I now to all that I have many times heard the voice of Great One. I have seen his leavings and—"

"I have seen *him*!" Musquash, rising on a wave of euphoria, stood and proclaimed with all the unabashed enthusiasm of an exuberant child who cannot bear to contain a secret. "Once, far away on the sacred isle of my forefathers, I came to a place in the marsh where Great Chief was using his fifth arm to suck up all the fresh water from the creek and tidal flat. Big he was. Yes! Bigger even than Onen'ia and Tsi'le'ni have said! And whiter than new snow at noon on a cloudless winter day! I watched him. I waited for him to go his way, but he did not go. He stood! He drank! And then, when he had sucked up so much water that fish and turtles and eels were all flapping and gasping on dry ground, I could wait and watch no more. Bravely I went before him. 'Great Chief,' said I to the white mammoth, 'in the name of all living things with whom you must share the gift of fresh water, I tell you that you must go from the land of my forefathers or I will take my lance and end your days, for wherever you walk, soon there is no water for the People.' And so, in fear of me, Great Chief went his way. But from that day to this, on the sacred isle of my forefathers, the creek and marsh are dead places. Great Chief has killed them! And so I think that one day we must hunt and kill him, because Moraq and the True People are right when they say that mammoths and man cannot share the same air. There is no longer room for both the People and Great Chief or his tusked kind within the sacred Circle of Life Ending and Life Beginning."

"Mmph!" Mowea'qua was indignant. "What kind of story is this? Great One would fear not such a little biting fly as you! And how can you, son of a shaman, not know that within the sacred Circle of Life Ending and Life Beginning, for all things room there must be, or room there will be for none!"

"Mmph!" The little boy mimicked the girl and folded his arms across his chest. "Nothing will be lost in the death of Great Chief, Mowea'qua. It is said by my people that he will live forever in the blood of those who kill and eat him. They will have his strength. They will have his courage. We should want to see him. We should hope that he is here, in this valley, so we can hunt him."

"My sons already possess strength and courage, as do all the brave hunters with whom I travel," said Ogeh'ma. "Soon we will put this valley behind us. Soon we will reach the Great Gathering. What need have men of mammoths when whales swim in the Great River of the North and caribou come to that good shore in endless numbers to give themselves to be meat for the People?"

The chief's question proved a heartening stimulus. Even under the red moon, Ne'gauni felt his mood lighten as others began to speak out in agreement and anticipation of the many good things that lay ahead for them once they reached the destination toward which Tôrnârssuk was leading them.

Yet Hasu'u shuddered as she continued to look across the band circle at Ogeh'ma. "I will be glad to reach this good camp, my father. In the meantime, I have no wish to see the Great One, be it alive or dead. Nor would I see any man of this band risk himself against such a beast. We have no need of its meat. Or of its strength and courage. Tôrnârssuk leads us. No man is stronger. No man is braver. Never has he failed to lead us to the best of hunting. May it be that Moraq is right! May it be that Great One and all mammoths have been driven from beneath the sky! May it be that they have been hunted to the last of their kind!"

A low rumbling of dissent came from Kinap as he turned his gaze to the red moon and warned guardedly, "Beware of what you wish for under such a sky, Headman's Woman. Who knows the mood or nature of the spirits that may be listening?"

The giant's gentle warning was not enough to satisfy Mowea'qua. The girl was furious. She was kneeling on the log now, the hood of her cape tossed back, her eyes sparking red in the glow of the moon, her fists knotted at her sides. "Your wish you must take back, Foolish Woman! Know not you what Old Tribe people say? On the day the last mammoth is hunted and killed, so, too, shall die the People! All people! Young. Old. Strong. Weak. Courageous. Fearful. One-legged! Two-legged! Matter it will not who you are or from what tribe or place you come—Forest or Grassland or Dawnland or Lakeland or Barrenland. All in the eyes of the forces of Creation will the same be. Enemies! Strangers! Defilers of the traditions of the Ancient Ones! Hunters who outside the sacred Circle of Life Ending and Life Beginning dare to place themselves! You must not kill all of a kind! Be it mammoth or mouse, mold spore or moth, its absence within the sacred circle will the balance of that circle tip until one day all within spill out to die. The forces of Creation will not this allow. Already the sacred circle is tipping. Already the forces of Creation are sending Winter and Fire to punish and warn the tribes. Heed these warnings must you or the People will be from the sacred circle cast out forever, replaced by a new kind of being, one who in arrogance walks not. And on that day the People will forever walk the wind in the country of the sky spirits, hunted by the ghost animals you have already driven from beneath the sky. Great ghost bears as big as mammoths and long-toothed lions and giant wolves will catch and devour you. Mammoths and giant bison will crush your bones. Beavers the size of bears will chew you up and spit you out into the Great Sky River, where drown you will amidst the stars. Again and again will you die! Again and again will you be reborn, only to be hunted and killed again. No Old Tribe magic or medicines will help you, because our kind have you also from the earth driven! We will hunt you in the spirit world, as you have hunted us! So, if care you for the suckling at your breast, Headman's Woman, or for anyone else within this camp, your wish you must take back, say I! Now, Stupid One, now!"

A gasp went out of every man, woman, and child within the circle.

Ne'gauni cringed. Mowea'qua had gone too far. He knew it. Sensed it in his spirit. Old Ko'ram knew it, too; he sat as rigid as an old bone. And even Kinap and the boy Musquash were speechless.

But the headman was not.

"You will not command, insult, or threaten my woman, Mowea'qua." Tôrnârssuk's statement was as heavy as the driftwood tree trunks that surrounded his band, and so stressed by anger and fatigue that every word stung across the night like an arrow shot from a bow too tightly strung. "Your behavior is an offense to the Ancestors, daughter of Kinap. The animals you speak of are as dead as your tribe, and yet, behold, the People live on."

"Not for long, say I!" cried the girl, her voice shrill. "Not if your foolish woman the Great One wishes dead!"

"Mowea'qua!" Kinap was on his feet. "You will be silent, or, by the forces of Creation whose wrath you may just have brought upon us by daring to speak for them, I vow that I will rip your tongue from your mouth and feed it to the dogs!"

"Not to my dogs," said Ningao. "I would allow no part of her body to be eaten by them. They are good dogs all. Obedient dogs. But what would they be if they ate of the flesh of Mowea'qua and her spirit lived on inside them? Do you know what my people say of her grandmother's kind? That they were spawned of a mating of man and wolf, a black wolf, a man gone blind in the endless cold and dark of a northern winter. With the return of the sun, when the man saw that he had sired beasts on an animal, he tried to kill them, but the black wolf and her children devoured him. And so it is that, in the dark of the moon, the beast children of the Old Tribe can become wolves at will. And always, remembering that their father would have slain them, they seek to dishonor his memory by hunting, devouring, and raping the women of the People whenever they come upon us unaware."

"And so it is that they have been justly hunted and slaughtered wherever they have been found, until now few of their fanged and furred and filthy kind remain in the world," added Moraq. "Although no man of the True People would ever foul his body by raping one of them!"

"My mother was also of the Old Tribe!" protested Musquash hotly, stepping close to Mowea'qua and dropping into a protective crouch beside her. "She had no fur, no fangs! She was not what you say. And Mowea'qua is not what you say! *I* am not what you—"

"Your true father was a great shaman," Kinap reminded him. "His powers enabled him to dilute your slave mother's blood with his own. You carry nothing of the look of her. You are not Old Tribe. You are of the People."

Ne'gauni was aware of Mowea'qua drawing deeper into her furs, staring at Kinap, her face distorted not only by its recent battering but by a quivering scowl that set her lower lip to trembling.

"You my true father are," she said to the giant in a voice so small and tremulous that it seemed to belong to another girl entirely. "A tattoo on my body you may not have placed to mark this truth, but your blood is my blood. Old Tribe I am through Kelet. Yes! But lies do Ningao and Moraq tell. Those of the Old Tribe do not the People hunt and devour! No! It is the People who the Old Tribe hunt! To drive us from the hunting grounds of our Ancestors, to raid our cache pits, to steal our women! Upon my grandmother's band did the People prey. Killed all did they. Except Kelet. A slave was she to them, pierced many times against her will by many men until her belly filled with life and a daughter of rape came from between her thighs . . . a daughter of the People. Tell them this, my father, for that daughter was my mother. And so of the People am I, through her and *you*."

Kinap was rumbling to himself as he always did when discomfited. "I no longer know what you are, Mowea'qua, but I will tell you now that I was not moved to tattoo the mark of my people into your skin to acknowledge you as my own because I regret the day I lay upon your mother almost as much as I regret the day of your birth. And yet, whatever you have become, I will fault myself for leaving you too long alone in the care of one who could have raised you to be no different than you are."

Ne'gauni heard Mowea'qua catch her breath and exhale a ragged little sob just before the widow Suda'li blurted, "You would make better daughters on me, Giant. Shorter girls. Pretty girls. Girls who would be submissive to their father."

Ne'gauni was taken aback by the brazenness of the widow's remark. No. It had not been a remark. It had been a proposition boldly given.

And accepted. "On you I will make sons," Kinap told her. "I have had enough of daughters."

Mowea'qua bit her lower lip and, for a moment, seemed to wither away into herself. The moment passed. Suddenly she was transformed. Scrambling to her feet, she flung back her cloak and turned her ire not on the widow or her father but on Tôrnârssuk and his Northerners.

"A wolf think you I am? Mmph! Furred and fanged? See you then if true this is!" She bent, took up the hem of her traveling tunic, peeled it over her head, and threw it vehemently into the circle. "The body of Mowea'qua behold!"

Ne'gauni gaped. Astounded. As was every other member of the band. In her moccasins and leggings, the girl stood in unflinching, splay-legged defiance upon the driftwood log. Her belly was flat and tight beneath the thong that supported her leggings. Her bared skin shone in the light of the red moon, as lush as the newly opened fruit of a fully ripe mountain ash, as smooth and sleek as the polished wood of the bow that Kinap had broken and hurled away earlier in the day. He gulped. His mouth was drier than before. Mowea'qua's face was bloated and darkening from her father's beating, but her body was beautiful. And she had breasts! Amazing breasts! Not the tight little sprouts of a young girl, but the firm, opulent roundings of a young woman, with nipples large and dark and peaking in the chill air.

Untying the thong that held her leggings, she kicked them off. She turned. Around and around. Smoothing her skin with her hands, she ran her fingers through her hair, then lowered her fingertips to the dark tufting just above and between her thighs. "Behold, say I! On this body there is fur only here, in this place, where belongs fur on a woman of the People."

Again Ne'gauni gulped. His loins were alive. Throbbing. Seeking. Mowea'qua? Impossible.

She was standing motionless now, still splay-legged, glowering at Tôrnârssuk and the Northerners as she declared, "Woman am I, not wolf, except in spirit! But on your chins and upper lips fur I see, men of the far Barrenlands who have many times shown yourselves eager to prey upon the People when lived you as raiders within this forest. Stand naked, say I. Let Mowea'qua see if your bodies are as furred as your faces! Mmph! Anxious to show yourselves you are not? Yah! When comes the dark of the moon, say I that if anyone is going to turn into an animal, it will be you!"

Ne'gauni gasped and, with the stunned silence of the band settling around him like a stone sinking into a peat bog, stared after Mowea'qua as she turned, leaped from the log, and ran off toward the lake . . . howling.

Chapter Seven

▼▼▼▼▼▼▼

She swam.

Angrily.

Defiantly.

Beneath the red moon, alone in the darkness, with her moccasins hastily deposited upon the beach, Mowea'qua arced back and forth through the cool shallows, alternately diving and surfacing like a restless river otter, but not half so boldly. She was careful not to venture beyond her depth, checking down now and then with her toes and fingertips to make certain that she could touch bottom. The Northerners might well believe that she was capable of turning into a wolf, but wolves were creatures of the land, and although Mowea'qua could swim, like them she felt no affinity for water.

Expelling bubbles of air as she propelled herself toward the surface, it pleased the girl to think of how her howling must have put everyone on edge. A shiver went up her back; the short, coarse, nearly invisible hairs at the base of her spine prickled as her senses quickened with a loathing born of generations of enmity and alienation. Let the Northerners who so arrogantly presumed to call themselves True People hold her in contempt because of her Old Tribe lineage! She was not ashamed to be thought of as kin to wolves. In the time beyond beginning all the People and Animals were of one tribe. The Northerners could deny it, and Kinap and Ne'gauni and Chief Ogeh'ma and all of his Dawnland band could agree with them, but she knew the truth: The blood of the ancient race ran in each and every one of them.

Surfacing, Mowea'qua released the remaining air in her lungs with a loud whoosh, then breathed in again, hungrily, deeply, filling her lungs with the cool air of night. Her hair, with the raven's feather still captive in her long braided forelock, streamed over her bare back as she paddled on, her gaze fixed on the beach and the circle of driftwood.

In the red glow of the full moon, she could see almost as clearly as in full sunlight. How strange the world appeared. Tritoned. Starkly red and black, gray in areas that stood between complete light and total shadow. No one seemed to have moved since she had run from the campsite. No one! Disappointment touched her. And annoyance. No doubt they were still talking among themselves. About her? About their endless fears?

"Mmph!" She would never understand their ways.

The People worried about being overheard by malevolent spirits and hid themselves under their sleeping furs as they whispered about intangibles that seemed to be no real threat to anyone; then they carelessly risked bringing Death to all the People by allowing one stupid woman to openly wish the unthinkable upon them! Chi'co'pee and Suda'li insulted her and the Old Tribe and no one spoke against them, but when she spoke out in defense of herself and her grandmother's people, her father threatened to deprive her of her tongue and the headman informed her that her behavior was an offense to the Ancestors. There was no fairness in this, or logic, as far as she could see. None at all.

Mowea'qua's brow furrowed as she scanned the beach. Musquash was visible in silhouette as a dark little mound atop the driftwood log from which she had leaped in anger, and she could see that her father was still standing tall among the other watchmen, a monolith among men.

"He will for me come," Mowea'qua assured herself. In his own good time. Kinap would come. By keeping herself apart, she would soon force him to call her back into the protection of the band and thus prove to her and the widow and everyone else that he had not meant the cruel things he had said to her this day.

"Loving my mother he does not regret! Strangling me at birth he would not have done! Mmph! And though upon me he has not imprinted the mark of his kind, never would he rip out my tongue!"

She shivered as she swam, certain that her beloved giant could never do such a cruel and hideous thing to anyone. And he had not had enough of her! He loved her. He cared about her. How could it be otherwise?

All through her childhood, all through the long, lonely moons of spring and summer and autumn, she had lived out her days and nights looking forward to the time of deep snow when her father would come to winter with her within Kelet's lodge. How her heart sang when she heard him calling out to her through the trees! How her spirit soared to see him tromping boldly toward her on his enormous snow walkers, his beloved face a shining knot of burn scars, his tongue alive with stories and news of the world beyond her part of the forest, his massive back and shoulders laden with surprises gathered on his yearly wanderings—gifts to bring joy to his Mowea'qua during his stay and afterward, when he went his way again, leaving her alone with her grandmother, promising to return. And always he had fulfilled his promise. Always.

"He *will* come," Mowea'qua assured herself again. On a night such as this, with the moon showing red and Wildfire burning to the north and the voice of a mammoth sounding in the valley along with wolves and owls and the rumblings of distant thunder, the giant would not allow his daughter to remain beyond the protective circle of the band, vulnerable to predators—and to drowning. At any moment he would come stomping down the beach. He would command her to come from the water. He would be angry. Very angry. He might even strike her again, but Mowea'qua, her temper cooled by her swim, was resigned to accepting punishment from him. Perhaps she deserved it? She could not say. Since the death of her grandmother, Kinap had changed in his manner toward her. The old openness between them was gone, and although she had been delighted to come from the deep forest to live with him among the People, she had long since despaired of trying to please him or the members of his tribe in the only ways she knew how: making medicine, which they would not use; hunting game, in a manner that proved alien and offensive to them; cooking and serving meat, which they set aside and somehow never found the appetite to eat; and talking talk that no one wished to hear.

Perhaps, of all the transgressions against her dignity, it was the latter that most exasperated Mowea'qua. She had been taught by her grandmother to speak always in the way of her heart, in the way of the Old Tribe, a way that assured a clear and direct pathway to understanding. Kinap had never objected to her Old Tribe ways before. He knew that it was natural for her to use language in much the same way she would use an awl or hammerstone to pierce a hide or shape a stone to some new purpose. Directly. Forcefully. Making no pretense as to what she was about lest she squander valuable time accomplishing her purpose. But now, living with him among the People, Kinap more often than not seemed a stranger, and she was beginning to understand that speech was more than a tool with which to facilitate forthright communication; indeed, sometimes it seemed as though words were used specifically to avoid it, as though they were not words at all but buffer stones meant to smooth and dull the edges of too sharp a truth or too disconcerting a meaning.

"Mmph!" she snorted and stroked outward. Maybe one day she would master the way of it. In the meantime it seemed such a waste of energy to send her tongue moving on and on around the meat of a subject when, in the end, the truth would have to be dealt with anyway. Still, she knew that her latest flare of temper and burst of straight talk had angered her father. Aching for his forgiveness and regretting the impetuosity of her tongue, if not the truthfulness of her words, she was determined to make amends. When he commanded her to come from the lake, she would emerge in a paced and dignified manner as befitted the daughter of a giant among men, a survivor of many deaths, a master of bow and drum. Everyone would see that she was obedient to his will, but they would also see that neither his threats nor his violence against her had succeeded in cowing her. Kinap would have no respect for such a daughter, even if the widow Suda'li believed otherwise.

"Yah!" The girl trembled with loathing of the other woman. "If any tongue trimming needs, it is the tongue of Suda'li! And whether I speak or speak not, truth does not change. A foolish woman *is* Hasu'u. A liar *is* Moraq. And

Tôrnârssuk cannot be as all-knowing as everyone thinks if he believes not in the great white mammoth!"

Mowea'qua kicked out in the water, brought her body around, and paddled in the opposite direction. The Great One was out there somewhere. She knew it. Felt it. If only the others could be brought to believe in the power and presence of the great white mammoth, they would not be so weighted by their many pointless fears. And maybe then Tôrnârssuk would allow himself an occasional smile.

Thoughts of the headman drifted through her mind as she swam laterally along the shore, still keeping an eye on the beach, wanting to be ready to respond to her father's first summons. Tôrnârssuk was powerful. Only Kinap was stronger. Yet men feared Tôrnârssuk. He was dangerous. Everyone knew it. Mowea'qua had heard of his murderous exploits as a raider and had seen other men turn up their necks and grin in the manner of submissive dogs when in his presence. Even so, he rarely raised his voice and often stood alone, quietly keeping his own thoughts, a man of few words, his manner as cold, distant, and bleak as the heart of winter. She did not know why his woman was so blissfully content in the gloom of his shadow, unless Hasu'u's affection for him was yet another confirmation of her innate stupidity. Yet, sometimes Mowea'qua would find herself watching him, and for no reason that she could explain, Tôrnârssuk's broad, pensive, long-eyed face was so compelling that she could not look away. Sometimes, as now, despite the chill of the water through which she swam, when she thought of him her loins flexed and grew so warm that it seemed as though an ember born of the distant Wildfire had somehow taken life and centered itself there.

She caught her breath. Something cold and slick had just slithered across her belly. A strand of water grass? An eel?

A fish? Imagining the gaping jaws of Waktcexi, the giant, many-headed, man-and-woman-eating water monster that swam its way through several of Kinap's tales about the time beyond beginning, she rolled frantically onto her back, kicking and stroking madly with her feet and arms until her buttocks scraped against the gravel of the sandbar.

Sputtering and gasping for air, Mowea'qua clambered backward onto solid ground. Shivering, she found her footing and hunkered low as, teeth chattering, she stared back across the shallows. The only wake she could see was her own. Relieved, she castigated herself for giving in to panic. The only monster swimming in the lake this night was swimming inside her own head. On the opposite beach, the band was still gathered inside the driftwood circle. Her heart gave a little lurch. She could no longer see Kinap standing tall amidst the other watchmen; he must have seated himself again.

Her heart sank.

Why was he not coming after her? Why? Unless all that he had said was true after all? Unless he no longer cared about his Old Tribe daughter? Unless, in Suda'li, he had at last found someone else to love?

"No!" She would not allow herself to believe that. "He *will* come! I will wait here for his call." Crossing her arms over her chest, she hugged herself tight for warmth and gritted her teeth to keep them from chattering. The cold waters of the lake had numbed her battered features, but now, exposed again to the wind and chill of night, her face was hurting, reminding her of the violence of her father's blow. "His own power he knows not." She made excuses for him. It was easy to do. She loved him so.

Wolves were calling again, far out on the peninsula. Mowea'qua cocked her head, listening as the low, ascending monotones rose into the night to touch a well of loneliness within her spirit and raise in her a response that she could neither fully understand nor deny.

Uncertainty shook her.

Maybe they were right about her. Maybe she was not of the People. Maybe she was a wolf after all.

▼▼▼▼▼

"Look at her. She mocks us. Sitting out there like a seal hauled up out of the water, naked, staring, daring us to come and take her." Moraq's voice was convulsed with anger, and with lust. "I say we go to her. I say we give her what she wants . . . then drown her before she calls out again to her cursed Old Tribe wolf people and invites them to come and try to eat this band."

"Never would Old Tribe people do this!" Musquash objected.

"No?" Moraq's query was pure provocation.

"No!" snapped the boy.

Ne'gauni stiffened as he stared expectantly across the band circle to where Kinap had seated himself again. With Sudal'li. Close. So close to the widow, in fact, that she seemed a part of him as he sat motionless within his bearskins, silent, his face and emotions hidden within his cowl. Ne'gauni trembled with frustration. Why did the man not speak out in agreement with his adopted son and in defense of his daughter? Granted, Mowea'qua's behavior had been so shocking and sexually provocative that Ne'gauni was still shaken by his own reaction to it, but surely no father could sit still for what Moraq was proposing. And yet Kinap was doing just that.

"You are so eager to bring Death into my camp these days." It was Tôrnârssuk, not the giant, who replied to Moraq. "First you offer to assist in the slaying of one who has proved to be a Dreamer. And now you would drown the wild one, but not before you force yourself between her thighs and invite all the men of this band to do the same. I will tell you this, old friend: I look forward to the day when we reach the Gathering of Many Tribes, for there will be more to distract you there on the shores of the Great River of the North—many willing women . . . many whales to kill."

"The Great River of the White Whales is yet far," slurred Moraq. "But Mowea'qua is near and asking to be—"

"Mowea'qua has accused me of being foolish, but in truth it is the daughter of Kinap who is a foolish and ignorant young woman," Hasu'u interrupted, with an earnestness that revealed the extent of her dismay at the unfolding situation. "I do not believe that she intended to insult me with her words any more than she meant to enflame you or any other man of this band by displaying her body, Moraq. Your words to her were cruel words. She wanted you to see that you were wrong about her and her Old Tribe Ancestors. She is one of us. A woman of the People."

"Mowea'qua will be my woman!" Musquash was on his feet again and bristling inside his furs. "Moraq will not drown her!"

"Nor will he force himself upon her." Ne'gauni was surprised at his outspokenness. Glaring across the darkness of the band circle, he speared Moraq with his gaze and was not sure of where to place his anger—at the feet of the Northerner because of his open expression of murderous lust, or on Kinap's lap because of his silence. "Men of the True People do not mate with women of the Old Tribe. Is that not what we have all heard you say, Moraq?"

The Northerner's head went down. Like a stag finding itself suddenly faced with a challenge from an unexpected source, he huffed warily as he took measure of his adversary out of guarded eyes. "That one has shown us all the body of a woman," he conceded tightly. Then, unwilling to fully yield to the younger man's attempt to dissuade him from his purpose, he added, "But in the light of the red moon, Dreamer, can any of us say just what we have seen? Out of her own mouth Mowea'qua has claimed the spirit of a wolf. And what I intend for her is no mating. It will be a punishment. A long overdue and final punishment. If our headman agrees to it."

"You cannot!" Hasu'u's exclamation was a plea to Tôrnârssuk.

All eyes were on the headman.

Ne'gauni gripped his crutches and pulled himself upright before Tôrnârssuk had a chance to make a pronouncement against the girl. "Kinap! You are Mowea'qua's father! Say something!"

"What would you have me say?" Weariness weighted the giant's words. And something else. Sadness. The deep and unutterable sorrow of a man who has at last conceded to a long-fought-against despair. "I have advised her. I have rebuked her. I have warned her. Again and again I have done these things. To what end? She refuses to submit to my will. All have seen this. So it must be that, out of consideration for one whom I would name as my new woman and out of responsibility to her sons, I will abide by the decision of my headman in this matter of a daughter who has dared to speak out against her own band."

"New woman? Suda'li? New sons? N'av and Ka'wo'ni?" Musquash squeaked as though all the breath in his body was being squeezed out of him by astonishment. "I . . . I will n-not share a f-fire circle with them! And Mowea'qua spoke out against n-no one. All that she s-said was true! How can it be wrong of huh-huh-her to warn us of—"

"Be silent, boy!" Tôrnârssuk spitted the child with his

command. "Sit down. You will do as your father bids you to do. Would you shame him as the wild one has done? Cannot even one of his children demonstrate obedience this night?"

Musquash plopped himself down on the driftwood log and crossed his legs with a resounding "Mmph!"

Ne'gauni winced. The boy had complied with the headman's command. That was good. But the unmistakable belligerence in his posture was not good. He was beginning to behave more and more like Mowea'qua.

Tôrnârssuk turned his gaze to the moon as he spoke slowly and somberly. "The daughter of Kinap has chosen to put herself outside the circle of the band this night. Be it so. Under a red moon, no one will speak her name. Under a red moon, no man will go out to her."

"And if she chooses to come back into the band circle?" Moraq pressed eagerly, hungrily, obviously already ravishing the girl within his mind.

"Under a red moon she will remain cast out. All backs will be turned to her. No word will be spoken. No woman will offer meat. No man will attempt to lie on her. And no further judgment or punishment will be contrived against her. Not in anger. Not under a red moon."

Ne'gauni felt suddenly light-headed with relief. Kinap had been right about Tôrnârssuk. He was a fair man. Even when considering punishment for Mowea'qua! He sighed as though reprieved from doom. He had no idea what he would have done if Tôrnârssuk had agreed to follow Moraq's lead out onto the sandbar, but he could not have stood passively by and allowed the girl to be raped and drowned. He held no affection for the daughter of Kinap, but although she had failed to save his leg, she *had* saved his life. Twice. Once in the deep woods when she found him near death in the creek. And again today when she risked her own life to stand up for him to the very men who now openly lusted to kill her. His mouth had gone dry again; he tried to work up spit enough to moisten his throat and failed. He could feel the tension of his fellow travelers focused beyond the band circle and upon the girl who crouched naked on the sandbar. In a world where females among the People were raised to behave with well-disciplined predictability, the future did not look promising for Kinap's intractable daughter. Perhaps it never really had. Nevertheless, Ne'gauni puzzled over how quickly nearly everyone had been willing to turn against the girl. Even Kinap had lost all patience with her. Was he the only man in all the world to care whether Mowea'qua lived or died?

It seemed so.

Ne'gauni could feel the dark thoughts and ill feelings of the band circulating within the circle until Moraq, still pressing for a chance at rape, asked the headman with malicious expectancy, "And afterwards, when Tatqeq has gone to rest beyond the western hills and the sun rises out of a new dawn, will we then decide punishment for her? Banishment or death? And, either way, will we then take her as she has all but asked to be taken?"

"I have told you, Moraq! You are too eager to bring Death into my camp! No such decisions will be made under a red moon!"

Ne'gauni was startled by the headman's pronouncement. Tôrnârssuk had shouted. Never before had he heard the man raise his voice to anyone.

A dog barked.

Pwaumó's baby fussed.

Moraq, taken aback by the headman's outburst, hunkered down into a posture of submission even as the exhalation that came through his clenched teeth betrayed his anger along with the fact that, if pressed too far, he was ready for a fight, even with Tôrnârssuk.

"Our headman has spoken wisdom!" declared old Ko'ram. With a sigh of great forbearance, he reached out to take hold of one of Ne'gauni's crutches and, steadying himself, huffed and grunted his way to his feet. Swaying a little, he cleared his throat with much hacking and working around of phlegm, then jabbed his chin skyward and shook his rattle at Moraq. "The bad spirits that bloody the face of the Spirit Moon are feeding upon this band. They speak through your mouth as surely as from the tongue of the daughter of Kinap!"

Ne'gauni wondered if his heart had just stopped. It seemed so. As he looked around, he suspected that the hearts of every other man and woman and child must have done the same thing. No one spoke. No one moved. No one seemed to be breathing. Even the dog and the baby had fallen quiet.

"My mouth?" Moraq was in no mood to accept what he obviously took to be an outrageous accusation. "It is the daughter of Kinap who has spoken against the—"

"Daughter of Kinap! Daughter of Kinap!" interrupted the old Wise Man. "You have made it clear enough to all what you would lead others to do to her this night! It cannot be. No! If you need to release into a woman so badly, Moraq, then take your man bone into your own hands and pleasure yourself. But I warn you! Under the watching eyes of Spirit Moon you risk making new life on yourself! And only the forces of Creation can say what would pour forth from the end of your man bone at the end of such an unnatural birthing! Or if your man bone would not explode from the bearing of it! So beware! All of you. No man must touch himself for pleasure or lie on a woman under a red moon!

No! And there has been too much talk in this camp! Much too much talk! But you cannot be blamed for where your thoughts have been leading you, Moraq. Nor can the daughter of Kinap be blamed for speaking and behaving as she has. It is my fault. All of it."

"Yours?" Ne'gauni was aghast.

"Yes, Dreamer, mine. I am old. Sometimes I forget that I am Wise Man and that others do not share in my inestimable store of knowledge! You are only Someday Shaman. You have much to learn and, in your ignorance, could not be expected to warn the band of what was to come. And since our headman is from cold and distant Barrenlands, he knows not the evil and seductive spells that are cast by Spirit Moon. I should have spoken sooner. And yet I see now that there is little need for me to speak at all. The wisdom of Tôrnârssuk has looked upon the red face of Spirit Moon. Our headman has seen the phantoms that dwell there. He has understood that Spirit Moon looks down upon the earth below, hungering for the meat of man, taking pleasure in making fools of the People, setting its spell upon us, leading us to war upon one another with words. And then, when all is said and done and we have slain our own kind in anger, it can send its phantoms down from the sky to feed upon our dead! And when they have eaten their fill of us, they will carry our blood and bones and flesh back to Spirit Moon so that it can feast upon us. If we allow it."

Once again there was dead silence within the band circle.

Ne'gauni stood transfixed. Marveling. Tôrnârssuk and the old man were facing one another. Neither man said a word. Yet somehow, squinting through the red stain of moon glow, he could make out their faces and knew they were conversing together, because he understood every word that they were not saying.

"Did you like my tale of terror, headman? Has it turned the mood of the band as you would have it turned?"

"You have done well, old man."

"Am I not clever? Am I not truly Wise One? Am I not the next best thing to a true shaman and fully worthy of my place within this band?"

"It is so."

"The wild girl will be safe enough for now."

"It seems so."

"You can deal with her tomorrow, when we have all cleared our heads of fatigue and Moraq's man bone has had a chance to cool, but in the meantime, Tôrnârssuk, I would remind you that Spirit Moon is watching. You must distract your people. You must show them your power. As I have shown you mine."

Ne'gauni blinked.

The communication between Tôrnârssuk and Ko'ram had ended as it had begun. In silence. And now, for the first time, Ne'gauni realized that, just as Kinap had not misjudged the fairness of Tôrnârssuk's nature, Mowea'qua had been right to believe in Ko'ram's innate wisdom. Frail and flatulent as the old man was, he was wise. Wise enough to have seen the violence toward which Moraq's mood was leading the band. Wise enough to have recognized Tôrnârssuk's unwillingness to be manipulated into acting in haste against Mowea'qua. And wise enough to have understood that what could not be achieved by a headman's command could be accomplished by a Wise Man's manipulation of fear of the unknown. Ne'gauni shook his head, dazed by what he had just seen transpire, for surely old Ko'ram had just saved Mowea'qua's life as certainly as he had placed secure footing under a headman who had been in imminent danger of losing control of his authority.

"Let there be no more harsh words spoken this night."

Tôrnârssuk's voice had returned to its usual low, even, and seemingly imperturbable flow. "Let not the red moon set shadows between Tôrnârssuk and Moraq. Too long have we walked the same trails and lived as brothers. Rise now. Ko'ram of the Dawnland has spoken wisdom to us. And now I say that a vigil must be kept. We must show the spirits of the red moon that we know no fear of them. Far have we come this day. Weary are we. But the People of the Forest and Dawnland and Barrenlands and Grasslands will dance and sing together this night to show our strength and unity as we drive back whatever phantoms may be watching us in the red glow of Spirit Moon!"

"Be it so!" Ne'gauni spoke out loudly, so buoyed by the headman's words that he barely noticed Ko'ram's elbow jab.

"Well spoken, Dreamer," acknowledged the old man as the band seemed to come to life before his eyes. Nodding and folding his arms across his chest, he added out of the side of his mouth, "Are you beginning to understand the way of the shaman's path?"

Ne'gauni had no chance to reply.

"What about Mowea'qua?"

Musquash's question hung in the air.

The boy was on his feet again, standing atop the driftwood log as combatively as Mowea'qua had done.

"She who has offended the Ancient Ones with her words and anger has chosen to place herself outside the circle of the band this night," replied Tôrnârssuk. "Until the dawn you will not disobey me again by speaking her name."

"B-but she wi-will be cuh-cuh-cold and loh-loh-lonely," stammered the boy. "And there are wuh-wuh-wolves out th-there."

"Then let her sing and dance with them," said the headman. "She is dead to us until the dawn."

"And after that?"

"The council will decide. Yes. The council will decide."

▼▼▼▼

And so they danced.

Under the red moon.

With wolves howling on the peninsula, loons calling on the lake, Wildfire dancing to the north, and visions of man-eating mammoths bloodying their minds, they leaped and whirled and stomped their feet as though they, like the wild girl on the sand spit, did not know the meaning of the word *fear*.

Tôrnârssuk stood apart. He had led his followers to the dance and then fallen out, electing to be one of four men who would continue to stand watch, each at a separate position around the perimeter of the band circle. Kanio'te to the north. Itiitoq to the west. Inaksak to the east. And the headman to the south.

What a sight and sound the dancers made!

They raised their arms and shook their fists at the clouded sky. They yipped and barked and howled until they put the wolves to shame and silence. And now, as they lifted their voices in the ancient war and hunt chants of their respective tribes, they turned up their eyes to all they could see of the veiled face of Spirit Moon and appeared to be spirits themselves. Dangerous spirits. No longer human.

Tôrnârssuk's brow came down. His right hand rose to finger the long line of his mouth. Before the dance had begun, he and each of his fellow Northerners had inserted into their pierced lower lips the polished ivory adornments that, when worn, made the men of the Barrenlands appear to be as impressively and ferociously fanged as the most dangerous carnivores. Then, at old Ko'ram's insistence, they joined with the others to take ceremonial dancing capes, noisemakers, and masks from the traveling packs they had earlier buried: masks of birds and beasts of land, sea, and air, each carved of wood in the style of the far north, painted with the blood of its maker, inlaid with rare stones, shells, and polished bone, festooned with human hair as well as with the pelts, antlers, and plumage of totem animals; noisemakers of shell and bone and the beaks and feet of seabirds, fashioned in the style of the Dawnland tribes; ritual capes of fur and feathers cut and sewn in the manner of the Forest People. The women, still covering their heads beneath their robes and sleeping skins, had hurried to bring forth and share the contents of their little gut-skin-lined bags of precious pigments. Soon, from these grease-and-spittle-moistened powders of rare clays, pounded roots, and superheated stones, the face of every man, woman, and child who did not own a mask was boldly patterned, each in the colors and style of his or her own fire circle. Even the Dreamer had stopped glowering long enough to allow Hasu'u to paint his face, and after old Ko'ram insisted on attaching his ankle janglers to the young man's wrists, Ne'gauni, with Hasu'u's assistance, was doing his best to take part in the dance.

Now, while Kinap beat his drum and Onen'ia's flute shrieked defiance at the sky and Chief Ogeh'ma raised his voice in a resounding forest chant, Tôrnârssuk watched in silence as Ko'ram managed once again to energize his old bones to dance and shake his rattle at Spirit Moon. He wondered if either the elder or his reluctant apprentice had even the slightest suspicion of the way in which he had led them to this moment.

Foolish, gullible old man grasping at your last chance at glory! Do you not see the danger in your dance? Sad, guileless, life-savaged young man so easily manipulated into believing your own fever-ridden dreams! Do you not see the deadly snares that await you on the pathway along which the old man would be your guide?

Tôrnârssuk shook his head.

If anything went wrong tonight—if North Wind rose again and brought with it the renewed threat of Wildfire, or if enemies survived in the valley and dared to attack the band, or if a man-crushing mammoth came out of the night to fulfill the ancient tales of terror—he would now be able to easily shift the weight of his responsibility onto the shoulders of those who had so unwisely dared to openly interpret the will of the spirits and speak in their headman's place.

Tôrnârssuk's brow furrowed.

A strange mood was on him. He held no animosity toward Ne'gauni or Ko'ram. Indeed, he was glad to see the young man smiling and participating in the dance. And he was grateful to the old man for inspiring him to suggest an activity that had redirected Moraq's lust for blood and sex while at the same time enabling his followers to feel as though they, and not the red moon, were in command of the night. And yet his heart was cold. So cold. And hard. Not toward the old man. Toward himself.

He should have been the one to command the dance! He was headman! He should have anticipated and acted upon his followers' need for diversion on such a night as this. And he should never have allowed the band to engage in open and undirected conversation under a red moon. Never! How could he have forgotten how easily the tongues of men and even of women and children could be transformed by fear into conduits along which words could run as poisonously as venom from the mouths of the vipers of the southern forests? And why had he failed to repudiate the slurs against Mowea'qua's lineage? The girl was unmanageable, but despite the wildness of her tongue and imagination, he doubted that she was an intentional liar. On the distant Barrenlands of his Ancestors, despite Moraq's and Ningao's horror stories to the contrary, it had been his experience that survivors of her grandmother's ancient race always fled from his people, as though his tribe, not theirs, was to be feared as kindred to animals.

Only once had it been different. Here, long ago, in this very valley. Tôrnârssuk remembered it well. He had been leading his fellow raiders along a timeworn game trail for several days. The woodland through which they had been traveling was dark and misted and interspersed with bog. Now and then they had felt themselves being watched and, after stopping to rest for the night, discovered little things missing. Small things. Unimportant things. Kamak's whale-bone spoon. Inaksak's bag of small trading shells. An old fish-hook that Itiitoq had been mending before the fire when he had fallen asleep. A carving that Avataut had been whittling to pass the time. Soon they had fallen to arguing among themselves, one man accusing the other of pilfering personal belongings. Then, awakened one night by the ferocious barking of the dogs, they saw a pair of thieves making off into the night with several lances and two quivers of arrows. They had followed in quick pursuit but lost them in the dark. Dawn found them hunting the careless interlopers. Easily picking up their trail and recognizing them as Old Tribe by the imprint of their moccasins, they tracked the thieves straight back to their filthy village of sticks and bones and attacked them with bow and lance, mocking them as they tried to flee, slaughtering men, women, and children as they ran screaming.

Tôrnârssuk's eyes narrowed. At his command they had left the dead for carrion. They had not touched the bodies, not even to retrieve their stolen weapons or belongings or bloodied lance points and arrows. Nor did they search out their victims' hunting camp for spoils; those of the Old Tribe were reputed to possess a dark and powerful and all-contaminating magic, but it was well known that they owned nothing else that any man of the True People could possibly covet for himself, except the sport to be had in killing them.

He felt no guilt. No regret. The life of a raider was what it was. Occasionally he had led his band to engage in peaceful trade, but only when discretion warranted caution among large or canny tribes. It was better to raid. Stealth and avarice sharpened a man's mind. The excitement to be had in such a life had fired his youthful imagination, challenged his restless spirit, and lured him south. He had reveled in it. Until recently. Now, with strands of white streaking his hair and far too many memories of close encounters with Death to allow him a peaceful night's sleep, the sheer weight of physical fatigue and concern for the welfare of his new family was calling him home.

For days now the old restlessness had been driving him, impelling him, filling his thoughts with memories of the wide open skies of the Barrenlands of his youth, and allowing his mind only one thought.

Return into the far country of your Ancestors.

While you still have a woman. While you still have a son. While you still have a band.

Return.

Before it is too late.

Sila is hunting you.

Return.

The word plagued him with need. The need to be out of the forest. The need to reach the Great River of the North.

The need to unite once more with those who had broken with him after the spring flood had so devastated his band. The need to admit to Avataut, most trusted hunt brother of his youth, that he had been right to head north on his own with only Armik at his side. The spirit names and magic amulets that he and his fellow raiders had brought with them from the hunting grounds of their Ancestors were losing power in this benighted land of endless trees. Too many of their women and captives and old friends had died along the raiding trail. The time had come for them to return to a peaceful life under the broad, cold, open skies of their homeland before the demons of lesser tribes caught up with them at last and consumed them to a man as penalty for all they had wrought within the Dawnland and the inland forests.

Tôrnârssuk's hand moved to rest over one of the many talismans that he wore around his neck. Of late he was sometimes as surprised as he was comforted to find that the amulet was still there. Still on its sinew cord. Still safe against his skin. Still in its central place of importance amidst the fetish bones, the strands of seal and bear and wolf teeth, the slender braid of Hasu'u's hair. Pale, uncarved, and unpainted, no larger than a molar ripped from the jaw of a man, the sacred stone had been worn smooth by the uncountable generations of holy men and warrior hunters who had cherished it as much as he ever since it had been presented to him by the angatkok of his father's village on the day he slew his first white bear and, in the killing, saved the holy man's life.

Tôrnârssuk's eyes focused inward. Once he would have sworn on his own life that the amulet was all-powerful. No more. The boy Musquash had inherited a similar stone from his shaman father and swore that such talismans brought power and wisdom to holy men of all tribes. His mouth tightened. He had pillaged the encampments of far too many posturing, ineffectual holy men to believe this. Not one of them had possessed an amulet like his or the boy's, and not one of them had been able to save himself or his people from the depredations of Tôrnârssuk's raiding band.

But the angatkok of his father's village had given him much more than a sacred talisman that day. When the holy man slipped on the ice and put him in the position of defending them both from a charging bear, Tôrnârssuk had been given the gift of his true spirit.

He stood very still, remembering, smelling the hot stink of his own fear, seeing in his mind's eye the way it had been for him when, in one heart-stopping instant, he had seen his first manifestation of Sila in the great white all-devouring bear spirit of the north as it called out to his soul.

> I come!
> I am Bear.
> I am Death.
> I will devour the man and give life and power to the
>   spirit of the hunter.
> I am Death.
> I am Bear.
> I come
> Unafraid!

He stood his ground. As he had stood then. Alone on burning bright snow. Alone beneath a burning bright sky. A young man, untested, with only a lance and a dagger to protect his life and the power of the fallen angatkok, he shouted to the spirit of the bear and, stunned, saw his own soul coming toward him in the skin of the animal. His strength.

His courage. His willingness to confront Death, to challenge Fear, to reach out and embrace Sila.

> *I stand to you, Bear!*
> *I, too, am Death.*
> *Though you devour me, I will eat your soul!*
> *I am Man.*
> *I stand*
> *Unafraid!*

And it had been so.

He had killed the bear and, in the act of killing it, had felt his youthful inexperience devoured and replaced by the predaceous hunting spirit of the animal. All saw the change in him. All were inspired by his courage. From that day he and the great white spirit of the north, Tôrnârssuk, White Bear, One Who Gives Power, were one. The name of the bear became his name, the first of many names that he would win and answer to with pride. The soul of the bear prowled his spirit. The soul of the bear protected and strengthened him. The soul of the bear roused within him an insatiable restlessness and a fearless curiosity that provoked him to challenge the will of other men, to mate with their women uncaring of whatever "cubs" he made on them as he went his way, roaming solitary at first, setting his footsteps out of the hunting grounds of his Ancestors, taking up the life of a raider so that he might see and "sap" the forested world that lay far to the south. Along the way, many a brave and restless young man recognized his power and chose to walk in the shade of a hunter whose spirit was one with the great white bear of the north. Soon he had a band of his own, loyal followers, captive women, a reputation to maintain among men and even among lesser carnivores, for it came to be said that his power was recognized by man and beast alike. Wolves and foxes were sometimes seen following his war band. Once a wolverine tracked them, and often there were ravens, for where White Bear walked, there was always meat for predators—human meat left behind to redden the snouts and fill the bellies of carrion eaters and bloody the beaks of ravens.

Tôrnârssuk braided his fingers around the smooth shaft of his lance. Many a long, cold winter had come and gone since the day the bear had given him the gift of its spirit and the angatkok had placed the sacred stone talisman of his Ancestors around his neck. Now, under the red moon, if the stone was speaking wisdom, it was telling him that he had seen too much of Death to still believe that either he or his followers were immune to it. And although he could feel the spirit of the white bear still prowling restlessly within his soul, it was a changed spirit. An older spirit. A spirit that sometimes frightened him because, for the past many moons, he had felt its once overwhelming power beginning to die within him.

His brow furrowed as he looked at his followers dancing within the bastioning walls of driftwood: at Hasu'u, holding her sleeping robe over her head as she danced with his infant in its cradleboard on her back; at Ne'gauni, doing his best to stay upright beside her; at Chief Ogeh'ma and his stringy wife and blanketed daughters; and at all the other men and women who put their trust in him. When had he come to care for them? Why did the beauty, gentleness, and all-abiding kindness of the Dawnland woman so touch his heart that sometimes he was certain that his love for her would blind him to every other reality? And the baby? Why did the life of this one tiny son mean so much to him when all the other children he had spawned and seen die or had merely abandoned along with the women who bore them upon the long raiding trail of his life had meant nothing? The death of the infant's captive mother had moved him to pity, but this, too, had been an emotion as alien as the ever-constricting, irrational bonds of kinship that he was now feeling toward followers who had only recently elected to walk at his side and were not even of his race: the foolish, flatulent old Wise Man and the giant storyteller and the flirtatious widow and the combative twins and the bold little boy named for a muskrat and the girl . . . the wild, gray-eyed girl.

He scanned down the beach and across the shallows. She was still there, crouching alone on the sandbar, waiting.

For what? Annoyance pricked him. Forgiveness by her father? Redemption by the band? He exhaled frustration. Mowea'qua deserved no consideration from the giant. She would receive neither exoneration nor compassion from her headman or her band. By all the cold, compassionless forces of Creation and Destruction that governed the order of his world, how the sight of her standing naked and wildly defiant had stirred the old voracious bear spirit within him tonight! He was hard again just thinking of it. And angry. Not at the girl. No. Mowea'qua had caused him to remember just who and what he was. His anger was with himself.

He should have struck the girl down then and there as punishment for her audacity! Hasu'u's gentle heart would surely have wept to see it, but since when had he allowed the feelings of a woman to determine his decisions? Ever since he had first set eyes on Hasu'u! This must stop! For her sake as much as for his own. The life of Mowea'qua was peripheral to his needs, expendable to his desires, and irrelevant unless it served the welfare of his band. He should have encouraged his men to follow Moraq's lead to the violent sexual release of tension that the girl's well-deserved mauling would have given them. And he should have joined them.

The White Bear of old would have done this! Tôrnârssuk, One Who Gives Power, should have understood the necessity of doing so! Tunraq, Guide and Guardian and Man Who Walks in Favor of the Spirits, should have demanded that he do no less! And Wíndigo, inheritor of the black and eternally bloodied cloak of Raven, Great Ghost Cannibal, Winter Chief of the manitou spirits of the forest, master of demons, lord over the Djeneta and Djigáha and immortal wolf woman of legend, would have enjoyed every moment!

A coldness touched him.

He was still in his prime, but the great bear spirit within his soul was surely growing old, indecisive, so soft of heart that he now found himself actually pitying the girl.

Moraq had seen weakness in him tonight. Others must have seen it, too. This must not happen again. Tomorrow the council would decide Mowea'qua's fate. Tomorrow he would abide by the judgment of other men and consent to deal with the girl in the only way she had left open to them—Moraq's way. Even if the giant were to find it within himself to speak on behalf of his daughter and ask for her life, he would not grant the man's request. After his recent confrontation with, and consideration given to, the excesses of the cripple, he could not allow himself to be seen as willing to yield to yet another open challenge to his authority. To do so would compromise his leadership and put the stability of the band at risk at a time when the people were already vulnerable to the deadly whims of Sila. Kinap would understand. Old Ko'ram would regretfully see the wisdom of it, as would Chief Ogeh'ma. The Dreamer would be in shock for a while. And later, lest Tôrnârssuk suffer any loss of affection from his wife, he would lay the final decision to end the girl's life in the lap of a council that would include Hasu'u's own father and brothers. She would be saddened, but she could not blame him for the death of the giant's daughter. Nor would he fault himself. He had openly warned his people that he would suffer no divisiveness among them. Mowea'qua should have listened.

His eyes narrowed as it occurred to him that in the tales of every people he had ever encountered, there was always a troublesome young female out to upset the order of the band. Invariably she was cast out. Invariably she returned as an evil haunting. Invariably some magic was worked to make her spirit disappear forever. And invariably, after she was killed in one unpleasant manner or another, she was held up to all young women as an example of how not to behave.

And now, as in some fable of old, Mowea'qua remained motionless on the sandbar, watching what little she could see of the dance, listening to the songs and sounds of the band, oblivious to the fact that this was to be the last night of her life.

A rush of unexpected empathy for the girl flushed the headman's face. Once he, too, had been wild. Once he, too, had boldly and recklessly challenged all who stood against him. Why did she not run away, as he had run when he saw that he had pressed his luck among his own people too far? Why did she not call upon the wolf within her spirit, as he had called upon the great white bear? Why did she not simply disappear into the night? Maybe she would find her own kind out there in the dark. Wolves or men, or whatever those of the Old Tribe truly were, if she stumbled upon them somewhere out there in the forest they would take her in, or kill her. Either way, he would not hunt her. He would be grateful to see her gone. He did not want to deal with her tomorrow.

"My headman?"

Tôrnârssuk winced, startled by a small voice and the feel of a small hand tugging at the fringes of his leggings. "What . . . ?"

"I will swim out to her and tell her to come back if you wish it so," Musquash volunteered.

"I have told you, boy. No man is to swim out to her. She has chosen to be where she is. You are not to speak her name."

The boy shrugged. "I am obedient. I have not spoken her name. And I am not a man. She must be very cold by now with no clothes to warm her, my headman. She must be sad. Very sad. And sorry."

"Join the others, Musquash. Remember that you are the son of a shaman. Dance. Sing. Show the phantoms of the red moon that you are bold and unafraid. Do this for your band. For the giant who names you Son. Go. Do as I say. Trouble me no more this night. I would be alone with my thoughts, for I, too, am sad. And I, too, am sorry. Tomorrow, at my hand, Mowea'qua will die."

Chapter Eight

v v v v v v v

We must run away."

Mowea'qua stared into darkness. Who had spoken? She could not quite make out the voice that had come sputtering out of the lake. Above her head, long, ever-widening bands of cloud had eaten the stars and all but consumed the moon. It was difficult for her to tell just where the sandbar ended and the water began.

"Kinap?"

Her heart leaped. It had to be Kinap! Who else would love her enough to come out to her across the water? Blue-mouthed and numb with cold, the girl stifled a sob of joy as, digging in her heels and bracing her palms on the cold, gravelly surface of the sandbar, she willed her stiff, chilled body to rise in shivering expectation.

He was coming for her at last!

She could not see him or hear the splash of his hands and feet above the din being raised by the band, but she was certain that he was coming, swimming underwater as she so often swam, moving like a river otter, arms extended, parting the water with his hands, surfacing only now and then to pull in a breath of air.

She trembled with relief. "Beginning was I to think that never would you come for me, my father. Thought I that—"

"Phhwoof!"

The girl jumped back, startled and frightened by the sound of something breaking the surface of the water at the very edge of the sandbar. She could see its form now, dark and sleek. Suddenly, panic bit at her throat. What was the matter with her? She could hear Kinap's story drum booming from the band circle. Whatever was coming toward her from the water could not be her father! It was something else. Something that did not appear human. Something that was not a man at all but . . .

"Waktcexi!" she cried and whirled to run.

"Wait! Mowea'qua! Wait! Do I look like a water monster to you?"

Recognizing the voice, she turned, squinted hard at the object of her terror, then dropped back into a crouch. Never had she felt so foolish. The chill air of night must have numbed her brain as well as her body. Hugging herself, she gritted her chattering teeth and felt fear replaced by disappointment as she realized that Kinap was not coming to bring her back to the band. At least not yet. And there was no many-headed water beast emerging from the shallows to devour her. The monster of her imagination was only Musquash coming from the lake headfirst, blowing water like a miniature version of one of the whales she had heard Chief Ogeh'ma speak of in his many stories of the Great River of the North. She frowned as she watched him scramble onto solid ground, surely no giant as he shook himself like a wet pup and hurried to kneel shivering before her, naked save for the little stone amulet that he always wore around his neck.

"You must listen to me, Mowea'qua. I have come to tell you that—"

She could not let him finish his statement. "You bring a message to me from my father!" she interrupted, her voice fairly singing as hope leaped high within her heart. "Ready am I. Yes! Return will I to the band. And promise will I to hold my tongue. Easy it will not be, say I, especially with Suda'li, but much thinking have I done, and say I now that never again will I speak to make Kinap ashamed or to—"

"You cannot return to the band!" It was the boy's turn to interrupt. "And you cannot stay here. You will die if you do."

Confusion brought a frown to the girl's face. The frown, in turn, roused a deep ache in her battered features. She did her best to ignore it. The boy looked so worried, so distraught. She could not understand why. "Look at me, say I, Musquash. Our father has beaten me. Complain I did not. Strong am I. No harm to me will a little cold air bring."

"It is not cold air that will harm you. It is the headman. Tomorrow Tôrnârssuk will call a council. He has already decided the outcome. He is going to kill you, Mowea'qua."

The words struck her like stones. Her consciousness went into a defensive knot, absorbed them, and, unwilling to grant them credibility, cast them away as unworthy of her consideration. "Never will Kinap allow this. Never! He will come, say I. Always my giant comes for his Mowea'qua. *Always*. See this you will. Before this night is over, he will come or call me back into the circle of the band. I will show him that I can obey. And so I wait."

Musquash exhaled an impatient huff and blew drops of lake water from the tip of his dripping nose. "Kinap will not come for you. Even if Tôrnârssuk had not forbidden it, he would not come."

"He will, say I, he will!"

"Sometimes, Mowea'qua, I think that maybe Kinap is right when he says that you learned nothing when you lived in the deep forest with your grandmother. Tonight you called the headman's woman foolish and stupid, but you are the stupid one. Listen! Kinap has taken up his drum again! And do you not hear the flute and noisemakers and singing of the band? Our father dances tonight! Yah! While you sit here cold and alone, how he dances! Even after others have spoken of how they will kill you, how he sings! Mmph! He thinks that he will help the others to drive bad phantoms from the red moon, but old Ko'ram has seen the truth: The bad spirits are not in the face of Spirit Moon. They are inside the band circle—inside the heads of Moraq and Ningao and all the others who speak against the daughter of Kinap. And inside your head, too, making you speak bad words . . . very bad words."

"Mmph! I spoke only truth, only warning. And when weary he is of dancing, Kinap will speak for me."

"The bad spirits are in his head, too, Mowea'qua! He has already spoken. He has said that he will not stand against the headman in any decision that is made against you. Only our Dreamer has spoken out for you, Mowea'qua, and the headman's woman, but now even they have forgotten you. They dance together. Everybody dances! Everybody sings! Only the headman stands apart. And our father sees nothing but Suda'li. He named her his woman tonight. She did not turn away. Her sons will be his sons. Tôrnârssuk's band is his band. He does not care about you . . . or me."

"Believe you I do not!" Mowea'qua's voice snagged in her throat. Musquash was a child. A six-year-old stripling only recently taken into her father's care. How could he possibly know what Kinap felt about her, his only child, or about anything or anyone else? A shaman's son the boy might be, but he had inherited none of his evil father's power nor any insight into magic or the hearts of men. He was not much more than a baby! She would not allow herself to believe him. And yet, remembering all that had transpired this day, she could not keep herself from believing and, with tears stinging her eyes, fought to keep her chin from quivering as she vehemently denied it. "Listen to you I will not. Wait here I will. All night if I must. Kinap will come to his Mowea'qua or call out to me, insisting that into the circle of the band I must return. See this you will, say I!"

"And say I, Stupid One, that whether you stay here or return into the band circle, after tomorrow's council, you will be killed. Unless we run away. I have taken your things and put them with mine, over there across the water and back in the trees, well away from the camp circle. No one noticed what I was about. No one saw me go. Everyone was too busy shouting and stomping at the moon. We can dress, take up our weapons, and be far away by dawnrise. If they cannot find us, they cannot kill us."

"Us?"

"I will not share a fire circle with Suda'li and her twins. And I will not leave you. No matter how foolish you are, Stupid One, I will be your man."

"Call me stupid you will not! And you are no man! You are a bog rat! A biting fly!"

"So you always say, Mowea'qua, but no one else cares about you tonight. And I am cold. Let us swim back to the beach, gather up our things, dry ourselves, and be on our way."

She shivered. Violently.

Across the shallows, the band danced on.

Within the forest, owls were no longer calling.

On the peninsula, the wolves were silent.

In the sky, the red moon had vanished behind gathering storm clouds, and, far to the north, thunder was rumbling.

Mowea'qua cocked her head. Old Ko'ram was right. Rain was coming. If Wildfire was still dancing to the north, her threat to the band would soon be washed away. "The sky spirits have heard and obeyed the voice of my Wounded One." She wondered why the utterance brought no gladness to her heart, only sadness, bittersweet. "Lives he to guide the band and command Wind and Fire only because of me."

"He is your Wounded One no longer, Mowea'qua. Your medicines have healed him. He is no longer Son of Asticou. He is Shaman. His dreams have won him a place of honor within the circle of Tôrnârssuk's band. Ne'gauni no longer needs you, Mowea'qua."

Tears were pooling in her eyes. She tried to blink them away; it was no use. They spilled onto her cheeks. She let them fall. The boy was right. Ne'gauni did not need her. He did even like her. She had given him back his life and yet, although the boy claimed that her Wounded One had spoken for her, she did not believe him. Ne'gauni would never forgive her for taking his leg. Never! He would always revile her. As her own father reviled her. The blood of the Old Tribe ran in her veins. They would never let her forget it.

"We must go, Mowea'qua."

She trembled. "Where?" she asked bleakly and could not understand how the utterance of one little word could hurt so much. The Old Tribe was no more. The People wanted no part of her. And if she fled Tôrnârssuk's band, she would never know the many wonders of the Great Gathering of Many Tribes, or see the Great River of the North, or hear whales of many colors singing to the stars, or see Kinap—or Ne'gauni—ever again.

"You must forget this band that thinks you are part wolf, Mowea'qua. The Four Winds will carry us where they will.

There are mammoths in this forest. I know there are! And you know what Kinap says: Even one mammoth in the hunting grounds of Man is a sign from the forces of Creation that all is well with the world. So you must not be afraid. I wear a sacred stone of the Ancient Ones. You have been given the gift of a feather from the wing of Raven. He is lord of earth and sky. He has told you what you must do. You must fly away with me, Mowea'qua! Together we will make a new band."

"Mmph. And just how and where will we 'fly,' a wolf woman and a baby bog rat?"

"Yah! Did your grandmother teach you nothing? Do you not know that the Dawnland People say that it was Muskrat and Wolf who saved the world? In the time beyond beginning, when Giant Beaver selfishly dammed up Water so that only he and his kind could drink, Wolf led Muskrat to the lodge of Giant Beaver. Wolf stood guard. Into the great lodge did Muskrat swim. Bold and unafraid, Muskrat dove deep. While Giant Beaver slept, Muskrat opened many holes in the stick walls of Giant Beaver's lodge, allowing Water to flow free again so that all of the Animals and People could drink once more and all green growing things could find life anew. Then, when Giant Beaver tried to run after Water and recapture her, Wolf chased him into the camps of Man, and Giant Beaver was killed to the last of his kind. So do not think you can hurt my feelings by calling me Muskrat. I am proud to name the bog rat Brother. As you should be proud to call wolf Sister. And know this! I am no baby, nor will I be a boy forever. I will protect you, Mowea'qua! I will keep you safe wherever we go!"

She flinched, then shivered, and not just from the cold. What was it that she had heard both Ne'gauni and Tôrnârssuk say? *"No one is ever safe. There are always enemies. Man or* muskrat, woman or wolf, the power of Sila hunts and brings Death to us all."

"Mmph! I am not afraid," declared the boy. "Maybe old Ko'ram has seen another truth. Maybe the bad spirits are not only in the face of Spirit Moon. Dangerous spirits! They feed upon the hearts and speak from the mouths of the people of Tôrnârssuk's band. And so I say again that we *must* run away, Mowea'qua. Those who would kill you tomorrow must not find you. We do not need them. We will seek the mammoths. They will show us the way through the forest to hunting grounds better than either of us has ever seen. How can it be otherwise? I have the sacred stone of the Ancient Ones! You have the feather of Raven! Wolf and Muskrat will walk together as in the time beyond beginning. Kinap no longer cares whether we live or die. Why should we care about him, or about any of the others? Let them follow Tôrnârssuk north! Let them seek and find whatever awaits them there!"

Part Two

SILA

▼▼▼▼▼▼▼

"No one has seen Sila; his place of being is a mystery, in that he is at once among us and unspeakably far away."

—NAJAGNEQ, ESKIMO SHAMAN
*Across Arctic America: Narrative
of the Fifth Thule Expedition*
Knud Rasmussen, 1927

Chapter One

▼▼▼▼▼▼▼

The hunter awoke.

He lay on his back, tense as an overstrung bow, staring into vaulted darkness, listening.

Yes!

It was there again.

Something—or someone—was moving outside.

He sat up, flung back his bed skins, reached for his lance, and, in an instant, was on his knees, stark naked and ready to take on all comers at the entrance to the conical summer lodge that he shared with his woman and small son. Impatiently backhanding the well-oiled seal-gut weather baffle out of his way, he peered into the night to see and hear . . .

Nothing.

Only darkness.

He uttered a low curse and went out, circling the tent, finding no sign of any of the usual thieving trespassers a man might expect to discover prowling about his campsite in the depths of night. No bear or fox, no marten or mouse, no stray dog nosing about the fire pit for leftovers. No man foolish enough to put his life at risk by breaking the honor code of the assembled tribes to pilfer another man's unguarded caches of meat and skins. And no sound at all except for the dull patter of the rain, the low rumble of thunder growling sullenly overhead, and the constant silken *shhh* of the great river.

He shivered, not only against the cool fall of raindrops upon his skin but in response to the instinctive unease he always felt in the dark.

What did you expect to find?

"White Bear." He snarled the name of his enemy as he slitted his eyes and continued to glare into the night, grinding his teeth until the muscles in his jaw bunched and crawled like serpents writhing beneath his skin.

Are you out there? Are you still alive? Despite all that I have done this day, are you still coming north?

"Avataut?"

He frowned, distracted by the sound of his woman's voice calling his name softly from within the tent. He did not answer; there was no need. She would interpret his lack of response as a command to remain silent and still. She would obey. Nuutlaq always obeyed. She would lie closemouthed and motionless on the caribou and sealskins that overlay their bed of spruce boughs, waiting to comply with whatever he might ask of her. After a few moments, if he did not summon her to some specific task, she would know that whatever had drawn him from their lodge did not concern her. She would feel no compunction to ask what had awakened him. She would simply readjust the sleeping furs over her short, blubbery body and, sucking her gums as was her habit these days, lull herself back to sleep without a word.

Avataut's wide, meaty lips tightened into a grimace of disgust. Not with his woman. No. Although Nuutlaq's breath of late was as sour as a residue of fish sludge left too long in an underused boiling bag, he found the woman to be the perfect wife: strong, uncomplaining, obedient to his every whim, fat enough to prove to everyone at the Great Gathering just how bounteously a man of the True People could provide for a wife, complacent when he now and then exchanged her with other men so that he could enjoy a little lively sex with their younger wives while they benefited from her excellence at sewing and all the other tasks demanded of her gender. And, best of all, she was totally unconcerned about anything that did not directly impact him, their son, or herself—in that order. How could he possibly be displeased with her? His dissatisfaction lay with the night.

If anything—or anyone—was prowling outside his lodge, darkness prevented him from seeing the intruder, even though his tent stood alone on much-coveted high ground. It had been White Bear's campsite when they first came to hunt and barter peacefully with the many bands that gathered each spring and summer along the Great River of the North. They had shared much meat and many women and good times in this place. Bountiful times. Boisterous times. Hunting had been so exceptionally good that there had been talk of raising a winter house and staying on through the time of the long cold. Tôrnârssuk had chafed against such talk. The restless ghost of the great white bear that prowled his spirit impelled him to move on. There were still unknown lands to see! Still unsuspecting tribes to harass and exploit! But before going his way with Avataut and those of the band who shared his impatience to resume the raiding life, he marked the campsite with a raven-feathered staff of bear bone, inscribing his name in deeply incised pictographs so those of his followers who chose to remain behind to savor the soft life a while longer would not forget that he intended to return the following spring to raise his lodge on this exact site again.

What arrogance.

If Tôrnârssuk wanted the site so badly, he should have returned to claim it long before now. Instead, after the flash flood, he had insisted on remaining in the deep forest with the injured members of his band, even after they finished mourning their dead. It was not wise for men to linger in a place where other men had died. The injured should have been left behind. He had said as much to White Bear, but somewhere along the trail south from the Great River of the North, bad spirits had begun to feed upon the man, sapping his enthusiasm for the raiding life, dulling his once-flawless judgment, weakening his once-merciless spirit.

Avataut shook his head. Maybe it was the death of Tôrnârssuk's woman in childbirth that had so enervated him. Who could say? It had been a bad death. Big with child as she was, Waseh'ya should have been left behind at the river with Nuutlaq and the other pregnant or nursing wives. In other times, better times, White Bear would not have hesitated to turn his back on her and go his way, or to do what was necessary for the good of the band. And, as one who had come to be called Tunraq, Guide and Guardian and Man Who Walks in the Favor of the Spirits, he should have foreseen the flood. Yes! If the power of Tôrnârssuk's combined amulets and spirit names had still been with him on that day, no man, woman, or dog would have drowned. And no captive would have gone unpunished after heaping shame upon the head of one who had been the headman's most loyal and trusted hunt brother.

Bitterness moved Avataut to anger. As a youth he had abandoned what was left of his ever-feuding band to walk proudly and unquestioningly in the shadow of one whom he believed to be invincible. As a mature man he had come to learn what all men must learn if they are to survive—that no man is invincible. Now, in rain and darkness, the knowledge did not sit well with him. In all their years together, White Bear had never claimed to be more than a man, but the stories of his valor preceded him. Others spoke of the great bear spirit that lived within him, and, for his own gain and vanity, he had encouraged them to believe it, to risk all for him, to yield all to him. And so Avataut had done. Gladly! To walk in the shadow of a man of infinite power was to bask in the reflected glory of that power and take no small measure of it into himself. Just as wolverines and foxes will follow wolves, and as eagles, hawks, and ravens will follow marauding bears or bands of human warriors to feast upon the leavings of these greater predators, so, too, had he found substantial rewards. He had found no cause to complain until, having perceived the core of fully human vulnerability within Tôrnârssuk, he could see nothing else.

He was frowning again, begrudging everything he had ever yielded to the man—including the joy of punishing the captive who had shamed him.

"Hasu'u."

The strange foreign Dawnland name with its oddly placed glottal stop was far too sweet upon his tongue. As always, when he thought of White Bear's young, soft-mouthed, doe-eyed captive, his loins warmed and stirred. By all the powers of this world and the next, why did he want her so when his heart was so bitter toward her? Had he forgotten the way she had humiliated him? A woman leaping into raging rapids with no apparent thought to her own safety! Crying out his name for all to hear! Then grabbing him by his hair and hauling him from the water as though he was not a man at all, but a limp hank of tangled river weed. Such appalling behavior on the part of a female should never have been tolerated among True People. It was unforgivable! True enough, as a man of the interior Barrenlands, he was not much of a swimmer. Nevertheless, he took great pride in the fact that during his first summer at the Great Gathering he had eagerly accepted the challenge from a small group of Northerners to balance himself in one of the lightweight skin boats of the upcoast whale hunters. Had he possessed a kayak of his own, he would have taken up his bow and lances and eagerly joined their flotilla when they went out in great numbers to hunt white whales. Instead he had gone out with the rest of his band when Tôrnârssuk had been goaded into joining the crew of one of the big, driftwood-ribbed, walrus-hide-covered umiaks. They had taken many whales, and he had discovered to his delight that he possessed a natural ability as a boatman. Indeed, he actually liked being on the water and was almost certain that he would have been able to wrest himself from the flood had Hasu'u not interfered. And even if he had failed, at least he would not have died embarrassed.

Better for a man of the True People to drown than to be saved by a woman! And better to walk alone than to continue to keep company with a headman who no longer walks in the favor of the spirits! Too many have died under the past moons while following in his shadow. I will not be one of them!

And so he had gone his way. Armik, the only other man in the band wise enough to recognize the danger inherent in remaining close to the contagion of a bad-spirit man, had joined him. Together they had set off for the Great River of the North. It had not been an easy journey. Although White Bear professed to hold no rancor toward them because of their decision to break with the band, he had denied them the use of even a single burden woman to carry their loads, cook their meat, or open herself to their sexual needs along the trail. When they finally arrived at the river, they had been as disheveled and irritable as a pair of blackfly-bitten moose in high rut. Although greeted with joy by the women and children they had left behind, it had taken them a while to secure again a place of honor within the encampment and convince Tôrnârssuk's former raiders that it was not they but White Bear who no longer walked in the favor of the spirits.

"I tell you, Spirit Sucker encamps with him these days to suck the life from his men, women, and dogs," he had warned. "To walk within the fall of his shadow is to be in danger of death. Bad spirits have eaten of his heart. He has lost stomach for all that is good in this life, for raiding, for stealing away the women and goods of those who are too weak to protect them! When he comes to the Great Gathering he must be shunned . . . driven away . . . perhaps even killed . . . for the good of all."

"Spirit Sucker comes to all men in time, Avataut, regardless of whom they name Headman."

"And Tôrnârssuk is the best of all men. It makes no difference if he wishes to make his lodge here by the river in peace or continue on as a raider. He will always be made welcome among those who have journeyed out of the far north at his side."

Avataut did not know what rankled him most, their loyalty to White Bear or their refusal to take his word. "Then you will welcome bad spirits along with him and invite Spirit Sucker to feed upon your sons and dogs and women!"

"We will see."

"We will wait."

"Under the Spearfish Moon he will come to the river as he has promised. By then the injured he cares for should be well enough to travel . . . or dead. We will guard his chosen campsite for him until then. If he comes bringing bad spirits, this will soon enough be evident to all."

The Spearfish Moon rose.

Salmon and shad, smelt and herring, and great sturgeon swam up the mighty river and its tributaries to spawn and be taken by hungry bears and wolves and foxes and hawks and eagles, and by the tritonged fishing spears and nets of the men, women, and children of the Great Gathering. All along the beach, drying frames were laden with spruce-skewered filets of fish. The smoke of meat-curing fires scented the air. And Avataut, with his own prodigious catch tended proudly by Nuutlaq, remembered his experiences of the previous summer with the kayakmen from upcoast and, wanting to join them on the river this season, began to cut willow branches and driftwood out of which to frame a sleek little hunting vessel of his own.

And still Tôrnârssuk did not come.

"Bad spirits must have eaten him by now, and all those foolish enough to stay at his side," Armik had said. "They should have had the good sense to turn their backs on him and come with us, Avataut. Look around. New bands are arriving every day, even True People like ourselves. Only White Bear's followers have no one to speak for us in council. You should be the one, Avataut. Yes! You should. Those True Men who have returned to the Great Gathering again this year from upcoast speak well of you, and I have overheard them say that only you are fit to be headman in Tôrnârssuk's place."

Avataut smiled as he recalled the comfort he had taken in Armik's opinion.

Others had not been as appreciative.

"We will wait."

"Under the Moon of Geese Coming Home our headman will return."

And soon the Moon of Geese Coming Home rose high in the springtime skies. The geese returned and, with them, waterfowl of all kind.

Avataut's arrows sang. The winged creatures of the sky listened and yielded their lives to him in great numbers. His skill with a bow had always been second only to that of Tôrnârssuk. Soon there was meat enough to share with Armik and any True Man who had a taste for such scrawny fare. There were feathers for fletching and fresh down for the lodge pillows, all in such abundance that, to every man at the Great Gathering whose hunting skills were not as good as his own, he gave freely of what they would have and asked nothing in return except good fellowship.

And still Tôrnârssuk did not return.

"Truly, Avataut, White Bear must be dead," assured Armik. "He would have been here by now were it not so."

"Perhaps," he conceded hopefully. As time continued to pass, when not hunting or tending his weapons and tool kit, by day he was on the beach working on his skin boat, soliciting advice from the growing number of kayakmen among his fellow Northerners and trading meat and feathers in exchange for knowledge.

"But why do you do wish to know these things and to build this kayak, Avataut of the Barrenlands, when you, an eater and hunter of land-dwelling meat, have only to wait in this good camp for the caribou to come from their summer feeding grounds to winter in this forest?"

"Because the whales will come to this good camp before the caribou. It would be an offense to the spirits of the game not to hunt them."

"But why hunt in the way of a kayakman, Avataut? Why

not go out as you did last summer with a crew of True Men on one of the big umiaks? The rest of your hunt brothers have said that when Tôrnârssuk returns they will do this as they did under the last Moon of Whales Coming Upriver. We think perhaps they believe that the big many-manned boats are safer than our little one-man kayaks, and, with White Bear to give them courage, they will not be afraid."

"White Bear gives courage only to bad spirits these days," he informed them. "And all hunters of the True People know that, whether hunting whale or caribou, alone or with many hunt brothers, no man is ever safe!"

The kayakmen nodded sagely at his last statement. "Truly we are of one People, Avataut of the Barrenlands. True People. Although we sing different songs and cut our garments out of different skins, caribou hunters and whale hunters speak the same tongue and are not afraid to look into the face of Sila and refuse to turn away."

And then, inevitably, since there had been talk of valor, there was more talk of Tôrnârssuk. Avataut had long since cast the words from his brain, but he could not forget that to a man the kayakmen lamented the news that bad spirits had fallen upon one whom they had come to admire above all men. And so, even as they praised "the Great White Bear of the North," he set himself to win that admiration for himself. It was not difficult. They grunted approval of his workmanship, eagerly instructing him in the many ways in which his little craft must be refined into a creation that would honor the spirits of the whales he intended to hunt from it. There were special amulets to be made and songs to be learned and taboos to be observed and new weapons to be fashioned. His own Barrenland hunters marveled at his newfound ambition and courage and conceded that not even Tôrnârssuk—

although he had boldly met the challenge of a sagacious old crew master from across the river and unflinchingly led his followers off whale hunting in an umiak—had sought to build his own kayak or shown the slightest inclination to venture onto the great river alone in a small boat.

"He was afraid," Avataut told his listeners. "I, Avataut, am not."

And so, by night, with his gradually evolving creation "sleeping" like a gestating infant on its stone platform on the beach close to the other kayaks, he often lay awake basking in the overwhelming joy he found in his ever-increasing status among his fellow Northerners as well as among the many bands and peoples assembled in the great camp. And often, while his woman and son lay dreaming, he rubbed his many amulets and prayed to the spirits of the Ancient Ones that Tôrnârssuk, the Great White Bear of the North, was dead.

The encampment swelled with newly arriving bands, each anxious to choose a good campsite, an optimum place to await the coming of the first whales into the great river. Many eyed the bear-bone stake rising out of high ground on the beach close to the bluffs. Many asked why the prime spot was not taken. The Northerners explained and warned all comers away—until, one day, a man not of the True People came to strike down the marker and claim the campsite as his own and Avataut found himself speaking out, striking down the bear-bone marker himself as he fought for and won what he had known then was meant to be his all along.

Again his jaw tightened until the muscles bunched and rose under the skin. He was headman of the Northerners now! At council he spoke for them among the other bands. The People called him Kwakwaje'sh, Wolverine.

His own True People smiled with pride in the name, as did he, for like a wolverine, he had proved himself fearless and powerful and predaceous enough to take for himself the den of the great White Bear of the North. No one spoke the name of Tôrnârssuk openly again. It was as though the man had died. White Bear's campsite and rank were his. Avataut had made them so!

His chest swelled with pride. Close to the beachside bluffs, his was the last and largest lodge in a line of tents raised by his fellow raiders and by two other small bands of Northerners who had recently joined them, but it was only the first in what was beginning to seem an endless array of shelters of varying shapes and sizes.

Truly the Great Gathering was not misnamed. There were bands assembled here from many diverse tribes, some from as far away as the great inland lakes, others from the southern forests, and still others from as far north as the Land of Little Trees, where men cut for trade the rare gray chert that many coveted as magic, for all knew that it was smoke turned into stone by sorcerers and that, when fashioned into arrowheads, it never missed its mark.

His brow furrowed.

In the light of day the encampment was an astounding place. So many people! True People. Forest People. Lakeland People. Grassland People. Dawnland People. All coming together along the wooded shores of the Great River of the North to trade and hunt. So much activity! So many fires! So much noise! So many children chasing one another about, harassing the dogs, ducking in and out of the many dugouts and kayaks and larger plank-and-skin-and-bark boats assembled on the beach, engaging in mock intertribal warfare, screeching and laughing at endless games. So many women of all shapes and sizes to be shared and enjoyed or admired from afar: some tattooed, some painted, some in high-peaked hats, others in tightly woven caps of grass, still others bareheaded and naked save for short little see-through skirts of fringes or feathers; all gossiping at the drying frames or at the cooking and rendering fires; some shyly flirting, others brazenly opening themselves to men in exchange for goods or for the obvious pleasure they took in attempting to prove their fecundity. And there were certainly enough men around to help them do that. Every day there was a constant parade of hunters coming and going from the sweat huts or ceremonial houses or family tents to hunt or fish or seek the portending of the mad shaman who made her lodge on the bluffs overlooking the river. In late afternoon, most men left their women and joined together in large rowdy groups within the big Man House to aggressively trade or gamble or engage in boisterous tests of hunting skills and contests of all sorts, everything from dice to shinny ball to wrestling matches to story-shouting competitions.

Avataut smiled at the overwhelming pleasure he found in his thoughts. In the light of the past many days, free of the dominating shadow of White Bear, there was nothing at which he, Wolverine, did not excel or at which he could not best even the strongest or cleverest of men. Hunters vied for his favor until, sometimes, he felt as though he had not only replaced but had actually *become* Tôrnârssuk.

His smile faded. The gash at the top of his head was throbbing as he scanned the darkness. It was the very shank of night. And now, standing naked in the rain, he could still feel the presence of the other man . . . still dominating . . . still powerful . . . still a threat.

Avataut's mouth pulled against his teeth.

He is still alive! I know it! I feel it!

He squinted off, unable to see much beyond the end of his nose. No light was visible in any of the nearby tents or on the lower span of beach. The weather was so foul that embers from the uncountable open-air fires had been gathered into protective pouches and brought inside individual lodges. No one was about. Not even the camp dogs were stirring. He shook his head. Normally, even by starlight or moonlight, his campsite yielded a commanding view of the beach and river, but tonight, with stars and moon devoured by storm clouds, only one thing was clear to him.

It is still raining!

He exhaled a hiss of anger. So much for his certainty that the storm would not come for at least another day. So much for attempting to prevent White Bear from coming north with his man-and-woman-and-dog-devouring spirits. North Wind had betrayed him! Great Spirit of All Deer had been offended by his unwillingness to pursue the wounded doe and conspired against him with the forces of Creation! All he could do now was hope that the shaman from the Cave of the Winds was wrong and that, for the sake of his band and all those along the river, White Bear was long dead or Wildfire had found and consumed him before the onset of Rain.

Ah! It must be so. What could the shaman truly know? She is female. Women have no power! I have been foolish to allow her words to lead my fear! I am Avataut! I am Wolverine! And yet . . .

His eyes narrowed. If Tôrnârssuk fulfilled his promise to return to the Great Gathering, there were some among his fellow Northerners who might choose to again name White Bear Headman—unless he staggered out of the forest badly burned with his surviving followers and dogs in the same condition, or dead. This would, of course, put truth to Avataut's warnings and assure his new and hard-won status. Or would it? He shuddered. There was something about White Bear. Something compelling. Something so forceful and commanding that, when in his presence, men automatically turned to him as to the sun on a clouded dawn.

Avataut felt suddenly tired beyond bearing. He had loped all the long way from the meadow. Confident of the route back through the forest and anxious to be safe on the shore of the great river in case North Wind turned and brought Wildfire his way, he had covered the distance in little more than half the time it had taken him to negotiate it when he had been unsure of the trail. Even so, returning to his campsite in the gray haze of a rain-sodden dusk, he had not arrived in time to take cover from the storm that so thoroughly made a mockery of all that he had tried to accomplish. Now lightning was illuminating the campsite and bluffs and the sprawl of the mighty river. He scowled but could still see . . .

No one. Nothing.

Yet, as the glow of lightning glimmered and faded, something caught Avataut's eyes. An irregularly shaped chunk of rock not much larger than his thumb lay on the ground less than a single step out from the entry to the lodge. He knelt and picked it up, glad that he had not stepped on it, for it was big enough to bruise a heel or turn an ankle. He frowned. It was not like Nuutlaq to keep the entrance to the lodge unswept. Even on days when he sat outside with his knapping tools assembled close by, busily reshaping or smoothing the edges of damaged lance points or arrowheads, she was after every errant scrap and splinter of stone that might fly off from his handiwork to trip a visitor or pierce through a moccasin or the pad of a dog's foot. He shook his head. Perhaps Ulik had been at some sort of stone-tossing game with the rowdy new friends he was making in the camp. He would have to talk to his son and woman about this in the morning.

Lightning flared again.

And in that bright instant between light and darkness, Avataut was startled to see that the object in his palm resembled one of his own fire-starting flints. His fingers curled inward as his hand moved up and down, defining the shape, texture, and weight of the stone. It could be his, he thought, but there was no way to be sure unless he checked his fire-starting bag to see if any of his flints were missing. It was possible that one or more could have fallen through a tear or a rip in the seams, but it was also unlikely. The lynx-skin carrying case was old and well worn, stolen from the cousin he had killed on the night he had broken into the man's tent to take Nuutlaq as his own. How delighted she had been by his willingness to take her forcibly from another man! Ever since that night, she tended the bag as though it were an extension of her feminine pride. The sinew threading had been replaced several times; the newest was tight and strong. The bag itself had been kept supple and sound. He was certain of this because, although confident of Nuutlaq's diligence, he checked the integrity of his traveling gear every time he prepared to set off from the encampment for even the shortest time. A man could never completely trust a woman, and he could never be careful enough when on the hunting or raiding trail. There was always danger. Always! That had been one of the few lessons that White Bear had not had to teach him in those long-gone days when they had first hunted and raided together as though they were brothers. And yet, now that he thought about it, when the wind had awakened him in the pale light of yesterday's dawn and inspired him to set fire to the distant meadow in the hope of assuring that he would never set eyes on White Bear again, he had been in such an impassioned hurry to accomplish his purpose that he had not bothered to . . .

Someone laughed.

Avataut looked up.

He caught his breath. Someone *was* there. Standing only a few paces off, motionless in the rain, a tall pale form all but hidden by the night.

"White Bear!" Avataut was on his feet in an instant. His heart was pounding. He dropped the flint and gripped his lance with both hands, held it out, threatening. "I will not yield this camp to you. Take your bad spirits and go away. I am headman now!"

"But for how long?"

Avataut's hands tightened on the shaft of his spear. He did not recognize the interloper's voice. It was deep, as Tôrnârssuk's voice was deep, but it was different in every other way, husky, identifiable as neither masculine nor feminine, oddly flat and yet, at the same time, somehow hollow in its resonant expression of mockery.

Again lightning flared.

Thunder cracked.

Avataut flinched. He heard footsteps now, the sudden slosh and suck of woven sandals as the intruder turned and hurried across sodden ground toward the bluffs. Following with his eyes, he saw the pale form scrambling up the zigzag trail to the wooded heights. Recognition dawned. He felt a deep chill.

"Inau!" The name of the shaman from the distant Cave of the Winds escaped his lips. Again he shivered. Violently. What was she doing prowling around his camp in the dead of night? As far as he knew, she never left the immediate surroundings of the solitary lodge of sod and whale bones that she had constructed against an ancient sand dune high on the bluffs. Others went to her, bringing choice cuts of meat or fish or prime furs or feathers in exchange for fetishes and prophecy. He had never done so. Nor would he!

There was something unnatural about Inau. Something that made his skin crawl. Sometimes, when she stood alone on the bluffs staring out across the river, he would find himself looking at her and would be unable to turn his eyes away. It was said among the Dawnland People that the woman was a seer and magic maker without whose songs the whales would not come into the great river from the distant sea. But Avataut did not believe this for a moment. Nor did any other Northerner he knew of. Since the time beyond beginning, bands of his own True People had been journeying across the Barrenlands to hunt white whales in the icy bays of a great salt sea that lay at the northernmost edge of the world. His own kinsmen had always been hunters of caribou, but the stories of those distant cousins who sought the great mammoths of the sea in tiny vessels made of the skins of seals were told in the winter dark. Ah, what stories they were! Tales to ignite the imagination and fill a young boy's dreams with images of blood and meat and glory. And in those dreams and ancient tales of death and valor, always a male shaman called the white whales. Never a woman. Never!

His mouth tightened in revulsion at the thought of the shaman's pale, bony, beaky face—too much like the skull of one of the great whales whose bones walled up her lodge and to whom she sang in the depth of night. And no matter how hot the day, her hair hung in a curtaining black cascade to below her knees, the thick strands overlying an ankle-length cloak made of ropes of sea shells and winter-white ermine and fox tails and owl feathers.

Lightning was again illuminating the clouds, a pale light this time, so transient that it was gone before Avataut could fully refocus on the bluff. Yet the light had lingered long enough to allow him to see that Inau had disappeared into the trees. He was relieved, and yet, at the same time, angered and discomfited by her trespass. Why had she come? Why had she spoken to mock him? A ripple of suspicion roused a shiver. What if she truly was a seer? What if she knew what he had been about this day? No! He would not believe it. No female could possess such power. On the off chance that she was watching from the wooded heights, he raised his right arm and belligerently shook his lance to warn her against future intrusions.

"I am not afraid of you!" he called out to her in the darkness. "Stay away!"

Lightning cracked the sky again.

Unsettled, he turned and went back into his lodge.

▼▼▼▼▼

Time.

Avataut could feel it passing with every slow and silently drawn breath, mocking him as the shaman from the Cave of the Winds had mocked him. Kneeling just inside the weather baffle, lance in hand, he did not know how long he remained on his knees, waiting.

For what?

Did he expect Inau to return? Or did he still expect the specter of Tôrnârssuk to come to him out of the storm?

Impatience pricked him. Or was it guilt?

"Never!" He had had enough of rain and storm-lit

darkness. With his mind in a tumult of self-serving justification of the treachery he had wrought against one beside whom he had once so proudly hunted as a brother, Avataut managed to shrug off any vestigial feelings of loyalty to his former headman. Closing the weather baffle, he laid down his lance, then reached for one of the old buckskins that Nuutlaq kept piled by the entryway for just such contingencies. After impatiently toweling himself off, he went to his side of the mattress, burrowed deep beneath the sleeping furs, and pulled Nuutlaq close for warmth.

"Eeeah!" she exclaimed. "You are so cold. And your hair is still wet!"

"It will dry. And you will warm me." Shivering violently, he bent his head. The wound in his scalp was no longer throbbing. He buried his face in his woman's breasts to avoid the foul scent of her breath, and slowly began to relax a little as he felt the warmth of her skin emanating into his own.

"I thought that you would kneel at the entrance to the lodge all night, my husband."

"Mmm."

"Listen. It is still raining." She sighed contentedly and began to massage his back with the heels of her strong, callused, stubby little hands. "With fire burning to the south all day, we thought the storm would never come."

He tensed. "Why do you remind me of this?" Indeed, why was she speaking to him at all? It was not like Nuutlaq to be so talkative. For the second time this night a ripple of suspicion roused a shiver. Did she, along with the madwoman on the bluffs, suspect what he had been up to this day? Did anyone—or everyone—in the great camp suspect? He cursed his luck if this was so. He had put them all at risk. But he had no regrets. His cause was just. What he had done had been for the good of his woman, son, and band, for the entire gathering. Yes! He had done it for them. Almost as much as for himself.

"I have been meaning to speak ever since you returned, my husband. You left camp so quickly and with so few words to me or anyone else. Not knowing into which part of the forest you had gone to hunt and speak to the spirits of the game, no one knew where to search for you. There was no way to warn you that Wildfire was dancing in the forest. Had she consumed you, my Wolverine would have been greatly missed by all who have come to name you Headman in this camp . . . and by this woman and our son."

"Mmm." So that was it. She wanted him to know how much she needed him. How much they all needed him. He would not criticize her for this.

"Many feared for you, Avataut."

"Mmm." This was pleasant news; he was relaxing again, smiling as he closed his eyes and felt the first incursions of sleep moving beneath his lids.

"And many feared that North Wind would turn and bring Wildfire to feed upon us."

His eyes batted open. He was tense again. "There was little chance of that," he snapped defensively.

"Little is more than none. The shaman from the Cave of the Winds saw our fear and sang to the rain spirits on our behalf. Inau is truly powerful, my husband. Rain has come at her command."

"Has it?" His mood had gone as dark as the interior of the lodge. Even if Nuutlaq's words were true, the madwoman would receive no thanks from him.

"Ah, Avataut, my heart sings with joy now that you are safely back and Armik and the other scouts have returned from downriver. Is it not good to recall the news they brought to us while you were away, my husband? Whales sighted off the great cliffs that rise out of deep water where the river opens to the sea! Many whales! White whales! Soon they will enter the river and the great hunt will begin. And this season, my Wolverine, you shall go out with the others in a fine sleek boat of your own! What you take shall be ours. All of it. With not a shred given in tribute to the boat master of the umiaks. Ah, Avataut, I am a caribou- and deer-eating woman, but truly I have come to savor the flesh of whales! And now my blood sings with pride, for my man is the best and the bravest of all men to seek this meat for me!"

Avataut made no reply. Normally talk of his intent to take his own little vessel out hunting whales on the great river set his own blood afire with pride. Now he was seething. He should have been the one to go off downriver with the scouts of the lesser tribes, but he had wanted to put the finishing touches on his kayak and so had chosen to stay behind. Only to be seduced into going to the meadow by the promise of North Wind. Only to see Rain ruin the wildfire he had set in hope of stopping White Bear forever in his tracks. And now news of the coming of the white whales utterly demeaned the value of the fawn he had brought to his woman across the miles. It was enough to make a man snarl and spit disgust, which he did.

Nuutlaq paid no heed. She yawned and enveloped her husband in her spongy embrace. "Now I can sleep again. My man is in my arms. Our son sleeps warm and content on his side of our lodge. The worst of the storm has moved to the south. Even now rain must be falling on the smoking land. That which brought us to fear for you and for ourselves will no longer be a danger to us."

"Or to anyone else," he added sourly.

She cuddled close, asking sleepily, "Do you think that he is still out there?"

"He . . . ?"

"You spoke his name. Tôrnârssuk's name. So fearfully you spoke it. And warned him away. For a moment I was certain that he had at last returned. Ah! Ever since the shaman Inau foresaw the coming of a great white bear and warned all to be on guard against it, his name has been a whispering in the minds of everyone who once named him Headman."

Avataut shivered again. Nuutlaq's body warmed his flesh. Her words chilled his soul. "No hunter in this camp needs a shaman, much less a woman, to warn him of the dangers of the white bears that come on the pack ice from the northern sea in season to hunt all the way down the coast as far as the shores of the great river and beyond."

"I do not speak of a bear, my husband." Nuutlaq was enjoying the conversation. Rarely did they find much cause to converse with one another. Now that they were doing so, she was not about to be put off by his obvious attempt at evasion. "I speak of a man. A man who once raised his lodge on this very spot and may yet return to claim it. A man within whose spirit prowls the spirit of a bear. A white bear. A man who is feared and yet—"

"I know of whom you speak!" Avataut's temper caught fire. He did not care about Nuutlaq's fears, nor did he wish to hear any more about them. He was male. She was female. He would take care of her or she would die. This was his concern, not hers. But it astounded him to realize that she had overheard him speak in a way that had brought her to believe that he was capable of being afraid. And by daring to tell him so to his face, she had shamed him. As the madwoman had attempted to shame him. And as Hasu'u had so thoroughly succeeded in doing.

Thoughts of Tôrnârssuk's captive roused a sudden and inexpressible convulsion of emotion in Avataut as he took hold of Nuutlaq's wrists, forced her arms back and down, and moved to straddle her. With memories of White Bear's woman flaring in his mind, his anger centered in his loins. Despite fatigue, he was hard and hot and throbbing, seeking—as was his way whenever with captive women on the raiding trail— to penetrate and overwhelm with a demonstration of his overriding male power and capacity to inflict pain. Pinning Nuutlaq's wrists to the bed furs, he rammed a knee between her thighs. "By the power of Sila, woman, if you fear any man in all of this world, you had best fear me!"

A little gasp of surprise went out of her. Nuutlaq could not remember Avataut ever before showing displeasure with her. Their eyes met. Even in the darkness she saw his rage and understood his intent. Something long dormant flexed and stirred within her. He had killed a man to win her. He had raped her afterward. In his cousin's lodge, with the dead man lying close, eyes blankly staring, brains spattered on the bed skins and blood seeping from his nose and mouth and ears, Avataut had held her down and, with the blood of the dead man slick beneath them, mounted her. He had smothered her cries with his mouth as he lanced her again and again with the driving heat of his maleness. What an honor it had been! To be stolen from another man! To be so forcefully mated! Few women were so desired. Her father and brothers had said as much. Her mother had been proud of the daughter who was the envy of every woman and girl in the band. And afterward—when not one of the cousin's brothers or uncles had been brave enough to challenge Avataut and had, instead, skulked away, dishonored—under the first moon beneath which they had shared a lodge, Avataut had raped her many times. Or so he thought. It had not really been rape. Not even the first time. She had enjoyed it far too much.

Now, feeling the fevered press of his need moving as though with a life of its own against her belly, for the first time in longer than she could remember, Nuutlaq's woman place was warm and moist and hungry to receive her man. Truly, she thought, he *was* like a wolverine! So strong! So bold! So eager to raid and steal and keep for himself all that weaker predators were unable to hold as their own. He was making her feel young again! Gone was Mother of Many who had seen all but one of her children die. Gone was Wife and Burden Carrier and Maker of Meat and Provider of Pelts and Hides and Sinew and Fat. Gone was the compliant receptacle she had allowed herself to become when younger women were not available to him and he entered and released into her with no more enthusiasm than he took in urination. Now, like the bride she had twice been, Nuutlaq was Eager Woman, trembling, gasping in anticipation as she opened her limbs and arched her hips to him, wondering what she could possibly have said to so change his manner toward her. She must think! She must remember!

"Ah!" she cried out with delight as he thrust deep. In an ecstasy of long-unsavored sensation, she remembered telling him that she had overheard him speaking fearfully of Tôrnârssuk. So that was it! Long ago similar words had provoked him to lust when, bored with her first husband, she had sought Avataut's gaze and told him that it was a pity he was not brave enough to take her from her man because, if he could summon enough courage to do so, he would become the best of all men in her eyes and she would open her thighs to his every pleasure. "Ah!" she gasped as he withdrew and, wanting it to be as it had once been between them, panted, "If White Bear comes to take back this fine camp into which you, the best of all men, have brought this woman, would you be afraid to fight him, my Wolverine? Would you be afraid to kill him . . . for me?"

"For you?" He found the premise pathetic, but saw through her attempt at flattery even as he misconstrued it as an effort to avoid rape. He thrust deep again. "So you still find me the best of all men?"

"Yes, my husband, yes! All say that this is so! You are Wolverine . . . bold . . . without fear!"

"And yet you fear that I will lose this prime camp to another man?"

"Not just to another. To Tôrnârssuk! He is White Bear! Only the best of all men could defeat him."

So, thought Avataut, even in his absence Tôrnârssuk somehow managed to make other men look small. He was so angry and frustrated that not even Nuutlaq's sour breath could distract him as he pulled back and again drove deep, wanting to prove his size, to savage her with it, to punish her for her lack of faith in him as he would punish White Bear's woman if he ever had a chance to take Hasu'u down and hold her beneath him like this.

Nuutlaq was moaning.

Within the darkness of the lodge, Ulik peered from beneath his sleeping furs. "Is my mother sick?"

"Go back to sleep! Your mother is my concern, not yours!"

The boy, only four winters old, made an utterance of hurt dismay, pulled the bed furs over his head, and said no more.

Avataut could not have cared less about his son. He was huge now. Surely not even White Bear could equal him! The head of his man bone was so engorged and sensitive that he could barely contain the swelling throb of liquid heat within it. Closing his eyes, he threw back his head, balanced on his

palms, and imagined himself pounding another woman . . .
White Bear's woman . . . young, beautiful, doe-eyed Hasu'u,
naked and sweated and writhing beneath him, her tawny
thighs splayed wide, glistening with . . .

The image was too much.

Now it was Avataut who cried out in ecstasy as he emptied himself into his woman in a release of such violent and
exhausting passion that, when it was spent, he collapsed
onto her and then rolled away to lie like a corpse, as though
he had died from the sheer pleasure of it.

▼▼▼▼▼

He slept.

And dreamed of a heart-struck doe being savaged by
wolves and bears, and then awoke, on his back, staring into
vaulted darkness, listening.

The rain had stopped.

The lodge was quiet save for the sound of Nuutlaq
sucking on her gums in her sleep and the soft, adenoidal
snoring of his son.

Time had passed since he had last awakened—a good
amount of it, judging by the texture of the night around him.
It was thinner. Softer. Almost transparent. And yet the first
blue haze of dawn had yet to seep into the interior of the
lodge. Sunrise and the full light of morning were still a while
off. Somewhere outside, a dog barked, and on the bluffs
above the Great River of the North, the shaman was singing
to white whales.

Avataut closed his eyes. He had no interest in the song of
Inau. It had long since become as the song of the great river
to him, a familiar thing, a smooth, darkly flowing sigh that
was, by its very nature, peripheral to all that was important

to him. Now, yawning, he drifted back into sleep and, dreaming of himself swimming with white whales, did not know that he spoke aloud or that he smiled as he smacked his lips and vowed, "I, Avataut, say this. I will take many whales! All True Men will praise me! I *am* the best of men. If Tôrnârssuk returns, I will kill him. And I will take his woman. Who is there to stop me?"

Chapter Two

▼▼▼▼▼▼▼

She was a wolf.

A black wolf. Wild. Free. As bold and savage as those wolves of old from whose loins it was said that she and her kind had sprung, Mowea'qua ran howling, calling back over her shoulder to Kinap.

"Follow me, my father! Come! Together we will run for-ever. Yes! No others need we! Follow, say I, follow!"

He did not hesitate.

Under the shadowing wings of ravens, across the vast gray Barrenlands of the wild girl's dream, the giant ran at his daughter's heels, no man at all, but wolf, huge, scar-faced, grizzled with age, yet as fleet of foot as a youth, and as strong.

The world spread out before them. Blue sky above. No clouds anywhere to be seen. The sun stood at the very apex of noon. A white sun. An Arctic sun. It was the cold, com-passionless eye of the Creator of All, and it stared down un-blinkingly at its shape-changing children as the girl and the giant raced on in the skins of wolves beneath the shadowing flight of ravens.

Kinap took the lead.

"Wait!" Mowea'qua called out to him.

He did not wait.

She extended her elongated, sleekly furred head and ran on after him. She kept her ears high and her eyes focused ahead. Her heart and lungs meted out only strength enough to sustain her long, four-legged, earth-eating stride. The rest of her energy she held in check for the hunt to come; there was no use in squandering it. Feeling for balance through the pads of her feet, Mowea'qua drew into her nostrils the coolness of a wind born not only of the restless tides of air that eternally swept both earth and sky, but of the speed of her movement as she cut forward through the air across a dreamscape that was as vast and glorious as any to be found when the world was new.

"Hay ya!" she cried.

It was the time beyond beginning!

She had left the world of warring tribes and bickering bands behind and entered the ancient tundral hunting grounds of the Ancestors! Her grandmother had described it many times. Here she would find no True People or Dawnland People or Forest People or Grassland People or People of the Inland Lakes. Here there would be no people at all! First Man and First Woman were yet to be born. And those of the Old Tribe were wolves, as her grandmother had always sworn, black wolves hunting and feeding among all other animals upon a treeless plain as they fought to maintain their place within the eternal Circle of Life Ending and Life Beginning.

The world was bending up ahead, curving away to a horizon rimmed by soaring mountains of ice. Mowea'qua followed Kinap up the slanting side of what seemed to be a massive sand dune. As he gained the top and continued to race along the hard-packed spine of the esker, she leaped onto the tallest of several monolithic boulders and stood alone, panting, exulting in the cold white splendor of the moment.

She was a wolf! Truly a wolf at last! Tongue lolling, ribs heaving, her body was aflame with a sensory excitement such as she had never known. Everything was brighter, clearer. She could focus so far ahead that she could make out the individual silver guard hairs on Kinap's tail as he loped along, headed for only he knew where. With no effort at all she heard insects gnawing away at some sort of softwood buried in the depths of the granular soil that underlay the boulder upon which she stood. She discerned the aroma of decomposing stone and picked up a strong fungal essence from the black lichens that grew beneath her feet. A hawk had perched here a while back; she could tell because, although he had left no stain of his passing upon the rock, she could smell the scurf and oil and mites that had clung to the skin between his feathers.

Cocking her head, she shuttered her eyes and sent a part of her vision focusing inward. Her olfactory senses sent intensely colorful and startling images to her brain. She could see as well as smell the foxes and tundral wolves and mice and voles and ground squirrels and marmots that all came to dig in the soft sand of the esker and shelter there at one time or another in their respective burrows beneath the great stone and the many boulders that surrounded it. With the power of this inner eye she saw as well the scented beetles and spiders and ants, all busy within the earth. And upon the land she sensed all that had passed this way before, and saw the vast herds of Barrenland caribou and the mighty brown bears and mightier mammoths and strange beasts that she did not know—huge fang-toothed cats and spotted lions, and deer of many kind, some with necks like cranes and humps on their backs and stubs for antlers, and others smaller, antlerless, with sweeping manes and tails and a grace and beauty of form that touched her heart so that she nearly wept to think that they were among the creatures that the People had hunted from beneath the sky.

Then, with a catch of startled breath, she felt the growing force of thunder rising from the earth and into the stone.

Her eyes opened wide. Her head went high.

Thunder roaring in the ground?

"Impossible!"

And yet, with another startled intake of breath, Mowea'qua realized that she was wrong. She could see the source of the thunder.

"Caribou!"

The herd was enormous. It was a tide, a living storm surge of flesh and blood and bone, of tossing antlers, pounding hooves, raised tails and snouts and slobbering jaws, all moving toward her from out of the towering white glacial massif that walled off the edge of the world.

She saw Kinap turn and begin to run toward her ahead of the living tide that was oversweeping the esker.

"Hurry!" she urged him on.

The caribou were closing on him.

No man could outrun them. Not even a giant.

But this was Mowea'qua's dream, and she called the terms that determined what could or could not be. Her father was no mere man. Nor was he only a giant. He was a wolf. A dark and dangerous wolf. No caribou could outrun him. And suddenly, at her will, as ravens circled overhead, Kinap was leaping up and out to take his place beside his daughter atop the monolith, and the two of them were standing side by side as the tumultuous sea of life streamed past them and poured on and away across the world.

Kinap threw back his head and howled.

Mowea'qua, delighting in their closeness, did the same. In the next moment, following his lead, she was leaping out, flying with ravens it seemed, hurling herself onto the back of a caribou straggler and, with Kinap still in the lead, biting and growling and exulting in the primordial savagery of their kill.

They ate together, father and daughter sharing all, savoring meat and blood and bone and innards almost as much as the filial camaraderie of their feast until, looking up, Mowea'qua saw the first of a large pack of feral dogs coming to contest for meat.

She snarled. Warned them away. The wolf in her had always hated dogs.

And yet they kept on coming.

Dog after dog they came . . . slavering . . . circling . . . closing around her . . . swarming like flies, biting flies . . . attacking her. She called out to her father for help, but to her horror, Kinap growled as he cast off the pelt in which he had been running. He was a part of the pack now, no longer wolf, but dog.

"It cannot be!" she sobbed.

"I am now what I have been born to be," he told her. "Too long have I allowed your kind to stand in the way of all that would pleasure me."

"Please, my father, this you cannot mean! Leave me to them you must not!"

"I will not leave you," he said. And he was as good as his word as he set himself to devour her.

"No!" she wept, flailing and kicking out at him in desperation. It was no use. He was too strong. Her own strength failed her. She withered beneath his predations.

Death would come for her now.

She knew it. Felt its approach. Again she sobbed, knowing that there was nothing she could do to save herself.

And then, in a single shadowing instant, the dream shifted.

Mowea'qua could not be sure just when Kinap and the other dogs turned tail and ran.

The world had gone quiet.

She was aware of an immense cold shadow falling over her and, summoning up the last of her strength, found just enough to raise her head and look up.

The dogs were gone.

There was no sign of Kinap.

The herd of caribou and the circling ravens had vanished.

Only Mowea'qua, all at once terrified and spellbound by the chilling beauty and power of that which stood over her, dared to hold her ground before the menacing great white bear of the north that, like the dogs before him, had come unbidden into her mind to claim sovereignty of her dream.

"I am the One Who Gives Power," said the bear, standing upright in the way of a man, with the sun at his back and a raven perching on his shoulder. "I am Wíndigo, Great Ghost Cannibal, Brother to Raven, Winter Chief of the manitous. I am Tunraq, Guardian and Guide into the world of spirits. You will walk with me now."

▼▼▼▼

"Mowea'qua! Do not cry out again! Wake up, Wolf Woman! You endanger us both. You must be still, I say! Your Muskrat will not leave you!"

"Muskrat . . . ?" Mowea'qua opened her eyes.

"I come!"

Startled by the high, breathy, declarative voice of the child, she raised her head to find herself sitting upright in a small lean-to with her arms wrapped about her knees. She blinked away sleep and, her mind still fogged with a residue of fading dreams, looked out to see what seemed to be Tôrnârssuk coming toward her.

"Ah!" Terror bit at the back of her throat, closing off her vocal cords and preventing a scream even as her heart gave an unexpected lurch of pleasure, then promptly sank with disappointment.

She shook her head.

White Bear was not coming for her.

She should be glad! He was Death! Her dream had just proclaimed him so. And yet she felt no sense of reprieve as her gaze cleared and her eyes fixed, not on a man at all, but on a skinny little boy hurrying from a nearby thicket behind which he had evidently just been relieving himself.

Mowea'qua frowned as Musquash paused before her. Over his traveling cape of muskrat pelts he had slung a baggy, hooded rain cloak of greased gut skins. It shone white and slick in the dank light of the rising sun as the boy puffed out his chest and flashed a reassuring smile while shaking his minuscule penis dry with one hand and tugging at his breechclout with the other.

"Did you miss me?" he asked.

She rolled her eyes. What a baby he was! "A gnat I would miss more!" She was not happy to see him and saw no reason to say otherwise. Indeed, recalling the circumstances that had brought them to this moment, she found the child about as welcome as the wad of spruce sap that had stuck to the bottom of her moccasin last night. Surely the boy was just as annoying and difficult to lose.

Mowea'qua's frown became a scowl. Her battered face felt tight and sore. Her own gut-skin rain cloak smelled of rancid bear and raccoon grease. The raven's feather that she had braided into her forelock the previous day lay sodden against her cheek. She peeled it loose and, absently smoothing it between the thumb and index finger of her right hand, peered from beneath the sagging front of the shelter of bent saplings and hastily unfurled moose hide under which she and the boy had spent the night huddled together.

The woodland was dark despite the light of the new day. Spruces in the main, heavy-armed, sag-headed. Branches bearded with long, blackish strands of tree lichens. And all standing close around the little shelter. Too close. Threatening somehow. Ominous in ways that Mowea'qua could not define. She scanned around. Everything was familiar. And nothing was familiar.

She held her breath, listening, waiting for the resident spirits of this part of the forest to speak to her in the morning wind and offer assurance that she was welcome and would come to no harm in this place.

But there was no wind.

There was no sound at all except for the occasional rhythmic plop of water dripping from the trees. If the kami were speaking, she could not hear their ancestral spirit voices. Nor had she heard them last night when she and the boy swam from the sandbar to retrieve the considerable pile of belongings that Musquash had managed to assemble secretly on the beach.

She exhaled softly, trembling as she recalled that second nighttime swim during which she had once again been moved to near panic by visions of water monsters rising from below to devour her. Now even the slightest movement of her aching body reminded her of just how far they had come since emerging from the water to hastily don their clothes, load up their pack frames, and hurry off into the darkness. The fear she had felt in the water had followed her. Not fear of beasts conjured from her father's tales, but a sure and all-too-tangible fear of the men who might soon be hunting her. Panic dogged her every step as she and the boy made their way deep into the benighted forest until, at last, the sounds of Tôrnârssuk's encampment could no longer be heard and the full power of a raging thunderstorm forced them to stop and take cover. Yet, even though they had weapons with them and the lean-to they had raised kept them dry enough to attempt to rest, they had not slept easily.

Now it was morning.

The forest was silent, so silent that, to the wild girl's intensely keen senses, it seemed to be holding its breath, or to have died. No, she thought, it was not dead. It was merely resting. The forest was, after all, a living entity, a vast and infinitely complex and all-enveloping sentient organism within which she was but one of many parts. No doubt it was as wearied and relieved as she to have seen the great storm come and go its way with its tumultuous downpours and fractious displays of lightning and violent spits of hail.

"It will be all right, Mowea'qua," said Musquash. "Do not look so sad. We have come far. Now we must be up and on our way again. In case we have been followed."

She cocked her head. The trees were misting yellow in the bilious sunlight. Her brow furrowed. On second thought, the forest did not look relieved to be free of the storm. It appeared as bruised and exhausted by it as she. Sadness coupled with hunger to form a hollow in her belly. "Has no one called out to us?"

"No one. Nor would they call, Mowea'qua. If they follow

us, they will come in silence. If they find us, they will want to kill you. But you must not worry. I will allow no harm to come to you. It is good that you have been able to sleep even though you cried out to our father and begged him to protect you. Kinap will not do this, Mowea'qua. He has made a new family with Suda'li. You must forget him. And you must learn to be quiet! I have kept watch over you all night. You are safe with me, but until Tôrnârssuk leads his followers away from the lake and north to the great river, we will have enemies in this forest."

"Mmph. Yes. I remember now. Bog Rat will protect Wolf Woman."

"And so!"

She cocked her head to the other side and looked at him out of speculatively lowered eyelids. "Go back should you, say I."

"Me?"

"Is there in this wood someone else to whom I should be speaking?"

"Go back?"

"Yes, Echo, go back now. If the way you can find."

He looked around. Worry tightened his face. He shrugged it off and replied hotly, "I could find my way if I wanted to, but I will not leave you alone."

"No one has sworn to kill you, Muskrat."

"But Tôrnârssuk has sworn to kill you, Mowea'qua. And so, to defend you against him, I will stay at your side. I am not afraid!"

"Yah!" She could not have said why she was suddenly so angry with him. He was so small! So confident! So full of bold pronouncements that would have seemed foolish even if he were twice his age and size. And he was willing to put himself forward to risk everything for her. She could not understand him. She had never been nice to him. Nor did she wish to be nice to him now. "You are a man not! A stubborn, arrogant little puffball are you!"

He was not in the least stung by the insult. Instead, he fisted up his hands and trotted in place, jabbing left and right and forward and back with a make-believe spear at conjured enemies. Then, leaping forward to snatch up one of the lances that stood upright beside the lean-to, he jabbed the air and boasted, "You will see how this puffball will confound our enemies!"

Mowea'qua was not amused. Images of her dream had not completely faded from her mind. Dogs leaping to the attack. Savage dogs. And Kinap one of them. Hurting her. Devouring her. No, she thought. She would not believe her father capable of that. Kinap might well have turned his back on her forever in despair of her constant defiance of his authority, but if others sought her death, he would have no hand in it. If others hunted her, he would not be among them. He could never be her enemy. Never! It was the other dream specter she must fear. The great white bear of the north. The enemy that had appeared within her dream at what had seemed to be the moment of her death, not to save her, but to escort her into the world of spirits. She wrapped her arms more tightly about her knees to keep from trembling. "Will you Tôrnârssuk fight and confound if he comes for us, Puffball?"

"As bravely as I fought the twin sons of Suda'li!"

"And end flat on your belly spitting leaves? Mmph! What good would this do me?"

"I can fight! I can win! Against any man!"

His audacity was beyond belief. "At yourself look! Like a

baby grouse you strut and boast with stains of your own body water steaming on the buckskin that covers your little boy bone! Fight against any man? Ha! Yourself you do not even know how to shake dry!"

Musquash cast a quick glance at his loin cover, blushed as red as a pine grosbeak, and just as quickly cast aside his lance and slapped his hands over the truth. Aghast, he stammered, "It is n-not what you th-th-think! It . . . it is . . . is only r-r-rain . . . r-raindrops!"

A coldness touched Mowea'qua's spirit. He looked so distraught, so ashamed, so utterly humiliated. She knew that she had at last managed to wound his pride. True, the boy had more than enough of that for both of them, but despite his tendency to bombast and his almost painful expressions of earnestness, he meant well for her. She had no doubt of that. And perhaps, now that she thought about it, her anger was not really with him at all. It was with herself. Because of her outburst of temper last night on the beach, she was Outcast and Orphan—and so was he. His loyalty shamed her. She should never have allowed him to put his own place at Kinap's fire or within the band at risk for her sake. Such selfishness was not worthy of his affection, much less of her father's love or of Ne'gauni's gratitude. Her lower lip and chin began to quiver. She was of the Old Tribe, and the Old Tribe was no more. The People wanted no part of her. Sitting here now, reflecting on her situation and the circumstances to which she had brought the boy, Mowea'qua could not blame them.

"You must not cry," Musquash said softly. He was crouching before her now, drawing the bottom edges of his rain cloak up over his thighs and fisting them into his lap to cover the telltale stain of his youthful inefficiency. "In the stories that Kinap tells of the Ancient Ones, Wolf Woman never cries."

Taken aback by his gentle admonition, Mowea'qua reached up and was surprised to find tears not only welling in her eyes but sliding down her cheeks. Disgusted with herself and confused by just how deeply she was moved by the boy's tender expression of concern, she fingered them impatiently away as she said, with a noticeable catch in her voice, "This is not a story, Muskrat."

"We will make it one!" declared the boy, bright-eyed and smiling once again. "Yes! It will be for us as it was in the time beyond beginning. And a fine story it will be. Muskrat and Mowea'qua will share many fine adventures together!" He lowered his voice and, excited, whispered a revelation. "There *are* mammoths in this forest. Last night, when you were deep asleep, I heard them rumbling with the thunder. I peeked out of the lean-to, Mowea'qua. I was very brave. There was nothing outside. Only rain and darkness. I started to duck back inside, and just as lightning flashed, I saw something. Something big! It was gone with the flash. But I think it was a mammoth, Mowea'qua . . . a white mountain of a mammoth passing with its herd in the night. It was Great Chief of all mammoths, Mowea'qua. It had to be!"

"Mmph! A figment of a dream it was! Another story!"

"No! No story! And, well, maybe a dream, but what if it was not? If it was Great Chief out there in the storm, then he is not the last of his kind, and so we will hunt him. We will eat him! His strength will be our strength. His wisdom will be our wisdom. You will see. It will be so, Mowea'qua."

"Sacred is the great one. Against him or any of his kind I will send no spear or arrow. Nor will you."

He wrinkled up his face to suppress annoyance with one whom he wished only to please. Then, affably, he gave one of his careless little shrugs and declared, "We will see. In the meantime we have the sacred stone of the Ancient Ones to grant us the strength of the Ancestors! We have the spirit that lives in the feather of Raven to guide us and grant us wisdom! The forces of Creation are smiling on us, Mowea'qua. I am sure of it!"

She envied his enthusiasm and might have been cheered by it had an owl not begun to *ooh* in the spruce wood.

A shiver went up Mowea'qua's back.

Another owl answered.

She went rigid. Owls were creatures of the night. Why would they be calling to one another in the light of the rising sun? Surely the prey they sought had taken refuge from their sharp beaks and questing talons long before now? Shivering again, she recalled how upset Goh'beet had been the night before when owls had spoken outside the periphery of the band circle. What if the People were right? What if owls were not birds at all? What if they truly were the ghosts of lost souls crying out to the living to remind them of the brevity of life?

"What is it, Mowea'qua? Why do you look so worried?"

"Owls . . . by day they speak . . ."

He made another face, this time to show how foolish he found her. "Storms must have kept them from hunting for most of last night. Now that Rain has gone its way with Lightning, Thunder, and Hail, Owl and his kind are out and about looking for a little something to eat so they can go back to sleep for the rest of the day and then hunt again tonight without their bellies growling to give them away. Truly, Mowea'qua, you must not be afraid. I am with you.

And I know a story about an owl. Yes! A story about a snowy white owl who set off alone to the edge of the world to seek Great Chief of all the mammoths and—"

"Yah! Alone are we! Hunted we may be! If the kami of this part of the forest are speaking, I cannot hear them. Things are for us not good, Puffball. A time this is not for stories!"

"Kinap says that all life is a story."

"Kinap is here not. Never again will his face we see." The statement brought a stab of pain to her heart. It was all she could do to keep herself from bursting into tears. Could it really be true? Would she never again see her beloved giant or hear his rumbling laughter or stand in awe at the soaring height of him as he danced and beat upon his drum and recounted the tales of the Ancient Ones for all who beheld and listened to him? And would she never again see Ne'gauni, her solemn, sad-eyed Wounded One, or walk proudly beside him, enjoying their endless jousts with words and knowing that, save for her Old Tribe healing magic, the spirit of his life would have left him long ago? And would she never stand with him and Kinap, exulting together at all of the many wonders to be found at the Great Gathering of Many Tribes on the shores of the River of the North in which whales of many colors swam, singing to the stars?

"You are crying again, Wolf Woman. In the stories that Kinap tells, Wolf Woman is never sad. Wolf Woman is never—"

"Enough!" She could bear his prattle no longer. Angry again, she snapped to her feet, inadvertently pulling the moose-hide cover of the lean-to up with her so that it hung from the top of her head and dropped around her shoulders. "Stare not at Mowea'qua, Puffball! Pick up that lance that you have so carelessly thrown aside. And then gather up your things. Linger here in the country of owls we must not, for now say these words do I: If a story this truly is, then afraid you had better be, because you are only a foolish little boy and this woman is no wolf, and only the kami can say how or when it will end for us!"

Chapter Three

▼▼▼▼▼▼▼

I tell you she is gone! Are we going to stand here and do nothing?"

Ne'gauni flinched at the angry snap of Moraq's voice. It was coming from somewhere down the beach and a good distance off, but it was a sound that he had no wish to wake to. Grimacing, it occurred to him that he was truly coming to loathe the man.

Sitting upright within the shelter that he and Kinap had hurriedly raised against last night's storm, he reached for his crutches, begrudging the beginning of a headache and the advent of morning.

He had not slept well. The previous night had been enough to put a corpse on edge. The threat of Wildfire. The rising of the red moon. Mowea'qua's daring and defiant run into the night. His confrontation with Moraq. The call to the spirit dance. The unexpected closeness of Hasu'u. And then the storm.

By all the forces of Creation, had he truly summoned it?

"No."

Ne'gauni could not bring himself to believe it. Old Ko'ram had waved aside his doubts and sworn to him that it was so.

He shook his head. At the first drop of rain and the first rumble of thunder, the old man had rammed an arm skyward, shaken his rattle, and hop-danced about in wind-loosing, caterwauling celebration of Someday Shaman's success.

"May the forces of Creation be praised! Truly I am Teacher! Truly our Dreamer has learned his lessons well! Truly Someday Shaman is now Shaman Indeed!"

Ne'gauni frowned. He was still ill-at-ease with Ko'ram's assertions and with his recollection of the way Kinap had then taken him aside. With an avuncular arm slung around his shoulders, the giant had advised that it would be to his advantage and that of his family not to argue with the old man. He was right, of course, but even so, Ne'gauni sensed a great yawning pitfall on the far side of taking credit for commanding the elements. What would happen if he was called upon to do so again and failed? Who would celebrate his newfound status then? Besides, he had no wish to take the giant's advice. Not then. Not now. Not ever again.

Things were not the same between them. After working feverishly together to erect the lean-to, dig up their water-damageable belongings, and drag everything they owned into the protection of their hastily contrived shelter, he had asked the storyteller one single question.

"How could you stand by and not speak out to defend Mowea'qua tonight?"

"You saw how she was."

"I did."

"You heard the things she said."

"I did."

"Then how can you ask me why I stood silent? This night I have seen for the first time what she really is, what I have been trying to deny to myself for nearly half a lifetime. And why do you suddenly care about her? You have never hidden your dislike of her wild ways."

"Whatever she is, Kinap, you have said yourself that you have made her so."

"By all the forces of Creation, Ne'gauni, she cut off your leg! How can you of all men find cause to defend her?"

"Because for whatever it may or may not be worth to me in the days and nights to come, Mowea'qua did save my life. And she stood up for me at the creek when the Northerners would have abandoned me or seen me slain. You said nothing. You stood there like a gut-wounded bear and did not even utter a growl in my defense. And, like it or not, Giant, you are not just any other man. Whether it brings pride or shame to your spirit, you are Mowea'qua's father."

"And whether it brings pride or shame to yours, I have come to this spot on the beach out of goodwill toward a cripple who cannot raise a shelter against this storm on his own! But, by the forces of Creation, I will not stay to hear insults from such as you." The giant, already in a mood as foul and inherently dangerous as the rising storm, had snatched up his sleeping robe and stalked off, making no secret of the fact that he intended to pass the night in the tent of the widow Suda'li.

"Go, then!" Ne'gauni had shouted after him. "I want none of your 'goodwill'! Find what comfort you can with that crow and her two weasels! But know that I will speak for Mowea'qua at the council tomorrow even if you will not!"

"You will be the only one to do so."

"No. I will not. Hasu'u has sworn to me that she will speak on Mowea'qua's behalf to the headman tonight."

The giant had paused, turned, retreated a few steps, and then growled a terse reply. "Women may say what they will to their men in the privacy of their lodges, Dreamer, but they cannot speak in council. Tôrnârssuk may listen to his wife tonight, but tomorrow he will be among men. Tomorrow he will do as he must for the good of the band. As will you. As must I."

"But she—"

Ne'gauni tensed. He could still hear his intended words of protest cut short by Kinap's furious, back-armed gesture of dismissal as the giant whirled on his heels and left him standing alone in the pounding rain. He shook his head. What kind of man turned his back on a friend who was only trying to help? What kind of man refused to speak for the life of his own daughter?

A man like my own brothers.

"Cowards all!" hissed Ne'gauni, remembering how, with lightning flashing, hail pummeling the beach, and the stink of ozone tainting the rain, he had scanned the beach, noting that everyone else had already taken shelter within the other hastily erected individual and family lean-tos. His brow furrowed. The Northerners had even brought their dogs inside. No one wanted to be exposed to the forces of Creation in such potentially deadly weather. No one.

Not even Mowea'qua.

And yet she had remained outside the circle of the band. Alone. For all intents and purposes already cast out. A terrible bleakness of spirit filled him. It had been the same for him last night. With his heart aching almost as badly as the stump of his left leg, he had fisted up his hands in frustration and be-grudgingly retreated into the lean-to. Upset and angered and confused by everything that had transpired under the light of the red moon, he had rummaged irritably among the carelessly piled belongings, impatiently seeking Mowea'qua's healing aids among her things. Unable to locate any of her belongings in the dark, he had sought his own medicine pouch and fingered into his mouth all that was left of its glutinous, pain-eating contents.

His mind still felt thick as he recalled lying awake, waiting for his pain to ebb and sleep to ease his troubled mind. And all the while he had half expected the girl to come creeping in out of the rain to bundle herself in her bed furs on her side of the lean-to. He would not have betrayed her presence to the rest of the band. Surely she knew that! He would have berated her. Ah, the choice words he would have used to describe the outrageous folly of her behavior as he warned her of what would happen to her if Moraq had his way tomorrow! But Mowea'qua had not returned to the beach.

Ne'gauni sighed. If Moraq was right, the girl had run away. Another folly! Did she imagine that she could not be tracked by those who would wish to punish her? His brow furrowed as, looking around, he realized that Musquash had not come in out of the weather. He had not seen the boy since the dancing had begun last night. Now, as then, logic told him that the child must have swum out to be with Mowea'qua. The boy was an exceptional swimmer. There was little reason to fear for his safety in the water. Nevertheless, the thought of the defiant little boy and the reckless girl huddling together all night against the storm did nothing to cheer him. And now, as penalty for his disobedience, Musquash would also face the judgment of the council.

Tôrnârssuk is headman, he reminded himself. *His will be the final word. If I speak as well for the girl today as she spoke for me yesterday, he will prove himself as fair a man as the giant has claimed.* He nodded. The words made him feel better. Until he recalled Kinap saying:

"To keep a band strong and invulnerable against its enemies, anything is fair, boy. Anything!"

"Dreamer! Awake! We come! It is time to counsel!"

Ne'gauni's hands tightened on his crutches. Old Ko'ram was calling him. He exhaled in resignation to the demands of the moment and knew that he might as well face the day and whatever it would bring. Positioning his twin staffs, he levered himself up and, keeping his upper body bent forward to accommodate the low height of the shelter, used his head to open his way out of the lean-to. A moment later he was squinting into a jaundiced sun and standing upright in the light of as dank and sullen-looking a morning as he had ever seen.

And there, standing before him, was a sight that nearly dropped him where he stood.

His eyes went wide.

Old Ko'ram was not there.

A gathering of predatory beasts awaited him.

Furred and fanged, broad of back and long of limb, they growled as they advanced, hulking forward yet somehow still walking upright in the way of men as they menaced him with slavering jaws and pale, lancet eyes that flashed hostile and murderous intent.

"Manitous!" he cried out in recognition of their phantom kind even as he realized with a sick, sinking feeling in his gut that he had seen them before. "Yes!" He could recall the exact moment. It had been just after the band first entered the valley and he felt himself being watched by imagined monsters lurking in the undergrowth. "Ah! You are real!" he shouted and, raising his left crutch, clasped it in both hands. "Back!" Using the crutch as a stave, he slashed and swung outward and across with all his strength until one of the demons leaped forward, ducked beneath his weapon, and yanked it so forcefully from his grip that his right knee buckled and he collapsed onto the sodden ground.

It was over.

He would never have a chance to speak in council. The manitous were still advancing, and deep within his brain the Darkness was growing, emerging like a warm little spider to cast its arms around his consciousness until, suddenly stinging, it gathered his thoughts into a poisonous black web of mind-numbing despair from which there was no escape, no reprieve.

▼▼▼▼

"Awake, Dreamer!"

Ne'gauni, shocked by the intensity of Tôrnârssuk's command, looked up to see, not phantoms from the world of spirits, but every adult male member of the band looking down at him aghast.

"Do we look like manitous to you?" demanded the headman.

Ne'gauni was appalled. "I . . . no . . . not now."

The headman, still holding the young man's crutch, shook his head dubiously and, only after a moment of consideration, extended it downward to him. "Perhaps the sun was in your eyes?"

Ne'gauni accepted his crutch and reached for its fallen mate. "I . . ."

"Is that how you see us? Not as men, but as manitous to be defended against? And after all that we have tolerated from you along this trail?"

For the second time this morning, Ne'gauni flinched at the invasive sound of Moraq's angry voice. And this time, as he pulled himself upright, when he met the Northerner's contemptuous glare he knew without a shadow of a doubt that he loathed the man.

"Your memory is short, Moraq of the North!" proclaimed old Ko'ram. "Can you have forgotten that it is our Dreamer who has summoned Rain to quench the threat of Wildfire? Or that our shaman has—"

"Maybe it was not us he was seeing?" The darkly posed query came from Kanio'te.

"What do you mean?" asked the old man.

"Tell him, Tôrnârssuk." Kanio'te was not a man given to ordering others, nor, as the son of a Dawnland hunt chief, did he fail for a moment to understand the order of command within the band; nevertheless, his brow was down and his expression stern as he faced the headman. "Tell our Wise Man what you told me last night as we stood watch. Tell him about the two-legged wolves who may still reside in this valley and against whose possible predations I and my fellow Dawnlanders have kept our lances and stone hurlers close all night despite the storm."

"Those wolves are no threat to any real man," slurred Moraq. "But then, Kanio'te, you are not of the True People, so it is only natural for you to be afraid."

Kanio'te stiffened. "I have told you before, Northerner, I *am* a real man. As are my people True People. If my sense of danger has been misplaced, it is only because I took you at your word when you spoke against the two-legged wolves in the insults regarding them that provoked the girl to anger last night."

"*I* provoked *her*?" Moraq laughed.

Tôrnârssuk's eyes narrowed as, ignoring Moraq, he informed Kanio'te, "I, too, have kept my weapons close all night. No man with loved ones to protect would have done otherwise."

The smirk that had followed Moraq's laugh vanished from his weather-cured face. He had been reprimanded and knew it.

"It is so," Kinap affirmed. "While Suda'li slept, her boys drew lots to see who would take first turn keeping watch with me."

Ne'gauni was angry. And hurt. The giant had named those he loved. Not Mowea'qua. Not Musquash. And surely not the one-legged young man who had shared his fire circle for the past few moons. He shook his head. It was aching again. The Darkness was gone, but he felt empty, lost, and confused. "Protect against what?" he asked. "Wildfire was surely drowned by the storm that came to us last night, and if there are mammoths in this valley, would they not have taken shelter from—"

"We speak not of mammoths, but of men," interrupted Tôrnârssuk. "We speak of the Old Tribe."

Ne'gauni was more confused than ever. "Last night you all said that Mowea'qua is all that is left of them."

"Yes." Inaksak pulled in a quick, shallow, nervous little breath, then exhaled it along with a hesitantly whispered acknowledgment. "But once, long ago, we fought them in this place."

"Fought?" Moraq's tone did nothing to disguise the fact that he found the premise ridiculous. "They ran before us. They died on our lances like feral dogs. And not one of them possessed courage enough to turn and even try to attack us."

"None of my dogs would have been so cowardly." Ningao offered his opinion with the pride of a father speaking of his children.

Ne'gauni was stunned. His eyes found the giant. "You knew of this?"

"I knew."

"And still you allowed Mowea'qua to remain outside the protection of the band circle all night, alone, without her garments or so much as a skinning knife with which to protect herself?"

Kinap shifted his weight restlessly. "That one has proved herself to be a survivor. She needs no garments. No weapons. You know the legend of her kind as well as any man. In the dark of the moon she is transformed into a—"

"This is not the dark of the moon!"

"It soon will be, Ne'gauni. And who can say that the pelt of a wolf will not sprout from her skin? Who can be sure that her teeth will not become weapons? Truly. She *is* one of them."

"Never." Ne'gauni could not believe what he was hearing from the giant. "And Musquash?" he pressed. "What about the boy? Have you no concern for him? Or are you going to stand there and tell me that he also sprouts fur and fangs in the dark of the moon?"

The giant stiffened. "I thought the boy was with you?"

"Why would he be? He names *you* father, not me."

A low rumbling of distress sounded at the back of Kinap's throat. "Musquash would not come to me in the tent of the widow. He has made no secret of his lack of affection for Suda'li and her boys."

"Perhaps because since naming her Woman you have forgotten that you have chosen to name him Son?" Ne'gauni wondered when he had last been so angry. On the overlook? No. Not even then.

"But is not the blood of the Old Tribe also in the boy?" asked Inaksak, his voice held low, his eyes full of worry.

"It is what he has always claimed," conceded Kinap, "but, in truth, I have never seen a sign of it in him." A tremor went through the giant as he set his cowled gaze toward the empty sandbar. "And yet now he has chosen to be with—"

"She is long gone," interrupted Moraq. "And the boy with her."

Chief Ogeh'ma clucked his tongue and swung his head ruefully from side to side. "It would seem that the girl has chosen her punishment. Perhaps it is for the best. Her wildness puts us all at risk, that much is certain, but I, for one, would find it difficult to stand by and see her life ended in the way that Moraq was suggesting last night. And I do not see how we can abandon the boy to his whims . . . or hers."

Moraq was nodding vigorously. "I say we hunt them both, take back the child, and make an end of the girl. Otherwise she could follow us all the way to the Great River of the North."

Rage was building in Ne'gauni. "I did not know that there were any 'real' men among the 'True' People who were so afraid of girls, Moraq."

The Wise Man was not the only one to see where this must lead, but he was the first to act on the need to intervene before Ne'gauni and Moraq came to blows. "It is the boy we must think of." He flung an arm skyward, shaking his rattle in furious indication of the importance of what he was about to say. It would only be long afterward that Ne'gauni would realize just how wise the old wind-maker truly was. "Have we all forgotten that Musquash is the son of a shaman?"

"The boy has no power," Moraq reminded him.

"Perhaps not . . . perhaps so," countered Ko'ram. "But if he comes to harm, would you, Moraq, be willing to stake your life on what terrible manner of punishment the spirits of his Ancestors might choose for those who have failed to protect the son of one who was an intermediary for them in this world below the sky from which they watch us even now?"

There was dead silence.

Moraq's face paled and tightened.

Ne'gauni relaxed a little as he felt the impact of the old man's question sweep through the assembly like the cold rush of an invisible storm comber.

"We must find him," said Inaksak.

"We must bring him back into the protection of the band," declared Ningao.

"And we must make sure that from now on we keep him close and as safe as possible!" Kamak was adamant.

"It will be so," assured Kinap.

"And the girl?" drawled Moraq. "What of the girl?"

"Yes! What of the girl?" Ne'gauni was livid. Rage nearly had control of him now. Moraq's murderous lust for Mowea'qua was still alive in his eyes. Nothing had changed with him since last night. Once again they were facing each other like a pair of stags, locking the invisible horns of their conflicting wills, each knowing that the other would not yield. But now, unlike last night, it was Ne'gauni who was snorting the heat of anger as he took the measure of his adversary and knew that if Moraq won this challenge, Mowea'qua would lose her life.

But it was not Moraq who spoke in answer to Ne'gauni's ferociously placed question.

It was Tôrnârssuk.

"You have both just decided what must be for her," he said quietly. "The girl cannot be allowed to continue to create dissension within this band. She has insulted my woman. She has challenged me and the wisdom of my hunters. She has threatened us all and openly risked calling down upon us the wrath of the Ancient Ones and the forces of Creation. Now, not only has she run away, she has taken a member of this band with her and, by so doing, encouraged him to disobey me and put his life at risk."

Ne'gauni's heart was racing. "If Musquash did follow Mowea'qua, it was not at her calling. The boy's affection for her is not welcome. We have all heard her openly call him Bog Rat and Biting Fly. She can barely stand the sight of him. She will not want him with her. Not now. Not ever!"

"Then surely his life is at risk," said Moraq. "It is obvious that she has worked some sort of Old Tribe magic on the boy. And perhaps even on you, Dreamer. Why else would either of you worry so much about her when even her own father does not care whether she lives or dies? I say that she has used her black wolf magic to summon the boy to be her slave or perhaps, under the dark of the moon, if hunting is not good for her, to be meat."

Ne'gauni moved to swing a crutch at the man, but Tôrnârssuk stepped in his way.

"There are many dangers for a small boy in this part of the forest, Dreamer," the headman told him obliquely. "We must find him. We must bring him back into the safety of the band circle. And now, as we assemble a search party, our new shaman must speak to the spirits of this place on our behalf. You must ask them to guide our steps to wherever the girl has taken him."

Ne'gauni felt as though a shard of ice had pierced his heart. "And what will happen to her when you find him?"

Tôrnârssuk's long eyes narrowed, in speculation or to contain up-welling emotions that now lay all but concealed within. Sadness. Resolve. Regret. All were visible as he replied solemnly, "You have called Rain. You have banished North Wind and Wildfire. Truly, Dreamer, it seems that you do walk upon the shaman's road. So send your invocations once again to the Four Winds, and if you care for the life of the giant's daughter, ask them to see to it that she is not with him when we find him."

Chapter Four

▼▼▼▼▼▼▼

Mowea'qua was feeling better.

She could not say why.

Perhaps it was because the sun was well up and, in response to its warmth and light, birds were singing and squirrels were chattering above her head. Or perhaps it was because every now and then the annoyingly persistent ground mist thinned just enough to grant her a view of the forest floor so that she could stride out without fear of tripping over a fallen branch or slogging across a span of accumulated rainwater and soaking her moccasins up to her ankles. Or perhaps it was because whenever she and the boy paused to pick their way over and around deadfall, they were almost always able to stuff their mouths with several varieties of a gift left to them by the departing thunderstorm—pale, tender, newly sprouted mushrooms. Or perhaps, although she was loath to consider it, she was feeling better simply because she had begun to suspect that foolish little Musquash might not be quite so foolish after all.

"Possible it is," Mowea'qua conceded to herself as she trudged along behind the boy, for she was so heavily weighted by her pack frame that it was impossible not to acknowledge the probability that her new opinion of him was correct.

Not until this morning had the girl been able to take a closer look at the many things that Musquash had brought from the lakeside encampment of the band. Somehow he had managed to select and bring absolutely everything they could possibly need to survive alone together within this strange and still forbidding woodland: the big, tightly rolled moose-hide lean-to cover; a pair of sleeping furs; rain capes and cool-weather cloaks; extra moccasins and fawn-skin socks; her bow drill and fire horn, packed with tinder stones; dried lichens for kindling; and moss wicks for use in the little soapstone oil lamp that he had tucked into her rolled bed fur. There was a packet of dried meat for the trail ahead—not much, but enough to sustain them so they would not be forced to stop and hunt before they felt themselves out of danger from those who might yet choose to hunt them. Her medicine and sewing bags were with them, the latter with her precious bone needles, thimbles, awls, hooking wand, and coils of sinew and fiber thread. Musquash had filled a good-sized rawhide parfleche with a carefully selected mix of useful tools, including her snare lines and nets, a pouch of hide scrapings and snippets of sinew for the making of glue, and another smaller bag with extra arrowheads and bowstrings. He had even thought to bring them each a pair of snow walkers for the eventual and inevitable onset of winter. On his back, along with his own belongings, he carried a brightly quilled deerskin sack of colored sticks-of-chance, beaver-teeth gaming pieces, and a hard little hair-stuffed moose-hide shinny ball, this so they could pass their time at play when there was no work to do.

"Mmph! Truly a child he is if thinks he that for us there

will be time for anything but work in the days and nights that lie ahead."

It was a bleak thought. Yet, as Mowea'qua walked on cautiously through the ground mist, stepping over and around stumps and blowdowns and sumps of standing rainwater, she allowed herself a tight little smile of satisfaction. Thanks to Musquash's foresight in bringing along her medicine bag, she had been able to medicate her face so that the movement of her battered features did not hurt too much. Also thanks to Musquash, she could look forward to donning dry socks and moccasins when they made camp this night. It pleased her to note that, also thanks to the boy, she was using the butt end of her favorite stone-headed bear-bone lance as a walking stick that allowed her to steady her movement beneath the weight of her pack. And not only was her burl-wood medicine bowl attached by a thong loop to one of the points of the antlers that framed the pack, but so was her quiver and Ne'gauni's bow.

"Yah hay!" the girl sang out defiantly. Somewhere along the way her feelings of sadness and betrayal had coalesced into something else entirely. She was angry. And absolutely certain that everything was going to be all right. She was determined to make it so! She and the boy would survive, out of pure spite if need be. And they *would* see Kinap again. She was certain of it. He was bound to weary of the widow Suda'li in time. Mowea'qua could not see how it could be otherwise. The woman had a mouth as sharp as the beak of a snapping turtle. Sooner or later Suda'li was going to forget herself and cut the giant with it, giving him cause to regret naming her his woman. At the end of the summer hunting season, when the Great Gathering disbanded and Ogeh'ma parted company with Tôrnârssuk, Kinap would do the same. He would leave the widow and return to his old way of life. He would seek out the daughter and adopted son whom he had abandoned. He would come back for them, tromping his way boldly through the trees as he had always done, calling out and promising that all would be as it had once been between them.

The girl's smile tightened against her teeth as, lost in thought, she trudged on after the boy into a broken stand of mixed hardwoods and conifers. She would forgive her father, of course, but not right away. Kinap deserved to be punished for his lapse of loyalty. She would find ways to make him squirm before she returned his affection and insisted that he incise her face with a tattoo that would at last mark her as his acknowledged offspring and as a daughter not only of the Old Tribe but of the People and of his tribe and band. In the meantime, while she proved to him that she was capable of being obedient to his will, it would do him good to see again just how strong and adaptable a daughter he had made.

She sighed. Until that day all she and the boy had to do was keep ahead of Tôrnârssuk and his death-dealing trackers—if, indeed, they were even on their trail. Once she was sure that they were not being hunted, they could relax and seek out an adequate campsite, raise a lodge, and set themselves to the considerable task of laying in meat and provisions enough to get them through the winter. Kinap would find them. Mowea'qua was certain of it. Had she not heard her grandmother claim that he could follow the trail of a single snowflake through the tumult of a blizzard? And did he not always return to his daughter in the winter? "Yes!" Always. Why should it be any different in the days and nights that lay ahead?

"Yah hay!" she sang out again as she lengthened her stride, for the ground mist was thinning once more, and, although stressed by the weight of her pack, Mowea'qua could find no words adequate to express the pleasure she was taking in her thoughts—especially when she again recalled that Musquash had actually been brazen enough to steal back her arrows and snatch up Ne'gauni's bow in the bargain. With the bow and their lances, they could now be virtually assured of bringing down enough big game to see them through the long time of the cold moons. When Kinap finally came to them, she would see to it that he feasted on deer, forest caribou, and perhaps even a rare woodland bison. "Yah hay, hay yah!" She chorused a jubilant refrain to her own earlier song of delight, salivating at memories of luscious chunks of fatty hump steak sizzling on bone spits over hardwood coals banked high in her grandmother's fire pit.

The boy turned, paused, and smiled back at her. "So you see it, too!"

"See what?" Mowea'qua asked, barely knowing that she spoke at all as she found herself wondering if Ne'gauni had missed his bow by now. If the band had elected to abandon its two runaways and, as she strongly suspected, had opted instead to simply pack up and move on to the great river without them, he must have done so when he gathered up his things. Ne'gauni had grown very attached to the bow since Kinap had made it for him and taught him to excel at the use of it. She knew that he would not take its absence lightly. But, upon discovering that the quiver of arrows that the giant had snatched from her and given to him was also missing, would he guess that the boy had stolen both and brought them to her in defiance of the headman's command that all name her Outcast? Would he keep silent and abide the loss out of concern for the child and some small measure of loyalty to one who had saved his life? Or would he speak out and add thievery to their offenses against the band?

"Look closer, Mowea'qua!"

"At what?" Cut by the edge of irritation in Musquash's voice, she stopped before a fallen branch that lay on the forest floor between them.

He gestured wide. "Can you not see or smell it? On the trees! On the bushes! On the ground itself! I thought I saw and caught a whiff of it last night just before we stopped, but I could not be sure in the dark and rain. And then, after sunrise, we were so busy packing up and moving on that I forgot all about it. But now here it is again!"

"It?"

"Sign!"

"Of what?" Puzzled, the girl looked around, grateful for the chance to stretch and reshift the position of her pack. A small smile returned to her face as the burning ache in her shoulders and lower back eased a little. Mowea'qua would not have admitted it to Musquash, but the weight of her load was brutal, and, rather than jettison any valuable belongings, she had been pacing herself by allowing the boy to break trail for some time now. It did not really matter which way they went, as long as it was not back to the lake and into the path of those who might be following them. Now, as she scanned her surroundings, she had no idea where she was, but through the trees she saw that the sun stood about midway up the sky. Her brows arched as the unblinking eye of the great Kami stared back at her through a netting of wind-torn branches. Its position told her what she needed to know, that she and the boy were headed northeast, away from the lake, into the morning, toward the distant edge of the world over which the great Kami, Creator of All Things, was born anew each day. She sighed. It seemed as good a direction as any in which to go.

"Well?" pressed Musquash.

Mowea'qua made a face. Just what was she supposed to see and smell? After the abuse the forest had taken from last night's storm it was as much of a tangled mess as her hair had been before her swim. The air was growing warm, moist, nearly as oppressive as the weight of her pack. And the light of the sun was bathing the world in a dull amber glow that yielded a complex and equally oppressive scent that made her think of insects she had seen entombed within globs of—

"Sap?"

"Yes!" affirmed Musquash. "You do smell it! It was all over my moccasins last night."

"And on mine," she remembered. "But since when in a forest walking is it unusual to step on sap?"

"Look around you, Mowea'qua! The trees are bleeding! Not just a little sap here and there, but from newly made wounds! Great and terrible wounds! In some places as though Giant Beaver himself had chewed them all down! And in others it is as though—"

"Fierce was the storm last night. Rain and Hail and Lightning have—"

"No! No storm has done this. Look! And take a deeper breath, then tell me again what you smell!"

"Mmph!" The girl's snorted imprecation was not intended to dismiss the boy's impassioned commands; it was a startled exclamation of disbelief and disapproval of the extent of her own carelessness. There *was* another smell in the air. Sour. Sharp. She sniffed it cautiously and realized, with a start, that it put her in mind of a mass of ill-digested stomach contents recently left behind by the passing end of a large herbivore. She turned, stared at the trees, and wondered how she could have failed to notice the freshly gouged trunks and broken branches, much less have ignored the shredded bark and sundered leaves and needles that lay upon the muddied earth over which she and the boy had been traveling. Musquash was right. The forest was wounded! And not by any storm.

Mowea'qua's eyes moved up and around. It was as though some monstrous and wholly unfettered source of madness had opened a pathway of destruction through this stretch of spruce woods. At first glance, it could have been said that a ferocious blast of wind had rampaged through the trees, but the wind had been down last night and, although strong during the last few days, had not been powerful enough to inflict the kind of damage that now met her gaze. As she continued to pivot on the balls of her feet, feeling the stickiness of resin beneath the smoked rawhide soles of her sodden summer moccasins, she noted that all around her saplings had been flattened or uprooted and partially debarked and shredded before being thrown high and scattered about like unwanted portions at a hunt feast. Some trees stood untouched while others were savaged, their branches broken and left splintered and dangling, tender end-shoots mangled or missing, trunks laid open in long, sap-oozing channels that ran vertically from root to crown as though ripped by giant claws.

The girl cocked her head. She recalled seeing black bears standing upright in the deep woods not far from her grandmother's lodge. Leaning into trees, they had blissfully rubbed and scratched themselves against rough bark, or had shaken down the late summer fruit of the forest, or snapped off branches to munch on tender leaves, or dug and ripped into tender bark until sap ran and the bear tongued it up in sloppy bliss. But no bear, not even the terrifying great white bear of her most recent dream, could have so devastated this space of woodland. Only one living creature that Mowea'qua knew of could have done this. And only reverently did she allow herself to speak its sacred name. "Mammoth."

"Many mammoths!" Musquash was ecstatic and, from the breathlessness of his tone, more than a little nervous, too. The boy was staring up and around now, hands on hips, turning on his heels. "You see, Mowea'qua, I was not dreaming. I did see them. Yah! To break down the tops of trees as tall as these, they must truly be giants! Taller than a hand-count of Kinaps standing one on top of the other. Is it so, do you think? Can they be as big as in my dream?"

The question startled her. "Yah yourself! Are not you the very same biting fly who last night boasted of facing down and warning away the great white mammoth himself when you were only a little gnat half the size you are now?"

"Yes. And was it not the best of stories?"

"Stories? Mmph! Truth I knew that tale could not be!"

"It was the truth! Well . . . almost the truth. Perhaps I did not really v-venture q-quite as c-close to him as I said I d-did."

"How close?"

He offered an embarrassed little shrug. "I hid when I saw him d-drinking on the f-far side of the m-m-marsh. From my hiding p-place I s-spoke to him only in a w-whisper. But he heard my w-words. He m-must have heard because he went his w-way, and never a-a-again was he s-seen on the s-sacred island."

"Mmph! And if found we are by those who may be hunting us, will you from them hide, too, and whisper them away when they come me to kill?"

"No! N-never! For y-you I w-would—"

"Silence yourself, Puffball! Stammering you are! Think you that I do not know that this you do only when of yourself you are unsure? Yah! And once again, say I, a time for stories this is not!"

"B-but the mammoths *are* here, Mowea'qua! As I said they would be. In this very place they slept and fed. Great Chief himself may be with them! And this is the second time that we have crossed their trail. First last night, and now this morning. Did I not tell you that the forces of Creation would be smiling on us?"

"Yes," Mowea'qua assented with a complete lack of enthusiasm. She was thoroughly disgusted. Still looking around, she chastised herself for wallowing so deeply in self-indulgent musings that she had been oblivious to her surroundings. And it irked her to realize that she had failed to notice mammoth sign when a mere wisp of a boy had been able to see and smell it even in the dark. She shook her head. The force of the rainstorm had washed away the tuskers' tracks and pulverized their droppings as well as diluted their urine, but even so the lingering acidic smell of their leavings was unmistakable. And there was something about the way they had so savagely tusked their way through the trees that troubled her.

She knelt.

"What are you doing?" asked the boy.

The girl did not answer. A deep sense of foreboding was upon her, and she could not say why. She had never actually seen a living tusker, but, in those last lingering days of winter before she had gone north with Kinap, she and her grandmother had come across sign of at least one mammoth on their hunting trails. Often she had stood with the old woman listening in awe to the voice of a Great One rumbling in the forest. She had not been afraid. Tuskers were sacred to the Old Tribe. Her grandmother had filled her childhood with stories about them and spent a lifetime patiently gathering and polishing the bones of their dead whenever she found them, this to honor their Ancestors as surely as she honored her own.

Mowea'qua reached to absently brush an errant strand of hair from her eyes. If she and the boy were to come upon a mammoth now, she would not fear it. No! Why should she? Had she not spent the nights and many a long winter day of her childhood warm and safe inside a big cozy lodge walled up with the tusks and bones of its kind? Just thinking of it raised a hot lump of longing in her throat. How she missed that secret place! How she ached to see again that hidden refuge deep within the sacred spruce grove close by the laughing tumult of the waterfall! How she yearned to enter once more into that dark and welcoming hollow of comfort within which her grandmother had spent her last days warming herself by the central fire while offering food and love and wisdom to a granddaughter who had, under that last moon, secretly yearned only to go her own way.

Regret was bitter within Mowea'qua's mouth. What an ungrateful and stupid girl she had been! If only she could tell Kelet how sorry she was! If only she could wish the old woman alive again! She would admit to her that she had been right to warn her foolish granddaughter that the world beyond their sacred grove was a dangerous and confounding place. And that no one of the Old Tribe was welcome in it.

"Yah!" Her hand tightened around the shaft of her bear-bone lance as she imagined herself there. Far away. In that safe haven of her girlhood. She saw the great shining tusks and ribs of long-dead mammoths arching upward to support the curve of the thatch-and-birchbark-covered roof. She could see herself lying on her bed furs, staring dreamily up at

the smoke hole across which, on sultry summer nights when
the vent flap was left open wide, mice were sometimes audacious enough to leap and squeak with joyous abandon in the
light of the moon and stars. She could see her four fine pairs
of snow walkers upended against the shadowy curve of the
convex wall, each pair of a different size and shape to accommodate varying terrain and surfaces of snow. And there were
her big woven fishing trap and her gathering and winnowing
baskets of willow slats and tightly coiled streamside grasses.
There were the many neatly stacked rolls of prime pelts and
hides that she had prepared and set aside for Kinap to trade
south at the end of winter. And there, relaxing in his jesses
on a perch high amidst the spiderwebbed rafters from which
hung stores of smoked meat and the ingredients of Old Tribe
magic, her old friend U'wo'hi'li, the fishing eagle, kept his
one good eye fixed on the place close to the entryway where
U'na'li the black wolf lay sleeping.

Sadness touched Mowea'qua. She had healed them both,
restoring sight to the nearly blinded raptor and returning life
to the wolf after she had found it mauled and left for dead by
a bear. During their last winter in the lodge, Kinap had set
the eagle free to rejoin its kind and had slain the wolf when
he mistakenly took it for one of a pack that had threatened
old Kelet. For a long time the girl had been angry with him
over that, but he had made a cloak for her out of the skin of
the black wolf, and now she wore the pelt of U'na'li to warm
her against the storms of life and cherished her memories of
the animal as intensely as she yearned to be safe within the
lodge of bones again. But, with a sigh, she knew that the
abandoned refuge was no doubt in ruins; mice must have
claimed it as their own long before now. With work and time
and luck, perhaps, she and the boy might someday come to

share a similar lodge. Even so, without Kelet or Kinap to share it with them, it seemed a lonely and unsatisfying prospect.

A cramp pulled at Mowea'qua's lower back. Fatigue was stinging her limbs. She ignored both and, concentrating on the moment at hand, fingered up a torn and muddied sprig of mangled spruce needles. Holding it close to her nostrils, she closed her eyes, breathed in the smell of mud and sap and crushed greenery, and—like the wolf in her dream—invited her olfactory senses to lead her to an inner knowledge that quite astounded her. "More than one scent is here. The earth of the forest floor speaks to say that Musquash was right: In this place *were* beavers. Yes, say I. Days ago came they this way, dragging newly cut young trees, bruising this earth as they passed over it. Then came mammoths. Only yesterday. Stronger is their scent. But, think I, perhaps not many mammoths. Perhaps one only. And eaten has this mammoth of this green food. Smell I on these spruce needles its spit and the scum that on its grinding teeth grows thick as moss. Yes. Fed here a while did this one great mammoth before moving on . . . hurrying . . . running . . . in fear, think I."

"Of the storm?"

"Perhaps." Mowea'qua chewed her lower lip. The boy's observation made sense. They had both done more than their share of wincing and cowering in fright as lightning bolts had clashed overhead in the storm last night. But now it was morning. The storm had gone its way. As had the beavers and the mammoth. Yet, as she remained on her knees, breathing in the smells of the muddied earth and the spruce bough and the surrounding forest, her nostrils were picking up another scent.

She tensed. It was a subtle scent, elusive, so tenuous that, even though it raised prickles of dread upon her skin, she could not be sure if it was real or a figment born of fear.

"What is it, Mowea'qua? You look so worried. What else besides the storm would make such a giant beast as a mammoth run in fear?"

Mowea'qua opened her eyes and stared up at the boy. He looked so small. So vulnerable. And all because of his misplaced affection for her. "Hunters," she told him quietly, rising to her feet with all her newly won confidence in their happy future evaporating as surely as the morning mists. "Human hunters. Men who the mammoth kind would hunt and slay to the last of their kind . . . along with us."

The boy considered her statement before he shook his head and shrugged in that careless and arrogant way of his, as though he possessed all the combined knowledge of all the wise men in the world and could therefore dismiss his companion's worries with no more than an eloquent upward stab of his skinny shoulders. "It cannot be! We have had most of a night's head start on those who would hunt us. If they have been in this place, it would mean that they are now walking ahead of us. How could they have come this far? And how could they have tracked us in the dark? Your nose is not yet healed from our father's beating, Mowea'qua. It must be tricking you."

▼▼▼▼▼

He was wrong.

And so was the girl.

But it would be a while before either of them knew it.

At Mowea'qua's insistence they veered from the path the mammoth had broken through the trees and moved on in silence into deeper woodland. They kept close together now. Holding their lances at the ready within the ever-gathering gloom, they made their way cautiously through the trees across a flat, sodden, strangely spongy land that smelled strongly of leaf mold and deep layers of rotting vegetation. Even the usually ebullient little Musquash was sobered by their surroundings, for this was a murky realm of bog pools and shifting mists within which the sun was lost to view above ancient stands of lichen-bearded spruce, through which the light of day filtered downward to the forest floor as though diffused through a membranous caul.

No birds sang.

No squirrels chattered.

The two travelers found it increasingly difficult to breathe. The air around them was thick, humid, yet at the same time oddly devoid of the ability to nourish them with life-sustaining oxygen as they walked on and on, listening with no small measure of concern to the downward *squoosh* and upward suck of their moccasins moving across the unpleasantly yielding surface of the muskeg.

"Walk warily," advised Mowea'qua. In that very instant—as though the forest itself had heard her words and wished to prove the wisdom of her advice to the boy—she found herself up to one knee in an oozing sink of muck from which she was hard-pressed to pull her leg free without yielding her moccasin to the sludge. "Yah!" she declared, standing on more or less solid ground again and, after smoothing mud from her moccasin, tightening and retying the laces. "From now on each step will we test with a jab of our lances!"

And it was so.

The going was slow.

Mowea'qua was not sure just when the land beneath her feet began to rise. Suddenly, it seemed, the ground was firmer. The bog pools appeared to be behind them. The trees no longer stood in suffocating ranks. Not only was the air once again infused with oxygen, but there was space and light enough to sustain pale, ground-covering lichens and bog laurel and rosemary and many green growing things whose forms were new to her and whose names she did not know. The girl might have been heartened by the change of scene had the boy not noticed the skull in the trees.

"Look, Mowea'qua. Do you see it?" he asked, pointing up.

She looked. And scowled. A defensive knot tightened in her belly as, craning her neck, she stared up at the massively antlered skull of a deer that had somehow come to be positioned high above the forest floor in a notch between a pair of up-reaching spruce branches.

"I will wager you my share of our end-of-day food that there is a lynx in this part of the forest," said Musquash.

"Old Ko'ram has bad habits taught you! Wager you I will not. Your end-of-day food you will need."

He shrugged. "In the deep woods on the sacred isle I once saw a lynx carry a fawn high into a tree so it could eat without being bothered by wolves."

"Mmph! A lion, not a lynx, would it take to drag the head of such a big buck so high into the trees."

He shrugged again. "I have never seen a lion."

"Nor have I. Except in dreams. Of them has Kinap told me. Seen them has he in the southern forests . . . cats as big as stags, with stabbing teeth as long as . . ." Mowea'qua let the words drift; if there were lions in this part of the forest, she did not wish to linger in it. "Come!" she commanded.

They went on.

Soon, to their amazement, they began to see other skulls positioned high in the trees. Deer. Raccoon. Hare. Even a triad of beaver skulls.

"Natural this cannot be," worried Mowea'qua as she cast

yet another apprehensive gaze into the trees. A chill went shivering up her spine. For some time now she had been doing her best to ignore the unsettling feeling that she and the boy were somehow being watched by the heads of the dead animals they were passing along the way to she knew not where. Now, staring up at another deer skull, she caught her breath and stopped dead in her tracks.

Something was moving within the gaping eye sockets of the skull.

Mowea'qua's blood ran cold.

"What is it?" asked Musquash, pausing beside her.

She gestured him to silence. The movement within the skull had stopped. Had she imagined it? No! There it was again! She swung her lance into readiness. As she squinted to fully sharpen her gaze, she could see a definite gray slur of motion within the black concavity of bone.

"What do you see?" Musquash pressed in a worried whisper as he positioned his own lance for whatever danger might now befall them.

"Something alive . . ." she warned. And then, suddenly, her face flushed hot with embarrassment. Relief flooded through her veins, and she only barely managed to withhold a short guffaw of mockery at her own expense.

"No lion that," observed Musquash with a chuckle as he lowered his lance.

"No," conceded Mowea'qua, glaring at the little gray mouse that had just emerged from the bony rim of one of the skull's eye sockets. It twitched its whiskers and stared irritably down at the two interlopers whose footfall had roused it from sleep. As it turned tail and disappeared back inside the skull, the girl shook her head. "A lion it might have been," she added defensively. Thoroughly annoyed with herself, she turned her eyes to the ground and stalked on, determined not to indulge further in flights of foolish fancy.

She found it impossible. They were entering another stretch of closed-canopy forest. She clenched her jaw and thrust out her chin. She would not allow her courage to fail her now, even though with every step into the gloom it was all she could do to keep from imagining herself being observed and stalked by all manner of predators, including Tôrnârssuk's hunting band as well as animals that had not drawn breath in this world since the time beyond beginning.

"Slow down, Mowea'qua! And look out! There is another bog pool up ahead."

She skirted the deceptively benign-looking morass of dark water and hurried on. The mists of morning had finally cleared completely, but the air was growing close again. Stifling. She wanted to be out from beneath the trees and under the open sky so badly that when the screech of a lynx came through the forest she did not even look around to place the sound but lowered her head and continued on undaunted.

"A lynx!" exclaimed Musquash. "I told you so!"

"Keep up and boast not, Puffball! For into the trees no lynx has carried the many skulls we have seen." Her mind was aflame. Not with visions of the lynx. No. As Mowea'qua lengthened her stride, she was visualizing every monstrous flesh-eating carnivore ever described in her grandmother's and Kinap's tales of the lost world of First Man and First Woman: giant maned lions and short-faced bears and enormous dagger-toothed leaping cats and strange wolves with jaws powerful enough to crack the tusks of mammoths.

"Mowea'qua, wait for me!"

"Keep up, say I! And your lance keep at the ready!"

But no lance could protect them from the predator that fell upon them now. Mici'cak, Master of Biting Blackflies, caught the scent of their sweat and set his droning, merciless, blood-sucking insect war bands upon them.

"Yah!" Mowea'qua cursed her minuscule attackers.

"Never have I seen so many!" Musquash was slapping at his hands and waving madly at the air in front of his face. "I think I would rather face a lion! At least I would know from what direction my enemy was coming and—"

"Talk not now! Stop. We must our packs take off. Quickly now. As I say you must do. Weapons have we to ward off this enemy!"

At the girl's direction, they rummaged hurriedly in their belongings and were soon slathering their faces with a thick layer of protective grease, pulling on their gloves, and setting off hastily to gather bits of lichen to stuff into their nostrils and ears.

"Is this necessary?" objected the boy.

"Only if you do not want Mici'cak and his warriors sucking at blood inside your head."

Musquash gulped once, fingered an insect from his eye, and obeyed without further hesitation.

"Yah!" Mowea'qua cursed again as, pinching a biting fly from the tip of her already wounded nose, she squished the offending insect into oblivion between her thumb and forefinger. "A mistake it was for you to try to feast on me, warrior of Mici'cak! Mmph!" She looked up into a swirling black cloud of hungry insects. "Go, suckers of blood and harriers of all warm-blooded beasts! Seek out the flesh of Lynx! In all of this part of the forest it cannot be that Musquash and Mowea'qua are the only food you and your winged kind find fit to eat!"

The boy pinched a fly from his own nose. "Now I know why I have heard it said that caribou, moose, deer, and the wolves and foxes that follow to feed upon them leave the deep woods and seek rivers and lakes in which to wade when Mici'cak is hunting."

"And so will we," the girl declared as she hefted her pack and slung it onto her back. "Come. If there are beaver in this forest, then some sort of deep water there must be ahead, say I. Find it we must before the warriors of Mici'cak bleed us dry and into our ears and eyes and noses bore in to lay their eggs."

The boy shuddered. "We should have stayed on the mammoth's trail." Puckering his mouth and brow, he took thoughtful measure of their surroundings. "I should not have listened to you, Mowea'qua. The Great One would have led us into country where Mici'cak and his followers do not feed so greedily. And it would have been easier going, since the way ahead was already opened for us."

"For us *and* those who would hunt us!"

"I have told you, Mowea'qua, that we have left them far behind. And even if we have not, I, too, am a hunter. I will protect you."

"You? Me protect? Mmph! Told you have I that no more than one of these little biting flies are you to me. So be still! Bother me not or I will on you step and grind into the ground and without you be relieved to go my own way!"

"You do not mean that."

"No?"

"No. I will not always be so little, Mowea'qua. And I *will* protect you. So call me Biting Fly if you like. Did neither your grandmother nor Kinap tell you that in all of this great forest biting flies bring down more meat than wolves or bears or the spears of men?"

"Mmph! You are only *one*, Biting Fly, not a great black blood-sucking cloud of them!"

"In time, with the right woman, this one biting fly will father many."

"Yah!" His audacity never failed to amaze and irritate her; this time it also roused her temper. "Do not at me look as your mate! Any children I may bear will not the spawn of flies or muskrats be!"

"Yah yourself. Someday you *will* be my woman. I have wished it on the sacred stone. All will be well for us in the days ahead. You will see! The spirits of the Ancient Ones have heard my wish! They will keep you safe. For me!"

She could not believe what she was hearing. Not even from Musquash. "Pick up your pack, say I! On our way we must be before the sun goes to its rest beyond the edge of the world and abandons us to darkness in this place."

He eyed the sky, turned, placed the source of daylight, then nodded with satisfaction. "Night will not come to us for a long time, Mowea'qua." Grinning with absolute confidence, he suddenly made for the nearest tree and clambered into its heights with all the speed and agility of a chipmunk.

"Come down!" the girl demanded, totally bewildered by his unexpected behavior.

Musquash did not come down.

"Come down, say I!" she insisted, surprised to feel a sharp pang of concern for his safety. "See you I cannot. Musquash! What think you to do up there?"

"What you should have thought to do long before now," he called down. "I will look around from the top of this tree and see if I can tell the best way for us to go. Wait down there in safety, Mowea'qua, until I return to you."

Mowea'qua jammed her thumbs under the shoulder straps of her pack and glowered. He was right, of course. She should have thought of it! Nevertheless, with biting flies swarming all around and her face now aching almost as badly as her back and shoulders, she was in no mood to concede the point. "There is no safety for either of us, say I," she mumbled resentfully, then called up to him with no attempt to hide her worry. "Careful you must be! How many times must you I remind that Sila hunts us all?"

"And so!" he called down again. "Yah hay, Mowea'qua! It is as I promised when we first set out! All will be well for us! The forest opens up just ahead!"

"Why not the entire world inform!" she grumbled as she looked around nervously, still conjuring lions, and worse.

A few moments later he was standing beside her, wide-eyed and breathless with excitement. "There is a marsh just beyond these trees! A big freshwater marsh. A stream flows into it. Beavers have dammed it to make a pond. The biggest beaver dam and pond I have ever seen! And in the middle of the pond is a beaver lodge that is . . . is . . ." He paused to spit invading blackflies from his mouth. Then, his manner suddenly subdued, he leaned close to reveal in a tone of wonderment, "Mowea'qua, this big dam and pond and beaver lodge are . . . are like . . . like nothing . . . like . . . like nothing you . . . you . . ."

"Like what?"

"Ah! Come! Follow me! You must see for yourself! Only then will you believe!"

▼▼▼▼▼

She saw.

And still Mowea'qua did not believe.

It was exactly as Musquash had said it would be.

The forest opened wide before them. A marsh lay ahead. And at the center of the marsh was a beaver pond and lodge.

"You see! You see!"

Mowea'qua could not bring herself to answer the boy. She could see well enough, but she was too amazed to speak. The marsh, lying as it did beneath open skies, stretched wide and welcoming, a broad span of grassy wetland encircled by bastioning walls of evergreens and hardwoods. But the beaver pond was no ordinary beaver pond. It was as big as a small lake, and all around its murky circumference willows, aspens, and birches had been felled and dragged into great tangled heaps within which, here and there, she could make out the dark moundings of muskrat nests.

The girl cocked her head. She could not see the dam from where she stood, nor could she hear the stream whose waters the beaver had captured to use for its own needs, but she noticed that well out from shore many large trees stood inundated. Apparently killed by rising water, they rose as signposts from sunstruck depths, each marking the space of once-dry land within which it had set seed and grown tall. The beat of the girl's heart quickened as she looked at the trees. Bleached white by the sun and blasted by wind and weather, they had long since been stripped of nearly all bark and branches and resembled nothing so much as the tusks of drowned mammoths reaching for the sky. She grimaced at the unpleasant comparison.

"Well?" Musquash, standing very close, looked up as he eagerly pressed the girl for a comment.

Mowea'qua gave him none. Even from where she stood she could easily make out the massive, cleanly whittled cut marks at the base of some of the closest fallen trees. Surely, she thought, no beaver could have made such incisions! If she were to wade out into the shallows to measure them, she was certain that they would be as long and wide as her fully extended hand. Yet, even as her eyes narrowed in thoughtful speculation, her nostrils widened, then closed defensively. The unmistakable glandular stink of water rodents was unnaturally strong all around her. In that moment a fish broke the surface of the water far out on the pond, and a startled heron took flight from atop the beaver lodge.

Mowea'qua caught her breath. Not at the sure, silent wing strokes of the gracefully ascending bird, but at the realization that there was something very strange about the beaver lodge upon which the bird had been perching. It was enormous! And it was assembled not only of meticulously arranged saplings, but of entire debranched tree trunks.

"Well?" Musquash nudged her with a demanding elbow as he again pressed for an answer. "What do you think?"

Mowea'qua took a sideward step away from him and, her eyes fixed on the pond and lodge, absently waved biting flies away from her face. "So great a lodge no beaver can have made. And trees of such size no beaver could chew down, much less drag off into the water!"

"No ordinary beavers," agreed Musquash, beaming up at her smugly. "It is Giant Beaver who has made this pond! It is Giant Beaver who has chewed down these trees! It is Giant Beaver who has dragged them off to dam up the stream and create this great pond so that he could raise up his mighty lodge in the center of it and be safe from all who would hunt and eat him and his giant beaver woman and giant beaver children. The stories say that he and his kind are as big as black bears! They could easily—"

"*Were* as big," Mowea'qua interrupted as she turned her gaze down to the boy. "No longer beneath the sky does Giant Beaver make his lodge for himself and his beaver women and children. To the last of their kind have they been hunted and eaten and skinned and rendered into fat by the People."

"Yah, giant's daughter, you cannot know this! Look at the size of the tooth marks on the trees and then look yet again. Some of those cut marks are fresh. So I think maybe the story I told you must be wrong. Giant Beaver and his kind still live beneath the sky and make their way with all the other animals and people in the sacred Circle of Life Ending and Life Beginning. And the sacred stone of the Ancestors has led us to him. Imagine it!"

"For what purpose, ask I?"

His smile did not waver as, trembling with suppressed excitement, he lowered his voice and shrugged off his pack. "To put the proper ending to the story, of course. Muskrat has once again led Wolf to the lodge of Giant Beaver. Now, while Halboredja the wandering sun walks high in the sky and Giant Beaver sleeps within his lodge, you, Wolf Woman, will stand guard with your lance and arrows while this Muskrat does what must be done before Giant Beaver's pond grows so big that it drowns the world and all of the people and animals in it."

Mowea'qua shook her head tiredly. She was in no mood for stories and hard-pressed to believe that even Musquash could be so bold. "No such thing will you do! If in that pond is truly a giant beaver, the last of his kind he could be. You cannot hunt the last of a kind, Muskrat! Would you, puffball that you are, tip the balance of the sacred Circle? Besides, it is too dangerous," she told him, staring across the pond, shivering at another possibility. "The builder of that giant lodge might not be a beaver at all. It could be . . . something bigger . . . something . . ." She would not allow herself to speak the dreaded name of the water monster Waktcexi.

"I will hunt!" declared the boy, oblivious to her warning. Plopping himself down onto a nearby fallen branch, he began to work away at the laces of his moccasins, loosening them, then kicking his feet free as he looked up at Mowea'qua with a purposeful gleam in his eyes. "You must not fear for your Muskrat, Wolf Woman. The one I seek eats not of the flesh of bog rats . . . or of boys." He popped to his feet and, in case any eavesdropping spirits were lurking about who might overhear and betray his intentions to his prey, cupped his hands around his mouth as he whispered to the girl, "I will swim deep. I will find a way into the great lodge. This kind of hunting I have done many times on the sacred island. Once, when I was hunted by enemies, I ran off and hid within a beaver lodge. The beavers did not betray me then. They will not betray me now. Somewhere within the great lodge there is a giant beaver who will offer his life for you today, Mowea'qua. I am sure of this. So stand guard, Wolf Woman. Be at the ready with your lance and arrows while Muskrat flushes the chosen one from his lodge. Soon we will have enough meat for many a long day and night! And if we are tracked and found by those who have sworn that such beasts no longer exist, we, the last two members of the Old Tribe, will serve them up the fat-rich tail of Giant Beaver and watch them choke to death on their own words."

Mowea'qua was so appalled that she stopped swatting at the blackflies that were droning around her face, trying to penetrate the thick layer of grease that covered her skin. The boy's premise should have pleased her. Strangely, it did not, even though she remembered only too well the contemptuous and dismissive manner in which Tôrnârssuk had spoken to her the night before:

"Your behavior is an offense to the Ancestors, daughter of Kinap. The animals you speak of are as dead as your tribe."

The words of the headman still burned her senses. Especially now when she knew that he was wrong. There *were* mammoths in this forest! And Musquash was right. As she looked across the water, she knew that only a giant beaver could have built the great lodge of trees in the middle of the pond. And beavers did not build lodges for themselves; they built for their families. The beaver in that pond was not the last of his kind. And as long as she and Musquash lived, the blood of the Old Tribe would live on in them.

As long as they lived.

And just how long would that be?

Anxiety crawled beneath her skin as, with a start, she saw that her bony little companion was actually pulling off his hunting shirt. "Stop, say I!" she commanded sharply. "Your clothes you will put back on before Mici'cak and his biting brothers eat you alive!"

"They will not touch me once I am in the water!"

"Into the water you will not go!"

"I must if I am to hunt for my woman!"

"Your woman I am not! And hunt for myself can I."

"No, Mowea'qua. It must be as it was in the story I told you of the time beyond beginning. Muskrat must hunt Giant Beaver and Wolf must stand guard. Only then can the world and people and animals be saved from—"

"This is a story not!" she interrupted, wondering if it was possible to be any more frustrated with the boy than she was now.

He was slapping flies from his arms and shoulders and belly as he clucked his tongue at her like a little sage. "You must not forget what Kinap has told us. All life is a story, Mowea'qua. We make it up as we go along! And what I do now our children will boast of to their children when they tell them stories of how we were banished from our band and sent out into the dark forest with the sacred stone of the Ancient Ones to save the people and the animals and—"

"Yah!" The exclamation exploded from her lips in a burst of pure exasperation. "Right was old Ko'ram! Bad spirits there were in the band of Tôrnârssuk. But they were not in Ne'gauni's head. Or mine or Moraq's or Kinap's. No! They are in yours."

He gave one of his shrugs. "We will see." Without another word he snatched up his lance and, wearing only his loin cover and dagger belt, turned and ran to the edge of the pond and dove in.

▼▼▼▼▼

Mowea'qua was not sure just how long she stood staring after him.

"Wrong was I about you, Bog Rat," she muttered. "Many things have you wisely taken from the camp of Tôrnârssuk, and clever were you to climb a tree to see the way ahead for us, but an arrogant little puffball you still are! And now more foolish are you than ever before, say I!"

She wanted to follow him. She wanted to swim out and drag him back to shore, by his hair if need be. She wanted him safely back on dry land so that she could forcefully sit him down, take hold of his scrawny shoulders, and shake him until at least some small semblance of sense came into his hard, stubborn, irrational little head.

"A boy cannot a giant beaver hope to slay! No! Too dangerous is this, say I! Much too dangerous! Stop you must I!"

And yet, despite her proclamation and the overwhelming intensity of her desire to fulfill it, Mowea'qua continued to stand as though rooted. A tremor of frustration shook her. When the boy had hurled himself headfirst into the pond and vanished beneath its surface, she had not thought twice about running after him. Instinctively casting aside her lance, she had shrugged off her pack and, fully clad and wearing her moccasins, boldly waded into the water with every intention of swimming after him. But now, up to her hips in the fetid shallows of the pond, with deep, dark water stretching away between her and the beaver's lodge, another instinct entirely was preventing her from taking another step forward.

Fear.

She shuddered as she recognized it as the same emotion that had overcome her the previous night when swimming to and from the sandbar—a cold, skin-prickling, scalp-tingling terror of submitting her body to deep, dark, unknown waters within which the many-headed monster of her father's tales might be waiting to rise and devour her.

Ashamed, Mowea'qua balled up her fists and told herself that in her own way she was being just as foolish as the boy. Was she not the very same girl who had, until only recently, spent her life hunting alone and unafraid in a now-distant forest realm of wolves and bears that could well have made meat of her had she shown the slightest sign of fear or carelessness?

"Yes!"

And was not logic now assuring her that if beavers had raised a lodge within this pond, it was not likely that there were flesh-eating monsters dwelling in it?

"Yes!"

And, even though she was a creature of the land and felt no affinity for water, it was not as though she could not swim. Perhaps not with the ease or agility of the audacious little bog rat who was passing himself off as a boy these days, but certainly well enough to get herself safely across deep water and out to the beaver lodge.

"Yes," she assured herself, certain that, once there, she could clamber out of the water and wait atop the structure for Musquash to come up for air, then grab him and tow him back to shore before he drowned or injured himself in his ridiculous attempt to hunt an animal so many times his own size!

But neither altruism nor logic was serving Mowea'qua now. The pond in which she stood stank of rotting vegetation. As she impatiently waved the ever-persistent blackflies away from her face, she stared down and cringed. The water was warm and of an unpleasant yellowish-green hue that made her suspect that it might not be water at all, but a lake of urine released from the bladders of the giant beavers that had created it. Her gorge rose. To make matters even more repellent, she had so thoroughly stirred up the muck at the bottom of the pond that, immersed nearly waist-high in a watery stew of mud, algae, drowned insects, floating leaves, and specks of unidentifiable flotsam that looked all too much like decomposing body waste, she could not see her own feet.

The girl's heart skipped a beat as something slithered around her right thigh and came in contact with the bare skin on the inside of her legging. She jumped and plunged her hands into the water, desperately reaching down to ward off that which had already swum away. A fish? An eel? The fin of a water monster seeking human prey? Or perhaps only a strand of pond weed or drifting beaver turd stirred by some unseen current? Mowea'qua did not intend to stand there waiting to find out.

Dread coupled with disgust and quickly turned to panic in the girl's breast as, afraid to take her eyes off open water, she began to back out of the revoltingly tepid pond as fast as she could, all the while imagining the gaping jaws—not of any fish or eel and surely not even of Giant Beaver himself—but of Waktcexi, the man-and-woman-devouring water monster of Kinap's tales.

"Yah!" she cried out as, without warning, the slime at the bottom of the pond oozed from beneath her heels and she went down on her rump with a splash.

Somewhere in the trees behind her, a raven cawed.

Mowea'qua barely heard the sound.

Staring wide-eyed across the water, she sat stunned in muddy shallows. Something was rising from the depths of the pond. Something was sending ripples pooling outward across the water. Something was breaking the surface close to the beaver lodge. Something . . .

"Waktcexi!" Mowea'qua cried the name of the beast and managed to leap to her feet just as she realized that the smoothly rounded dark head emerging from the water was far too small to be the dreaded monster of her father's tales. Indeed, with a sigh of relief, she relaxed as she saw that the beast that had just surfaced was no monster at all. It was only Musquash coming up for a breath of air.

The girl rolled her eyes and vented a moan at the extent of her own foolishness. The boy was turning toward her now, aggressively treading water as he raised his lance high and waved it in an exuberant indication of his intent. She did not wave back. Instead, she huffed anger and ferociously gestured him back to shore.

"Return!" she called out to him. "Return now, say I!"

Musquash offered no reply to Mowea'qua's imperative summons. Instead, he waved again, more exuberantly than before, then promptly turned back toward the beaver lodge and somersaulted into a dive.

Mowea'qua watched him slide beneath the surface until all she could see of him was his upturned feet moving in a series of quick, forceful kicks. Then even the tips of his toes were gone, and the only thing that betrayed his presence in the pond was the rapidly diminishing circle of ripples that emanated from his point of entry into the murky depths. She shook her head. And to think that she had always taken pride in her own brave heart! The boy's appalling audacity put her to shame. The brazen little bog rat had, by his own admission, hesitated to approach the great white mammoth, but that was long ago and he was older now. Truly he knew no fear! No fear at all!

The girl stiffened.

A branch had snapped in the woods out of which she and the boy had come.

Mowea'qua caught her breath. Fear of water monsters had prevented her from swimming after Musquash. Fatigue had so dulled her senses that she failed to recognize mammoth sign earlier in the day. Nevertheless, she was a skilled hunter who had worked her own solitary traplines far too long not to react instantly to the stark reality and potential threat of unknown footfall when she heard it.

She whirled and stared straight ahead. If something was moving within the shadows between the trees, Mowea'qua could not see it. Yet, somehow, she could feel its presence. And, as the hackles rose on the back of her neck, she knew that it was watching her.

A deer it could be. Or a raccoon or skunk or squirrel. Or something even so small and harmless as a bird or mouse!

Hope was sweet. And all too fleeting in the face of common sense.

A lion could it also be. Or a bear. Or a pack of wolves. Or men . . . many men . . . all on my trail . . . all my death seeking!

Adrenaline was coursing through Mowea'qua's veins. Lamenting the careless impetuosity that had allowed her to cast aside her lance and leave her bow and arrows lying out of reach at the edge of the forest next to her discarded pack, she stood to her full height. What else could she do? She wanted to run. Indeed, she thought, if Tôrnârssuk and his long-eyed Northerners had tracked her down, she would have to run from them, for surely she would not stand passively to the kind of death that Musquash had sworn they had in mind for her! But if there was a hungry lion or bear or a pack of wolves out there in the trees, any attempt at flight on her part would be seen by these predators as an admission of vulnerability and taken as an invitation to immediate attack. Her heart was pounding. And to think that she had called the headman's woman stupid! Surely not even bland, dull-eyed Hasu'u would be foolish enough to wantonly deprive herself of weapons when walking alone in the forest!

"Yah!" She hissed the exclamation through clenched teeth and, glaring combatively into the trees at she knew not what, forced herself to assume the age-old defensive posture of a prey animal in desperate need of making itself appear big and bold and dangerous to the eyes of any carnivore that might be stalking it. Splaying her legs in a stance of belligerence, she arched her shoulders, held her head high and slightly forward, extended her arms outward at her sides, spread her hands wide, and fixed her gloved fingers into the rigid, inwardly curling appearance of claws. With any luck at all, if Tôrnârssuk and his Northerners were watching, they might just be impressed enough to change their minds about killing such a brave and potentially useful young woman, and if any large predatory animals were lurking in the shadows, they would turn away to seek an easier kill.

Hope was once again sweet within her, and more fleeting than before.

The girl tensed.

Deep within the trees, a raven called. A pair of owls answered. And, all at once, other birds were sounding in raucous and imperative response.

Mowea'qua cocked her head. She could make out the individual voices of Jay and Crow, of Hawk and Eagle. But there was something subtly wrong about the sounds. Something unnatural, and therefore ominous. She shivered. As the crescendoing chorus of croaks and cries decrescendoed into silence, she found herself thinking, not of birds at all, but of gathering wolves summoning one another into a pack for the purpose of joining together in a major kill.

And then she saw them.

Not wolves. Not birds. Not lions. Not bears. And surely not men.

They were coming from the trees.

Did Mowea'qua's heart stop at the sight of them? It seemed so. Never had she seen such beasts. Never! They were maned and muscular in the way of forest bison, yet they came slouching cautiously forward in the way of wolves or lynx on the prowl, and even the smallest among them seemed to be as big and dark and thickly furred as a black bear. Her eyes widened with disbelief. As they ambled toward her, they were walking more or less erect on hairy, misshapen hind limbs and extending their furless snouts to scent the air, enabling her to see the livid blue and bloodred skin around the sunken black eye sockets of their small, hideous, impossibly elongated heads.

Mowea'qua willed herself to remain perfectly still. It was no easy feat with blackflies hovering around her face, yet she succeeded because everything about the approaching beasts named them Meat Eaters and Dangerous. And there were so many of them! A big, hulking grayback led the first rank of three; no doubt from its size and apparent strength it was the leader of the pack. There were four more directly behind. With a sick feeling in her belly, she could see several more, hunkering half-hidden within the shadows between the trees.

She swallowed. Hard. A lump the size of her fist seemed to have lodged in her throat. She tried to gulp it down. It was no use. It was the very embodiment of terror. The beasts were closing on her! Every nerve ending in her body was screaming that she must flee or die. Looking desperately to her left and then to her right, she realized with abject despair that she and Musquash had managed to emerge from the forest onto the only good-sized stretch of open ground; everywhere else the shoreline of the pond was lost in a tangle of drowned and fallen trees. There was nowhere to run—except into the advancing ranks of the beasts, or into the pond itself. And within those dark and murky waters another monster, Waktcexi of legend, might well be waiting to devour her.

Her heart was racing now. Light-headed with dread, the girl nearly swooned. The beasts had seen her fear and were reacting to it. Those in the shadows were rising and emerging purposefully into the light of day while the others grouped into a single advancing rank, with those on each end moving ahead of the others.

Mowea'qua's worst fear was realized. They were hunting as wolves would hunt, or as men, intelligently communicating with one another in subtle ways as they positioned themselves into a living snare line. Even if she were to race forward and force a successful feint through the first rank, the second rank would surely close to prevent her escape into the forest. And if she continued to stand her ground, they would all too soon fall upon her and tear her to pieces where she stood. Either way, she would be meat. And soon, if

Musquash managed to escape the jaws of Waktcexi, he would come from the pond and wonder where she had gone. He would call her name. Again and again he would call it. There would be no reply. She would have been dragged off and devoured. And later, if the boy proved to be a clever enough tracker, she suspected that he would find her head stashed high in the branches of a nearby tree.

The thought roused an unexpected emotion in the girl. Indignation. Surely, she thought wildly, this was not the purpose for which her mother had given birth to her and her old grandmother Kelet had nurtured her and Kinap had come each winter with gifts and stories and outpourings of paternal affection—all so that she could one day be ripped to shreds by predators, her bones splintered for the marrow within, her innards devoured, her skull stripped of flesh and transformed into a nesting place for rodents! She would not believe it! She *could* not believe it!

A sudden bright burst of insight rocked Mowea'qua on her feet. She gasped. The kami had not abandoned her after all! The spirit of old grandmother Kelet herself had come out of thin air to stir her mind into a memory of the two of them standing on a snowbank watching as a fleeing hare suddenly found courage enough to turn tail, charge, and violently kick out at the face of an attacking lynx. She saw fur fly. She saw blood spatter. She heard the pained screech of the startled lynx and saw the predator whirl away to abandon the chase, bounding off to lick its wounds while the hare, unharmed, stood watching, stunned and trembling but still alive.

Now it was Mowea'qua who stood stunned and trembling. The kami had just shown her what she must do. If she was to save her life, she must be as Hare to Lynx, clever and daring and courageous enough to do the unexpected in the face of Death. She must prove to the advancing beasts that she was more than meat standing on the bone waiting to be taken and easily transformed into a midday meal. She must show them that she was Mowea'qua, descendant of wolves, born of the Old Tribe, daughter of a giant among the People, a girl like no other, prey such as they had never seen, a living force to be reckoned with—only with utmost caution.

"Away!" she commanded them. "Back into the trees go you! Meat I will not be this day or any other!" The boldness of the proclamation fired her spirit. Raising her arms and beating at the air with her fists in a symbolic statement of what she would do to any predator that dared to come near, Mowea'qua threw back her head and followed her words with a warning howl that would have put the largest and most powerful of wolves to shame.

The beasts stopped dead in their tracks.

The girl almost wept with relief. Her ploy was working! "To the kami and to the ghost of Grandmother Kelet and to the bold and clever spirit of Hare all praises be!" she cried in thanksgiving. Realizing that she had not quite managed to appear dangerous enough to cause her would-be devourers to turn away in search of less aggressive prey, she loosed another bloodcurdling howl.

They held their ground.

"Go!" Mowea'qua screeched at them.

The beasts did not go.

"Yah!" Annoyed with their refusal to obey, she feigned a quick charge, only a few short steps, then stopped, stomped her feet forcefully up and down, leaped high, whirled about, and came down hard on her heels into a crouch, barking and snarling and showing her teeth as she slapped at her thighs as though they were war drums.

And still the beasts stood unmoving. Watching. Taking slow and thoughtful measure as, growling among themselves, they appeared to be deciding if their chosen prey was still worth the effort of an attack. And then, with a shake of its maned head, the big grayback humped up its hairy shoulders and, the decision apparently made, began to lead the others forward again.

Mowea'qua's heart went cold.

They were coming toward her so quickly now!

So much for bluff and bluster! She had been as bold and brave as she knew how to be, but Lynx, although temporarily brought to pause by her bombast, had just turned on Hare, and Mowea'qua knew that she was about to be brought down and devoured. Her eyes widened and her face blanched with terror and revulsion.

The beasts were so close she could smell them.

"Carrion eaters!" she exclaimed. Suddenly bewildered, she recognized something more than the stink of carnivorous animals that had recently feasted upon long-dead and putrid flesh. There was another scent emanating from the beasts. Subtle. Elusive. It was the same smell that her nostrils had picked up on the spruce bough back in the grove within which she and the boy had come upon mammoth sign—the smell not of Animal, but of Man.

"No." She shook her head, certain that her senses must be as frayed as her nerves, because now, for the first time, she could see the beasts clearly. And clearly they were not human.

They were monsters.

How strange, she thought as she stared at them in horrified fascination. Never in his many tales of the supernatural denizens of the forest deeps had Kinap ever described such beasts as these. If they had ears, they were laid back and hidden within their filthy manes. Save for the shining, impossibly blue and red flesh around their sunken eyes and furless snouts, their heads were as long-haired as mammoths were said to be, and the pelt of each animal was dull, sickly looking, as though it grew from malnourished skin, even though there was scarcely a scurf-dusted strand that was not clotted with dried blood and the grisly residue of recent kills.

It was the sight and scent of blood and gore that tore the moment for Mowea'qua. Horror overwhelmed her, a horror so intense that not even fear of Waktcexi could keep her from turning and running for her life straight into the pond.

It was too late.

Pain flared across her upper back as she felt her shoulders struck hard from behind. There was no time to react. No time to cry out in protest. Jarred into near insensibility, she stared down in shock just in time to see the surface of the water coming up to meet her as she was propelled forward and facedown into the shallows.

A beast was on top of her. Straddling her. Hurting her. Flailing madly with her arms, Mowea'qua fought to be free. It was no use. The thing had settled itself onto the small of her back. She could feel the sharply questing claw-tips of its broad, heavy, uncompromising paws raking through her hair and down the sides of her scalp as it mercilessly pressed her face into the muck at the bottom of the pond. Was she screaming? It seemed so. A strange, grotesquely hollow and distorted sound was bubbling wildly all around her as, unable to prevent herself from breathing in, water and muck flooded into her lungs and seared her sinuses. The pain was excruciating. The weakness that followed was instantaneous. Her body went limp as her mind expanded into a wholly undifferentiated white-hot brightness, then seemed to sink into itself as, totally helpless, she felt herself being dragged from the water by her ankles.

Now she would die.

Now she would be meat.

Mowea'qua was sure of it.

A shudder went through her. What little remained to her of consciousness was ebbing. She let it go. It was best not to feel, much less imagine, what must come to her now.

Chapter Five

▼▼▼▼▼▼▼

The power of the sacred stone was guiding him.

Musquash was sure of it!

The water was cooler and clearer this far out from shore. He liked the feel of it against his skin. Swimming with the ease of his totem animal, he propelled himself deep, squinting ahead and fingering his way along the intricately aligned timbers of the lodge's vast underwater foundation until, exhaling bubbles in startled disbelief, on his very first dive he found a way in.

It was quiet.

So quiet.

The boy treaded water as, with one hand gripping the rim of the entrance platform, he looked up and around, then ahead into a timbered corridor. It was dark, dank, a long, gray, wattle-walled tube leading mysteriously off into the interior of the great lodge. Batting water from his eyelashes, he saw that daylight was filtering in from somewhere up ahead—not much light, to be sure, but enough to enable him to see that Giant Beaver was not waiting in ambush, poised to slap him into oblivion with a single downward smash of its mighty tail the moment he dared emerge from the water. Relieved, he sent his lance sliding quietly forward onto the hard-packed mud floor of the entrance platform, then hauled himself out of the pond.

He crouched, motionless, fighting back the impulse to shake himself like a wet pup emerging from a creek. Silence was vital to him now. He breathed as quietly as he could, straining to hear even the slightest sound that might betray the movement of a large animal coming toward him down the tunnel from the central chamber of the lodge.

Giant Beaver was in there somewhere!

Giant Beaver Woman was with him!

Together the giant twosome would protect their giant beaver children against anything—or anyone—seeking to bring them harm.

Musquash's eyebrows arched. If Giant Beaver's young were last year's brood, they would be nearly as big as their parents by now. But, unless his swim had disturbed the water enough to alert his prey to the presence of an intruder in the pond, they would all be sleeping now. The knowledge was soothing. He had made a considerable effort to move smoothly through the depths, making no more of a stir than a muskrat or diving bird might have done when swimming in search of fish. He doubted that he had disturbed his prey. Indeed, it pleased him to think of them lying on their raised platform, their fat, sleekly furred bodies cushioned by a thick mattressing of shredded bark, soft moss, and grasses, each animal dreaming of how the entire family would come forth at dusk to forage for food and tend to the endless repairs and additions to the lodge and the dam that fortressed the watery refuge. The boy allowed himself a smile. He had no wish to wake his prey—until the time was right.

His hand went to the dagger that hung from his belt in a sheath of smoke-cured rawhide. It was a beautifully knapped, double-edged stone blade the length of his palm. Exquisitely hafted into a sinew-bound grip of polished antler, it fit his hand so perfectly that it seemed a natural extension of his arm. Kinap had made it for him. Musquash's smile inverted into a scowl. He would forever treasure the gift of such an excellent knife, but the loyalty of its maker would have been appreciated far more.

Resentment darkened the boy's mood. He did not want to think of the giant. Not now. Not ever again! And yet how could he think of anything else? If Kinap had not chosen to side with the Northerners against his own daughter, Mowea'qua would not have lost her temper and run away and he would not be here, outcast for her sake, hunting giant beavers in this far and unknown part of the forest. His brow furrowed. He had so wanted to talk reason to the man, but just as he had tried and failed to soften the headman's heart toward Mowea'qua, so had he also been unsuccessful in his attempt to make the giant understand just how wrong he was about her.

Musquash's free hand sought the amulet at his neck. He reminded himself that the ancestral spirits within the sacred stone must have had a good reason for denying him success with either man. He had thought so long and hard about what he must say and do. He had pressed the little talisman to his heart. He had asked the Ancient Ones within the stone to affirm his intent. They had not spoken in direct reply, but he had been filled with such a strong and righteous certainty of purpose that he had no doubt they approved his intent.

And so, before swimming out to join the girl on the sandbar last night, Musquash had sought out the giant. He was so sure that Kinap would listen to reason. If it was obvious to old Ko'ram that bad spirits walked with Tôrnârssuk's band, it must be obvious to Kinap, too. The time had come for the giant to gather up his little family and break company with the Northerners and the Dawnland people. There was no need for harm to come to Mowea'qua. They had only to wait until the others fell asleep, then take up their belongings and go on their way. It seemed such a perfect solution. Failing to find Kinap amidst the circling dancers and noticing the silence of his drum, the boy looked for him in the darkness on the far side of the band circle and found him "dancing" in place while the widow Suda'li knelt before him, worshiping his exposed man bone. Or feeding off it?

Now, as then, Musquash blinked, revolted. Until that moment he had forgotten all about Suda'li. Had Kinap not been sighing and moving his hips in obvious pleasure, he would have charged forward to rescue the giant from the murmuring predations of the penis-eating widow. Instead, unseen by the twosome, he had stood by in shock, scarcely able to believe what he was seeing, watching wide-eyed as he overheard every impassioned word whispered between the giant and the woman.

"Ah, Suda'li, to what are you leading me?"

"Pleasure . . . diversion on such a night as this . . . as I have promised."

"And I have told you, woman, we cannot couple this night. Ah . . . you must stop. It is forbidden. I must return to the others. The beat of my drum gives strength to their dance. There can be no mating between us . . . not between any man or woman . . . not under a red moon . . . and not while my daughter is—"

"Do not speak of her. Not now! Not when we are like this together. Ah, giant, your strength makes this lonely widow feel so safe, so bold, so hungry for you. Has no woman ever pleasured you in this way? Ah, do not draw away. Allow my hands and mouth to caress and lead you to what is no true mating, no true coupling, for surely no new life can come of this. Only pleasure will we share. And is it not good for you like this? Yes! It *is* good. Your body cannot lie to Suda'li. How big you are! How alive to my tongue and touch! Ah, my giant, what else does a man truly need apart from a willing woman to pleasure him in all ways? An ugly, half-wild daughter who shames you? A puny, ungrateful little stick of a foundling who is not of your own blood? Forget them! Abide by the council's decision on the girl tomorrow with no regret! Tell the foundling that he must make his own way with the crippled shaman from now on. No man could have done more for them than you have done. And how have they rewarded you? All three have challenged you! Forget them, I say, and from this night, under this red moon, begin life anew with Suda'li! I will give you sons to make you forget that you ever had a daughter or found need to name a foundling as your own."

Musquash's face flushed. He did not want to recall more. And yet he did. A sudden orgasmic spasm had gone through the giant as, with his hands pressing the widow's eager face into his thrusting, shivering loins, Kinap had thrown back his cowled head and gasped a repudiation of his children and of all and anything that might ever come between him and his pleasure-giving new wife. And Musquash, sickened and at a complete loss to understand what could be even remotely enjoyable in allowing a woman to gulp down his man bone, had turned away and sought a place in which to retch unseen.

Afterwards, confused and cut to the quick by the giant's unexpected rejection, he had gone secretly and systematically about the camp gathering up and setting aside all that he and Mowea'qua would need to survive alone together in the forest. This accomplished, he had swum out to join her on the sandbar. He had not looked back. There had been no need. In the bloodred light of the Spirit Moon, Kinap had chosen with whom he would walk and place his loyalty when the sun rose again over the edge of the world, and it would not be with Musquash or Mowea'qua, or even with Ne'gauni.

The boy's mouth tightened. He could not imagine how the man was going to urinate, much less make sons, without a penis, but, even though the giant had bruised his spirit, Musquash could not fault him for his lack of loyalty; Musquash was, after all, only a foundling, and the giant had once put his own life at risk to save him from death at the hands of his father's many enemies on the sacred island. After doing such an extraordinary thing, Kinap owed him no further allegiance; indeed, thought the boy, it was he who would forever owe the giant a debt of gratitude. Even so, Musquash's heart remained hard toward the man. He could not fathom or ever forgive his willingness to abandon his own daughter.

"I will never be such a man," he murmured to himself. "Never!"

Bitterness refocused the boy's thoughts. His fingers moved to slip the slender thong noose that held the knife sheath closed. From this moment, until he found and flushed his intended prey into the light of day, the blade must be ready to be drawn and used at an instant's notice. Unlike those who knew not the meaning of the word *loyalty*, he would make good on his promise to Mowea'qua.

His heart gave a little thunk as he thought of the gray-eyed girl who awaited his return to shore. Mowea'qua was so like his Old Tribe mother in appearance! She was young and vulnerable and beautiful to his eyes, as his mother had been young and vulnerable and beautiful on that long-gone day when they had laughed and danced and played together in the surf of the sacred island for the last time. If only he had refused to obey her when their enemies had suddenly come for them! If only he had not run for his life and remained hidden when she commanded him to do so! If only he had not abandoned her! He might have saved her! He might at least have tried!

Musquash clenched his jaws. What was done was done. He could sit here forever wishing that it had not happened. He could pine away into a pile of bones with regret over not behaving differently when it had. Either way, brooding would not change anything, and surely it could not bring his mother back to him. She had died that day. He had seen her flayed alive, her soft skin peeled back and taken as a cloak by the whirling witch-of-a-shaman who took her life. And, while his own spirit wilted away into some silent inner place of near-mindless refuge from which it had not emerged until old Kelet had finally coaxed it forth with love, he had seen his mother's spirit sundered forever as her killers hacked her body into pieces and threw her away into the sea to be food for fishes.

The boy trembled. He could not go back in time to make it right for her, or for himself. Nor could he look forward to taking revenge upon her murderers with his own two hands, for he had seen them slain at last winter's end by Kinap and a combined force of Tôrnârssuk's Northerners and Ogeh'ma and his Dawnland sons. There was a certain grim, albeit not quite soul-settling, satisfaction in this, but true comfort could be found only when, as now, Musquash swore to himself that he would forever honor his mother's memory in the way he chose to live the life she had given him.

Never again would he fail to protect a loved one!

Never again would he run from a challenge, no matter how dangerous to himself!

And so he was determined to look after Mowea'qua. How could he do less for her? The blood of the Old Tribe ran in her veins. When he looked into her wide, mist-colored eyes, he saw his mother's eyes looking back at him. It was as though the Ancient Ones had sent her into his life as a gift to his troubled spirit. Through his loyalty to the giant's daughter he could make good on his vow to his mother. Here was another like her, another Old Tribe woman to care for and love. He would provide her with meat, all she could eat. He would see to it that she was robed in the warmest pelts, all of the finest quality. The spirits within the sacred stone amulet would help him to protect her from danger, and, no matter the cost to him, he would never abandon her.

"Never!"

A little thrill of resolve went walking up Musquash's back. He could hear movement deep within the tunnel now. A low, huffing sound, then the scrape of something heavy being dragged across the floor of the inner chamber. The boy's heart leaped. Giant Beaver was astir! The time had come for him to do what he had come to do. He must act now! He must act quickly! He must find his way into the lair of the beast. And, no matter what happened, for Mowea'qua's sake he must not allow himself to be afraid.

Curling his hand around the sacred stone, he gave the amulet a quick, hard, imperative little squeeze—in case the ancestral spirits within had dozed off while he had crouched in the gloom ruminating over the past. "Be with me now, Ancient Ones," he implored and, without hesitation, reached for his lance, then made his way cautiously across the entrance chamber and into the tunnel itself.

▼▼▼▼

He did not look back.

On and on he went, amazed that he was soon able to stand with room to spare.

Truly, he marveled, keeping his lance fixed ahead and his thoughts to himself lest his words be overheard by his prey, *it is exactly as the stories say! Giant Beaver must be as big as a black bear! And even more clever is he in the way he makes his den for himself and his kind!*

The beavers had laid down many layers of mud to smooth their passage back and forth across the floor of the tunnel. Despite the heavy dampness of the air within the lodge, the mud had dried to a smooth, slick, chalky-smelling veneer. As Musquash made his way ever deeper into the passageway, he could feel the thin surface layer cracking under his feet and, even in the gloom, saw that his dripping hair, breechclout, and moccasins were leaving a trail of footprints and water spots. Had he been worried in the least about being followed, this would have troubled him, but it was quiet in the entrance chamber out of which he had just come, and the dryness of the tunnel floor was a sure sign that this portion of the lodge had not been used in a very long time. He did not find this unusual. Indeed, it was proof to him of all that he had ever heard about his prey.

Giant Beaver was wise!

Giant Beaver was wary!

Giant Beaver was Supreme Father and Chief and Teacher of all the beaver kind!

Despite the arrogant and ignorant proclamations of northern unbelievers such as Tôrnârssuk, Moraq, and Ningao, Giant Beaver had not been hunted from beneath the sky! Giant Beaver dwelled with Mammoth in this valley.

Since the time beyond beginning, they had fed together and grown huge upon the leaves and bark and sap of trees and upon the grasses and green growing things within this forest. Just as Great Chief of all tuskers downed mighty branches and tore down saplings to feed himself and his mammoth herd, Giant Beaver raised his mighty lodge in exactly the same way in which he had taught his smaller relatives among the beaver and muskrat clans to do.

And so, recalling past forays into the lodges of Giant Beaver's smaller relations, Musquash smiled as he moved silently onward, confident that there would be several openings into and out of his prey's hidden domain. Some of these Giant Beaver would use often; they would be strong with his scent and slippery with fresh mud and water brought in on his fur as the great one went his way into and out of the pond. Others, like this long-unused tunnel, Giant Beaver would hold in reserve for emergencies so that little or no scent of him or of his family would betray their presence to even the cleverest and most persistent of hunters.

But I am the cleverest and most persistent hunter of all! The spirits of the Ancient Ones are with me in the sacred stone of my Ancestors. Giant Beaver will not escape! Soon, as in the time beyond beginning, this Muskrat will take his lance and drive Giant Beaver into the light of day, where Wolf Woman will be waiting with her bow and arrows!

The boy's thoughts were so heady that he could actually see the arrows flying as he imagined Mowea'qua exclaiming in delight at his boldness and brilliance as a hunter.

Then, directly ahead, the tunnel forked.

His smile faded.

He paused. Stared. Pondered.

Right or left? Which way now?

Unsure, he gave the amulet another little squeeze. The

spirits within the stone did not deign to speak to him, but, suddenly, insight flared. A magical communication from the Ancient Ones? Or the inner voice of past experience? Either way, Musquash knew what he must do.

He proceeded a little way into each passageway. Both were dry. The tunnel to his left led off into darkness. The tunnel to his right appeared to be angling upward into the lodge and was faintly awash in the dull haze of daylight. He kept to his right.

Moving warily, Musquash sought the light. He held his lance positioned forward and at the ready. The floor beneath his feet remained dry, but it was definitely leading him upward. His heart began to pound. It was the way of the beaver kind to construct their sleeping chambers high within their lodges to more easily access fresh air; the light that was filtering downward into the mountainous dome was probably coming from an air duct.

Find the source of air and light, and find Giant Beaver's chamber!

The boy was smiling again as he kept on his way. The tunnel forked twice more. Each time he followed the light. Only once was he brought short by a dead-end passage. Here he offered a silent salute to the wisdom and cleverness of Giant Beaver's skill in fortification; then, congratulating himself on his own cleverness, he backtracked and continued on with his spirit singing in anticipation of the kill to come.

And then he was there.

The tunnel ended before him, not in another fork or leafy dead-end wall of woven branches and saplings, but in an opening into what seemed to be a vast hollow. Shivering with excitement, Musquash stood poised at the entry. The smell of a living animal was strong in the air. He breathed it in eagerly, defining to himself the scents of warm skin and fur and glandular secretions and of partially masticated vegetation and of . . .

Deep within the hollow, something sighed.

Something big!

"Giant Beaver!" exclaimed the boy as he gripped his lance and wondered why he suddenly felt so small.

A long, low groan followed the sigh out of the depths of the chamber as, in a great whoosh of sound, something of immense size shifted its weight and slapped the floor with such force that the lodge was shaken to its foundation.

Musquash shook along with it.

Terrified, he stood his ground, frozen with dread amidst ominously creaking timbers that seemed about to come crashing down onto his head. But the structure remained standing. As did Musquash. After a moment, with the riled water of the pond sloshing angrily against the exterior walls of the lodge and the last structural vibrations shivering away beneath his feet, the boy remembered to breathe.

He stood very still.

Whatever had just groaned and slapped the floor of the inner chamber was silent now.

Musquash waited for it to moan or move again and, when it did not, felt a little taller. But only a little. Giant Beaver was waiting for him! Summoning what was left of his tattered courage, he told himself that he must not be afraid. He had his lance. He had his dagger. The spirits of the Ancient Ones were with him inside the sacred stone amulet of his Ancestors. If life was, indeed, a story that each man and woman must invent along the many forked trails of day-to-day existence, then this was his chance to begin creating the best tale of all. He must not hesitate! He had boasted to Mowea'qua that he was bold and clever enough to find his way into the very heart of the lodge of Giant Beaver. And this he had done! Now it was time to prove the rest of the boast, not only to the girl, but to himself.

I will be as brave as Muskrat in the ancient story of the time beyond beginning! I will charge into the chamber of Giant Beaver! I will startle my prey! I will drive Giant Beaver into the light of day, straight into Wolf Woman's waiting lance and arrows!

It sounded easy enough. Especially when he reminded himself that he was set to take on a beaver, not a bear or great spotted lion such as those described in the ancient tales of the time beyond beginning. Granted, the animal might well be as big as a mammoth, but even so, Giant Beaver was only a beaver after all!

Once again his thoughts were so heady that he could see arrows flying as he imagined his prey flushed from cover and brought down.

Soon Mowea'qua will have much meat! Soon Mowea'qua will have much fat to smooth her skin and burn in her oil lamp! Soon Mowea'qua will have the fine thick pelt of Giant Beaver to make into a sleeping robe! Because of Musquash she will have these many fine things. And never again will she call me Bog Rat and Puffball and Biting Fly. No! After today, Mowea'qua will look at me and smile with pride as she names me Man!

He was feeling much taller now.

Until another deep and dolorous sigh came from depths of the inner chamber and, with one downward thunk of its mighty tail, Giant Beaver again set the underpinnings of the lodge to trembling.

Musquash felt suddenly small again. Very small. His vision of flying arrows and easily vanquished prey gave way to an unwelcome, albeit far more realistic, perception of that which he had set himself to slay. He tried to swallow down

apprehension but did not succeed as, for the first time, it occurred to him that perhaps Mowea'qua had been right to
warn him that what he proposed to do was far too dangerous.
A water rodent the size of a mammoth could snap his spine
with one swipe of its enormous tail. Its great digging claws
and gnawing teeth could disembowel him just as easily as the
claws or teeth of any carnivore. And what if Giant Beaver
was not alone in his chamber? What if an entire band of
bead-eyed, flat-tailed, mouse-whiskered giants was lying in
wait for him to blunder into their lair?

His eyes narrowed. It was too much to consider. He had
sworn to protect and provide for Mowea'qua. He had promised her the meat and fat and fur of Giant Beaver. This she
would have from him. Besides, he thought, he had come too
far to turn back now.

"I am Musquash, son of Squam, born to the Old Tribe and
to the People! I will continue my quest. I will drive Giant
Beaver from his lodge. For Mowea'qua I will do this. And
like Muskrat in the story of the time beyond beginning, I will
not be afraid!"

But he *was* afraid.

And disgusted with himself.

Wanting to feel tall again, he gave the sacred stone amulet
yet another imperative squeeze. "Spirits of the Ancient Ones,
hear me. You have been with me this far; do not desert me
now!"

The words seemed to work magic. On the spirits within
the stone? Or on the boy who spoke them? Musquash did not
think to ask as, positioning his lance in both hands, he lowered his head and charged into the inner chamber.

"Yah! Behold! Death comes to Giant Beaver! For Mowea'qua he comes! To honor the memory of an Old Tribe
woman he comes! Bravely he comes! Asking Giant Beaver

to yield his life to the needs of others, Muskrat comes! As in the ancient story!"

His scream died in his throat.

Halfway across the sunlit chamber, his heart pounding and his blood hot for the chase to come, Musquash came to a screeching halt.

Giant Beaver was there!

Just as in the ancient story!

Facing him, lying alone and motionless within the shadows at the very back of its secret hollow, the animal was as big as any bear that ever menaced a man or boy beneath the sky.

The boy stared, stunned by the immensity of the beast.

Giant Beaver stared back, stunned by the audacity of the boy.

Neither moved.

Neither breathed.

The moment held them captive. Predator and prey. An animal born of a dying age. A boy born at the dawning of a new epoch. Past and Future. What did they see in each other's eyes? Life and Death held in eternal balance—the primordial kinship of hunter and hunted poised together on the rim of the ever-turning Circle of Life Ending and Life Beginning, each knowing that one must now flee or fall before the other as surely as darkness must yield to dawn in order to assure the birth of a new day.

Musquash's hands flexed on the haft of his spear. Squinting into the gloom, he took in the height and curve of Giant Beaver's massive back and shoulders, the glint of its dark little ratlike eyes set wide in its sloping rodent face, and the dull sheen of its inwardly curling brown claws and tusklike yellow front teeth. He gulped. Each of the latter, although worn and broken, was easily as long and thick as his forearm. A shiver went through him. Cold. So cold! He recognized it for what it was and would have no part of it.

"I am not afraid!" The words rang so boldly that he actually believed them. "I greet you, Great Father of All the Beaver Clan." He spoke the obligatory formal salutation of predator to prey as he had heard it spoken many times in one variant or another by hunters on the sacred island and by Northerners and men of the Dawnland. "I am Muskrat. I have come to put an ending to the ancient story. Bravely have I come. Cleverest of All Hunters am I! And now, as in the time beyond beginning, you must flee before me into the light of day. Wolf Woman is waiting. Together we will give you a death that will make your spirit and the spirits of your beaver woman and children sing with pride! Your meat will give us strength! Your fat and fur will give us warmth! You will live on in us and in the stories we will tell of you as we honor your name all of our days."

If Giant Beaver was impressed or intimidated or even annoyed by the proclamation, the animal gave no sign; it remained motionless.

Somewhere outside the lodge, a startled bittern broke the silence of the marsh with a fearful cry and savaged the air with the beat of its powerful wings as it took flight. Its sudden running ascent from the shallows rippled the waters of the pond and sent waves slapping against the lodge.

And still Giant Beaver did not move.

Musquash found this odd. The call of a frightened bittern never failed to put him on edge. Bitterns were such cautious, secretive, and brave-hearted birds; normally, when startled, they did not cry out or take flight as did herons or other wading birds. Instead, concealed within the reed beds within which they fed, they stood stock-still, turned their beaks bravely skyward, and waited for danger to pass them by as they swayed their large brown bodies slowly to and fro in as good an imitation of a waving reed or cattail as the boy had ever seen.

He frowned. Something had panicked the bittern into flight. A flesh-eating animal on the prowl? A carnivore big enough to pose a threat to a bird as large as a bittern? A shadow drifted across his mind. It had a shape. At first it was that of a mammoth, and then of a lion, and then of a lynx, and then of a group of men led by a giant, Northerners and Dawnlanders, all moving stealthily through the mists of a skull-festooned forest in search of human prey.

The boy's jaw tightened. He did not like where his thoughts were leading him. He would not follow! Kinap and the others were probably halfway to the great river by now. Mowea'qua had her bear-bone lance as well as Ne'gauni's bow and her own arrows to use against lynx, or even lions. She would be safe until he returned to protect her. And yet, as he found himself listening to the gradually subsiding slosh of waves raised by the bittern, Musquash remained uneasy. Staring into the gloom with his eyes still fixed on his prey, he could not understand why Giant Beaver had yet to so much as lift his head or swivel an ear or whisker in a display of concern for his situation.

"Just what kind of beast are you?" he asked. "How can you show no fear of me? I may look like a boy, but I have spoken truth to you. I am Muskrat. As in the ancient story, I have come to you as Death this day!"

Giant Beaver remained unimpressed, and immobile.

Musquash was shaken by a rush of frustration. His blood was once again up for the chase. Impatience was heating it. His mind was working out the best approach to what must now be done. He must get the beast to rise! Poke it! Prod it! Pierce it! Hurt it! A giant beaver it was, but it was still a beaver, cousin to a rat, and, unless cornered, rats ran when danger threatened. His mouth tightened into a grimace of resolve. He would not stand in its way! Once the beast was up and moving, he would grant Giant Beaver whatever room was available in such a confined space and, allowing it access to its best hope of escape, leap aside when it ran in panic for the nearest exit.

He stepped to his right, giving his prey a clear view of the passageway through which he had just come. Somewhere in the gloom at the back of the chamber there was another; the boy was sure of it, but the knowledge was irrelevant to him now. "There," he said to Giant Beaver. "At least one way is clear to you." Raising his lance in both hands, he held it high above his head—a statement of his intent, a warning of what must happen when the weapon was lowered, or an unspoken benediction of what was to come. He had no idea. He was done with thinking. It was time to act. Before he lost his nerve.

"Yah!" cried Musquash as he brought the weapon down fast, extending it well ahead of himself as he advanced steadfastly across the chamber into the gloom, jabbing forward and to his left and right, threatening his prey with every step. "Rise, Giant Beaver!"

Giant Beaver did not rise.

"As in the time beyond beginning, you must flee before Muskrat!"

Giant Beaver did not flee.

The boy paused. He was deep into shadow now, to one side of his prey, but within poking distance, a dangerous place to be—for both of them.

And yet the animal did not move.

Musquash was confounded. It was so dark in the shadows. And there was an unpleasant smell. He puckered up his face, looked straight into the eyes of his prey, and demanded, "Why do you lie there like a slug on a bed of moss? Have you never seen a lance before? I could kill you with it now! But that would not be as it was in the ancient story! So move! Go! Seek the light of day! Mowea'qua is waiting!"

Giant Beaver did not move.

Musquash had had enough. He made good on his threat. One good jab. Straight into the shoulder. Not too deep. Just enough to prick skin, draw a little blood, and win the animal's attention.

Giant Beaver cried out.

At last! A reaction! Musquash was jubilant.

Until his prey rolled up its eyes, heaved a shivering sigh, and collapsed onto its side.

Musquash stared in disbelief. "What are you doing? Get up! This is not as in the ancient story!"

Giant Beaver trembled.

The boy lowered his spear. His nose was telling him what his eyes had only just begun to see. And now he was trembling, too, because he knew that from this moment on nothing was going to be as in the ancient story.

Giant Beaver was old. Giant Beaver was sick. Giant Beaver was wasted away to skin and bones beneath a time-ravaged pelt that was as grizzled as a snow-blasted mountain. Whatever strength had moved the beast to rise and shake the foundations of its watery world only moments before was gone from it now. Like the mystical time beyond beginning that had spawned its kind and all the wondrous animals that had once walked with it beneath the sky, Giant Beaver was dying.

"No," said the boy. "The story cannot end like this. There must be a chase! Giant Beaver must be driven into the waiting arrows of Wolf Woman! Giant Beaver must be strong! Giant Beaver must be as bold and brave as the biggest and most dangerous of his kind! How else will Mowea'qua be impressed by the bravery of her Muskrat?"

The animal shuddered and wheezed, a long and terrible sound.

And the boy, recognizing that sound, was stunned. His lance clattered to the floor. He dropped to his knees beside his prey and, leaning forward, saw his image mirrored in a fixed and glazing eye. Truly, he had come to Giant Beaver as Death this day.

"Ah!" exclaimed Musquash as a sudden coldness filled him. Something had just shifted and darkened, not only within the great lodge, but within the boy himself. A living force of some kind. Invisible. Powerful. And then, like a sigh of lamentation, it was gone, leaving in the wake of its passage an aching sense of absence, of bruising emptiness, of something precious and irredeemable lost to the world forever.

Disconcerted, Musquash looked around the inner chamber and, for the first time, recognized it for what it was—a sad and solitary abode for a sad and solitary creature. There was no giant beaver woman! There were no giant beaver children! All the tunnels that led into the heart of the lodge would be dry, for long had it been since the giant beaver woman and all of Giant Beaver's children had set their spirits free to walk the wind and Giant Beaver, in his loneliness, had lost heart to live and crawled inside to die alone.

The boy's throat constricted. He should have known! He should have seen! Every sign was there to tell him. Mowea'qua had warned him that it might be so. But his arrogance and need to impress her had blinded him to the truth.

Giant Beaver was alone. Not only in this lodge. Not only

in this pond. Not only in this part of the forest. In all the world beneath the sky Giant Beaver was alone, the last of his kind!

And Musquash had killed him.

Tears stung his eyes. He was suddenly tired. So achingly, overwhelmingly tired that he slumped forward, pressed himself against the great one's side, and closed his eyes, listening for a heartbeat and hearing instead a cold and lonely wind murmuring across a distant world . . . a world of endless storm and cloud and blowing snow where mountains of ice rose up to walk like giants across an eternally frozen land upon which Mowea'qua stood alone, a black wolf, not a woman, wailing,

"You must not kill all of a kind! Its absence within the sacred circle will the balance of that circle tip until all within spill out to die. On that day the People will forever walk the wind in the country of the sky spirits! Ghost bears and lions and giant wolves will catch and devour you. Mammoth and bison your bones will crush. Giant Beaver will chew you up and spit you out into the Great Sky River, where drown you will amidst the stars. Again and again will you die! Again and again will you be reborn, only to be hunted and killed again and again . . . and again . . . and again . . . and . . ."

He followed the words into sleep.

Dreamless.

Dark.

Until the darkness thinned and he saw himself within the sacred Circle of Life Ending and Life Beginning. Something was shaking it, hard. Something was tipping it, mercilessly, spilling him out as though he were no more than a tiny bit of unwanted chaff being tossed from a winnowing basket.

He fell.

And fell.

Into the Great Sky River.

Alone, he was swept away among the stars until, lost and cold and fearing what was to come, a great sadness woke him.

Someone was weeping.

Musquash sat up with a start. His cheeks were hot and wet with tears. The sobs had been his own! The entire lodge was shaking! And from somewhere deep within the passageway that had led him into the inner chamber, someone was calling his name.

Chapter Six

▼▼▼▼▼▼▼

K inap! Ah! He has found us! Run, Mowea'qua! Run!
Run!"

The boy's cry of dismay and warning rang across the
marsh.

Tôrnârssuk was not pleased.

He stood at the edge of the pond glaring across the shallows to the deep water around the great mound of the beaver
lodge. The boy had just clambered through an air vent and,
after shrieking his warning, plunged headfirst into the pond
with the giant in pursuit, angrily tossing branches in every
direction.

There was a great splash as Kinap hit the water.

Tôrnârssuk cringed. As though the boy's cry had not
been bad enough! As loud as the cry of the bittern he had inadvertently startled into flight while leading the search party
through the reeds, it had no doubt been heard for a distance
equal to half a day's walk through the trees in any direction.
This was not good. Not good at all. There were other hunters
in the forest this day. Instinct named them Enemy.

"It seems the girl was right again. The boy *is* a bog rat.
Hiding from us inside a beaver lodge! It is what a muskrat

would do, you know, swim out to steal the stores of beavers and—"

"Enough." Tôrnârssuk was rankled by Kanio'te's quietly spoken but unsolicited commentary on a species of animal the Dawnland People admired for no reason that he or any of his fellow Northerners could understand. The boy's ability to swim was well known. But since last night Mowea'qua had been proved right about other things. There was at least one mammoth in this forest. And only a beaver such as those monstrous creatures spoken of in the ancient tales was capable of constructing a lodge of the size that rose from the middle of the pond across which Kinap was now swimming toward shore, dragging the boy—fighting and flailing all the way—facedown by his hair.

Moraq, standing to the headman's right, crossed his arms over his chest and leered in amusement. "That ought to keep the whelp quiet for a while."

Tôrnârssuk was not amused. "The *boy* is a shaman's son," he reminded coolly.

"That shaman is long dead, and that boy is *trouble*."

Tôrnârssuk's brow came down. Moraq was so quick to speak his mind these days, too quick, and almost always when his opinions varied from those of his headman. But the man was right this time. The boy *was* trouble. Musquash's disappearance had necessitated a search that put good men at risk. And, after seeing the skulls in the trees and twice crossing the tracks of unknown hunters on the trail of the runaways, the sobs of the child had raised the hackles on every man in the search party, especially when they saw from where they were coming.

No man wanted to seek him there. Tôrnârssuk and his Northerners could not swim. The men of the Dawnland

were still mumbling amongst themselves about the size of
the beaver lodge and taking it as proof of the existence of
water monsters. After a few moments, Kinap, frustrated by
their refusal to enter the water, had stripped off his clothes
and hurled himself into the pond.

The giant was coming from the water now.

Kinap threw the boy onto the mud at the headman's feet
and stood over the child, calling out for his clothes and
shaking himself dry as he whipped the long queue of his
single black braid about as though it were a dead eel attached
to the curve of his otherwise bald and hideously scarred
head.

Choking and gasping, Musquash lay still for a moment,
then made a grab for his dagger.

Tôrnârssuk stepped on his hand.

The boy looked up, his dark eyes flashing, his handsome,
finely boned face contorted with hatred.

"We will go back now," the headman said coldly. "Get
up."

The boy remained motionless, still glaring.

"Get up!" Kinap's command held an unstated warning of
what would happen if the boy did not obey. With Kanio'te
handing him his garments, Kinap quickly pulled on his
bearskin cloak and, arranging the cowl around his head, hid
his disfigurement within it.

Tôrnârssuk was grateful for the man's consideration. The
storyteller had to know that even the bravest and most stoic
of men were made light-headed by the sight of him, and that
women frightened their little ones into a healthy respect of
fire by warning them that if they were not cautious around
the family cooking and rendering fires they would end their
days looking like Kinap. The giant's scars were unsettling, at

once a tribute to his ability to endure and survive the most appalling pain and a reminder of just how vulnerable even such a man as Kinap was to the unforgiving whims of the forces of Creation and the many cruel and impetuous faces of Sila. His jaw tightened. Had it not been for the storm last night, they might all have learned the agonizing lesson that the giant had learned long ago—what it was like to dance in the burning embrace of Wildfire.

"I cannot get up!" Musquash declared. "Take your foot off my hand!"

Tôrnârssuk looked down at the boy. Musquash was still glaring at him. The headman raised a speculative brow, kept his foot where it was, and pressed down, hard enough to make the child wince. "You disobeyed me last night. You will not command me now. Nor will you disobey me again."

"Mmph! I have not disobeyed you. You said that no *man* was to swim out to Mowea'qua. I am not a man. I am a boy."

"A boy who has been forbidden to speak her name."

"Under a red moon," Musquash reminded him, his tone surly and sour enough to curdle the air. "It is day! There is no moon in the sky now! And even if there were, I would never stop speaking her name. Never!" The declaration made, he tucked up his knees, rolled hard to his right, and, with all his strength behind the move, jerked his hand free and leaped to his feet and bolted off, screaming, "Run, Mowea'qua! They have come for you. Run!"

Kinap had the boy by his hair again, swept him high and held him dangling, one giant hand against the child's face to silence him until . . . "Yah! He bites!"

Once again Musquash was thrown at the headman's feet.

"A biting fly . . . again as the girl has said," observed Kanio'te.

Tôrnârssuk eyed the man with open censure. "You and your Dawnland father and brother have made no secret of your disapproval of our intent for the girl, but you have chosen to walk with us, Kanio'te. Do not again force me to remind you that we are of one band now, with one purpose . . . the good of all."

The Dawnlander's face tightened.

Tôrnârssuk knelt beside the gasping boy. "You must not shout or try to run away again, Musquash, or we will gag and hobble you. You and the girl have led us far. Too far. So get on your feet. Go and gather your clothes from wherever you have left them. The blackflies have already gone to their day-end rest. The moon will rise soon enough. Though we may have to sleep in the bogs, I will not pass the night in this part of the forest."

"Are we to leave her behind, then . . . to *them*?" Moraq's query sliced the moment with a cutting edge of frustration and a hunger that betrayed his lust.

Tôrnârssuk did not look at the man as he replied, "She has chosen with whom she will walk. From what we saw of the footprints along the trail, they may have been made by those of her own kind. Perhaps it is just as well."

"For her, not for us," countered Ningao. "I say it is a trick. All of it! How can the footprints we saw be Old Tribe? They are all dead. We killed them long ago. Here. In this very valley."

"We did not kill them all," Moraq reminded him. "Tôrnârssuk saw no value in the chase. They could still be here. Still a threat. Still—"

"Listen to yourself!" Ningao interrupted, shaking his head. "She has used her Old Tribe magic on us all as surely as she has used it on the boy! She thinks she can frighten us away with skulls in the trees and false footprints placed all along the beach and leading off into the forest! She is probably watching us now, hiding out there inside the—"

"The lodge of the water monster that our headman said did not exist?" Moraq finished the man's supposition.

Tôrnârssuk tensed as, beside him, the boy looked up at Moraq, pinch-faced.

"The 'monster' is dead," Musquash informed them. "I have slain it. For her. As in the ancient story."

"Ha!" Moraq was not about to believe a word of it.

"The 'monster' is no monster," said Kinap tersely. "It is a beaver. As in the tales of old, a giant animal, but only a beaver nonetheless. And it *is* dead. Of old age, from the look and stink of it. There was no sign of the girl in its lodge. I saw only Musquash's tracks in the dried mud of the passageways, as easy to follow as the trail the two runaways left on their way through—"

"Mowea'qua is your daughter," Moraq interrupted. "We cannot trust you to tell us the truth in matters concerning her."

"I have led you this far," the giant reminded him.

"For the boy," stressed Moraq.

"No," said Kinap. "For Mowea'qua. So that I may kill her with my own hands. For what she has done . . . for all that she has said . . . for the risk at which she has put my son and my new woman and all who have taken her into this band as one of their own. She is my daughter no longer."

"And I am not your son," said Musquash.

"You must not speak so!" It was Inaksak. "You are the true son of a great shaman, little boy. Kinap honors this in you. As do we all. No man in this band will allow you to come to harm, Musquash. But you must not speak so rudely to your elders. Such talk would be taken badly in any northern camp. And in any northern band a boy would be honored that a man such as Kinap did not turn away when that boy named him Father."

"I am not a Northerner. No longer do I name Kinap Father. And Mowea'qua is all the band I need or want."

"Be it so," rumbled the giant as he rammed his limbs into his leggings and began to pull on his moccasins. "And so, say I, all the more reason for me to hunt her. By the forces of Creation, I curse the day I first took pity on a woman of her kind, for surely the forces of Creation have cursed me in return! Everything bad that has ever come into my life has come because of them. If they are out there, I will find them—and *her*—and finish forever what I should never have begun."

Tôrnârssuk rose, sensing something in the giant that disturbed him—dark, dangerous, a tide of emotion that must be stopped now before it swept through them all. "We have the boy, Giant. We must now return to the lakeside camp. Our women are waiting. We still have a long journey ahead of us and cannot squander our days and nights if we are to reach the Gathering of Many Tribes before whales return into the Great River of the North and others reap our share of meat and fat."

"You are Headman. You must do as you see fit for the good of the band . . . as must I," growled Kinap.

"You cannot go alone." Inaksak was openly concerned for one whom he had come to admire. "As big as you are and as fine a hand-to-hand fighter, you saw the number of footprints on the beach. Despite what Ningao says, they look real enough to me. If the girl has gone off with those of the Old Tribe—"

"Then by the forces of Creation that you so revere, I will join you, Kinap!" Moraq was beaming. "And we will both finish something that should never have been left behind to dog the trail of our days!"

"Old Tribe?" Musquash, not understanding the flow of the conversation, turned the words, then caught his breath. "The skulls in the trees! They were real, not magic. Mowea'qua did not place them there. And there were no footprints on the beach before we came through the trees to rest here." He was on his feet again, turning slowly, looking dazed as he scanned around. "Where are my things? My pack . . . my clothes . . . my bow and arrows?"

"I think they have taken her by force." The announcement came from Kamak as he and Ningao rejoined the search party. "We have been checking the tracks back there in the trees . . . all male, from the look of them. If the girl is with them, she is not walking on her own. Put together with the drag marks we found . . ."

"Drag marks?" Musquash sounded sick.

"They have stolen her!" declared Ningao.

"And the boy's belongings!" injected Moraq in a righteous blast of indignation. "As they once robbed us! Do you remember how it was, Tôrnârssuk? The way they sneaked around our camp, watching us, coming in the night or in the mists, taking little things, then bigger things—better things— until we had to put an end to them after they made off with our weapons and put our women and dogs at risk?"

Tôrnârssuk's gut tightened. "I remember."

"Well?" pressed Moraq. "Now we have a chance to finish them! Will we make an end of them or not? Or will we stand here clacking our gums like weak and fearful old women who are afraid to decide what should and must be done for the good of all?"

"I say we go after them!" Ningao offered his opinion freely.

"Ningao may be right," agreed Kamak. "If we do not pursue and punish them, which one of us can say whose woman may be taken next?"

"Do you imagine that they would truly follow us back to the lakeside camp?" asked Kanio'te.

"And all the way to the Great River of the North!" insisted Moraq. "Would you risk your wife, Dawnlander? Or Kinap's Suda'li? Or Ningao's Tsi'le'ni? Or your mother and sisters? And to those who walk in the crude and filthy moccasins of the Old Tribe? I cannot speak for you. But it is unthinkable to me! I will not be so dishonored!"

Tôrnârssuk eyed his followers. How quickly their mood had changed. They were seasoned hunters and hardened fighters to a man. It was one thing to ask them to abandon a female whose irrational and dangerous behavior had put them all at risk, but another thing entirely to ask them to walk off and leave her behind when they had just been given every reason to suspect that she had been stolen from them. There was not a man present, including himself, who did not feel his pride assaulted and his manhood demeaned by the girl's abduction. Mowea'qua was of their band. When they found her they would kill her as punishment for her offenses against them, for this was their right and obligation. But no others might touch her!

"Well?" Moraq pressed again.

Tôrnârssuk's head went high. "We will do as we have always done: hunt and slay to the last man all who would dishonor us."

Moraq was beaming again. "So the great white bear of the north still walks in your skin, Tôrnârssuk. I was beginning to wonder if it had died in you."

The headman's right hand tightened around the shaft of his spear. Something had gone suddenly hard and cold within his heart. "Do not make that mistake again," he warned as his left hand rose to press the amulet that lay against his chest beneath his hunting shirt. Perhaps there was power in the stone after all? Moraq was right. The spirit of the great white bear of the north was alive within him once more. And too long had it been since he had taken pleasure in killing a man . . . or savaging a woman.

Chapter Seven

▼▼▼▼▼▼▼

Pain.

It was the only reality.

The beast was hurting her so!

Mowea'qua turned her head to one side. She lay still, naked, jaws clenched tight beneath her buckskin gag, eyes so swollen that she could not open them to see. It was just as well. She did not want to see. She was doing all she could to will reality away. And failing. She sobbed. It was impossible!

The grayback was on her again, as it had been on her when she awakened to find herself sprawled on her belly with water exploding out of her lungs and consciousness returning with brutal clarity. If only she could forget! If only she had not survived to remember!

But, somehow, she was still alive.

The grayback had beaten, savaged, and perhaps even blinded her, but neither it nor its pack had made meat of her. Yet.

And so now, flat on her back, Mowea'qua kicked out. Hard. The movement was pure reflex. The power behind it surprised her. As did the angry screech of pain that came from the beast as it recoiled, then, growling, impatiently moved in again to reposition itself for what she had come to consider far worse than any manner of killing could possibly have been.

She flinched at the invasiveness of its touch, then, trembling, felt the forward press of its need and knew what must follow. The animal was powerful. Tireless! She had no strength left to defend against its predations. None. For an untold space of time since she had been dragged from the pond, pummeled into submission, opened to the beast's furious rutting, and then pierced in turn by every member of the pack, the grayback had been carrying her slung over its shoulders like a dead deer. Now, at last, it had stopped. To relieve itself. And to pierce her again, this time snarling when the others came close, denying them further access to her woman place, asserting its dominance over the pack. As it was now asserting its dominance over her.

Mowea'qua did not have to see the beast's face to know which one of the pack was on her. She knew the grayback's scent. Foul! She knew its touch. Merciless! She knew the press of its weight. Overwhelming! She knew the oily stink of its hair. She knew the ugly vocalizations it made. And sometimes, as now, she imagined that it was speaking to her.

"A gift from the kami are you. A gift cannot deny itself to those to whom it has been given! Open yourself . . . female must take male . . . again and again . . . until new life is made . . . like this!"

"No!" she cried, but the gag muffled her protest even as the beast stunned her with a downward bash of its brow to her forehead.

Mowea'qua went limp.

The grayback, fevered by that singularly focused purpose that the girl had come to dread more than she had ever feared death, took full advantage of her weakness. It turned her, reached forward to grip her by the inner thighs, then pulled her hips up and back as, opening her to the ferocious forward thrust of its loins, it pierced her to the core with a lance of flesh and fire.

Mowea'qua slumped forward. With her cheek pressed to a forest floor still sodden from last night's storm, she felt tears seep through her swollen eyelids into the cool surface of the earth. Surely, she thought, the kami of her Ancestors had deserted her at last. Never had she been so cruelly bent to the will of another. Never! Even when Kinap had struck her down and broken her heart along with her bow, she had not allowed him to see just how much he had hurt her. She had fought to maintain her dignity. She had managed to keep her pride. And later, when he commanded her to take the feather of Raven from her hair, she had refused. Looking back now, it seemed such a small concession to have been asked to make in return for his favor. But it *would* have been a concession, and by refusing to make it, she—who had been raised to see concession as weakness— had been so sure that she would win his respect.

A moan escaped through the binding of Mowea'qua's gag. If only the beast would cease its pounding! In a daze of pain, her eyes batted open, the barest of slits, just enough to permit the fading light of day to enter. The world on the far side of her lashes was as blurred as her mind. A shadow lay across the upper half of her face; somehow it had weight, substance. Squinting through it, it was a moment before she realized that it was not a shadow at all. It was the feather of Raven; still attached to her forelock, it was as bent and battered as she.

A sob formed again at the back of the girl's throat. What

good was Kinap's respect now? What good was her pride? By the time her father wearied of the widow Suda'li and remembered that he had abandoned a daughter who loved and needed him, that daughter would be long dead. And even if little Musquash had come from the pond, found her missing, and raced back to the lakeside camp to alert Kinap to her situation and bring him to rescue her, she was sure that the giant would come too late.

Another sob shook her. What if the boy had not survived his swim? Or, overconfident little biting fly that he was, what if he had flown after her on his own and blundered into her captors' midst? Perhaps this was why the beasts had not eaten her? Perhaps, while some of them sated themselves on her body, others occupied themselves elsewhere? Perhaps their bellies were already full . . . of the meat of an all-too-valiant little boy?

Mowea'qua's heart sank. If Musquash was dead, his death was her fault. If he was still alive, it was in spite of her. Either way, she would never see the boy again. There would be no reunion with Kinap. There would be no big lodge raised in the heart of the forest. Hump steaks would never sizzle over a fire pit across which her father would look at her with pride as she told stories of her bold adventures apart from the band that had so cruelly cast her out and dishonored her ancient lineage. Perhaps one day Kinap would seek her out. Musquash might be with him. She would hope for that. The boy would speak kindly of her. And then, together, finding no sign of her bones and failing to see her skull placed with others in the trees, they would go on their way, never knowing that they had found the place where the beasts had slain and devoured her.

Still again she moaned. She would never have a chance to thank Musquash for his loyal heart, or to tell her father that he had been right about the feather of Raven. It *had* been a bad omen. She should have obeyed him! She should have cast it away!

Now, with the beast pumping away at her backside, she gritted her teeth and tried to find strength enough to raise an arm and pull the feather from her hair. Failing, she lay inert, exhausted, crying softly until, slowly, it occurred to her that it was against all odds for the feather to still be twined in her hair. Yet there it was! And here she was. Against all odds, still alive and, although powerless to stop the beast's invasion of her body, in possession of enough Old Tribe pride to will herself to stop crying and to scream instead against her fate.

It did not matter that the scream was muffled by her gag. Mowea'qua could feel its resonance in every fiber of her being and was certain that the grayback must feel it, too. She wanted the beast to feel it! She wanted it to know that even though it ravaged and might eventually kill her, it would never break her will.

It was sating itself now, clasping her tighter than before as, apparently excited by the resistance it felt in her body, it began to grunt quick, breathy little bursts of air and shiver liquid heat deep into her woman place.

Mowea'qua was overcome by outrage. She knew that the beast was mating with her. As the entire pack had mated with her. As though she, too, were a beast. It was unnatural! Unthinkable! Unbearable! And yet it went on and on until, once again, she was sobbing.

How could the People have abandoned her to such a moment as this? The indignity and unfairness of it was as hurtful as the penetration of the beast! What had she done that was so unforgivable? Spoken words of warning to a stupid woman whose foolish wish had put the sacred Circle of Life at risk?

Refused to take a feather from her hair? Shouted at the headman in defense of her own kind and named him and his followers Liars when they defamed the Old Tribe? Yes, to all! But why was this so terrible? Hasu'u was the one who had offended the forces of Creation! No one had sought to punish the headman's woman or repudiate her Dawnland people!

Mowea'qua was shaking with righteous indignation. And with despair. What good were her questions? What good were her tears? The People would not come to rescue a daughter of the Old Tribe. The Northerners would just as soon see her dead, and her own father had stood by and said that he would abide by any decision they made concerning her.

Now, with the grayback still at her backside, her vision cleared just enough to grant her a blurred view of shaggy dark forms hunkering close all around. She gasped. The pack was waiting! Soon the beasts would take turns on her again.

Did she scream in horror of what was to come? No. She lay dazed, her body shaken by the ongoing predation of the grayback, her insides hurting so much that, when she thought of the others moving in, she knew there was only one thing left for her to do. She must call upon Old Tribe magic. It would not save her from the mauling that was to come, but it would help her maintain what was left to her of Old Tribe strength and dignity and pride in the face of continued degradation. For what was magic if not the invisible force of faith and will working together to overcome the staggering adversities of the forces of Creation? And what if little Musquash was right after all? What if life truly was a story that each man and woman must create along the way? The boy, as daring as his totem animal, might well have already ended his story as a warrior fighting to the death against beasts and water monsters. And all to prove his love for one who had never spoken so much as a kind word to him. Her heart ached to think of it. And then her spirit soared.

Even though no living man or woman would witness the boy's heroism, the Ancient Ones would sing the praises of Musquash's brave heart. The Ancestors would see to it that the boy lived on forever among the stars. But what would the end of Mowea'qua's story be? What would the Ancestors think of a daughter of the Old Tribe who allowed a child to follow her to his death and then, at the end of her own life, forgot the meaning of courage?

She drew in a quick and sobering breath. The answer was obvious. The Ancient Ones would hold her in as much contempt as she now held herself. When the end of her story came, her spirit would live on in the beasts that devoured her, and the only stars she would ever see would be through their eyes. Yet, even then, might she not have some hope of punishing those who had brought her to such a shameful end? Might she not make of her spirit a perpetual ache in their teeth and bellies, an oozing canker on their tongues, an ever-festering burr in their paws, an eternally suppurating ulcer at the tip of their male bones so that not one of them—especially the grayback—could ever mate again?

"Yes!" Mowea'qua was so energized by hatred and by her need to harm the beast that she barely heard the sound of her own voice as she finally found strength enough in her arms to reach up with one hand and force down her gag as she began to claw at the ground with the other hand, elbowing down as hard as she could, pulling herself forward, desperately trying to separate herself from the grayback as she screamed at the top of her lungs. "Put to this story an end! Finish it! And me! Death I would have! Now! Now! *Now!*"

▼▼▼▼

"I say we give her what she asks for!"

"Hold your arrows and lower your bow, Moraq," commanded Tôrnârssuk, his voice held so low that it was barely audible as the search party crouched within the trees, well downwind of those they had been tracking for hours. "I will tell you when it is right for us to make our move."

"She is Kinap's daughter. The kill should be his. And the honor of it. Is this still what you want, Giant?"

Kinap ignored the malicious undertones of Moraq's whispered query as he and the others stared fixedly through the undergrowth, observing the rape of Mowea'qua.

Musquash was shaking. "They are hurting her!"

A dark roll of laughter bubbled at the back of Moraq's throat. "As we should have done last night."

Kanio'te's brow furrowed as his head swung slowly from side to side in troubled contemplation. "They use her to a man. It is not the way of the Dawnland People to misuse a woman so."

"She is no woman," slurred Ningao. "She is one of them . . . by her own admission."

There were tears in Musquash's eyes. He backhanded them away. "Just what *are* they?"

Moraq raised a jaundiced brow. "Do you not recognize your own kind when you see them? They are Old Tribe thieves. Filthy, hairy, woman-stealing rapists. Are they not exactly as we described them?"

"And so it is as I assured you," rumbled the giant restively, giving the boy no chance to reply. "No matter what Musquash says, as you can see, the blood of the Old Tribe cannot flow in the boy's veins."

"That has been obvious from the day you first came to walk with us," agreed Kamak.

"Look," said Inaksak, pointing off. "There are your things, Muskrat, and hers . . . stolen, as we knew they would be."

"I care not for my things!" The boy burst to his feet, his face contorting as tears overflowed his eyes and spilled onto his cheeks. "We cannot just sit here! We must help Mowea'qua before she is—"

Kinap reached out, jerked the boy down, and, snarling, pulled him close. "She has chosen this. Soon she will die, if not at their hands, then at ours. And so you will shut your mouth and keep it shut before you betray our presence to those whom we hunt."

"They are finishing with their sport for now," observed Kamak. "Look there. Do you see the big one in gray wolf-skins driving the others away from her? You could never get me off a woman as easily as that!"

"They are not True Men," noted Moraq. "And the gray is clearly master of the pack. When we kill him the others will scatter like rabbits."

"Look!" Inaksak was pointing again. "They are preparing to move on."

Ningao was scowling. "The girl lies as limp as a torn old buckskin doll, and as silent. Is she still alive, do you think?"

"Enough for our purpose," Moraq assured him.

Tôrnârssuk's long mouth had gone white over his teeth as, slowly, he rose and gestured to the others to do the same. "Come. The sun has long since gone to its rest. It is the time without shadow. Soon darkness will come and the moon will rise. Those who have dared to steal a woman of our band will return with her to their denning site before then. We will follow. We will fall upon them there. And finish them to the last of their kind."

"As we should have done long ago, eh, White Bear?"

Moraq's goad hung in the air.

Tôrnârssuk appeared to ignore it.

▼▼▼▼

They had come far.

In ever-gathering darkness.

Through endless tides of constantly shifting pain.

Mowea'qua moaned. It all seemed a dream to her now. A nightmare even worse than that which had awakened her after her first night spent as a runaway within the forest. The grayback had bundled her in her wolfskin cloak and was again carrying her, head slung down over its shoulders. Since the cloak was only that, her flanks and limbs remained exposed; the dank, chill air of dusk was biting at her bare skin. The warm seep of blood and semen was sticky on her inner thighs. Even though her eyes were closed, she could feel the woods closing all around.

Dark.

Somnolent.

Brooding.

Dangerous.

She shivered. What was Danger to her now? What worse fate could possibly befall her than that which had already come to make a mockery of her once-brave spirit?

Birds were chortling somewhere near. Raven and Owl, Crow and Jay, Hawk and Eagle. Predators and carrion eaters all! There were no songbirds in Mowea'qua's dream. Nor were there men, yet every now and then she heard low masculine murmurs and muted male laughter. This made no sense to her, no sense at all, but such was the way of dreams, and, drifting in delirium, Mowea'qua did not question it.

She was a wolf again!

A black wolf. No longer wild. No longer running free. She was a captive now, snared and helpless in an invisible net woven by the sheer brute force of bolder, far more savage beasts than those wolves of old from whom her grandmother had sworn that she and all of their kind took descent. Her paws twitched. She moaned again. She did not want to be a wolf. She wanted to be a girl again, Kinap's daughter, back at the lakeside camp, safe within the protection of the band, her head obediently covered under the red moon, her hostile words of warning to the People and Northerners never spoken, and the feather of Raven never braided into her hair.

Tears were burning her eyes. She could not change what had happened. She could only regret it. It all seemed so distant. Unreal. As much a part of her ongoing nightmare as everything else that had happened since her defiant swim out to the sandbar under the bloodred glow of the Spirit Moon. Yet now, as the grayback paused and unceremoniously dumped her onto a pile of some sort of sour-smelling skins, she knew that what she was experiencing was no dream. Pain told her. Still again she moaned and, in a daze, uttered a pathetic little howl of longing to be free of it.

"Silence!"

Mowea'qua caught her breath. The command had been spoken by a human voice. A female voice! Old. Ragged. A throaty croak that now uttered an implicit warning.

"Silent we must all be in this world of enemies."

With the grayback standing close, Mowea'qua squinted ahead. Her eyelids were still so swollen that she could barely see the dark shaggy form that was moving toward her, advancing ghostlike through the blue haze of twilight. She cocked her head. Was it a woman or beast or spirit? She could not be sure. Whatever it was, it was not alone. An exceedingly fat, high-rumped, pigeon-toed dog was gamboling ahead of it on a lead. Her vision swam. Through a veil of mist, it seemed, she saw the figure steady its gait with a tall staff as, straining against the pull of the dog, it approached across a wide clearing set amidst a circle of branchless trees and large, scabrous-looking mounds.

She started.

There were beasts hunkering in small groups around the mounds! And was that a column of smoke rising from the largest mound? She could not see the smoke clearly enough to be sure, but, breathing in, she could smell it and, with it, the rich, heady aroma of roasting meat. The scent was unexpected. As was the realization that the mounds were lodges of some kind and that someone, or *something*, must be cooking up a meal inside the largest of them.

Confused, she cocked her head, unable to find logic in what she was seeing or smelling. The scent of roasting meat was undeniable. Deer? Hare? Raccoon? Perhaps all three? Or perhaps bear? Long had it been since she had eaten of the latter, for bear, sacred to the Old Tribe, were so rare in the forest within which she had dwelled with her grandmother that she could not quite remember the ritual of the bear feast. Nevertheless, the mouth-watering scent of bear flesh remained as a haunting in her nostrils. Salivating, she knew that what she was smelling now was close to that, definitely red and rich and mammal and surely not the lighter, less nourishing flesh of fish or fowl. A feast of some sort, she thought, and then her mind ran wild.

"Ah!" she gasped as an image of little Musquash being spit-roasted over a cooking fire maintained by beasts had her certain that she must be dreaming after all. The beasts were animals! They could not live in lodges like men! They could not cook their kills! In the time beyond beginning when the People and Animals were all of one tribe, Man stole from Lightning the secret of summoning Fire and had kept that secret to himself and the People ever since. No Animal knew the way of it!

Yet surely smoke was rising from the big mound, and the smell of roasting flesh was strong in her nostrils. Along with another, far less pleasant scent—the all-pervasive stink of the beasts themselves and of an encampment that had been occupied far too long.

"Encampment?" Mowea'qua turned the word. How could this be? Straining to focus her gaze, she saw that the mounds were indeed lodges. Low, arching, broad-based structures, each was encircled by a tangling of what could only be mammoth tusks and thatched with bark and boughs laced down with wide strips of thong that were in turn overlaid with large, dark hides. To one side of each lodge stood a totem post. The skull of a large animal was fixed atop each post. Bear? It seemed so. With her clouded vision she could not be sure, but each skull was crowned with a circlet of what she could only guess to be its own claws and teeth, then adorned with long, feathered stringers of some sort of spirit offerings: bits of dried meat, perhaps, and berries, leaves, even freshwater shells and small bones—she could hear the latter clicking in the rising wind of evening.

A chill went through Mowea'qua. If only she could see with clarity! If only she could gather in her thoughts and think clearly again! There was something familiar here. And disturbing. Something about the shape of the lodges. Something about the sight of mammoth tusks heaped around them.

Something about the way the structures and the skull-topped totem posts were arranged in a circle. And something about the slow, measured way in which the specter was approaching with the fat dog straining at the end of its leash.

Mowea'qua's head was aching. Her vision was swimming again. The specter was very close. Its actual form was hidden within a thick tenting of what appeared to be bear and beaver skins, but she could see its bare bony feet and its gnarled hands and recognized its gait as that of a human being of advanced age whose wisdom wisely counseled a fear of falling. The girl's heart leaped. So had her grandmother walked in the depth of winter whenever she was inspired to bundle herself in her furs and venture from the lodge with U'na'li, the wolf, on a lead. And now, as the specter paused before Mowea'qua and jerked the fat dog up short on its leash, although the girl could not see the apparition's face, she sobbed in recognition, "Grandmother?"

"Mmph. Yes. A grandmother was I. But no longer. The last of my spawn are dead."

Mowea'qua nearly swooned. Now, at last, it all made sense. The kami had not abandoned her after all. She had called to Death, and Death had come! Sila, it seemed, had chosen to walk in the form of her grandmother this day; until this moment, she would not have thought it possible. "Dead, then, am I?"

"Mmph. Old Tribe are you."

"Yes!"

"Strong must you be."

"Yes!"

"And yielding."

"Yielding . . . ?"

"Passive. Accepting. Opening yourself to the forces of

Creation. Enduring all. Bearing many! As the Old Tribe must endure. And now hope again to survive. In you!"

Mowea'qua did not understand. The Old Tribe was no more. How could it endure? How could she be dead and still be advised to survive? And what more could she possibly be expected to bear than she had already borne under the cruel press of the beasts? Doubt began to stir her mind. Never before had old Kelet come from the realm of the Ancient Ones to actually stand before her and speak aloud outside of her mind. Yet here she was beneath the fading sky, smelling of unwashed skin and fur and rancid oil, speaking in the voice of a stranger and offering advice that raised the hackles on Mowea'qua's bare skin.

Something was not right. The girl sensed it in her bones. She had called out to Death, yes. But had she not also called upon Old Tribe magic to help her maintain Old Tribe strength and dignity and pride in the face of Death? Yes! So why would her beloved grandmother come to her now and, at the moment of her death, advise her to forfeit what little was left to her of these Old Tribe virtues, when Kelet herself had, through her teachings, made them central to her granddaughter's very being?

"Yah!" Mowea'qua's musings were cut short as, without warning, the specter released the leash and urged the fat dog to the attack. The animal did not hesitate for so much as a second. Mowea'qua raised her arms to ward it off. Too late. The dog was on her, grunting and rooting and nosing beneath her crossed wrists to land sloppy licks all over her face. Then, having tasted of her skin, it sagged across her thighs, turned itself belly up, extended all four paws skyward, and, wriggling on its back, begged a belly rub as though from an old friend. Amazed, Mowea'qua reached down to tickle the ursine chest and belly and saw that the dog was no dog at all. It was a bear, a cub as big as an overfed camp dog, but a cub all the same.

"Mmph," snorted the specter. "The totem of this band recognizes her as one of our own."

"Told you I it would be so. There was no missing it when first we saw her upon the trail . . . not once we saw her eyes. Truly, say I, a gift from the kami is she to us."

Mowea'qua gasped. The grayback had just spoken! This time she had not imagined it. Her mind was reeling, so much so that when the cub began to mouth her fingers she took no notice until it crunched down, hard. She cried out in pain, pulled back her hand, and, with the bear moving to nuzzle her in earnest apology, stared at a small puncture wound in the side of her thumb. It was not much of a cut, but it was bleeding. And it hurt. "Bleed not do the dead!" she declared, glowering up at the specter. "Nor do the dead pain feel."

"Life is pain," said the specter dourly. "No use to us would another corpse be."

Mowea'qua's eyes narrowed. "My grandmother you cannot be!"

"Never said I that I was."

"She is Great Grandmother of Many," informed the grayback. "Old she is. And wise. In times gone long away a breeder. As will you be now for us."

"A woman cannot with beasts breed!"

The grayback laughed. "Beasts? Is this what think you we are? Mmph! Then what in your own eyes are you? And why did you into the night run away to be one with us?"

Mowea'qua was stunned, not only by the questions, but by the sound of a man's laughter coming from the mouth of an animal. She turned up her gaze to the grayback. Her vision was still swimming, but it was much clearer now, and, for the first time, she saw her captor for what it truly was. It was not a beast. Nor was it a man. Somehow, impossibly, it was both!

And now, leering, it lowered itself to its haunches and stared straight into her face. "Yes! Look! See! And know!"

Once again Mowea'qua's mind was reeling. She could see now that the grayback was neither maned nor furred. It was fully clothed, as a man would be clothed, but not in garments that any man she had ever known would willingly place against his own skin. Its hunting shirt and leggings were of the vilest, most crudely cut and sewn pelts of bear and beaver, and its overcape consisted of a collection of the most decrepit-looking gray wolf tails she had ever seen. In the presence of Great Grandmother of Many, it had parted the wild tanglings of its filthy black hair and tossed the long unkempt strands back over its shoulders to reveal its face. A long face. Manlike. Broad across a prominent brow. Nose high-bridged. Cheekbones wide and round above cascading upper lip hair that flowed greasily into an equally oily waist-length beard. Had it not been leering at her—and had she not remembered the feel of its teeth nipping at the tender skin of her breasts and belly and inner thighs—she might have assumed that it had no mouth.

Mowea'qua cringed.

It was showing its teeth. Large, flat, serrate-edged, scum-rimmed teeth, with the long, prominently distended canines of a carnivore. Her gorge rose. All that she could see of its skin was smeared red and blue with grease paint. And its eyes were as pale and sharp and piercing as the stone head of her bear-bone lance.

She gasped.

It had gray eyes!

Eyes the color of mist!

Grandmother Kelet's eyes!

Old Tribe eyes!

Unnatural eyes!

As her own eyes were always said to be.

"No!" she cried. "This cannot be!"

"No? See you in my eyes the truth of what is between us. Our blood is one blood. Wolves our ancestors were in the time beyond beginning. Long ago in this valley Strangers slew many of our tribe. Now they have returned. With their loud singing. With their drums. With their dogs. With their many females and young they flaunt their arrogance in this forest that we a refuge have made in a world overrun by their kind. Saw you did we when first the noise of these Strangers drew us beyond the falls. Followed you did we. Sang out to you in the wolf song of the Ancient Ones did we. When into the night you ran alone, howling in answer to our call, knew we that a gift from the kami of our kind were you! No life-bearing females have we left among us. So each man in the hunting band has with his life filled you. Now those men who have stayed behind to guard the village will come into you. Again and again will you open yourself until with new life you swell! What you bear will not the issue of one be, but of all, in the way of the Old Tribe."

Somewhere a raven called.

Far away.

In another world, it seemed.

Tears were running down Mowea'qua's cheeks. "Into the night I did not run to be with you! And Old Tribe you cannot be! Old Tribe people would not stink as you stink! Old Tribe people were beautiful in all ways! In all skills and magic were they versed! Grandmother Kelet told me this. Old Tribe people would not steal from other tribes! Old

Tribe people would not hurt others as you have hurt me! Old Tribe people would—"

"Do as they must to survive," interrupted the specter. "A fool or a liar was your grandmother. The Old Tribe is as you see. Behold, your Old Tribe brothers and sisters come now to greet you."

Mowea'qua stiffened. It was as the old one said. The beasts that had been hunkering before the mounds had risen. They were coming forward. And others were emerging from the mounds. Children—filthy, wild-haired, monstrous children. All male, from the look of them. And, accompanying them, a single sickly-looking young female walking slope-shouldered, hang-headed, and heavy-footed, with a fur-swathed infant held to bared breasts.

"With the birth of that infant was her womb cast out, along with caul and cord," informed Great Grandmother of Many with about as much empathy as she might have shown to an oft-used heating stone that had cracked in too many places and thus outlived its usefulness in the family boiling bag. "Birth fever eats her spirit. Die soon she will. In her place will you now breed new life for us."

Mowea'qua was shivering uncontrollably. The others were pausing before her. Pale-eyed. Narrow-faced. All as wild-haired as she. Her hands drifted upward through the chaos of her own hair to touch her face—her long, narrow, pale-eyed face. Understanding dawned as horror within her spirit. The grayback was right. She *was* one of them! And now, appalled, she saw that the young female was trying to force a nipple into the mouth of the infant. But the baby could not take suck. It was dead. Long dead! Its tiny corpse was rigid. And it was not swathed in furs. It *was* furred! As furred as the cub of any bear or . . . wolf.

"Ah!" Mowea'qua cried out again as the infamies that Moraq and Ningao had spoken against her ancient lineage suddenly beat within her brain.

Spawned of the mating of man and wolf!

The beast children of the Old Tribe become wolves at will, hunting, devouring, and raping the women of the People whenever they come upon them unaware!

And so it is that they have been justly hunted and slaughtered wherever they are found, until now few of their fanged and furred and filthy kind remain in the world!

It was true! All of it!

Was it any wonder that the People and the Northerners looked upon her with such disdain and revulsion?

Old Kelet had lied to her! Kinap had tried to tell her, but even he, storyteller that he was, had not had stomach enough to give her the entire truth of it. Her grandmother had chosen to raise her alone within the dark heart of the great inland forest, not to protect and nurture her proud and ancient Old Tribe heritage, but to shield her from the devastating truth and everlasting shame of it!

Again a raven called.

Closer now.

Another answered.

Closer still.

The grayback tensed.

As did the old one. "Thought I that all guardians were called in from the forest to mate now with the new woman among us?"

"It is so," replied the grayback. "As you see."

"Mmph," snorted Great Grandmother of Many, scanning nervously around. "Ravens grow restless. As do I. Ending is the day. Guardians must come forward. Let each complete now what must be done with our new woman in the way of the Old Tribe, beneath the sky, before the rising of the red moon. And then, think I, we must break down this longtime good camp and move on. In case she has been followed."

"No one for her will come," assured the grayback with a blatant huff of confidence. "Watched and waited long did we before our move we made. No one wants her . . . except her own kind."

Mowea'qua felt sick. Musquash had wanted her. Enough to risk everything to be at her side. Hugging the cub, she hoped that the little boy was safe and far away and that he would never learn the truth of his own kind. Never!

The female and young were standing stock-still, tense with expectation, staring sharp-eyed, pitiless. The males were closing a circle around her as, in apparent agreement to some unspoken consensual ranking among the pack, the first of those who had not yet pierced her began to free its male bone.

Mowea'qua did not move. A strange calm had come over her. As she stared at the approaching beasts, it occurred to her that if she were to bolt and run, she might just make it into the trees before she was caught. But whether she fled or stayed, it would be the same for her. One by one they would fall upon her until, like the pack of feral dogs that had savaged her in last night's dream, they devoured—if not her flesh—then surely her spirit. Already she could feel it happening; her will to live was gone. She had no wish to call it back. No one would come to rescue her. She was where she had chosen to be. With the Old Tribe. Among her own kind at last.

She closed her eyes. Again she wished for Death. This time it came.

▼▼▼▼▼

As in the dream it came.

She did not see the rain of arrows, stones, and lances that fell upon the village. She did not hear the startled shouts of men or the screams and squeals of terrified women and children as Tôrnârssuk and the search party broke from the trees. A stone flung from a trithonged hurler struck her brow even as the grayback went down, clutching the arrow in his neck, and her latest assailant slumped forward, deadweight now, a lance in his back. Stunned, with her mind adrift under what seemed to be the shadowing wings of ravens, she heard wolves howling and raptors shrieking all around as a dog came close . . . a huge black dog . . . slavering and then tearing at her throat . . . killing her as it spoke in the voice of a man.

"It ends here for you, daughter. As it should have ended on the day you were born!"

"No! Kinap! No!"

"Heed the boy, Giant. No need for a father to finish off his own. Not when a band brother is willing to step in and—"

"Get away from her, Moraq!"

"Stand aside, Musquash. Now! Ah! Get off me, boy! Can you not take hold of this child, Kamak? Did I not tell you to keep the boy back from this?"

"Ah! Here. I have named him Son. I will take him. And now, Moraq, if you would have it so, finish her as you see fit, as we have finished the others. I will look no more upon her kind."

The tearing sensation at her throat ceased. Mowea'qua gasped for air; there seemed none left for her in all the fading world as the voice of the boy raged on, sobbing now.

"I am no son of yours, Kinap! No son of yours! You have

killed children! And a bear cub! And an old woman! What 'kind' are you? Not a man! No! Stop, Moraq! Stop . . . stop . . ."

The words faded.

A shadow was pressing her. Hurting her. Invading her as the grayback had invaded her. Driving deep between her thighs as savagely as any beast.

Somewhere close by, a man echoed Musquash's plea and transposed it into a command.

Someone laughed, a low and ugly sound.

And then a warm, heavy weight fell upon her, and the world went dark.

Mowea'qua welcomed the darkness; there was no pain in it, no distress, only quiet. Deep. Mindless. And then not even that. Until, once again, voices roused her to the peripheries of consciousness and she was aware of the smell of blood, hot and wet on her face.

"Tôrnârssuk . . . you have killed him, Tôrnârssuk!"

"And so. Leave him with the others, Ningao."

"But he is one of our own, a man of the True People."

"Leave him, I say!"

"For carrion? With the bodies of Old Tribe beasts?"

"You must not argue with our headman, Ningao. Among my father's Dawnland People, no True Man would shame himself or offend the spirits of his Ancestors by setting himself to copulate with a dying woman! Tôrnârssuk was right to call him off. And to kill him. Moraq should have obeyed. As must you. Come. Leave him where he lies beside the girl. We should not linger here among the dead."

"Wait, Kanio'te. All of you. Wait! What about Mowea'qua?"

"What about her, Musquash?"

"She is not dead, Tôrnârssuk!"

"She is dead to us."

"No," cried the boy. "I will not leave her here to die! Even if you carry me off, I will find a way to come back for her! And if, by abandoning her, you cause her spirit to walk the wind, the forces of Creation will curse you, for they have chosen the way in which to punish her and have left her with her life!"

The voices stopped.

Mowea'qua was aware of someone kneeling over her and, managing to pull in a ragged breath, strained to open her eyes. The feather of Raven lay across her lids. She could not see through it. It was just as well, she thought, for she was certain it must now be as in her dream: The dogs that had ravaged her and the beloved father who had betrayed her had been driven off by a greater power. She had no wish to look into the face of Sila as it spoke out of the mouth of the great white bear of the north.

"The boy is right."

"Tôrnârssuk, you cannot listen to a child!"

"Would you challenge me again, Ningao?"

"No, White Bear!"

"Good. I would not raise my hand to end the life of another band brother this day. So do not forget again that I *am* Tôrnârssuk, White Bear, One Who Gives Power. I am Tunraq, Guardian and Guide into the world of spirits. I am Wíndigo, Great Ghost Cannibal, Winter Chief of the manitous, War Chief of this band and Brother to Raven. Behold. There is a sign here for us. The spirits have given the feather of Raven into the care of this woman. I, Brother to Raven, cannot do less than care for her. So come. We will take her with us. The great river is far and the journey ahead of us is yet long. And I have seen enough of Death this day."

Part Three

SHADOW OF THE RED MOON

▼▼▼▼▼▼▼

Shadows fall
My spirit trembles
I will walk toward the Day!
Raven follows
My spirit trembles
I will walk toward the Day!
Night is coming
My spirit trembles
I will not look back!

Chapter One

▼▼▼▼▼▼▼

In the time beyond beginning there was a whale. A white whale. Only this. No moon. No sun. No solid ground. Only a vast, dark sea with one whale singing in it. Imagine it, Avataut, one lonely whale calling down the stars, capturing the music of starlight in the spray of its breath, and out of this light singing all things into being."

"One whale?" The hunter smirked at what he took to be his hunt brother's folly. "What kind of tale is this that you would tell me, Armik?" he asked as they walked together along the river strand toward the big communal Man House. "In the time beyond beginning there were no whales, no dark seas, nor were there stars to light that darkness. There was only Wind and Sky and Earth Below. From a mating of these things was First Caribou born. From its cast antlers did the True People take life to leap and dance with Wind upon the skin of Earth beneath Ever-Watching Sky. All True Men of the Barrenlands know this!"

"Yes, Avataut, yes," agreed Armik, "but we are far from the Barrenlands. Long has it been since we danced the dance of life beneath the sky as our Ancestors danced it in rhythm with the movement of the great herds. And long has it been since the antlered children of First Caribou were our main source of meat. We hunt in new ways. We take a new kind of meat. And we make our lives among hunters whose ancestors are not our own."

"So?"

"The tale I tell of First Whale is a shaman's song, Avataut! A Dawnland song of Creation. Different from our own Creation song, I know, but, I would wager, not so very different from the tales your new friends among the kayakmen tell. The song of the white whale! The song of Inau!"

"I care not for the songs of women."

"She is more than woman, Avataut. She is Shaman! And the song of First Whale is the same song she sings each night on the bluffs when she calls the whales to return into the great river and give their lives to all who have come to this far shore in hope of a good hunt. Never have I understood the meaning of its many words until the Dawnlanders among the scouts translated for me when we went downriver together in their long, bark-covered canoes. It is a song of great power. And the whales are coming, Avataut! I saw them from the great cliffs. Many whales! Any day now we will see them on this shore. Soon you will have a chance to see if they will yield their life spirits to you when you go out to them in the new skin boat that you have made."

"You, too, will see! You will be close at my side!"

"Uh, yes, Avataut, yes. In one of the umiaks, yes, if you wish it so. But in truth, my hunt brother, I am not at ease in any boat. And ever since the night of the red moon, I have been thinking that maybe we should pay the shaman Inau a visit this season."

"Why? She is not of our tribe."

"Out of respect."

"She is not my mother."

"Out of gratitude, then."

"For what?"

"For . . . for taking the blood from the face of the moon . . . for calling the whales!"

"Every man at this Great Gathering asked the cloud spirits to wash the blood from the moon! And every man at this Great Gathering asks the spirits of his Ancestors to speak to the spirits of the whales, Armik. I do not believe that they answer the call of a woman . . . least of all a woman of the lesser tribes."

"Ah, but, Avataut, we cannot be sure of that. All say that her spirit singing is like no other! And her dancing, too! All say that those who enter her lodge of bones enter also into the belly of the world, through the open maw of First Whale, into the very womb of Mother Below. There, in darkness, they are bathed in magic smokes of many colors and given amulets drawn from a magic sack! Amulets to protect a man when he is on the water! Ah, Avataut, all say that spirit birds appear at her bidding to carry her words on behalf of the hunters upward into the sky country of the Ancestors! And in exchange for meat and pelts and fat for her lamp, she will call upon the spirits and ask them to speak through her to predict the way the hunt will go for any man of any tribe assembled on the beach!"

"Will she? How generous of her," slurred Avataut. "Men of the lesser tribes may well believe in her magic, Armik, but True Men heed not the warnings of women, and True Men know that portendings and amulets cannot be bought with offerings of meat! These things are gifts freely given by the spirits and must come to a True Man as they will!"

"Yes, Avataut, yes, but . . ."

Avataut lengthened his stride, wanting to put Armik

behind him so he could proceed to their destination without further unwelcome distraction. Talk of the female shaman never failed to put him on edge. He did not like to think about the woman. In his mind's eye he invariably saw her as he had seen her on the night of the thunderstorm, a pale form scrambling up the rain-sodden trail to the top of the wooded bluffs above his campsite.

He grimaced. What had she been doing there in the midst of the storm, prowling around his tent, murmuring and mocking him out of the darkness? He shook his head. He would not ask himself that question again. There was no point. Again and again he had pondered it and had yet to come up with a satisfactory answer. Nor was he sure that he really wanted one. Especially now! After spending most of the day fasting and resting in preparation for tonight's contests of strength and wit, his mood was as high and buoyant and strong with purpose as an eagle soaring on a summer wind. He wanted nothing, least of all thoughts of Inau, to bring it down.

A tremor of expectation went through Avataut. What a time he was going to have in the Man House tonight! He was determined to make it so. Last night, to the delight of his fellow Northerners and the kayakmen among them, he had twice bested at wrestling a young braggart only newly arrived at the Great Gathering with a small trading band from the distant lake country. He had come away with an elaborate earring of bright copper beads and a stringer of birchbark makuks filled with valuable and much-coveted crystallized sweet sap. He had shared these packets of sap with his bandsmen and the kayakmen. After cracking the rock-hard contents with a stone picked up from the curb of the fire pit, he had passed out the fragments, holding back only a few small chips for himself and his woman and son. For this act of generosity he had been praised almost as highly as he had been exalted for winning the earring. Among those born of the unforgiving northern barrens, only the best and most successful of hunters could afford to be generous. Indeed, generosity ranked second only to courage as a mark of a man's worth. And sweet sap from the southern forests and copper from the inland lakes were both viewed as rare and wondrous things. To a man, the Northerners agreed that the braggart had been a fool to risk losing his trading supply of sweet sap, and an absolute idiot to allow himself to be taunted into wagering his earring to an obviously superior man.

Avataut's broad face split with a grin. It was his plan to best the man again tonight. And this time for an even showier and far sweeter prize! Indeed, he was looking forward to another chance to put the newcomer in his place. The man was a hothead as well as a sullen loser. Unwilling to accept defeat, he had shamelessly offered trail weariness as an excuse for his losses and, stalking angrily from the Man House, had sworn to return the following night to win back his earring and even his score with Avataut at any game of the Northerner's choosing.

Avataut squared his shoulders as he walked on across the stony strand. Armik was still plodding along at his side. Having finally picked up on his headman's unwillingness to make conversation, he had settled into a thoughtful, lip-chewing silence. Avataut was glad.

The sun was setting. Its long, tender, day-end rays were warm against his back, almost as sweet to his body as the foreigner's candied tree sap had been sweet to his mouth. Nevertheless, he was anxious for the day to end so that the feasting and challenges of the night could begin. How he loved the rowdy camaraderie that he found within the Man

House at the end of each day! The laughter! The songs! The stories! The good-natured taunting and tests of strength and skill! His spirit swelled with pleasure just to think of it. The renewed sense of kinship between him and the former bandsmen of Tôrnârssuk was intoxicating. With the exception of the boatmen among the Northerners, all True Men named him Headman, and even the kayakmen sought his judgment in matters not dealing specifically with boats. Men of the lesser tribes deferred to him in subtle ways, invariably stepping aside when he entered the Man House and yielding to him and his bandsmen the best place by the feast fire.

Avataut's stomach made a leap and a gurgle as though in response to his thoughts. He and Armik were both bringing freshly caught salmon to add to the day-end feast, eight fine fish speared in the cool pink haze of this morning's mists. With a shrug of his broad, blocky shoulders, he shifted the weight of his six salmon so that they hung in a more centered and comfortable position on his back. The fish, suspended from a gill noose looped around his left shoulder, were all as long as little Ulik, his four-summers-old son, was tall and, since they remained ungutted so that the edible portion of the innards could be savored by all, were nearly as fat. Although Nuutlaq and Irqi, Armik's woman, had spent the day guarding the salmon and keeping them cool in the band's weir pool, the eyes of the fish had sunken and their scaled sides had long since lost the luminosity of life. Nevertheless, when the skin was peeled away, the oily flesh would be even richer with flavor than the eyes, tongues, and guts, and so Avataut was not pleased by the thought of sharing any of it with men of lesser tribes. But share it he would. He would flaunt his generosity as headman of the True People as surely as he would flaunt his winning of the copper earring. His fellow Northerners would expect nothing less of him.

His smile broadened. He was wearing the adornment now, not only because the big loop of rare shiny beads pleased him so much—which it did—but also because if the young hothead who had lost it to him was actually brazen enough to show his face tonight and make good on his vow to attempt to win it back, Avataut intended to prod the braggart's injured pride until the fool was so hot to prove himself that he would rise to any challenge. Any challenge at all!

He laughed.

Armik looked at him from beneath furrowed brows. Avataut ignored his hunt brother's questioning gaze and kept on walking, happily basking in the certainty that when he responded to the hothead's challenge with a proposal that they engage in a northern-style fist duel, the newcomer, having no idea what the "game" involved, would readily accept. And on any terms.

Avataut's smile settled into a leer. He could hardly wait for the moment. How his fellow Northerners would roar with approval! What pride they would take in their headman's cleverness, audacity, and willingness to spice the night with a display of a True Man's courage! And how they would guffaw at the newcomer's expense, for they would know what only hunters of the far northern barrens knew—that only the very bravest of men, even among the True People, could long stand to the challenge of a fist duel. Tôrnârssuk had been a master at the game, and Avataut knew his way around it, but once the fall of the dice went against a contender, most readily conceded defeat, for the dice determined not only the number of blows and to which part of the body they must be struck, but which of the protagonists must be the first to face his opponent's fist with no attempt at self-defense until the full number of hits was given. The contest was, therefore, not a game of skill or strength, but a test of a man's ability to stand to the threat of pain, injury, or, sometimes, even death. It was won by the last man standing, or lost by the first man to turn away. And since Avataut now found himself in the enviable position of answering the hothead's challenge to name the game of his choice tonight, the first throw of the dice would be his.

A chuckle rose at the back of his throat. "Yes!" he exclaimed and, laughing again, felt his beautifully carved and subtly weighted gaming pieces of caribou bone lying in the little auk-skin bag that he had attached to a thong sewn to the side of his hunting shirt. These dice would fall in his favor. In his skilled hands they always did, even when now and then at less risky games he found it wise to yield a play here and there to divert suspicion from the fact that he was such an excellent cheat. Tonight, however, once the young braggart agreed to the terms of the game, Avataut was determined to drop him with the first blow. Why put off the inevitable when he intended to claim as his prize not only the pleasure to be had in shaming the man, but the hothead's young wife in the bargain? The woman of the braggart was not much to look at by the standards of his own tribe; like most females not of the True People, she was too long of limb and spare of teat for a True Man's taste, but when the hothead's band first came into the great encampment, her tight little buttocks had caught Avataut's eye and given him an erection even as it occurred to him that she appeared docile and strong enough to make a serviceable camp drudge for Nuutlaq. Not since Tôrnârssuk's captive, Hasu'u, had he seen a female posterior more inviting and promising for his purposes. As an additional bonus, the woman had fine big teeth and wide bone-cracking jaws that put him in mind of his namesake animal, the wolverine. Nuutlaq would be grateful to have such a strong young subordinate to boss around and take over the endless task of chewing sinew and hides to softness at their fire circle; as it was, she had been mumbling about sore gums all day, and the little bite of sweet sap he had shared with her had given her a toothache.

"Noatak and Itqilik went up onto the bluffs last night with several hunters of the inland tribes."

Avataut stopped dead in his tracks. His smile sagged into a glower as Armik's announcement drove all thoughts of women and contests within the Man House straight out of his head. "Onto the bluffs, you say? Men of *my* band?"

"Yes, Avataut, to see with their own eyes the dance of the shaman from the Cave of the Winds. To hear her song. To listen to the tales she tells. To feel her power."

"Women have no power."

"This woman is different." Armik seemed to shrink a little inside his clothes as, with the sunset breeze ruffling the fur trim at the shoulder seams of his buckskin summer tunic, he looked around as though afraid of being overheard. Then, leaning close to Avataut, he reminded him in a timorous whisper, "On the night of the red moon we all heard the shaman on the bluff sing down Rain, Avataut! We all saw her command Wind and Storm to take the blood from the face of the moon and to seek out and vanquish Wildfire lest, on some whim of the forces of Creation, she send her flaming fire children to burn up all living things when you were away from the encampment and yourself in danger of—"

"I was not in danger!" Avataut interrupted defensively. He was bristling now as, with his mood suddenly brought down from the sunny daydream heights in which it had been so smugly soaring, he felt his cherished status as headman being eroded by the reputation of another. By a *woman*. It was intolerable! "For a day and a night and all of another day I made spirit quest alone. And unafraid. All know this! And while I was away from the great river, I, too, called out to North Wind. Yes! Many times did I lift my voice to the spirits of the Ancient Ones and ask them to keep all within this great encampment safe from Wildfire. With me, Avataut, Wolverine, Headman of the True People, no True Man has cause to seek power elsewhere!"

He paused, made momentarily breathless by his own audacity. Armik was staring at him, wide-eyed and gape-jawed. He was certain from his hunt brother's expression that he had impressed the man. And he had not lied in order to do so. No! Every word he had spoken was the truth. A man of the True People would be no True Man at all if he did not know that it was not wise to lie in matters of the spirits. It was like lingering with the dead. Dangerous! He *had* gone on a spirit quest. Yes! He *had* gone alone. Yes! He had *not* been afraid to commit to the purpose of his quest. And he *had* asked the Ancient Ones to keep his band safe from Wildfire. Yet, with a rising lump of frustration in his throat, he knew all too well that these truths masked another truth, one that he would not admit to any man: that it was no whim of the forces of Creation but he, Avataut, Wolverine, Headman of the True People, who had willingly put the lives of every man, dog, woman, and child at the Great Gathering at risk when, in a dread-driven panic over the shaman's dream of the coming of a white bear, he had set Wildfire loose upon the meadow in hope of killing that "bear" and, with it, his fear of it forever.

Fear.

His jaw clenched. As did his fists. Since that long-gone day on the meadow, he had caged his fear of Tôrnârssuk's return in a shell of his own arrogance. No one need know of it. No one! Least of all Armik, in whose unflagging loyalty and admiration he had come to see a reflection of his own excellence. Tôrnârssuk was most likely dead. If not, the man would be shunned when he returned to the Great River of the White Whales. Avataut had made certain of that! And if, by some unforeseen chance, he and White Bear ever came face to face again, the wolverine in Avataut's spirit had grown so bold that he now saw himself as infinitely more powerful and clever than any bear. Surely, he thought, only the best of all men could have taken Tôrnârssuk's place and overshadowed his reputation within the Great Gathering! If White Bear returned, Wolverine would drive him off or kill him. Indeed, he almost looked forward to the day! And so, lest he be seen as ever having been afraid—and therefore weak—in the eyes of any man, he glared at Armik and repeated his proclamation, more strongly than before. "I *have* commanded Wind and Wildfire to work my will! No man can say otherwise! As long as I am headman of the True People, Armik, no True Man has cause to seek power elsewhere!"

Armik gulped audibly and seemed to shrink a little deeper into his furs. "But, Avataut, you are Headman, *not* Shaman, *not* Tunraq, *not* Angatkok. And I have been thinking these past days and nights that, before a hunt for white whales upon the great river, perhaps even True Men have need of magic makers and shamans to ease their fears of what may or may not come to them. Was it not always so when we walked with the one whose name we no longer speak? Do you not remember how it was before bad spirits came to weaken him? Have you forgotten how he put on his raven mask and donned the skin of the great white bear and sang for us the many spirit songs of our Ancestors as he led us all in spirit dances? Ah, truly, Avataut, he was all things to us: headman and tunraq and angatkok and—"

Avataut was so shaken by a sudden wave of righteous

indignation that his eyes bulged as though they might pop from their sockets. For a moment he could not speak. The moment passed. "After all the moons and suns that have risen and set since we broke from his bad-luck band to strike off on our own! After all the distances we have traveled as hunt brothers! After all the camps and feasts and women we have shared! And after I have fought for and won for myself and all other True Men on this shore the best campsites in all this Great Gathering, how can you—the first man to say that I should be headman in his place—still speak of him and honor his name above mine?"

Armik shrank still deeper into his furs. "No, Avataut, no! I do not honor him! I fear him! Ever since the shaman on the bluffs foretold the coming of a white bear I have been dreaming troubled dreams. Bad dreams. Very bad. About you. About me. About the hunt to come. About going out onto the great river again in boats. Only to a true shaman does a man dare speak of these dreams. And so I have come to think that if we were to bring gifts to her as others do, she might work some magic on our behalf. Ah, Avataut, if the white bear returns, he will bring his bad spirits with him, and neither he nor they will be pleased to hear all that we have said about him in his absence. He will want his campsite back. And I think, Avataut, that what a white bear wants, a white bear will take, even from a wolverine."

"You think too much. And not enough! Where there is meat, so, too, there are bears. Black. Brown. Some even the color of the sun. And sometimes, when the winters are as long and cold as the last, bears as pale as the sea ice that carries them south. You and I know this! We need no shaman to tell us. Already black bears have begun to compete with us for fish along the tributary streams. Was it not so this morning when we went for salmon at the weir pool? Yes!

And I will tell you this, Armik: If that white bear with whom we once walked as a brother returns to take from me what I have made my own, I will drive him off or kill him. This I have sworn! For my woman and son and all who have named me Headman in his place! And if you, a man of the True People, no longer possess stomach enough to stand with me and trust in my power, then I say to you now that you have been taking your ease at the trading circles and cooking fires of too many foreigners these days and are no longer fit to carry the two knives of a True Man. Forest People, Grassland People, Dawnland People, Lakeland People: Their ways are not our ways. Their thoughts are not our thoughts. And their shamans are not our shamans; they cannot speak for us!"

Armik's sun-browned face flushed red. "Always we have stood together, Avataut. Always we have shared our women and our meat. Always will it be so. But, Avataut, still I say, you are *not* shaman, and a man has need of a shaman's insight and blessings before he gives his spirit to the hunt. And I must ask, are you not even a little bit curious? Would you not like to see just what it is about the shaman on the bluffs that causes all to say that she is more than a mere woman . . . that at night her spirit leaves her body to fly with nighthawks across the sky, to swim with fish and seals and whales within the great river, and to wander the forest and encampment, seeing many things . . . secret things . . . knowing what is in the hearts of all, man and beast alike?"

A chill went up Avataut's spine. The sun had just gone down behind the bluffs. Suddenly, almost painfully, he was aware of the absence of its warmth. The last long, cool gray shadows of the dying day were sliding down the river strand to set his mind racing back to the night of the thunderstorm. He remembered standing naked in the rain. He heard the crack of thunder. He saw the flare of lightning and, recalling its livid glow, tensed at the memory of the mocking words and laughter of the woman called Inau. For the second time since setting off for the Man House, in his mind's eye he saw her pale form scrambling up the rain-sodden trail to the wooded bluffs. Now, feeling himself watched, he turned and stared back along the strand.

She was there.

Armik pivoted on his heels and, following his hunt brother's gaze, gasped the shaman's name. "Inau!"

Avataut scowled up at the figure on the heights. She was there all right, motionless in the dark, a tall pale form barely visible against the blackness of the trees; had it not been for the stark white glow of her cloak of winter furs and feathers, she would not have been visible at all. A knot tightened in his belly. He knew now, as he had known on the night of the thunderstorm, that it was the woman and surely no spirit that he had glimpsed and heard prowling around his tent in the midst of the downpour. Why had she come? What had she seen? What did she know of all that he had done that day on the meadow to cancel his fear of the return to the great encampment of a man who might subvert his hard-won position as headman among his people? *Nothing,* he told himself. *She can know nothing!*

"Ho, Avataut!" Inau called out to him in his own tongue. "After you have won the woman and shamed the bragger from the Lakeland tribe, Wolverine, amulets have I for you and your hunt brother! And warnings! Many warnings!"

"Woman?" asked Armik, amazed and openly puzzled. "What woman, Avataut? And how does she know about the challenge given by the hothead from the Lakeland tribe? Ah!" His voice fairly squeaked as he forced it into a whisper. "You see! You see! She *is* different! She *is* shaman, Avataut! She *is*! And she does have power! How else would she know your

True Man name, and the name given you by the men of the lesser tribes?"

Rattled, Avataut spat the first reply that came into his head. "I am headman of the Northerners. All hunters in this encampment know my names!"

"But how would *she* know them? She who never descends from the bluffs except in spirit to—"

"She comes from the bluffs. With my own eyes I have seen her. And you know as well as I that many seek her out in her lodge of bones. Men of the lesser tribes must have spoken of me and pointed me out to her as headman of the True People. And you have told me yourself that Itqilik and Noatak were with her on the bluffs last night."

"In the dark. They could not point you out to her in the dark, Avataut!"

"There was a moon last night!"

"Yes, Avataut, but—"

"In the light of tonight's moon you must come to me!"

Both men winced at the shaman's shouted invitation.

But Inau's words struck Avataut like a blow rent by a battle club. He was glowering now. His stance was one of pure belligerence. Although the edge of the long forested bluff upon which the woman stood was a good fifty paces away, he and Armik had been speaking in lowered voices. Yet she had heard every word. She must have heard! How else would she have known where to join in on the conversation? How? He gulped incredulity along with vexation. And just how had she known that he intended to dupe the hothead into wagering his woman? It was impossible! A lucky guess. A mere coincidence.

Armik gave him a meaningful nudge with his elbow. "You see! She stands there, far away, but her spirit is near . . . here beside us, listening . . . knowing our thoughts!"

And in that moment, as though picking up on those thoughts and wishing to affirm them, the shaman spoke out again. "You must not be afraid to join your hunt brother in my lodge of bones tonight, Armik. You must bring meat to me in exchange for spirit wisdom. A fresh haunch of deer I will have from you. Ah, perhaps I ask too much? It is too early to say. The doe broke and ran, did she not, Avataut? A pity. A great pity. For her. For the fawn. For us both, perhaps. But since you have come safely away from the flame children of your servant Wildfire, I will accept an offering of whatever meat you and your hunt brother will wish to share with me this night. Why do you stand staring at me gape-mouthed, Avataut? Have you lost another flint?"

▼▼▼▼▼

Avataut won the hothead's woman.

Easily.

But the pleasure of the contest was ruined and the shaming of the braggart brought little satisfaction.

The words of the shaman were embedded in his brain. They irritated his consciousness even more than the smoky interior of the unvented Man House had irritated his eyes and sinuses. Now, needing air, he stood alone outside the Man House, pulling in deep cool breaths of the night, but neither these nor the low, usually soothing *shhh* of the river were enough to drive the words of Inau out of his head.

How did she know about the doe? How? And by what trick of the tongue did she come to name Wildfire as my servant? A bat winged low overhead, scooping insects, tearing Avataut's thoughts as neatly and silently as it tore the invisible substance of the night. At his back, within the Man House out of which he had just come, the activities of the night were winding down. He could hear the rise and fall of voices and smell the acrid, greasy, end-of-feast smoke that was seeping through the gaps in the loosely stitched seams of the many joined skins that covered the roof of the great longhouse. A bat swooped low again, a light flurrying of all-but-invisible wings, gone in an instant, yet eliciting in Avataut an immediate and innate revulsion as he slapped at thin air and turned instinctively in the direction in which the creature had flown.

Glaring toward the bluffs, he found himself staring into starlit darkness. Inau was up there, silent in her lodge of bones. Later she would sing. Much later. Sometime in the depth of night, when everyone within the great encampment lay asleep in that darkest of hours before dawn, when the moon had set and moisture from the great river rose and condensed in the air to conceal all but the very brightest pinpoints of starlight, she would emerge, as was her way, to stand above the river and call out to the whales.

His jaw tightened. He was never fully at ease in the dark. And he did not want to think of the woman. Let the darkness keep her! Soon the moon would rise nearly full again; its light would transform the night, brightening and redefining the world. Maybe he would feel better then. He doubted it. Inau's words would probably still be biting at his brain. They had followed him out of the Man House as doggedly as they had followed him into it. No matter what he did, he could not shake them off. Even now they were on him like a pack of dogs at a marrowbone, pulling his thoughts this way and that, depriving him of every shred of joy in his victory over the hothead as surely as they had robbed him of appetite when he had joined the other hunters of the assembled tribes for the evening meal.

How did she know that I would goad the hothead into wagering his woman? And how did she know that I would win her?

Avataut scowled. He shook his head. Angrily. Like one of the imagined dogs in his brain he shook it from side to side, hard and fast, harrying his thoughts of the shaman as tenaciously as her words had been harrying him until he succeeded in scattering them at last.

"Ha!" he exclaimed, breathing a little more easily now, glad to be outside, under the open sky, no longer within the Man House. And yet, once again, a bat dipped low, and with the passage of its wings, his thoughts fell back into the great vaulted room. Wide. Dark. Redolent of the smell of sweat and oiled skin and of meat being boiled and roasted. A room so thick with smoke from the unvented central cooking fire that the air took on a gritty texture, stinging the eyes and making them smart and tear even as it flavored every bite of the food they ate.

And, appetite or no appetite, how Avataut had eaten! Too much. Even for a man who answered to the name Wolverine. He vented a belch. It did little good. His belly remained heavy. His throat was tight and sour with the need to heave. Just thinking of the food of lesser tribes was enough to make a man of the True People want to puke, and tonight, after contributing his salmon to the communal food pile, he had forced himself to eat more than his share of the main body of the feast. How could he have done otherwise? The amount of food a man was able to consume at any one sitting was as much a test of his strength as any other challenge. And tonight's feast, provided in the main by the braggart's newly arrived trading party and several other equally small bands that were welcoming their long-awaited inland cousins with a great show of goodwill, had been a test indeed.

He felt bilious just thinking about it. He had wolfed down the flesh of deer and rabbit and fish and fowl, nearly all of it slow-cooked in the manner of the Lake People: some spit-roasted until the outer flesh was blackened and stiff and thick as a scab; some simmered in stone-heated boiling bags to which nuts and roots and berries and various green growing things had also been added; some wrapped in leaves, then packed in mud and buried deep in the coals to be baked during the progression of the meal. Along with meat, he had partaken of other food, some of it indescribable, most of it vile: sour cakes of pounded fat and pulverized seeds that stuck between his teeth; servings of soft and pithy cooked grains that resembled larvae but had none of the flavor or crunch; dried wedges of some sort of bitter orange fruit; and a dark, odd-tasting drink made of the steeped gratings of a fibrous root. Other than fragments of rock-hard sweet sap that were passed around for all to enjoy, not a single morsel of the feast had been to the taste of a True Man, who preferred his berries fresh and his meat raw, barely seared, or, if it must be preserved, wind-dried or fermented by long burial in specially prepared cache pits. And yet, lest he be found squeamish, Avataut, as headman of the True People, had eaten everything that was presented to him until the braggart himself came close to offer a nominally seared haunch of deer.

"I regret that there are no little unborn fingerling children of flesh-eating flies wriggling in the meat of this doe, Headman of Northerners. I have heard it said that such insect food is as sweet to your people as the sap of the a'nina'tig tree is to mine. Still, we have seen to it that, other than a charring away of hair, the flesh of this haunch has remained uncooked. Can it be true that hunters of the northern barrens prefer it so? Is it not revolting to you?"

Avataut could still hear the young man's words. Insult? Or an attempt at congeniality? He had no idea. After nearly a lifetime spent trading and raiding among the inland tribes, he could understand their words well enough, but their ways remained a mystery. As he had stared at the haunch, other words had flared bright at the back of his mind. The shaman's words. Inau had asked for a haunch of deer. "What kind of trick is this?" he had snarled at the braggart. Certain of a conspiracy between the madwoman on the bluff and the braggart in the Man House, he waved away as intolerable the only cut of meat that would normally have been palatable to him.

"What ails you, Northerner?" The hothead had fairly purred with satisfaction at having riled his intended opponent. "Does your belly quail at the prospect of more food? Have I not heard correctly when it is said that the stomachs of you Eaters of Raw Flesh are without bottom? Or would you claim gut sickness and, by so doing, attempt to find a way to shrink back with honor from my last challenge? Ha! There is no way I will let you do that, Friend. That is a chief's earring that you have won from me, and I will have it back. So if you will not eat, then you must name the contest of your choice as you consented to do last night. Unless, of course, Avataut of the Far North is afraid to stand to a better man?"

"Avataut of the Far North is not afraid to stand to any man!" he declared now, as hotly as he had declared then when, rising, he had named the contest, and the terms. And now, as then, he broke into a cold sweat. He had lied. He *was* afraid. Of one man. Of Tôrnârssuk. No, he thought. No more! He had vanquished that fear. Long ago.

His brow came down. He had a vague recollection of the braggart's bandsmen shouting in angry protest of the severity of the game even as Armik and the kayakmen and his own bandsmen guffawed in surprise and clapped their hands in raucous approval of his selection of "a True Man's sport." Wagers were made. On him. On the braggart. Frowning, Avataut could not recall what they were. He remembered only that as he fingered the bone gaming pieces from the auk-skin bag and shook them between his hands, his thoughts had not been on the game at all. They had been on the shaman, on the haunch of deer, on the heart-struck doe that had run from the meadow, on the fire that he had made and commanded as though it were his servant, and on the flint he had found and cast away on the night of the thunderstorm. He had looked for it the next morning. There had been no sign of it. Nor had any of his own fire-starting stones been missing.

How did she know about the flint? Unless she put it outside my tent for me to step on! But why would she do that? Why? Unless . . .

"Throw the dice, Northerner!"

His brow furrowed at the sharply recalled command. Who had spoken to urge on the game? Avataut did not have the slightest idea. Annoyed, he ran his fingers back through his hair and, trying to remember, succeeded only in rousing pain from the newly scabbed laceration that the claws of Raven had opened in his scalp when he had come onto the meadow. Try as he might, he could conjure no recollection of throwing the dice. He knew only that he had apparently made a single wild throw. A reckless throw. It troubled him to think of it now, for he knew that it could have come up badly for him. Very badly. A low number of first hits to his opponent might have been decreed and the places on the body to be struck shown to be inconsequential—foot or thigh, toe or finger, or even one buttock or the other. If that had happened, the hothead could easily have stood to the blows, gloating until the next throw of the dice came his way. If the braggart had then managed to roll high and come up with a series of head or belly strikes, Avataut would have lost all assurance of winning. He was strong, he was brave, he was older and more experienced at hand-to-hand fighting than his challenger, but even the best of men could take only so many punches to the gut and face without passing out or being stunned into forfeiting the contest. Yet the dice had fallen his way. Pure luck. His mind had still been on Inau, as it was now.

What does she know? What can she know? And what would the men of this gathering say—or do—if she told them that the caribou may not return to the river crossings this autumn because I may well have incurred the wrath of Great Spirit of All Deer by not pursuing a heart-struck doe into the forest? And what would they say—or do—if she told them that it was I who gave life to Wildfire and put them all at risk because I was afraid to face Tôrnârssuk? How long would they name me Headman then?

"The dice have spoken! Five hits! Two to the belly. Three to the head. Do you stand or turn away?"

He remembered the words. Who had called out the decree of the dice so that it could then be translated into the many dialects of those gathered in the great, smoky room? Armik. Yes. He remembered that much.

"I stand!"

The words of the braggart still rang in his head. As did the loud and merciless goading of those who had teased and taunted the young challenger into showing everyone just what he was made of. And so he had. Without hesitation. Without the remotest suspicion that he was about to fall to a foul, he had stood to Avataut's blows without a whimper. And, although his kinsmen called out to him and implored him to yield the game, he took all five before he fell.

"Mmm," Avataut mumbled to himself, conceding the hothead's bravery as he absently rubbed the bruised knuckles of his right hand. *Perhaps I should not have hit him quite so hard. Perhaps . . .*

The crunch of footsteps on the strand intruded into his thoughts.

"Northerner!"

Avataut turned, startled to see that the whale-skin entryway of the Man House had been laid back. Light was streaming out of the interior. It ribboned the strand in soft yellow, illuminating a small group of approaching men. He recognized the Lakeland traders. Lean men, slight of build, as light on their feet as foxes, they walked amidst the tantalizing clicking of their many copper bracelets and the copper-beaded fringing of their leggings. As they paused before him, he coveted their adornments and, responding to a pang of pure, mean-spirited envy, could not resist *tsk*ing his tongue at the sight of the unconscious braggart, head lolling forward, moccasined feet dragging as two of his kinsmen supported him by his arms.

"So he has still to regain his wits, if he had any to begin with," observed Avataut, drawling open disparagement of the young man in his own careless version of the trader's tongue. "He will think twice before he challenges a True Man again."

They reacted as one, stiffening at the insult, but only one spoke for the other five—slowly, pointedly, obviously wanting every word to be understood.

"We will not forget this night, Northerner. And though we will honor our brother's debt to you, we will not forget the dishonorable way in which it was won."

Avataut looked the man up and down. They were of the same height, but where he, as a man of the far north, was as sturdy and barrel-chested and muscular as Kwakwaje'sh, the wolverine, the trader was as slim, sinewy, and as long of back and limb as a fox of the inland forests. And no young fox at that. He appeared to be well past his middle years, perhaps as much as a season or two beyond thirty, but still impressive for a man of the lesser tribes. Although he had the ugly, high-bridged nose and prominent eyes of his race, his face was attractively painted in vertical bands of deep blue, a rare and expensive pigment. His long, thick forebraids were bound in the luxurious pelts of young river otters and adorned with feathers, shells, and copper beads. Looped around his left ear was an earring identical to the one wagered and lost by the braggart. And his elaborately fringed buckskin hunting shirt, leggings, and knee-high moccasins were decorated and painted to match his face and hair. At any other time, the trader and raider in Avataut's spirit would have been piqued to single the man out as a future mark; now, distracted by the manner in which he had just been addressed, he huffed annoyance and warned, "Do not threaten me."

"In the Lakeland country of Sebec, my father, chief of the Copper People, such 'games' as you and your kind have called this night are not 'played' to pass an evening or entertain visitors for casual and friendly sport. They are prerequisite to war."

"War?" Avataut turned the word. On either side of him the Lakeland men glared at him, squint-eyed, pinch-mouthed, painted chins jabbing outward, their manner as imperious as hawks looking down their long beaky noses at potential prey. The audacity of them! They, too, were impressively attired, but, having just come from the Man House, into which, by the laws of the Great Gathering, no man of the People bore arms of any kind, not one of them had so much as a dagger on him.

Avataut made no attempt to keep his contempt from showing on his face as, thinking of the two fighting blades that lay secreted beneath his shirt according to the custom of True Men, he slurred, "Why would I wish to make war with such as you? Your band is small. Your people are not True People. Anything I want from you I could take at will, by force, at any time. But this I have not done. No man of the lesser tribes can say that Avataut does not honor the laws of this great camp. If I have offended you tonight, so be it. You cannot understand the ways of a True Man."

"You are mistaken, Avataut of the Far North," said the spokesman for the traders. "No man can live outside the fall of his shadow. Your reputation as a raider and thief walks ahead of you. And so I tell you now that if you are to continue to dwell in peace among the many bands of the People who have been hunting and trading on the shores of the Great River of the White Whales since the time beyond beginning, it would be wise of you to understand *our* ways, for although you and your Northerners have wintered on this shore and others of your kind come here to hunt the white whales, you will forever be strangers in this land . . . a race apart."

Avataut knew that the last three words had been intended as an insult. He took them as a compliment. *A race apart*. Yes! As though a True Man would ever wish to be considered anything else! Nevertheless, he was irked. The man was as arrogant and undeserving of his respect as the braggart. So he demanded, "Who are you to speak so to me? Has someone of great rank among the many bands of the lesser tribes died and named you Chief over all? If so, I have not heard of it! Under many a moon have my people camped on this shore. Under many a sun have we hunted alongside men of many bands and tribes. We have learned to speak in many tongues. We have shared meat. We have shared women. It is you, Newcomer, who are a stranger in this place!"

An openly restive and resentful murmuring went through the traders. As the injured hothead moaned, the spokesman fixed an icy gaze on Avataut. "I am Táwoda, eldest son of Sebec, brother of the one whom you have shamed this night," he informed him. "My brother, Nak'w, is young. In the way of youth, he has been full of himself. In the way of youth, he has sought to test himself against one whose strength and fighting skills he found cause to admire. And in the full arrogance of youth he actually believed he could beat you! It would have been enough for you to have led him along, to have done a little teaching through the 'game' at which he sought to best you, to have brought him to a confrontation with the limitations that arrogance puts on a man's ability to truly achieve his aims. But no. This was not enough for you. You led him, yes, and then, when he followed, you chose to break not only his arrogance but the man himself. You have shattered his jaw and nose along with his pride. He will be long in healing. As my memories of you and the ways of your kind will long remain an open wound within my mind."

Avataut's eyes narrowed. "Your brother challenged me. I answered his challenge. So do not attempt to solicit my sympathy. You cannot whine your way out of his debt to me. I will have my prize."

Táwoda's aquiline features went as tight as the newly stretched skin of a drum. "As I have said, Northerner, the sons of Sebec pay their debts. The woman my brother has wagered and lost to you will be needed to tend his injuries tonight. I will bring her to your camp with the rising of the sun. After that, let there be no more words between us."

"You lose as sourly as he does."

"Yes." As the eldest son of Sebec walked on, he added darkly, "You would be wise to remember this."

Avataut knew a warning when he heard one. He chose to dismiss it without comment. Having come from a man of a lesser tribe, it was unworthy of a True Man's consideration.

Yet, as he watched the Lakeland traders move on down the strand, he considered them. How ungrateful they were! How unappreciative of his benevolence toward them! He could have insisted that Táwoda bring the braggart's woman to him immediately. It was his right to do so. She belonged to him now, just as the hothead's copper earring and birchbark packets of sweet sap belonged to him. But, truth be told, his right hand still hurt and he was simply too full of food to even think about taking on a new woman now.

He loosed another belch and, arching his back, rubbed his distended sides and belly. He could no longer see the traders. Darkness had absorbed them even before they left the strand and turned into the forest, carrying the braggart toward the far part of the encampment in which they had raised their tents beneath the trees. A fitting choice of campsite, he thought, for a race of men unfit to live beneath the open sky.

A dog barked.

Another echoed it.

And another.

The sounds came from deep within the trees.

A male voice shouted the animals to silence.

Then, after a sharp yelp, all was quiet again save for the low whisper of the river, the sporadic sigh of the night wind rising in the trees, the occasional whine of an insect, and the soft rise and fall of voices in the Man House. Until a woman uttered a single high, sorrowful wail.

Avataut smiled. The sound pleased him. The cry had come from the hothead's woman. He was sure of it. The traders must have reached their campsite and, after silencing their pathetically small and obnoxiously yappy pack dogs, informed the braggart's wife that her man had gambled her away to a "stranger."

Stupid woman, he thought. *You should raise your voice in celebration, not lamentation. At dawn tomorrow you will have a better man, a True Man!*

"Ha! Listen to that! When next that woman wails, it will be with pleasure and under the press of a real man, eh, Avataut?"

He blinked, surprised by Armik's question as, for the second time since coming from the Man House, the crunch of footsteps on the stony strand caused him to turn. His brows arched. His hunt brother was coming toward him. In the light that was pouring from the entrance, he could see Armik's short, sturdy form striding forthrightly ahead of several taller, equally burly men. Avataut recognized them as Grasslanders. A rough and rowdy crowd. Almost as rough and rowdy as his own Northerners. To a man they shaved their heads, leaving only a single braided forelock in which was worn the flight feather of a golden eagle. As though this was not striking enough, their faces appeared to be adorned with bleeding wounds, for their method of scarification was unusual. And impressive. Instead of the conventional manner of tattooing in which the skin was left smooth after being superficially pricked and impregnated with patterns of color created by ash and various plant juices, the Grassland men scarred themselves so aggressively that the resultant bold, intricate "tattooing" rose high and glossy beneath the thick, luminous pigment of fresh grease and bloodred clay with which it was painted each day. Indeed, these men came as close to intimidating Avataut as any men he had ever known. Still, they were not raiders, they were traders, and since they were not True Men and had not threatened him in any way, he did not respect them enough to recall their individual names or specific band affiliations. Yet, instinctively, he stood to his full height and threw out

his chest at their approach and was not displeased when he
saw that they were beaming at him as they spoke approvingly
in their own tongue, a dialect so similar to that of many of
the forest bands with whom he had traded over the years that
he had no trouble understanding it.

"Well done, Northerner!"

"That one needed to be trounced, and thoroughly!"

"Have you ever seen a youth so arrogant?"

"You have given him something to think about while he
is on the mend."

"He will be a better man for the besting you gave him. I
would wager my own woman on that!"

"Come, Wolverine, join us while others go to their sleep
in the Man House. The night is still young. We have decided
to bring leftovers from tonight's feast to the shaman on the
bluffs. And salt from the sacred springs of our Ancestors, and
also a sack of precious red clay, for all know that the sacred
blood of the earth that gave birth to all People is in it. These
are rare gifts. Fitting gifts for a shaman. And we have heard
much of her power since we have been in this camp. So now
we would seek that power for ourselves, for success in our
trading here, and for a good journey home to our distant
families. So I say again, join us, Wolverine. It has been told
to us by this hunt brother of yours that you have yet to visit
the sacred lodge of the holy one on the bluff."

"I seek not the counsel of women," Avataut replied
coolly, guardedly, and with a politeness he had not deigned
to show to Armik earlier. The Grasslanders were looming
over him, six men in all, each as big and slope-shouldered as
a forest bison. He eyed them thoughtfully. A wolverine he
might well be, and a better man than any male not born to
the True People, but, unlike the surly, blue-faced Lakeland
traders, these men of the Grasslands were not only big and

bold, they had a reputation as quick-tempered fighters despite their affable ways. He had no wish to offend them. Their approval and willingness to walk with him as though they were of one band and tribe could only further enhance his status in the eyes of others. Besides, with his knuckles sore and his stomach as full as it was, he was not sure this would be a good time to provoke them, even though they were unarmed and he had two knives strapped to his side beneath his hunting shirt.

"Inau is more than a woman, Avataut of the North!"

"Is she, Grasslander? So I keep hearing from my hunt brother here. Is that not right, Loose Tongue?"

"It is true, Avataut!" Armik cringed at what he had just been called and took the words as his headman had intended him to take them—as a rebuke for speaking about a bandsman to those not of his own tribe. Nevertheless, Armik was by nature a single-minded man and, having seen his chance to press his earlier position, was not about to let it pass. "I was telling the Grasslanders here that everything is exactly as the shaman said it would be. Truly! Avataut, we *should* seek her magic. Spirit power *is* hers! How else could she have known that you were going to challenge the braggart in the Man House tonight?"

"It was common knowledge around the encampment after he invited me to do so last night."

"But not even I knew that you would stake your winnings and ask him to match the bet by wagering his woman!"

Avataut's brows arched toward his hairline. "I have looked openly at that woman. Many have seen this. And what many have seen with their eyes many will speak of with their tongues. The one you name Shaman must have heard talk."

"But what about the haunch of deer, Avataut? How did

she know that this kind of meat would be offered to you as a portion of the night's feast in the Man House?"

"Many things were offered to me as a portion of tonight's feast in the Man House, Armik. And much deer meat is always eaten in this camp." Avataut was beginning to feel less edgy about the shaman; indeed, he was grateful to Armik for pressing him with so many questions. His answers concerning her so-called power made sense to him.

But Armik was not having any of them. "But still, Avataut, have you not won the bragger's woman just as she said you would? And look here, slung over my shoulder is the haunch of deer she asked for! Can you imagine it? When you waved it away at the feast, it was passed down the line to these Grasslanders here, and after you went out, word went around the Man House that they were going to add it to the gifts they intended to bring the shaman on the bluff. So I have taken it upon myself to win it back for you from these good men in a game of stick toss."

"Why?" The question curdled sourly in his mouth; he was feeling edgy again.

"So that we can bring it to her in your name, Avataut, as she has requested. A haunch of deer in exchange for magic smoke and songs and words of wisdom and warning and the amulets of power that she has already made for us to assure the favor of the spirits on the hunt to come."

"Ah!" the Grasslanders exclaimed in unison.

Then one of their number stepped from among the ranks and, reaching out in a broadly fraternal gesture, slung a long, powerful arm around Avataut's burly shoulders. "Then you *must* come with us, Avataut of the North! If a shaman has made talismans of power for you, you cannot spurn their magic! This would be an offense to the forces of Creation. A dangerous thing! If men were to learn of it, they would hesitate to trade with such a man, and the hunt might turn badly for all who share this camp with you. So come, Northerner! You *must* walk with us. I, Chaksa, cannot allow you to refuse. Come! Together we will discover the power of Inau."

▼▼▼▼▼

She was waiting.

In darkness and firelight the shaman worked her magic.

High on the bluffs, within a sacred bone-and-wood-braced hollow dug deep into the side of an ancient river dune, she made her lodge and carved her talismans and raised her fire and sacred smoke. They sought her there, as she had bid them seek her.

Somewhere along the way, not even realizing that he did so, Avataut took the lead. Under the stars he led the others on, moving under the shimmering luminescence of the Great Sky River, following a narrow trail marked out by skeletal rows of the vertebrae of whales and worn smooth by the moccasins of the many men of many tribes who had gone before them onto the heights to seek the power of Inau.

The light of a single torch glowed ahead.

Avataut paused.

Armik and the Grasslanders stopped close at his back.

They stood together in silence.

Avataut's head went high. The first glow of the rising moon was beginning to sheen the river and show silver through breaks in the trees. Directly in front of him, the flat, hard-packed earth of the bluff-top trail opened onto a broad, stony, semicircular expanse of elongated grass-furred knolls. His heartbeat quickened. There was something strange here. Unexpected. Something of the smell and feel of his distant birthplace. Something of the far north. Something of a land only newly laid bare beneath the sky and yet old somehow, older than time itself. He could not grasp what his senses were telling him. How could he? As a man of his own time, he could not know that the broken expanse of knolls had once lain at the bottom of a great inland sea or that it was, like the bluffs themselves, part of a vast primordial floodplain shaped by tumultuous outpourings of meltwater from the same continent-spanning ice sheet that had scraped the land of his ancestors to bedrock and whose easternmost edge once stood a mile high upon this shore before it melted and ran wild to its death in the great river and ocean beyond.

"Look, Northerner. The shaman's lodge lies there, just ahead, where the torch burns at the crest of the biggest knoll."

Avataut's brow furrowed. Chaksa was right. And wrong. The smell of burning hanks of dune grass and fat-impregnated hide was overriding the subtler, more elusive scent of the past. He was glad for the distraction; the other smell had unnerved him. But he could see no torch. The light that had led him along the bluff top was emanating from a circular opening in the rounded peak of the knoll; a steady, softly diffused light, it radiated upward and spilled down the long grassy shoulders of the hillock, illuminating what seemed to be a facing of whitish stone at the front of the knoll. Again a chord of memory struck within him, for many were the times that he had returned across the snowy barrens of his ancestral hunting grounds, guided home by the glow of oil lamps shedding light through the semitransparent seal-gut window coverings at the top of the mounded, snow-covered, underground winter lodges of his own people.

"You see, Avataut!" Armik was gulping pure enthusiasm. "It is as Noatak and Itqilik have said. She does make her lodge inside the belly of Mother Below . . . just as do our own

True People in winter. So you see? We are not so different. She *can* speak for us!"

Avataut made no comment. He did not appreciate his hunt brother's exuberant observation, even though he knew that at least a portion of what the man said was true. A well-made underground lodge, with its structural supports framed against and excavated deep into the leeward side of a hill or dune, was a warm retreat from winter winds and storms. With a long, stone-lined entrance tunnel serving as a cold trap and elevated inner rooms walled and roofed with wood and bone and thickly chinked with moss and sod, when the oil lamps were burning and the interiors glowed with light there was no better refuge from the brutal weather of the time of the long dark. In spring and summer, however, during protracted periods of rain and melting snow, spacious, often multiroomed interiors that were warm and snug under winter's insulating layers of snow and frozen earth turned into dripping domiciles fit only for mold and worms and burrowing ground-dwelling rodents that wriggled in and out of the oozing walls. Indeed, he thought, his opinion of the shaman Inau was now more negatively fixed in his mind than before, for only a madwoman would choose to dwell in an underground winter lodge all year round.

"Look, Avataut, look!" Armik's exclamation was subdued by awe.

A light was now showing low on the flank of the large central knoll. Small. Flickering. It was growing larger and brighter with every passing moment. Just as Avataut recognized it as the burning head of a torch being carried forward from far back within the entrance corridor of the shaman's lodge, a pale form emerged from that corridor on hands and knees, held out the torch, then rose to stand tall and beckon them all forward.

"Come!" The shaman Inau's deep, husky, strangely hollow voice resonated in the language of the People from the Land of Grass as she spoke out in invitation. "I welcome you!"

The Grasslanders murmured in amazement.

"You see," said Chaksa to Avataut. "Your hunt brother and the others are right. Her power *is* great. How else would she know the language of my Ancestors and choose to speak it now, in the dark, not knowing who comes to her, or the origins of my tribe?"

Avataut held his tongue. There was no point in speaking, much less in arguing the point. Chaksa and his fellow Grasslanders were already hurrying forward. They would believe what they chose to believe—perhaps what they needed to believe?

His brow came down. Moonlight was silvering the entire bluff top now. Mating with the sparking glow given off by the shaman's torch, it gave everything within his line of sight an eerie, otherworldly glow. He did not like this place. He liked even less the fact that he had been coerced into coming here, albeit in a most congenial fashion. His jaw clenched. As the Grasslanders moved away from him toward the shaman's knoll, he watched their bald heads shining in the moonlight, pale and smooth as eggs.

Avataut shook his head. It took no magic to identify the tribal affiliation of Chaksa and his men; no other people that he had ever seen or heard of shaved their entire skulls. And, since Inau had been coming to the Great Gathering for as many seasons as anyone could remember, he would have been surprised if she, a professed shaman, had not made the effort to master at least a rudimentary knowledge of the tongues of those who sought her wisdom. It was a useful skill, one that Tôrnârssuk had urged all his followers to learn, for it had been his favorite tactic to feign ignorance of any language other than his own when trading among the lesser tribes. What a fine sport he had led his bandsmen to! A game as stimulating and satisfying to the spirit as the contest Avataut had tricked the Lakeland braggart into tonight! What pure pleasure it had been to boldly enter the hunting territory of another band, ostensibly to trade, claiming ignorance of the language of their host, pretending goodwill, winning confidence, while all the while listening to unguarded conversations that inevitably led to the discovery of the secrets and weaknesses of the band. How many hidden caches of prime meat and pelts and stone for fashioning into spearheads and arrowheads had they stolen for themselves when the ruse of trading was done? And how many young girls had they savaged after discovering the hiding places in the woods to which they had been sent with cautious elders to dwell until the traders went their way? Far too many to count, for such were the benefits to be gained when walking in the shadow of White Bear's wisdom in the days and nights when he was feared as Wíndigo, Great Ghost Cannibal of the North, and his name and the reputation of his bandsmen struck terror into the hearts of peaceful forest and coastal tribes . . . before bad spirits had come to feed within his head and sap the courage from his veins.

"Come, Avataut, we must follow the Grasslanders!"

Avataut flinched, startled by the sharpness of Armik's tone. "Must?" He did not like the sound of the word. No man had ever told White Bear what he must or must not do. No man would have dared.

"This haunch of deer grows heavy, Avataut." Armik was making no attempt to conceal his impatience. "We must bring it to Inau. Look. She is waiting for us. We cannot refuse to bring meat to her, Avataut. The Grasslanders are right, I think. We cannot insult a shaman by refusing to accept her talismans! Our success on the hunt may depend on these things. Come, I say! Now we will see her power with our own eyes! Now we will learn all that she knows about our hopes and dreams, about our future and our past! You must not be afraid to seek her power, Avataut. You—"

"Afraid? Is that what you think?" Avataut boomed in sudden anger, his voice so loud that it thundered across the bluff as though born of a storm cloud. "I fear no women, be they of this world or of the world beyond!"

"Then come to me, Avataut, Headman of Northerners, if you are not afraid." Inau was beckoning again. Insolently. Tauntingly. Her voice was as cool and lambent as the silver light of the moon, as low and mellifluous as the whispering sigh of the great river. And then, as an afterthought, it seemed, she added lightly, "And you, too, Armik, hunt brother of Wolverine. Yes! Why do you hesitate? You must come to the lodge of Inau! Here there is magic!"

Armik caught his breath. He was openly enchanted. Without another word to Avataut he leaned into the weight of the haunch and loped off toward the knolls. In a moment he was at the heels of the Grasslanders, eager as a hungry dog hoping to catch its share of any scraps that might be thrown to its pack at a hunt feast.

Avataut glowered as, once again, a bat winged low. He felt a slur of air, then winced at actual contact with the creature as its wings brushed the top of his head, rousing pain in the scabbed-over wound that the raven had made in his scalp on the day he set Wildfire loose upon the meadow. But why think of that now? He swatted hard at the bat. Too late. His hand sliced thin air. The bat had flown far ahead. He could see it clearly in the moonlight as it winged on in the wake of the seekers of Inau's magic.

His gut tightened. What was it that he had heard the Dawnland people say about bats? That they were bird and mouse melded into one animal, living proof of the duality of flesh and spirit. Light and dark. Earth and sky. Male and female. Like Tatqeq in his own people's stories of the moon, bats were a coalescence of opposites, intangible, there one moment, gone the next, moving in silence as surely as the dark and mysterious tides that stirred the waters of the great ocean, ever ebbing and flowing, an eternal source of wonder and power and magic.

"Magic indeed!" Avataut hissed frustration. With his mood shifting from undefined restlessness into an intensely focused anxiety to have this night over and done with, he set his footsteps belligerently in the rivering light of the moon, following Armik, the Grasslanders, and the bat toward the torchlit knoll where Inau was waiting. "Now we will see!" he muttered to himself. "And now I will know! What she knows. What she does not know. Yes! Now! I *will* see with my own eyes what this Inau is made of!"

▼▼▼▼▼

They went before him.

Into darkness.

Into silence.

Into the yawning mouth of a great whale.

Avataut paused. He looked to his left and right, then craned back his head. The sun- and weather-whitened skulls of two enormous sea beasts had been placed upright to face each other from either side of the entrance into the shaman's knoll. The lower jaw of each whale was open and had been laid flat upon the ground to form a long, single-toothed threshold. The teeth were enormous. The size of the skulls strained credulity. No whale he had ever seen or hunted or even dreamed of had been so big. He swallowed. Hard. And stepped between them, into a vestibule of bone.

Shivers prickled up Avataut's back. Again he paused to scan up and around. The skulls of the two great sperm whales towered over him, blocking off much of the light of the stars and moon, making him feel small and vulnerable despite his two knives.

Somewhere behind him, something moved.

Avataut whirled, half expecting to see the jaws of the paired skeletal heads snap shut behind him. When they did not, he exhaled relief, rolled his eyes in despair of his overly active imagination, then faced forward again, certain that he had heard only a whoosh of wind or the wing beat of another bat or the scuttling of some small animal or insect in the dune grass. The skulls of the whales were only that— inanimate bones! And old bones at that, worn smooth by endless seasons of weather and windblown sand. Rodents had long since chewed away any sharp edges. Moss grew in patches on those sections of the skulls that faced north, and lichens bearded the eye sockets.

A wind gusted across the bluff.

Avataut caught his breath. The lichens in the eye sockets of the great skulls were swaying as though imbued with life. Was it possible, he wondered, that the spirits of great whales could linger about their bones though their carcasses had been sundered and hauled far from the waters within which they swam when they were alive? If this was so, then even if the shaman within the knoll possessed no power, the life force remaining within these skeletons did. And so, thinking of the hunt to come and of what it would be like to be upon the water in a small skin boat with such whales as these swimming nearby, he said, "Hear me, Great Bones. I, Avataut of the Barrenlands, Wolverine, now headman of all Northerners, honor you and your children and the ancestors of all whales."

The wind dropped.

Had the whale spirits heard him and accepted—or rejected—his words of deference?

A wave of impatience went through Avataut. A man could never be sure of such things. It was best not to think about them.

Four short, definitive paces brought him to the actual entry into the ancient loess dune within which Inau had made her lodge. Again he paused. The damp, chalky smell of calcareous sand and clay and decomposing stone was strong in this place, as were the scents of moss and moldering dune grass. Avataut frowned. He found the smells unpleasant, but not nearly as unpleasant as the appearance of the arching, whalebone-braced opening into the maw of the hillock. It was wide enough to admit a good-sized man with shoulder and elbow room to spare, but it was so low that, in order to enter it, he was going to have to kneel and bend forward until his chin was almost on the ground.

Suspicion rubbed against the grain of his pride. A woman who was strong enough to drag the skulls of great whales from the beach and position them upright on the bluff was surely strong enough to have dug a decent-sized entry tunnel into her underground lodge. He huffed annoyance as suspicion clarified into understanding. This crawl space was more than an insulating cold trap built to keep chill winds at bay and store wet garments during inclement weather. This passageway had been deliberately designed to force submission to the will of the one who had fashioned it! All those who entered the shaman's realm must first bend their knees in obeisance and bow their heads in respect to Inau.

"Ha!" exclaimed Avataut, but it was not a laugh that

escaped his lips; it was an ejaculation of unadulterated indignation. He would as soon eat the leavings of the camp dogs as show obeisance to a woman! His hands curled into fists. The others had already followed her inside. It was too late for him to turn back. If he did, Armik would be convinced that he was afraid. And the Grasslanders might later find cause to accuse him of offending the forces of Creation.

And so he knelt. Defiantly. He bent his head. Combatively. He was Avataut of the Barrenlands, Headman of All Northerners, and what he was doing now would serve his own purpose, not that of the female shaman. If she *was* shaman! And so, growling in disbelief of her powers, he reminded himself that he was Kwakwaje'sh, Wolverine, and in the spirit of that most pugnacious of animals muscled his way into the abode of Inau as brashly as he would have broken into a hidden cache pit.

Darkness greeted him.

Utter and complete darkness.

He clenched his teeth. The others had already exited the entryway, leaving him to make his way after them in pitch blackness while they followed the light of the shaman's torch upward into the main portion of the lodge. He could not see the end of his nose, much less make out the contours of the passage that stretched out before him, but experience told him that if this winter house was anything like those with which he was familiar, the crawl space would not be overly long, and, at its end, there would be a ladder or large stepping stone affording access up into the main portion of the lodge.

He heaved a sigh. It was so dark! The shaman must have bid the others close the plank hatch that opened the way into her living space. Why would she do that? This was not the depth of winter when starving carnivores or marauding raiders might well attempt to force access into her lodge in hope of stealing her stores of meat and fat and precious kindling. And if she possessed only normal insight she must know or at least suspect that he was following the others. At her invitation! Common courtesy should have dictated that the hatch be left open so that light could shine downward into the crawl space and ease his passage through it.

Avataut glared straight ahead. Into the dark. Into the cursed dark! No moon or starlight or soft night glow of clouds would dispel the gloom in which he found himself now. He had entered the black realm of moles and worms. The darkness that surrounded him was as thick and oily as the fluid at the center of an eye, and as it pressed in upon him as though with a weight of its own, he fought back an old aversion to being alone and confined in total darkness. A childhood folly! An irrational fear that no grown man should ever own to, least of all one who answered to the names of Headman and Wolverine!

Once again suspicion raked his senses. Had the shaman deliberately led him into the dark? Could she know his fear of it? No! It was impossible. He would not believe it. No one knew of his feelings. How could they? He had all but forgotten them himself, and yet here was the old dread again, nearly as intense as on that black winter day when he had been stitched up inside a sealskin, buried alive, and left to die under the snow.

So long ago! An infant's memory! A childhood terror he might never have understood or overcome had his father's wizened old sister not explained its underlying cause to him when he came sobbing once too often from nightmares in which he saw himself as a larva buried deep beneath the winter snow—helpless and cold and alone, pupating in darkness, arms and limbs bound fast, with no way to reach light and air. Until Old Auntie came to save him—until Old

Auntie dug him up and drove off the carrion-eating birds and animals that had come to root him out of the snow and feed upon him.

Avataut's mouth tightened at the memory.

There had been a feud. A murderous feud between his maternal and paternal relatives. Old Auntie told him what she knew of it. It was not much. She could not recall the exact cause of disaffection between the two clans, but there had been dog killing and woman stealing involved, and because of these things enmity ran deep and dark as heart blood between his father's and mother's bands.

And so, Old Auntie said, in the time of the long dark soon after Avataut was born, his mother looked with hard eyes at the child she had borne to a man of a hated clan and decided to kill it lest it someday grow to become an enemy of her own people. But Old Auntie, wise in the way of the women of her own clan, guessed what the new mother was about to do, followed her out from camp, and fought with her in the winter dark to rescue the infant she had buried alive in the snow.

What a fight it had been, Old Auntie said. Hair pulling! Face scratching! Eye gouging! Screeching and clawing at one another like a pair of lynx until everyone in the band rushed out to see the cause of the melee. Old Auntie told them. And although Avataut's mother dug him up and took him from the sealskin that had smothered his cries, Avataut's father would hear none of her protestations of innocence. And he would not believe her accusations against Old Auntie. As though his own sister would ever try to harm his child! No one would believe such a tale!

And so, Old Auntie said, in the light of a green aurora she helped her brother dig the snow pit in which he buried his wife. With her own two feet, Old Auntie danced and tromped on the snow beneath which the woman, bound hand and foot, was left to die—but not before Old Auntie opened a gash in her own thumb and spattered the snow with a generous offering of blood so that the flesh eaters of the far north would be enticed to come and feed upon the woman as they would surely have come to feed upon her son.

Late that night, Old Auntie said, Avataut's father led a punitive raid against his dead wife's clan. This had been a very good thing, Old Auntie vowed, because when all the would-be baby killer's relatives were slain, the blood feud was over and Avataut's band was rich in meat and hides and captives and dogs and many other good things that made life a thing to be savored. Afterward Old Auntie was rewarded, for she, a barren, unmarriageable female relegated by her brother's marriage to a subservient place within his lodge after a lifetime of service to him, had come to dwell once more in a position of honor at his fire. And there she stayed, happily abusing her slaves, begrudgingly attending Avataut, and outliving her brother's subsequent wife when the young woman died in agony of no known cause within a moon of displacing Old Auntie at the family lodge fire.

Avataut's brow furrowed. The memories were as oppressive as the darkness of the passageway. Old Auntie was never kind to him. Not even once. She made beautiful garments and moccasins for him, but the clothes were deliberately cut to chafe his skin, and the footwear blistered his feet until they bled. She set special cuts of meat and fat aside for him, boasting to all of her generosity to her brother's son, then smirked when her offerings made his guts quiver and his bowels lurch and run.

He never complained. Never. He was a sickly child in Old Auntie's care. She made it clear to him that he gave her good cause to taunt him as she saw fit, to insult his mother's deceased clan at will, and to gag him, bind him, and bury him alive in the snow to be food for carrion eaters if he ever spoke so much as a single word of criticism about her to his father. In the end her petty cruelties made him strong, clever at avoiding them, and determined to prove his worth to his father, band, and clan. He learned to hunt for himself earlier than most, made his own meat from the scant flesh of the rodents and birds he snared, and would have fashioned his own clothes had this not been seen as woman's work. And then, late in his fourth autumn, soon after his father took a new wife and Old Auntie was caught baiting the bride's meat with tightly curled slivers of dried bone that would surely have straightened in her belly to pierce her intestine and produce a slow and agonizing death, it had been Avataut's turn to smirk.

His lips compressed against his teeth. He was still smirking when his father forced Old Auntie to gulp down the meat she had intended to serve as Death to his bride. And he was smirking still when he followed along at his father's heels as Old Auntie was dragged kicking and screaming out from camp by her thinning hair to be bound hand and foot and buried alive in the as-yet-unfrozen topmost layer of the permafrost. With his own two hands Avataut helped his father dig the shallow pit into which Old Auntie was thrown. With his own two feet he danced upon the grave. With one of his own side daggers he gashed his thumb and let it bleed onto the peaty mound beneath which Old Auntie lay. And although he was young and small and afraid of the dark, he crept from camp that night, hunkered on a nearby rise, and smirked as he watched carrion eaters dig up Old Auntie and devour her.

No one mourned Old Auntie. When the time of the long dark descended again upon the Barrenlands, Avataut suffered badly from the old nightmare in which he saw himself buried alive, suffocating in darkness beneath the snow, but when the earth at last rolled her snow-whitened face toward spring and the sun rose again to light the land, his bad dreams ceased.

Life was better for him. His father's bride grew big with child. She had little regard for the offspring of her husband's former wife, but the clothes and moccasins she made for him did not chafe his skin or cause his feet to blister, and the food she cooked for him did not make him sick. Then, in his fifth autumn, when the caribou were many upon the land and the bands dispersed after the last big communal hunt, she vanished into the fogs of dawn, abandoning Avataut and her husband and baby daughter to run off with one of Avataut's uncles.

A new feud began, bloodier and darker in its intent than the first. And even as his father strangled the female offspring of his unfaithful wife and prepared to go forth on a raid from which he would not return, he gave his son one lasting piece of advice. "Never trust a woman, Avataut. Use their kind as a man must, but never trust them! Never!"

"Are you with us, Avataut?"

Startled, Avataut flinched. A light had just flared and then faded into the blackness at the very back of the crawl space. Armik's call had come out of the light and disappeared along with it. Somehow his words continued to stir the darkness. Somehow they made it thin a little. Avataut's thoughts of the past thinned with it; he was glad to let them fade. "I am with you," he called back and, moving forward on his hands and knees, reminded himself that, although he still disliked being alone in darkness, he had always come safely through it. He might not like the memories it was capable of rousing in him, but now, as he moved deeper into it, he was not afraid.

He could hear voices. Male. Female. Low. Purposeful.

He went on.

And on.

The voices fell away into a single low, threnodic humming.

And then, suddenly, he blundered into something solid and knew that he was at the end of the crawl space. His hands felt upward along two upright, smoothly hewn wooden posts. He did not have to see them to recognize them: the sides of a ladder. He felt along its length and width, defining its sinew-joined structure, then placed his feet on the bottom rung and began to climb until, reaching up, he felt the bottom of the plank hatch.

Why is it closed? Why have I been left behind to blunder along in the dark?

His questions angered him. He thought of Old Auntie—cruel, manipulative, clever, but, like all women, not clever enough! He shoved up as hard as he could on the closed hatch and, to the explosive accompaniment of the hatch cover crashing backward onto the planks of the floor above, clambered out of the darkness into the dimly lit living space of the shaman Inau.

▼▼▼▼▼

The room opened wide before him.

He could barely see it. A rainbow-hued pall of smoke laked before him, wafting diaphanously upward and outward from several large stone oil lamps that were burning at various places on the floor.

Later Avataut would remember the moment.

Later he would suspect that there was something in the

smoke, something potent, some insidious mind-eating essence rising out of burning herbs and oils and fungi steeped in some secret potion born of the shaman's craft.

Magic?

Later Armik and the others would assure him that this was surely so.

Now, with his eyes smarting and his throat constricting against the invasion of lung-searing irritants, Avataut knew only that his head was reeling. Lest he lose balance and fall flat on his face, he hunkered quickly down on his heels, steadying himself with outstretched hands.

He squinted into the pall. The smoke was even thicker than that which had stung his eyes and flavored his food in the Man House. And it stank. Of what he could not say. He could barely make out the forms of Armik and Chaksa and the other Grasslanders seated cross-legged in a circle, each man well apart from the others, hands resting on bent knees, faces upturned, expressions set and rapt. They did not speak to welcome him. They did not look his way. Indeed, they had not been moved in the slightest by the cacophonous clatter of his entrance. To a man, they were entranced.

And Avataut saw why.

Inau was dancing within their circle.

And, truly, she was more than a woman.

She had the head of a white whale!

He stared.

Inau whirled.

His head whirled with her.

She spun, in the direction of the rising sun, around and around she spun. With her arms upraised, her whale's head thrown back, her black braids flying wide, and all the white ropes of fur and shell and feathers that composed her robe opening and closing to reveal fleeting glimpses of the form beneath, the shaman danced.

Avataut leaned forward and did his best to focus his gaze as he tried to make sense of what he was seeing. It was impossible. There was no sense to be found in it. A woman could not have the head of a whale! Yet, through shifting smoke and flickering lamplight, he saw the long and bulbous brow, the cetacean features, the beaked snout, the wide lipless mouth and round glinting eyes. His own eyes widened. Inau might well have the head of a whale, but the glimpses he was catching of her body revealed the form of a fully human being. And that form was beautiful! His loins stirred at the sight of woman revealed, embraced by smoke, defined in lamplight . . . so long of limb . . . so smooth and taut of belly and flank . . . so narrow of hip . . . so tender of breast, each tiny mounding as firm and upturned as that of a young girl . . . and the gentle rise of her pubic bone so softly furred above her childlike penis that the hairs were barely visible at all and . . .

Penis?

Breasts?

"Impossible!" he cried, aghast.

Inau danced on.

Avataut's head was throbbing. Just what was dancing before him in the rainbow smoke? Woman? Man? Or something else, something not quite human, an androgyny, a legendary creature born of Tatqeq the moon, an amalgamation of genders, male and female melded into one being, a mate unto itself? The premise shook him. He would not believe it. Not for a moment. And yet he could not deny that she had the head of a whale! How could this be? How!

The thrum he had first heard when in the crawl space was

coming out of the open whale jaws of the dancing shaman now. Out of the smoke. Out of the soft rainbow light of the oil lamps. Out of the gaping mouths of Avataut's hunt brother and Chaksa and the other Grasslanders. And, somehow, the sound was entering him, filling him, expanding within his head until it poured out of his own mouth, taking his spirit along with it.

Whirling him away.

Spinning him away.

Sucking him out of his body and hurling him across vast undifferentiated spaces and multicolored distances that could not be measured any more than they could be fully perceived . . . until, with a start, he came hurtling back to the moment, to the place in which he had been crouching motionless all along.

Blinking, nauseated, thick-headed, Avataut tasted the backwash of hallucinogens and had no idea what they were or where they had taken him or if all that he had just seen and experienced had been real or part of a dream.

Disoriented, he looked around.

The smoke was down.

The others were gone.

The shaman was kneeling in the middle of the room with a basket of woven sea grass at her side and all her oil lamps arranged around her in a circle. The largest of these, a broad, dark, concave stone, was positioned in front of her. A fire burned in the concavity of the dark stone. Not a tiny oil-fed flame fluttering in complacent containment at the end of a moss wick as in the other lamps. No. The dark stone hosted a true fire, a dancing, full-bodied entity of heat and light that was feeding aggressively on the shaman's offerings of bits of wood and bone and grass drawn from the basket at her side.

A queasy, uneasy feeling sent shivers running along

Avataut's arms and back. The fire in the dark stone was swaying and waving its many flaming arms as though casting about in hope of leaping from the stone to take on new life elsewhere. The sight of it disturbed him; he could not say why. Perhaps it was the brightness of its light? Whatever it was, it made his head ache hotly behind his eyes. He closed his lids, scrunched them tight to relieve pain and, when he opened them again, was startled to find himself back at the meadow.

A raven cawed.

He winced against the sound and, hearing the scrape of flints, looked down, amazed to see his hands holding and working his fire-starting stones.

He saw sparks flash bright in yellow grass.

He felt North Wind at his back as he watched it breathe hot new life into ready tinder.

And, as Wildfire leaped high in sun-seared grass and danced away across the burning meadow toward the high green bastioning wall of the summer-dry forest, he saw a wounded doe looking back at him out of the trees as a great white bear came pounding toward him.

"Aiyah!" cried Avataut. Pivoting on the moccasined balls of his feet, he would have gone scrambling madly down the ladder into the darkness of the crawl space had not the sound of laughter arrested his movement.

He turned toward the sound.

He was back inside the shaman's lodge again! His hands were empty. There was no doe. There was no bear. There was no burning meadow. The only fire that burned did so within the confines of the shaman's stone lamps. All that he had just seen was inside his head, no more than memories roused by fatigue, like his recollections of Old Auntie. A good night's sleep would banish them. He blinked again, his head still aching, but as he stared across the room his vision was now almost hurtfully clear.

The shaman was staring back at him.

Their eyes met. Held.

"What have you seen in the smoke of the fires of Inau, Avataut of the Barrenlands?" asked the whale-headed woman as, placing a small, polished, cylindrical piece of bone into the concavity of the dark stone, her eyes continued to pinion him out of the round openings of . . .

Relief coursed through him. "A mask!" he exclaimed and, naming himself Fool, realized that this was what he had been seeing all along. In the blur of smoke and whirling robes, he must have imagined a penis where there was none. And Inau did not have the head of a whale! She was wearing a mask, a grotesque and intricately carved representation of the head of a whale, but only a mask all the same.

"Are you so certain that this is all you have seen?" she pressed in a voice as low and sinuous as the smoke of her lamps. Before he could answer, she reached to a fiber cord that hung from one side of the mask and gave it a sharp downward tug.

For the second time in only moments, Avataut cried out, startled. The hinged jaws of the shaman's mask had just snapped open to reveal rows of sharp white teeth painted bloodred. Inside the gaping mouth was a second, much smaller mask. He recoiled at the sight of it. It was made to look like a bat, and, just as the jaws of the larger mask fell open, it appeared to fly out of the mouth of the whale with wings flapping and its own bloody-toothed jaws snapping ferociously open and shut. And all the while the wearer behind both masks screeched as though about to fly to the attack herself.

Avataut cringed. "What trickery is this?"

Inau laughed, deep in her throat. The sound was as unpleasant as the masks she wore, and as intricately made. A complex and subtle braiding of opposites, it was all at once masculine and feminine, animal and human, mellifluous as the sigh of the great river and treacherous as that river's deepest and most dangerous undercurrents.

Avataut lowered his head. The room seemed to be spinning slightly. He was tired. The day had been long. The night longer. Fatigue was heavy on his spirit. And yet he sensed that there was danger for him here. He felt it in the marrow of his bones.

"Come closer," invited the shaman. "Do not be afraid, Avataut of the Barrenlands. Inau has been waiting. I knew that you would come."

"Did you?" His tone was as surly and defensive as his mood. "And so you left me to find my way alone in the dark while you greeted lesser men with smoke and tricks!"

"You—who once walked as hunt brother to Tôrnârssuk, as loyal follower of Wíndigo, Great Ghost Cannibal, Tunraq and White Bear of the North—surely you need no one to light your way through the darkness of the way you would go in this world? The light of your avarice and arrogance shines ahead of you along the trail you have chosen to follow, Wolverine, Bold Hunter Who Raids the Camps and Steals the Denning Sites of Others."

Indignant, Avataut was on his feet in an instant, shaky, but stronger now, his senses sharpened by a sudden rush of anger. "I have come at your invitation, Shaman—if that is what you are. To placate a band brother and hunters from the far Grasslands I have come. For promised amulets, for words of wisdom—not for smoke and tricks, and not for insults!"

"Smoke and tricks? Is this not what Man would have of Shaman? And how has Inau insulted you, Kwakwaje'sh? I have merely spoken the name that you have made your own in this encampment, Wolverine. Are the attributes of that animal not also yours? Are you not bold? Are you not powerful? Are you not cunning in your greed to possess the best meat, the finest skins and women and adornment? Have you not taken by force and guile all that you have ever desired for yourself in this life? And have not lesser men stood aside and celebrated these qualities in you ever since you dared claim as your own all that one who once walked as headman in your place left behind on the shores of the great river for others to guard until his return?"

Avataut's face flushed as hot as his temper. The shaman's queries were as pointed and barbed as fishhooks, baited with tones pitched to grease his pride. But he had not missed the derision that had underlain every word. He would not rise to such lures! To do so would risk being snagged on the very truths in which he took so much pride and against which he found no need to defend himself, least of all against the disapproving slurs of a woman.

"Unlike you, Inau, I wear no mask, nor do I hide myself in smoke or skulk about the great encampment in the night, concealing myself in darkness. I have come before you as I am. Boldly and openly have I come! Only when taking on the war shirt of a raider does Avataut choose to hide his face behind a battle mask made to frighten and confuse those whom he would bend to his will or send running in panic before him. So do not think that you can sit inside your circle of smoking lamps and manipulate me with your female wiles! I am not a man of the lesser tribes! It is Avataut of the Barrenlands, Headman of All Northerners, Kwakwaje'sh, Wolverine, a man of the True People, who stands before you! I have dared to hunt white whales on the Great River of the North with no blessing from you. I am not afraid to do so again! The spirits of my Ancestors are with me. The Ancient Ones will protect me. I will not be intimidated by the masks you wear! In your mouth, the honor of my name has been twisted back upon itself and transformed into dishonor. I will not stay to hear further insults from you."

"Man will hear what Man will hear. Man will see what Man will see. Go if you will, Wolverine. Return into the dark. Or stay and accept the wisdom of Inau. Either way, that which you fear will follow."

Avataut froze. "What say you?"

"Come. Enter the circle of light. Kneel before the sacred fire of Inau. A talisman awaits you. And a warning."

"Of . . . what?" he asked cautiously, holding his ground on the rough-hewn surface of the plank floor, unsure if it or he was trembling.

"Wolverines do not go forth upon the water, Avataut of the Barrenlands."

Avataut's heart leaped. He did not like where this was going; he did not like it all. "This wolverine goes where he pleases," he informed Inau. "It is the nature of his kind."

The shaman's masked head went high. "Beware, Avataut of the Barrenlands. With the rising of tomorrow's sun you must fast. You must sweat in the sweat lodge of your band. You must cleanse your body and spirit of the avaricious nature of Kwakwaje'sh, for when it is time for you to go forth onto the waters of the great river, you must go, not with boldness and arrogance, but with humility and caution to guide the strokes of your oar and the flight of your lances. And in the days and nights to come, before and after the hunt, you must do nothing to offend the spirits of the whales or the dignity of any man who would take sustenance from their lives."

"Be cautious on the hunt? Fast and sweat? Do nothing to offend the spirits of the game?" Relief coursed through him once again. "I need no shaman to give me such advice! There is not a man alive who does not know that. Ha! It is as I told my hunt brother Armik. It *was* a waste of good meat to bring that haunch of deer to you. Women have no power!"

"Woman?" Again Inau laughed. The same laugh as before. Low. Mocking. All at once masculine and feminine, animal and human, soft and melodious as the sigh of the great river, and dangerous as that river's deepest and most treacherous undercurrents. "Can Avataut still doubt all that his eyes have seen within the lodge of Inau?"

"Darkness and smoke and masks! Tricks! Deception! This is what I have seen!"

"All must come through darkness to find the light of life. All must learn to see through the smokes and mists that arise to obscure the dangers that lie along the paths of our lives. And all know that the masks of this shaman reveal the true face of Inau, of one born of Darkness and Light, of Water and Air, of Earth and Sky, of Flesh and Spirit. Inau is Male. Inau is Female. Inau is two halves made Whole. Inau is Complete. Inau is a gift to the People from the Four Winds and the forces of Creation. In all this world there is none like Inau, for I alone am capable of communing with the spirits of all for the good of all in full understanding of the needs of all. And I tell you now, Avataut of the Barrenlands, that while others sleep, my spirit sounds the river deeps and sings with great whales even as it sees into the hearts and dreams of men as surely as a bat sees its way through the dark, ever-shifting channels of the night."

The statement jolted him. Deep within his spirit something lurched, plummeted, then grabbed at his guts and twisted them into a hard, defensive knot. It was a fisting of pure animal instinct, a primal distrust of all that could not be readily understood or accepted as wholly natural within the boundaries that had always ordered his world—and could therefore, by their very nature, be perceived only as threatening to his place within that world. What had he seen dancing in the rainbow smoke of the shaman's lodge? A true offspring of Tatqeq the moon, a being of mystical power born somehow by magic to undeserving tribes, or only another clever female like Old Auntie, attempting to manipulate the minds of men in order to secure meat and shelter for herself in a world in which unmarriageable women lived out their lives in constant dread of losing the protection of band and tribe?

"Inau has been watching you, Wolverine."

His eyes flashed. The fist in his belly tightened. "And just what do you think you have seen?"

"Wildfire dancing to the command of Man."

He was stunned.

Silence settled between them, heavy, palpable.

Inau sat dead still within it.

Avataut broke a sweat. His heart was hammering. His blood was pounding, throbbing in the wound that Raven had gouged into his scalp that morning on the meadow when he had, indeed, set Wildfire loose to obey his command.

"Yes," sighed Inau and reached for a twin-tonged fire prod that lay beside the sea-grass basket. "Truth speaks in your eyes and in the silence that you cannot bring yourself to fill with denial. And so, Avataut of the Barrenlands, I tell you again that you must heed the warnings of Inau, for if you do not, the greed of Wolverine will be his undoing as he continues to subvert and grasp for himself the power of a much greater spirit."

Avataut was shaking. "Of what do you accuse me! Of what 'spirit' do you speak?"

"I speak of that which you fear."

"You speak in circles! In riddles! In guesses and assumptions!"

She stiffened at the sharpness of his tone and, using the fire prod to raise something from the flames that were now dying within the dark stone, said quietly, "Of all the animals that hunt upon the sacred skin of Mother Below, there is only one whom the wolverine fears. And of all the spirits that walk the dreams of Avataut, there is only one that rouses him from sleep and sends him in a naked panic into rain and darkness."

Avataut had no time to react to her statement, for in that moment, without warning, she suddenly pitched the object from the tonged end of the fire prod and sent it hurtling across the room. Directly at him. He sidestepped. Too late. Surprised to find himself still dizzy, he lost his balance and went down hard on one knee just as the object struck him in the chest and then fell, landing like a stone before him.

"Pick it up!" commanded Inau. "Shaman has made it for Avataut of the Barrenlands out of smoke and dreams and blood and bone. It is cut into the image of what you fear. Fire has not destroyed it. Wind and Storm have not vanquished it. Flood has not swept it away. And the words of Wolverine have not diminished it. Take it. Acknowledge its power . . . and the power of Inau."

Avataut stared down. At a charred piece of polished bone not much larger than one of his thumbs. His blood ran cold. He could not bring himself to touch it. It was a fetish, as he had expected, and, although blackened, its shape was undeniable. It had been carved into the perfect likeness of a great white bear on the prowl.

"It will come," vowed Inau.

The name of Tôrnârssuk burned at the back of Avataut's brain. Slowly, fighting down outrage, he reached out and forced himself to snatch up the fetish, then dropped it as it seared his hand.

"Beware, Wolverine. The great white bear of the north devours all those who fail to stand to its presence with the respect and honor due its kind."

Avataut had had enough. All around, the oil lamps were now guttering; the smell of burned fat and herbs was strong in the air. Shadows were filling the lodge. Blue. Purple. Heavy with the residue of smoke. Glaring at the shaman, it was now Avataut who spoke a warning, and a justification. "If White Bear returns to the Great River of the North it will be as I have said—bad spirits will come with him and Misfortune will walk at his side."

"For whom? You? Or for him because of you?"

"For all who are foolish enough to stand with him and name him Headman in my place!" he declared. Unable to stomach another moment of her goading, he rose, turned, and went his way, back down the ladder, into the darkness.

Chapter Two

▼▼▼▼▼▼▼

They followed Tôrnârssuk north.

Solemnly and steadfastly, with Kinap leading them in bold new songs of pride born of valor and victory over Old Tribe enemies, they followed their headman out of the Valley of the Spirit Moon and into the high, rolling, heavily forested hills that lay beyond.

No one looked back.

Except Ne'gauni.

"What is it, Shaman Indeed?" asked old Ko'ram, bent and huffing under the weight of his pack frame as he paused beside the young man and followed his gaze down into the lowlands out of which they had just come. "What do you see?"

Ne'gauni offered no reply. He could see the falls from here, and the sheer cliffs of the overlook from which they had glimpsed the smoke of Wildfire and heard the trumpeting of tuskers and the crack of distant lightning. Loons were calling on Big Lake, as sad and lonely a sound by day as on the night the valley resonated with the cries of wolves and beasts and mammoths and the lake glowed bloodred in the light of the Spirit Moon. He tensed. He had foreseen the threat of Wildfire. Perhaps he truly was Shaman? Perhaps old Ko'ram was right when he said that he had called down Rain, for surely it seemed that Rain *had* come at his command to vanquish Fire, and the beasts that he had imagined upon the trail had proved to be real. But he had not foreseen their threat to Mowea'qua. And if he was truly Dreamer, truly Shaman Indeed, he should have seen! He should have known! He should have warned her!

"Why do you fall behind?"

Ne'gauni turned, his reverie shattered by Tôrnârssuk's impatient shout. He frowned. The headman's words had been more accusation than query, and the man did not appear in the least happy as he elbowed his way irritably back through the band.

"What is this, Ne'gauni?" Tôrnârssuk demanded as he came to take an imperious stand before the young cripple and the old man. "Come! You cannot stand here looking back! We have a long journey ahead of us. The band needs to see its Dreamer striding out with confidence today, and to hear its Wise Man lifting his voice and joining the others in song. The Great River of the North awaits. Tell him, old man. He must turn his eyes to the future, not to the past. The smokes and flames and phantoms of his dreams lie behind us now."

"Yes, yes," gushed Ko'ram. "Come, Ne'gauni, we will join the others now. Surely what our headman says must be so."

Ne'gauni stood his ground. He looked at Tôrnârssuk out of troubled eyes. "Is it so?"

Tôrnârssuk's eyes narrowed; his mouth moved into an expression of grim mockery. "You are said to be Shaman. You tell me."

"I cannot."

"And so you stand like a stone unable to decide which

way to go! What troubles you, Ne'gauni? Do your dreams no longer point the way? Do imaginary spiders and mice no longer run around inside your head to sting and gnaw your spirit with whispered warnings? Or, given all that has happened since the rising of the Spirit Moon, are you afraid to speak out and take a man's responsibility for where your so-called portendings might lead us all?"

Ne'gauni flushed, embarrassed and defensive. "I have not dreamed, by day or night, since you led the searchers into the forest and returned. Indeed, I have not been able to sleep at all, but I am not afraid, Tôrnârssuk, to tell you that I hesitate to follow you to the north. I still sense danger for us there."

"Still?" exclaimed old Ko'ram, aghast.

"Good!" countered the headman. "A man who does not sense danger is a threat to himself and to all who walk with him as brothers and sisters of his band. The presence of danger on the trails of life is as sure as night following day. You of all men, Ne'gauni, should have learned this and made your peace with it long before now. So come, Man Who Walks Ahead in Dreams to Foresee Danger for the People, walk forward with confidence and do not forget again that it is said by the Wise Men of your tribe that the Circle of Life turns forward, never back. A man cannot stand in one place within it. Life will not allow it. What has been, has been. What will be, will be. What is, is! How we plan for and confront the dangers that await us in our tomorrows will determine the outcome of what must inevitably become our yesterdays. Was it not so for us on the shores of Big Lake in the Valley of the Spirit Moon? Danger anticipated. Danger faced. Danger vanquished. Yes! So sing out, Dreamer! Join in the giant's song that lightens the steps of my band and honors the bold hearts of those hunters who went forth with this White Bear to slaughter old enemies and retrieve a dead shaman's son. The sun is high! You are young! This moment is good for us all! So savor it, Ne'gauni! Danger awaits us wherever we go. My people have a name for it. We call it Sila. And in the end it will eat us all and spit us out upon the Four Winds to be reborn again!"

Ne'gauni shivered. The sun was warm on his back, but still he shivered, unable to find anything to savor in the moment as the headman turned and walked away, leaving his words hanging invisibly in the air behind him, bitter as oak gall, cold as the north wind. "Not all of us will be reborn," the young man mumbled to himself. "Not those whose spirits you have sundered along with their bodies and left behind to bleed and rot along with—"

"Enough!" Old Ko'ram jabbed his rattle in Ne'gauni's face and shook it furiously. "Do not remind our headman of that! He is not the same since returning to the band with the wild girl. Others sing, but he does not. Look at him, Ne'gauni! Listen to how he twists his words! A blind man could see that his spirit is more troubled than on the night of the red moon when Mowea'qua howled with wolves and defied the will of the band by running off into the darkness!"

The statement struck a sudden and unexpected response within Ne'gauni. He caught his breath and then called out after the headman, "Tôrnârssuk . . . wait!"

Tôrnârssuk paused, turned, questioned the young man with raised brows.

"I have not thanked you," explained Ne'gauni.

"For what?" asked the headman.

"For forgiving Mowea'qua, for bringing her back to the band, for placing her in the protection of your own family fire circle . . . and for killing Moraq along with the rest of the beasts."

Tôrnârssuk went rigid. "I have not forgiven her. The

spirit of Raven spoke to me and prevented me from killing her. I will care for her until we reach the Great Gathering of Many Tribes and, if she still lives, will trade her there to the first man willing to barter for her. And as for the man you speak of, he was no beast. He was a True Man! He was a brother of my band and of my heart. His death leaves yet another cold dark hollow in my spirit that will never be filled. So do not speak to dishonor him. Or utter his name again. It is forbidden!"

"By the forces of Creation, Ne'gauni," wheezed old Ko'ram as the headman whirled in a barely contained fury and stalked off to reclaim his place at the head of the band. "Have you lost your wits along with your leg? To speak the name of a dead man! Ah! Would you summon that spirit from the world beyond this world and put us all in the path of his vengeance? Have you not heard of the way the headman cut that one's throat from ear to ear and opened him from crotch to gullet before leaving his body with those of the Old Tribe beasts? A terrible death! A dishonoring! And now, because of your careless tongue, if that spirit has heard its name and follows your utterance back into the world to harm any of Tôrnârssuk's people, the headman will be able to lay the responsibility for this on your shoulders. You must guard what you say, Ne'gauni, else you end your days sharing the dead man's fate as penalty for your indiscretion! And then who would be Shaman Indeed for this band? And whom would Teacher teach after a lifetime of searching for a pupil?"

Ne'gauni stifled a reply. He was still so frustrated over not having had a hand in Moraq's death that he shook whenever he thought of it. How he would have savored looking into the Northerner's hateful eyes at the moment the headman slew him. What profound and infinite pleasure he would have taken in driving his own dagger deep into the man's throat, in turning the blade, in silencing the vicious tongue and canceling forever the threat he had posed to Mowea'qua. But old Ko'ram was right to castigate him for forgetting the ancient taboo against naming the dead. How could he have done so? Lack of sleep? Worry over the runaways? A combination of both? It did not matter. There was no excuse for his lapse of judgment. Moraq's name had not been spoken since the search party had returned to the lakeside camp and told of how he had been slain as punishment for challenging the headman and setting himself to perform an unspeakable act upon what had, at the time, appeared to be a dead woman. No one would mourn such a man. In keeping with the ways of the Northerners, his weapons had been gathered and broken, his dogs brained, and all that he owned heaped into a pile and burned lest, through his possessions, Moraq's spirit somehow find access back into the world of the living to avenge himself upon the man who had killed him and on the bandsmen who had stood by and watched him die.

"Come!" urged old Ko'ram emphatically as he looped an arm through the crook of Ne'gauni's elbow and began to pull him along in the footsteps of the others. "Tôrnârssuk is right. We cannot stay here! It is dangerous to linger in the country of the dead. We must go on to the Great River of the North. And we must not look back."

Ne'gauni allowed himself to be led until, suddenly, he jammed the tips of his crutches down against the ground and jerked the old man to a tottering halt. "Wait! What did he mean—'if she lives'?"

Ko'ram looked surprised. "Exactly that. If she lives. Have the daughters of Ogeh'ma and Segub'un been keeping you so distracted with their gifts and mindless giggles that you have not seen the way it is with Mowea'qua?"

Ne'gauni felt the blood rush to his face. "They are

nothing to me. Am I to be faulted because they have taken it upon themselves to bring meat and drink to me now that I no longer share the giant's fire? If I allowed it, they would shadow me as surely as Mowea'qua ever did! And Hasu'u has assured me that she will soon be well and trailing along at my side once again."

The old man *tsk*ed. "Hasu'u's kind heart allows her to see only what she wishes to see, but how can you, Shaman Indeed, not see that Mowea'qua lies like a corpse on the headman's drag frame? She will not eat. She will not drink. Poor child, so cruelly used, so badly torn. Not a word has she spoken since her return. Not a word. Not even to the boy. In truth, it would have been better for that wild and willful girl if she had died out there with her own kind under the Spirit Moon."

Ne'gauni was appalled. "How can you say this?"

The old man looked nervously around and, only when he was convinced that no one—not even a bird or squirrel or errant insect—was within earshot, leaned close to the young man and whispered, "A man and two fine dogs have died because of her, Ne'gauni. And by returning her to the band, the headman has gone back on his word and defied the will of the council regarding her. This is not good. Not good at all."

"He obeys a sign given to him by the spirit of Raven."

"Mmm. Yes. The feather of Raven. A gift to Mowea'qua and a sign to Tôrnârssuk from the dark spirit, from one who is known as Trickster to our people."

Ne'gauni's brow came down. "To those of the Barrenlands Raven is One Who Survives."

"And to all People Raven is Eater of the Dead!" snapped old Ko'ram. "Think, Dreamer! Think, Shaman Indeed! Think and remember that Raven shadows the tribes to feast upon the leavings of our hunts and, in starving times, to feast upon *us* when we are forced to leave our dead behind. What kind of omen is this feather that has come from the dark spirit Raven to Mowea'qua and Tôrnârssuk? Death has followed it. And now, in this band where our headman himself takes on the mask of Raven when he is out raiding and slaughtering his many enemies, what can such a sign mean to us peaceful dwellers of the forest and Dawnland?"

"That his enemies are no longer a threat to us," said Ne'gauni strongly, for surely the answer made sense to him and should have been obvious to the old man as well. Yet, even as he took comfort in this moment of self-assurance, his brow knotted over the scarred bridge of his nose. Ko'ram was going on and on about the feather, but somehow Ne'gauni was no longer hearing his words. He was remembering, reflecting inward, seeing Mowea'qua as she had been that day upon the trail before they reached the overlook, one moment striding aggressively ahead of him with her nose in the air, the next on her knees, fingering up the flight feather of a raven and exclaiming in delight as she held it up for his observation. What had she said? The words came back to him in a rush.

"Look, Ne'gauni. A sign it is from the kami! A gift from the Old Tribe spirits of the forest! An omen, think I. A shaman could us tell if it is for good or bad."

Shaman! The word slapped his senses. Now, as then, deep within his brain, something shifted, darkened, then went very bright. The brightness burned him. Hurt him. He closed his eyes, shook his head, tried to clear it, and, only half succeeding, batted open his lids to stare ahead in disbelief.

Old Ko'ram was not at his side.

Mowea'qua was no longer there.

Another woman was kneeling in her place. A pregnant woman. A chill swept through him as he stared at her. Her head was down. He could not see her face through the fall of her hair. And yet he knew her. He had seen her before. In another daydream. He recognized her garments, the worn leggings, high-cut moccasins, buckskin dress with generous fringing to foil the blood-sucking insect war bands of Mici'cak, Master of Biting Blackflies, and the finely worked blue quill-work banding stitched down the sides of her sleeves and leggings. And now, as in the moment when he had first seen her, she was turning up her face to him.

He pulled in a ragged breath. He had no wish to see what he knew he must see. He tried to wrench his gaze away. Too late. She was staring at him. But how could this be when she had no face? No face at all! No eyes. No nose. And, where a mouth should be, only a gaping wound that gushed blood and fire and warning words.

"My people have gone to the north. You should not journey there."

"Ah!" he gasped as, desperately trying to find logic where there was none, his strong sense of reason overrode confusion to put logic where he thought it must be. The vision was fading. The details were blurring. Only the face remained clear. And now it had features. He had given it features. Mowea'qua's features! Not as they had been that day on the trail when she discovered the feather of Raven or as they had been when she stood naked and beautiful and defiant before the entire band in the bloodred glow of the red moon, but as they were now. Swollen! Battered! Unrecognizable!

"Ne'gauni?"

He did not answer Ko'ram. He felt sick. The old man was steadying him on his crutches as he stood staggered by the realization that he should have recognized the vision for what it was when it had first come to him. "If I was truly a shaman I would have seen."

"Seen what, Ne'gauni?"

"I would have known!"

"Known what, Ne'gauni?"

"That the danger I sensed ahead of us was for Mowea'qua. I should have foreseen that she would run away. I should have warned her of what awaited her in the forest under the Spirit Moon. I should have—"

"What?" interrupted the old man, obviously at the end of his patience. "I tell you, Dreamer, you have much to learn before Teacher can bring you to master the complexities of the way of the shaman's road. There are many twists. Many turns. The way ahead can only rarely be clearly seen. So let us obey the headman and follow the band and worry no more about Mowea'qua."

"She saved my life, old man."

"And took your leg!" Ko'ram waggled a bony forefinger at him. "Beware, Shaman Indeed, that girl may have powers we know not of. Her face and form may resemble a female of the People, but do not be misled. Her eyes and manner betray the truth of what she is. Eyes the color of the forest seen through mist. Unnatural! Willful and wild as a wolf. Intolerable!"

Ne'gauni flinched. A pang of guilt shot through him. How many times had he thought exactly the same things of her? Too many to count. Yet now he found himself recalling the way she had spoken in his defense at the stream on the far side of the falls. How defiantly she had stood with the wind at her back and sunlight glancing through the black chaos of her hair to illuminate her as yet unmarred face as her eyes glared molten verification of her ancient race and implacability of spirit. The old man was right. No one he had ever known had eyes like Mowea'qua's. No one! Old Tribe eyes? Evidently so. Manitou eyes? Ko'ram could believe this if he wished. As for Ne'gauni, he fixed the old man with a glare that he could only hope came close to matching the girl's implacability as he said, "Wild and willful she may be, but Mowea'qua did save my life and has chosen to defend me to the headman when others fell silent and you could bring yourself to do nothing but clutch your rattle and cut copious bursts of stinking wind! Believe what you will of her, old man, but I will never again speak against her name."

"Wisely spoken, young Dreamer, because whether you wish to hear it or not, she is one of them—Old Tribe—not one of us, never one of us, and I have heard it said that it is possible that she has used her manitou power to call down the warring spirits of the red moon to destroy the one who dared speak against her on the night she ran away. And I have heard it said that she has used her Old Tribe magic to work some sort of enchantment on our headman's judgment regarding her. And I have heard it said that, if she lives, she may yet bring Spirit Sucker to feed upon us all."

"Who dares to speak so?"

Ko'ram sucked in his lips, chewed on them worriedly as he looked around again, then, along with a tight-buttocked squeak of escaping flatulence, admitted sheepishly, "I do, Ne'gauni. I dare to speak so! I may not be Shaman, but I *am* Wise Man. And I tell you now that although the band walks with newfound pride and confidence today as it sings and celebrates the success of Tôrnârssuk's raid against old enemies, it would have been better for us all if the search party had been content to return to camp with only the boy, better if the wild girl and the Old Tribe village had never been found, and perhaps better still if Mowea'qua had never been born. There will be more trouble because of her. I can feel it in my bones!"

▼▼▼▼▼

Sun.

Shadow.

Light.

Dark.

The girl's consciousness drifted in and out of each until, at last, she batted open her swollen eyes and stared up at the blur that was the shifting canopy of the treetops.

Another dawn? Another day? Another dusk?

Mowea'qua closed her eyes.

What matter?

She was too weary to care. The forest went on and on forever. She did not want to see it. She did not want to see anything ever again.

Or hear the singing of the band.

And yet the song that had drawn her up out of she knew not where continued as relentlessly as the forest. Verse after endless verse. Refrain after endless refrain. Even the children were singing, and every now and then a dog would raise its head to bark or howl, enthusiastically asserting its right to participate in the revelry of its human pack as the travelers walked on, rejoicing in the success of the search party and exulting in chanted tales of bravery and of the glorious slaughter to which their headman had led them.

Mowea'qua cringed.

Kinap was pounding his drum with a cadence of such furious power that both her heart and spirit were bruised by it. Onen'ia's flute shrieked like an eagle gone mad as it soared upon the wild wind of the Dawnlander's improvised melody.

And old Ko'ram was now screeching and shaking his turtle-shell rattle and deer-hoof ankle janglers more aggressively than he had ever done before.

Mowea'qua wished that the old Wise Man would cease his caterwauling. She wished that the drum and flute would fall silent. And she wished that the singing would stop. The words raked her mind. They recalled too much. Far too much.

Gray eyes staring through the mists of bog and grove and valley.

Go away!

Beasts closing all around.

Stay away!

A ghostlike form advancing through the blue haze of twilight with a bear cub on a lead.

I do not know you!

A spectral face leering over her, bearded, fanged, gloating. *"Strong must you be. And yielding. Our blood is one blood. You are one of us now."*

"No!" she sobbed. "Not one of you am I. Not Old Tribe! Not a beast! Not one of you! Never one of you! Never!"

"Mowea'qua? Are you dreaming, Mowea'qua, or are you awake at last?"

"Ah . . ." A moan escaped the girl's lips as the tremulous piping of Musquash's question drew her thoughts away from that bloodied place of terror to which the singing of the band had led her mind. She was grateful. Her memories were too terrible to hold. Still, she made no attempt to answer the child's query. It hurt too much to speak; even breathing was an agony, and her unintended exclamations had set fire to her throat. How could it be otherwise when someone had nearly crushed it?

Kinap!

A sob shook her. The resultant pain was almost too much to bear, but no more so than the memory of her beloved giant bending over her, strangling her, choking the life out of her as he swore that he should have ended that life on the day she was born. He was right, of course. As Moraq had been right on the night of the Spirit Moon. Everything he had said about her lineage was true. She knew that now. No matter how she wished to deny it, she had seen the truth of what she was and understood why her father had not come to see her since she had been returned to the band. Kinap had meant what he said out there in the village of the beasts. He wanted her dead. She could not blame him.

"You must not cry, Mowea'qua. Please. It hurts my heart to see you cry."

She trembled at the boy's statement. *Crying am I? So it must be.* She could feel his fingertips gently brushing warm moisture from her cheeks. *Tears?* The tip of her tongue tasted salt as it moved to explore the corners of her partially open lips. *Yes. Definitely tears.*

Mowea'qua lay still, licking them away, allowing the child to continue his soothing ministrations as she felt herself being jostled along on the big drag frame upon which she was being pulled by a pair of the headman's strongest dogs. Even when the boy's hand moved from her face, she did not have to look up to know that he was still staring down at her, watching her as he walked at her side, worrying over her, a different boy entirely from the obnoxious child who had so courageously set himself to dog her steps on the night she had chosen to defy the headman and the entire band. No longer was he bold little Bog Rat or brazen Biting Fly or arrogant Puffball. He had become a sad-eyed, tight-lipped shadow of his former self, no longer Muskrat at all, but Mushroom, a pale, tender wisp of a sprout who resembled nothing so much as one of the fragile little fungi that had been a gift to them from the thunderstorm when they had walked together in the bogs.

"You must forgive me, Mowea'qua," he said. "I have done a terrible thing. I tipped the basket. I did not mean to tip it, but I did, and because of me we both nearly went spilling out across the Great Sky River. But perhaps the forces of Creation are not so angry at me after all. We are together! Those who stole you away from me are dead and can never hurt you again. I will take care of you. You will heal and grow strong. And I will not leave you, Mowea'qua, not ever again! On my life and on the sacred stone of my father's Ancestors, this I promise you! This I vow!"

Again she trembled. Tipped the basket? What did he mean? And what terrible thing could he possibly have done, except to ally himself with her? She had no idea. And she hurt too much to worry over it. It was enough to be weighted by the knowledge that the boy's loyalty to her remained unchanged. She could not understand why, and she certainly did not care whether he stayed at her side or went his way and never looked at her again. All that mattered was that he was safe within the protection of the band, still alive, not meat in the jaws of the water monster Waktcexi, not trampled under the crushing feet of mammoths, not drowned in the fetid depths of the pond of Giant Beaver, not roasted alive and devoured by beasts, and not killed by the war club of Tôrnârssuk as punishment for running off after her under the bloodred glare of the Spirit Moon. Another sob shook her; she welcomed the pain. It was her due. She accepted it and, as she thought of all that might have befallen young Musquash because of her, knew that she deserved no less.

The boy spoke again, low, earnestly. "Mowea'qua, can you hear me? You must hear me! I have overheard Suda'li whispering to the giant that even though the headman brought you back to the band, you will soon die and we will all be well rid of you. But I will not believe this! You must prove her wrong, Mowea'qua. You must remember the mammoths! You must remember the sign they left for us in the forest on the night they rumbled with thunder in the dark woods. You *must* remember, Mowea'qua. Great Chief is out there with his herd. I know he is! And though Giant Beaver and all of his kind are dead forever, as long as even one great tusker walks in the forest you will get better and all will be well with the band and with the world. It is what you said. It is what you swore was true. Ah, Mowea'qua, will you not talk to me?"

Mowea'qua's hands fisted at her sides. She refused to speak. She refused to listen. She did not want to think of mammoths. Or of thunder rumbling in the dark forest. Or of the beaver pond upon whose vile shores she had been taken captive and mated by beasts. And yet his words brought it all back. Her head swam. Weakness rose in her as a tide that swept her mercifully away from the moment. Away from the drag frame. Away from the watching eyes of the child. Away from the pain of her battered body. Away into the dark and silent refuge that she was learning to make of her mind, into a soft, sheltering, shadowy retreat within which there was no present, no future, and no past, no past at all.

Until . . .

"Do not lose yourself in the Darkness, Mowea'qua. I have never found it a good place to be. Come back to us."

Her lids flickered. So heavy. She had neither the strength nor the inclination to open them as she wondered dully, *Who speaks now to me?*

"I would have gone with the others if they had allowed it. I want you to know that, Mowea'qua. I want you to know that I would have fought for you if I had been given the chance."

Ne'gauni!

"The Great River of the North still lies ahead of us, Mowea'qua. And we have whales to see! Whales of many colors. Whales as big as mammoths. Whales singing to the sun and moon and stars! We will see them together, you and I. It will be so. You will see!"

She trembled again. Violently. Pain flared within every nerve ending of her body, and yet, somehow, it was her spirit that was bleeding.

"Come away, He Walks Ahead in Dreams to Foresee Danger for the People. You must not blame yourself for what has befallen this disobedient girl. You are Shaman, not Warrior. She will come to her senses or not. Allow her to rest. Walk with me and my sisters awhile. We have made soft new rabbit-skin pads for the armrests of your crutches. You must try them out and see if they do not ease your way far better than the ones she made for you."

"I thank you, Nee'nah, but no. I will stay with Mowea'qua. Until she is better. As she once stayed with me."

"It is all right, Brother of My Heart. Look. See how Musquash now curls up like a pup asleep at Mowea'qua's side? I will watch them both until she wakes. Go. Walk with my sisters if it pleases you."

"It pleases me to walk with Mowea'qua, Hasu'u. And with you. Always it pleases me to walk with you."

Mowea'qua lay very still. She could feel Musquash at her side. So small. So warm. Breathing deeply in his sleep. But her thoughts were far from the boy. A sudden, thoroughly unexpected emotion was stirring within her breast. Jealousy? Indignation? Ne'gauni was *her* Wounded One, not Hasu'u's, not Nee'nah's!

The voices fell away.

Mowea'qua's consciousness fell away with them until, gradually, she became aware of a lack of movement. The drag frame had been set down. Dogs were barking and children were laughing. She could hear the twin sons of Suda'li squabbling and, awash in a sense of coolness and shadow, batted open her eyes to stare up at a worried-looking Hasu'u.

"Ah! You are awake, Mowea'qua! This is good. Very good! Rain clouds are gathering. Night will come soon. We are raising the shelters in which to pass the darkness. My mother is preparing more of the alder wash for your eyes. Have you need of willow stalks to ease your pain? Do you think you can chew them? Musquash and Ne'gauni are off gathering new shoots along the creek. If your mouth and throat are still tender, we will pound them in water and make a drink for you to sip. I have porcupine quills through which you can suck. Now, try to sit up. You will feel better for it."

Mowea'qua stared at the older woman. At Tôrnârssuk's beautiful, compassionate Dawnland woman. She did not want to look at her. Looking at her made her think of him. And thinking of him recalled the dream and the terror, the great white bear of the north towering over her, the dogs ravaging her, the snarling black wolf who was her father falling upon her to rip the very life out of her. Her breath snagged in her throat. Pain flared. A moan escaped her lips as she closed her eyes and, with a defiant grimace, willed herself back into mindlessness. She did not want to think! She did not want to remember all that had befallen her. She wanted to be dead . . . back in the Old Tribe village with Moraq and the beasts . . . where she belonged.

"No! I will not allow this. You will not defy me! Or anyone else. Ever again!"

Mowea'qua opened her eyes with a start as, amazed by the anger in Hasu'u's voice, she found herself pulled upright by her shoulders and shaken so hard that her vision cleared.

"You will listen to me, Mowea'qua, for I tell you now that it is you, not I, who is Stupid Woman!" Hasu'u's tattooed face was set. Her eyes were flashing. "I am a headman's wife and a chieftain's daughter, and you would be wise to listen to me, for you have been placed in my care. You have lain on this drag frame steeping in self-pity long enough. I know that you hurt. I know that your spirit aches. And if I thought that it would help you or anyone else in this band, I would strike your father a blow with my own hand for the pain that his betrayal has brought you. But you have brought this betrayal upon your own head, Mowea'qua! Do you imagine that you are the first woman to be spurned by one you love or mauled and forcefully mated against your will? Ask Tsi'le'ni, Ningao's woman, if you would hear a tale of sorrow! Ask me, for I, too, have been a captive and abandoned by one who was once dearer to my heart than any man I had ever known before Tôrnârssuk. But that is behind me now. As it is behind you. You will heal, Mowea'qua. As I have healed. As Tsi'le'ni has healed. So heed me, new sister of my fire circle. Tôrnârssuk has saved your life. You will not throw back into his face this gift that he has given to you at a greater cost to himself than he may know. A man of the True People is dead because of the dissension you caused between him and his headman. You will not moan! You will not complain! You will be obedient to my will and to that of the band. I will hear no more worried whispers against my man's judgment because of you. And if it is true, as you say it is when you cry out of your dreams, that you are 'not one of them, not Old Tribe, not a beast,' now is your chance to prove it, not only for your own sake, Mowea'qua, but for his!"

Chapter Three

▼▼▼▼▼▼▼

It rained that night.

A soft and steady summer rain, a gentle settling down upon the forest of great, gray, heavy hanks of moisture-laden cloud borne inland from the distant sea. Lightning shivered in the darkness, a dull and fleeting gleam. Thunder rumbled high in the cloud mass, a deep and restive sound; like an old man grumbling in his sleep, there was no apparent threat in it.

And yet, while old Ko'ram snored and farted and clutched his rattle close to his scrawny chest in the tent he shared with Onen'ia and Goh'beet, while the children of the band dreamed of valorous bloodshed, while the dogs tucked noses beneath tails and hunched together in a single sodden, furry clump, not all the travelers were able to sleep. Some lay awake in their shelters, listening to the rain, talking low, murmuring as restively as the thunder.

All about the raid on the Old Tribe village.

And all about how it would be when Tôrnârssuk brought them at last to the Great River of the North.

▼▼▼▼▼

"It will be all and more than we have ever imagined," enthused Kanio'te to Pwaumó as they bundled together inside their little tent with their teething baby sleeping fitfully between them. "As Tôrnârssuk has shown himself to be all and more than we have ever heard said of him!"

"For many a long moon I have found him to be a competent leader," conceded Pwaumó. "For a Northerner."

"You should have seen him on the raid, woman! The man is as implacable as the great white bear of the north for which he has been named, and as hungry for the blood of his enemies as Raven. If only you could have seen us as we went forth together! The Northerners all in their war masks, the giant bellowing his rage, our lances and arrows flying and our braining clubs striking terror to those who ran and fell before us! Ah, Pwaumó, never before has my blood burned as in the moment when we broke from the trees and shouted our intent to kill them all. There was no stopping us! We were invincible! Especially the giant! Truly, Tôrnârssuk is One Who Gives Power!"

"And takes life as he sees fit. Without benefit of counsel. To kill one of his own men, Kanio'te, to leave that man's body behind, unmourned and—"

"That man asked to die! We all saw it! We all agreed that the headman was right to finish him, for surely his constant challenges and behavior with the girl marked him as unfit to live among us. Ah, Pwaumó, when we come to the Great Gathering, other bands will stand aside and defer to us because we walk with Tôrnârssuk. They will fear us, woman! Imagine it! Forest and Grassland and Lakeland People fearing Dawnlanders! And all because we have wisely chosen to ally ourselves with one whose reputation as a warrior and raider justly walks before him. There will not be a man at the gathering who will not hunt and trade with us far more generously than he would ever have done had we come to the great river simply as another band from the coast."

She lay very still. "Is this good, my husband?"

"Of course this is good! Now you will have a chance to own a copper bead or two to add to the shells of your dancing collar! Is this not what you have always longed for and what I have been unable to afford? Perhaps I will find a good blank of rare graystone out of which to knap a new lance head. And if we are not too late in the season, there may still be sweet sap to be traded for. Would it not be a fine thing to have a stringer of duckbills filled with sweetness for our little one to teethe on?"

"Yes, my husband, but I speak not of ducksuckles or rare stones or precious copper beads. I ask if it is good to be feared by others."

"Better to have others fear us than to stand passively by while more aggressive men take for themselves and their families the best hunting and bartering grounds."

She exhaled a gentle repudiation. "You sound more and more like a Northerner these days, my husband."

"We have been traveling with them long enough for me to have come to respect their ways."

"But you and Onen'ia are sons of Chief Ogeh'ma. You are Dawnland men, Kanio'te. You have always chosen to echo the words of your father, words that wisely speak caution against the ways of those who make unnecessary threats against other men or bands or tribes."

"Unnecessary? Had my father been wise enough to call the other Dawnland chiefs into an alliance and make a few 'unnecessary' threats against the shamans of the Far Island, we would never have been forced to pay them tribute in meat and hides and women in order to avoid the endless threat of their curses! And those who died back there in that foul Old Tribe village were not men. Not women. Not children. They were beasts, Pwaumó. Filthy, thieving, unnatural things. It was necessary to kill them. You should be thankful that they are dead and no longer a threat to us."

"And yet the headman has seen fit to bring at least one of them back into the band."

"The wild girl? Yes. He will trade her at the Great Gathering. The profit he makes will be shared with the men of the raiding band. This he has vowed. It will be a good thing for us, Pwaumó, a gift from Raven and the generous spirit of White Bear!"

"The giant will not object to seeing his daughter sold off from the band?"

"He would have killed her with his own hand back at the village. As would any man of us. If Tôrnârssuk had asked it."

"And the boy? It is said that he is also of the blood of the Old Tribe."

"No one believes it except the child himself."

"Even so, my husband, if the headman were to ask it, would you raise your lance against him? Against a child?"

A long, shallow, restless sigh went out of Kanio'te.

"I am my father's son, Pwaumó, and a Dawnlander, but on the raid I learned what, in my heart, I have perhaps known all along. I have never been less than a True Man. When Ogeh'ma has eaten his fill of white whales and caribou on the shores of the Great River of the North and sets our band to return to the Dawnland, we will not go with him, my woman. I will walk and fight alongside Tôrnârssuk, if he will have me. And whatever White Bear asks of me, I will do."

▼▼▼▼▼

"I am afraid," whispered Musquash. On his knees within the shelter that he and Ne'gauni had raised and now shared, he stuck his face out into the rain, cast a gloomy gaze at the intermittently glowing underbelly of the clouds, then glowered across the benighted encampment to fasten his gaze on the headman's tent.

"Come inside, boy. The night grows cold and you are letting in a draft," yawned Ne'gauni from within the depths of the lean-to. "And just what do you fear, you who always boasts of never being afraid of anything?"

Musquash did not move. "I do not fear for myself. I fear for Mowea'qua."

"Mmm. Of course. It is good to know that some things in this band remain unchanged."

"The last time there was thunder and rain in the forest I was with her to keep her safe and warm. I should be with her now."

"Come inside," repeated the young man, stifling another yawn. "If Tôrnârssuk wanted you hovering around inside his tent, he would not have sent you off to spend the night with me. Hasu'u will tend to Mowea'qua's needs. You can be sure of that. And Mowea'qua is safer with the headman than she was with you, Musquash. So come and lie down beside me and get some rest. It has been a long day."

"I promised to take care of her."

"You have tried your best."

"My best was not good enough," said the boy with a catch in his voice as he closed the tent flap. "If I had not left her alone on the shores of the pond of Giant Beaver, I would have been able to take up my lance and my dagger and—"

"You would have been killed or taken captive yourself."

"What matter? I would have been with her! I could have saved her from—"

"She had her own lance. And her own dagger. And *my*

bow. All thanks to you. With these things, had it been possible, she should have been able to save herself."

"I am sorry about stealing your bow, Ne'gauni."

"Are you? I wonder. I will make another, but it will not be easy. I must find the right kind of wood, and when I do, it will be sappy at this time of year, so I will have to smoke it slowly to cure it and drive the insects from it before I can even begin the shaping. Ah, boy, you have cost me a fine weapon!"

"I would have brought it back to you when the raid was over, but everything the Old Tribe thieves had touched was left behind with the dead . . . except Mowea'qua."

"Yes. And so you did save her. Every man who recounts the story of the raid says the same thing. Had you not followed the search party into the village of the beasts and leaped into the fray on Mowea'qua's behalf, Kinap would have ended her life before Tôrnârssuk had a chance to interpret the sign left to him by Raven."

"Do not speak of the giant. He is worse than any 'beast.' He has killed children, Ne'gauni! I saw him!"

"Are you so sure, boy, now that you have seen the adults among those 'children' with your own eyes and witnessed what they did to Mowea'qua?"

"They were dirty and hairy and stinking, and I am glad that the bad ones who hurt her are dead. But I do not think they were beasts, Ne'gauni. They were *people*. Old Tribe People. And their children screamed as they died."

"Enemies . . . thieving, raping enemies. Do you imagine that they would not have made you and the children of this band scream if they had chosen to attack us? Enough talk, boy. Tôrnârssuk has brought you and Mowea'qua back to the band alive. Be grateful. Go to sleep. And rest content for a while."

▼▼▼▼

"I tell you Tôrnârssuk has been reborn and this band has been reborn with him!" declared Ningao as a little laugh of pure pleasure rippled through him. He was tired. His eyes ached for want of sleep. He had a bone bruise on his left heel. But he was ecstatic. Lying beside his woman inside the tent he shared with her and his favorite dog, he tussled the head of the animal and spoke to it as though it was as capable of understanding his words as his wife. "It was so good to see our headman as a warrior again, Skinny One! Do you remember how it was in the days and nights when we were raiders, moving across the land like a pack of wolves setting ourselves to prey upon the weak and the stupid? Ah! No. You came to us later. But you would have enjoyed the life, Skinny One! It was good. Dangerous. Never was there a day or night when our hearts did not pound or our blood run high with the excitement of it!"

Tsi'le'ni sent a hand to fondle the upright ears of the dog. "It is good that our man is so pleased with his return to the old raiding ways of his band," she said to the animal. "But do you not regret the killing of two dogs of your own pack, Skinny One?"

"Ah, no, woman," Ningao spoke for the dog. "Skinny One understands that there was need for them to die."

"Does he?" Tsi'le'ni's question was a gentle reproof. "It seemed to this woman a shameful thing to stand by in silence while the lives of two strong, healthy animals were ended, and one of them a breeder with pups in her belly."

"They were *his* dogs, my woman," Ningao reminded her with lowered voice. "It would have been shameful to allow them to live and risk having them possessed by the spirit of the one who named them his. Such dogs would have been a danger to their pack and a threat to our band."

"Do you truly believe that a slain man can live on in his

dogs, Ningao? And do you not mourn the death of one who was long a hunt brother to you upon the trail?"

"Ah, no, Tsi'le'ni. If you had seen the way he was on the raid—the way he snarled in defiance of the headman and fell upon the wild girl when the killing was done—you might well say that he already was a dog. Although no dog of mine would ever behave like such an animal, eh, Skinny One?"

Tsi'le'ni's hand strayed from the dog to rest lovingly on the face of the man. Darkness hid the worry that creased her low, narrow brow but did nothing to mask the concern in her voice when she asked, "How are defiant dogs so different from raiding wolves . . . or men, my husband?"

Now it was Ningao who sighed, impatient with the question, yet tender in his response to the woman. "You are not of the True People, Tsi'le'ni. I cannot expect you to understand. But I tell you now that I thank the giant's wild daughter for running off and awakening the great white bear in Tôrnârssuk's spirit, for surely it has inspired the rest of us to remember that we are True Men. Even the Dawnland hunter, Kanio'te, felt joy in the attack when we fell upon the Old Tribe village. Yes! I saw it in his eyes, and in the ease and excitement with which he joined us. And you should have seen the giant Grasslander! In truth, my woman, I have never seen even a Barrenland man as mad with the need to kill!"

"As mad to kill as on the day your band saw fit to pierce my father with arrows and take me and my mother and this big skinny dog as captives?"

"Ah!" he gasped, startled and instantly apologetic. "Forgive me, Tsi'le'ni, I had forgotten that day. I—"

A soft chuckle at his expense bubbled at the back of her throat. "Do not be so distraught. It is forgiven, Ningao. Long ago forgiven. I was not sorry to see him die. I was glad. He was as cruel as that dog-of-a-man Tôrnârssuk so rightly slew in the Valley of the Spirit Moon. My only regret is that on the day my father died, when I came to walk with your band, I was taken first by Avataut and not by you."

"Ah! Avataut! A bold hunter. A brave fighter. But not man enough to win the heart of my beautiful Tsi'le'ni!"

"I am far from beautiful, Ningao."

"To my eyes there is no woman more so, even among the finest women of the True People. Your skin is smooth and soft. Your body is strong and supple and round in all the places that make a man smile! Your hair shines in sunlight with the brown sheen of the tail feathers of a spruce grouse. Your—"

"My ears are too big. My nose is too wide. My lips are too small. My eyebrows mate in the middle of my face. And there is a dimple in the middle of my chin deep enough for troutlings to hatch in. Even among the Forest People it could be fairly said that this big skinny dog of yours has a prettier face than mine!"

"A man does not mate with his dog, Tsi'le'ni!"

"Avataut might."

"Ha! What kind of words are these?"

"True words!"

"No, woman. Avataut may no longer walk with us, but he was once a hunt brother to all True Men within this band. He will be so again. You cannot blame him for wanting you. We all wanted you in those first days of your captivity. I more than any. You were a new woman, never before mated; this is exciting to any man."

"Tôrnârssuk did not touch me. You sought to pleasure me as well as yourself. The others merely sated their man need. But Avataut hurt me, Ningao. Deliberately. And mocked me while he did so."

"Ah, my woman, Avataut has always been rough and greedy at his pleasures. It is his way. Still, I say again that we were once hunt brothers and it will be good to see him and hunt with him again when we reach the Great Gathering."

She shuddered. "I do not look forward to that day, Ningao."

"Why? He has a woman of his own at the big river, and if I know Avataut, he will be enjoying the wives and sisters and daughters and captives of any man willing to share them. But you are my all-the-time woman now, Tsi'le'ni, and I will not share you with any man!"

She exhaled a little breath, relieved and pleased by his words, yet still concerned enough to ask, "Have you forgotten that on the day Avataut parted with Tôrnârssuk to go north with Armik, he would not look at us after I refused to journey with him as his burden woman and chose to stay with you instead?"

"Tôrnârssuk allowed you to make that choice."

"Yes, Ningao, but Avataut was so angry. So offended! Not since Hasu'u dragged him from the floodwaters have I seen such a hateful look in a man's eyes."

"Ah, foolish woman, you must not trouble yourself over things that happened so long ago and so far away. Avataut has probably forgotten all about them. I know that I nearly have." This said, he slung an arm around her and, with the dog settling down between them, closed his eyes and told his wife to do the same. "We must sleep, my woman. The Great River of the North lies ahead. Wind and Storm and Wildfire and woman-stealing Old Tribe thieves have threatened us to no avail. We walk with Tôrnârssuk. Remember this, Tsi'le'ni. And be glad. All will be well for us. I feel it in my heart! The white bear in our headman's spirit has been reborn, and, truly, he is One Who Gives Power."

▼▼▼▼▼

"They say that Tôrnârssuk allowed you to take the lead in the killing." Suda'li's voice was a throaty purr of pride as she lay naked, poised on an elbow alongside the giant, stroking the bare skin of his massive chest, focusing her gaze on a face whose monstrous burn scars were mercifully concealed by the darkness of their shelter. "Ah, my giant, the story songs of your power have fired my heart toward you. Is it true? Would you alone have killed all the Old Tribe beasts had the headman and the others not insisted on taking their turn at the pleasure of it?"

"Pleasure?" Kinap, lying motionless on his back, turned the word and, only after a moment, conceded flatly, almost incredulously, "Yes. It was that."

"How powerful you are, my giant, in body and deeds and will." She sent a hand downward, smoothing and massaging his belly and hips and flanks. "I was foolish to fear for you. I was foolish to think that you might not return to protect me and my sons on the long dark trail that still lies ahead. But you are a survivor, one who is in favor with the forces of Creation. In all of this forest there is no one the equal of Kinap. Not even Tôrnârssuk is as big or strong."

"Had he not stopped me, I would have killed her." His voice was as dark as the night, as deep and rumbling with latent power as the thunder. "My own daughter . . ."

"And so you should have done had it been his will." She leaned forward, kissed his face, swung her breasts back and forth against him until she knew that he must feel them peaking hard against his skin. "Only the bravest of men would have been able to find it within himself to do what my giant was willing to do for the good of the band."

"Yes . . . for the good of the band."

Outside in the rain, a baby began to cry in one of the other tents.

"Pwaumó's girl. Always fussing." Suda'li moved closer to the giant. "My sons are asleep. They do not fuss . . . much. We need not wake them, Kinap." Her hand was searching, finding, enclosing, manipulating. "There are other sons yet to be born sleeping here, in your woman pleaser. Mmm . . . so warm . . . so big . . . truly a giant. If anything were to happen to you before we reach the Great River of the North, who in all this world could ever fill me as you fill me, my giant?"

He lay unmoving, unresponsive. "If the boy had not intervened, I would have crushed the throat of my only child, Suda'li."

"I will give you other children. Sons! Do not worry over what might have been with Mowea'qua. If she lives, the headman has sworn to find a man for her when we reach the Great Gathering of Many Tribes, and because you are her father we will claim the bulk of whatever goods White Bear takes in trade for her. She will soon enough be out of our lives . . . someone else's burden . . . someone else's trouble."

Chapter Four

▼▼▼▼▼▼

The sky cleared.

The band rose with the dawn, broke down the dripping camp, and moved on, but not before Tôrnârssuk took a moment to look Mowea'qua up and down as Hasu'u helped the girl settle herself on the drag frame.

"Her color is better this morning," observed the headman's woman, smiling as she rose and hefted her little Tiguak onto one hip. "She has taken broth. She will live. I am sure of it. Ah, and look! Here is Musquash coming to join us again. Has Ne'gauni no need of you, boy?"

"I have helped him to break down our tent and pack up his things. He will be along when your sisters stop fussing over him."

"Be polite when you speak of my sisters, child. They and my mother have kindly provided you with the clothes upon your back since your own garments—and everything else you saw fit to sneak out of this band without our headman's permission, I might add—have been lost and you refuse to wear hand-me-downs from the widow Suda'li's twins."

"I would go naked first!"

Tôrnârssuk ignored the boy. He was too intent on

scowling down at Mowea'qua as he spoke to his wife. "I see that the feather of Raven is still in the rat's nest of her hair."

"I have washed and salved her body, man of my heart, but she has been in so much discomfort that I have not sought to further distress her by untangling her hair."

His scowl was not in the least alleviated. "When you do, see to it that the feather remains where it is so that all may see it and remember why she is still alive."

Hasu'u rubbed little Tiguak's back and beamed at her man with love. "I am glad that Raven has spoken to you, man of my heart, and gladder still that he singled out Mowea'qua as one of his own and guided you to bring her back to us."

"Would that the rest of the band shared your enthusiasm, Hasu'u," he said tightly. "Your Dawnland people are right. Raven *is* Trickster. And I am not amused by his latest jest. Look at her. Those who went out in search of her expect to receive a reward for sparing this one's life, but no True Man at the Great Gathering will barter for such a wild and broken thing."

"I will barter for her," said Musquash.

"You are no man at all!" Tôrnârssuk put the boy sharply in his place. "And even if you were, you have left yourself nothing of your own with which to trade."

The boy shrank inside his oversized shirt.

The headman ignored the child and continued speaking to his woman as though he had not been distracted from the flow of their conversation. "I doubt if any man of the lesser tribes will find cause to part with even the least of his trade goods in exchange for such a female as this one, and once it is seen that she is of the Old Tribe, I will probably have to pay many more times her worth in prime pelts just to be rid of the beast!"

Mowea'qua flinched as, sitting bolt upright amidst the tumbling furs that Hasu'u had placed over her to keep away the chill air of morning, she opened her eyes and half sobbed, "Not one of them am I! No! Not a beast! Not like them! Not, say I! Not!"

The headman's face contorted with anger. "No? What could possibly have happened to change your mind? You were so proud of your ancient Old Tribe lineage back there on the shores of Big Lake in the light of the Spirit Moon! So proud that you stripped yourself naked and ran off howling like a wolf to prove to us all that you were, indeed, one of them!"

The girl was seared by the virulence of his sarcasm. Her battered face fell. Her lower lip quivered. As tears filled her eyes, she pulled one of the bed furs up over her face so that no one could see her cry.

"You must not speak so to my Mowea'qua!" protested Musquash. "She is not a beast! She—"

"She is not your Mowea'qua," interrupted the headman, deliberately withering the little boy with the adamance of his tone. "And if she is not a beast, she has yet to prove it to me!" This said, after a short, definitive huff to vent his temper, the headman leaned in to plant a kiss on the head of his baby son and another on the brow of his wife. "We must journey on, Hasu'u. Let me know when you begin to feel tired and I will call a rest for the band. And take the skin of the great white bear of the north off the drag frame! It was a gift to you from my heart and spirit. A thing of power to protect you. How can you allow it to be sullied by her touch? Does it mean so little to you?"

Hasu'u was visibly flustered. "I . . . I have placed all of the big furs on the drag frame this morning, man of my heart. It is easier to carry them thus, spread out beneath the girl and as blankets for her, with the dogs to pull their weight."

His face was a mask, taut as a drumskin stretched over carved bone, but anger was boiling black behind his eyes as he reached down, snatched up the big white pelt, and slung it around his shoulders. It was so large that it covered his fully loaded pack frame with ease, and the long forearms and huge white paws of the great bear hung down over his chest. He glared at Mowea'qua. As she cringed on the drag frame, haplessly pulling up the nearest furs to cover her nakedness, his features twisted. There was no anger in his eyes now, only irony. And perhaps disgust. "Wolfskins! Do you see that, Hasu'u? Instead of lynx or forest lion or wood bison, she grasps at the pelts of wolves. They are her kin. Let them warm her. And perhaps, as long as she remains in this band, it is good that I take up the skin of this great white bear again and wear it to remind me of who I am and what I must be in the days and nights that lie ahead!"

This said, not realizing that he had brought not only the girl but his wife to tears, he turned and walked off, gesturing and speaking impatiently to everyone he passed. "Come! Ningao! Kamak! Arnaktark! Inaksak and Itiitoq! And you, Giant, and men and women and children of the Dawnland, let us be on our way. The great encampment is yet far. And the white whales will not wait for us forever."

▼▼▼▼▼

Dawn ripened into a misty morning that, in its turn, ripened into a warm day alive with the breath of soft, fair-weather breezes that were just strong enough to keep away the war bands of Mici'cak, Master of Biting Flies, while carrying a soothing touch of coolness along with the sounds of

songbirds and squirrels and, now and then, the hammering
of a woodpecker and the shrieking of a hawk in the high
canopy of the trees.

The contour of the forest floor, level now for the most
part, allowed easy and comparatively relaxed movement as
the band advanced through a world of sun-dappled silver
birches and evergreen shade. Here and there they crossed a
creek and paused to drink and fill their water flasks and eat
of whatever traveling rations the individuals among the
band had set apart for themselves. At one streamside pool,
Segub'un and her daughters cast their nets and brought up
enough fish to make a small feast for all. And afterward,
when the band moved on after thanking the spirits of the fish
and returning their bones to the water so that they could be
reborn, lest the travelers have time to reflect on the cold, unspoken realization that the last time they had fished in a
streamside pool Moraq had been with them, Hasu'u led them
in a light and joyful walking-along song.

> *"Together we go!*
> *Hay ya, ya! Hay ya, ya!*
> *The day is sweet and our bellies are full!*
> *Together we go! Together we go!*
> *Hay ya, ya! Hay ya, ya!"*

The headman raised an eyebrow and, appreciating the
wisdom of his wife, picked up on the leading stanza and followed it with encouraging words of his own.

> *"Together we go!*
> *Hay ya, ya! Hay ya, ya!*
> *The great river waits.*

Together we go! Together we go!
Hay ya, ya! Hay ya, ya!"

Ningao joined in.

"Together we go!
Hay ya, ya! Hay ya, ya!
Strong dogs and True Men of Dawnland and Barrens.
Together we go! Together we go!
Hay ya, ya! Hay ya, ya!"

Tsi'le'ni, eyeing her dog-loving husband askance, clucked her tongue before singing with loving but obviously strained forbearance.

"Together we go!
Hay ya, ya! Hay ya, ya!
Women and little ones along with the dogs!
Together we go! Together we go!
Hay ya, ya! Hay ya, ya!"

Kamak laughed and pointed good-naturedly at Ningao as he sang out,

"Together we go!
Hay ya, ya! Hay ya, ya!
With man who will soon sleep alone with his dogs!
Together we go! Together we go!
Hay ya, ya! Hay ya, ya!"

It was an unexpected but fairly and well-placed barb. Even Tôrnârssuk allowed himself an exhalation of mirth as the women tittered and elbowed one another knowingly and N'av and Ka'wo'ni, who did not really understand the joke at all, hooted and danced around merrily anyway.

Ningao the dog lover, giving his woman an apologetic shrug, felt bound to add another line in hope of forgiveness for his inadvertent oversight.

"Together we go!
Hay ya, ya! Hay ya, ya!
This man with a woman second to none!
Together we go! Together we go!
Hay ya, ya! Hay ya, ya!"

Tsi'le'ni blushed and bowed her head lest others see the color of her embarrassment and pride.

The women *aahed* their appreciation of the compliment. Several of the men did the same and exchanged amused glances as Kamak pointed at Ningao again, this time as though to say, *Well spoken! She will sleep with you again now!*

Old Ko'ram, realizing that his deafness was depriving him of most of the impromptu words that the others were singing between the refrains, looked around with no small measure of befuddlement and frustration. To compensate for his failing hearing, he joined in on the song with extra fervor. High-stepping with great exaggeration, he shook his rattle at the treetops and danced ahead of Ne'gauni in an ankle-jangling, wind-cutting forward hop while booming out his own self-serving verse lest others doubt for a moment that he was still a man of power and major importance to the band.

"Together we go!
Hay ya, ya! Hay ya, ya!
With Wise Man and Teacher all are bold in our steps!

Together we go! Together we go!
Hay ya, ya! Hay ya, ya!"

Ne'gauni, leaning into his crutches and irritated by the way Nee'nah's newly made rabbit-fur brace pads were beginning to lump up beneath his armpits, was annoyed even more by the lingering noxiousness of Ko'ram's rising flatulence than by the arrogance of the old man's bombast. Grimacing, he could not resist singing out a dour refrain and verse of his own.

"Together we go!
Hay ya, ya! Hay ya, ya!
Steeped in high wind and low!
Endlessly I go! Endlessly I go!
Hay ya, ya! Hay ya, ya!
Endlessly I go!"

There was dead silence.

Everyone stopped. Everyone exchanged startled looks. Some repressed smiles at the terse and unexpected humor in the young man's verse. All looked away from the old man in embarrassment for him.

Ko'ram, having heard only the last of the young man's refrain, stopped, puzzled by the band's sudden pause and totally perplexed by the way his twin grandsons were hooting with laughter as they danced in and out amongst the trees in imitation of the old man's hop step, each loosing loud pops of wind out of their mouths. He frowned, suspecting but not entirely willing to believe what he was seeing.

"Suda'li, look to your sons," commanded the headman, not in the least amused by their antics.

Nor was Hasu'u. She had gone rigid as she stood close to

Mowea'qua's drag frame with Musquash at her side. Her head was high as her eyes sought Ne'gauni, her expression openly rebuking him for what she had obviously taken as callous disrespect of an elder.

Ne'gauni hung his head and, less in contrition than in regret over having displeased the headman's woman, muttered, "Sorry."

Old Ko'ram was still frowning. Obviously confused, he watched the others moving on and, grasping at what he mistakenly took to be understanding of the moment, turned to Ne'gauni, shook his rattle in the young man's face, and scolded, "Shame! Dreamer must not allow himself to be mocked! And did you see the way the headman's woman looked at you? She is not pleased with you. Have I taught you nothing? You must sing the refrains as given, Shaman Indeed! This song in which Hasu'u leads us is a very old song. Very old. Everyone knows the way of it. It is the 'together we go' song, not the 'endlessly I go' song. What words are these? There is no such song as 'endlessly I go'! No such song at all! What were you thinking to make it up? It implies that the trail will never end for you. A terrible thought! It makes these old bones tired just to think of it. Truly, Man Who Walks Ahead in Dreams to Foresee Danger for the People, even Mowea'qua knows better than to change a refrain once it is given to us by the Ancestors."

"Yes, Ko'ram," Ne'gauni acknowledged as he swung out with his crutches again, wishing that he had not been so impetuous as to cast away the old moss-stuffed rabbit skins that Mowea'qua had made for him to bind around the braces. He had been able to adjust those as he wished, and, once secured, they had not lumped up to form abrasive ridges that only added to the already unavoidable discomfort caused by the press of his weight against the staffs.

His brow came down as, staring ahead with resolve, he lengthened his stride, annoyed to find Nee'nah and her sisters, Chi'co'pee and Ane'pemin'an, falling back to walk with him, smiling their eager-to-please smiles, asking if there was anything he needed. He grunted a negative response and ignored them. He was remembering another trail, another part of the forest, a wild tangled wood of blowdowns and lichen-scabbed rock and patchy areas of leafy ground cover through which Mowea'qua had gone striding out beside him, willful as North Wind, telling him all about the correct way in which to sing. As though she knew everything! As though she had not a fear in all the world!

A tremor of remorse went through him. Now, as then, the pungent scent of the ancient boreal forest was strong around him, no longer unseasonably dry but moist from recent rain and intensely fragrant with the smell of balsam and a fragile, far more subtle and sweeter scent that assured him that shinleaf and pipsissewa flowers were still in bloom. The combined fragrances were heady, soothing. He breathed them in as though they could be food for him, nourishment, a balm for his troubled spirit. Watching the band moving ahead through sun-streaked shadows between the trees, his eyes fastened on the drag frame. His heart ached for the girl who lay motionless upon it, changed utterly from the girl he had known on the far side of the falls, before the rising of the Spirit Moon, a lifetime ago.

▼▼▼▼▼

They went on until the shadows they cast upon the forest floor grew long and wide. As the sun slipped away unseen beyond the summits of distant western hills, a stag appeared in a clearing ahead. With a single shot from his bow, the headman felled the animal before anyone else had even seen it.

Here, in the clearing, the men came together to butcher the stag lest female hands and knives dishonor its gender at a time when its spirit still lingered in the world of the living. Before the first cut was made, the hunters of the Barrenlands and Grassland and Dawnland solemnly circled the body of the stag and raised their faces to the sky so that the spirit of the deer and the forces of Creation would know that they shared their headman's gratitude as he spoke the traditional litany of thanksgiving.

"Great Father of Forest Deer, your antlers are like trees of many branches. Many are the fawns that must have sheltered beneath them. Your flanks are high and your limbs are long and sleek as the thin white clouds that race across the wide face of the sky to avoid being caught by following storms. These flanks and limbs must have lifted you to many a mating on many a doe and carried you swiftly from the jaws of your enemies. We thank you for coming to us. We thank you for forswearing the making of fawns and the mating of does and the bold running from your enemies. We thank you for choosing to make of your life a gift to this band. We thank you for honoring the arrow of this man."

As the deer was skinned and gutted and portioned, the women searched for standing deadwood with which to make a fire. Soon, even before darkness had settled upon the forest, flames were leaping high and the smell of roasting meat scented the night as Tôrnârssuk and his followers fell to the feast, sharing the organ meat, slicing off choice cuts, cracking the bones, and using marrow scoops to scrape sweet, oily marrow from the joints.

"We thank the forces of Creation for seeing us safely upon this long trail to the Great River of White Whales with a headman who can make such a shot as that which was accepted by the generous heart of this stag, whose blood and flesh and heart meat now strengthen us for the journey ahead!" said Chief Ogeh'ma, nodding approval of the surfeit of his meal. "May it be that someday all Dawnland men will learn from the men of the north to be masters of this fine skill of shooting little lances from bent branches! Try as I might, I have yet to find the way of it."

"And may we men of the Barrenlands learn to use the long toggle-headed harpoons that we have seen your Dawnland cousins among the seal and walrus and whale hunters at the great river use," the headman returned.

Kanio'te sat a little straighter. "It is good for men of the Dawnland and Barrenlands to walk and hunt together."

"And Grassland men with them," added Suda'li from the woman's side of the fire. "Kinap could teach you the use of the bow and arrow, Ogeh'ma. He has learned well on past journeys among other bands of Northerners."

"Well enough," rumbled the giant.

"Your skill with our weapons equals our own," said Inaksak. "We all say it of you, Storyteller. And your skill as a fighting man . . . no Northerner would question it after—"

"Do not speak of it!" the giant interrupted with a growl as he threw the section of marrowbone he had been gnawing on into the fire. "It is done! Behind us! Finished!"

"And so," agreed Kanio'te eagerly. "True Men of the Barrenlands, True Men of the Dawnland and Grassland, together we have proved that we are like the giant's bow: two kinds of wood embraced in sinew, all three stronger together than when apart."

"In the time beyond beginning the People were all of one tribe," Musquash reminded them pointedly from where he sat at the foot of Mowea'qua's drag frame, back from the fire, well apart from the other boys.

"Not all people," N'av countered with a sneer and, as his

twin chortled agreement, gave a sideward jerk of his head to indicate Mowea'qua.

"She is not a people." Ka'wo'ni smirked. "She is Old Tribe. She is—"

"Mowea'qua is Chosen Sister of Raven!" Hasu'u was on her feet, glaring at the twins as though she would set them both ablaze with her eyes. "Speak against her and speak against the will of Tôrnârssuk. Would you do that, grandsons of Ko'ram, sons of one who has already been eaten by a white bear?"

Chapter Five

▼▼▼▼▼▼▼

That night Mowea'qua dreamed that she was a wolf again.

A black wolf. Wild. Running free. Bold and fearless as those wolves of old from whose loins Grandmother Kelet had sworn that she and her kind had sprung in the long-gone time beyond beginning when the People and Animals were all of one tribe.

Voices entered the dream.

Male. Low. Rumbling discontent. "I tell you, woman of my heart, it was *my* place to repudiate the sons of Suda'li. You must not speak out for me like that again. Ever! It unmans me in the eyes of my men. I am White Bear! I am Raven! I am Wíndigo, Great Ghost Cannibal of the North, and Tunraq, One Who Gives Power to all who follow me! All know this!"

Female. Low. Dulcet. Pleading. "Forgive me, man of my heart. I meant no offense, but it was not the first time I have heard words spoken against the girl since you brought her back to us, and in truth, I have begun to fear that—"

"Truth? Have you ever spoken anything less than that to me or any other man or woman or child of this band, Hasu'u?

And what has your loyalty to truth ever won for you, woman? Or for anyone? Fear all you like! The girl will live or she will die. It matters not to me. Look at her. She twitches and whimpers in her sleep like an animal."

"She is in pain, man of my heart."

"She *is* pain! I should never have brought her back to the band. Never."

"But, man of my heart, how could you do otherwise when Raven left a sign for you to—"

"Ah. Yes. I had almost forgotten. The feather. A sign."

Mowea'qua shrugged off the voices and ran on, deeper into her dream, howling now, or so it seemed, as she had howled on the shores of Big Lake under the bloodred glow of the Spirit Moon, calling back over her shoulder to Kinap.

"Follow me, my father! Come! Together we will run forever. Yes! No others need we! Follow, say I, follow!"

And, in this dream as in the other, he obliged, no man at all, but wolf, huge, scarred, grayed with age, yet as fleet as any youth, and many times as strong. In this dream, however, Mowea'qua saw that he was not alone. A dog ran with him, a lean, lithe, ferret-faced bitch with ears laid back and pink teats dripping milk. A pair of gangly pups bounded at her side. As ferret-faced as their mother, the twins were *yarf*ing and snarling, lifting bloody snouts to show their needle-sharp milk teeth as they raced ahead to nip at Mowea'qua's heels, viciously tearing her flesh to the bone.

"Yah!" she cried and, forced to stop, turned on the dream trail to kick the pups so hard she sent them flying. Their yelps of pain brought a smile to her face. She had hurt them. She was glad! She turned and ran on, casting a backward glance over her shoulder, certain that she would see Kinap following. Her smile turned upside down. He had paused alongside the bitch dog, both of them nosing at her pups, checking for injuries. A flaring of hope brought a smile back to Mowea'qua's face as she found herself wondering if the scent of the pups might not bring Kinap the wolf to his senses. Perhaps, instead of commiserating with the spawn of some other male, he would remember where his blood loyalty lay and devour the vicious little curs as penalty for attacking his daughter. And then, realizing that their dog mother was no worthy mate for such a magnificent wolf as he, Kinap would turn on the bitch and devour her, too. It was what he did so well—turning on those whom he brought to love and trust him!

Mowea'qua trembled as a wave of disappointment washed through her. It was not to be. Even in dreams she could not have things her way. The pups were up and running after her again. Kinap and his bitch were following. Her heart sank. The expressions on their faces affirmed what she already knew: Her father had chosen with whom he would run, and it was not with her. He was no wolf! He was not even a man of the People! He was a dog, and if he and his ferret-faced bitch and her twins caught up with her, Mowea'qua was certain that she would be the one to be devoured.

Angered and hurt by his betrayal, she turned her gaze ahead again and defiantly lengthened her stride. Let him follow! Let him try to catch her! She would not allow it! She was a wild wolf, not a dog broken to the will of man. And so she ran full out, deeper into the dark hemorrhagic shadows of the bloodred dream forest, inwardly rejoicing in her wildness, uncaring of the livid, somehow lecherous gaze of the Spirit Moon. Leaping and burrowing and forcing her way over and under and through the undergrowth, she went on and on until, at last, she broke free of the scrub and came to an abrupt pause.

Breathless, panting, Mowea'qua stood stunned by the

eye-searing intensity of daylight that she saw emanating from the vast gray dreamscape that lay ahead.

The forest stood silent at her back.

The Spirit Moon had vanished from the sky.

It was as though she had, by magic, broken through an invisible barrier of some sort to find herself alone on a gentle rise, facing into an even gentler wind, with an entirely new world stretching out before her. And yet, although she had never set foot in this world, Mowea'qua recognized it instantly.

It was the world of the time beyond beginning.

It was the world of Grandmother Kelet's stories.

It was the world of past dreamings, of wide, boulder-strewn, perpetually frozen earth and stunted, oddly shaped trees and enormous fields of never-melting snow that shone white beneath brazen skies across which a single raven was now circling, a mote against the sun, cawing, beckoning her to follow.

"Mowea'qua!"

She shivered at the sound of her name. "Yes!" she cried and, throwing caution to the wind, lifted her paws and loped forward in eager response to Raven's summons.

How beautiful was the world of the time beyond beginning! How welcoming! It was a vast, boundless, rolling tundral plain across which Kinap and his bitch and pups could never catch her. She was young. They were not. She was free. They had the pups and each other to worry over. She could outdistance them with ease. The certainty inspired her to throw back her head and howl. And yet, strangely, she found only sadness in the sound and a loneliness so bleak that all joy was sapped from the moment.

Storm clouds were beginning to gather on the horizon.

Mowea'qua paused, stared ahead, and shivered a little, for the air around her had grown suddenly cold. And now, for the first time, she felt the thud of footfall trembling in the permafrost and saw that she was not alone on the great gray plain.

Something was plodding on toward the clouds.

Something.

She squinted and tried to see more clearly.

Whatever it was, it was huge. It was silent. It was all at once awesome and somehow terrible to behold in the stark bone whiteness of its soaring height and mass and the length and upward curl of its enormous tusks.

"The white mammoth!" she cried out in startled amazement.

"Yes, Mowea'qua, it is real. It is good that you dream of it. I have seen it! I know I have."

She winced, disconcerted by the intrusion of a light and familiar voice into her dream.

Someone else spoke, murmured low, impatiently. "Go back to your place of sleep beside our Dreamer, boy. We have no need of you here."

"But she is crying, Tôrnârssuk."

"Go, boy."

"But the sisters of your woman have spread their sleeping furs beside Ne'gauni. I do not think they want me there."

"Then seek out the giant. You belong at his fire."

"No more!"

"Then lie down by the old Wise Man. He sleeps alone tonight."

"He smells, Headman."

"Then find your own place, boy, before you wake my son! Close by if you wish it so, but trouble me and my woman no more!"

"Yes. All right. But I will not sleep, Headman. If Mowea'qua needs me I will not be far. Just over there. By that big stone. I will not leave her. Can you hear me, Wolf Woman? Muskrat will not leave you ever again!"

"You will not call her that name again within this band!"

"No, Headman's Woman, never again . . . if you wish it so."

The voices fell away.

Mowea'qua shifted restlessly under the wolfskins beneath which she was sleeping. They seemed heavier than before, as though someone had added another to their number. The additional warmth was welcome. She snuggled deeper into it and, briefly, was aware of a deep, burning, bruising ache within her loins. The awareness passed. A dream muskrat had just found a perch on her shoulder. He nuzzled her cheek; his whiskers tickled. She waved him away and, as she felt him scamper off down her arm, found herself fully back inside her dream again.

Something had changed within it.

The mammoth had vanished.

The sun had disappeared behind the storm clouds.

Or perhaps the mammoth had been transformed into cloud? She could not be sure, but the clouds were much closer than before. Thunderheads now, they filled the sky, threatening with flat underbellies black as night and boiling white crowns so bright it hurt to look at them. And far ahead, at the base of a low, snow-blasted, utterly treeless range of hills, Mowea'qua could now see a hunting camp—a single tent, no more than a crude pit hut, before which a man and a woman, each hidden inside snow-crusted furs, were crouching opposite each other on either side of a stone-curbed fire. They were cooking something. She could smell it. Mowea'qua's heart quickened. Her nostrils widened. She drew in the scent of something wonderful. Bear meat! Sacred meat! The best meat of all!

The couple had seen her.

Lightning flashed on the far side of the little hills.

The couple appeared to be conversing. Then one of them rose, beckoned.

A rush of expectancy swept through Mowea'qua. They were offering shelter from the impending storm, and they were going to share their feast with her. She was certain of it. Her belly lurched in response to the rich, fatty scent of the bear meat, and, inside her dream, she remembered that she had refused to eat so much as a morsel of the stag at the feast fire of Tôrnârssuk's band. She would eat now, in her dream. On her own terms. At the fire of First Man and First Woman she would eat, and be honored to do so!

Something touched her brow.

Raindrops?

It seemed so as, sighing in blissful anticipation of a meal, Mowea'qua moved eagerly forward into her dream, drawing into her wolf nostrils the high, heady smell of fire-seared flesh along with the bittersweet coolness of a wind born of the constant tides of subfreezing air that, according to old Kelet's stories, eternally swept the earth and sky of the time beyond beginning.

"Ah," she exhaled, relaxing ever deeper into her dream. Once again she had left the world of ever-warring tribes and battling bands behind. Once again she had entered the most ancient hunting grounds of the Ancestors. And this time First Man and First Woman were waiting for her, inviting her to shelter with them and share forever the warmth of their fire upon this treeless plain that lay so safely hidden away at the very center of the Eternal Circle of Life Ending and Life Beginning.

"Safe? Of course we are not safe! Go to sleep, woman of my heart. Stop fussing over the girl. And after all these many moons of sharing my life with me, how can you ask such a question when I have told you again and again that, no matter where we go or what we do, we will always walk forever in the shadow of Sila!"

Mowea'qua winced at the angry whisper; the words had cut sharply through her dream. She recognized their source. They were Tôrnârssuk's words. White Bear's words. The words of Raven. She did not want to hear them. She did not want to think of him. She did not want to remember where she was or why she shared the sleeping space of the headman and his woman. She wanted to be back inside her dream before she recalled the night of the Spirit Moon and the fury of the storm and the horror of all that had happened to her after.

It was too late.

She was back inside her dream again, but once again everything was different. The country of the Ancient Ones was shifting beneath her feet, bending, curving away toward the storm clouds that now towered over a horizon rimmed by soaring, tumultuous mountains of ice. She caught her breath. How beautiful were those mountains! So beautiful that, as though drawn forward by that beauty, the entire world of the Ancestors was moving toward them, leaving her behind as it carried the little hunting camp and the cooking fire and the beckoning couple with it . . . away from her.

"No!" she called out. "Wait! Hungry am I. Journey with you forever would I! Wait! Please, wait!"

And then, suddenly, as in another dream, she was racing forward up the side of what seemed to be a massive sand dune. Only this time she had to fight for every step; the sand was slipping and slumping and rivering away like water beneath her feet. She fought for purchase, fell, rose, and ran on, only to slip and fall and then rise and run on again and again until she gained the top and loped along the hard-packed spine of the esker. She did not look back. Instinct told her that she had put her father and his bitch dog and pups far behind. They could not hurt her now. Soon she would be with First Man and First Woman, and no one would ever be able to hurt her again, for theirs was the realm of the spirits, and no living men or dogs or wolves could venture there.

"Mowea'qua? Can you hear me, girl?"

She stopped, brought short by the soft voice of a worried woman and by a sudden deep and almost unbearable sadness. "Not a girl . . . a wolf," she mumbled out of her dream. For a moment, she could have sworn that she heard Hasu'u saying that this was not so. The moment passed and, with it, the sense of sadness.

A great boulder lay ahead.

Mowea'qua leaped out and, with her four strong dream-wolf paws, grappled and scraped her way to stand alone on its smooth, lichen-scabbed peak, looking ahead, exulting in the cold white splendor of a new moment.

Now she saw what she had seen before, in other dreams, not only the land that was as old as time but all the animals that had ever moved across it: vast herds of caribou and long-horned bison; high-shouldered, short-faced brown bears and mighty mammoths and fang-toothed cats and lions, spotted and maned; deer of many kinds, some with tall necks and great lumps on their backs and only stubs for antlers, and others smaller, higher of flank, antlerless, with sweeping manes and tails and a grace and speed and beauty that never failed to touch her heart, so that she nearly wept to think that they were among the creatures that the People had hunted from beneath the sky.

Then, with a catch of breath, just as she saw a giant beaver ambling on his way, old from the look of him and as big as any brown bear, she was shaken off the boulder by the force of thunder murmuring all around.

Shocked, Mowea'qua found herself on her hands and knees, still inside her dream but no longer a wolf, no longer at the base of the monolith, nor at the bottom of the great sand dune. She was herself again, back in the be-nighted forest under the bloodred glow of the Spirit Moon. And somewhere close by, a drum was beating. No—it was not a drum. It was the pounding of her heart. She looked around and saw that she was in a clearing with dark trees standing all around. Just ahead was the one-tent hunting camp of First Man and First Woman. They were there, crouching before their stone-curbed fire, poking at the meat they were roasting as casually as though they had never left the Barrenlands.

Mowea'qua rose shakily to her feet.

First Man and First Woman set down their fire prods and rose as one to stand facing her from either side of the fire, motionless, completely hidden within their snowy furs.

Mowea'qua cocked her head to the other side. She wished she could see their faces. Indeed, it seemed important for her to see their faces. Her belly tightened, but not with hunger. There was something familiar here, something that, although she could not quite place it, had every nerve ending in her body on end and screaming that there was danger for her here. Something to be feared. But what?

Again she cocked her head. The scent of roasting flesh was strong now. Very strong. No longer pleasant. There was the stink of burning hair and gut meat in it. And something had just begun to cry, the high, pitiful, mewling of a small animal.

Mowea'qua's brow furrowed. Her throat hurt. As her hands rose to cross over her neck, she suspected that she herself might be uttering the terrible cry, but even as the thought crossed her mind, it was gone. Her gaze locked on the fire. Her eyes widened. She saw that the cry was coming from within the ring of stones, from some hapless blackened thing trussed on a spit over the flames upon which it was being roasted alive. A coldness filled her. And then, with recognition, a terrible rush of heat.

"Musquash!" she sobbed.

"You must be silent, Mowea'qua. The child has finally fallen asleep. Would you wake the entire camp?"

Who speaks to me?

It did not matter. The male voice had already fallen away into the flushed confusion of her mind as, lost within the rising terror of her dream, Mowea'qua saw the stones around the fire begin to move.

She gaped.

The stones were not stones. They were living beings awakening from motionless slumber, stretching now, rising to reveal themselves, furred and fanged, Old Tribe beasts leering with savage and purely sexual intent as the grayback took form among them and, standing upright to display its maleness, growled as it spoke.

"You are one of us."

"No!" Mowea'qua choked back a scream. "A beast I am not! Mate me you will not! No! Never again! No!"

The beasts stood unmoving, devouring her with their eyes, distracting her as, somehow, the grayback managed to come forward and circle around her unseen. She felt the exhalation of its breath just as it grabbed her from behind and reached around to cover her mouth with a smothering paw. "You will not scream."

She reached up, dug her fingers into the massive hand and tried to pry it loose, to no avail. He held her so tightly that she could barely breathe as, staring ahead, mad with dread, she saw First Woman coming toward her.

Slowly.

Surely.

One measured step at a time, advancing through the circle of beasts, First Woman came. Shedding her garment as she might have shed an outer skin, she came. Walking lightly, revealing a body as lithe and furred as any wolf's, she came. Not fully animal, not fully human, a being born of another time and another world, staring fixedly back at Mowea'qua out of eyes that were the color of the forest seen through mist, she came. Clutching a dead bear cub to one furred breast, she came. And then, pausing and holding out the cub so that Mowea'qua could see that it was the same fat, sweet-natured, trusting little cub that had offered her the one moment of comfort she had known while a captive in the village of the beasts, First Woman laughed the ugly, inhuman beast laugh of Grandmother of All and spoke out of a face that was a pale elongated oval within the wild raven-feathered chaos of her black hair.

"Do you not know me, Mowea'qua?"

"No!" sobbed the girl to First Woman, her cry smothered by the hand of the beast as she shook her head in furious denial of the dream creature that was herself. Hideous! Unnatural! All at once wolf and woman! Everything that Moraq had said of her kind and more!

"You must not fight me, girl," the beast whispered, his breath warm at the back of her neck as he enfolded her in his arms and, smothering her with one paw, took her down with the other and held her close, still whispering. "There is no need to cry, not here, not now, not with me."

Mowea'qua was not crying. She was weeping. She was sobbing in great convulsive gulps. The beast had her again!

She could feel the naked power of his warm body pressed to hers. How could this be? Her head was swimming. She could not breathe. She could not think. The grayback was dead! Tôrnârssuk had killed him. As he had killed Moraq and led Kinap and his followers to kill all the beasts in the Old Tribe village. And yet here she was again, with the beast alive again, hurting her again.

"Be gentle with her, man of my heart, as you have always been gentle with me, or she will forevermore be afraid to open herself to a man and will never make a barterable wife!"

Mowea'qua winced at the intensity of Hasu'u's whispered warning, and then winced again at the equally intense and angry whisper of the headman that followed it.

"Can you truly imagine that I would take her, woman? Now? So soon after others have mauled her?"

"I . . . I meant no offense, man of my heart. I only—"

"Look at me, Mowea'qua!"

The dream shattered. In an instant. Mowea'qua batted open her eyes to find herself in the embrace, not of the grayback, not of any beast at all, but of a man who enfolded her in the warmth of his arms as they lay together beneath the pelts of wolves and the skin of the great white bear of the north.

"Do not fight me, girl," said Tôrnârssuk. "Raven has placed you in my care. Though you are of the Old Tribe, I have sworn to name you Sister as long as you walk with my band."

Her chin was quivering. Tears were welling in her eyes, sliding down her cheeks, hot, so hot.

He took his hand from her mouth, fingered away her tears as Musquash had done earlier, then traced his fingers gently back and forth across her features, communicating tenderness as a compassionate father might to an errant and frightened child, as Kinap had done, so long ago, in another world it seemed. "You need have no fear of me, Mowea'qua. You have brought enough pain upon yourself. I will not add to it."

Relief swept through her, and gratitude, and a deeper, subtler, far more intense and complex emotion, one that she would not recognize until the dawn and perhaps not even then. "Not one of them am I," she whimpered, wishing it was true, wanting him to believe it was true, wanting it so much that she reached up and flung her arms around his neck, hugging him tight. "Glad am I that you have killed them all! Not Old Tribe am I! Not! Lies my grandmother told me! All lies, say I! Run away I should not have done! Not from you. Not from White Bear who has come again to save me from the beasts of my dreams. Forgive me, Headman. Please forgive! Please! Obedient I will be to you! Always and forever!"

He sighed. Held her. Stroked her. "Rest content, Mowea'qua. Go to sleep in my arms and know that this old White Bear will do all within his power to keep the beasts from your dreams."

She trembled, snuggled close, and closed her eyes again. Sleep came. Sudden. Dreamless. Obedient.

▼▼▼▼▼

A gust of wind skittered softly across the clearing.

An ember popped in the banked fire pit over which the stag had been roasted.

And in the increasing chill of the forest night, with the moon rising above the trees, while Mowea'qua slept, quiet at last in the arms of the great white bear of the north, Hasu'u whispered a gentle admonition to Tôrnârssuk as she lay nursing the headman's son close at his back.

"You must not say that you are old, man of my heart."

"No? Would you put words into my mouth again this day, woman?"

"No, man of my heart, no! But—"

"I am no longer young, Hasu'u."

"A young man could not be as you are now, Tôrnârssuk."

"And what am I now, woman?"

"All that men have ever said of you and more."

"And so?"

"Ah, man of my heart, you are Wíndigo, Great Ghost Cannibal, whose name brings fear to the hearts of those who would foolishly stand against you or attempt to compromise the integrity of this band. You are Tunraq and Angatkok and Raven, Guide and Guardian and One Who Survives to walk strong in the favor of the spirits along the many trails of life. You are Tôrnârssuk, Great White Bear of the North, who gives power to those who set their footsteps in yours and bravely follow wherever your tracks may lead."

"I know my names, Hasu'u."

"Yes, but do you know that above all these names, in my heart, above all, you are True Man . . . strong and wise and courageous enough to follow the will of Raven and risk being kind to such a poor battered thing as the giant's daughter, even though others may still question the wisdom of it?"

"Kind?" He turned the word wearily, obliquely. The others were right to question him, for surely he was still questioning himself. He wondered what his woman would say if she knew that his kindness to Mowea'qua had nothing to do with willingness to follow the will of a totem spirit. He wondered what she would say if he told her that the feather of Raven had *not* spoken to him, that he had not taken it as a sign but had used it as an excuse to justify his weakness and inability to do what he knew he should have done.

He closed his eyes. And cringed. Blood. Death. He saw

them still. And smelled the hot, rankly sweet stench of them. The raid on the Old Tribe village had not been the glorious battle that Kanio'te and his fellow Northerners had been recounting to the women and children of the band. The attack had put none of them at any real risk. Like most of the raids of old, it had been a rush to slaughter. Nothing more. Nothing less. The band of filthy, degraded Old Tribe men, women, and children in that stinking village had not been prepared to fight; given the chance, they would have fled, but killing them had revitalized his men and awakened the spirit of a warrior in Kanio'te, and perhaps even in the boy Musquash. Yet, for the first time in his life, the great white bear within Tôrnârssuk's spirit had taken no pleasure in killing. None. Once his sense of outrage was satisfied and his lance and arrows had been released, he stood back and watched Moraq, the giant, and the others do their worst. He had experienced neither excitement nor satisfaction, nor even the vaguest sense of justification. He had simply stood by and watched, wondering why he felt so tired, so weighted down as though by some invisible and inexplicably crushing burden, overwhelmed by a sick, sinking sense of revulsion such as a man might feel when, after gorging himself to excess at a hunt feast, he is sure that one more swallow will cause him to puke up all the rest.

Moraq had seen.

Moraq had known.

Moraq had challenged him.

Once too often.

Only then had the old bear in Tôrnârssuk's spirit awakened. In defense of the ravaged girl? Or in defense of his own pride and position as leader of the band? Strangely, he had no idea. He knew only that Moraq had died at his hand as penalty for misjudging him. Afterward, the sense of weariness and revulsion had returned, and he could not bring himself to kill the girl. He still could not understand why. She had done nothing to make him believe that she had earned back her right to live, but perhaps, with Moraq's blood hot on his face and Moraq's innards exposed and stinking in the air, he simply did not have stomach enough of his own to remember that he was a True Man and finish what the Old Tribe beasts had begun.

A tremor went through him. He could hear Hasu'u's soft and even breathing as Tiguak sucked and sighed at her breast. A gentle sound. A loving sound. It made him feel suddenly weary again, almost unbearably weighted by responsibility, and yet filled with a depth of love for the child and for the woman that shook him to his very soul.

High above the clearing, a shooting star streaked white against the night and was quickly gone. Tôrnârssuk's gaze was drawn upward through an opening in the sleeping furs that covered him and his family and the wild girl. Had the star made a sound as it fell? A slight hiss? He could have sworn that it had. As though somewhere, hidden away within the vast span of stars and darkness above his head, some huge and invisible and potentially malevolent spirit had just sucked its breath in through its teeth in awe of the meteor's bright and transient passage.

Sila.

Tôrnârssuk shivered, acknowledged its presence, and drew deeper into the warm heaviness of the skin of the great white bear. The falling star had left a faint streak of lingering, milky blue light fading in its wake. His eyes followed it westward to where the moon, in pale profile now, was settling benignly into the crowns of the trees at the far side of the clearing. The Spirit Moon that had risen on the night of the thunderstorm was gone, vanished by the grace of rain along with the threat of wildfire; he hoped never again to see its red and bloated face, although he conceded that memories of it would haunt him in the days and nights to come, for soon enough the band would reach the burned land and he would have to lead his followers across it to the Great River of the North or journey far out of the way to avoid it. No one would be willing to accept such a delay. Himself included! The white whales would not wait for the coming of his band. The best of the trading goods were most likely bartered away already, and everyone was anxious to meet with old friends and relatives again. But what the flaming children of Wildfire had left behind after their vicious dance in the bloodred glow of the Spirit Moon would not be a pleasant sight.

Kinap was a living testimony to that. And Tôrnârssuk had seen such burned land before, long ago, crossing the barrens as a child with his family band, coming into the interior after summering on the coast, seeking the caribou, finding none because the feeding grounds had been charred and blackened for as far as the eye could see. Not a tree left standing. Not a sprig of lichen left to boil for soup. And all living things that could not run or fly away gone to ashes or scorched to bone in dead-end gullies and beneath stones and within thickets where they had tried in vain to hide.

Again he shivered. The night air was growing colder. Markedly so. If the wind stopped its errant gusting, there might well be frost before dawn. Tôrnârssuk had no complaint. He liked the feel of cold air on his face as he kept his gaze drifting across the round little space of open sky above the clearing.

It was so good to be able to see the sky again! Even when he had led the band down from the overlook to encamp on the shores of Big Lake, with Wildfire threatening and Spirit Moon leering down at them, he had looked up and across the starlit water, inwardly rejoicing at the temporary absence of forest towering above his head, shutting off the sky. By all the spirit powers of this world and the world beyond, how he had come to loathe the suffocating confines of the forest! Avataut had been right all along. A man of the True People needed to see the sky if he were to draw sustenance from the air. He did that now, pulled in a deep, cooling, lung-expanding breath of the increasingly chill air of night and held it captive until, expelling it slowly, he felt his head clear and his spirit sing for the first time in longer than he could remember.

All signs of the falling star were gone now. He could follow along the sweeping curve of the Great Sky River as it flowed endlessly across the arching black vault of the firmament, sparkling like a stream of countless tiny chips of sun-struck ice hurled high against the face of the night. Sila was up there somewhere, curled in darkness, hiding behind the stars, sleeping perhaps, the Unseen and Unknowable Force, the Eternal Enemy, waiting. Tôrnârssuk breathed in again, strangely at ease with the certainty that they would meet again somewhere along the trail of life, he and Sila, as they had met so many times before. And one day or night, Sila, in whatever form the Eternal One chose to show itself, would best him and spit him out upon the Four Winds. But now, warm within the skin of the great bear that had given him its spirit so many winters ago, with his woman and son close at his back and his belly and blood enriched by the meat of the stag he had taken with a single shot this day, Tôrnârssuk made out the bright stars that defined the bodies of Big Bear Forever Walks the Sky, and Little Bear Who Follows, and, close to that ever wandering pair, One Who Stands Still.

He smiled. It was good to see old friends again! When, from beneath the cursed cover of the trees, a Barrenlands man could look to the night sky and find comfort in the knowledge that he could follow the path of the Big and Little Bears to the One Who Stands Still, by the constancy of that one never-moving star, he could find his way home to the land of his Ancestors far to the north.

He breathed in again, savored the chill air of night again, and, with his mind now wandering from thoughts of Sila and walking contentedly among the stars, assured himself he was closer to the barrens tonight than he had been the night before or the night before that. Soon the band would reach the Great River of the North, and when the hunting there was done and the Dawnlanders and the Grasslander and the one-legged young Dreamer from the inland forest were content again among their own people, he and his fellow North-erners would pack up their dogs and drag frames and take their women and little ones to find their way across the mighty water so that they might begin at last the final journey home.

Tôrnârssuk's heart quickened to think of it. Old compan-ions would join with him. Armik! And Avataut! Bold, brave Avataut, most trusted hunt brother of his youth! The man's spirit had always been as restless and as hungry for adventure as his own. But they were older now. Wiser now. How joyous the moment would be when they met again on the beach close to the bluffs above the river. He would take down his raven-feathered, meticulously incised bear-bone staff and re-claim the last campsite he had made on that shore, and then he and Avataut would embrace again as men. They would breathe in the warm living scent of trust and fellowship and affection they had always known for one another, and they would exchange tales of all that had gone between them since they had parted company after the flood.

And someday soon, after they had hunted and shared the

meat of white whales and were at last on the far shore of the Great River of the North, Tôrnârssuk would lead Avataut and Armik and any other Northerner who wished to take up with his band into the very heart of the interior. He would seek out bands of his father's people with whom they would be welcome to settle to live in harmony, peacefully, no longer raiders or even traders who so often and unnecessarily incurred the wrath of Sila. Once again they would live as their forefathers, as hunters and gatherers wisely content to cautiously follow the seasons and the ancient movements of the game under summer skies that never saw the setting of the sun and in winter camps in which the children would play and his beautiful Dawnland woman would lead others in songs of joy beneath perpetually star-strewn skies and benevolent moons and dancing rivers of multicolored light. And soon a day would come when, in the traditional way of fathers and sons of the north since the time beyond beginning, Tôrnârssuk and Tiguak would go off to wander together across the barrens just as Big Bear Forever Walks the Sky and Little Bear Who Follows wandered across the night. He would teach his son all that he knew, and take him to all the hunting grounds he had known as a boy. The burned land he had seen as a child would surely be healed by then, and lichen and scrub growth and little groves of fragrant trees no taller than a woman would be thick upon the tundra, as would be the caribou.

He lay very still, closed his eyes, overcome by an intensity of wanting that made the Barrenlands of his youth seem suddenly farther away than ever before. Why had he ever left them? What had he gained by it? Had it not been for the way his arrow had arced and flown to take the life of the stag today, he would have been convinced that, despite the successful slaughter in the Old Tribe village, the spirit names and magic amulets he had brought with him from the hunting grounds of his Ancestors had lost all power in this land of endless trees. So many had died along the raiding trail. So many! And now Moraq was dead also, slain by his hand. It still unsettled him to think of it.

The girl in his embrace stirred slightly, curled warm and childlike in the crook of his arm. He was grateful for her movement; it refocused his thoughts. How slim she was, tall as a man, yes, but slender, and so deeply bruised and hurt by her ordeal. Hasu'u had bathed and oiled Mowea'qua's injuries, but he could smell the subtle scent of battered and torn tissue, the strong medicinal scent of pulverized balsam mixed into some sort of animal fat, and the residual scent of rape. He drew the girl closer as the pity he had felt toward her on the night she had crouched out on the sandbar waiting in vain for the giant to come for her stirred in him again. As did the memory of her standing naked and splay-legged and wildly defiant in the bloodred glow of the Spirit Moon. In that one singular display of righteous indignation, Mowea'qua had disproved all of Moraq's and Ningao's slurs against her lineage. What a body the girl had! All woman! It still stirred the man in him to think of it, and, to his surprise, he could feel the once voracious spirit of the great white bear stirring in him as well as, with his loins warming with man need, he allowed one hand to stroke downward over her side and along her flank. She murmured, curled closer, so childlike, so trusting, that, remembering how cruelly she had been ravaged, his loins cooled as he withdrew his hand from her side and, feeling pity again, reached up to stroke her hair.

It was in that moment that Tôrnârssuk encountered the feather of Raven and, with a start, realized that the totem spirit of One Who Survives was speaking to him after all. He lay nearly motionless, fingering the long sleek shaft of the broken feather, straightening it, smoothing it, inviting it to communicate understanding. If the girl, beaten and broken and pathetic as she was now, could still manage to arouse the great white bear spirit within him, he should thank her, not growl at her in anger or feel annoyance with himself for having saved her life! Everything that Mowea'qua had done on the night of the Spirit Moon had resulted in reawakening the power of the spirit of the great white bear within him. His followers had all seen the change in him. It had inspired his men to success upon the raid, lightened their steps on the trek out of the Valley of the Red Moon, and put song to their voices as they journeyed ever forward toward the Great River of the North.

Tôrnârssuk was smiling again. His free hand moved to rest over the talismans he wore around his neck. The sacred amulet that the angatkok had given him when he saved the holy man's life and slew the great white bear was still there, still in its central place of importance amidst the fetish bones and strands of seal and bear and wolf teeth and the cherished slender braid of his beloved Hasu'u's hair. There *was* power in the sacred stone! He could feel it now as he had felt it on that long-gone day after he had seen his first manifestation of Sila coming toward him in the body of a bear and had stood his ground before it. Alone on burning bright snow. Alone beneath a burning bright sky. Alone, a young man untested, telling himself that he was not afraid.

"I stand to you, Bear! Though you devour me, I will eat your soul!"

Had he shouted those words at Sila? Yes! It seemed only yesterday. And yet a lifetime of yesterdays lay between that cardinal moment and this dark, quiet, somnolent night within which he now lay, as safe and marginally content as any man could ever hope to be, with his wife and son and the wild girl warm together inside the skin of the great white bear whom he had devoured that day, and whose soul was with him still.

He opened his eyes and stared up at the stars. Big Bear Forever Walks the Sky and Little Bear Who Follows were still wandering on their slow, ponderous, untroubled way along the endless pathway across the darkness. The Great Sky River was still flowing eternally across the arching black vault of the night. And if Sila was still up there hiding amidst the stars, Tôrnârssuk could no longer see it or even feel its presence. But there, to the north, was One Who Stands Still, and, trembling a little, he knew that by the constancy of that one star he would soon find his way home to the land of his Ancestors.

And so, still smiling, Tôrnârssuk moved to draw his woman and son into the same protective embrace within which he held the sleeping girl. Hasu'u was right, he thought as he felt his beautiful beloved snuggle close to his heart. He *was* Wíndigo, Great Ghost Cannibal, whose name brought fear to the hearts of those who foolishly chose to stand against him or attempted to compromise the integrity of this band! He was Tunraq and Angatkok and Raven, Guide and Guardian and One Who Survives! He was Tôrnârssuk, Great White Bear of the North, One Who Gives Power to those who chose to set their footsteps in his and follow wherever his tracks would lead. And, above all, he was a man of the True People, strong and wise and courageous enough to risk being kind!

He closed his eyes, and as he drifted into untroubled sleep for the first time in more moons than any man could be asked to remember, the Great River of the North had never seemed closer and Sila had never seemed so far away.

Chapter Six

▼▼▼▼▼▼▼

Everything had changed.

For the better!

Ne'gauni was sure of it even before he pushed back his sleeping furs. Feeling stronger and more rested than he had felt in longer than he could remember, he attributed his sense of well-being to the meat of the stag on which he had feasted on the previous night of camaraderie among the band. Gone was the old sense of gloom, the prescience of unnatural and dangerous darkness looming ahead. He could not have said why, but he was actually smiling—until, shivering at the unexpected chill air of morning, he looked around, his sense of well-being dashed.

Things *had* changed, that much was certain, but whether they had changed for the better, he could no longer say. The forest all around was discolored by frost. With a sinking feeling in his gut, he found himself looking into the wistfully smiling face of Nee'nah.

"It is early for the first white breath of winter, yes, Dreamer?" she asked, sighing the words, crouching close before him.

He saw no reason to answer. Early frost? Late frost? What

matter? The wind must have dropped late last night along with the temperature of the air. This did not surprise him. He was beginning to understand that this far north the weather spirits behaved according to their own impetuous and often pernicious whims, following vague and ever shifting patterns that no man could possibly understand, not even one presumed to be Shaman.

"Did you sleep well?" Nee'nah sighed again.

Ne'gauni did not smile back, not at Nee'nah nor at her sisters, Ane'pemin'an and Chi'co'pee, who crouched beside her. He found their faces to be like three intrusive little moons aligned in a row before him, each round and smooth, each vaguely resembling Hasu'u's but not one of them even half as beautiful. He exhaled his own wistful sigh. No woman could equal the loveliness of Chief Ogeh'ma's and Segub'un's firstborn daughter. None in all this world or the world beyond! He sighed again and knew that his thoughts carried an adamance of feeling that bordered on belligerence as he stared past the threesome toward the headman's sleeping space, where the graceful, slender, doe-eyed one who owned his heart was busily snapping her family's bed skins and wiping them free of frost with a little brush of spruce needles. Musquash was assisting her. And, to his surprise and infinite relief, he saw that Mowea'qua was on her feet, helping.

"The headman should have had us raise our tents last night," said Chi'co'pee, seeing where his glance had gone and wrinkling her nose in disapproval of the disheveled girl. "We would not have been awakened by her cries."

"You cannot blame her for having bad dreams, sister," said Nee'nah.

"If she was an obedient daughter, as are we, she need not be suffering from lack of sleep. Besides, she is fortunate to be still alive."

"I, for one, had little need of sleep last night." Ane'pem-in'an's statement had the sound of a smirk. "And, warm beneath these shared furs, I needed no tent to keep me warm against the frost."

"The sun will soon show its face to warm the land, and the band along with it," Ne'gauni assured them, vaguely annoyed, barely knowing that he spoke at all as his eyes drank in the welcome sight of Mowea'qua up and off the drag frame.

"Ah, listen, our shaman portends the sunrise and speaks prophecy to us . . . just to us!" swooned Chi'co'pee.

He rolled his eyes. Prophecy? The sky was clear overhead. Unless this was to be a day like no other in all of Creation, only the youngest babies in the band would not be able to hazard a guess that the sun was bound to follow the dawn and soon show its face in the sky. Irked, he reached for his crutches, disdained the fussily offered assistance of Hasu'u's sisters, and rose, drawing his sleeping fur up with him. Slinging it around his shoulders, he scanned the clearing.

Everyone was already up, preparing to move on, talking happily together as they busied themselves at their various tasks, reenergized as he had been, it seemed, by the meat of the stag and a night's good talk and rest and the excellent progress they had made on yesterday's trail. But although Ne'gauni was aware of others looking his way, he could focus his gaze on only one thing.

Mowea'qua.

He was so glad to see her moving about again that, quite unexplainably, tears smarted in his eyes and a great hot lump formed at the back of his throat. He gulped it down and could not keep himself from watching her almost greedily, smiling a little as he did so. Hasu'u had apparently given the girl a pair of the headman's moccasins and one of his traveling shirts to wear; her own garments, cut for her much smaller frame, would never have fit the giant's daughter. Somehow the oversized footwear and the broad lines and straight cut of the shirt made Mowea'qua appear like a lanky youngster playing dress-up in a parent's clothes. His smile vanished and an unexpected tenderness touched his heart as he saw how pale and tired and fragile she looked as she shuffled about in her big shoes, her uncombed hair still a wild, raven-feathered tangle around her battered face.

"I will bring water from the creek to refresh my Dreamer," said Nee'nah.

"No! I will bring it!" insisted Ane'pemin'an.

"No, I will do it!" snapped Chi'co'pee. "Our Shaman Indeed cannot be allowed to go thirsty!"

Ne'gauni let them go without so much as a word. As though he could have stopped them! The three unmarried daughters of Chief Ogeh'ma and Segub'un came and went as they pleased and were so eager to please him that they were pulling on their garments and half tripping over the lacings of their untied moccasins as they hurried off, giggling, winning the surprised glances of brothers and parents and the interested appraisal of the Northerners and everyone else in the band along the way.

His jaw clenched. He was blushing and knew it. He had not asked for their attendance to what they perceived to be his needs. He had not invited them to spread their sleeping furs so close to his last night. And he had definitely not solicited their brazen offer of additional under-the-sleeping-furs body warmth when, sometime toward dawn, he had awakened to find them naked beside him.

His blush deepened. He stood defensively taller and pulled his sleeping fur closer around himself as he wrapped his arms around his chest. He had mated with one of them. He had no idea which one. It was a blur to him now, an extraordinary and embarrassing blur. All part of waking from a dream of sexual release to find that it was no dream at all and that his maleness was buried bone deep in moist, hot, flexing woman. He had withdrawn, of course, immediately, and angrily shoved the three unmarried daughters of Chief Ogeh'ma and Segub'un out from beneath his bed furs, but by then it had been too late to call back that part of himself that he had not intended to share with them.

He grimaced. How could Chi'co'pee complain about Mowca'qua's occasional outcries when she and her sisters had stayed close to him all night, giggling together until, at last, they had all fallen back to sleep? Now, aware of being observed by the band as the sisters tittered off to the creek, his blush deepened as he cast a sideward glance to where Segub'un and Ogeh'ma were snapping out their own family furs, grinning at each other in a way that confirmed their earlier assurance that they would be honored if the new shaman found ease with any one or all of their daughters.

His grimace tightened into a glower. They had not meant "all." He knew that as surely as he knew that of their four daughters there was only one with whom he wanted to share his bed furs and his manhood and his very life to the ending of his days. And she was coming toward him now.

"It is good," said Hasu'u.

"What is good?"

"Truly you are my Little Brother now."

He cursed the flush of heat that flamed on his face.

"It *is* good, Ne'gauni," Hasu'u assured him again, this time with a light and loving little laugh. "Whichever one of my sisters you may choose, you will find a loyal woman in her. And if, when we reach the Great Gathering, you find another who pleases you more, Nee'nah, Ane'pemin'an, and

Chi'co'pee will be held in much esteem and seen by all men of the Dawnland as potential wives of great value because they have each first walked with a shaman, however briefly."

Ne'gauni was irked by her choice of words. Her sisters had not exactly "walked" with him when they chose to strip naked and crawl eagerly beneath his bed furs last night, but he could not bring himself to say as much lest she be offended and take his words as an insult to her sisters. So he shrugged and said instead, "I still do not feel much like a shaman, Hasu'u."

She dimpled. "From what I have just heard of my sisters' whispers as they rushed by me in their hurry to please you yet again, they would not agree. It takes a true magic man to satisfy three hungry new women in one night!"

He gaped like a stunned fish, then cursed himself for doing so, for his expression brought yet another laugh to the lips of the headman's woman, a laugh as melodious and loving as the first. "Ah, Ne'gauni, after all that we have been through together, sometimes I forget that we are both still young! And you, needing scarcely more than three hands to sum the winters you have seen, I think that perhaps before last night you had never emptied the heat of passion into a woman. Ah, Little Brother, do not be ashamed to give freely or to take without constraint all pleasure of the body and heart so that one day you may come to find one with whom you may share the depth of love that I feel for the one man of my heart . . . Tôrnârssuk."

Had she dashed a flask of icy water into his face, he could not have been more chilled by the all-too-familiar ache of disappointment that came to him whenever he remembered that she could never be his. And yet, after she leaned in to kiss his cheek and turned to walk back to where she had left Mowea'qua and Musquash attending little Tiguak, he knew a deeper chill. A sudden and totally unexpected chill. The old sense of gloom was back, and with it the unwelcome prescience of something dark and dangerous looming ahead.

Tôrnârssuk was kneeling amidst his family's pack frames, busily strapping the side packs onto his dogs. He was smiling! Mowea'qua was standing close by, looking at him with an expression of open adoration on her face. And, to Ne'gauni's absolute amazement, she was combing her hair.

"You see," grumbled old Ko'ram, coming close to shake his rattle in the low, slow, insidiously warning way of a conspirator who has seen doom on the horizon, "what did I tell you? No good will come of this. No good at all! That one should have been left behind to die with the beasts with whom she belongs. And if you do not believe me, then beware, Shaman Indeed, for soon will come the dark of the moon, and who knows what dark powers will be loosed upon us then or what will be waiting for us, because of her, when at last we reach the Great River of the North!"

Part Four

RIVER OF THE WHITE WHALES

▼▼▼▼▼▼▼

Who has heard the Voice of Dawn?
The Stars have heard
And the Great One, rising from the Deep.
Now I, too, have heard
The Way is Made ready before me!
I stretch forth my Hands. I go toward the Dawn!
I am not afraid.

Chapter One

▼▼▼▼▼▼▼

There was blood in the river.

The blood of white whales!

Avataut laughed, rejoicing to see it so.

Along with teeming flocks of predatory birds wheeling overhead, shrieking in anticipation of feasting on the leavings of the hunt, the white whales had returned at last to the Great River of the North in pods that numbered beyond counting. He could see them now, schooling out along the shallows over the sandbars and shoals. Had it not been for the excited shouts of children and the calls going out among the people of the Great Gathering, he knew that he would have been able to hear them, too, for of all the whales that swam into the river from the great deeps of ocean that lay beyond, the white whales were the only ones that sang in quite so sweet or loud a song.

"Avataut! Come!" Armik was hurrying up the beach from the river's edge, elbowing his way past others running in the opposite direction, panting and flushed with excitement. "Nuligak has already been called to lead the kayakmen. And look! Do you see the red sail? Umak has returned! He has brought his crew and his big umiak from across the river and has come with the dawn to make first kill! Already his harpoons are flying. Already the floats are out. Kupuk has told me to tell you that you must join them on the water now. And quickly. The time of fasting and making spirit songs and readying our boats and whaling tools is done. They will see what you, a Barrenlands man, can do this day, Avataut! Now, at last, you have the chance to put your kayak to a true test!"

"And you yours!"

"I . . . uh . . . I have been keeping watch for the coming of the whales with the others most of the night, Avataut, and Irqi is not feeling so well this morning. I think I will sit with her awhile. But you go! I will wait. I will watch. I will—"

"You will not sit by with your woman while I risk my life on the river! You will join me! I will have no man of my band show weakness before a hunt!"

"But, Avataut, I am the only man of your band to have joined you in the making of a boat."

"And what was the point of that if you are afraid to use it and stand quivering in your moccasins at the thought of venturing onto the water? Why did you drag me up onto the bluff with men of lesser tribes the other night if you have not come away feeling confident that Inau made the proper magic or gave you whatever advice you thought you needed to make you feel like a True Man again?"

Embarrassment took the flush of excitement from Armik's face almost as quickly as resentment tightened his features. Nuutlaq had just come from Avataut's lodge, shoving E'ya, the young woman Avataut had won from the braggart, in front of her. Although E'ya could not understand a word of the northern tongue and, from the look of her black eye and swollen mouth, was suffering at Nuutlaq's hand because of it, he knew by Nuutlaq's evasive gaze that she had heard every word her man had said. To be demeaned within full earshot of a female, especially such a wanton gossip as Nuutlaq, was intolerable. In no time at all every Northerner on the beach would hear through his wife how the hunt brother of Avataut had been insulted. And so Armik said, hotly and defensively, "I am a True Man, Avataut. Again and again I have shown this. And as the hunt brother closest to your spirit, I have tried to share your enthusiasm to learn new ways. Still, I am a man of the inland barrens and have made no secret to you of my feelings of discomfort in a boat. Tôrnârssuk himself was no different. He also—"

Avataut made no attempt to withhold the vicious, backhanded swipe that dropped Armik where he stood. "Are you afraid, then, as he was afraid? You will not speak his name again, Armik! Go! Gather what you need! I will see you on the water, or you will walk with my band no more!"

▼▼▼▼

Avataut was shaking with excitement as, without a glance over his shoulder to see whether or not Armik was back on his feet and following, he raced down the beach to where his kayak awaited him.

Most of the boats were already off their stands and being carried into the river by their owners. The morning was cold, unusually so. There was frost on the beach; the footprints of the kayakmen remained behind them on the gravel of the strand, and a thin spittle of ice was visible breaking up along the shore. Those men who were not quite ready to depart were all pulling on their waterproof gut-skin hunting coats. Nuligak, already dressed and ready to heft his craft, was beaming at Avataut with a good-natured but decidedly wicked gleam in his eyes.

"Never have I seen so many whales!" declared the burly little man who had helped Avataut more than any other to make and understand the way of his kayak. "Stay close to me. If you dare. Do as I do. If you can. Allow the great river to speak to you. Handle your boat as respectfully as when we last went out together, and, if the spirits of the whales are willing, your women and son will sing with joy and pride tonight. Come! Now we will see if a hunter born to the barrens does indeed have the heart of a True Man!"

"Yes!" replied Avataut, beaming back at the man as he reached out to give him a friendly but wickedly hard slap on the back. "Now we will see!" So it was to be a challenge! All the better. He was ready for it.

As Nuligak hefted his boat and headed off with the others, Avataut turned to his own little craft. Everything he needed was already with the kayak. The harpoon lines were secured, the bladder-skin floats inflated and in place. Hanging from the wooden harpoon rest he had carved into the shape of a stalking wolverine before attaching it to the prow were all the special little fetish bags and feathers and bits of driftwood, shell, bone, and pebbles he had found on recent solitary walks along the shore, each of a special shape or color or texture that had called to his eyes and spoken to his spirit, promising to strengthen or guide him or grant him wisdom on the hunt. What need had he of the fetishes of Inau, when the spirits of the river and sky spoke to him? His lightweight paddle, smoothed to the sleekness of a woman's flanks and incised, like his harpoons and the kayak itself, with his mark—an abstract of a wolverine—was lying beside the craft on the stone blocks. His two wooden harpoons were in the rest, each longer than he was tall, each affixed with barbed, intricately carved walrus-tusk heads designed not only to pierce skin and fat and hold fast within a whale but also to allow the attached lines to toggle around freely without breaking or compromising either the hunter or his position among the other kayaks.

Avataut's heart was pounding with excitement and anticipation as he reached into the interior of the craft and pulled up the hooded gut-skin hunting shirt that Nuutlaq, instructed by Nuligak, had sewn for him with such care, using thread of the finest, most delicate sinew and grass to sew the seams with stitches so small that each was nearly invisible. According to the kayakman, if his boat was turned over and he went into the water, the stalks of grass in the stitching would swell and make the shirt completely impervious to water.

"We will see," he said and, drawing in a deep, intoxicating breath of the morning, committed himself to the hunt.

▼▼▼▼▼

They took whales.

Many whales!

In lean sleek kayaks of many colors and wallowing fat umiaks with patterned and colored sails and even in big bark canoes that pitched frighteningly among the swells, they took whales.

Many whales!

The children hurried to the bluff tops. The women and people of the various inland bands and tribes joined them. They stood together, but not too close to the encampment of the shaman Inau lest their shouting and jumping up and down offend her as she stood apart, her work as Caller of Whales complete. But every now and then someone offered up her name in joyous thanksgiving because all knew that her magic songs had summoned the whales.

Many whales!

It was done in the old way, with the kayakmen striking out singly or in pairs, paddling with all the power at each man's command until a great flotilla was formed, the boats moving steadily and swiftly out into deep water beyond the whales. Then, turning as one, the kayakmen began to howl like wolves, madly beating and churning the water with their paddles, herding the whales, driving the now-frantic animals toward shore, over shoals well known to the hunters, until, confused and desperate, the whales hurled themselves onto sandbars where they floundered in the shallows, surrounded by the human wolves of the river.

And one wolverine.

▼▼▼▼▼

She watched him.

From the place she had made her own high upon the bluffs, Inau watched. She—who was both woman and man and defined the duality of her nature as feminine only because of an innate inclination toward a grace of movement rarely seen in males—could not take her eyes from the river.

Her head went high. The wind was cold off the water. Very cold. Unseasonably so. It carried the smell of melting pack ice breaking up off distant headlands, of saltwater mixing with fresh. From much closer in toward shore, she could discern the rich red scent of the blood of whales and the smell of the wet hides and wood and bark of the boats along with the high rank stink of the hunters' adrenaline, and that of their prey.

The shaman's nostrils expanded. She continued to draw in the essence of the wind and the river and the increasingly strong scent of the hunt, pulling it deep into herself through the intricate open-work carving of her mask. How she yearned to feel the cool breath of the morning against her bare skin! She was in need of refreshment after being up until nearly dawn, confined with latecomers to her lodge, listening to their fears, making the magic they sought in smoke and song and dance, speaking the ancient hunt wisdom that they already knew in their hearts, reaffirming with cautionary words their inherent belief in their own ability to succeed, and, through this subtle reawakening of faith in themselves, assuring them that they would be less vulnerable to the whims of the forces of Creation on the hunt today.

But now others were near. So many others: men, women, children, even a few dogs, all standing at the edge of the bluffs. All observing the hunt. All keeping a respectful distance, save for a few who, now and again, cautiously tiptoed close to lay a gift of some sort at her feet as they whispered a reverent "thank you" for calling the whales. And so Inau dared not remove the mask. She wore it for them, as she had worn it for those who came to her lodge last night and every night since she had returned to the Great Gathering of Many Tribes. The mask was a necessary part of the magic.

Her head went high. She must not let them know that behind the feathers and chiseled wood and whalebone, behind the bright paint and cavernous snapping jaws and dangerous-looking rows of teeth, the face of the shaman from the Cave of the Winds was, unlike her body, wholly unremarkable. A totally unmagical face. Neither beautiful nor homely, its plain features were, perhaps in their own way, a mask, for they betrayed not a single facet of her character and even less of her bifaceted gender; indeed, she remembered now that on the night of the thunderstorm she had been brought to a startled pause by the unexpected image of her face reflected up to her in a pool of rainwater set momentarily alight by a white flash of lightning.

She had walked on, disconcerted, for although well past her thirtieth summer, an old woman by anyone's standards, the face that had looked back at Inau from the pool had appeared to be that of a child at the brink of puberty. Still no furrows in the brow or temple or at the sides of the mouth. Still no down-pulling at the corners of the lips. Still no darkening or puffing of the skin beneath the eyes. Perhaps, she wondered now, the loneliness of the life decreed by her Differentness had inured her to the emotional stresses that so altered the faces of others over time. She could not be sure. She had never known hunger, or any excess of physical pain, or grief over losing one who was dear to her—a mother, a father, a sister or brother, a husband or wife, a child, or even a friend.

The mother who bore her had refused to suckle her.

The father who sired her had denied she was his.

Had she not come squalling into the world in the midst of a Great Gathering, on this very shore, with many bands and tribes assembled all around, waiting for the coming of white whales during a summer when it seemed they would never return to the river, she would have been wrapped with caul and cord and birth sack to smother in the moss that had absorbed her mother's blood. Her father fled the gathering at first sight of her, out of shame or fear—no one knew which. Her mother followed him, abandoning the newborn to beg his forgiveness for presenting him with such an impossibility of a child. She was found hanged some days later, by her own hand or by that of her infant's father, no one was sure. No one could even recall her name, or his, for they had come late to the river, seeking to camp and hunt with relatives, none of whom had ever arrived. But everyone at that summer's gathering was convinced of one thing: the hanged woman and runaway man had been foolish to flee from what the elders at once perceived as a blessing from the forces of Creation. For with the newborn's first cries, the white whales returned at last into the Great River of the North to give themselves to be meat for the People.

And so the infant was welcomed with awe and joyous acclamation by the People. A council was called. A name was chosen for the child: Inau. The Gift. An ancient name. A genderless name. A rare and magical name said to have been called up out of shaman dreams, a primal and eternal whispering at the peripheries of mankind's consciousness, an echo of the past reminding of the time beyond all beginning, when, in an effort to end Its eternal loneliness, the sacred One had created the world above and the world below and all the magical forces therein out of Itself.

Darkness and Light. Sun and Moon. Earth and Sky. Water and Ice. Wind and Fire. Flesh and Spirit. Male and Female and every Living Thing above the land or below it: All were made in that singular moment of Creation, born out of the Perfect Whole, who, although made a little less lonely, drew back and remained as It had been and always would be, the sacred One.

And always, just as the ancient primal memories came whispering back through the shaman dreams of the People to remind them of how the world had been in the time beyond all beginning, every now and then as the generations passed a child would be born to affirm to the People the everlasting perfection of the sacred One out of whom all things were made.

And so Inau, born with the external sexual organ of a male and the genital orifice of a female, had not been spurned and despised as unnatural. She was seen as Complete, as Two Halves Made Whole, as a Perfect Creation born in the image of the sacred One, a Gift to be entrusted to the shamans of the Cave of Winds, where she had been taken to be raised and instructed until the time came for her to return each summer to the Great River of the North to call the whales from the sea so that they would give themselves to be food for the People, and to commune with the spirits of all for the good of all in full understanding of the needs of all.

Now, still breathing in deeply, Inau was all at once chilled and soothed by the cold air of morning and by the scent of the blood of life and death coming off the river. With or without her mask, she had no doubt that she was all that she had been born to be. Surely she had only to look at her body to know the truth of her Differentness. And, since the last of the elders in the Cave of the Winds had set their spirits free of their bones to roam the wind forever, she was as lonely in her solitary existence as the sacred One had been in the time beyond beginning. Nevertheless, she had learned long ago that, despite her body, no one looking at her face could recognize it as belonging to the Gift or fully accept it as the framework for a rare intelligence and a storehouse for the wealth of acquired knowledge and wisdom that could only come after the passage of many years.

And so, like all shamans, Inau wore a mask, the stark and frightening whalebone mask that hid the deceptive banality of her face and cleverly concealed the second and equally fearsome bat mask within. Each animal shared her duality of nature in its own way: the bat, furred and suckling its young like any warm-blooded creature of the earth even though it must fly into the night to hunt on the wings of a bird; and the whale, making its life in the water even though it must rise from the depths with the fins of a fish to breathe air like a creature of the land. The mask defined her to the People. Like the whale and the bat, she existed in two worlds, not fully at home in either and yet master and mistress of both. When coupled with elusive glimpses of her body, the sight of a masked Inau was enough to set fear and revulsion and outright awe in the bravest men. Fear was important; it bred respect. Revulsion and awe were both necessary; in equal measure they maintained the distance prerequisite to creating the illusion of magic.

And magic was everything.

Magic *was* Inau. Magic *was* the Gift. Magic gave meaning to her life through the heart it gave to the People each time she created the illusion of a living power beyond themselves. She could never give them the gift of children to enrich and empower their number upon the hunt. She could never give them the gift of meat lest, in taking up the weapons of a man, that part of her duality that was woman defile the weapons of all hunters. And so she gave them the one gift she could, the gift no one else could give: the wonder of Herself and of the Magic that came through her to give them faith in a power beyond this world that could be beseeched and made to heed their hopes and dreams, and thus became a living power within them that enabled them to dare to presume that they had hope of controlling that power and, with it, the inexorable onslaught of the forces of Creation that skeined through their lives, culling them as mercilessly as the hunters were now culling the whales.

The wind gusted hard off the river. The smell of blood was very strong now. The blood of whales. And perhaps more than a little of the blood of men mixed in? Inau shivered as she quickly drew the furred and feathered roping of her cloak close around herself. She stood as tall and straight as she could, like a combatant facing into the wind, wanting to appear impervious to the elements so that no one watching her would guess that the shaman from the Cave of the Winds was as vulnerable to the forces of Creation as any man, woman, or child—or whale.

She stared out across the water. How brave were the men in their fragile watercraft! She would never have such courage! The whales that were not grounded in the shallows and taking harpoons with pitiable cries were circling and sounding and rising with great sprays and thrashing the water all around. Inau's heart leaped in wonder and gratitude at the glorious sacrifice the whales were making for the People, and soared with gladness to know that the wisdom inherent in her spirit had given courage to the hunters through the gift of her magic. Yet her own spirit felt small in her now, and as her eyes held once more on the man in the kayak with the unusually high harpoon rest attached to its prow, the emotions of her flesh were strong.

Too strong.

Avataut. Kwakwaje'sh. Wolverine.

His name slurred across her tongue; she would not speak it. She loathed the man. How bold he was! How rash! How willing to risk himself to prove his valor amidst the tumult of the waves and the thrashing bodies of the whales, shouting out above all the rest, looking to his left and right to see if others were observing his excellence.

Self-serving. Vain. As full of himself as one of the seal-bladder tow floats is filled with hot air!

Inau's mouth twisted with disapproval of what she considered to be the worst qualities in a man. Avataut had two women and a son depending on his safe return. His new woman was young and his fat little boy was already making a good attempt at stoning birds with the other boys; both would be seen as useful to any band and would be taken to the fire circles of others if Avataut perished on the hunt. As for the man's corpulent, aging wife with her suppurating gums, her rotting teeth, a breath foul enough to drop a gull from the sky, and a nasty, superior attitude toward all other women, she would be fortunate if anyone were willing to toss her scraps enough to allow her to live through the coming winter. And then there was Armik, his fellow bandsman, close to Avataut on the river now, loyal to a fault, fighting his dread of being on the water, trying so hard to please his friend and headman that he was risking his life to do so.

For what purpose?

The ways of men were often as the ways of wolves, she thought. One must lead, others must follow. For the good of the pack. Still, Inau questioned the placement of Armik's loyalty, for although she had witnessed Avataut strutting proud in his occasional grand gestures of generosity to his followers, his propensity toward showing off that generosity marked it as self-serving in her eyes. Since coming onto the bluff, not once had she seen him look to his hunt brother's struggling little boat, ill balanced now not by any fault of construction or misarrangement of hunting equipment but by the fearful tension of the man within. If Armik was lost to the river, she doubted that Avataut would notice unless someone called it to his attention or until the man came up missing later on. And even then, somehow, she was sure that, in keeping with his character, the news of Armik's death would not adversely affect him, unless it was seen by others as a mark against his own reputation as a leader of men.

Inau's eyes narrowed behind her mask. She had disliked the shrewd-eyed, blocky-bodied, meaty-mouthed North-erner from the moment she first set eyes on him over two summers before. He was cocky, openly avaricious, with a ten-dency toward brooding petulance whenever he was crossed; she had seen the wolverine in him even then. Always skulking back when not in the foreground of his headman's attention, covertly measuring the movements of others, watching for weaknesses, speculating on how he could use those weaknesses to his own advantage, and, whenever the opportunity arose, taking advantage with no concern over how his actions would affect those from whom he took whatever he could get away with.

Yet, in those long-gone days, Avataut, like his hunt brother Armik, had not been above deferring to another man. A better man. All who had come to the Great Gathering with the one called White Bear had been deferent when walking in that man's sobering, compelling, and overpowering shadow, Avataut even more so than the rest. She often wondered what had happened to prevent White Bear's return to the great river. Bad spirits, as Avataut claimed? Perhaps. Whatever the cause, Wolverine feared White Bear's return. But why did he fear it? Because, as he so passionately asserted, he genuinely believed the man and the bad-luck-bringing spirits that walked at his side to be a danger to all assembled at the Great Gathering? Or because he knew in his deceptive, avaricious, manipulative heart that the status he had won for himself in the other man's absence would be eclipsed by the return of that superior man?

Whatever his reason, Avataut's fear was real. Now, as Inau saw him lever back to hurl another harpoon, oblivious to the way his little craft was being tossed about by the waves amidst the bodies of leaping and sounding whales, it was hard to believe that the man was afraid of anything. But he was. She knew he was.

Sometimes she could smell it on him when he passed to and fro along the beach below the bluffs or came from his lodge in the depth of night to stand alone with a single torch to light the little space in which he stood, as though he feared the night itself. He would stare southward into the darkness, mumbling to himself, rubbing his amulets and fetishes, wishing White Bear dead, consumed by the dread that had become increasingly apparent to her after she had warned of the ice floes she had seen drifting off the headlands while en route to the Great Gathering from the Cave of the Winds, and of a large white bear and cub that she had seen not far downriver, swimming together in slub ice, feasting on seals along the shore. Often after that, she would hear him down on the beach working aggressively on his kayak with other Northerners, defaming and warning against the return of his former headman at every opportunity. As the days passed she had continued to watch him, fascinated and amazed that others did not see that it was as though he was fattening and growing stronger every time he demeaned the reputation and cautioned against the deadly spirit power of one he had once spoken of as a beloved hunt brother.

Beloved.

Inau suppressed a laugh.

Though I live my entire life as lonely and apart as the sacred One, may no man or woman ever love me as Wolverine professed to love White Bear!

She knew all too well what he had done in his attempt to finalize that love and cancel forever the threat that White Bear's return posed to him. No man or woman or child spoke the name of Tôrnârssuk now. Avataut had them all afraid to speak it. If the man ever did return to reclaim his campsite on the shore of the Great River of the North, thanks to his hunt brother Avataut he would be driven off or perhaps even killed as though he were in fact a great white bear come to threaten the safety of the People. But even this had not been enough to satisfy the spirit of the wolverine within Avataut.

On a dawn not long ago, she had watched him go from

the encampment with North Wind blowing hard at his back. So tense. So wary. So furtive. Not at all like a man said to be setting out to commune with the spirits of the game. He had paused and looked back, not once but several times, his expression strained, his eyes wild with intent, until he had disappeared into the forest, headed south.

Why?

What need had he to leave camp that morning? Why should he have been in the least concerned about securing any other kind of game than the white whales that the scouts were even then seeking downriver? Smoke had eventually given her her answer. She had watched it building to the south and had known that he had set Wildfire loose within the forest. Even so, she had not wanted to believe it. Surely no man would be willing to put at risk every man, woman, and child at the Great Gathering—including his own wife and son—and every living thing that stood in the path of those flames to secure his position as headman of the Northerners in the campsite he had usurped from his former hunt brother and headman.

And so Inau had contrived a test for him: the flint. The small, dark, fire-starting stone. She had taken it from her own collection of flints and placed it at the entrance to his lodge after he had returned to it in the storm. She had waited patiently on the trail to the bluffs where the view of his campsite was the most advantageous for her purpose and, between clashes of lightning, had rattled the scrub growth, knowing he would be awakened—if he slept at all—and drawn out to see who, or what, was trespassing around his tent. She had not been disappointed. He had come out. He had circled the tent in the rain. And the words he had spoken to the night and his reaction to the flint had told her what she did not want to know.

Her face tightened with anger toward him.

The forces of Creation were free to set Wildfire loose upon the land to work their will. Man was not! How many creatures had died to assure the arrogance of his intent? Apart from White Bear and his band, how many other men, women, children, and dogs had been out there in the unseasonably dry forest, dwelling in small isolated hunting camps or perhaps even journeying toward the Great River of the North? And even if they had managed to come unscathed through the fire, it would not change the fact that wherever Wildfire and her flaming children danced, they consumed trees, grasses, lichens, fungi, and all green growing things that would otherwise be food for the animals that, in turn, would be food for the People. It took no shamanic insight or wisdom to know that the ripple effect of Wildfire's dance of devastation was like a stone striking the surface of a pond, felt by everything that lived upon or touched the surrounding land. Even now the animals and people that had called the burned land home would be abandoning ancestral hunting and feeding grounds to invade the hunting and feeding grounds of others.

Inau shivered a little, grateful that she had been able to convince the storm to come inland that night. She wondered how long the forest would lie wounded before it healed. Too long, she thought, and was resolved to make Avataut pay for what he had done. Ever since the night of the thunderstorm, she had set herself to harry him. It gave her pleasure to do so. Although it had crossed her mind to call a council and formally accuse him of deliberately offending the forces of Creation and putting the gathering at risk, she had decided against it. For what Avataut had done there would be no forgiveness. For what he had done his band would suffer. And, although Inau was Shaman and entitled to sit with chiefs and headmen in judgment upon wrongdoers, as the Gift it was her calling to smooth the way of the People along the trails of life, not to create enmity between them.

She stood a little taller, confident that Avataut would one day be seen by others for what he was. Until that day she would goad him. Taunt him. Perhaps even inspire him to leave the Great Gathering when he had taken from it all he desired. She was certainly finding it easy enough to keep him on edge with her subtle and never-ending hints of her knowledge of his perfidy. She almost laughed to think of the way she had all but forced him to come into her lodge with the Grasslanders the other night, confusing him in darkness and smoke and magic made of the sickening essence of the sacred fungi that could eat a man's mind and allow a shaman to lead his thoughts where she would.

He had refused the fetish of the white bear, but not before she managed to burn him with it and warn him out of the pure generosity of her spirit that he must beware lest the voracious greed and arrogance of his nature take on a life of its own and begin to feed upon him. He had not chosen to listen; or, rather, he had listened but refused to believe. So she had watched him retreat from her and hurry off into the darkness that seemed to upset him so. When he had gone, she retrieved the amulet, and in the predawn light, while he slept with his foul-breathed woman and fat little son, she crept to his lodge and placed it at the entranceway where she had placed the flint on the night of the thunderstorm. His son found it in the morning and would have made a plaything of it had Avataut not snatched it away. She could still see the twisted expression on his face as he glared up at the bluffs and shook his fist in her direction. And then, as she had watched openly from the heights above his camp, he had hunkered before his tent, called for his woman to bring him his knapping tools, and, after gouging out the eyes and drilling a hole through the center of the fetish with his mouth awl, he whittled a splinter off the side of one of his lances and drove it into the fetish, into the heart of the little carving of a white bear. This done, he had risen and, looking to where she stood, shouted out in pure belligerence as he held up the blinded, heart-wounded amulet for her to see.

"Behold! I am not afraid of your magic. I have blinded and cut the heart out of the bear that you would have follow me at every turn. Now I will bury it!"

And so she had watched as he dug a little pit in the hard-packed surface of the loess dune just outside his lodge and tossed the talisman into it. This done, he had kicked gravel and sand back on top of it, then ground it into the dune with his heel, burying it in that tiny, shallow grave as no doubt he would have loved to bury her and the man who might yet come north to remind Wolverine that of all the animals in the world below the sky, White Bear was the most powerful.

"Shaman . . . ?"

Inau looked down.

A young girl stood before her. About eleven summers old, from the look of her. Wan. Trail weary. Bedraggled to the point of appearing pitiable. Fear shone in her eyes, and she could not keep her teeth from clicking or her knees from knocking as she asked, breathless with awe, "Are you a woman or a whale?"

"I am neither. I am Inau, Shaman, a gift to the People."

The girl's dark eyes held steady. They were the only

bright and pretty thing about her, for her tattered blue-quilled buckskins were as blackened by soot as her face and hands, and she reeked as though having come through a pall of smoke. "My grandfather says that you are so big and strong with magic that you could make us all disappear, so unimportant are we."

Inau found herself frowning. The child might well be afraid, but she was obviously not shy. Out on the river, the sound of the hunt was very loud now, frenzied. Downriver, close to where some of the whales were being dragged to be butchered upon the widest beach along the shore, one of the hunters from the inland forest was waving his arms and lance frantically. Someone else, a Grasslander by his size and the shine of his nearly bald head, was shouting. She could not make out the words above the voice of the little girl.

"My people have no gifts to bring for magic and so they are afraid to come to you, Inau Shaman. But someone had to come. So while they rest back there in the trees after our long journey, I have come to you. We have need of a healer. We have come so far, Inau Shaman. So very, very far. My mother is lost to Wildfire, and the baby inside her, too. We loosed the dogs, but they ran away and did not come back. And my little brother is so badly burned he must surely die without your magic."

"Burned . . . ?" Inau turned the word, her mind running briefly back to her thoughts of Wildfire and the burned land, but even as she spoke she saw that Avataut had handed over his float lines to Armik and was now paddling madly away from the hunt, downriver and in toward the shore, where many men were hurriedly gathering and shouting out the alert.

"Bear!"

She saw it. In the dark gray rush of one of the deep water channels. Black nose up. Great paws treading water. Facing toward shore. Drawing in the scent of blood and meat. A bear. A white bear!

"Hold!" Avataut was screaming, giving his boat to the current as he aimed his harpoon. "This kill is mine!"

Chapter Two

▼▼▼▼▼▼▼

The band journeyed on.

To everyone's surprise, it was Tôrnârssuk who led them in song. Barrenland songs—bold, joyous songs about a land most of them had never seen. Songs about rivers of light and falling stars and endless herds of caribou moving back and forth across a vast and rolling hunting ground that stretched out forever beneath the sky. His voice was as rich as the songs he sang, in his language and the tongue of the People so that all might understand and follow along when Ningao and Kamak and Inaksak and the other Northerners joined in the ancient refrains, surprised and delighted to see their headman relaxed and happy as he had not been in far too long. At the headman's request, Kinap punctuated the rhythms with the sounding of his drum, and Onen'ia played his flute in a way that made it seem as though a magical bird was singing with the travelers, and old Ko'ram was asked to shake his rattle and deer-hoof ankle janglers and screech like a lynx whenever the mood moved him, which was often.

Ne'gauni was amazed. Not by the old man's screeching; he was used to it by now. And not by the headman's songs, even though he, like everyone else, was surprised to hear

Tôrnârssuk singing, pleased to know that the man could actually be happy as other men were happy, and stimulated by heady, rousing Barrenland rhythms. No, Ne'gauni was amazed by the change in Mowea'qua.

She was walking on her own, close to Tôrnârssuk, between him and Hasu'u, quiet and obedient as the dogs that plodded along complacently pulling the headman's drag frame and carrying his side packs. She still wore Tôrnârssuk's hunt shirt, but someone had found her a pair of leggings and moccasins that fit, and she had not only combed out the wild tangling of her hair and rubbed it with earth to make it shine, but she had also smoothed out the feather of Raven, braced the broken shaft with a twisting of grass, and rebraided it into her forelock.

"Do you see? She is almost beautiful again," said Musquash on a sigh. Falling back from the head of the column, he strode out beside Ne'gauni as the young man walked along, shadowed once again by the three unmarried daughters of Chief Ogeh'ma and Segub'un.

"Even when the bruises fade and the swelling goes down on that one's face, she will never be beautiful." Chi'co'pee gave her opinion freely, lightly, taking pleasure, as she always did, in demeaning Mowea'qua.

"She is now Chosen Sister of Raven, my sister, so be careful what you say of one whom our headman has taken into his protection," warned Nee'nah.

"Besides, Chi'co'pee, although you are half her size, among all the women in this band only your moccasins were big enough to fit her big feet!" chided Ane'pemin'an.

"You are all three ugly," declared Musquash, his expression soured not only by his dislike of the sisters but by the fact that he had just come up behind old Ko'ram and fallen into the wake of his latest wind.

"What did you say?" asked the old man, huffing more than a little as he fell back a few steps, using his need to be a part of the conversation as an excuse to slow down and catch his breath.

"I said that my Mowea'qua looks beautiful!"

Ko'ram looked down at the boy, shook his head to show his disapproval of the statement, then squinted ahead to settle his gaze on the giant's daughter as he wheezed, "The sooner we reach the great river and trade her out of the band the better."

"You still say that!" Ne'gauni snapped, infinitely annoyed, for it was now apparent to him that no matter what Mowea'qua did, the old man had set his heart against her.

"Our Wise Man *is* a wise man," injected Chi'co'pee. "The widow Suda'li says that Mowea'qua may yet prove to be—"

"That woman eats penises!" interrupted Musquash in a sudden fury. "I do not want to hear what she says!"

Ne'gauni stared at the boy, startled and at a loss to understand his invective against the widow. Musquash, red-faced with anger, ran off to assume the place he had taken as his own at the head of the band, close to where Mowea'qua walked between Tôrnârssuk and his woman.

Old Ko'ram came to halt. After impatiently gesturing the three sisters to move on ahead, he rested his hands on his hips and leaned forward, a little blue around the mouth and nostrils as, still wheezing, he pointed to Mowea'qua with a stab of his chin. "Do you see that?" he asked Ne'gauni. "Do you see the way she has put herself between them?"

Ne'gauni was stunned. "What?"

"Are you deaf as well as blind? No matter how she may comb her hair or attempt to change her ways and appear like an obedient woman of the People, Mowea'qua cannot help being what she is. Too much of the blood of the Old Tribe is in her. Her eyes speak the truth of it. A wolf prowls her spirit. She will be a danger to this band as long as she is with us. Already, by putting herself between the headman and his woman, she is making new trouble. Look, Dreamer, look and listen! You do not need a shaman's eyes or ears to see or hear the truth of it! See how only one night spent with Mowea'qua beneath his bed skins has made Tôrnârssuk sing out as though reborn! The woman who holds your heart cannot be happy about that! Indeed, Hasu'u must be ashamed after so many moons of trying her best to bring a song to his lips and failing."

"No one holds my heart!" The lie burst from Ne'gauni's lips unbidden. The blush that flamed upon his scarred face named him Liar. "The headman sings for the same reasons that we all sing! He knows that he has led us well. The Great River of the North is no longer far, we have bested enemies in the forest, and—"

The old man huffed a dismissive snort. "You still have so much to learn, Dreamer, so much to learn! I sometimes wonder if there is life and breath enough left in me to teach it all!"

▼▼▼▼▼

Hasu'u was worried.

The frosty morning had yielded to a mild day. Tôrnârssuk was singing. The band was joining in. In the cradleboard on her back little Tiguak was swaying to the unaccustomed rhythm of his father's song and sounding out with a happy baby's gurgles and shouts as he did his best to be a part of the music his fellow travelers were making.

And still she worried.

At her side, Mowea'qua was keeping up, head down, quiet, bent slightly forward under the pack roll she had insisted on carrying, lost in thought, walking so close to the headman that she seemed to be a part of him. Hasu'u felt so sorry for the girl that she was half moved to tears every time she looked at her, but at least she could take heart in the fact that Mowea'qua was on her feet again, and that the fear she had shown of Tôrnârssuk last night was gone.

She sighed and leaned into the weight of the cradleboard as her heart swelled with love for Tôrnârssuk. It was a rare man who could bring himself to be gentle with Mowea'qua after all she had said and done and provoked on the night of the Spirit Moon. But he was a rare man. She knew it. She had always known it. And so she worried now, not only because she was certain that, despite the current mood of the band, there were those who were still uneasy about his decision to bring the girl back from the raid, but also because for one fleeting moment of flaming, irrational jealousy, she had also doubted him.

Lying with her back to him last night, nursing his infant, feeling him moving and breathing restlessly as he drew the sobbing girl into the warmth of his embrace, Hasu'u had been overcome by the devastating certainty that he had rescued Mowea'qua not out of kindness, but out of lust. She knew only too well that it was his right to take another woman anytime he chose to do so, and as a hunt chief's daughter and a headman's woman she would never dishonor him, or herself, by challenging that right. So she had lain very still, achingly aware of him lying with another apart from her, asking herself why he would not desire to couple with Mowea'qua?

The girl was young. She had wantonly displayed her body when she had run off to the sandbar, a nubile, opulent, new woman's body, sleek and tight with youth. Every man in the band had wanted to take her down and forcibly penetrate her that night. She had seen it in their eyes. Even in old Ko'ram's eyes, and in her father's eyes, and in Ne'gauni's eyes as he had stared, gape-jawed and salivating. Why not Tôrnârssuk? He was a man, after all, and had been a raider for many a long year before he had taken her to be his woman; the experience of rape was not unknown to him. Perhaps, after so many moons of living with only one quiet, steadfast, baby-suckling woman to adore him, the predacious male spirit of the great white bear that had once impelled him to behavior she preferred not to think of had awakened in him the need to take his male prerogative with a new woman, a more exciting and much younger woman, to penetrate and punish Mowea'qua even as Moraq would have punished her and, through her pain, pleasure himself.

Hasu'u leaned harder into the weight of the cradleboard, deliberately rousing pain in the skin of her forehead as her browband pressed into it. How could she have dishonored him, and herself, with such thoughts? How? They were sworn to one another, always and forever, without equivocation. How could she have doubted for a moment that he would not hold to the vow he had made on that long-gone night when he held her in his arms and, joined with her for the first time, vowed to be her man and to cherish her, and her alone, for all the days and nights that they drew breath together? And how could she ever have thought him capable of inflicting additional pain on Mowea'qua when the girl had already been ravaged into near insensibility and so hurt and torn that it was unlikely that she would ever be able to open herself willingly to a man, unless the forces of Creation smiled upon her and gave her a husband who would be patient enough to teach her to find pleasure in that which had brought her only pain?

Hasu'u sighed again, distraught. Her hastily spoken

words cautioning Tôrnârssuk against rape had angered him. And rightly so. She leaned even harder into the weight of the cradleboard, worrying, wondering if he would forgive her.

"Are you sure you would not rather lie down and be carried on a drag frame, girl? I know you must still be in pain."

Hasu'u looked to Tôrnârssuk, startled out of her unhappy reverie by his question to Mowea'qua.

The girl looked up, her face washed and clean now, her hair shining, the feather of Raven a black sheen amidst the dark fall of the meticulously plaited forelock that fell forward across her shoulder and down over the rise of her buckskin-covered breasts. "Chosen Sister of Raven grows stronger in her headman's shadow," replied Mowea'qua, her eyes soft on Tôrnârssuk's face as she added, "Slow down the band I will not. Rest will I when my headman rests. Always and forever."

Hasu'u's eyebrows arched to her browband. Her mood shifted, instantly. What was this? Obedience? Or adoration? Obviously Mowea'qua had taken to heart the stern advice she had given her this morning as the band had prepared to move on.

"Look at you," Hasu'u remembered saying to the girl as the little boy, Musquash, had hovered close. "This will not do, Mowea'qua! Is it any wonder that some members of this band are whispering in concern of our headman's judgment in saving your life and bringing you into his protection? No man at the Great Gathering of Many Tribes will want such a creature as you. If you do not want to be taken for a beast, you cannot continue to give the appearance of one. So before we journey another step toward the Great River of the North, we must begin to 'unbeast' you. I will do what I can to find clothes for you. Musquash, fetch me that little deerskin bag from the side of my pack frame. My comb is in it. I will untangle Mowea'qua's hair and make her at least presentable as the new sister of our headman's circle before we continue on."

"Mowea'qua does not like to comb her hair," the boy had informed sullenly.

Hasu'u remembered declaring, with no attempt to hide her annoyance, "Is it so? Well! She does not have to comb it. I will comb it for her. And from this day, little boy, if you care for this poor battered girl as much as you say you do, you must help her to understand that she must learn to be obedient and do as she is told . . . for her own good as well as for the good of the band."

"No one this must tell me," Mowea'qua had replied quietly. "Chosen Sister of Raven am I. Whatever he says, I will do . . . gladly. Give me the comb."

Hasu'u gave a little start as, again coming out of a reverie, she noticed that Musquash was back walking beside Mowea'qua, trying to take her hand. It was no use. The girl twisted her fingers free of his grasp and looked down at him with a withering glance.

"Away, little boy. No longer with you will I walk."

"I am not a little boy!" protested the child, cut to the quick by her unexpected repudiation. "I am Muskrat. I have killed Giant Beaver for you! I have fought for my Mowea'qua! Just like in the story. Well, almost like in the story. Bravely I have fought. Against Tôrnârssuk himself!"

The girl's face worked with revulsion. "In you is the blood of Old Tribe beasts! Away go you! Of the People am I. Yes! Chosen Sister of Raven am I! Yes! Of Tôrnârssuk's band am I! Always and forever!"

"No, Mowea'qua," Hasu'u corrected compassionately, perhaps with a little more emphasis than was fully necessary.

"Only until a man is found for you at the Great River of the North."

The girl's eyes went wide and wild with fear. "Chosen Sister of Raven am I. Not to be mated! No! Never to be mated again! Never!"

"Tell her, man of my heart," urged Hasu'u. "Tell her that Chosen Sister of Raven must also be Obedient Sister of Raven. Tell her that when we reach the Great River of the North she will become the woman of another."

But Tôrnârssuk did not tell her.

He was frowning ahead, raising his face into the wind.

They had reached the burned land at last.

▼▼▼▼▼

"Now we will see what Wildfire has done," rumbled Kinap.

And it was so.

They went on. Into appalling devastation.

It was as Tôrnârssuk remembered. Only worse. Wildfire had danced through forest in this land, not across barrens, and the ancient trees stood gaunt and black and silent, their branches reaching out like the burned arms of slain men held forever in some cruel and grotesque moment of a dance. Each was as charred as the earth and, after the last rain, reeking of its own death.

"I think maybe we should go back and go around," said Goh'beet, pausing, holding her baby close, shivering a little.

"Go back? Go around?" Chief Ogeh'ma was openly disgusted by the woman's suggestion. "How can we know how far we would have to journey? And over what kind of country? Am I the only one here hungry for the meat of white whales?"

"I agree," said Kamak. "I say we go on. The river cannot be so far away now. What say you, Tôrnârssuk?"

"A few days' walk . . . if we continue straight on," replied the headman. His face set and grim, without another word he led his followers to do just that.

▼▼▼▼

The caws of ravens drew them on. Peevish. Coarse. The sound of greedy birds squawking and fighting over meat.

"Look!" Ka'wo'ni was pointing. "There they are! There must be a whole hand-count of them up ahead!"

"Come! Hurry!" cried N'av. "What can they be eating? Whatever it is, it looks big! Let us see!" Already he was bounding off after his brother toward a grove of blackened deadfall at the flank of a long, charred rise that might have offered shelter to some hapless creature at the height of the fire.

The boys ran on, waving their arms madly, screeching and hooting and making good work of driving the ravens off their find of a meal. The birds ascended in a sullen fury of black wings, and only then, with the carrion eaters' feast revealed, did the twins pause, hunch up a little, and proceed with caution.

"Hold!" commanded Tôrnârssuk.

The boys obeyed, instantly and without question.

As did the rest of the band.

"Ah!" exclaimed old Ko'ram, squinching up his eyes. "What could have been so huge when it walked upon the land? Or are these old eyes tricking me?"

"We will see." Tôrnârssuk slowly led them forward, only to pause again, not wanting to believe what he saw.

"Mammoths!" exclaimed Musquash.

There was not a man, woman, or child in the band who did not suck in his or her breath in awe and amazement as they came to stand before the burned and blackened tusks and skeletal remains of three mammoths, all in a heap where they had collapsed over the calf they had apparently tried to protect when they had all died together.

"There is still some unburned hair and hide and flesh on the underside of the flanks and ribs," observed Kanio'te, his lean face showing revulsion at the smell of rotting meat and the sound and sight of feeding insects. A single raven winged out of a cavernous rib cage.

"You were wrong, Headman!" declared Ka'wo'ni.

"Yes!" agreed N'av. "You were wrong, Tôrnârssuk. There are mammoths in the forest!"

"Were," corrected Ka'wo'ni. "Maybe these are the last of their kind in all of this forest."

"There is no more forest," said N'av. "It is all burned up!"

"There is a forest, stupid," countered Ka'wo'ni. "Behind us. Ahead of us. Only—"

"You will be silent!" Kinap rumbled to the twins.

At the giant's side, Suda'li looked up. "They meant no offense!" she told him, her tone one of vaguely guarded rebuke as she defended her own. "They only speak the obvious."

"They speak too much and much too freely," growled Kinap.

Tôrnârssuk's face showed no emotion. He was staring at the mammoths. His mind was in turmoil. He was thinking of Moraq. Somehow the dead man he had slain as penalty for challenging him once too often was at his side. Smirking. Breathing cold, caustic words at the nape of his neck and into his ear.

You were wrong. Again. And now all who have followed you and put their trust and lives into your hands have seen that you were wrong.

He shuddered. Was the ghostly voice real or imagined? He was not sure. Either way, it was right. Great tuskers *did* still exist! And not just in the dreams of the People, as he had sworn on the night of the Spirit Moon—and, in the swearing, named Mowea'qua Liar and set her up for all the pain and degradation that had come to her since. What else had he been wrong about? He shrugged off the question; this was not the time for it. Not here. Not now. Not in this burned, dead land when the great river still lay far ahead and all the happiness and joyful expectation he had experienced the other night was gone. Again he shuddered, imagined his own bones lying on the ground alongside those of the mammoths, and wondered if he was seeing a vision of his own death in the bones of the giants.

Mowea'qua, standing close, was shivering as she pressed against the headman's side. "Na'v and Ka'wo'ni could right be, say I. Maybe all the world is now like this burned forest . . . a dead place stretching on and on forever . . . if that is the Great One lying there, as Hasu'u wished under the Spirit Moon."

Hasu'u paled.

Ne'gauni moved forward, visibly shaken as he reminded the band, "We all saw the boundaries of the dancing ground of Wildfire from the overlook. There *were* boundaries. Beyond this stretch of burned land we will find forest again and, beyond the forest, the great river. All the world has not died."

"Can you be sure, Dreamer?" asked Nee'nah, following close on his heels to stand beside him even as she was followed by her sisters.

"Have you not all named me Shaman Indeed?"

"Yes!" sighed the three unmarried daughters of Chief Ogeh'ma and Segub'un.

"It is so!" affirmed Ko'ram with a rousing shake of his rattle.

"Look! Here!"

The cry came from Musquash, who, to everyone's amazement, had somehow managed to run forward unnoticed. Having scooted deep inside the largest of the arching rib cages, it was he who had disturbed the raven feeding within and was now peeking out, holding his nose even as he smiled and proclaimed, "It is a stinking bad place inside these mammoths! Phew! The meat and skin were roasted by the heat of Wildfire, but it has all gone smelly soft and full of wiggly fly babies. Still, underneath the meat there is skin and hair! Much hair!" He held out a fistful of long strands. "Look. Here is some! And it is not scorched. It is all brown, like this, the color of balsam bark. None of it is white! Great Chief of All Mammoths is not here. He walks in another part of the forest."

"How can you know this, boy?" asked Hasu'u.

"Because I saw him on the night Wildfire danced under the Spirit Moon," revealed Musquash proudly, hopping outside of the skeleton and tossing the hair of mammoths to the mild wind of the day. "When Mowea'qua and I were together in the dark woods, we found sign of Great Chief everywhere. Much sap sticking on our moccasins. Torn trees where he had been ripping at the bark with his big, long teeth. And then, during the big storm, when lightning was flashing white in the trees and thunder was roaring, he roared, too, and I saw him, standing tall as a mountain, white as the lightning. Tell them, Mowea'qua! Tell them!"

Tôrnârssuk was startled to find that the girl had sought his hand and curled her fingers into his palm as she suddenly drew herself to her full height, pulled in a deep and steadying breath, and, with her head high and the raven feather in her forelock catching the light of the sun, spoke forthrightly.

"To tell there is nothing. Frightened little boys can many things think they see in a dark and stormy forest when, say I, nothing is there except themselves and the trees and the beasts who follow to fall upon them and hurt and kill them if they can. We should have run away not that night, say I. Sorry am I for this, more than ever I can say. Yet say this will I. Wrong was I to speak out against our headman's words and Hasu'u's, too. Right she is to fear the power of Great Chief. Big is he. Small are we. And wise is Tôrnârssuk. And right. No mammoths were there in the Valley of the Spirit Moon. No sign of them, say I. And if these mammoths that here lie dead are in the world the last of their kind, then again Tôrnârssuk is right. It matters not! Stand we here together. Alive. With a good camp and good hunting awaiting us on the shores of the Great River of the North. The sacred Circle of Life Ending and Life Beginning turns on. In it we still are, even if these mammoths are not!"

There was stunned silence.

Tôrnârssuk heard a murmuring go through the band. Saw glances of surprise and approval exchanged. The girl had spoken out for him, and spoken well. Not like an Old Tribe beast at all. It was obvious that those who had only moments ago been uncertain of his judgment in bringing her back into the protection of the band were now reassessing their earlier opinions. Only Ko'ram was glaring at her in that hard, fixed, inflexible way of the very old who believe that they alone have found Truth and, even though it is again and again disproved to them before their very eyes, will not let it go or yield to another. Ko'ram disliked Mowea'qua. Tôrnârssuk doubted the man could ever bring himself to forgive her behavior on the night of the Spirit Moon, or forget that the blood of the Old Tribe ran in her veins. And yet Ko'ram and everyone else could discount it in the boy because the child had inherited the appearance of the People and none of the look of his partial Old Tribe ancestry. Would they have been so forgiving of him if he had gray eyes like the girl, or was not the son of a shaman? He doubted it.

He frowned. Musquash looked lost, hurt, betrayed by the girl's unexpected repudiation of his claims, standing there in his borrowed clothes and moccasins, his mouth turning down in a funny, quivering little twist that betrayed the fact that he was trying hard not to cry.

Tôrnârssuk felt sorry for him. He admired the child. Musquash had suffered much in his young life and was strong, not weaker, for it. Any man would be proud to name such a youngster Son.

The cawing of ravens drew his eyes skyward. The birds were returning, circling overheard, impatient to return to their feast. He exhaled resolve. Raven had been speaking to him on matters concerning Mowea'qua. He had been listening. He might as well listen now. The winged brothers and sisters of Raven were clearly telling him that it was time to move on. He had no regret. He did not want to linger in this place.

"The great river will not come to us," he said and, striding out, gestured his people forward.

A coldness was on him now. He shifted the weight of his pack frame across his upper back and thought of the skin of the great white bear that he carried rolled up and balanced across the antler frame. If the spirit of that great white bear was inside him now, he could not feel it. He felt tired. Older than Ko'ram must feel. Despite Mowea'qua's words of confidence in him and the looks of approval he had received from his followers, he could not shake the certainty that he had been wrong about the mammoths. Mowea'qua could twist his words all she liked, and others might even be willing to abide that twisting, but he *had* been wrong, and although logic told him now that this should not matter to him or to those who had for so long prospered under his leadership, he knew that it did. He had made too many errors in judgment lately. Major errors. Others might be willing to overlook them, but Tôrnârssuk was not.

▼▼▼▼▼

It was cold again that night. And clear. Under the stars the journeyers raised their lean-tos and bundled in to sleep.

Sometime well before dawn, Mowea'qua awoke, sweated and breathless from her dreams. She had seen herself as a wolf again. Wild. Running out across that endless land in which she knew she would find the beasts and become one of them again.

"No!" she gasped, willed herself awake, and, feeling trapped in the warm darkness of the headman's lean-to, threw back her bed furs and crept out into the dark.

Trembling and in need of air, she crouched before the little shelter clad only in her hunt shirt, feeling the cold surface of the burned land beneath her bare feet, breathing in and out again and again until her heart ceased racing and, shivering in the cold, she knew that she was indeed awake, a woman, not a wolf.

The stars above her head were bright.

So bright!

Mowea'qua turned up her face and looked for the moon, but it had either gone to its rest or turned its face from the world below, and she could not find it in any of its endlessly changing phases. Inside the lean-to, little Tiguak was fussing softly. Hungry, no doubt. The son of the headman was almost always hungry; he would be a big man, strong like his father, she had heard the other women of the band say. She heard Hasu'u shush the little one and begin to hum to it, as she always did when the baby needed soothing. She listened to Woman Who Sings Always and cocked her head, understanding how Hasu'u had won her name but not really sure if she found the woman's almost endless humming and singing pleasing or irritating. It never seemed to bother Tôrnârssuk or anyone else, and she had enjoyed it once, but since coming into the protection of White Bear there was not much about Hasu'u that did not rub against the grain of her temperament. She wondered now how the headman could sleep next to a woman who hummed to his baby so much.

She sighed, shivered again. It was so cold! Her teeth were clattering. She wished Hasu'u would stop humming. She would not be able to go back to sleep as long as the woman was humming. Again she sighed. Her bladder and bowels felt heavy and full; she had neglected to empty herself after tonight's cold meal, and she had eaten heartily. She rose and moved away from the lean-to, seeking a place downwind and away from the rest of the tents to relieve herself before returning to sleep. Maybe by the time she was done, Hasu'u would have stopped humming.

She did not go far.

Squatting, she spread the edges of the headman's hunt shirt out around herself lest she soil it, and relaxed into the pleasantness of elimination. Whatever salves Hasu'u and Segub'un had given her to slather onto and into her woman place were as fine as any medicine she and old Kelet had ever made; it no longer hurt or burned when she urinated. Now, looking up at the stars, she was feeling so much better than she would have thought possible only this morning and found herself wondering what it was about the stars that caused the Northerners to love the sight of them so. Seen though the stark, denuded branches of burned trees, they looked so far away, cold and lonely without the moon to keep them company in all that high, black space of sky.

She started.

A wolf was howling!

She froze, listened as the song of the solitary animal rose and fell within the night.

Her bowel tensed. Her mind was racing. Was she dreaming again? The terrible dream? She put out her hands, stared at them in the starlight. A little stab of relief leaped within her. Her hands were hands. Not paws. She was still Mowea'qua. Not a wolf. Not a beast!

She rose, her elimination complete. She would go back to the lean-to. Even if Hasu'u was still humming, it seemed a safer place, warm and snug with Tôrnârssuk in it, although she would not sleep; she would lie awake lest in her dreams she become a wolf again—and perhaps this time be unable to wake.

She caught her breath.

Other wolves were joining the solitary singer now. The hackles on her back rose and shivered up her nape and over her scalp and down her arms. She turned, frightened—of the wolves or of herself, she could not say. Was she dreaming? She could not say! The lean-tos seemed suddenly so far away, and the rising ululations of the wolves were ascending into the night from all around until it seemed that wolves must be everywhere.

They were singing.

They were calling.

They were closing in.

And then, in a moment of rising terror and stark panic, she saw him.

The great white bear.

As in her dreams.

He was standing upright like a man at the top of a little rise at the peripheries of the camp, just outside the trees, with his back to her under the full vault of the open sky.

A sob of relief broke from her throat.

"White Bear!" Mowea'qua called as she ran to him, her arms spread wide, the lacings on her hunt shirt loose and open, her hair flying wild in the dark of the moon. He would save her from wolves. And he would keep her from becoming a wolf. He always did.

▼▼▼▼▼

He turned, startled.

The girl was running toward him.

And then, suddenly, she stopped. Stared. Cocked her head.

"Tôrnârssuk?"

"And so," he said, unsettled by the sight of her, her hunt shirt thrown wide, her body and breasts revealed in starlight, shining, sweated from her run, giving off the scent of fear, and of woman. "Who did you think you would find?"

"White Bear."

"Then you have found me."

She was trembling violently. "Do not let them take me!"

"Who?"

"Wolves . . . beasts . . . safe keep me from them . . . as before, White Bear, as before. With them I do not want to run. Again never! Not a wolf am I, not a beast, not Old Tribe! Not!"

His brow furrowed. She was shaking so hard with cold and terror that he instinctively opened wide the skin of the great white bear in which he had wrapped himself when he had come naked from his sleeping place beside Hasu'u to seek the cold dark solitude of the night. Tormented by the sense of inadequacy that had been with him ever since the band had come across the mammoths, he had been unable to sleep. Maybe the stars would speak to him! Maybe the sight of Big Bear Walks Forever Across the Sky and Little Bear Who Follows would give him a sense of comfort. Maybe he would see Sila hiding in the bright star run of the Sky River and tell it to leave him in peace, just for a little while. Now, as he enfolded the girl in the bearskin and drew her close, it was as though her presence was what he had been seeking, the answer to his need, for as she slipped her arms around him and pressed her bare, trembling body against his, in yielding to Mowea'qua the comfort she sought from him, Tôrnârssuk found that he was also comforted.

And so he held her, sent his hands beneath her hunt shirt to stroke her, tenderly, lovingly. The wolves fell silent, their need to call out to one another across the burned land satisfied for this night. He was grateful. The girl noticed the absence of sound, and as he smoothed the sweat from the soft warm skin of her back and arms she began to relax, to murmur with gratitude, to sigh a little and sway against him, sleepy now as she responded instinctively to his touch, mindlessly it seemed, murmuring with pleasure in his handling as he drew her down and, together, they lay upon the burned land within the skin of the great white bear.

She nestled close, trusting, assuming no intent on his part other than to rest with her, to sleep beneath the stars in which he and his fellow Northerners found such comfort. "Stay here will we, then," she whispered. "Mowea'qua with White Bear . . . sleep safe now from wolves . . . with you."

He knew that Mowea'qua intended no seduction. He knew that coupling had become both repellent and frightening to her. But now, lying naked with her fast asleep against him within the embrace of the skin of the great white bear, Tôrnârssuk felt the spirit of that bear alive in him, hungry, prowling restlessly, centering itself in that part of him that he knew he would not deny tonight. Not for the first time, Mowea'qua had aroused man need in him, and now, recalling Hasu'u as much as giving him permission to rape her, a hot core of anger toward his wife focused his desire. His beloved woman had shown herself to be not in the least offended by the thought of him pleasuring himself between thighs other than her own. So why should he deny himself? If Mowea'qua was to be weaned from her terror of coupling, he might as well be the man to do the weaning, now and gently, giving her pleasure where she had known only pain so that she would not be hostile when the time came to accept a man of her own when at last they reached the Great Gathering.

And so he moved, slowly, bending over her to begin that which he knew would bring, instead of pain, an awakening to pleasure as he mouthed her body . . . slowly, so slowly . . . exhaling the warmth of his breath onto her skin until she sighed and moved beneath him in her sleep. Now, gently, he sought her woman place and, with his tongue, awoke to his touch that soft, tender height of flesh that, apart from her breasts, conveyed a woman's first sensation of joy with a man. It peaked at the explorations of his tongue . . . sweet, moist, responsive.

She gasped, suddenly awake, startled.

He drew back, poised over her, looked down to see her rapt expression of wonderment. "I will stop if you wish it so," he told her. "I do not want you to be afraid."

She shivered beneath him, not from the cold, for it was very warm now beneath the skin of the great white bear.

"Afraid?" Mowea'qua spoke the word as though it made no sense to her. "With White Bear Mowea'qua is not afraid."

The starlight was enough to illuminate her features, showing him the curve of her long soft mouth, lips drawn back to reveal small, serrate-edged teeth and sharply defined canines. Against the skin of the white bear, her hair was a wild black shadow that accentuated the unusual elongated oval of a face made angular by the rise of broad cheekbones and the graceful arch of dark eyebrows above pale eyes in which the stars were reflected back to him, as though, somehow, the night sky was also there, within the woman.

Now it was Tôrnârssuk who shivered, for it struck him that there truly was something unnatural about her face, so different, as though all the peoples of all the tribes in all the world had come together to meld themselves into this one creation. Disconcerted, he whispered, "What are you, Mowea'qua . . . just what are you?"

"See you what I am. As you have said. Chosen Sister of Raven. Your woman now."

"Until the river."

"Always and forever."

"No." And in the dark of the moon, under the black vault of the night, in the skin of the great white bear of the north, Tôrnârssuk came down upon the woman who was named for the wolf. "Now."

And so it was done.

He was both patient Guide and ardent Seeker, leading through pleasure into pain and then beyond until the girl caught fire beneath him, and together they danced the dance of life making, rising and falling to its burning rhythms until at last it was completed for them both. She burrowed her face into the hollow of his throat and clung to him, whispering, her voice less sound than a nascent shadow tremulous and redolent of lingering fear. "Yah! Are we *both* beasts, then, Tôrnârssuk?"

He understood at once and told her tenderly, "No, Mowea'qua, we are not beasts. We are White Bear and Wolf Woman, man and woman together, as it has been since the time beyond beginning when the Animals and People were of one tribe."

A shudder went through her. She pressed still closer as she implored, "Mark me then you must, Tôrnârssuk. Place upon my face the tattoo mark of your band so all will know when we come to the Great River of the North that of your band am I . . . not beast . . . not Old Tribe . . . a True Woman."

He did not miss the desperation in her voice. Nor did he fail to understand its cause. "Be at ease, Mowea'qua. If it will please you, yes, tomorrow when we break camp at day's end I will mark you as a woman of the People. Sleep now. Dawn cannot be far away."

She sighed, relaxed into a sudden blissfulness of heart and mind that allowed her to fall asleep almost instantly within his arms.

He held her, stroked her absently, thought that with the right patterning of traditional band tattooing to offset the color of her eyes, she might not be so readily identifiable as Old Tribe; it would be easier thus to find a man for her at the Great Gathering. Especially now when he knew that he could say with confidence to any man that she was a pleasure to lie on.

He closed his eyes. Tried to sleep. No use. He had found release within the girl and was glad that he had been able to bring her to know that never again need she fear opening herself to any man who sought to come into her as a man and not as a beast. Yet he remained dissatisfied, unfulfilled, and on edge. It was Hasu'u he loved. It was Hasu'u he wanted. It was Hasu'u he had imagined beneath him as he drove deep into the girl and filled her with the shivering wet heat of his maleness. And yet he had broken his vow to her tonight.

He sat up, restless again, achingly unhappy. Would she care? It certainly had not seemed so the other night. His jaw tightened. Why should she care? He might well be still capable of rising to the lead of a young woman lying naked against him beneath his bed furs in the night, but he was not the man he once was, not the leader he once was; there were too many questions in his mind.

He huffed impatience. Or was it disgust? He turned his gaze upward, looking at the stars, thinking about the day, worrying about what tomorrow would bring to his band as they moved on across this burned land of dead mammoths and moonless skies beneath which, once again, he could sense Sila watching him from among the stars.

Mocking him.

Waiting for him.

"Ah!" he exclaimed in disgust and lay back, pulling the skin of the great white bear of the north over himself and Mowea'qua. *Tomorrow will bring what tomorrow will bring!* he thought and, suddenly exhausted, drifted off to sleep fully overwhelmed by the realization that he must get his followers to the Great Gathering. True enough, he knew better than most that in all of life there was no guarantee of safety for any man, woman, or child, but there, on the shores of the Great River of the North among many bands and old and trusted friends like Avataut, he would at least find a haven of relative safety for them, since he knew in his heart that he was no longer fit to lead.

▼▼▼▼▼

He did not see Hasu'u duck back into their lean-to, after standing disconsolate for many long moments.

He did not see Ne'gauni, sitting unseen and unable to sleep at the entrance to his own lean-to, within which the three unmarried daughters of Chief Ogeh'ma and Segub'un were snoring.

The young man did not move. He stared, shocked, angry, and jealous. It was the latter emotion that confused him. Jealous? Of Tôrnârssuk because he had coupled with Mowea'qua? Impossible. And yet, he had to admit, there had been moments in the past, albeit fleeting, when he not only had been able to tolerate the girl but had sensed something rare and perhaps even wonderful in her otherwise head-strong and self-serving nature. The admission disturbed him. He must have been wrong! He reminded himself with infinite annoyance that although he had somehow managed to accumulate three women whom he could, if he wished, call his own, whereas only a moon ago he had none, it was Hasu'u who owned his heart, no matter how he might deny it to old Ko'ram or to anyone else, especially himself.

He wrapped his forearms around his knee and tried to calm his anger. She had seen! Wolves had called. Hasu'u had come from the lean-to. And she had seen the man of her heart, Tôrnârssuk, and Mowea'qua together, wrapped up in the big bearskin, moving beneath it; had they been stark naked and lying on top of it their coupling would not have been any more obvious. Hasu'u had watched. Motionless. And then, without a sound, turned away. He had held his breath, listening, expecting to hear her sobs, but then he had exhaled harshly, reminding himself that Hasu'u was a hunt chief's daughter. She would not cry. Her heart might bleed and her spirit wail inside her, but no one would ever see Hasu'u cry.

Ne'gauni hissed through his teeth. His anger was worse than before. The white mound of the bearskin was motionless now. He knew that Tôrnârssuk and Mowea'qua must have fallen asleep. But he could not understand how the headman could even look at another woman, much less a thing like Mowea'qua, when he already possessed the finest woman in the world.

"By the forces of Creation, would that a lightning bolt would come from the sky to strike them both dead!" He shook as he spoke the imploration, softly lest he wake the band with the intensity of a curse that he wanted to shout to the infinite.

"No, Ne'gauni, no. You must not ill wish her. Not her. Not my Mowea'qua."

Ne'gauni squinted into the dark. Musquash was coming toward him from where he had apparently been sitting not far away. "Your love is wasted," he said as the boy dropped to his knees before him. "Have you not seen the truth of this with your own eyes this night?"

"The wolves woke me. I have seen. But what have I seen, Ne'gauni? Her heart is not his. It . . . it will be for me. S-someday." He hung his head. "I am a boy. Tôrnârssuk is a man, an old man, I think. He will not live forever."

Chapter Three

▼▼▼▼▼▼▼

Avataut had killed the white bear.

He had killed it with one harpoon, and at a distance from his kayak, an amazing strike, and everyone on the beach and bluffs had stood in awe of him when he hauled the beast onto dry land and opened it from throat to crotch and hunkered down to eat its heart.

If only it was Tôrnârssuk's heart!

It pleased him to think it as he walked back and forth along the beach under the bright sun, although somehow the other man seemed less important to him now, less threatening. Perhaps he had actually killed him when he had buried the amulet. Or blinded him. Or robbed him of the heart to come north. Whatever he had done, Avataut felt better for it. Let Inau stand on the heights and collect her share of whale meat and fat from grateful hunters, and let her glower down at him, as she was doing now. He had sent Nuutlaq to her with a cutting of the meat of the great white bear, intending to shame her with it after all the insults she had heaped upon him. He hoped she choked on it. He had no need of her magic. His reputation had never been better, or his luck.

Armik had managed to tow his whales to shore for him. Three whales! And a white bear! All in one day! Armik had taken none and was still tight-lipped and glassy-eyed over what he considered a spirit-eating ordeal. Avataut scanned the beach. Fires were burning everywhere along the shore as the fat of the white whales was being rendered into precious oil. Women were working joyfully together with their children at the many meat-making tasks assigned specifically to their gender. All parts of the whales were being harvested, with small cuttings of flesh and blubber and sweet tender skin being eaten raw and larger portions boiled, roasted, and sliced up to be air-dried and preserved for winter rations.

Avataut laughed as Armik came toward him, still glum and green. "You will go out again onto the river and hunt again. It will be better for you next time."

"Is there not enough meat in this camp already?"

"There is never enough meat. The hunters will sweat tonight. Rejoice in the success of the hunt tonight. All True Men in this camp who were on the river and took whales will join us. Maybe you should stay with your woman. Maybe you are not True Man enough."

"True Man enough to bring your whales to the beach for you. True Man enough to respect the spirits of the game. Do you still do this, Avataut? The bear you killed—it was female. It had a cub. Now that cub will starve."

"Then be a True Man. Hunt it. Kill it. Eat its heart. It should be about the right size for you."

▼▼▼▼

Inau watched from the bluff.

"It has been a good hunt for the whale hunters this season."

She turned at the sound of a male voice. Táwoda was

standing behind her. She nodded. His features appeared strained; not even his blue face paint could hide the worry or fatigue in his eyes. "But the season has not been kind for some of you who have not come to hunt whales. How fares your brother?"

"He is the same," replied the man of the Copper People from the Inland Lakes. "Since the night of the challenges in the Man House the bleeding from his ears has stopped, but the dark centers of his eyes will neither widen nor contract when light is held to them. He lies staring, unseeing, like a corpse breathing. We all fear for his spirit and request that you continue to speak to the forces of Creation on his behalf. You have only to ask of us what you will have in return. Here, at this Great Gathering, I speak for only my own small band of traders, but we have many hunting allies in this camp, and in the country of our tribe we are rich in many things and in the metal that many value and—"

Inau raised a hand, signaling that she would hear no more. "Shaman has no need of copper. Soon I will be returning to the Cave of the Winds. It has been gift enough to my spirit to hear that, even though one of your own has been struck down, you have not been so concerned with your personal grief that you have failed to be generous in the gifts of salve and comfort that you have brought to the burned boy of the little band that walks in blue-quilled garments. Such generosity is a gift to my spirit."

"We have been fortunate to have brought enough to share."

"Not to trade?"

"The burned boy's band has come to this gathering with nothing except the pain and sadness that they have suffered at the burning flame hands of Wildfire. The sons of Sebec would not take advantage of them. We would not ask them to barter what little they have in exchange for what they need so badly, especially when we can well afford to freely offer it. I have heard it said that it is the same of Inau. That you come each summer to call the whales for all who would hunt them, not only for those who can afford to bring gifts in exchange for your magic."

Behind her mask, Inau's face tightened. Táwoda was a man she could respect, but unlike him, she dared not reveal the soft center of her heart. He was a hunter, one who could provide meat for his own fire. She was the Gift; her duality of nature forbade her female half the use of a man's weapons, while her male half precluded the possibility of taking a husband to provide her with meat for her fire. And so the Gift was dependent upon the gifts of others. But, in truth, she needed little to sustain her; the largest portion of all that was brought to her found its way by "magic" back down to the beach and into the encampments of those hunters upon whom the whales chose not to smile. Even now her drag frame was packed, ready to be hauled home, to the Cave of the Winds.

Inau turned back to the river and set her gaze upon the beach. Her eyes narrowed. It had been a good hunt this season. Why then the sense of unease? Why the feeling that all was not well among the many who were even now feasting as they worked to set by the richness of their harvest? She shuddered. Perhaps it was because, although she could not see him, she knew that Avataut was there.

▼▼▼▼▼

There was too much talk going on in the sweat lodge.

Much too much!

Avataut might have enjoyed it had it been about him. Annoyed, he sucked air through the woven grasswork of the little smoke filter that he and all the others wore over the lower halves of their faces, held in place by fiber loops around their ears.

One of the crewmen of the big umiak was gesturing and, to Avataut's mind, exaggerating the difficulty he and his men had had in maneuvering among the smaller boats today. Something about the sail coming around wrong to the wind. He knew nothing of sails and cared less. The big umiak needed a crew to make it leap upon the water; in his estimation none of the men who sailed and rowed it could shine singularly in the eyes of any other man like an individual kayakman.

In the dull glow of the dark interior, lit only by a central fire, the Northerners sat naked in a circle, each adding his own small share of green wood to the fire now and then to make it smoke. With the vent hole closed, the room seemed a cage for smoke; it smelled strongly of the scent of the men, wet with the cleansing liquid of their own sweat and urine.

"I have heard it said that Tôrnârssuk will not come to the river this summer."

Avataut went rigid at the sound of the name. He looked across the fire at Umak, master of the big umiak, and held his tongue and temper only because he had not forgotten that the northern water hunter was a man of great rank among the boatmen. In the ancestral traditions of Umak's people, his ancient name linked him directly with First Man and First Woman. Umak had been the first to suggest that Avataut might have the makings of a kayakman. And it was Umak who had taken him and Tôrnârssuk hunting in his umiak when they were last together at the great river. So, straining to be polite, he said to the older man, "You are only recently returned to this shore, Father of the Big Boat. The one you speak of has become a bad-spirit man. It is not good to set his name loose upon the air."

Umak set his gaze across the fire and through the smoke to settle upon Avataut. "Then it is true? He will not come to the river? Too bad. My heart sang in his presence. My spirit was made stronger for knowing him. He was brave when we hunted together on the water and had a natural skill with a harpoon unusual for a man born to the inland barrens."

Avataut was riled. "Harpoon or lance, all men of the inland barrens have a feel for the use of these! And have you not seen me on the river? Have you not seen me take whale and bear? I, Avataut, am as at ease in a kayak as in my own skin! If the one who made your spirit strong appeared brave when out on the big boat with you last summer, he wore a false face so that you would not see that he was afraid."

"Then it was a good face," said Umak sternly. "I could not see through it. Any more than he or you or any man could see through mine. We were strong for each other that day. Strong for our people. It was good. Our strength moved the wind. Our strength honored the whales."

There was a tension in the sweat lodge that had not been there before. Avataut was suddenly aware of his nakedness. He felt smaller. Demeaned. Vulnerable to the scrutiny of many eyes that had seen only the strength in him until this moment.

"I am sad to hear that bad spirits have chosen to walk with him," said Umak, still looking straight at Avataut, still speaking of Tôrnârssuk. "Truly, the spirit of the white bear of the north was alive in his skin. Maybe it will eat the bad spirits. Maybe he will still come to the river in time to take a few whales. When the spirit of the great white bear chooses a man, he—"

"I have been chosen!" Avataut reminded him, sitting very straight now, throwing out his chest, slapping his hands down hard and wide upon his thighs. "All saw me kill the white bear that would have come from the river to steal the meat of whales and threaten the people of the Great Gathering. All saw me hurl my harpoon—"

"From a safe distance," Umak interrupted pointedly. There was no hostility in his voice, but clearly he spoke with the mild, confident authority of a proven hunter and respected elder intending to put an upstart in his place. "It is said that the one who has not returned to hunt whales this summer killed his bear close in, face to face, with only one of his two knives . . . like a True Man!"

"Say what you will!" Avataut wondered if he had ever been so angry. "I will not stay to listen to such insults from an old man."

▼▼▼▼▼

He was shaking.

The wind was cold off the river as he emerged from the sweat lodge. Avataut took its chill as yet another personal insult. Reaching down to snatch up the robe he had left outside, he slung the sealskins around himself and stomped back to his campsite.

He ignored the respectful greetings he received along the way from the many guardians of the whale meat who were posted along the shore. Indeed, he barely saw them or anything else until he dropped to his knees before the little grave he had made for the fetish of the white bear.

He stared down, half expecting to find it disturbed.

"Are you still there? Or have you risen to walk about this camp and make a mockery of all that I have become in your absence?" The idea irked him. It was not possible! Or was it?

Bare-handed, he sent his fingers questing into the loess gravel to seek and find what he had thought never to look upon again.

His face contorted. Something had pricked him. He cursed, knowing that his thumb must have encountered the sharp tip of the tiny lance he had made to pierce the heart of the fetish. He felt something else now. Smooth. Inoffensive. The long sinew cord on which Inau had strung the amulet. His fingers closed on it, pulled it up; the carving of the little white bear followed and rolled into the hollow of his hand, glinting up at him, white in the light of the stars.

He could not explain the emotion that went through him as he stared at it. "So you are still here. I have blinded you. I have driven a piece of my own lance into your heart. I have buried you. And still you follow me." He growled, like a bear, he thought. "So be it!" he declared as he reached up and hung the fetish around his neck. "I will keep you close. Where I can watch you."

Somewhere, far out on the river, whales were crying for their dead.

Avataut knelt back. Listened. To his right, the skin of the bear he had slain was stretched wide on the drying frame that Nuutlaq and E'ya had made. They had already fleshed it; soon it would be cured. Soon he would wear it. Then all would know without doubt that he, Avataut of the North, Headman, was White Bear now!

Chapter Four

▼▼▼▼▼▼▼

Crossing the burned land was proving a mistake.

Tôrnârssuk was not certain when he first realized it, but it was apparent to him now that his was not the only heart to be chilled by the charred and blackened land. Signs of Death were everywhere, small, quiet deaths: here a bit of the fur of a squirrel's tail caught on a branch in the moment the animal had leaped away into the explosion of a firestorm, there a pile of heat-fractured mouse bones, or the remains of a fox not clever enough to run in time, or the seared body of a rabbit, confused by heat and flame, leaping high and in circles until it could breathe and leap no more.

He sighed as he walked on, feeling physically strong but emotionally exhausted, regretting the impetuosity that had brought him to lie with Mowea'qua, recalling the bad omens of the night of the Spirit Moon. The band had come so far. The people were tired; he could see it in them now. Although no one complained, there was a strained, dogged persistence and a weary resignation to their steps. Little Musquash, downcast and forlorn, walked on alone, perhaps looking for signs of the great white mammoth, avoiding Mowea'qua now, even though Tôrnârssuk caught him now and then looking after her with such hurt and longing that it was enough to make a grown man cry out of pity for the child's smashed dream of winning her affection. As for Mowea'qua, she walked steadfastly at his side, smiling up at him now and then with an expression of open adoration in her eyes that he would just as soon not see, babbling on about little things he cared nothing about. But when he told her to keep her eyes on the way ahead, she obeyed. It was his beloved Hasu'u who was strangely silent, introspective, and truculent.

"Your song would cheer us all, woman of my heart," he said to her. "Sing for us, Hasu'u. Lead the band in song."

"I am weary of this long trail and have no heart to sing," she said and, without looking at him, leaned into her pack frame and continued on, moving ahead to walk on her own without breaking stride.

Tôrnârssuk kept his own pace. He would not go after her. Not after this morning! Not after she had come from their tent to find him and Mowea'qua already packing up the drag frame and, although the scent of their coupling was strong as musk on them both, behaved as though it did not matter to her, as though his spending the night outside their tent wrapped up naked inside his bearskin with his man bone working another woman was the most natural thing in the world.

"Mowea'qua and I have been one together," he had informed her tersely, defensively, putting on a good show of cold, blustering, forthright arrogance lest she see how much her lack of concern was hurting him.

Hasu'u had stood unmoving, silent, her face as emotionless as a stone.

"Is this acceptable to you, then?" How flat his voice had been. How controlled. Not really a question at all. And surely not the pained croak of incredulity that he had feared it might be. Remembering it now, he wondered if his tone had not been rude, contemptuous even, brazen as a gaming piece tossed onto a buckskin playing cloth at the high point of a game when the contestant who has thrown it knows that he has already won enough throws to win the game. *Here. Take it as it falls! I have had all I need of you. How you fare in this game matters not to me! I win, no matter what you do!* He remembered staring raptor-eyed at her after placing that question, wanting her to grow red-faced and teary-eyed with jealousy, wanting her to sob out a reminder that he had broken his vow to take no other woman as long as either of them drew breath. It was a vow that should have meant everything to her, as it did to him . . . even though he had broken it.

But Hasu'u had not become teary-eyed. Her face had not reddened. She had raised high her beautiful head and replied without hesitation. "It is acceptable."

Tôrnârssuk flinched as he walked on, thinking, *Of course it is acceptable! She does not care with whom I lie. She has hidden well until now her lack of respect for me. But after all, is it not said that not even a True Man can know the heart of a woman? Perhaps she only agreed to walk with me as my woman out of a need to replace her own dead infant with my son, for surely even when we were first together I was not the man I was when in my youth.*

His heart hardened. Not toward her. Toward himself. Hasu'u was showing fatigue as she walked ahead of him, her posture straining for a dignity of bearing that had always come naturally and without effort to her before. The difficulties of the trail were beginning to tell on her; it was proving to be a long and bitter way to the Great River of the North. How he wished he could shorten the distance for her! How he wished he could put a song in her heart again! How he—

"Sing will I," Mowea'qua eagerly volunteered.

"It is Hasu'u's songs that bring heart to the people," he told her.

"Learning her songs am I." Smiling, Mowea'qua began to sing as best she could out of her damaged throat until he reached out and laid a hand on her shoulder.

"Be silent, girl. You have not the voice for it."

▼▼▼▼▼

The day wearied on.

Ne'gauni, in a dark and sullen mood, saw the girl fall back to stand momentarily aside as she bent to retie the lacings of her moccasins. He could hear her humming. One of Hasu'u's songs. The sound raked his senses. Lengthening his pace until he was standing next to her, he stood over her, unable to keep himself from saying angrily, "You will not sing her songs. They are *her* songs. A gift to the band only when she chooses to share them. You are Chosen *Sister* of Raven, not Tôrnârssuk's woman. He is Hasu'u's man, not yours. Do not forget that. When we reach the great river he will find a new man for you. And then she will be happy again and sing for us all, rejoicing in the fact that we are finally rid of you."

Mowea'qua, her laces secured, straightened and stared unblinkingly at Ne'gauni, deeply hurt by his words, and yet angry, too, so angry that, wanting to hurt him back, she vented wishful thinking as though it were a fact she might boast of. "It is Hasu'u he will trade at the great river! Not Mowea'qua, say I. Never!"

He was stunned. "He would not do that."

She turned up her nose. "No? See we will. At the great river!"

He stood glaring after her as she stalked back to the

headman's side, head high, back straight as a lance. Like a raider, he thought, going off to battle an enemy.

"You need not look at her when you have us to please you, Dreamer," purred Chi'co'pee, coming up behind him.

He stiffened, his face aflame, as he realized that all three of the unmarried daughters of Chief Ogeh'ma and Segub'un had come upon him unannounced and uninvited. "Go away!" he shouted at Hasu'u's sisters. "Find another man! Can you not see that I do not want you . . . or her . . . or any woman save . . . Ah, what use is it! Go away, I say! I cannot bear to look at you!"

▼▼▼▼▼

It was nearly dusk when the body of the woman was found by Goh'beet's daughters as they ambled along at their mother's side, playing kick-the-cone with a blackened little remnant of what had once been a living forest. The corpse was badly charred, barely recognizable as human, and they might have passed it by, taking it for the remains of a deer, had it not been for a bit of blue quillwork washed clean of the ashes that were all that remained of her dress.

Ne'gauni stared, silent, troubled, remembering. "This I have seen," he said. "In the Darkness . . . this woman . . . this burned woman in a blue-quilled dress."

No one spoke.

A wind was moving through the blackened wood, creaking in the skeletons of the trees, cold, a winter wind in summer, moving across the burned land, raising its scent, the scent of Death.

"Maybe the world *has* died," sighed Goh'beet.

"Maybe we are all that is left alive in it," said Tsi'le'ni.

"Maybe we are not alive at all?" suggested Suda'li.

It was old Ko'ram, wheezing beneath the weight of his

pack, who broke the terrible solemnity of the moment. "Let this burned land be a lesson to all," he warned as he jabbed his rattle skyward. "We must remember this moment! We must draw courage from it, not fear, not doubt! Our fate could have been that of this poor burned woman had our headman not led us wisely and our shaman not seen her in his dreams and warned us of the dangers of the way ahead. All know this! And so now, as we continue forth together toward the Gathering of Many Tribes on the shores of the Great River of the North, all must remember. All must rejoice! All must be glad!"

▼▼▼▼▼

Glad?

Ne'gauni did not understand how any of them could be glad.

He stood his ground, close to old Ko'ram, watching the band file by.

They spoke words of parting to the woman in the blue-quilled dress. Quiet, respectful words, words of sympathy and hope that her family lived on somewhere far from the burned land and that her death had not been painful and that her spirit was now reunited with the Ancient Ones in the world beyond this world.

Ne'gauni shifted restlessly on his crutches.

Ko'ram took no notice as, with a sudden snort of annoyance, he extended a foot to trip his two grandsons as they walked by so engrossed in shoving and poking at one another that they half knocked him over.

The twins went sprawling.

Old Ko'ram harrumphed with satisfaction, then, after swaying a little on his feet, moved to totter over them like an old hawk poised to strike at them with beak and talons. "The spirits of the Ancient Ones are watching you!" Shaking his rattle ferociously over them, he gave each boy a kick that set his ankle janglers madly clicking. "To walk by Wise Man and Shaman Indeed without so much as a word of respect! To argue and make sport of one another on such a day as this! What will our headman think of you? Have you no respect for the dead woman in the forest, or for your elders? No. I think you do not. I saw you taunting Goh'beet's girls this morning. And I saw you put burrs under Musquash's pack straps. And he a shaman's son, and now a boy proven unafraid in battle against bigger monsters than the two of you. Is this behavior respectful of the ways of others? Is it mindful of your place within the band?"

"Musquash is not respectful!" protested Na'v. "He ran off after the wolf girl on the night of the Spirit Moon. He will not share the tent of Kinap. And now he sleeps where he will at night, alone."

"He is disobedient!" added Na'v.

"He is the son of a great and feared shaman. The band can make allowances for his occasional lapses of good sense. What is your excuse?"

"We are Wise Man's grandsons!" the boys cheeked out in unison.

The old man fixed them with shrewd eyes. "Then maybe I should not brain you . . . yet. What do you think, Dreamer?"

"You would not do that . . . would you?"

"Yes! And why should I not do that? I am Wise Man. I am Grandfather. It is my right to brain them. Tôrnârssuk would allow me this privilege. And maybe Kinap would be grateful to have such noisy and disrespectful boys gone from the tent that he now shares with their mother. Unless . . . mmm . . . unless, of course, they were to show respect to their Wise Man and Grandfather by taking up this elder's pack frame and carrying it as our headman so wisely had them do when we were traveling together to the overlook!"

"But, Grandfather—"

"But, Grandfather, we—"

"Wise Man will hear no buts from such as you! And wise boys who do not wish to be brained and burned and left behind with the dead will obey their elders when they walk within the fall of the shadow of White Bear. You have heard the stories of how our headman led the others on the raid. Merciless! That is what Tôrnârssuk is to his enemies and to those who challenge his will or are disrespectful to the elders of his band. So get up! Here. Take my hand. Show some respect to Wise Man and perhaps he will not brain you after all. Yes. Now take this elder's burden. Good! Ah, that is a relief to these old bones. Now go, both of you. Walk with your mother awhile and do not trouble me—or Musquash or Goh'beet's daughters—again."

"You are hard on them," observed Ne'gauni, leaning on his crutches and staring after the flustered twosome as they staggered off with the old man's pack in search of sympathy from Suda'li.

"Someone must be hard on them," grumbled Ko'ram, "lest they grow into savages like Moraq and—"

"Do not speak his name," said Ne'gauni sharply, his mood inexplicably uneasy. "What kind of Wise Man are you? We need heartening in this burned and blackened land of dead women and mammoths and obnoxious little boys, not—"

"Ah!" Ko'ram wilted down onto the ground along with the exclamation, clucking his tongue in self-admonition as he wrapped his arms around his puny knees and, hugging his rattle, rocked himself like a miserable and repentant child. "I am an old man. I did not think. I . . . I . . . did not remember."

"Then think now and stop stammering like Musquash

when he is caught at one of his exaggerations!" Ne'gauni fairly shouted the words as anger flashed in his eyes. "You are always telling me what to say and what to do! Get up! Shake your rattle! Jangle your ankle clappers! Cut some wind! It may well be what you do best. And as we join the others, raise your old croak of a voice in song! A Wise Man's song! A song to lift the spirits of this band! A song to give us back the heart to leave this cursed burned land behind and reach the great river!"

The old man made no effort to suppress a shudder that caused an audible clacking, not only of his now stationary rattle and ankle janglers but of what was left to him of his teeth. "So much to teach you . . ."

"What?"

"I tell you, Shaman Indeed, maybe you were right. Maybe we should not go north. Maybe . . ."

"What?"

"Ah, Ne'gauni, for many a moon we have traveled together with these Northerners in peace, but the signs . . . the omens . . . Ah, it is said that he is a cannibal, you know, our White Bear, our Raven, Great Ghost Cannibal, yes, Winter Chief of the manitous."

"He has killed the only manitous in this forest. Back there under the Spirit Moon."

"No . . . one of them is with us still!"

"So you say. Maybe you are right. I do not know."

"It is good!"

"What is good? That I do not know whether Mowea'qua is a manitou or not?"

"That I have been able to be Teacher for a while. Ah . . . it has been so good to be Teacher . . . to see you learn . . . to . . . Ah, Ne'gauni, you must seek another."

"Another what?"

"There is so much you have yet to learn . . . so much . . .
Would you take my rattle for a moment and shake it over me,
Dreamer? My spirit seems to be leaving me . . ."

"Ko'ram?"

No answer.

He was gone.

▼▼▼▼

"We will mourn," said Tôrnârssuk grimly. "Five days."

"It is right to do so according to the customs of his
people," agreed Kinap as the Dawnlanders nodded solemnly
and began to go about looking for whatever suitable burned
wood they could find with which to raise a bier for Ko'ram.
To a man, the Northerners shifted restlessly and turned away.

Ne'gauni stood in shock.

Old Ko'ram had died so quickly, so unexpectedly, so quietly, that, standing there with the old man's rattle in his
hand, he had no chance to even try to call his spirit back. It
had left his body, leaving no trace of flatulence as might have
been expected, just a soft extended exhalation of breath that
was not summoned back into the little heap of buckskin-clad
skin and bones that sat with folded knees upon the trail, eyes
opened wide and staring off, an expression of surprise upon
his face.

"You will say the words," said Kinap.

Ne'gauni looked up at the cowled giant. "Words?"

"Shaman words."

"I . . . I do not know what to say."

"The spirits will speak in you."

"Will they, Kinap?"

"If you are Shaman, you will know what to say."

▼▼▼▼

It was dark by the time they raised a scaffold for the old Wise Man and wrapped him in his sleeping robe and piled all his belongings around him.

Gifts were brought. Small, private, thoughtful little offerings from each individual who had walked with him upon the long trail out of the forest toward the Great River of the North, and packets of food to keep him from going hungry on his spirit journey to the world beyond this world.

"Will he need a dog to drag his burdens in the land of the sky spirits?" asked Ningao, genuinely concerned and uncertain of the Dawnland protocol as he made a good attempt not to sound as though he hoped for a negative answer.

"It is not the Dawnland way," replied Chief Ogeh'ma. "But we thank you, Northerner. In the way of the Wise Man that he was, he will find willing spirits to help him make his way in the world beyond this world."

"His son, the father of my boys, will be waiting for him," Suda'li reminded them. "They will embrace. They will rejoice to see one another again. Our Wise Man will not carry his burdens alone in the country of the sky spirits."

Ne'gauni reached up to lay the rattle on the bier. "He will need this." He smiled as a bittersweet memory put words on his tongue, words that old Ko'ram had spoken to him at the stream on the far side of the falls and overlook, when he had been much younger, it seemed. "I return this to you, Teacher. 'A Wise Man must make a proper noise when he calls upon the spirits!' "

"He has his deer-hoof ankle janglers to win their attention," said Tôrnârssuk. "The rattle is yours. It was his dying gift to you. A sign to you of his faith that you are all that he hoped. You must take it . . . Shaman."

▼▼▼▼▼

And so the songs of mourning were made.

And so the dances of mourning were danced.

Loud songs. Joyous and reverent dances. For as the band gathered around the bier, it was not so much to lament a man's passing as to celebrate a life. Ko'ram's life had been long and rich, and although he had outlived his only son, he had left two grandsons behind him in the world, and he had accomplished one rare and wonderful thing: He had become Teacher. And as Teacher, he had made a shaman.

And so Ne'gauni stood and shook his rattle at the sky and thanked the old man for the gift of his knowledge and of the noisemaker. From some deep and silent place within himself, out of the Darkness, born as Light upon his tongue it seemed, a song came, and words. He knew not what he said or if indeed he spoke at all. And after the stars had moved across the firmament four times, he collapsed, exhausted, onto his bed furs and fell fast asleep.

▼▼▼▼▼

"You are truly Shaman now, Ne'gauni."

He opened his eyes. Musquash was squatting beside him. Behind him the stars were still shining, each in a different position from when he had seen it last. Soon would come the dawn.

The boy shivered. "I am glad it is not to be me," he said.

"So you said once before."

"Under the Spirit Moon . . . a long time ago."

"Yes."

"You really saw her before, Ne'gauni? The burned-up woman? In your dreams?"

Now it was Ne'gauni who shivered. "I saw her. Not in dreams, I think, but in the Darkness, a woman with blue quills on her dress. She had no face. I thought at first I had seen

Hasu'u. And then Mowea'qua. But I think now that she was a warning for them." Again he shivered, recalling the vision, and the one that had followed it, of himself fleeing across a flaming world of endless trees, with the wind driving him on, a furious wind, mating with Fire, feeding the flames. Somewhere ahead a man ran before him, looking back over his shoulder as he ran, no longer faceless as in the primary vision, but sharp-eyed and heavy-jawed and meaty, a Northerner's face, a laughing stranger disappearing into the Darkness beyond the flames as, somewhere far ahead, a mammoth trumpeted, its voice the sound of thunder, its footsteps shaking the earth.

"Ne'gauni . . . ?"

Musquash's voice seemed so far away. He could not answer. He saw himself fall, rise, stagger against the wind as all around him the forest burned and the wind laughed and a woman screamed and animals and people fled ahead of the flames only to be consumed as, burning, he fell again and plummeted alone into the Darkness.

"Ne'gauni!"

He shook his head. The vision was gone. The boy's face was very close to his, worried, intent, like a pale round moon hanging in thin air against the stars.

"You were in the shaman place . . . inside your head . . . or maybe far away?" asked the boy. "Are you back?"

"I am back."

"What did you see?"

"What has been. What will be. I do not know."

"But the burned-up woman was in your dream again?"

"Yes." Sadness touched him, a sense of loneliness and grief, not for himself but for her, the faceless woman in the blue-quilled dress. "Why was there no warning for her, no one to see to her safety? Or did she burn for us . . . so we would know of the danger even as it consumed her? I do not understand. Was her life worth so much less than any of ours?"

Musquash sighed and settled back on his haunches, then took something from around his neck and solemnly reached up to hand it to Ne'gauni. "Maybe this should be for you. Maybe it will tell you. It does not speak to me."

Ne'gauni held out his palm and looked at what the boy placed in the hollow of his hand. It was a small thing. A tiny amulet strung on a simple cord of braided sinew. A white pebble worn smooth by constant handling. He felt a sudden rush of recognition. "The sacred stone of your father and his father's father for untold generations before him. You cannot give this to me, Musquash."

"All true shamans have them. It will speak to you. It will speak of hope and of all good things. My mother told me so."

"Then keep it, boy, and cherish your memories of her and of her promises. Would that I had some small talisman like this from my own mother."

"Did she never give you anything to keep?"

"My life, and the wish that I come back to her one day from my adventures as a trader with gifts for her and tales to make my people sing with pride."

"You will do that," said the boy.

"No. It would not make her or any of them sing with pride to see a scar-faced, one-legged cripple return to them from the northern forest. And they would not be pleased to know that the fine copper-headed lance that was a gift to me from her father, Chief Sebec of the Copper People, was stolen. An amulet would have been better. A small thing. Less coveted. Easier to keep."

"But you would come to them as Shaman, Ne'gauni! And

wearing the sacred stone of the Ancient Ones. Surely that would make them sing with pride."

"Perhaps. I do not know. I have my own pride. I would not want them to see me as I am now. And I will not wear your amulet, boy. It is for you to keep."

"But I am not a shaman, Ne'gauni. The sacred stone will never speak to me."

"It will if you are worthy of it. If you do not force it. If you do not dishonor it, or yourself."

The words set a storm of emotion loose within the boy. He was suddenly as an aspen, quaking. "But I *have* dishonored it, Ne'gauni! And myself. I have! I have killed Giant Beaver! He was the last of his kind. I have tipped the sacred Circle of Life Ending and Life Beginning! And now we are all falling out, all of us, all the dirty little children in the Old Tribe village and the bad hairy men and women, and the poor burned-up blue-quilled woman, and the mammoths in the forest, and now old Ko'ram, too! It is my fault, Ne'gauni, all of it my fault! And now Mowea'qua hates me. She will not ever be my woman. Unless I find the great white mammoth! Then she would know that I am worthy, a better man than any man. I know he is there, Ne'gauni. I did see him! I did!"

"In the Valley of the Spirit Moon."

"Yes! But I still see him in my dreams, Ne'gauni. So big! So white! Watching me as he did on that night in the thunderstorm. Maybe it is a sign? Maybe he is following us. Watching us even now. If I could find him again and hunt him and bring his meat to the band, everything would be all right again. It would, Ne'gauni, I know it would! And then Mowea'qua could call me Bog Rat and Biting Fly and Puffball again, or whatever she wanted. I would not mind!"

Ne'gauni found himself reaching out, pulling the sobbing

boy close, holding him like a brother, like a son, as he gently placed the amulet back around his slender neck. "Keep the stone, boy. The forces of Creation have given it to you, not to me. Be worthy of it and it will speak to you when the time is right. Keep asking. You will find the mammoth."

"Do you think so, Ne'gauni? Do you really think so?"

"If it is there, if it is following . . . if you want it badly enough . . . if you keep asking on the stone . . . perhaps." He did not tell the boy what was truly in his heart. That the stone was worthless. Tôrnârssuk wore one. And look where its powers were leading him.

Chapter Five

▼▼▼▼▼▼▼

The burned land lay behind them.

Before noon on the fifth day after mourning for old Ko'ram, Tôrnârssuk led his followers into the forest once again. It was beautiful to them now, and not even the Northerners among them complained of not being able to see the sky.

They went on steadily, quietly, into low hills fragrant with evergreens until Chief Ogeh'ma spoke out and asked them all to stop as he paused, raised his head, and squinted his deeply lidded eyes, breathing in with an expression on his face akin to that of a starving man scenting out a roasting haunch of his favorite meat. "Do you smell it?"

"Smell what, my father?" asked Chi'co'pee, walking at his side with her sisters and mother again. "Rain?"

His lined face split with a grin. "Rain? Yes! It could be rain. The air grows moist. My scars speak of thunderclouds in the making maybe. And the wind has for some time now been gusting as though trying to decide which way to blow. But my nose tells me something else. There is water up ahead. Big water. Moving water. Fresh water. By all the powers in this world and the world beyond, I think that this man may yet have hope of sinking his teeth into the meat of white whales!"

▼▼▼▼▼

They went on.

Expectant now.

Aware of the texture of the air and of every sound and scent that came to them as they moved through the trees until, cresting a rise, they saw a break in the forest up ahead. Even before they stepped out of the woods and set their eyes upon what they had so long yearned to see, they could feel its power.

The Great River of the North lay ahead and far below, a vast enormity of flowing water, gray under a brooding and overcast sky, a river so wide that in places they could barely make out the far and wooded highlands on the opposite shore.

Even those who had seen it before exhaled in wonder at its immensity and shivered a little in response to its beauty as Tôrnârssuk raised his arms in salutation to the river and voiced a variant of the ancient invocation to the dawn, to new beginnings:

"The Great River awaits us!
Who has heard the Voice of this River?
Who has heard the Voice of Dawn?
Stars have heard.
And Sun and Moon.
And Great One, rising from the Deep.
Now I, too, have heard.
The Way is made ready before me!
I stretch forth my hands.
I go toward the Dawn!

I go toward the River!
I am not afraid."

No one spoke.

Then, one by one, following the lead of their headman, the men, women, and even the littlest children raised their arms and echoed their headman's greeting to the living force of the great river.

It was Mowea'qua who broke the spell of the moment.

"Look!" she cried, pointing to where a huge dark form was leaping out of the river, hurling itself into the sky, arcing high as it blew a waterfall upward out of its head, then dove into the deeps with the flukes of its enormous tail raised high for a moment before they hit the water with a resounding slap that sent white spray flying as the great body disappeared into the deeps. "Never so large a fish have I seen! How big must it be if it can be seen jumping from so far away, ask I?"

"That is no fish, girl!" exclaimed Ogeh'ma as he and every other man and woman who had been to the river before broke into laughter. "That, Mowea'qua, was a whale!"

▼▼▼▼

"Where is the Great Gathering?" asked N'av.

"When will we see all the many people and get good things for ourselves in trade?" Ka'wo'ni piped up.

Suda'li was beaming at her boys. "Soon!" she said. "Soon!"

"The place of the Great Gathering is downriver . . . around that sweep of shore over there," said Tôrnârssuk. "Before we go there, we must make ourselves ready."

"For what?" asked the twins in unison.

"To greet old friends."

▼▼▼▼

Ne'gauni watched them.

They were intent, laying out their belongings, painting their faces, putting on ear and nose rings and lip plugs, donning their finest clothes and necklaces and anklets and bracelets of shells and feathers and beads of bone. It seemed that even the dogs and drag frames and cradleboards were to be adorned with shells, feathers, and charms of all kinds.

Ne'gauni stood watching. He saw Kinap arguing with Suda'li, rumbling low, moving the woman forcibly aside as he knelt to rummage in a carrying pack, pulled out some finery apparently belonging to the twins, who were already dressed, then rose and stomped angrily to where Musquash was hunkering nearby in his ill-fitting hand-me-downs.

"You will wear these," commanded the giant.

"I want nothing from you," said the boy.

"You will wear these," said the giant again, dropping the soft garments, fringed moccasins, and a finely twisted cape of rabbit skins at Musquash's feet. "Better on your back and feet than wrapped up uselessly in a traveling pack. They are yours now. Na'v and Ka'wo'ni have more than they can use."

"I do not want anything of theirs."

"Nor do they or their mother wish you to have anything of theirs, but I will not stand by in silence and see any member of this band, least of all one whom I once named Son, disgrace our headman when we come into the Great Gathering today."

The boy looked up at the giant, pinch-faced. "You are not my father. Go away. I do not have to do what you say."

Kinap stood over Musquash, huge and dark in his black bearskins, rumbling like a thunderstorm. "Wear the clothes or leave the clothes, then. If you dishonor yourself and the band again, boy, it will be on your own head."

Ne'gauni said nothing; he was close enough to have

overheard their words but not to have been drawn into the conservation until, with a start, he saw that the giant was coming toward him.

"For you," said Kinap as he slung a bow and quiver of arrows from around his shoulder and, with them, an otter-skin carrying case. "I have been refitting the bow and its carrying case for you. It and the arrows will replace that which you have lost because of my foolish children."

Ne'gauni felt a stab of surprise. He did not know what to say. He and the giant had rarely spoken since the night of the Spirit Moon, and ever since the raid he could barely bring himself to look at the man.

"Go ahead. Take it!" insisted Kinap. "Shaman you may well be, Ne'gauni, but you are still a man, and a man must have a weapon he can use with pride so that other men may see his skill and yield him their respect."

"I . . . I cannot."

"What? Are you like the boy, then? Wanting nothing from me? Because of how it is between me and Mowea'qua? Yah! What is done is done, Ne'gauni! So take the bow from one whom you once considered a friend. Do not dishonor the spirits of the wood and bone that have been bent to serve your hand, for now that I have altered this bow, it no longer will yield to mine. And see if you can make the boy put on the clothes I have brought him. And then look to yourself, Ne'gauni, and for the honor of this band remember your new rank and responsibilities! Even Mowea'qua has remembered how to comb her hair!"

Ne'gauni stood with the bow and quiver in one hand, watching the giant plod off, still not knowing what to say. Even the most cursory look at the bow revealed it to be a rare and wonderful thing, much finer even than the beautiful ash bow Musquash had stolen and been forced to leave behind in the Old Tribe village. The giant must have been reworking it for some time, for it could have been no easy thing to reshape a composite bow made in the style of Kinap's Grassland People, a creation of layers of glue-laminated wood and bison horn strengthened with sinew wrapping. Deceptively light and slender, it would propel his arrows with the strength and speed not of a scar-faced, one-legged cripple but of the giant who had refashioned it for him. He peered into the quiver and caught his breath in wonder at the exquisitely fletched stone-headed arrows couched within. Truly this bow was fit for the finest hunter, for the headman himself, for Shaman Indeed, He Walks Ahead in Dreams to Foresee Danger for the People. But, looking down at his clothes, he knew that Kinap was right about his appearance. He must look disreputable in his old trail-worn garments, but he had no better clothes, and he surely possessed no shaman's regalia apart from old Ko'ram's rattle. He raised it, eyed it thoughtfully; it looked about as impressive as he felt.

"Get dressed, Dreamer! Paint your face! Feather your hair! We must honor the river and the Great Gathering with our best appearance this day! How else will others be impressed and agree to trade and hunt with us?"

Ne'gauni frowned at the headman's command. Tôrnârssuk was coming toward him, moving aggressively past Musquash without glancing at the boy. Carrying a tawny brown bearskin over one arm, he was wearing his finest sealskins and the white bearskin cloak. His raven raiding mask was set high above his brow, as a headdress; worn this way, it would be a sign to those at the Great Gathering that, despite a reputation that he knew walked ahead of him, he came before them as a man of peace this day, not a raider. He looked big. Bold. Powerful. Dangerous. And angry. Ne'gauni took an unintended step back.

"What is this? You recoil like a frightened girl. Are you not Shaman of this band, Dreamer?"

Ne'gauni winced. There was a sharp, unexpected edge to Tôrnârssuk's voice, an irritable impatience, a weariness visible around the man's eyes, and a bitter, downward twist to the set of his mouth.

"Well? Are you Shaman or not?"

Ne'gauni steadied himself against the unexpected storm of the man's impatience. "The spirits seem to have willed it."

"And so! But they do not seem to have willed you into a decent hunting shirt or leggings, or even a robe worthy of your rank. You cannot go to the river with my band, not looking like this!"

"I have nothing better, Tôrnârssuk."

"You do now. Hasu'u has asked me to bring this to you. The brown bearskin is one of my own. You will find other useful things wrapped within it. She has been going about the band, asking for and taking contributions for you. There is something from everyone here. It is fitting. You have spoken well for us along the trail."

Ne'gauni was staggered, not only by the generosity of his fellow travelers but by the weight of the gift as it was laid across his outstretched forearms, balanced on his crutches.

Tôrnârssuk nodded. "Dress yourself, then. Use the red ocher in the paint sack for your face. There is bear fat in a seal-gut packet, and a shell and stone with which to mix the colorant. It will be a sign to all of your recent rebirth into your new life as Dreamer. Make whatever pattern pleases you, but do it quickly. I will have my followers safe at the river before dark."

Safe.

Later Ne'gauni would remember that Tôrnârssuk had used the word. The word he never used. The word he mocked. The one word upon which they had, perhaps, always been in agreement.

No man is ever safe. There is always Danger. Always Enemies.

But now, before he could gather in his thoughts, Ne'gauni deemed it necessary to lower his head, accepting the headman's gift and consenting to his wishes regarding it. When he raised his head again, he was distracted by the sight of Hasu'u standing off a ways with Tiguak in her arms.

How beautiful she was! Dressed this day not in her simple traveling clothes, and not as he had first seen her so long ago in the traditional Dawnland woman's dress of feathered skirt and necklaces of shells and brightly colored bird beaks and feathers, but as a Northern woman, a headman's wife, in the finest seal and caribou skins, with her face tattooed in the way of the women of her husband's band.

Their eyes met. Held. Did she smile at him? It seemed so. Such a sad smile! As though, having gathered in the gifts that marked his new life as a shaman, she was saying good-bye to the callow youth she had first known when she had come to his father's village as his brother's bride, and to the young man she had been reunited with along the trail to the Great River of the North. And now, with a sudden catch in his throat, he saw that she was holding the baby as though certain that she would soon lose him forever, and he realized that there was another reason for her sad smile, another reason for her to say good-bye.

Anger flamed in him.

Tôrnârssuk had already turned and begun to walk away.

"Wait," Ne'gauni called him back.

The headman turned, his eyes questioning.

"You cannot do it, Tôrnârssuk!"

"Do what?"

Ne'gauni moved to him, lowered his voice; he did not want the one who owned his heart to hear. "You cannot trade Hasu'u away. For the sake of her pride, if you care for her at all, you cannot trade her out of the band."

"Why would I do that? Have you seen something in your Dreamer's head that I should know about? Have I not warned you about withholding your dreams from me? Why would I trade my wife? Who would feed my son? Goh'beet? Some milk woman borrowed out of a band I do not know? What kind of vision is this, Dreamer?"

"No vision! No dream!"

"Then leave me to lead the band as I must lead it now. Change into your new garments. Paint your face. And trouble me no more this day unless you would speak to me as Shaman!"

Ne'gauni stood, shaken, confused. What had just happened? Mowea'qua had told him that Tôrnârssuk intended to trade Hasu'u. For all her wild, reckless, and unpredictable ways, as far as he knew Mowea'qua had never lied to him. Why, then, would the headman pretend not to know what he was talking about just now? He had never known Tôrnârssuk to lie. Why would he do so now? Unless, perhaps, he did not want Hasu'u to know until the very last moment that he intended to give her away? Why would he do this? Hasu'u was a Dawnland woman. A hunt chief's daughter. Surely, although Tôrnârssuk was a man of the Barrenlands and not born to the ways of the People of the Forest and the coast, he must know that Hasu'u would never utter a word to protest any decision he might make regarding her, no matter how deeply she might be hurt by that decision. To do so would be to dishonor him and herself.

Ne'gauni heaved an exhalation of pure frustration. He was Shaman Indeed. Everyone said so. And after all that had happened along the trail, even he believed it now. Why, then, did he stand here holding his new shaman gifts with his mind swimming around like a fish in a weir pool, befuddled? If he truly was Shaman and worthy of these gifts, he should be able to look a man or woman in the eyes and see into their spirit and know the way of their thoughts. He should understand!

Ahead, under the lowering sky, Tôrnârssuk had reached the place where Hasu'u was standing, waiting for him with Tiguak hefted on one hip. Ne'gauni stiffened. The headman was reaching out to his woman, or to the baby, he could not be sure, for in that moment Mowea'qua rose from where she had been sitting on her pack frame, combing her hair.

He caught his breath.

Never would he have imagined it possible. Musquash was wrong. The girl was not beautiful. She was more than that. She was captivating, spectacular, magnificent. In body paint and finery generously given by the Dawnland women, with her breasts bared in the style of the coast, she stood tall and opulent and as desirable as she had appeared on the night of the Spirit Moon. And now, as Ne'gauni found himself gawking, he saw her move to stand between Tôrnârssuk and Hasu'u. As Hasu'u lowered her head, turned, and walked slowly away with the baby, Mowea'qua looked toward Ne'gauni and smiled.

He did not smile back.

Nor did Musquash, who had come to stand at his side.

"Look," said the little boy. "Tôrnârssuk has marked her

face. There, around her eyes and across her brow, he has used needles and ashes to make the black pattern of his tribe. She is truly his new woman now. An always-and-forever woman. Do you see?"

"Yes, I see," said Ne'gauni as he turned away, and, remembering what he had seen in the dark of the moon and believing himself to be Shaman Indeed, had no idea that he did not see at all.

Chapter Six

▼▼▼▼▼▼▼

W e will go to the river!"

Tôrnârssuk's declaration roused a cheer from the assembled band.

As the headman stood before them, his heart swelled with pride. Not in himself for having brought them this far. His pride was in them for having managed to survive the journey despite him. If there was a weakness to be found in any of them, he thought, it lay in their mistaken loyalty to him. But soon he would make it right for them. Now, as they met his gaze with eager, expectant faces, he loved them all, and even had they not been in their finest raiment, he would have found them glorious.

"Let the flute play and the drum sound and our voices rise in song as our shaman shakes his rattle at the sky so that all at the Great Gathering may know that we come to them in friendship, without guile, to trade and to hunt on the shore of the Great River of the North!"

And the voices went up as one.

Although Ne'gauni's was tinged with anger.

And Hasu'u's had lost the lightness that had once made others compare it to that of a songbird in joyous flight.

Her sisters had no trouble sounding out like happy birds shrilling their excitement, for although the three unmarried daughters of Chief Ogeh'ma and Segub'un had been spurned by Ne'gauni, at the urging of their mother and sister and the other women of the band they had dressed and painted themselves in hope of catching the eyes of more appreciative men at the Great Gathering.

"You are beautiful, my dear ones," Hasu'u said, falling back to smile assurance.

"As are you, sister," replied Nee'nah. "We will all find good men."

"All? As though I would want another. Even now." Her face tightened. "I am content with Tôrnârssuk . . . and will be more so when Mowea'qua is traded away. Does she not look like a woman of the People in all the fine things I have managed to put together for her? The blue jay feathers I have been collecting along the trail, and the marten skin, and the little freshwater shells that—"

"Ah, Hasu'u!" Nee'nah interrupted. "Has he not told you? Have you not seen the way he has marked her?"

"To make her more acceptable to others . . . so her eyes will not be so—"

"Did he tell you this?"

"No, Ane'pemin'an. He has no need to tell me. He has vowed a reward to those who were with him on the raid into the Old Tribe Village. All know this. Besides, you are all three Dawnland women and must know that I, as a hunt chief's daughter and a headman's woman, would not ask my man the way of his mind in such a thing."

"But he has been one with her, Hasu'u!"

"To gentle her out of her fear of mating."

The three younger women exchanged looks of amazement.

"He will keep her, Hasu'u," revealed Nee'nah.

"We heard her tell Ne'gauni," explained Ane'pemin'an.

"It is you who will be traded at the Great Gathering so that he may share the profits to reward his fellow raiders as he has promised," added Chi'co'pee. "He will not break his vow to them."

Hasu'u was finding it difficult to breathe. "And Tiguak?"

"Maybe he will let you keep him," said Nee'nah, offering what she intended as a warming ray of hope.

Hasu'u was not warmed. "No," she said. "He would never give up one whom he truly loves. He will never part with his son."

▼▼▼▼▼

Walking beside Tôrnârssuk at the head of the band, Mowea'qua looked up at the headman, worrying more than a little. "Trade me away not will you now? Now that you have marked me?"

He eyed her thoughtfully. Of all the things he could curse himself for, gentling of the wild wolf within her Old Tribe spirit was no longer one of them. She would make some man an admirable mate; but he would not worry her with this now, and so he told her the one truth that he knew would be acceptable to her, at least for now. "Never would I barter you away to a man to whom you do not wish to go, Mowea'qua."

"Your woman am I. Always and forever. Almost four hand-counts old is Hasu'u. Four! Admitted so to me did she. Mmph! Not yet even three hand-counts old am I. Helpful to her can I be when she soon comes to dodder and complain of aching bones. If keep such an old woman as her you still want to do."

Tôrnârssuk did not look at her. How young she truly was, he thought, and, in the way of the young, so blithely and

mercilessly aware of no one's needs or desires but her own.
"We will see, Mowea'qua, we will see," he said evasively.
"Walk with the women now. I will lead the men ahead. We
are almost to the overview."

"Mmph!"

He raised a brow at the impudent sound she made, but
she obeyed and fell back as he walked ahead, gesturing his
fellow hunters forward to look down on the teeming encampment on the shores of the great river.

He stood in silence. Thunderclouds were massing on the
horizon. Ogeh'ma had been right about the rain. The old,
terrible sense of sadness and inadequacy overwhelmed him
again. Everything was exactly as he had hoped . . . and
feared.

The Great Gathering was larger than anything he had
imagined, but he was too late! The whales had already come
into the river and had been butchered all along the shore.
His people had followed him all this way only to be rewarded
with the dregs of the long-anticipated kill.

At his side, Chief Ogeh'ma was nodding philosophically.
"It is still good. You have hunt brothers among the whale
hunters. They will be willing to share, yes? Maybe in exchange for one or more of my daughters? If they are only half
the man you are, my girls will be honored to join with them
in that good and sheltering camp."

Tôrnârssuk did not reply at once. His right hand had
moved upward to rest over the sacred stone. Its power had
abandoned him. He was sure of it now. How could it be otherwise? Too many had died under his leadership. He could not
allow this to go on. Now, as he gestured the band forward
once again, he knew what he must do. Chief Ogeh'ma had
told him.

"Your daughters will find good men among my hunt

brothers in that camp," he said to Ogeh'ma. As he fell into step with the wiry little Dawnland man, he thought of his old and trusted friend Avataut. Hasu'u had saved his life. Now Avataut would save hers. And his. It would be so good to see him! He would tell him that he had been right in his judgment to return to the river. Then he would give him the sacred stone of the Ancient Ones and tell him that he must be Headman now.

Chapter Seven

▼▼▼▼▼▼▼

He comes! White Bear comes!"

Avataut levered himself off E'ya and, naked save for his fetish necklaces, stumbled outside. Thunder was rumbling in the increasing cloud cover. Had he imagined the words that had ruined his coupling? No. There was Armik, still talking.

"Tôrnârssuk returns, Avataut!" The man was gray-faced, shaking as though he, and not Avataut, was standing naked in the cold wind. "With Kamak and Inaksak and Itiitoq and Arnaktark and . . . and with Dawnlanders, and a one-legged shaman and a giant walking before him pounding on a drum. Can you not hear the drum, Avataut? Tôrnârssuk returns! He is not dead!"

Avataut was stunned. He had been so preoccupied in his pounding of E'ya that he must have gone deaf to all but the intensity of his own need. The woman would not respond to him. No matter how hard he worked her, no matter how he mocked the weakness of the braggart who had so foolishly risked her in a wager that he could not have hoped to win, she lay like a corpse, taking, never giving, never really yielding. He shivered, infinitely annoyed. With her. With himself. He heard the drumming now, far away but coming closer, mixing with the intermittent sound of thunder. Someone was playing a flute. Others were singing. Still someone else was using a rattle to emphasize the high points of the song. He recognized the rhythm; it was the old Barrenlands salutation to the dawn, the song all Northerners sang to honor the spirits of the game and to intimidate potential enemies and impress old friends when entering new hunting grounds. He knew the song well. Tôrnârssuk had taught it to him.

Avataut felt suddenly sick, light-headed with dread, but he would not show it, not even for a moment, not to any man, least of all to Armik, who was now staring with wide-eyed incredulity at the fetish of the white bear that hung with all the others around his neck. "At what do you look with such interest?"

"At an amulet I have not seen you wear before. Did the shaman on the bluffs give you that? Or have you carved it for yourself? A speared and blinded image of a bear . . . a white bear." Armik was glowering and nodding in acceptance of an unwelcome insight. "So you *have* been afraid of his return!"

"Ahhh!" Avataut snarled the wordless epithet and swiped the air with the back of his hand as though he could slap away the other man's accusation. He should have left the amulet buried in the ground. By bringing it out into the light of day he must have released its power. "Ahhh!" Again he cursed, this time focusing his invective on the talisman and on the shaman who had made it. She *did* have the gift of magic! And so did her cursed amulet! He had stabbed the thing through the heart with a sliver from his own lance and still he had not killed it. He had blinded it. He had buried it and ground it beneath his heel as he consigned it to what he had thought would be eternal darkness inside the dune. And still the one in whose image it had been made was coming for him. He was still alive! After all he had done, all he had risked, he was still alive! "Tôrnârssuk!" He launched the name from his mouth as though it were an ill-made lance that he would hurl and shatter forever against an invisible stone.

"Yes!" affirmed Armik, angry. "Tôrnârssuk! And you said he would not come!"

"*I* said?" Avataut skewered the man with indignation. "You were the one who kept goading me on about it!" His face twisted in a virulent fury, as did his voice as he raised it in a high, malicious, womanish parody of Armik's all-too-well-remembered words: " 'Ah, Avataut, Avataut, White Bear must be dead! Ah, Avataut, Avataut, surely he would have come to the river long before now were this not so. Ah, Avataut, Avataut, bad spirits must have eaten him! Ah, Avataut, Avataut, only you are worthy to take his place and speak for us in council! Ah, please, Avataut, please, please, please take his place! Take his campsite! Take up all the meat and hides that he has cached for his return! Take his reputation! Turn his name into something to be feared so that if he ever returns to this good camp, those who once knew and respected him will crush him as though he were a viper come among them from the southern forest! Take! Take! Take, Avataut, take! And when you have taken all the risk and won all the glory that was once his, do not forget to give me my fair share of it!' "

"I never said that . . . not that last part, anyway."

"You might as well have said it, for surely from the first day we arrived in this place you have been walking close, trying to breathe in the life force from my shadow, trying to take some small part of its power for yourself. As though you could!"

Armik's features congested. Anger, frustration, resentment: All three emotions burned in his eyes. He shrugged, miserable in the moment but not in the least contrite. "I have been a good hunt brother to you, Avataut. You have no cause to make sport of demeaning me. I could have chosen to stay with Tôrnârssuk's band. I did not. I chose to walk with you instead. I have named you Headman. I have shared with you the meat and hides that we took from his cache pit. So what do we do now that he is back?"

Avataut glared down from the high ground of his capacious campsite—Tôrnârssuk's campsite—and squinted nervously toward the beach, from which the sounds of drumbeat and singing were coming. There were so many tents and drying frames and fire circles set up now that he could not see to the shore. He was suddenly scowling. "Where is everyone?"

"The word has gone out, Avataut. You have been so preoccupied with boning the braggart's woman that you have failed to hear it. Some of the women and elderly have taken their children and are hiding in their tents. Everyone else has gone down to the beach to warn Tôrnârssuk away . . . or to kill him if he refuses to go. You should see your Nuutlaq, down there with Ulik, her toothache all forgotten, clamoring for a kill, telling your boy that Wolverine will soon come and may well make his son proud of him again this day by slaying his second white bear! No one will allow Tôrnârssuk to bring his man-and-woman-and-dog-eating bad spirits into this good camp, not after all the warnings you have given them."

"As it should be!" declared Avataut. Relief rippled through him, and pride, and even affection for Nuutlaq because of her ferocious esteem for him. His blood was running hot, heady, despite the cool wind. Then, distracted, he turned his gaze back to his hunt brother to see that Armik was taking measure of him in the manner of a long submissive dog that has just perceived weakness in an abusive master and is wondering if the time has come to leap to the attack and make things even, or end the relationship entirely, and in its own favor. "What is this?" Avataut demanded, taken aback, putting a growl to the query.

"Are you going to just stand here? I thought you would surely want to be there, Kwakwaje'sh, to make a fight of it, an end of it, because even if he is driven out, he will still be White Bear and there is always a chance that he will come back . . . in the night . . . in the dark when no one is expecting—"

"E'ya, bring me my hunt shirt and moccasins . . . now!" Avataut shouted over his shoulder at the woman in his tent, but his eyes never left Armik's face. He had been challenged and knew it, just as he knew now that Inau had been right. That which he feared had followed. And, strangely, he was glad. His hand rose to encircle the amulet at his neck; his fingers curled around it, pressed inward until the sharp tip of the little lance with which he had pierced the heart of the fetish penetrated his palm. His jaw tightened. The muscles bunched and rose to stress his skin. And still he pressed. Hard. Blood rose, oozed down his wrist. He stared at it. The pain was nothing to him. He released the amulet and raised his hand to suck the blood from his wound. His fear was gone.

Armik's head went high. "Listen!"

Avataut's eyes narrowed. The drumming had stopped. The flute and rattle were silent. No one was singing now. If thunder was rolling in the heavy, slate-gray underbelly of the clouds, he could no longer hear it above the shouting of angry, frightened people. His mind was working, fast, so fast that his thoughts were running out ahead of him even as E'ya brought his clothes and he snatched them from her, snarling her back and away. He jammed his feet into his moccasins and jerked his hunt shirt impatiently over his head. Knowing that when next he set eyes on Tôrnârssuk he must be wearing more than this, in four long strides he was at the largest of Nuutlaq's drying frames, pulling the uncured raw hide of the white bear free. He slung the heavy skin around his shoulders as he stalked back for his spear and bow and quiver, then, remembering that his two daggers were already secured inside his shirt, decided that a pair of lances would do. Snatching them up, he began to jog down toward the beach, hoping that Inau was watching from the bluffs.

He was Avataut! He was Headman of the Northerners! He was Wolverine, and well named, for not only had he proved himself fearless and powerful and predaceous enough to take for himself the den of the great White Bear of the North, but he would now show everyone at the Great Gathering that he could keep it. He had killed his own white bear! And now, in the skin of that bear, he would at last go forth to meet his fear on common ground and slay it!

▼▼▼▼▼

Tôrnârssuk did not understand.

He had been looking forward to a warm reception.

He had expected to see Avataut and Armik hurrying forward at the head of an advancing throng to welcome him back to the Great Gathering. He had expected all his former hunt brothers and their women and little ones to be with them, smiling, eager to greet the new members of his band, anxious to form a congenial escort to accompany him to the fine campsite and well-stocked cache pits he had set aside as his own so long ago. Here they would feast! Here they would relax! Here they would talk the good talk of men who have been long apart and relish a prolonged reunion. And later, when they had eaten all they could eat and exchanged all the stories they could tell and had grown comfortable in one another's company once again, before he withdrew to sleep content with his beloved Hasu'u in his arms and the dangers of the trail behind them at last, he would yield the sacred stone and his authority as headman to a better man. And let Avataut lie awake in the night, looking for Sila among the stars.

It had not happened.

Tôrnârssuk could not understand it.

Nothing was as he expected.

Walking into the Great Gathering was proving to be like walking into a thunderstorm.

He stopped amidst the angry crowd, looked for a familiar or friendly face, and, finding none, signaled his followers to stop. They obeyed. Instantly. They had journeyed long and far enough together to behave as one. There was not a man among them who did not anticipate and act immediately upon the half-circling swing of his head that communicated the need to form a protective circle around the women and children, as musk oxen did on the barrenlands when wolves were closing for a kill.

There was danger here.

They all knew it. Sensed it. Every nerve ending in Tôrnârssuk's body was screaming caution. And every face in the gathering crowd was assuring him that his concern was well placed. But why? What had put the expressions of open hostility on those faces, and so much anger and fear in their eyes?

He could not understand it!

At first, coming through the trees, he had nodded his head in friendly greeting to the few strangers he had passed in little family camps in the woods. He had been startled when they had run in panic at the sight of him. And then, coming farther, he had been puzzled when men he did not know stepped back into the shadows to stand glaring after him while women cowered and hid their little ones from his sight, and a man he had never seen before sobbed and accused him of summoning Wildfire to consume his woman and devour the spirit of his son. Shocked and offended, Tôrnârssuk had not deigned to comment on such a hideous accusation; with memories of the burned woman all too fresh in his mind and after all he had seen of the devastation fire could bring, he was the last man to accuse of being careless with it. Never had he disrespected the potential of its murderous impetuosity. Never! He calmed down after a while, although he heard Ne'gauni muttering about the burned woman and Suda'li huffing over the rudeness of strangers. The back talk calmed him as it reminded him that these people were indeed strangers, perhaps newcomers unused to the proprieties of the Great Gathering. Once on the beach and in the encampment proper, he would find the greeting he sought among his fellow Northerners.

But then, suddenly it seemed, a crowd had begun to form, men, women, children, everyone yelling at him to go back, screeching like the ravens that had converged over the bodies of the mammoths in the burned land. He knew now that he should have listened and led the band to retreat, at least until he could have made some sense of what was happening, but it was too late now for regrets. He had brought his followers through the trees. They were already on the beach. Surrounded.

"Go!"

"Go away!"

"You are not welcome on the shores of the great river!"

Tôrnârssuk's brows arched. It was the latter statement

that took him by surprise. It was common knowledge among all tribes that everyone who came in goodwill to the Great Gathering was welcome to trade and hunt and exchange women and dogs among the many bands assembled there. So it had been since the time beyond beginning. Why should it be different now? A man would have to break the ancient peace or willfully offend the spirits of the game or of the land and water and sky before he would be cast out. And he had done neither.

"Go, we say!"

"Go back to the land of dark spirits from which you come!"

It was the same two shouted voices. Tôrnârssuk could not see who had spoken, for the shouts had come from deep within the crowd, but he understood the words well enough. Although not spoken in the tongue of the True People, the dialect was common among the languages of the Forest People. Suspicion pricked his gut. Perhaps they recognized and remembered him as Raider. As a man who had spent a lifetime amusing himself in securing a reputation that set the ice of dread congealing in the blood of men whenever storytellers recounted his exploits around the lodge fires in the winter dark, he could not expect to be greeted always with happy and receptive hearts. Still, many raiders moved across the land these days, bartering when it served them, plundering when it did not. And he had not come to the great river today as he had come in the past. Today he came with his raiding mask turned back, his weapons sheathed, his face and eyes exposed so that all could see the guileless intent of the spirit that dwelled within, his heart open to all men.

"Go!"

"No! Stay! A better bear is coming to devour you!"

Tôrnârssuk flinched. "Nuutlaq . . . ?" Yes. He could see

Avataut's woman now, elbowing her way forward through the throng, her working clothes splotched with stains from the whale fat that she and the other women had obviously been rendering; the very air reeked of it. A good scent, he thought. Rich. Promising bright winter fires in the oil lamps and nourishing traveling rations and skin-soothing lubricant. And yet the sight of Nuutlaq coming toward him soured it; he had always found something essentially gluttonous in Nuutlaq's nature. Her appearance proved his earlier opinion. She had been plump when he had last seen her. She was fat now, no visible muscle, all blubber. Her small facial features were almost lost in the puffy rounds of her cheeks, and one side of her jaw was swollen, as from a festering tooth. He stared at her as she stopped a safe distance away, looking him up and down, still inside the safety of the crowd. He wondered why she looked so smug, so hostile, so expectant, as she used to look after hauling up a fish from a winter stream, throwing it onto the ice, smiling as she readied herself to smash in its brains with her snow beater.

"Where is your man, woman of Avataut?" he asked and would have added a congenial word about looking forward to seeing an old friend had she not snapped at him first.

"You are not worthy to speak his name, Bringer of Bad Spirits! Why have you come back? What trouble would you bring to us? All in this camp know what you are! You are not welcome here."

"What is happening, Tôrnârssuk?" asked Ningao in a lowered voice.

He had no idea, absolutely no idea, but Kinap was now towering rigid as a tree to one side of him, and he could feel the tension in every member of his band, even in the dogs.

"My two sons are long dead . . . drowned in the flood you led them to! And my poor dear friend, Amayersuk, drowned with them . . . washed away . . . never an honoring for her poor lost spirit : . . or for my sons . . . or for the dogs . . . all the poor drowned dogs! Avataut told us how it was. Yes! Avataut and Armik. They have told us all!"

He flinched at the woman's words as she came forward to stand beside Nuutlaq. He remembered her face, not her name, and was ashamed; he should have remembered her name. "Your sons were mourned," he told her quietly, offering the only comfort he could, for although he knew the names of her sons, he could not speak the names of the dead lest he dishonor them. "They died bravely. As did the others who drowned with them that day. Their spirits were honored. For five days. And also the spirits of the dogs." Out of respect for his two hunt brothers, Avataut and Armik, whose faces he had yet to see in the crowd, Tôrnârssuk did not add that they had been so shaken by the devastation of the flood that they had chosen to break company with his band and go their own way, and had not stayed to honor the dead.

"Yah!" Still another woman came forward. "And my daughter Waseh'ya! Have you mourned for her as you mourned for your dogs and your dead hunters, she who should never have left this camp, big as she was with child, and bigger still with ideas that you would care for her? Yah! Where are our dead, Tôrnârssuk? How can you come back to face us without our dead? Why should you live when they do not? Yah! If you were to bring back from the land of the sky spirits all who have died while walking with you along the raiding trail, there would be no room for the living in this world beneath the sky!"

Somewhere there were words. Tôrnârssuk could not find them. Under another moon, many a long summer ago, a younger White Bear would have snapped back a snarling retort. He would have said that life without death was impossible. Women died in childbirth. Men died on the hunt and on the raiding trail. Better that than to grow old and weak in the bladder and bones and brain, as they must be to speak to him as they were speaking now. But he did not say these things. He felt the weight of the deaths they spoke of and now, staring into the crowd, began to pick out familiar faces, hunt brothers and their women, and Umak, master of the big whaling boat he remembered from the last time he was in this place. He had once thought that the man might one day be a friend. No more. Umak was watching him, studying him, stone-eyed like all the others, as though taking measure of a stranger. No—as though Tôrnârssuk had somehow just returned from the land of the dead and was readying to journey there again and take them all with him.

He did not understand.

He had once found such joy in this camp, such easy camaraderie among men of all tribes. What had happened since he had been away? Why was he being met not as a friend, returning to them openhanded with drag frames laden with fine pelts for trade and nubile women in search of husbands, but as an adversary as dangerous as the animal in whose skin he walked?

He could not understand.

Thunder was rumbling almost constantly now. The wind was no longer gusting. It was blowing hard and steadily; there was a storm in it. The bellies of the clouds had gone black, ugly, mammular. Even the sky seemed unhappy at his arrival. Rain was beginning to fall in large cold drops as irregular as the hammering of his heart.

"Where is Moraq?"

Tôrnârssuk flinched. Who asked? He did not know. Someone else had begun to shout, but this time not at him.

"Aiee! Is that you, Segub'un? And your man, Chief Ogeh'ma! Aiee! It is so!" Yet another woman was keening from out of the crowd. "How have you, dear cousin, and your daughters and sons come to fall into the man-and-woman-and-dog-eating shadow of a bad-spirit bringer? Aiee!"

"Who dares to name my headman this!" It was Kinap, his voice rumbling out of his cowl as threateningly as the thunder before he turned his head slightly and whispered out of the side of his mouth to Ne'gauni, "Wake up, Dreamer! Our headman appears to have died standing on his feet. We need you, Ne'gauni. You must be Shaman Indeed and move forward to warn these comers back with whatever magic you can make before it is too late for all of us!"

"I . . . uh . . ."

"Old Ko'ram will guide you." Hasu'u's voice was, like the giant's, a whisper, but it was strong and steady at the young man's back. "Do not be afraid. Open your heart to his spirit, Little Brother. He will be with you now. Make him proud. Show us all what I have always known—that you were born to be Shaman!"

"I . . . uh . . . I . . ."

"Shake the rattle, boy!" whispered Kinap.

Tôrnârssuk's head was spinning as he cast a sideward glance to see the young man standing as rigid as the giant in his new garments, his face set ahead, his scar invisible in a blazing smear of red ocher greasepaint, his hands so rigid on his crutches that the knuckles showed white. He winced, startled and ashamed. Ne'gauni was terrified. As well he should be. Kinap was right: Their headman *had* gone dead on his feet. And now, because of his inadequacy, a one-legged callow dreamer of a youth was being asked to perform as a man and told that the very life of the band depended on it.

It was intolerable!

Tôrnârssuk's eyes widened. There were men amidst the throng showing weapons now. Lances. Braining clubs. How was it that he had just noticed this? Truly, he thought, he was no longer fit to lead! But lead he must. And would. He had brought his followers into danger. Now he would lead them out of it, wisely and cautiously, for although he knew the fighting skill and hearts of his men, they were greatly outnumbered and if forced to fight would be hard-pressed to reach their weapons. Only he and his Northerners carried two knives concealed and at the ready beneath their tunics, but what were daggers to the reach of lances and braining clubs? With women and little ones among them, he did not like the odds. But there was nothing to do but own to them. Sila had come out of hiding among the stars and was waiting here on the shores of the Great River of the North to challenge him once again out of he knew not how many pairs of eyes. He stared back, shook himself like a weary dog coming out of an icy creek, and, surprised to find himself refreshed, found his voice at last.

"When last I left the Great Gathering, True Men and men of the People did not stand back in silence while their women came forward to speak insults to those who came among them asking only welcome where welcome was due. I, Tôrnârssuk, White Bear and Raven, Tunraq, Guide and Guardian and one who has always sought to bring power to those who have of their own free will chosen to walk with me, will take my band and go. We will not dishonor ourselves by lingering in such a place." He turned. "Go!" he commanded the band.

"But, Headman," wheedled the widow Suda'li as she laid a hand on his forearm to stay his movement, "you have spoken of the wealth in meat and hides you left behind in your cache pits, and there are goods to be traded for, fought for, if—"

"Go!" Tôrnârssuk ordered the woman, appalled by the

extent of her stupidity and greed as he turned her forcefully and shoved her ahead of him along with the others. "What I left here is nothing to me!" he hissed through his teeth. "Trade is nothing to me! The band is all. Go! Go! Before they fall upon us to take all we own, all that matters, all . . . perhaps even our lives!"

"No!"

The word had not come from the giant.

Nor had it come from the mouth of any of the women in the crowd.

A man had spoken it.

Tôrnârssuk froze. He knew the voice! Relief flooded through him, intense and so welcome that, as he turned again, certain he was about to face a welcoming friend at last, he was smiling as he spoke the name. "Avataut!"

"And so!" replied the man who had opened a way for himself through the crowd and now stood surrounded by several tall Grasslanders and a gathering of Northerners, who were still flocking around him like gulls settling around the one kayak on the river that has proved a consistent source of meat for them.

Again Tôrnârssuk froze. His smile vanished. A shiver went up his back. His blood ran cold. For a moment, just for a moment as he had turned, he could have sworn that he was looking at himself. Then, in the shadow beneath the head of the bear that was worn forward over the face of the man, he saw the familiar meaty features of Avataut. How could this be? The white bear was *his* power totem. No man of his band would presume to wear the skin of that animal. No man! Especially a hunt brother as close to his spirit as Avataut. Until—or unless—he was dead.

Lightning stung the sky over the river, a long, multi-veined, horizontal snag that left the air yellow and acrid with the stink of ozone. A restlessness ran through the people assembled on the shore. Again Tôrnârssuk shivered. Waited for the thunder. It came, a massive blast. It shook him. He fought for breath.

And yet, ahead of him, Avataut was standing with arms outstretched, exulting in the storm, his bearskin a livid yellow in the lingering, bruising glow of the lightning.

Within the little circle of the band, Goh'beet's baby began to squall along with the weather. Tiguak joined in. Segub'un linked an arm through the crook of Ogeh'ma's elbow and, looking at Avataut and then at Tôrnârssuk, trembled as she whispered to her man, "How can this be? Can there be room for two such men in all of the sacred Circle of Life Ending and Life Beginning?"

In that moment, hearing those words, Tôrnârssuk felt the spirit of the great white bear die in him. At last he understood. It was over for him. It had been for some time. While he had been hard-pressed to find the strength of will to bring his band safely through flood and fire to this encampment, where all he wanted was to live and hunt in peace with his beloved woman and child, Avataut had been thriving in this very camp, fattening his woman on the best meat and winning a loyal and impressive following of his own. Just as the great white bear of the north had once come to him to define his life, so another bear had come to Avataut to redefine his. No longer was his old friend Wolverine. Avataut was White Bear now.

And White Bear was speaking. "No," Avataut said again, coming forward now, bold as the storm that was growing around him. "It cannot be, Tôrnârssuk. Raven cannot be allowed to fly from this Great Gathering. Who is to say that he will not circle around and return with all his bad spirits flying with him once again?"

"Bad spirits . . . ?"

"As you have seen, Tôrnârssuk, all have heard of the bad spirits that have followed you along the trail since you have been away . . . the many deaths . . . so many bad things a man cannot recount. And behold, you come to us now with a one-legged holy man and a giant with a face that . . . there are no words for such a face. And what magic can a cripple work for the good of any save twisted and broken things like himself? Surely bad spirits dog your steps, Tôrnârssuk!"

Kinap quickly lowered his head and reached to pull up the cowl that had blown back in the wind. "The bad spirits that took my face and claimed the leg of this young Dreamer were encountered long before either of us ever came to walk with Tôrnârssuk. He has led us well. We have not hungered nor gone thirsty. We have found shelter from Wildfire."

"Nothing twisted is there about my Wounded One! His dreams are straight in the way they lead the People!" snapped Mowea'qua. "And my giant's face is—"

"The face of a survivor . . . a man of power . . . a man who has long ago danced with Wildfire and lived to tell the tale," said Ne'gauni coldly, but strongly, speaking out for one who had spoken out for him.

Avataut was shifting restlessly inside his bearskin, eyeing the group, until, slowly, "Where is Moraq?"

Tôrnârssuk was suddenly tired. So tired. He waited. Not one of his band spoke up to reveal the truth. Their silence condemned him in his own mind. How fine they were, all of them! He did not deserve their loyalty. Nor had he deserved Moraq's. The man had been right to challenge him. Perhaps, if he had listened, Moraq would still be alive. He cringed, thought of what the man had set himself to do to Mowea'qua. He could not have allowed that. And yet he could not forget abandoning his body to the Valley of the Spirit Moon, leaving a True Man to rot and fall prey to carrion eaters along with the bodies of slain beasts who, for all their vileness, were not beasts, but men, women, children.

He hung his head. Ashamed. Then, raising it again, he looked into Avataut's face, into an old friend's face. The man he remembered was there, staring at him from beneath the head of the bear. Hard. Clever. Manipulative. Qualities he had always admired. But would they serve him now? "My band has come far, Avataut," he said, not for himself but for his followers. "You have hunt brothers among those who walk with me. And the others are good men and women, and children, not of the True People, Avataut, but of the Dawn- land and Grassland and Forest tribes. The Four Winds have swept us together upon the same trail. They have come far with me, all of us seeking the Great Gathering. Whatever bad spirits have shadowed me were with me before they chose to pitch their tents in my encampments. You know this, Avataut, for you saw these spirits before I knew they were there and named them for what they were and chose to walk away. Let others do so now. Let my followers seek out their own people here on the shores of the great river as they had hoped to do. I will take my woman and son and return to the barrenlands of our Ancestors and—"

"Ah, Tôrnârssuk!" Avataut interrupted, his gaze, hidden in the shadows beneath the head of the bear, no longer on Tôrnârssuk at all. He had settled his eyes on Hasu'u, and al- though she flinched and looked away, he kept them there. Fixed. Piercing. A raptor's eyes. As his words were a raptor's words as he said, softly, with a leading edge of kindness that was not kind at all, "Would you risk your woman to the bad spirits that walk with you, Tôrnârssuk? And your son, if it need not be so?"

The question stabbed Tôrnârssuk, and yet, although his

heart was bleeding, he said, "Never." He waited for Hasu'u to step forward and stand beside him, to raise her beautiful Dawnland face to all at the Great Gathering and say that she was his woman always and forever and would walk with him wherever he went, whatever the risk.

But Hasu'u did not speak.

▼▼▼▼

Moments passed.

A few breaths of time, no more than that.

The rain was spitting sleet.

Avataut barely noticed. Under the projecting snout of the bearskin his face was dry and his eyes were locked on Hasu'u. He could not look away, not from her proud stance or the determined set of her face, staring straight ahead, revealing nothing, and yet, to a man with the piercing and acquisitive gaze of a wolverine, revealing everything.

His mouth tightened. She was as he remembered. In all this world beneath the sky, he thought, there was no woman to equal Hasu'u. None! How brave and stubborn she still was for the sake of her foolish Dawnland pride, and still as beautiful as the doe on the meadow before he had slain her fawn and struck her through her heart! And to think that he had almost given up hope of possessing her, or of punishing her for that day, so long ago, when she had dragged him from the floodwaters by his hair and shamed him before the entire band by saving his life. And here she was, back in that life again, having no idea how much he hated her and ached to own her so that he could break her pride even as he was now breaking Tôrnârssuk as payment for his failure to punish her for the sake of a hunt brother's dignity.

Avataut's eyes moved from the woman to Tôrnârssuk. How magnificent he was, still strong, but too fatigued to mask the weariness in his troubled eyes. It thrilled him to see it. The White Bear of old would never have betrayed such weakness to another man. Clearly Tôrnârssuk was not the man he once was. The spirit of the great white bear had left him. Gone was the insatiable drive for pure, self-serving, unforgiving power that had so fired Avataut's own soul. He felt only disgust for the man now, and a small measure of that for himself for ever having feared his return.

The wind turned, dropped, then turned again to blow harder than before. Avataut lowered his head. Rain was falling laterally now, blowing under the snout of the bearskin to sting his face. The uncured hide was growing heavy with accumulated water; it weighted him and was beginning to smell. Close at his side, Chaksa and the Grasslanders moved a discreet step or two away, pretending not to notice, but they were growing noticeably restless and uncomfortable in the downpour, as were his fellow Northerners and everyone else on the beach.

"Kill him, Avataut!" urged Nuutlaq. "Fight him! Show him who is White Bear now . . . before his bad spirits bring another flood and sweep us all away, and with us all the meat and fat and skin that we have taken from the white whales!"

Lightning stung the clouds again. Thunder followed. And a warning from Kinap.

"Beware. The White Bear with whom this man walks will not be so easy to kill."

There was a rumbling from the Northerners who walked with Tôrnârssuk.

"A man-slaying on this beach will break the ancient peace of the Great Gathering," Chief Ogeh'ma reminded them, standing straight and commanding between his two taller sons. In his Dawnland raiment and with his many shell-adorned braids whipping and clicking in the wind before his face, he gave the illusion of being a man of formidable size as well as heart.

"White whales lie dead on this beach!" The declaration came from within the crowd. "All who have seen fit to bring bared weapons onto this sacred shore have offended the spirits of the whales who have come into the Great River of the North to give their lives to the People, to sacrifice themselves to the hunters so that they may sustain the life of the People as they have seen fit to do since the time beyond beginning and shall continue to do . . . only as long as the People hold sacred the lives of their own kind in the same way that the whales hold sacred the lives of their own children."

Who spoke? The voice was muffled by the growling of thunder, but Avataut cursed it. He had forgotten the ancient proscription, as, from all appearances, had half the hunters on the strand. He was sure that neither he nor any man who felt the need to protect his own against potentially dangerous interlopers appreciated being reminded of it now. Besides, he could have sworn that he had recognized the voice as belonging to Inau. No! It was impossible. She would not come from the bluffs. Not by day. Not during the height of a thunderstorm. And never without her mask. Yet he spun on his heels, looking for her, noticing several men leaving the beach, hunched up against now pounding rain. Inau was not with them. With the head of a whale she would stand out in any crowd. He grimaced, shivered off revulsion at the thought of the shaman, and, turning back to face Tôrnârssuk, caught the eye of a tall, sodden, crudely cloaked, baby-faced man standing close to Táwoda and a pair of traders from the Lakeland. Their blue face paint was streaming down their faces in the rain, revealing the hawkish lines of their features. He made no attempt to hold their gaze; he felt only contempt for them. No doubt their eyes were fixed on his copper earring. As though they would ever get it back! Word had gone out around the encampment this morning that their braggart of a brother was dying. Did they expect Avataut to make some sort of gesture of regret by returning what he had fairly won? Well, *cleverly* won; that was better than fair! He would keep the earring. He would wear it to the spirit world and show it off to the Ancient Ones when the time came; it was one of the finest things he owned.

Again lightning flashed. Very close. Thunder cracked the air, and when its growling settled down, the rain had lessened a little. Avataut could hear the river moving behind the crowd, well down the strand, for they were gathered far above the high-water mark here, behind man-tall windrows of driftwood piled up by past floods. The river was racing now, engorged with runoff from countless streams and tributaries. Suspicion flared in his brain. What if Nuutlaq was right? What if Tôrnârssuk was summoning bad spirits to make the river rise to drown them all? Logic counseled otherwise. Ningao and the other Northerners were murmuring restively at Tôrnârssuk's back; the giant looked nervous, hulking up like a gathering storm cloud with rainwater channeling off his well-oiled black bearskins. Tôrnârssuk had not moved; indeed, his tense and worried expression brought a smile to Avataut's face. It seemed some things did not change. Like Armik, who was evidently making himself invisible within the crowd lest his duplicity toward an old white bear be discovered, Tôrnârssuk and all his fellow Northerners from the inland barrens were afraid of deep, fast-running water. It was a weakness in every one of them—Avataut puffed himself up inside the skin of the bear—except in him.

"I again ask welcome for my followers in this Great

Gathering," said Tôrnârssuk, his voice raised now as he spoke formally to everyone on the beach. "They have come to you with their weapons sheathed. They have come singing, announcing their arrival so that all may know that they come without guile, with their hands open to trade, their spirits eager to hunt, and with young women among them who seek husbands among you. And so I ask those who know the name of Chief Ogeh'ma and his Dawnland family to welcome him now. And so I ask those who know the name of Kinap the Storyteller from the Land of Grass and of his woman Suda'li and her Dawnland sons to welcome them now. And so I ask those who know the name of Ne'gauni, He Walks Ahead in Dreams to Foresee Danger for the People, who is son of Asticou, chief among the Forest People, and of Wawautaésie, daughter of Chief Sebec of the Lakeland People, to offer him welcome. And so I ask that all who know these brave men of the Barrenlands who have returned with me to offer them welcome at this Great Gathering and shelter from this storm."

Even in the cold rain Avataut felt his face flush with jealousy. How eloquent was Tôrnârssuk! How compelling! Even now, with only the slightest effort, he could still be the man he was. If he believed he could be. Even now he was gesturing his Northerners graciously forward, naming them to a man, honoring them. And then, before any could speak, he turned, stepped forward to Avataut, and reached out to place his hands open upon his hunt brother's shoulders.

"And now from you, Avataut, most trusted of my hunt brothers, from you who have in my long absence safeguarded and kept my bear-bone staff high over my caches, from you who saw bad spirits following me long before I was able to see them for myself, from you whom the great white bear of the north has honored with the gift of its spirit even as he has withdrawn that gift from me, from you, Avataut, who knows the name of Hasu'u and of Tiguak, I ask welcome for my woman and son into this Great Gathering and into your lodge, where you may cherish them as your own."

Hasu'u caught her breath.

Segub'un clasped her hands over her face.

"And you, Tôrnârssuk, of whom do you and the bad spirits who walk with you ask welcome?" pressed Avataut, enjoying the moment far too much.

Tôrnârssuk did not hesitate. He had made his decision. For the good of the band. For the ones he loved. And now, looking directly at Avataut, needing desperately in this moment to see a friend, for the first time in his life he failed to recognize the face of Sila looking back at him out of Avataut's eyes. "I will ask welcome of no man. I will hunt solitary again. I am content in the knowledge that my son and the woman of my heart and those whom I have brought to this Great Gathering will be away from the bad spirits that walk with me and under the protection of Avataut, White Bear now, and Headman of the Northerners on the shores of the Great River of the North." This said, he reached back, slung off his bearskin, turned, and moved to place it around Hasu'u's shoulders. "You will walk with a new White Bear now, woman of my heart. It will be better for you. As safe as anything can be in this life. You will find heart to sing again. Is this acceptable to you?"

The falling rain concealed the tears that were standing in Hasu'u's eyes. Her agony of spirit was so great that she could not speak. He was giving her away to one who was little more than a stranger. As her sisters had warned her he would! And this she could have borne, this she could have willed herself to endure, as long as she knew in her heart that he was doing so because she had failed to please him. But she could not bear this! Not this! Not even a hunt chief's daughter, a headman's wife, a woman born to generations of Dawnland women, could be expected to stand by and accept in silence her man's decision to walk the wind forever . . . for this was what he was doing to save the band, to save her, to save Tiguak! But from what? How could he not know how well he had led them? How could he not know that all who walked within the fall of his shadow did so with pride, and slept well in the night knowing that he was there to guide them, with wisdom, with caution, with concern for their every step and their every need? No man could be right in every decision he made. Not even Tôrnârssuk. She must tell him this. Ah! She *had* failed him! Why had she not told him before? No bad spirits were following him. Indeed, the only bad spirits that she had seen in this camp were staring at her now out of Avataut's eyes. She would not look at him. She would look at Tôrnârssuk. She would stand here now and put the skin of the great white bear back on his shoulders where it belonged, and even though it broke with the traditions of every woman of her tribe who had ever lived, she would tell him that he was wrong. Wrong! And if he walked out of this camp alone, she would not stay in it. She would follow him and tell him that it was *not* acceptable for him to leave her behind. She was his woman. His always-and-forever woman. And he would always be White Bear in her eyes. Always. And so, raising her head high, she fought to find breath, to tell him everything that was in her heart, but as she began to speak, another spoke in her place.

"No!" Mowea'qua shouted as she stepped out to stand beside the headman and declare ferociously, "Yah! Only one White Bear is there in this camp! You, Avataut, you wear only a dead skin. Tôrnârssuk carries the spirit of a living bear inside him. This White Bear, this Tôrnârssuk, I will follow. No other!"

Avataut looked her up and down. There was much woman here. Young. Different. Intriguing. Beautiful. And Trouble for any man who claimed her as his own; he was sure of this the moment he saw the raven feather affixed to her forelock and found himself pinioned by unnaturally pale eyes glaring out of an elongated face tattooed from temple to temple in a wide, abstract pattern depicting the wings of a raven in flight. It was a startling tattoo, made in the style with which Tôrnârssuk incised everything he owned—as were the intricate, entwining spirals that adorned Hasu'u's perfect face—but, whereas Hasu'u's tattoo was as delicate and subtly made as she, the raven tattoo was as bold as the young woman who wore it. And it was only newly made; he could tell by the way the skin was red and slightly swollen between the incisings. Still, if it stressed her, she showed no sign of it, for although she was obviously no Northerner, the young woman wore Tôrnârssuk's mark with pride. No, he thought, she wore it with a defiance that unsettled him as surely as she had unsettled Tôrnârssuk's followers.

His brow came down. Squinting through the waterfall of rain that was channeling down over the snout of his bearskin, he could see that they were all exchanging glances, murmuring restlessly, angrily, defensively. The audacious young woman had stirred loyalty in them! And now, before one of his own followers spoke out to inform Tôrnârssuk that he had no need to yield his caches and campsite to a trusted hunt brother when that hunt brother had long since taken them for himself, Avataut knew he must act quickly or lose all he hoped to gain in this moment. As much as he ached simply to lever back with his lance and plunge it straight into

Tôrnârssuk's heart and cancel the threat of the man forever, he knew that he dared not. If Tôrnârssuk's blood was spilled on this beach, Ningao and Kamak and Inaksak and the others in his band would not stand still for it. They would fight. Outnumbered, with their weapons out of reach except for the daggers of the Northerners among them, they would fall, and if, by some quirk in the schemings of the forces of Creation, the white whales failed to return to the river next summer, Inau would blame Avataut. He was certain of that. And so, with his mind working fast, as it did so well when he found himself suddenly stressed and impatient to achieve his aims, he set his gaze on the girl with the raven feather in her hair and the wings of a raven tattooed across her face and said, "I see that Tôrnârssuk has marked you as one of his own. You must honor him. He has brought you into a good camp and to a hunt brother who will accept you as his own."

"Chosen Sister of Raven am I. Obedient Woman of Tôrnârssuk! Where Tôrnârssuk walks there also walks this woman, always and forever."

"No," countered Tôrnârssuk, his voice weighted by fatigue and sadness and a resignation that was painful to hear. "You will be silent, Chosen Sister of Raven. You will be Obedient Woman. As Hasu'u has always been an obedient woman. Take example from her. Learn from her. Do not dishonor me or yourself or your band before Avataut. You are his woman now. He is the White Bear with whom you will walk."

Avataut saw the girl's face expand with a tension that made it seem as though the skin lying over her unusual features must tear and rip wide to expose the bones beneath; it was not easy for her to be obedient. Hasu'u would be easy to break; looking at her now, he could see that her spirit was already bleeding. But Chosen Sister of Raven would be malleable in no man's hands. He would trade her or brain her, as her behavior indicated. Surely he had no need of a fourth woman at his fire, regardless of the status such ownership would convey. Besides, with Hasu'u now his to take and command, he had all he wanted, except for one thing. And now that, too, was to be his.

A smile tugged at Avataut's mouth. He suppressed it. He would smile later, when he had Hasu'u to himself. Now, increasingly uncomfortable within the heavy, saturated skin of the white bear and anxious to retreat into the warmth of his lodge, he was growing impatient. "Go," he commanded Tôrnârssuk. "Take your bad spirits with you. Go, I say! Go back to the Barrenlands and let no man, woman, or dog in this camp set eyes on you again. Go, I say! And be grateful that we have left you with your life. It is time your followers were out of the weather."

"He will return! He will come back in the night and bring his bad spirits with him! He cannot go far away enough not to be a danger to us! You cannot just let him walk away!"

Nuutlaq's warning stung the air, so imperative, so high and shrill and tightly wound by her need to see violence done that, when a lightning bolt struck far out on the river, the following clap of thunder seemed an affirmation of her intent sent by the forces of Creation themselves.

And suddenly, in this moment of pure inspiration, Avataut knew what he must do.

Tôrnârssuk stood resolute, solemn. "I will not return, Avataut," he said. "For love of my people, for my woman and son, I will not return."

"No," said Avataut.

Before he could say another word, the giant took a

threatening step forward. "No man in this camp will raise a hand against my headman," Kinap rumbled, more dangerous and threatening than the thunderstorm.

"No man," echoed Kanio'te, who was echoed in turn by every man in his band.

"I know your face . . ."

Avataut, distracted, turned his gaze to the one-legged young holy man who had just spoken as though out of a daze. The red ocher on his face was running like blood, revealing a raised white scar that zigzagged across his keen, hawkish, once-handsome face. Something in Avataut's gut tightened. The scar on the would-be shaman's face looked like one of the lightning bolts that had been snagging the clouds, and he did not like the way the young man was looking at him out of unblinking eyes, somehow not seeing him at all and yet seeing straight through him. But what power could he have—scarred, crippled, so young and inexperienced that when he had been called upon to shake his rattle and act like a shaman for the good of his band, he had stood gaping like a fish out of water, unable to form a single cogent word? And who was the rat-faced child standing beside him, clutching something in his hands, squeezing it, staring up at him now as though he wished to make him disappear?

Ignoring the disturbing and irrelevant twosome, Avataut set his gaze back on Tôrnârssuk. The spirit of Wolverine was alive in him now. Hungry. Greedy. Anxious to despoil and take for himself that which belonged to one who had once been a far more dangerous predator than even he was now. He would kill Tôrnârssuk—and, in the killing, shame him. And yet never would it be said of him that he had caused his enemy's blood to flow upon this sacred beach, or that he had raised a hand against him except to proclaim the manner in which he would surely now die. And so he raised his arms, lances high, and said to the assembly on the beach, "This man, this Tôrnârssuk, we have been hunt brothers. I, Avataut, now Headman of All Northerners, swear on my own name that Tôrnârssuk is a man of his word. Who can say why bad spirits have chosen to walk with him? It is not for him to know this, or change it, except to know that those who walk with him are shadowed by these spirits and suffer and die because of them. So it must be that for the good of all, he will take these bad spirits and go. And so it must be, so that all who fear these spirits may rest in the night without fear of his return, that he will take a kayak and commit himself and these bad spirits to the life force of the Great River of the North. The river is running fast and wild as a herd of caribou in stampede this day. It will carry him far. Perhaps so far that he and his bad spirits will be swept past the great black cliffs and out into the sea beyond. They will not return. This Great Gathering will not see them again."

The crowd was stunned.

Tôrnârssuk's fellow Northerners were openly appalled.

"No, Tôrnârssuk, do not consent to this." Kinap was adamant, reaching back for his spears until Avataut's lance came forward to push a warning point into the man's bearskins.

"It must be!" Avataut raised his voice, just a little.

"It cannot be!"

Avataut no longer felt like smiling as Chief Ogeh'ma's contradiction struck him like a slap.

"We will take our women and children and go from this camp—fighting our way if it must be so, dying if it must be so—but you will not consign that man, our Headman, our Tunraq, our Guide and Guardian, to the great river. We have hunted together! We have fought together! We have survived the dance of Wildfire in the Valley of the Spirit Moon!

We have shared meat and song and the joy of life together, and the sadness of mourning our dead together, a sadness that must come to all within the sacred Circle of Life Ending and Life Beginning! Spirits have walked with us—good spirits, not bad—and strong have we been together, all of us strong, young and old together, because we have chosen to name Tôrnârssuk Headman!"

Tôrnârssuk remained motionless. His voice was as cold as the rain as he said, "Your words are as the sun would be to me on this day, Ogeh'ma. Warm. Welcome. And yet I say to you now that I choose the shade. We have come far. Now, at last, there are men who will make your daughters smile when they welcome them as wives at this Great Gathering. The meat of white whales will sweeten and oil your mouth. The children of this band will no longer be at risk from such threats as we have encountered along the trail. Tunraq I have been to you, Guide and Guardian, but I have not been One Who Walks Strong in the Power of the Spirits for many a long moon. There will be no more blood spilled because of me. I accept Avataut's conditions. The band is all to me. You and your family are all to me. Do not dishonor me by refusing to accept my decision. You are a Dawnland chief, Ogeh'ma. You know as well I that were this your encampment and a man were to come to you carrying the reputation of one not in favor with the spirits, you would do exactly as Avataut is doing—drive him out for the good of all."

"Mmph!"

"You will be silent, Mowea'qua! You will honor me by remembering your vow to be Obedient Woman!"

Now, more than ever, Avataut was finding it difficult to repress a smile. "Then it will be," he said and withdrew the point of his lance from the giant's chest. "We will all honor

Tôrnârssuk as he takes the bad spirits from the Great Gathering out of concern for us all!"

"It will be so," said Tôrnârssuk.

For the first time since Tôrnârssuk had come onto the beach with his followers, Avataut saw an emotion other than sadness and resignation on his old hunt brother's face: fear. Yes! As he had known he would see it. A Barrenland man's instinctive fear of wide, deep, fast-running water. "I know, my brother, I know," he consoled. "It is a bitter thing you must do. But you and I have always said that as True Men it is good to face our fears. To look into the face of Sila. To overcome it. Or to be consumed. Either way, unafraid! Men of the True People. Running bold and wild in the sacred Circle of Life Ending and Life Beginning. So come, we will go to the shore. I have a hunt brother who will be honored to give you his kayak."

Chapter Eight

▼▼▼▼▼▼

Not everyone walked down the beach.

A few were turning away, some heading toward the bluffs, others back into the woods. Perhaps they did not want to see a brave man die, or perhaps they simply had had enough of the weather.

Ne'gauni could not move.

At his side, Musquash was crying, lips blue in the cold rain. "I have tipped the basket! We are all spilling out! All spilling out! Ah, here, Ne'gauni! Here! You must take it! It is not for me!"

Ne'gauni stood numb, rooted in wet gravel.

The boy was off, leaping over the windrows of driftwood, hurrying after Mowea'qua, grasping at her hand.

"You cannot be that man's woman, Mowea'qua! He is bad! There is a beast in his eyes! We must run away again! It is not safe for you here, Mowea'qua! We must run away!"

"Away go you! Obedient Woman am I! Go! Think you that I would Tôrnârssuk dishonor? Now? Away, say I!"

"I will not leave you, Mowea'qua. Ah, Mowea'qua, you are crying again. You must not cry! It can still be as in the story! Muskrat and Wolf Woman together and—"

"Yah!" She flailed back at him as hard as she could, knocking him flat. "Go!" she sobbed. "Make of your life a story! Find the white mammoth! Go! Wolf Woman is dead! I care not what you do!"

Ne'gauni saw the boy fall, heard the girl's shouted words, and yet saw nothing, heard nothing. He was lost in the Darkness again, part of another world. A light flared inside his head. Hot. Bright. It was a single flame until, suddenly, it burst wide, then imploded, setting fire to every quadrant of his body.

Did he cry out? It seemed so. He stared. Inward. Unable to move. Unable to speak. He had seen this light before. He knew this fire. And somehow, not for the first time, his spirit was loose within himself, a two-legged being, trapped, desperately seeking a way out, running, screaming down the branching corridors of his own veins and arteries until, beating for freedom within the great pulsing inner chamber of the drum that was his own heart, he at last broke free and ran on, only to find that—although in his vision he could move on two strong limbs—he was not free at all.

Across a flaming world of endless trees he ran. And ran. The wind drove him on, a furious wind, mating with Fire, feeding the flames. Somewhere ahead a man ran before him, looking back over his shoulder as he ran, faceless, a laughing stranger disappearing into the Darkness beyond the flames as a mammoth trumpeted, its voice the sound of thunder, its footsteps shaking the earth. He fell. Rose. Staggered against the wind. Then ran on again as all around him the forest burned and the wind laughed and a woman in a blue-quilled dress screamed and animals and people fled ahead of the flames only to be consumed as, burning, in agony, he fell again and plummeted alone into the Darkness, sobbing and calling out for the wind to turn and the rain to come.

And now it was raining.

A hand pressed his shoulder. "Ne'gauni . . . ? Son of the hunt chief Asticou and Wawautaésie, daughter of Chief Sebec of the Lakeland People?"

The voice swam in the Darkness.

Swam in the cold rain, and yet, behind his eyes, Wildfire was still dancing and, far ahead, the faceless stranger was still looking back at him, no longer faceless now, but meaty-mouthed and cruel-eyed as he ran on boldly, like an animal running wild in the sacred Circle of Life Ending and Life Beginning.

"Avataut!" he exclaimed, and the man turned and laughed at him again, but he was no longer running; he was walking down the beach in the skin of a great white bear, leading Tôrnârssuk to his death. "I know your face!"

"Ne'gauni . . . ?"

The Darkness left him. In an instant. As it always did. He stood shaken, blinking, shivering in the cold rain, seeing everything so clearly that it hurt him to his very soul, hearing with an intensity that cut him to the quick as Hasu'u raised her voice in the high, keening ululation of one yearning to give the strength of all-encompassing love to another who loved her in equal measure and must soon die and be lost to her forever. And suddenly he understood. So much! Too much! The realization of the depth of his own selfishness half drowned him in remorse. To have wanted her so much that he could not see past his own yearnings to value as she valued the one and only man worthy of her love. And yet he knew now that, despite the smallness of his own soul, the spirits had tried to work through him, to speak through him. The fear of going north, the strange, half-seen visions of terror and death glimpsed in the Darkness: All had been for Tôrnârssuk, who, in his unrelenting longing to bring his woman and son and band to a safe camp at last, had brought them here to the Great River of the North where Sila had been waiting, not for them, but for him all along.

"Always danger . . . always enemies . . . always. Why did I not see the danger to him before now?" He looked down, shaking his head, befuddled . . . until he saw the sacred stone, looped by its sinew thong to one of the sodden foxtails that decorated the fine brown bearskin robe that Tôrnârssuk had given to him as a gift in his attempt to make him look like a shaman.

"Ne'gauni?"

The voice pressed him. He was aware of a hand resting lightly on his shoulder. A man he did not know was looking at him with great concern, great consideration.

"I am Táwoda, eldest son of your grandfather, Sebec, chief of the Lakeland People. I am your mother's brother, Ne'gauni. Wawautaésie would be proud to know that she has borne a shaman. But she would not be pleased to see her son standing in a cold rain. Come. I am honored to welcome you into my band. Shelter with me in my camp until the storm is over. You should rest. Tomorrow we will take my wounded brother home and, as we go, serve as escort to Inau as she begins her return journey to the Cave of the Winds. We have no wish to linger in this place. There are bad spirits here."

"Now the bad spirits will go away," said a little girl in a pinch-faced passion of hatred, holding a deerskin over her head as she ran by.

"Hurry, child, or we will miss the joy to be found in it!"

Ne'gauni reached out and took hold of the arm of a man who would have hurried past him. "Take no joy in the death of any man, stranger . . . least of all in that man, for there is no better in—"

"Bah! You would protect him when he has set his dark

spirits out across the land to send Wildfire to burn up my wife and unborn child? And my son?" He paused, cast an eye at Táwoda, recognizing him for the first time. "Your salves were much appreciated, friend, but only this morning his life spirit ran away from his body. So slow to die. He could no longer bear his pain."

Ne'gauni felt himself jerked almost off balance as the man tore his arm free of his grasp and, without another word, was off down the beach with his little daughter hurrying after him, but not before his roughly made rain cape blew back and Ne'gauni caught sight of the blue quillwork at the seams of his hunt shirt. "It was not Tôrnârssuk who set Wildfire loose within the forest!" he called after him. "It was Avataut! I saw him!"

Lightning stung the sky. Thunder overrode Ne'gauni's words.

But Táwoda heard. "Is this true, Ne'gauni?"

"This is true!"

"But how could you have seen?"

"I *am* Shaman Indeed," acknowledged the young man with no small sense of wonder. With his hand curling around the sacred stone, he looked around for Musquash to thank him for his gift, but the boy was nowhere to be seen.

"Come," said Táwoda. "We must go to the bluffs. There is someone who must know of this!"

▼▼▼▼▼

Armik lifted his kayak from the stones upon which it rested and laid it upon the gravel of the now ice-rimed and wave-whipped shore. He stared down at it expressionlessly. Although Avataut had never had a good word to say about it, Armik knew that it was well made, although it had taken a battering on the shoals at the height of the last hunt and, although still watertight, would need minor refittings here and there before he would be comfortable taking it out again. Not that he wanted to. Indeed, he would just as soon never go out on the river in it or any other boat again. And so he had no complaint to offer when Tôrnârssuk moved toward it.

"Why not give him your own kayak, Avataut? It is bigger. There will be more room for all the bad spirits that he will be bringing with him."

Umak's sarcasm brought a resentful lift to Avataut's brow until he heard snickering from the assembled people on the beach.

Tôrnârssuk said nothing. Asked for nothing. Together with Armik, he carried the little boat to the water's edge. Avataut handed him the paddle without a word. He took it and, whatever terror he felt in the moment, allowed himself to show none of it as he stepped into the kayak. He hoped no one saw him flinch when Avataut gave the little boat a hard shove, out into the dangerous current.

Paddling hard, he tried to keep the prow heading outward rather than downriver, thinking defiantly that perhaps he might actually make the far shore. The cloud cover seemed to be lifting somewhat over those distant hills. He reminded himself with grim irony that the barrenlands of his Ancestors lay beyond those hills. He had intended to go there all along—although not by boat, and never in his wildest dreams had he ever imagined that he would be making this, his final journey, alone.

Hasu'u was still lifting her voice in that terrible, wonderful sound that spoke her love and her need to give him courage. The rest of the band had joined her. It was difficult to listen. It was everything to listen! They were no longer ululating; they were singing, loud, as bold and wildly as the river. They sang the same song they had sung with such joy and hope when approaching the river, and Kinap was pounding on his drum as Onen'ia's flute shrieked like an eagle to the ancient rhythms of the invocation to the dawn, to new beginnings . . . and now to new places to run in the sacred Circle of Life Beginning . . . and Life Ending.

Be strong! sang the song to him.

Come boldly! challenged the flute.

Be unafraid! commanded the drum.

"Yes!" cried Tôrnârssuk, but the sound that tore from his throat was not a cry. It was a shout of pure and triumphant consent to whatever the forces of Creation would decide for him this day. He threw back his head and raised his arms to the sky and, releasing his spirit to the will of Wind and Storm and wild Water, imagined himself running once more with the caribou across the barrenlands of his youth, with wolves keeping apace and the great white bear of the north on his heels.

"I come!
Who has heard the Voice of Dawn?
The Stars have heard
And the Great One, rising from the Deep
Now I, too, have heard
The Way is Made ready before me!
I stretch forth my Hands. I go toward the Dawn!
I come!
I am not afraid!"

"Tôrnârssuk!"

It was Mowea'qua who screamed his name.

"He will not come back!" snapped Avataut, annoyed with her and overjoyed by the sight of the river sweeping on without a sign of Tôrnârssuk on it.

The singing stopped. The drum and the flute fell as silent as the crowd, and, overhead, the clouds seemed to be noticeably thinner.

"Never have I seen so brave a man," said Umak as he gestured to his crew and stalked off up the beach to where his umiak lay at rest. "I have had enough of this Great Gathering. I think bad spirits are here. And the storm is lifting on the far shore. It speaks to me. Come, it says. Maybe we will find Tôrnârssuk downriver there."

"Yes, say I, yes!" Mowea'qua was already running after them. "Me you will take!"

Umak paused, eyed her thoughtfully. "You are Avataut's now . . . and the river is dangerous, even for us now."

"Afraid I am not!"

"Take her!" Avataut shouted up the beach. "I do not want her. She carries too much of his mark. And if you follow Tôrnârssuk, I warn you, the river will eat you, too!"

Mowea'qua was already clambering onto the big broadbeamed boat, calling out to Hasu'u. "Come! For once, Hasu'u, do not think about what you should do. Do it . . . come!"

It was too late.

Avataut had Hasu'u by the arm. "You will not shame me again."

"When have I ever shamed you, Avataut? I saved your life! You owe me mine. Let me go!"

"Is the other woman coming?" Umak called.

"She is mine, Umak. I will keep her. And if you find Tôrnârssuk alive, tell him if he ever returns to the Great Gathering with his bad spirits I will cut her throat and throw his son into the river before he ever sets eyes on them again!"

"I will tell him that, Bad Spirit!" assured Umak as several

of his men pushed the big boat into the downstream race of the river and were hauled aboard.

Avataut stared after them a moment, then whirled around to declare to the hushed assembly on the beach, "Let the river have them! Let the storm current sweep them all out into endless sea! They will not come back! He will not come back!"

Ningao looked to his fellow Northerners. "Tôrnârssuk has always been a hard man to kill."

"And he does not like water," added Kamak. "Maybe it will be offended and spit him out on that far shore."

Avataut was growling under the snout of the white bear and wringing out one of the sodden bear paws. The weight of the forelimb, although devoid of bone and flesh, was suddenly unbearably heavy. He shrugged it back and, with the rain now reduced to a drizzle, stood facing into the cool wind, wondering why everyone was looking at him as though at a stranger. "I have driven Bad-Spirit Bringer from this great encampment. I will stay no more on this beach to listen to ungrateful mumblings."

"Wait." Hasu'u's word was not a command. Her face had gone blank. "What is that you wear among your other amulets . . . a fetish of a white bear . . . speared through its heart?"

Avataut felt only contempt for her. "To keep him from returning!" He gave her the truth, then added what a part of him still believed to be the truth. "For the good of all who have come to hunt and trade in the Great Gathering! To keep his bad spirits from following him and—"

"And by his return revealing to all how small a wolverine can appear when setting itself to follow in the shadow of a great white bear!"

Save for the run of the river and an occasional, now

almost somnolent roll of thunder in the clouds, all was quiet on the beach as the shaman Inau came from the bluffs to stand before Avataut in her whalebone mask and her robes of shell and fur and feathers, with Ne'gauni and Táwoda and the traders walking grim-faced beside her.

Avataut wondered if the world had just shifted beneath his feet. He was not sure. No one else seemed to be shaking.

"I warned you what must be for you, Wolverine, Kwakwa-je'sh, if you would not heed the wisdom of Inau," said the shaman. "You who once walked as hunt brother to Tôrnârssuk, as loyal follower of Wíndigo, Great Ghost Cannibal, Tunraq and White Bear of the North, in his absence the light of your avarice and arrogance has shone ahead of you along the trail you have chosen to follow, Wolverine, Bold Hunter Who Raids the Camps and Steals the Denning Sites of Others, Man Who Sends Wildfire Dancing Ahead of Him in the Forest to Hunt and Slay Enemies He Is Afraid to Face Himself, no matter how many must suffer for his fear."

"You cannot accuse me of that, Inau! All have seen here today that I was not afraid to face him . . . to fight him . . . to—"

"Profane the sanctity of the sacred gathering . . . to bring weapons onto this beach."

He glared at her. "Who knew what danger he brought to us? The risk was worth all to—"

"And what of the risk of fire?" Ne'gauni fairly hurled the words.

Avataut laughed. "You would put the blame of this on me? You? A one-legged shaman? I quake in fear of you! Your accusations mean nothing. They can have no power. And even if it were true, to keep the Great Gathering safe from bad spirits no man could be faulted for risking—"

"Nothing is safe in all this world, Avataut. Sila hunts us

all," Inau interrupted coldly. "Such is the teaching of your own people. And no man may value himself above the band or tribe . . . much less take it upon himself to risk the band or tribe without first gaining the approval of a council."

"No council would have approved what I did on the meadow! No council would have had the audacity to even begin to see the need of it or—" His words stopped of their own accord. He could not believe he had actually spoken them.

Inau raised her arms. "I am Shaman. It is not my place to say more in this. There are headmen here from many bands, representatives of many tribes, good men all. You will speak together. You will decide what must be for a man who has risked all of you . . . who has brought Wildfire to dance in the forest and claim we know not how many lives . . . who has lured men to sport and injured them irrevocably for the pleasure of shaming them and winning their goods and their women . . . for a man whose presence here has profaned the sanctity of this sacred gathering, to which I will call the whales no more."

Chapter Nine

▼▼▼▼▼▼▼

He waited.

There, on the beach, close to where the boats lay at rest, he waited with Armik, as he had been commanded to wait. The beach was deserted now.

"You should run," he said.

"Am I not your hunt brother, Avataut? Look. Táwoda and the one-legged holy man are leaving the Man House and heading for the bluffs. The others from the inland lakes are up there now with the shaman. They will be leaving together now for the Cave of the Winds. It was what they planned before, or so I heard. The decision of the council will come soon. I do not think Inau wants to be here to take responsibility for it . . . nor do I."

Avataut glowered at him. "So you will run off after all? Abandon all that we have won for ourselves in this good encampment?"

"It is not so good for us anymore, Avataut. We have forfeited everything. You know that. So go. Do not stay. The rain has stopped. The sky has cleared. The river grows calm again. The storm has blown off. I suggest we blow away with it. If you do not, I would wager that you will not live to see the dawn. "

Avataut shook his head. "They have left us both unbound, unguarded, hoping we will run and shame ourselves and prove our fear by being unable to face what they will do to us as punishment."

"Take your big kayak and cross the river, Avataut. Why do you still care if they think you are afraid?"

"Because I am Avataut . . . not Armik."

"Ah, yes. You are Avataut. Wolverine. And White Bear now. It is such a big river. A man could lose himself along that shore. It is what I would do if I still had my kayak—go downriver, be carried by the deep current. Now that it is calm, you could go far, very far. You would never be found."

Avataut cocked his head; he was beginning to like what he heard. "So steal another. We will go together. Go. Now. Go, I say! Steal a boat, a better one than your last. Or have you no stomach for risk, even now?"

"I am not facing what you are here, Avataut. I had nothing to do with the fire, or with the challenge to the braggart in the Man House, and as far as anyone knows, I brought no weapons onto this shore. And unlike you, my woman is still talking to me. And you should forget Hasu'u and E'ya. No doubt E'ya has run back to the braggart's side, brainless as he now is, thanks to you. As for Hasu'u, she will seek protection from any man but you. Still, perhaps I should go. Yes. I will. I will go now. I will gather up my pack frame and take my woman and head north. True Men do not belong in this forest country. Tôrnârssuk was right about that. So take your kayak and go, Avataut. Now. While it is still light enough to see your way past the shoals into deep water."

Still glowering, Avataut watched him go. "You are no True Man, Armik!" he called.

"We will see, old friend. We will see!"

Disgusted, he pulled the bearskin up over his shoulders. He eyed the sky. It would be dark soon. Armik was right. It was time to go.

▼▼▼▼

The kayak sang upon the swell, prow high, the wolverine harpoon rest shining wet in the swell.

He was past the shoals and into deep water sooner than he would have dared imagine. He smiled. It seemed a different river than the one that had carried Tôrnârssuk. No storm-tossed wind-whipped tumult here. Only the sure race of cold, cold water running swift and deep, carrying him to safety. He paddled steadily. The bearskin was still heavy around his shoulders and it stank with damp, but it kept him warm in the cold air of twilight.

He was not sure just when he noticed a lack of response, a sluggishness in the craft. There was no doubt about the feel of cold and wet around his feet and limbs. At first he thought it was only the interior of the kayak swelling up a little with a natural and tolerable level of saturation, for he was not wearing any of the fine waterproof garments Nuutlaq had sewn for the hunt. Without these, it was only to be expected that he feel discomfort, wetness even.

Off to his right, the surface of the water appeared rougher—wind track or current, or perhaps whales. He squinted ahead, dug in with the paddle . . . too late.

Something big rose beneath the kayak.

Lifted it.

He felt the slick skin bottom of his craft slip off another, smoother skin. Suddenly there was a great sound, a whoosh and then a slap explosive as thunder, and the kayak was falling through a spray of spume.

He never saw the whale, if it was a whale, but he had a glimpse of something enormous and gray and mottled with what seemed to be little bits of bone. For a moment he recalled the man-eating water monster that the storytellers among the People spoke of, Waktcexi. Trapped upside down in the kayak, the bearskin wrapped around him like a caul, he thought that he might like to be eaten. It would be better than drowning in the dark with the cold depths of the Great River of the North closing over him, enfolding him, pressing him, taking him down, down into the dark . . . into the cursed dark . . . with the words of the shaman Inau going down with him.

"I know what you fear, Avataut of the Barrenlands! Beware! Do nothing to offend the spirits of the whales or the dignity of any man who would take sustenance from their lives. And heed my warning: Wolverines do not go upon the water!"

▼▼▼▼▼

No one saw him die.

But many days later—long after the shaman Inau had closed up her lodge of whalebones forever and, in the company of the one-legged young holy man and his newly found family, journeyed toward the Cave of the Winds from which she would not return, and long after the widow Suda'li had been spurned by the giant and had taken her twins to dwell in the lodge of Chaksa of the Grassland—the wolverine harpoon rest of Avataut's kayak was found by the giant as he searched in vain for the true son of his heart, Musquash, along the shore. Sometime after that the man in the blue-quilled hunt shirt drove a white bear cub from feeding on all that remained of a man wrapped up in the skin of a female bear.

And later still it was Hasu'u who asked to clean the bones when Nuutlaq refused to touch them and, wrapping them in the tattered bearskin, honored them in the way of her Dawn-land tribe by burying them deep in a loess dune close to the base of the bluffs upon which the shaman Inau had once maintained her lodge of whalebones. She sang for him, and for her missing man, for he had yet to be found, and her words were kind and filled with hope, as was the way of her heart, inspiring her listeners to believe that perhaps Kwak-waje'sh had found cause enough at the end of his life to risk himself at last for another, to seek Tôrnârssuk, to find his hunt brother, beg his forgiveness, and bring him back to his woman and his son and his band. It was this hope that Hasu'u sent across the water with the last of the kayakmen to leave the river at the end of that summer, a hope to be shared with Mowea'qua, so that she might never abandon their search for the man of both their hearts.

Armik never spoke of it. He was long gone by then. Sometimes, when hunkering alone by his fire, while his woman cooked his meat and his children played, his thoughts drifted back and he smiled and wondered if Avataut had known at the end that he had killed him. It need not have been, of course. At that last moment on the beach, the wolverine in Avataut's spirit might have given himself the gift of life and assured Tôrnârssuk's death when Umak had suggested that he yield to Tôrnârssuk his own larger kayak and thus give his old hunt brother some small chance of sur-vival. He had refused. How was Avataut to know that one whom he had so demeaned and misjudged had used one of his daggers to slice open a seam in the bottom of his kayak? And so Avataut had died. And Armik smiled. And was glad.

Far away, in the Valley of the Spirit Moon, a small boy with the heart of a giant picked through the leavings and took what he needed to survive from the abandoned village of the Old Tribe, and under the shadowing wings of ravens, set his feet forward again in the sacred Circle of Life Ending and Life Beginning.

The white mammoth walked before him.

And the story had just begun.

Author's Note

▼▼▼▼▼▼▼

Some five thousand years ago, the vast, continent-spanning ice sheets of the Pleistocene lay in retreat. During that long, warm, postglacial epoch known as the Altithermal, or Great Warming, a two-thousand-year-long drought settled over the Great Plains and the Great Basin of North America. To the north and along the northwest and northeast coasts, however, the warmer, drier climate proved a boon. Small bands of nomadic hunters—in the tradition of their Ice Age ancestors who pursued the great herds of the Pleistocene out of Asia to people the New World—began to follow the game and the advancing tree line ever northward. Everywhere patterns of culture were shifting, changing, with various peoples coming into contact, enriching, competing, and even warring with one another. And then, some three thousand years ago, in response to subtle perturbations in the orbit of the planet and the fluctuating radiant energy of the sun, the climate changed. The world went cold once again. And the cold stayed. Winters were brutal. The northern forests began to die back. Summer thunderstorms set fire to the deadwood and to lichens that were the main sustenance of the caribou. Thousands of acres were consumed, destroying the feeding grounds of game and the hunting grounds of the People. Man was forced to adapt or die.

Spirit Moon, like the previous novels in the FIRST AMERICANS saga, has been set in these tumultuous and ever-changing times.

Once again, the cannibal phantoms, mysterious beasts, and werewolflike people depicted in the storyline are drawn from the mythology of Northeast Woodland, Canadian Maritime, and Inuit cultures. More than ever, ongoing research has solidified my belief that these legends not only recount the earliest migrations of man into and across the North American continent, but also affirm the purely human predilection for demonizing the unknown.

The Old Tribe is an ancient proto-Ainu race that may soon be proved to have entered the Americas at the dawn of time; surely their culture is here and well represented, and intriguing three-thousand-year-old carvings of little Mowea'quas, or "wolf women," have inspired my creation of that character. The True People are the Paleo-Inuit, who were advancing their hunting range southward into the cooling subarctic forests, bringing with them a new weapon, the bow and arrow, which was destined to revolutionize the hunting techniques of native Americans as surely as the toggle-headed harpoon invented by Maritime peoples would change their way of taking whales and seal and walrus.

The encounter of Muskrat and Giant Beaver is not unlike a creation tale of the Naskapi Indians, a tale that has caused this author to believe without doubt that *Castoroides ohioensis*—all seven to nine feet in length of him—did not pass into extinction at the end of the Ice Age at all but, along with mammoths and mastodons, shared the woodland environs with the native peoples until relatively modern times. Algonkian-speaking tribes from Maine to the barrenlands of

Canada have recounted tales of "five-legged," big-toothed, shaggy monsters that slept standing upright, gouged down trees, and sucked up so much water from lakes and ponds that they, as in the story of Snowy Owl, had to be hunted and destroyed to the last of their kind. I do not believe these "shaggy monster" stories are about bears, as scholars continue to insist. A mammoth's trunk could be seen as a fifth leg, and elephants consume some fifty gallons of water per day. Since the bones of mammoths and mastodons are regularly hauled up in the nets of fishing trawlers off the Canadian Maritimes and the coast of Maine, we know they inhabited this region, and, from studies done by Russian scientists working on Wrangell Island in 1994, we also know that mammoths were alive and grazing on that Arctic refuge only two thousand years ago, proving the assertions of native peoples and putting truth to the claim of Inuits across the Arctic of having encountered living mammoths.

Mound houses such as Inau's are found across the Arctic. On the Great Plains the Pawnee continued to occupy them into the twentieth century, a connection, I believe, with ancient cultural and racial roots lying far to the north. The salt deposits and red clay spoken of by Chaksa of the Grassland People make this historical connection with deposits traded north in ancient and modern times out of Nebraska's "sacred hills." As for the dual sexual nature of the shaman Inau, androgyny is represented in all ancient religions and has its place in trans-Arctic shamanism as well.

My thanks, again, to Dr. Richard Michael Gramly, Clovis Project director at Richley Clovis Cache in Wenatchee, Washington, curator of the Great Lakes Artifact Repository, Buffalo, New York, and the organizer of the American Association of Amateur Archaeology, for all the books and his continued enthusiasm for the series.

Thanks, too, to Dr. Joseph P. Perlow for information so graciously and generously shared on medical matters relating to the healing of fractured bones amongst Paleo-Indian hunters—and of this author!

Thanks, too, to D.C. Waldorf for all the knowledge shared on stone knapping and also for the inspiration given in the exquisite reproduction Clovis points and the arrowhead of Ramah chert. Truly, the latter stone is "smoke transformed," a magic thing of rare, complete, and utterly honest beauty.

And last, once again, thank you to George Engel, president of Book Creations, Inc., for your patience; and to Elizabeth Tinsley, editor extraordinaire . . . and with a sense of humor, too!

Joan Lesley Hamilton Cline
aka William Sarabande
Fawnskin, California